ANGEL

PAVEMENT

Other Phoenix Fiction titles from Chicago

Angel Pavement

J. B. PRIESTLEY

The University of Chicago Press

The University of Chicago Press, Chicago 60637

Copyright 1930 by J. B. Priestley, renewed 1958
All rights reserved. Published 1930
Phoenix Fiction edition 1983
Printed in the United States of America

90 89 88 87 86 85 84 83   1 2 3 4 5

Library of Congress Cataloging in Publication Data

Priestley, J. B. (John Boynton), 1894–
    Angel pavement.

    (Phoenix fiction series)
    I. Title.   II. Series.
[PR6031.R6A7   1983]   813'.912   83-1385
ISBN 0-226-68210-2 (pbk.)

To

C. S. EVANS

*because he is not only a good friend and a fine publisher,
but also because he is a London man and will know
what I am getting at in this London novel.*

Angel Pavement

*

Prologue

Epilogue

*

Prologue

SHE came gliding along London's broadest street, and then halted, swaying gently. She was a steamship of some 3,500 tons, flying the flag of one of the new Baltic states. The Tower Bridge cleared itself of midgets and toy vehicles and raised its two arms, and then she passed underneath, accompanied by cheerfully impudent tugs, and after some manœuvring and hooting and shouting, finally came to rest alongside Hay's Wharf. The fine autumn afternoon was losing its bright gold and turning into smoke and distant fading flame, so that it seemed for a moment as if all London bridges were burning down. Then the flare of the day died out, leaving behind a quiet light, untroubled as yet by the dusk. On the wharf, men in caps lent a hand with ropes and a gangway, contrived to spit ironically, as if they knew what all this fuss was worth, and then retired to group themselves in the background, like a shabby and faintly derisive chorus; and men in bowler hats arrived from nowhere, carrying dispatch cases, notebooks, bundles of papers, to exchange mysterious jokes with the ship's officers above; and two men in blue helmets, large and solid men, took their stand in the very middle of the scene and appeared to tell the ship, with a glance or two, that she could stay where she was for the time being because nothing against her was known so far to the police. The ship, for her part, began to think about discharging her mixed cargo.

This cargo was so mixed that it included the man who now emerged from the saloon, came yawning on to the deck, and looked down upon Hay's Wharf. This solitary passenger was a man of medium height but of a massive build, square and bulky about the shoulders, and thick-chested. He might have been forty-five; he might have been nearly fifty; it was difficult to tell his exact age. His face was

1

somewhat unusual, if only because it began by being almost bald at the top, then threw out two very bushy eyebrows, and finally achieved a tremendous moustache, drooping a little by reason of its very length and thickness; a moustache in a thousand, with something rhetorical, even theatrical, about it. He wore, carelessly, a suit of excellent grey cloth but of a foreign cut and none too well-fitting. This passenger had come with the ship from the Baltic state that owned her, but there was something about his appearance, in spite of his clothes, his moustache, that suggested he was really a native of this island. But that is perhaps all it did suggest. He was one of those men who are difficult to place. The sight of him did not call up any particular background, and you could not easily imagine him either at work or at home. He had come from the Baltic to the Thames, but it might just as well have been from any place to any other place. As he stood there, straddling at ease, a thick figure of a man but not slow and heavy, with his gleaming bald front and giant moustache, looking down at the wharf quite incuriously, he seemed a man who was neither coming home nor leaving it, and yet not a simple traveller, and this gave him a faint piratical air.

"Lon-don, eh?" cried a voice at his elbow. It came from the second mate, a small natty youngster not unlike a pale and well-brushed monkey. "Vairy nice, eh?"

"All right."

"You com' 'ere, Misdair Colsbee? You stay 'ere?" The second mate liked to air his English and had not had much opportunity of doing so during the voyage.

"Yes, I stay here," replied Mr. Golspie, for that was the name the second officer was trying to pronounce. "That is," he boomed, as an afterthought, "if there's anything doing."

"You leef 'ere, in Lon-don?" pursued the other, who had missed the force of the last remark.

"No, I don't. I don't live anywhere. That's me." And Mr. Golspie said this with a kind of grim relish, as if to suggest that he might pop up anywhere, and that when he did, something or somebody had better look out. He might have been one of the quieter buccaneers sailing into harbour.

Then, nodding amiably, he stepped forward, looked up and down the wharf again, and returned to the saloon, where he took a cigar from the box the captain had bought at the entrance to the Kiel Canal, and helped himself to a drink from one of the many bottles that overflowed from the sideboard to the table. It had been a convivial voyage. Mr. Golspie and the captain were old acquaintances who had been able to do one another various good turns. The captain had promised to make Mr. Golspie very comfortable, and one way of making Mr. Golspie very comfortable was to lay in and then promptly bring out a sound stock of whisky, cognac, vodka, and other liquors. There had been nothing one-sided about this arrangement, for the captain had been able to keep pace with his guest, even though his progress had not had the same steady dignity. The captain, who had once served in the Russian Imperial Navy and had only resigned from it by escaping in his shirt and trousers over the side one night, was apt to turn fantastic in his drink. On two nights out of the three, during the voyage, he had insisted upon declaiming a long speech from Goethe's *Faust* in four different languages, to show that he was a man of culture. And on the night before they had entered the Thames Estuary, the previous night, in fact, he had gone further than that, for he had laughed a great deal, sung four songs that Mr. Golspie could not understand at all, told a long story apparently in Russian, cried a little, and shaken Mr. Golspie's hand so hard and so often that as he thought about it all now, over his cigar in the saloon that seemed so strangely still, Mr. Golspie could almost feel the ache again in his hand. Mr. Golspie himself did not perform any of these antics; he merely mellowed as the evening waned and the bottles were emptied; and he was mellowing now, early though it was, for he and the captain had sat a long time over lunch. Apparently, however,

Mr. Golspie did not consider that he was sufficiently mellow, for he now helped himself to another drink.

The men in bowler hats were by this time on board. Some of them were interviewing the captain. Others were interested in Mr. Golspie, for they had to decide whether he was fit to land in the island of his birth. His relations with these officials were quite amiable, but they did not prevent him from expressing his views.

"Regulations! Of course they're regulations!" he boomed through the great moustache, mellow but pugnacious. "But that doesn't mean they're not a lot o' damned nonsense. There's more palaver getting into England now than there was getting into Russia and Turkey before the blasted war. And we used to laugh at 'em. Backward countries we used to call 'em. Passports!" Here he laughed, then tapped the young man on the lapel of his blue serge coat. "Never kept a rogue out yet, never. Only wants a bit of cleverness. All they do is to make trouble for honest men—fellows like me, wanting to do a bit of good to trade. Isn't that right? You bet it is."

He then saw the customs officers, who dipped a hand here and there in his two steamer trunks and three battered suitcases.

"I expect you'd like to get away," said one of them, beginning to chalk up his approval of the luggage.

Mr. Golspie watched him with idle benevolence, looking quite unlike a man who has two hundred and fifty cigars cunningly stowed away in a steamer trunk. "Not this time. No hurry, for once. I'm staying aboard to pick a bit of dinner with the skipper here." He waved a hand, presumably to indicate the city that lay all round them. "It can wait."

"What can?" And the young man gave a final flourish of chalk.

"London can," replied Mr. Golspie. "All of it."

The young man laughed, not because he thought this last remark very witty, but because this passenger suddenly reminded him of a comedian he had once seen at the Finsbury Park Empire. "Well, I dare say it can. It's been waiting a long time."

Left to himself, with his cigars all safe, Mr. Golspie ruminated for a minute or two, then climbed to the upper deck, perhaps to decide what it was that had been waiting so long.

He found himself staring at the immense panorama of the Pool. Dusk was falling; the river rippled darkly; and the fleet of barges across the way was almost shapeless. There was, however, enough daylight lingering on the north bank, where the black piles and the whitewashed wharf edge above them still stood out sharply, to give shape and character to the waterfront. Over on the right, the grey stones of the Tower were faintly luminous, as if they had contrived to store away a little of their centuries of sunlight. The white pillars of the Custom House were as plain as peeled wands. Nearer still, two church spires thrust themselves above the blur of stone and smoke and vague flickering lights: one was as blanched and graceful as if it had been made of twisted paper, a salute to Heaven from the City; the other was abrupt and dark, a despairing appeal, the finger of a hand flung out to the sky. Mr. Golspie, after a brief glance, ignored the pair of them. They in their turn, however, were dominated by the severely rectangular building to the left, boldly fronting the river and looking over London Bridge with a hundred eyes, a grim Assyrian bulk of stone. It challenged Mr. Golspie's memory, so that he regarded it intently. It was there when he was last in London, but was new then. Adelaide House, that was it. But he still continued to look at it, and with respect, for the challenge remained, though not to the memory. Both the blind eyes and the lighted eyes of its innumerable windows seemed to answer his stare and to tell him that he did not amount to very much, not here in London. Then his gaze swept over the bridge to what could be seen beyond. The Cold Storage place, and then, cavernous, immense, the great black arch of Cannon Street Station, and high above, far beyond, not in the city but in the sky and still softly shining in the darkening air, a ball and a cross. It was the very top of St. Paul's, seen above the roof of Cannon Street Station. Mr. Golspie recognised it with pleasure, and even half sung, half hummed, the line of a song that came back to him, something about "St. Paul's with its grand old Dome." Good luck to St. Paul's! It did not challenge him: it was simply there, keeping an eye on everything but interfering with nobody. And somehow this glimpse of St. Paul's suddenly made him realise that this was the genuine old monster, London. He felt the whole mass of it, spouting and fuming and roaring away. He realised something else too, namely, the fact that he was still wearing his old brown slippers, the ones that Hortensia had given him. He had arrived, had crept right into the very heart of London, wearing his old brown slippers. He had slipped two hundred and fifty cigars past their noses, and had not even changed into his shoes. James Golspie was surveying London in his slippers, and London was not knowing, not caring—just yet. These thoughts gave him enormous pleasure, bringing with them a fine feeling of cunning and strength: he could have shaken hands with himself; if there had been a mirror handy he would probably have exchanged a wink with his reflection.

He walked round the deck. Lights were flickering on along the wharf, immediately giving the unlit entrances a sombre air of mystery. A few men down there were heaving and shouting, but there was little to see. Mr. Golspie continued his walk, then stopped to look across and over London Bridge at the near waterfront, the south bank. Such lighting as there was on this side was very gay. High up on the first building past the bridge, coloured lights revolved about an illuminated bottle, to the glory of Booth's Gin, and further along, a stabbing gleam of crimson finally spelt itself into Sandeman's Port. Mr. Golspie regarded both these writings on the wall with admiration and sympathy. The sight of London Bridge itself too, pleased him now, for all the buses had turned on their lights and were streaming across like a flood of molten gold. They brought another stream of pleasant images into Mr. Golspie's mind, a bright if broken pageant of convivial London: double whiskies in crimson-shaded bars; smoking hot steaks and chops and a white cloth on a little corner table; the glitter and velvet of the music-halls; knowing gossip, the fine reek of Havanas, round a club fender and fat leather chairs; pretty girls, a bit stiff perhaps (though not as stiff as they used to be) but very pretty and not so deep as the foreign ones, coming out of shops and offices, with evenings to spend and not much else: he saw it all and he liked the look of it. There was a size, a richness, about London. You could find any-thing or anybody you wanted in it, and you could also hide in it. He had been a fool to stay away so long. But, anyhow, here he was. He took a long and wide and exultant look at the place.

Dinner that night was very good indeed, the best the boat had given him. Mr. Golspie and the captain shared it with the chief engineer, who came beaming and shining from the depths, and the first mate, usually a very wooden fellow, for ever brooding over some mysterious domestic tragedy in Riga, but now for once gigan-tically social and cheerful. The steward, the one with the cropped head and gold tooth, lavished his all upon them. Bottles that had not been emptied before were emptied now, together with some that were produced for the first time. The talk, so far as Mr. Golspie had any part in it, was conducted in a fantastic mixture of English, German, and the ship's own Baltic language, a mixture it would be impossible to reproduce here, but it went very well, smashing its way through the entanglements of irregular verbs and doubtful substantives, for nothing removes the curse of Babel like food, drink, and good-fellowship. All four grew expansive, bellowed confidences, roared through the fog of cigar smoke, threw back their heads to laugh, and were gods for an hour.

"Very soon we shall meet again," said the captain to Mr. Golspie, clinking glasses for the third time. "Is that not so, my friend?"

"Leave it to me, my boy," replied Mr. Golspie, very flushed, with tiny beads of perspiration on that massive bald front of his.

"You come back when you have finished your business here in London?"

"As to that, I can't say. If I can, I will."

"That is good," said the captain. Then he looked very deep, and put a finger as big as a pork sausage to his forehead. "And now you will tell us what this business is, eh? In secret. We will not tell."

The chief engineer tugged at the ends of his moustache, which was nearly as large as Mr. Golspie's, and tried to look even deeper than the captain, like the repository of innumerable commercial secrets.

"I say this," cried the huge first mate, who was in no condition now to wait until his opinion had been asked. "I say this. It is good business. It is for the good of our country. I drink to you," he shouted, and promptly did so, with the result that he immediately remembered that disastrous affair at Riga, and sat silent, with the tears in his eyes, for the next twenty minutes.

"Well, I'll tell you," said Mr. Golspie, taking out his cigar and looking at it very knowingly, as if it was a fellow conspirator. "There's no need to make a mystery of it. D'you remember Mikorsky? Wait a minute. Not the little fellow with the office in Danzig, but the big fellow with the beard, in the timber trade. That's the one. Remember him?"

The captain did, and was evidently so pleased by this effort of memory that he appeared to conduct several bars of one of the stormier symphonies. The mate remembered, too, but only nodded, his tearful blue eyes being still fixed on that tragic interior in Riga. The chief engineer did not remember Mikorsky, and, in what seemed nothing less than mental anguish, repeated the name in twenty different tones, beginning very high and ending in a despairing bass.

"I've done one or two little jobs for him," Mr. Golspie continued, "during the time I had a bit of a pull. We'd a night or two together, too. I met him one day, not a month ago, and he said he was just going down into the country, to see his cousin, and I ought to go with him. So I did. I'd nothing better to do. Hot as hell it was down there, too, and I was bitten to death. This cousin of Mikorsky's was in the furniture end of the timber trade, and he'd invented a new process, machine, treatment, everything, for turning out veneers and inlays. And labour costs next to nothing down there. I asked where all this stuff was going. Well, they'd got orders from Germany and Czecho-Slovakia and Austria and a chance of something in Paris. 'What's it going to cost in London?' I said, showing 'em one of their lines, and they told me. It sounded all right to me, but I didn't say anything. Not then. I went away and made a few enquiries. I found out what they were paying for this sort of stuff in Bethnal Green and Hoxton and those parts, in London, you know, where the furniture's made ——"

"Bednal Green, yes," said the chief engineer proudly. "My uncle Stefan was there, yes, old Stefan in Bednal Green. Socialist," he added, as a melancholy afterthought.

"He was, was he?" Mr. Golspie boomed, with a certain brutal heartiness characteristic of him. "Well, good luck to him! I'll get on with the tale. They were paying half as much again for the same sort o' stuff, veneers and inlays, not a bit better, here in London. Couldn't get it where it was produced so cheap, y'see? Didn't look about 'em. They're getting slow here. There's something in this for me, I said to myself, and off I went down there again, to see this other Mikorsky, the cousin. I wanted to know how much of this stuff I could have every month, various lines, and the prices. They told me, and guaranteed it. We had a few drinks on it, and I walk out, with a contract in my pocket, so much of this, that, and the other, at so much, whenever I liked to take it up, and me the sole agent for Great Britain."

"Very good business," said the captain, with a grave judicial air, in spite of his rather goggly eyes. "And now, you sell it all, eh? You make big profit?"

"What I do is to find somebody who's in the way of selling it, somebody who's in this line o' business, and then go in with 'em." Mr. Golspie refreshed himself noisily. "And if I haven't laid my hand on somebody by this time the day after to-morrow, my name's not Jimmy Golspie."

"Make plenty of money, be rich, eh?"

"No, it's too honest. But I'll pick a bit up, to be going on with."

"Ah no, no!" cried the captain, reaching over and patting Mr. Golspie on the shoulder. "You make plenty, here in London. Ho-ho, yes! Plenty! Money here in London—oh!—" And he held out his hands as if he expected the Bank of England to be emptied into them.

"Not so much as you think," said Mr. Golspie, shaking his head very slowly. "Oh no, not at all. They may have it, but it's all tied up. It's not—er—shir—circulating. I tell you, they're slow here, they're slow."

"You think they sleep?"

"That's right. Half asleep, most of 'em."

"Ho-ho," roared the captain. "And you will put them awake?"

"One or two, p'rhaps, I might be able to shake up a bit. If not, I'm on the move again. And I'll have to be on the move now, boys. I told that steward's mate—the fellow that plays the concertina— to go and get me a taxi and take my traps ashore. It ought to be there, at the corner, any minute now. All right then. Just a last one for luck."

They were having this last one, with some formality, when the man returned to say that the taxi was waiting. Mr. Golspie led the way to the deck, and then stopped near the gangway to say good-bye.

"Now for it," he cried, more for his own benefit than for his listeners'. "Straight back into the old rabbit warren. God, what a place! Millions and millions, and most of 'em don't know they're born yet! Eyes and tails, that's all they are, diving in and out of their little holes. The good old rabbit warren. Look at it! Ah, well, it's no good looking at it here because you can't see it. But I've been looking at it. What a place! Well, Chief—well, Captain—this is where I go."

"And the beautiful daughter, the little Lena?" the captain inquired. "Is she here, waiting for you?"

"Not yet. She's still in Paris, with her aunt, but she'll be coming over as soon as I've settled down. Golspie and Daughter, that'll be the style of the firm then, and we'll see what London makes of it. And—my God—if I don't waken some of 'em up, she will, the artful little devil! But she'll have to behave here. Yes, she'll have to behave. Well, Captain, keep her afloat, and remember me to all the girls and boys at the other end, and let's meet again next time you're over. Drop me a line to the office here. I'll tell 'em where to find me. Where the devil's the lad? Oh, he's there, is he? Has he taken everything ashore? Right you are! So long!"

After a final wave of the hand, Mr. Golspie, a very massive figure now in his huge ulster, made a slow, steady, and very dignified progress down the gangway. When he found himself treading at last the stones of London, he turned his head and nodded, then strode off more briskly to the corner of Battle Bridge Lane, where the taxi was waiting. Two minutes later, he had gone hooting into the lights and shadows of the city, which sent whirling past the windows a crazy frieze, glimmering, glittering, darkening, of shops, taverns, theatre doors, hoardings, church porches, crimson and gold segments of buses, little lighted interiors of saloon cars, railings and doorsteps and lace curtains, mounds and chocolate, thousands of cigarette packets, beer and buns and aspirin and wreaths and coffins, and faces, faces, more and more faces, strange, meaningless and without end. But the lights that came flashing in found a tiny answering gleam in Mr. Golspie's eyes; and when they had gone, in the double darkness of the cab and the shadow of that great moustache, he grinned. London neither knew nor cared; nevertheless, there it was: Mr. James Golspie had arrived.

Chapter One

THEY ARRIVE

I

MANY people who think they know the City well have been
compelled to admit that they do not know Angel Pavement.
You could go wandering half a dozen times between Bunhill Fields
and London Wall, or across from Barbican to Broad Street Station,
and yet miss Angel Pavement. Some of the street maps of the district omit it altogether; taxi-drivers often do not even pretend to
know it; policemen are frequently not sure; and only postmen who
are caught within half a dozen streets of it are triumphantly positive. This all suggests that Angel Pavement is of no great importance.
Everybody knows Finsbury Pavement, which is not very far away,
because Finsbury Pavement is a street of considerable length and
breadth, full of shops, warehouses, and offices, to say nothing of
buses and trams, for it is a real thoroughfare. Angel Pavement is
not a real thoroughfare, and its length and breadth are inconsider-
able. You might bombard the postal districts of E. C. 1 and E. C. 2
with letters for years, and yet never have to address anything to
Angel Pavement. The little street is old, and has its fair share of
sooty stone and greasy walls, crumbling brick and rotting woodwork, but somehow it has never found itself on the stage of history.
Kings, princes, great bishops, have never troubled it; murders it
may have seen, but they have all belonged to private life; and no
literary masterpiece has ever been written under one of its roofs.
The guide-books, the volumes on London's byways, have not a word
to say about it, and those motor-coaches, complete with guide, that

roam about the City in the early evening never go near it. The guide himself, who knows all about Henry the Eighth and Wren and Dickens and is so highly educated that he can still talk with an Oxford accent at the very top of his voice, could probably tell you nothing about Angel Pavement.

It is a typical City side-street, except that it is shorter, narrower, and dingier than most. At one time it was probably a real thoroughfare, but now only pedestrians can escape at the western end, and they do this by descending the six steps at the corner. For anything larger and less nimble than a pedestrian, Angel Pavement is a *cul de sac*, for all that end, apart from the steps, is blocked up by *Chase & Cohen: Carnival Novelties*, and not even by the front of Chase & Cohen but by their sooty, mouldering, dusty-windowed back. Chase & Cohen do not believe it is worth while offering Angel Pavement any of their carnival novelties—many of which are given away, with a thirty shilling dinner and dance, in the West End every gala night—and so they turn the other way, not letting Angel Pavement have so much as a glimpse of a pierrot hat or a false nose. Perhaps this is as well, for if the pavementeers could see pierrot hats and false noses every day, there is no telling what might happen.

What you do see there, however, is something quite different. Turning into Angel Pavement from that crazy jumble and jangle of buses, lorries, drays, private cars, and desperate bicycles, the main road, you see on the right, first a nondescript blackened building that is really the side of a shop and a number of offices; then *The Pavement Dining Rooms: R. Ditton, Propr.*, with R. Ditton's usual window display of three cocoanut buns, two oranges, four bottles of cherry cider picturesquely grouped, and if not the boiled ham, the meat-and-potato pie; then a squashed little house or bundle of single offices that is hopelessly to let; and then the bar of the *White Horse*, where you have the choice of any number of mellowed whiskies or fine sparkling ales, to be consumed on or off the premises, and if on, then either publicly or privately. You are now halfway down the street, and could easily throw a stone through one of

Chase & Cohen's windows, which is precisely what somebody, mad-
dened perhaps by the thought of the Carnival Novelties, has already
done. On the other side, the southern side, the left-hand side when
you turn in from the outer world, you begin, rather splendidly, with
Dunbury & Co.: Incandescent Gas Fittings, and two windows almost
bright with sample fittings. Then you arrive at *T. Benenden: Tobacconist,* whose window is filled with dummy packets of cigarettes
and tobacco that have long ceased even to pretend they have anything better than air in them; though there are also, as witnesses to
T. Benenden's enterprise, one or two little bowls of dry and dusty
stuff that mutter, in faded letters, "Our Own Mixture, Cool Sweet
Smoking, Why not Try it?" To reach T. Benenden's little counter,
you go through the street doorway and then turn through another
door on the left. The stairs in front of you—and very dark and dirty
they are, too—belong to *C. Warstein: Tailors' Trimmings.* Next to
T. Benenden and C. Warstein is a door, a large, stout, old door
from which most of the paint has flaked and shredded away. This
door has no name on it, and nobody, not even T. Benenden, has
seen it open or knows what there is behind it. There it is, a door,
and it does nothing but gather dust and cobwebs and occasionally
drop another flake of dried paint on the worn step below. Perhaps
it leads into another world. Perhaps it will open, one morning, to
admit an angel, who, after looking up and down the little street for
a moment, will suddenly blow the last trumpet. Perhaps that is the
real reason why the street is called Angel Pavement. What is certain, however, is that this door has no concern with the building
next to it and above it, the real neighbour of T. Benenden and
C. Warstein and known to the postal authorities as No. 8, Angel
Pavement.

No. 8, once a four-storey dwelling-house where some merchant-
alderman lived snugly on his East India dividends, is now a little
hive of commerce. For the last few years, it has contrived to keep
an old lady and a companion (unpaid) in reasonable comfort at The
Palms Private Hotel, Torquay, and, in addition, to furnish the old

lady's youngest niece with an allowance of two pounds a week in order that she might continue to share a studio just off the Fulham Road and attempt to design scenery for plays that are always about to be produced at the Everyman Theatre, Hampstead. It has also indirectly paid the golf-club subscription and caddie fees of the junior partner of Fulton, Gregg & Fulton, the solicitors, who are responsible for the letting and the rents. As for the tenants themselves, their names may be found on each side of the squat doorway. The ground floor is occupied by the *Kwik-Work Razor Blade Co., Ltd.*, the first floor by *Twigg & Dersingham*, and the upper floors by the *Universal Hosiery Co.*, the *London and Counties Supply Stores*, and, at the very top, keeping its eye on everybody, the *National Mercantile Enquiry Agency*, which seems to be content with the possession of a front attic.

This does not mean that we have now finished with No. 8, Angel Pavement. It is for the sake of No. 8 that we have come to Angel Pavement at all, but not for the whole of No. 8, but only for the first floor. No doubt a number of tales, perhaps huge violent epics, could be started, jumped into life, merely by opening the door of the *Kwik-Work Razor Blade Co., Ltd.*, or by trudging up the stairs to the *Universal Hosiery Co.* and the *London and Counties Supply Stores*, or by looking up at the grimy skylight, and giving a shout to the *National Mercantile Enquiry Agency*; but we must keep to the less mysterious but more respectable first floor—and *Twigg & Dersingham*.

II

On this particular morning in autumn, Mrs. Cross was rather later than usual. That did not matter very much because it was not one of the floor-washing mornings, but just one of the ordinary dust-round-and-sweep-up-a-bit mornings. But somebody, one of the interfering sort, had left a note for her in the general office, that is, the room just behind the frosted glass partitions and the sort of ticket

office window with *Enquiries* on it, and this note said: *Mrs. Cross.
What about turning this room out for a change? Thank you! !*

"An' thank *you!*" said Mrs. Cross, quite aloud and with grim
irony, as she tore up this note and popped it in the top of the stove.
To show that she was not the kind of woman to be dictated to in
this fashion, she immediately went and gave the other room, Mr.
Dersingham's private office, a thoroughly good sweeping and dust-
ing. Having done that, she waddled straight across the general office
to the other room, which, with its long counter and cupboards and
drawers and samples of wood and litter, was the one she liked least,
being always in a terrible mess. On her way, she completely ignored
the general office, did not even give it a look, just as if it were full
of people in the habit of leaving notes. Her back told it very plainly
that she would clean up the office in her own way. Once in the other
room, the nasty one, she felt so pleased about this rebuff that she
set to work with a will, and for the next ten minutes was enveloped
in a cloud of dust. By the time she had finished, there may have
been very few articles in the room that were free from dust, but
nearly all of them had at least exchanged their old dust for another
variety that came perhaps from quite a distant corner. Then she
thrust back a wisp of grey hair from her swollen face, on which
time and trouble had first sketched a few lines and then deepened
them by puffing out the surrounding flesh; she dragged her swollen
feet across to the discarded leather office chair in the corner; she
flopped into the chair and put her swollen hands—for though she
said with some truth that she worked her fingers to the bone, hot
water and soap and wet scrubbing brushes had piled sodden, nerve-
less flesh on those bones—in her lap, and rested. Immediately she
plunged into a fierce reverie, in which the figure of Mr. Cross, who
suffered from rheumatoid arthritis, the two rooms between the City
Road and the black Regent's Canal that were her home, Mrs. Tom-
linson, the woman she was going to clean for later in the morning,
and the image of a pound of stewing steak, all played their parts.
Then she returned to the general office.

This time, she noticed its existence, and what she saw suddenly gave her a little fright. She had been a bit too hasty (her old fault) about that note. It really did want a good tidying. She had neglected it a bit lately, because for the last three mornings she had been late, all because she was not getting her proper sleep, and all because Mrs. Williams and her husband on the next floor had got a loud speaker, one of them little horns, and it was not only a loud speaker but also a late speaker, and in fact would speak your head off. And if she didn't get on with this office a bit, the one that left that note would be complaining to Mr. Dersingham, and then that might mean another job gone, all due to hastiness. She had better be putting her hastiness behind a brush and duster. And, as if to give her a final push, a clock somewhere outside sounded the half-hour. Half-past eight!—well, now she would have to bustle round.

She was still bustling round—though, to be accurate, she was only engaged in passing a languid, duster-holding hand over the tin cover of the typewriter—when Messrs. Twigg & Dersingham's next employee arrived, and their day really began. The frosted glass door that opened from the little space in which enquirers were kept waiting for a few minutes, now swung back to admit into the general office the body of a boy about fifteen, whose eyes were focussed upon a paper, folded into a very small compass, that he held about four inches away from them. This was the office boy or very junior clerk, Stanley Poole, who had just come all the way from Hackney, which remained with him as a combined flavour of cocoa and bread dipped in bacon fat that still haunted his palate. His body, which was small and thin but sufficiently tough, and was crowned by a snub nose, some freckles, greyish-greenish eyes, and some unbrushed sandy hair, had been in the service of Twigg & Dersingham for the last twenty minutes, when it had boarded a tram and a bus and had walked down several streets. Now it had arrived in the office. But his mind had not yet begun the day's work. Even now, when the very threshold had been passed, it was still in the wilds of Mexico, enjoying the heroic and exhilarating companionship of Jack Dash-

wood and Dick Robinson, the Boy Aviators, the terror of all
Mexican bandits.

"So you've come," said Mrs. Cross, putting back that wisp of hair
again. "It's about time I was 'opping it if you've come."

Stanley looked up and nodded. With a sigh, he withdrew from the
world of the Boy Aviators and the Mexican bandits. He tried to fold
his paper into a still smaller compass, before cramming it into his
pocket.

"Read, read, read!" cried Mrs. Cross derisively. "Some of yer's
always at it. What they find to put in all the time beats me. What's
that yer reading now? Murders, I'll bet."

" 'Tisn't," replied Stanley, balancing himself on one leg for no
particular reason that we can discover. "It's a boys' paper." He made
this announcement with a kind of sullen reluctance, not because he
was really a sullen lad, but simply because he had discovered that
when his elders asked these questions, they were usually not in
search of information, but were trying to get at him.

"Penny bloods, them things is."

" 'Tisn't," said Stanley, balancing himself on the other leg now.
"This is tuppence. I buy it ev'ry week, have done ever since it come
out. *Boy's Companion*, it's called. It's got the best tales in," he added,
in a sudden burst of confidence. "All about boys who fly in airplanes
an' go to Mexico an' Russia an' all over an' have advenshers!"

"Advenshers! They'd be better off at 'ome—with their advenshers!
You'll be wantin' to go an' 'ave advenshers yerself next—and then
what will yer poor mother say?"

But this only goaded Stanley into making new and even more
dangerous admissions. "I'm going to try and be a detective," he
mumbled.

"Well now, did y'ever!" cried Mrs. Cross, at once shocked and
delighted. "A detective! I never 'eard of such a thing! What d'yer
come 'ere for if yer want to be a detective. There's no detectin' 'ere.
Go on with yer! 'Ere, yer not big enough, and yer never will be

either, 'cos yer'd 'ave to be a pleeceman first before they'd let yer be a detective, and they'd never 'ave yer as a pleeceman."

"You can be detective without being a bobby first," replied Stanley scornfully. He had gone into this question, and was not to be put off by a mere outsider like Mrs. Cross. " 'Sides, you can be a private detective an' find jewels an' shadder people. That's what I'd like to do—shadder people."

"What's that? Follerin' 'em about, is it? Oh, that's nasty work, that is. Shadderin'! I'd shadder yer if I caught yer at it, my words I would." And Mrs. Cross took up her brush and dust-pan and gave them a fierce little shake, almost as if she had just caught *them* at it. "Now you just get on with yer work like a good boy, and don't you go tellin' anybody else yer want to be shadderin' else yer'll be gettin' yerself into trouble. Yer can't expect people to 'ave any patience with shadderers. If Mr. Dersingham knew what was goin' on in that 'ead of yours, 'e'd tell yer to go straight 'ome and 'ave nothing more to do with yer, and yer'd find yerself shadderin' for another job, and that's all the shadderin' *you'd* get."

Stanley turned away, and then pulled a face, not so much at Mrs. Cross as at the whole narrow school of thought represented at this moment by Mrs. Cross. He went to the letter-box and brought back the morning's post, which he placed on the nearest high desk. There he remembered something, and looked with a grin at Mrs. Cross, who was now having a final bustle round.

"Did you see that note left for you?" he inquired.

Mrs. Cross suspended operations at once. "Yes, I did see it, and if yer want to know where it is, I can tell yer, 'cos it's in that stove." She struck an attitude that suggested a counsel for the prosecution of the high-handed type. "And oo, might I ask, left that there note? Oo wrote it? Just you tell me that, that's all?"

"Miss Matfield wrote it."

"An' I thought as much. Soon as I set eyes on it, I knew. Miss Matfield wrote it! Miss Matfield!" Her irony was now so terrible that she shook all over with it, and her head seemed in danger of falling off. "And 'ow long, might I ask, 'as Miss Matfield been in this office, doin' 'er typewriting? 'Ow long? Two munce. All right— three munce. An' 'ow long 'ave I been cleaning for Twiggs and Dersingham's, coming 'ere ev'ry morning, week in an' week out, to clean this office? Yer don't know. No, yer don't know, and yer Miss Matfield doesn't know. Well, I'll tell yer. I've been cleaning for Twiggs and Dersingham's for seven years, I 'ave. It wasn't this Mr. Dersingham that started me, it was 'is uncle, old Mr. Dersingham, 'im oo's dead now—an' a nice old gentleman 'e was, too, nicer than this one an' a better 'ead on 'im to my way of thinking—and when this Mr. Dersingham took on, 'e sent for me and said, 'You keep on cleaning, Mrs. Cross, and I'll pay yer whatever my uncle did,' that's what 'e said to me in that very room there, and I said, 'Much obliged, sir, and the very best attention as always,' and 'e said, 'I'm sure it will, Mrs. Cross.' Typewriters! Coming and going so fast I can't be bothered learning their names. If there's been one 'ere since I started, there's been eight or ten or a dozen. Miss Matfield! Now when she comes in, just give 'er a message from me," she cried, thoroughly reckless by this time. "Just say to 'er: 'Mrs. Cross 'as seen the note left and only asks oo is cleaning this office, Miss Matfield or 'er, and if 'er, then them oo's been doing it for seven years, week in and week out, knows their own business better than them oo's only been typewriting 'ere for three munce, and so Mrs. Cross'll thank 'er to keep 'er notes to 'erself in future till they're asked for.' Just you tell 'er that, boy. And I'll say good-morning."

With that, Mrs. Cross unfastened her apron and gathered up her things with great dignity, gave Stanley a final shake of the head, and waddled out, closing the outer door behind her, a moment later, with a decisive bang.

Left to himself, Stanley, with the contemptuous air of a man who is meant for better things, began his morning's work. After taking off the two typewriter covers, dumping a few books on the high desks, and filling up all the ink-pots and putting out clean sheets of blotting paper (which duty was a little fad of Mr. Smeeth's), he remembered that he was a creature with a soul. So, grasping a short round ruler in such a way that it remotely resembled a revolver, he crouched behind Mr. Smeeth's high stool for a few tense moments, then sprang out, pointing his gun at the place where the great criminal's bottom waistcoat button would have been, and said hoarsely: "Put 'em up, Diamond Jack. No, you don't! Not a move!" He gave a warning flourish of the gun, then said casually, over his shoulder, to one of his assistants or a few police sergeants or somebody like that, "Take him away." And that was the end of Diamond Jack, and yet another triumph for S. Poole, the young detective whose exploits were rivalling even those of the Boy Aviators. And having thus refreshed himself, Stanley replaced the round ruler and condescended to perform one or two more of those monotonous and trifling actions that Messrs. Twigg & Dersingham demanded of him at this hour of the morning. These left him ample time for thought, and he began to wonder if he would be able to get out during the morning. Once outside the office—even though he was only going to the post office or the railway goods department or some firm not four streets away—he could enjoy himself, for the affairs of Twigg & Dersingham faded to a grey thread of routine; he plunged at once into the drama of London's underworld; and as he hopped and dodged about the crowded streets, like a sandy-haired sparrow, he was able to do some marvellous shadowing. There also loomed already, early as it was, a problem that would become more and more disturbing as the long morning wore on and he became hungrier and hungrier. This was the problem of where to go and what to buy for lunch, for which his mother allowed him a shilling every day. He always ate his breakfast so quickly that his stomach forgot about it almost at once and left him hollow inside by ten o'clock and absolutely aching by twelve. He often wondered what would happen to him if, instead of being the first to go to lunch, at half past twelve, he was the last, and had to wait until about half past one. There are innumerable ways of spending a shilling on lunch, from the downright solid way of blowing the lot on sausage or fried liver and

mashed potatoes, say at the *Pavement Dining Rooms*, to the immediately delightful but rather unsatisfying method of spreading it out,
buying a jam tart here, a banana there, and some milk chocolate
somewhere else; and Stanley knew them all.

He was trifling with the thought of trying the nearest Lyons again,
and was actually searching his memory to discover the exact price of
a portion of Lancashire Hot-pot in that establishment, when he was
interrupted by the arrival of a colleague. This was Turgis, the clerk,
who might be described as Stanley's senior or Mr. Smeeth's junior.
He was in his early twenties, a thinnish, awkward young man, with
a rather long neck, poor shoulders, and large, clumsy hands and feet.
You would not say he was ugly, but on the other hand you would
probably admit, after reflection, that it would have been better for
him if he had been actually uglier. As it was, he was just unprepossessing. You would not have noticed him in a crowd—and a great
deal of his time was spent in a crowd—but if your attention had
been called to him, you would have given him one glance and then
decided that that was enough. He was obviously neither sick nor
starved, yet something about his appearance, a total lack of colour
and bloom, a slight pastiness and spottiness, the faint grey film that
seemed to cover and subdue him, suggested that all the food he ate
was wrong, all the rooms he sat in, beds he slept in, and clothes he
wore, were wrong, and that he lived in a world without sun and
clean rain and wandering sweet air. His features were not good nor
yet too bad. He had rather full brown eyes that might have been
called pretty if they had been set in a girl's face; a fairly large nose
that should have been masterful but somehow was not; a small, still
babyish mouth, usually open, and revealing several big and irregular
teeth; and a drooping rather than retreating chin. His blue serge
suit bulged and bagged and sagged and shone, and had obviously
done all these things five days after it had left the multiple cheap
tailors' shop, in the window of which a companion suit, clothing the
wax model of a light-weight champion, still maliciously challenged

Turgis with its smooth surface and sharp creases every time he sneaked past it. His soft collar was crumpled, his tie a little frayed, and there was a pulpy look about his shoes. Any sensible woman could have compelled him to improve his appearance almost beyond recognition within a week, and it was quite clear that no sensible woman took any interest in him.

"Morning, Stanley," he said, not very cheerfully.

"Hello," said Stanley, in the toneless voice of one who expects nothing.

Turgis went over to his own high desk, pulled a blotting-pad out of the drawer, put a book or two on his desk, examined a note he had left on his pad, reminding him to "ring Whishaws first thing," and then spent a melancholy five minutes at the telephone.

"Will I have to call there this morning?" Stanley asked hopefully, when Turgis had rung off.

"No, they're sending somebody. Good job, too! We don't want you off half the morning. You'll stop in and do a bit of work, my son, for a change. Do you good."

"What work?" demanded Stanley, with scorn.

"By jingo, I like that!" cried Turgis. "There's plenty to do, if you'll only look for it instead of dodging it. You ask Smeethy, he'll find you some. Haven't you got enough? You can do some of mine, if you like. I've got more than I want."

Stanley changed the subject. "I say," he began, grinning, "you ought to have heard old Ma Cross on about that note. She let herself go all right, didn't she just! Oo, you ought to have heard her."

"What did she say?" Turgis inquired. But he did it very languidly, just to show that what amused small fry like Stanley might not amuse him.

At that moment, however, they heard the outer door opening, and the next moment the cause of all the trouble, Miss Matfield herself, walked in. She flung down a library book, her large handbag, and a pair of gloves on her table, then marched over to her hook and removed her coat and hat, while the other two waited in silence. They were both rather frightened of Miss Matfield. Even Mr. Smeeth and Mr. Dersingham himself were rather frightened of Miss Matfield.

"*Good* morning," she cried, looking from one to the other of them, and, as usual, putting a disturbingly ironical inflection into her tones. "Are we all very well this morning? Well, I'm not," and here, her voice changed. "O Lord! I thought I'd never get here. That bus journey gets fouler every morning, slower and slower and fouler and fouler." She sat down opposite her machine, but took no notice of it.

"You ought to try the Tube," Turgis suggested, not very boldly or hopefully. He had made this suggestion before. Everything had been said before, and they all knew it.

"Oh, I can't bear the Tube." Once more she seemed to annihilate the whole vast organisation.

It was now Stanley's turn. "Oo, I like it. I think it's exciting. I wish they had 'em where we live."

Miss Matfield was now busy rummaging in her handbag, and all she said was "Curse!" rather like a villain in an old-fashioned melodrama. It is only these strictly modern young ladies, who live their own life by pounding a typewriter all day and then retiring to tiny bed-sitting rooms in clubs, these beings who are supposed to be the inheritors of the earth, who can afford to talk like villains in old-fashioned melodramas. Miss Matfield, after a final and unsuccessful rummage, said "Curse!" again, then closed the bag with a sharp snap, seized her gloves, and marched them over to her coat. The other two said nothing, but looked at her. What they saw was a girl of twenty-seven or twenty-eight, or even twenty-nine, with dark bobbed hair, decided eyebrows, a smouldering eye, a jutting nose, a mouth that was a discontented crimson curve, and a firm round chin that was ready to double itself at any moment. She was not pretty, but she might have been handsome if somebody had kept telling her she was pretty. She was a trifle taller and bigger-

boned than the average girl of her class and type, with a good neck
and good shoulders, but her figure as a whole—and it was plain to
the view in her belted orange-coloured jumper, her short dark skirt,
and artfully silky stockings—was perhaps too top-heavy, too masterful in the bust for the flattened calves below, to please everybody.
(Including that distant and wistful connoisseur, Turgis, who by
making an effort at times was able to see her as a female figure and
not as a personality.) For the rest, her face, her voice, her manner,
all pointed to the conclusion that Lilian Matfield nursed some huge,
some overwhelming grievance against life, but though she gave
tongue to a thousand little grievances every day, she never mentioned the monster. But there it was, raging away, when she was
complaining or being bitter about everything; and there it was,
raging away more furiously than ever, when she was being bright
and jolly, which was not often, and hardly at all during business
hours.

"The char must have got my note," she announced on her return
to her table, "but I must say she doesn't seem to have done much
about it. Look at that. This is the foulest office I've ever worked in.
She never makes any attempt to clean it properly. All she's done now
is to walk round with a duster. And we've got to spend all day in
the beastly place, all filthy, just because she won't take the least
trouble. Well, I'm going to make a row about it."

"She got it all right," cried Stanley, delighted to be important and
to make a little trouble for somebody. "You ought to have heard
her. Didn't she go on!" And, in order to show exactly how she did
go on, he opened his mouth and his eyes still wider. But then he
stopped. The outer door had been opened, and feet were being wiped.
That meant that Mr. Smeeth had arrived, and Mr. Smeeth liked to
find Stanley busy during these first few minutes. So Stanley broke
off, and dashed at a bit of work he had saved for this moment.

"*Good* morning, everybody," said Mr. Smeeth, putting down his
hat and his folded newspaper, and then rubbing his hands. "It's getting a bit nippy in the mornings now, isn't it? Real autumn weather."

III

You could tell at once, by the way in which Mr. Smeeth entered
the office that his attitude towards Twigg & Dersingham was quite
different from that of his young colleagues. They came because they
had to come; even if they rushed in, there was still a faint air of
reluctance about them; and there was something in their demeanour
that suggested they knew quite well that they were shedding a part
of themselves, and that the most valuable part, leaving it behind,
somewhere near the street door, where it would wait for them to
pick it up again when the day's work was done. In short, Messrs.
Twigg & Dersingham had merely hired their services. But Mr.
Smeeth obviously thought of himself as a real factor of the entity
known as Twigg & Dersingham: he was their Mr. Smeeth. When
he entered the office, he did not dwindle, he grew; he was more
himself than he was in the street outside. Thus, he had a gratitude,
a zest, an eagerness, that could not be found in the others, resenting
as they did at heart the temporary loss of their larger and brighter
selves. They merely came to earn their money, more or less. Mr.
Smeeth came to work.

His appearance was deceptive. He looked what he ought to have
been, in the opinion of a few thousand hasty and foolish observers
of this life, and what he was not—a grey drudge. They could easily
see him as a drab ageing fellow for ever toiling away at figures of
no importance, as a creature of the little foggy City street, of crusted
ink-pots and dusty ledgers and day books, as a typical troglodyte of
this dingy and absurd civilisation. Angel Pavement and its kind, too
hot and airless in summer, too raw in winter, too wet in spring, and
too smoky and foggy in autumn, assisted by long hours of artificial
light, by hasty breakfasts and illusory lunches, by walks in boots
made of sodden cardboard and rides in germ-haunted buses, by fuss
all day and worry at night, had blanched the whole man, had
thinned his hair and turned it grey, wrinkled his forehead and the

space at each side of his short grey moustache, put eyeglasses at one end of his nose and slightly sharpened and reddened the other end and given him a prominent Adam's apple, drooping shoulders and a narrow chest, pains in his joints, a perpetual slight cough, and a hay-fevered look at least one week out of every ten. Nevertheless, he was not a grey drudge. He did not toil on hopelessly. On the contrary, his days at the office were filled with important and exciting events, all the more important and exciting because they were there in the light, for just beyond them, all round them, was the darkness in which lurked the one great fear, the fear that he might take part no longer in these events, that he might lose his job. Once he stopped being Twigg & Dersingham's cashier, what was he? He avoided the question by day, but sometimes at night, when he could not sleep, it came to him with all its force and dreadfully illuminated the darkness with little pictures of shabby and broken men, trudging round from office to office, haunting the Labour Exchanges and the newspaper rooms of Free Libraries, and gradually sinking into the workhouse and the gutter.

This fear only threw into brighter relief his present position. He had spent years making neat little columns of figures, entering up ledgers and then balancing them, but this was not drudgery to him. He was a man of figures. He could handle them with astonishing dexterity and certainty. In their small but perfected world, he moved with complete confidence and enjoyed himself. If you only took time and trouble enough, the figures would always work out and balance up, unlike life, which you could not possibly manipulate so that it would work out and balance up. Moreover, he loved the importance, the dignity, of his position. Thirty-five years had passed since he was an office boy, like Stanley, but a trifle smaller and younger; he was a boy from a poor home; and in those days a clerkship in the City still meant something, cashiers and chief clerks still wore silk hats, and to occupy a safe stool and receive your hundred and fifty a year was to have arrived. Mr. Smeeth was now a cashier himself and he was still enjoying his arrival. Somewhere at the back of his mind, that little office boy still lived, to mark the wonder of it. Going round to the bank, where he was known and respected and told it was a fine day or a wet day, was part of the routine of his work, but even now it was something more than that, something to be tasted by the mind and relished. The "Good-morning, Mr. Smeeth," of the bank cashiers at the counter still gave him a secret little thrill. And, unless the day had gone very badly indeed, he never concluded it, locking the ledger, the cash book, and the japanned box for petty cash, away in the safe and then filling and lighting his pipe, without being warmed by a feeling that he, Herbert Norman Smeeth, once a mere urchin, then office boy and junior clerk to Willoughby, Tyce & Bragg, then a clerk with the Imperial Trading Co., then for two War years a lance-corporal in the orderly room of the depot of the Middlesex Regiment, and now Twigg & Dersingham's cashier for the last ten years, had triumphantly arrived. It was, when you came to think of it—as he had once boldly ventured to point out to a friendly fellow boarder at Channel View, Eastbourne (they had stayed up rather late, after their wives had gone upstairs, to split a bottle of beer and exchange confidences)—quite a romance, in its way. And the fear that grew in the dark and came closer to the edge of it to whisper to him, that fear did not make it any less of a romance.

Mr. Smeeth now unlocked the safe, took out his books and the petty cashbox, looked over the correspondence and attended to that part meant for him, made a note that Brown & Gorstein, and North-Western and Trades Furnishing Co., and Nickman & Sons had not fulfilled their promises and sent cheques, dealt with the two small cheques that some other people had sent, gave Miss Matfield three letters to type, asked Turgis to telephone to Briggs Brothers and the London and North-Eastern Railway, delighted Stanley by giving him a message to take out, and, in short, plunged into the day's work and set Twigg & Dersingham in motion, even though Twigg had been quiet and unstirring for years in Streatham Cemetery, and the present Mr. Dersingham was only in motion yet on the District Railway, on his way to the office.

Stanley disappeared, as usual, like a shell from a gun, before Mr. Smeeth could possibly change his mind; Miss Matfield contemptuously rattled off her letters (the little *ping* of the typewriter bell sounding like a repeated ironical exclamation); Turgis talked down the telephone rather gloomily; and Mr. Smeeth made the neatest little figures, sometimes in pencil, sometimes in 'ink, and opened more and more books on his high desk. And for ten minutes or so, no word was spoken that had not immediate reference to the affairs of the office.

They were interrupted by the entrance of yet another employee of the firm. This was Goath, the senior traveller, whose job it was to visit all the cabinet-makers in London and the home counties and to persuade them to buy the veneers and inlays of Messrs. Twigg & Dersingham. He entered in the usual fashion, came trailing in, with one large flat foot feeling reluctantly for the new bit of ground and the other large flat foot equally reluctantly taking leave of the old bit of ground. He was smoking the usual cigarette, which left a faint and fading spurt of smoke vanishing happily into nothing behind him. He wore the same shapeless old overcoat, bagging monstrously at the pockets, and he wore it in the same way, that is, almost hanging off his drooping shoulders. The familiar dusty bowler hat was tilted, not cheerfully but depressingly, back from his furrowed and pimply forehead. He did what he always did. He turned upon the activities of the office a dull and knowing eye, an eye like a wet morning in February, just as damp and grey and hopeless, and at once these activities seemed to dwindle, to shrink from it. Mr. Dersingham had often said to Mr. Smeeth, and Mr. Smeeth had often said to Mr. Dersingham, that what Goath didn't know about selling inlays and veneers and the like was not worth knowing. But when you looked at him standing there, it seemed as if what he did know was also not worth knowing: it had had such a bad effect upon him. Everything about Goath was the same as

usual except his appearance at this hour, on this day, for Goath only
called at the office, his base of operations, on certain days and this
was not one of them.

"Busy are'n'cher," said Goath. It was not an inquiry. It was not
a greeting. It was a kind of gloomy sneer.

Mr. Smeeth laid down his pen. "Hello, what are you doing here?"

"Told to come," replied Goath. "Mr. Dersingham told me to come
in this morning—wanted to see me."

"Oh, did he?" It was obvious from Mr. Smeeth's tone that he did
not like the look of this, quite apart from not liking the look of
Mr. Goath, for which he can hardly be blamed.

"He did. Why he did, I don't know," Goath continued drearily,
"so don't ask me because I can't tell you. He simply said, 'Come
here first thing in the morning the day after to-morrow'—that's this
morning now—and I've come. And I've got here too early, into the
bargain."

"Mr. Dersingham didn't tell me anything about it," said Mr.
Smeeth, with the air of a man who liked to be told something
about it.

Goath gave a ferocious pull at the last half inch of his cigarette
and made a horrible hissing noise. "He wanted to make it a surprise
—a pleasant little surprise for you all—that's it." And as he said this
he tried to make Miss Matfield, who had just got up from her machine, accept a friendly leer, but all that it encountered was a stare
like a high wall with broken glass along the top.

Mr. Smeeth ran a finger backwards and forwards along his lower
lip, a trick of his in a reflective moment. Now that he had looked
at it a little longer, he plainly liked it still less. But then, after a short
pause, he brightened up. "Perhaps he's got some new stuff to show
you? Perhaps he wants to ask you something about it?"

"Haven't heard of anything new. I'd have heard. It always gets
round; everything gets round: 'No good showing us that,' they say.
'Show us some of this new stuff. That's what we want,' they tell you.
That's what they say, soon enough. And they don't know what they

want, not half their time, they don't. There's fellers making furniture now—*and* making money out of it—who don't know a good bit of wood from a bit of oilcloth. How they get away with it," Goath concluded mournfully, "beats me."

"That's right, Goath," said Mr. Smeeth. "It beats me, too. It's cheek that does it, really, that's my opinion—cheek, and a bit of luck. But honestly now, how are things going? You've been on the North London round this time, haven't you? How's it going? Better than last time, eh?"

"No," the other replied, with all the satisfaction of the confirmed pessimist. "Worse." He took off his bowler hat and for once examined it with the distaste it deserved. "Much worse."

Mr. Smeeth's face fell at once, and he made a tut-tut-tutting noise. "That's bad."

"Bloody bad, I call it, if Ethel here'll excuse me."

Miss Matfield turned on him at once. "My name is Matfield," she told him. "If you want to say 'bloody' you can, for all I care, but I'm not 'Ethel here' or Ethel anywhere else, and I don't intend to be."

"I'm crushed," said Goath, putting on a faint and entirely repulsive air of vocal dandyism, "quite crushed." But, being in his fifties, indeed, having apparently been in them almost longer than anybody else has ever been, and a hardened offender, he was not crushed.

"That's all right, Miss Matfield," Mr. Smeeth told her, uncomfortably. And he gave Goath a warning little frown.

"Well, as I was saying," Goath continued, "things are rotten. I've been in the trade thirty years, and I've never known 'em worse. If the price is right, then the stuff's wrong. And if the stuff's right, the price's wrong. And it's mostly the price. They want it cheap now, want it given away, no mistake about it, though the money they're getting for the finished article is more than ever. You look at what furniture's fetching now, retail, and then go and hear some of 'em talk—make you sick. It would—make you sick."

"I believe you," Mr. Smeeth assured him earnestly. Then he hesitated. "But—after all—somebody must be selling veneers, even if the inlays have gone out a bit. I mean, they've got to buy it from somebody, haven't they?"

"Well, whether they have or they haven't, all I can say is, they're not buying it from *me*. And I've been going to some of 'em for twenty years. Yes, I have, young feller," he added, for some unaccountable reason catching the eye of Turgis and talking to him quite sternly, "for twenty years. I was calling on some of them houses—Moses & Stott, f'r'instance—when you was a baby or nothing at all."

"It's a long time, isn't it, Mr. Goath?" replied Turgis, proud to be noticed by such terrific seniority and rather proud, too, to think that though he might not be anybody of much importance even now, at least he was more than a baby or nothing at all.

"You're right, young feller," said Mr. Goath with heavy patronage, "it *is* a long time. Hello! Is this him?"

But the person who had just opened the outer door and was now standing at the other side of the frosted glass partition was obviously not Mr. Dersingham, so Turgis, in the absence of Stanley, went out to discover the caller's business.

"Good-morning," said a brisk but ingratiating voice. "Any typewriter supplies? Ribbons, carbons, wax stencil sheets, brushes, rubbers?"

"Not this morning, thank you," said Turgis.

"Rubbers, brushes, stencil sheets, best quality papers, carbons? Ribbons?"

"No, not this morning."

"Well," said the voice, a little less brisk and ingratiating now, "if you should want any typewriter supplies any time, here's my card. Good-morning."

"It's surprising the number of those chaps we get round," said Mr. Smeeth, rather sadly, "all trying to sell the same bits of things. If you bought anything, what would it amount to? A shilling or two, that's all. It beats me how they make anything out of it. Smart, well-dressed chaps too, some of them. I don't know how they do it, I really don't."

"You'd think that chap was making thousands a year," said Turgis, speaking in an aggrieved tone, as if somehow his own shabbiness came into the question. "He's always all dressed up, spats and everything. He comes round here about once a fortnight and we've never bought anything from him yet."

"He's 'oping, that's what he's doing, just 'oping, like me," Mr. Goath remarked grimly. "Only it doesn't run to spats with me. I'd better try 'em, then I might get a big order or two. 'Here's old Goath with spats on,' they'd be saying up Bethnal Green way. 'We'll have to give him an order now.' P'r'aps they would. And then again, p'r'aps they wouldn't. Ah well—" and he yawned hugely and kept his eyes closed even after the yawn was done—"I dunno, I dunno, I dunno." He sent this rumbling away into the mournful distance. "Fact is, some of these mornings my inside's all wrong, dead rotten. Doctor says it's liver—that's all because I take a drop of whisky— but I say it's 'eart. And whether it's 'eart or liver, I'm going to sit down."

The room sank into a kind of mild sadness, rather like that of the atmosphere outside, where rich autumn had been bleached and deadened into a mere smokiness and gathering grey twilight, in which the occasional smell of a sodden dead leaf came like a remembrance of another world, as startling as a spent arrow from some battle still raging in the sun.

The faces of the three men—Mr. Smeeth's grey oval, Goath's purpled pulp, Turgis's tarnished youth—sank with the room, were half frozen into immobility, and seemed for a moment or two to be vacant, staring into nothing. Miss Matfield, who had risen from her table, saw it all for one queer second tangled with a whole jumble of deathly images: they were all under a spell, powerless to stir while the sky rained soot, dust poured from every crevice, and cobwebs wound about them. She wanted to scream. Instead, quite without thinking, she swept off her table a little brass box crammed with paper fasteners, and the clatter it made restored her to her normal senses.

"Sorry!" she cried harshly, stooping.

"And I should think so," said Goath.

"That should be Mr. Dersingham," said Mr. Smeeth, cocking an ear towards the approaching footsteps.

Mr. Dersingham put his head inside the general office. "Good morning, everybody," he cried. "You're here then, Goath. Are the letters in my room, Turgis? All right then, I'll just have a peep at them, and then I want to see you, Goath, and you too, Smeeth. I'll give you a shout when I'm ready. Stanley about? . . . All right—doesn't matter if he isn't. Send him in when he comes. I've forgotten to buy some cigarettes. I may want you in about five minutes, Miss Matfield. And if a man called Bronse rings up for me, don't put him through. Tell him I'm out. Oh—and I say—Smeeth, just make out a what-you-call-it, will you—a statement of outstanding accounts —you know, just rough and ready? I shall want that. Anything come this morning? It doesn't matter, though; you can tell me later."

"And if I know anything," Mr. Goath mumbled, when the head of Mr. Dersingham had been withdrawn, "that won't take you long, Smeeth—telling how much you've got in this morning."

"It won't," said Mr. Smeeth cheerlessly.

IV

Seated at his table, looking through the morning's letters, as he was now, Howard Brompont Dersingham might have been accepted as a typical specimen of the smart younger City man. At a first glance, he seemed the brother of all those smart younger City men who figure in advertisements, wearing unique collars, ties, suits, examining the infallible watch, or looking at a vision of less successful men who have never taken the particular correspondence course. He looked much too good for Angel Pavement, where business is merely business and a rather haphazard and dusty affair at that. He would not have seemed out of place in one of those sky-scrapers filled with terrifically efficient and successful operatives and administratives, in those regions where business is not at all a hap-hazard and dusty affair and takes on a solemn air, even a mystical tinge, as if it really explained the universe. It appeared absurd that such a fellow and all his concerns should be sandwiched between the *Kwik-Work Razor Blade Co.* and the *London and Counties Supply Stores.*

Another glance or two, however, would reveal the fact that he was only a rough, weakly unfinished sketch of the type. The hard-boiled eye, the chiselled nose, the severely controlled mouth, the masterful chin, all these were missing, and in their place were ordi-nary masculine English features, neither very good nor very bad, very strong nor very weak. Mr. Dersingham was a year or two under forty, tallish, fairly well-built but beginning to sag a little; his hair, which was now rapidly taking leave of him, was light brown, and his eyes light blue, and they neither sparkled nor pierced but just regarded the world blandly and amiably; he had retained one of those short pruned moustaches that crept under the noses of so many subalterns during the War; and he looked clean, healthy and kind, but a trifle flabby and none too intelligent. It was only after the War, during which he had assisted, with rapidly diminish-ing enthusiasm, one of the new battalions of the Royal Fusiliers, that he had joined his uncle at Twigg & Dersingham's. Before the War he had tried various things with no particular success, though he liked to suggest that the War had almost ruined his prospects. (In strict fact, it had improved them, for his uncle would never have taken him into the business, and left it to him when he died, if he had not taken pity on him as a returned hero.) It had been the intention of his parents to send Howard Bromport to Oxford or Cambridge, but they had lost money suddenly and Howard Bromport, no scholar, had failed to obtain a scholarship, so he had been compelled to stroll into business. In spirit, however, he went on to the university, and thus he became one of those men who are haunted by a lost Oxford or Cambridge career. These are not the scholars or the brilliant athletes who have been denied their chance of distinction, but simply the fellows who have been robbed of an opportunity of acquiring more striped ties, college blazers, and tobacco jars decorated with college coats-of-arms, in short, the fervent freshmen who never had the freshman nonsense knocked out of them. They it is who turn into the essential public school "old boys." Dersingham was a tremendous "old boy." He never missed a reunion, never failed to renew his stock of school ties. The public school spirit worked for ever in him. He was always ready to do the decent thing—and this was not hard, for he was really a decent, kindly soul, stupid though he might be—not for your sake, not for his own, but "for the sake of the old school." Strictly speaking, that school, Worrell (one of the second-class public schools, fatally second-class but terrifically public school) is not very old, but it has turned out so many fellows like Dersingham that it has acquired, by verbal association, the antiquity of Eton. Perhaps the shortest definition of Dersingham—and he himself would have asked for no other—was that he was an old Worrelian.

He did not play games very well and was not even a good judge of them, but he liked nothing better than solemn long discussions about them, in which minor pedantries could be thrashed out to the bitter end. Still, he played golf nearly every week-end, a little lawn tennis, and when the Charlatans had to turn out a third side at cricket, he sometimes turned out with them, as a possible slow bowler. (For four weeks every year he dropped the old Worrelian and wore the Charlatan tie.) He smoked considerable quantities of *Sahib Straight Cut Virginia* cigarettes, drank steadily but not too much for reasonable health and decency, delighted in detective and adventure stories, humorous anecdotes, jigging easy tunes, musical comedies, and good loud talk in which everybody agreed with everybody else except about things that could not matter very much to anybody, disliked literature, art and music, cranks and fanatics of every kind, most foreigners, anything or anybody really mean or cruel (when he could see the meanness and cruelty), and all the opinions that newspaper editors asked him to dislike. He had one or two real friends, a host of acquaintances, and a wife and two children whom he did not understand but of whom he was genuinely fond.

And now, after glancing through the letters, most of which were merely offers to sell him something he did not want, he sat on, stroking his ruddy cheek, looking puzzled and feeling puzzled. After a few minutes of this, he took a sheet of paper and carefully made some notes upon it. He did this all the more carefully because he felt that somehow by writing down what was already in his head, he was really grappling hard with the problem. Having frowned at these notes for another minute or so, he shook himself, set his face in hard business-like lines, reached out for a cigarette and then remembered that there were none, and rang the bell.

Miss Matfield appeared, or rather a notebook and pencil appeared, with a shadow of Miss Matfield in charge of them.

"I'm sorry, Miss Matfield," said Mr. Dersingham, with true old Worrelian courtesy. "I'd forgotten I'd told you to come in. I think I'd better see Mr. Smeeth and Mr. Goath first, and you can take down some letters afterwards. Will you ask them to come in—and then—er—just carry on with something, eh?"

"Very well," said Miss Matfield.

"Good!" said Mr. Dersingham. He never felt sure how he ought to handle Miss Matfield, quite apart from the fact that she seemed to him a rather formidable sort of girl. Her father, he knew, was a doctor, only a doctor in the country now, miles from anywhere, but he had once played scrum half with the Alsations. Ordering about the daughter of a scrum half of the Alsations, just as if she was some ordinary little tuppenny-ha'penny typist, was a ticklish business. And that was why Mr. Dersingham added "Good!": it meant that he knew all about the surgery and the Alsations.

"You fellows had better sit down," he said to Smeeth and Goath.

"We may be some time over this. That's right. Now wait a minute. Let me see, Goath, you're making—what? Two hundred, plus commission, that's it, isn't it? And you, Smeeth, what are you getting now? Three-fifteen, isn't it?"

Mr. Smeeth, troubled, admitted that it was. He had seen what was coming all along, had seen it for days and days and horrible nights.

"And what am I making?" Mr. Dersingham gave a short and embarrassed laugh. "Well, you can imagine for yourself, Goath, and you know well enough, Smeeth. Just lately I've been making nothing, not a bean. Just paying expenses, that's all."

"Er," Mr. Goath began with a pessimistic rumble.

"Just a minute. Don't think I'm beginning like this because I think you fellows are not earning all you make. I know you are. There's no question about that. But we've got to go into it all, haven't we?— got to see where we stand. I'll tell you in strict confidence that if it hadn't been for my wife having a little money of her own, I couldn't have carried on as long as I have done. You've only to look at the figures to see that for yourselves."

Here he stopped long enough to give Mr. Goath a chance of describing the state of the cabinet-making and wholesale furnishing trades. As we have heard him already, we do not want to hear him again. It is sufficient to say that his theme was that if the price was right, the stuff wasn't, and if the stuff was right, the price wasn't, and that this theme was elaborated by many variations in the minor key. And something in the nature of a second subject, repeated continually in the bass, was added by the statement that the speaker had been thirty years in the trade. To all of which Mr. Dersingham and Mr. Smeeth listened with gloomy attention.

"Well," said Mr. Dersingham, looking at his miserable little notes, "we'll have to go into all that later on. We're getting the wood from all the same people we dealt with in my uncle's time—and in some cases we're getting it on better terms than he did, isn't that so, Smeeth?"

"Ah, but there's more competition now, a lot more," said Goath dejectedly. "More and more competition, that's the way it is. Some of these people in the trade must be cutting it as fine as that"—and he waggled a very dirty thumb-nail—"to get orders. Nearly giving it away. Pay when you like, too. Foreigners," he added darkly, "that's what we're up against now, foreigners, coming over here to unload the stuff like mad. I met one coming out of Nickman's only yesterday morning, coming out as I was going in, and looking as pleased with himself as if he'd just backed a dozen winners. German he was. Speaking English as good as you and me, and dressed all up to the nines, but German all over him. And he had backed the winners all right, you bet he had. Got a pocket full of orders, he had. What's the good of having a war, I say, if it only means Germans coming over here and pinching trade right under our noses. Cor!— makes me sick—thirty years in the trade and tramping round week in and week out, and nothing doin' two-thirds o' the time, not a thing, and foreigners coming here with fur coats on—fur coats! Taking the bread right out of your mouth, that's all they're doing."

"Quite so, Goath," cried Mr. Dersingham. "I don't say I'm not with you there. But we can buy from Germany, just the same, and have been doing for some time, but it's beginning to look as if we can't compete. That's what I was going to talk about, to begin with. We shall have to try and do some cutting, too. It's our only chance. And the only way to do that—I think you fellows will agree, especially you, Smeeth—is to reduce expenses. The—er—what's-its-name —er—overhead charges are too big." Having found this word "overhead," so suggestive of big business, of keen men piling up fortunes in forty-two storey buildings, Mr. Dersingham clutched at it thankfully: it was a floating plank on the wide ocean of puzzle and muddle into which he had suddenly been plunged. "That's it. The first thing, the very first thing, we've got to do is to reduce the overheads in this business."

Mr. Smeeth tried to look very brisk and business-like, but he seemed greyer than ever and there was a mournful droop in his voice. "Well, we can try, sir. But it won't be easy. We're spending as little as we can, here in the office."

"Dash it all, Smeeth, I know that." Mr. Dersingham rubbed his cheek irritably. "But we shall have to spend less. I don't want to do it—I want to do the decent thing by everybody here—but you see how it is, don't you? Must cut something down. Now look here, to begin with, there's Turgis. What's he getting? A hundred and seventy-five, isn't he? And Miss Matfield? We started her at three pounds a week, didn't we?"

"That's right, Mr. Dersingham. It was less than she'd been getting before, but she said she'd start at that with us, and then we'd see about giving her a rise when she'd settled down with us. She's a very capable girl, very capable, and very intelligent, too, much better than the last we had; no comparison at all."

"And Turgis? What about him?"

"I can't really grumble, sir," replied Mr. Smeeth. "He does his best. He's a bit careless sometimes, I'll admit, and he's not to be trusted far with figures yet—you remember the terrible mess he made of the books when I was on my holidays this year?—but as these boys go nowadays, he's as good as the next. He doesn't take the interest in his work and in the firm that I did when I was his age, but then they don't these days, and that's all you can say about it. Miss Matfield's just the same, for that matter. She does her work all right, but she's not *interested*, doesn't think of herself, you might say, as one of the firm, but just comes in the morning, does what she's told to do, and then goes in the evening."

"Thinking about young men, that's what they are, all these type-writers," said Goath. "Young men and dancing and going to the pickshers, that's what's running in their 'eads, and you can't expect anything else of 'em, not in *my* opinion. Cheeky with it, they are, too."

"Well, I'm sorry, Smeeth, I really am, but I don't see anything else for it. One of them will have to go, either Turgis or Miss Matfield. We can't spare you, Smeeth——"

"Thank you, sir." And as he said it—quite simply and not with any touch of irony—Mr. Smeeth looked still greyer. Indeed, he shook a little.

"No question of it at all," Mr. Dersingham continued heartily, "absolutely none. But we'll have to get rid of one of these two and divide the work between us. I'll do something. I'll begin to type my own letters. I'll have a good shot at it anyhow. It's a question now whether you'd rather keep Turgis and let him do some of the letters or keep Miss Matfield and divide his work between the two of you. Stanley might do a bit more, too, if he's got any sense. In any case, we must have a boy, so there's no question of getting rid of him. Now what d'you think, Smeeth? Turgis or Miss Matfield? Nothing much in it, I know, but you ought to decide. You'll have most of the extra work yourself, I expect, when it gets down to brass tacks, though, mind you, I'm going to do a lot more myself, if I've time, in the office."

Mr. Smeeth did not feel quite so bad as he had felt a minute ago, but he felt bad enough. He tried to give all his attention to the immediate problem, which was serious enough for him, for he knew very well that it was he who would have to do most of the extra work, but, try as he would, his mind wandered darkly. He could not pretend to himself now that such pitiful economies as these could stop the rot. He had seen it coming for months. The firm, his position, his very living, they were all crumbling away together. The next thing would be that he would have to accept a cut in his salary. And the next thing after that would be finding himself outside, in Angel Pavement, with a hat on his head and no salary, no office, nothing. He hesitated, stammering something, rather painfully.

"I didn't want to spring it on you," said Mr. Dersingham, "and I suppose you'd really like a day or two to think it over."

"Wouldn't think a minute if I was you," said Mr. Goath. "Get rid of the girl, right away, without 'esitation. They never should have started girls in the City. The place has never been right since. Powderin' noses! Cups o' tea! You don't know where y'are."

"I would like to think it over, Mr. Dersingham," Mr. Smeeth told him slowly. "I don't want to get rid of the wrong one."

"I'd like to get it settled to-day while we're at it, but you think it over between now and five o'clock, and then we'll have another talk about it. All right then." And Mr. Dersingham examined his notes again, and then looked very severe. "The next thing is this question of what-d'you-call-it—these rotters who won't pay up. You've made out a statement, have you?"

But there was a knock at the door, and Stanley sidled in, a card in his hand. "Somebody wants to see you, sir."

"I'm busy. Who is it? Shut the door." He examined the card. "Never heard of this chap. Look at this, Goath. Anybody you know? What does he want?"

"Wanted to speak to you, sir," replied Stanley, looking very mysterious and important, with a hint of the "shadderer" in his manner. "Very important. That's what he said."

"I'll bet he did," said Mr. Dersingham, with a grin at the other two. "Probably wants to sell me some ridiculous office gadget. If he did, though, he'd probably have something about it on his card. This is a private card. Golspie, Golspie? No, I don't know him. Look here, Stanley, just tell him I'm having a discussion—no, a thingumty—a conference, just now, but if it's something really important, not trying to sell me typewriters and files and muck, I'll see him soon. He can either call again or he can wait there. Tell him that."

Mr. Golspie decided to wait.

v

He was still waiting there, sitting in the little chair beside the door and behind the partition, ten minutes later. Sometimes, Stanley and Turgis and Miss Matfield heard him stir and clear his throat. They also caught the fragrance of the excellent cigar he was smoking. Its fumes seemed to turn the office into a dull little box and their duties into the most mechanical and trivial tasks. There was something rich and adventurous about that drifting luxuriant smoke. It unsettled them.

"Who is he?" Turgis whispered. "What's he like?"

Stanley crept nearer and curved a hand round his mouth. "He's biggish and broad and got a big moustache," he whispered in reply. "D'you know what I bet he is?"

"No, I give it up."

"Inspector from Scotland Yard."

"You've got 'em on the brain, you little chump," said Turgis. "Course he isn't."

"Well, I'll betcher. He looks just like one. You go and have a look at him."

But Turgis was saved from the necessity, for the visitor suddenly marched into the office itself.

"Where's that boy?" he demanded. "Oh, look here, just go in again and tell Mr. What's-it ——"

"Mr. Dersingham, sir," said Stanley brightly, proud to serve Scotland Yard or anybody who suggested it.

"Mr. Dersingham. Tell him I can't wait much longer—I'm not used to hanging about like this—and that if I go, *I go*, for good and all, and then he'll be sorry. D'you get that? All right then, trot off and speak out. Wait a minute, though. He doesn't know what I want, doesn't know who I am, so I'd better show him I'm not going to waste his time." He took something out of the small despatch case he was carrying, and the others recognised it at once as a sample book of veneers and inlays, a few square inches of each specimen wood, thin as cardboard, being fastened to each stout page. "Now give him this, tell him to look it over, and say that's what I've come to talk about. D'you understand?"

Having thus despatched the boy, Mr. Golspie stood there at ease, his feet wide apart, his big chest thrown out, coolly enjoying his cigar. It was one of the strictest rules of the place that casual callers were not allowed beyond the partition, and Turgis ought to have ordered him out of the office at once. But somehow Turgis felt that this was not a man to be ordered out of the office by him.

"Not much of a place this, I must say," Mr. Golspie observed, looking about him, then addressing Turgis. "But they keep you pretty busy, eh?"

"Well, they do and they don't," Turgis mumbled. "I mean to say, sometimes we're busy and sometimes we're not. It all depends, you see."

"I don't see, but I'll take your word for it. Must be a dark hole, this, a bit later on, when you get the fogs. Too dark for my taste. Not enough air either. I like plenty of air, though God knows it's not worth having when you get it, in this neighbourhood. What do they call this street? Angel Pavement, isn't it? That's a dam' queer name for a street, though I've known queerer names in my time. How did it get it, d'you know?"

Turgis admitted that he didn't.

"Didn't suppose you would," the stranger told him. "Perhaps this young lady knows. They know everything nowadays."

Miss Matfield looked up. "No, I don't know," she replied, with a hint of distaste in her tone. Then she bent her eyes to her work again. "And I don't care."

"No, you don't care," said Mr. Golspie, bluff, hearty, and completely unabashed. "I don't suppose you care tuppence about the whole concern. Why should you, anyhow? I wouldn't, if I were a good-lookin' girl, not tuppence."

Miss Matfield looked up again, this time wearily, wrinkling various parts of her face. Then she brought to bear upon this intruder the full force of her contemptuous gaze, which would instantly have routed Turgis, Mr. Smeeth, or Mr. Dersingham, and a great many other people of her acquaintance. On this objectionable man it had no effect at all. He stared hard at her, and then smiled, or rather grinned broadly. Defeated by such complete insensitiveness, Miss Matfield made a gesture of annoyance, and then went on with her work, without looking up again.

"Now what the devil's that boy doing in there!" Mr. Golspie boomed to Turgis. "You'd better go and see if they've killed him. You needn't, though. He's coming."

He came, followed by Mr. Smeeth, who said: "I'm sorry you've been kept waiting. Mr. Dersingham can see you now."

They waited until they heard the door close behind him before any of them spoke again.

"What does he want, Mr. Smeeth?" asked Turgis.

"I don't know what he wants exactly, Turgis," Mr. Smeeth replied. "I take it he wants to sell us some stuff. He sent some good samples in; really first-class Mr. Dersingham and Goath said it was. I don't pretend to know much about it. But I expect the price will put it out of the question."

"He's a funny sort of chap, isn't he?"

"A loathsome brute!" cried Miss Matfield from her machine. "Imagine working for a man like that! Ghastly!"

Mr. Smeeth regarded her thoughtfully, and then, after telling Stanley to get on with his work and if he hadn't any work to go and find some, he turned to regard Turgis equally thoughtfully. One of them had to go. Should he put it to them now? Miss Matfield would probably not care very much—it was hard to imagine her caring, though she had been anxious enough to get the job—whereas Turgis, who had an oldish poverty-stricken father somewhere up in the Midlands, lived in lodgings here in London, and was lucky if he had five pounds in all the world, would be very hard hit and would not easily find another job. It would have to be Miss Matfield. Yet Miss Matfield, who had a good education behind her, was the more promising worker of the two, and would take over some of Turgis's work and be glad to do it. Well, well, this wanted a bit more thinking about, and, in the meantime, there were a hundred and one little things to be done.

The three in Mr. Dersingham's room remained there for the next half hour, giving no sign of their existence beyond an occasional rumble of voices. At the end of that time, the door opened, louder voices and a fresh reek of cigars invaded the general office, and Mr. Dersingham called out: "I say, Smeeth, we're all going out. Shan't be back before lunch. I'll give you a ring if I'm going to be any later." And then they were gone, leaving Mr. Smeeth and Turgis staring at one another. The various lunch hours, beginning with Stanley's (he went to the *Pavement Dining Rooms* and had sausage and mash, after all), came and went, the afternoon wore on, and still there was no message from Mr. Dersingham or Goath. The crescendo of the last hour of the day, when Stanley turned berserk with the copying press and Turgis snarled at the telephone and then yelled into it, had begun when the message actually did arrive.

"Hello! Is that you, ol' man—I mean, Smeeth? Dersingham speakin'." Even through the telephone, a strangeness, a certain richness, could be remarked in Mr. Dersingham's voice. He seemed quite excited.

"Smeeth speaking, Mr. Dersingham."

"Good, very good. Well, look here, Smeeth, I shan't be back this afternoon. Nothing important, is there? You just carry on then—and then—er—you know, finish off, sign anything that wants signing, then finish off, lock up, go home."

"That'll be all right, Mr. Dersingham. There's nothing very important. But what about that business we talked about this morning? Yes, Turgis and Miss Matfield?"

"All done with," and the telephone seemed to chuckle. "No need to bother about that, not the slightest. Turgis stays. Miss Matfield stays. D'you know, Smeeth, that that girl's father played scrum half with the Alsations? He did—same fella, Matfield. No, she stays. Both stay."

"I'm very glad, sir," said Mr. Smeeth, who really was glad, though perhaps he was mostly puzzled. There seemed to be no sense in all this.

"Explain ev'rything in the morning, Smeeth," continued the voice of Mr. Dersingham. "Only person who goes is Goath."

"What! I didn't catch that, sir."

"Goath, Goath. We've done with him. Goath's finished with. Don't want to see him again. If he comes for his money, pay him at once, d'you understand, Smeeth, at once, up to end of month. Then tell him—to clear—right out, right out."

"But—but what's happened, Mr. Dersingham? I don't understand."

"Explain ev'rything in the morning. But you understand about Goath, eh? Pay the blighter off if he comes, finish with him. You understand that, eh? Righto. Carry on then, ol' man."

Bewildered, Mr. Smeeth laid down the receiver and walked over to his desk. He had hardly time to collect his thoughts and to begin to wonder whether he ought to say something to the others, when the door flew open, almost like a vertical trap-door, to shoot into the middle of the office, where it suddenly stopped dead, the figure of a man. It was Goath. His ancient overcoat was still hanging from his shoulders as if it hardly belonged to him, but, on the other hand, his bowler hat, instead of being at the back of his head, was now tilted forward, giving him an unusual and almost sinister look. His face was purpler than ever; his eyes were glaring; and his mouth was opening and shutting, as if he were an indignant fish. To say of Goath that he had been drinking was to say nothing, for he was obviously always drinking, but this time he had plainly had more than usual or had been mixing his liquors. And his appearance, his manner, everything about him, was so extraordinary that everybody in the office stopped work at once to look at him.

"Smeeth," the apparition cried in a thick, hoarse voice, "you pay me my money, d'y'ear. Sala'y to end of mun' an' commission to yesserday. I've finished wi' Twigg an' Dersi'am, finished, finished—com-pletely." Here he produced a magnificent cutting gesture that nearly upset his balance. "I've finished wi' them. They finished wi' me. All over."

"Mr. Dersingham's just told me, Goath," said Mr. Smeeth, looking at him in astonishment. "And I'll give you your money if you really want it now——"

"Mus' 'ave it. Finished—com-pletely, com-pletely."

"But what's happened?"

"I'll tell you what's 'appened," replied Goath with tremendous solemnity, lowering his head so far that it looked as if his hat would fall off. "Go—Golspie, tha's wha's 'appened—Gol-sss-pie."

"Who's that? Do you mean——"

"Feller came s'mornin'."

"But what about him?"

Goath now threw back his head and looked defiant. "Mister Wha'sit bloody Gol-spie," he announced with great deliberation, "tha's the feller. An' he's a—devil. I tol' him, I tol' him 'Thirry years—thirry *years*—in the trade, tha's me.' An' wha' did he say to tha'? Wha' did he bloody well say?"

"Here, old man, steady, steady," Mr. Smeeth cautioned him.

"Don't mind me," said Miss Matfield coolly. "Go on, Mr. Goath. What did he say? Tell us all about it."

"Never mind wha' he said," cried Goath aggressively, glaring round at them all. "Does'n' ma'er wha' *'e* said. Who is 'e? Where's 'e come from? With 'is drinks an' cigars! All ri'—very nice—drinks an' cigars—but anybody can buy drinks an' cigars, an' *do* buy drinks an' cigar *and* big lunches. It's wha' *I* say—thirry years, don' forge' tha', thirry years—wha' *I* say tha' ma'ers. An' I say—wha's the game?—where's 'e get this stuff from?—who tol' 'im to come here?"

"Yes, but what's this chap doing?" Mr. Smeeth asked. "That's what I want to know."

"Bullyin' an' twistin', tha's wha' 'e's doin'," replied Goath promptly, taking off his hat. "An' he's got Mr. Dersi'am like tha', jus' like tha'." And, to the intense delight of Stanley, one hand fell heavily on the hat. "It's jus' like wha's it—y'know—wha's it, wha's it?" And to show what he did mean, Goath glared harder than ever and then wiggled his fingers in front of his eyes, directing them at Miss Matfield, who let out a sudden peal of laughter.

"Hypnotism," suggested Turgis.

"Tha's ri', boy, tha's ri'. Hyp-no-tism. Jus' like tha'. But not me," he continued, speaking very slowly and more distinctly now, "not me. I tell 'em what I think. Begins tellin' me I oughter to do this an' oughter do that, an' I won't 'ave it. I know the trade an' I speak my mind. An' another thing. If I don't like a feller, I don't like 'im, and that finishes it. That feller comes 'ere, very well, I don't, I finish."

"Is he coming here?" demanded Mr. Smeeth.

"You'll see, you'll see, Smeeth. I say no more. Finish. You just let me 'ave my money."

"All right, Goath," said Mr. Smeeth, who had been jotting down some figures for the last minute or two. "I won't keep you a minute. Then you'd better get straight home, old man——"

"Have no 'ome," Goath announced. "Lodgings." He lurched up to the desk, which was high enough for him to rest his elbows on the edge of it. "That's the way, Smeeth, a nice lil cheque. I tell you, Smeeth, ol' man, you've always been decent to me, an' now I'm sorry for you."

"Well, I'm sorry too, Goath, and I must say I don't understand what's happening at all. Mr. Dersingham rang up and told me you were leaving. Are you sure it's not all a mistake? I mean, you chaps seem to have—er—had rather a lot to-day, you know, and in the morning you might all feel different about it."

With an effort Goath stood erect, and then held out his hand to Mr. Smeeth. "No, no, I've finished. Shake hands, ol' man. See you again sometime. Meet some day—still in the trade, y'know, can't change after thirty years—have to stick to the trade. Goo'-bye, all." And Goath, after removing the dent from his hat with one fierce jab, crammed it on the back of his head and, with a final wave of the hand, departed.

"Well, this beats me," Mr. Smeeth confessed. "I can't make head or tail of it, I really can't."

"It looks as if that other chap is taking his place, don't you think?" said Turgis. "Though I must say he didn't look as if he wanted that sort of job. I mean, he looked too smart and bossy."

"No, I don't think that's it," Mr. Smeeth told him.

"Thank the Lord, we've seen the last of Mr. Goath, anyhow!" cried Miss Matfield fervently. "I loathed the sight of him, he always looked so dirty and dilapidated. I'm sure he was a rotten man to have going round calling on people."

"But what if the other chap comes?" said Turgis, grinning. "You didn't like the look of him, did you?"

"I should think not! I never thought of that." She groaned as she stuck another sheet of paper into the typewriter. "What a life!"

"That's right, let's get finished. Turgis, Stanley, come on, get a move on," said Mr. Smeeth sharply. And down below, in Angel Pavement, now a deep narrow pool of darkness sharply spangled with electric lights, you could hear a little host of other people finishing for the night, a final clatter of typewriters, a banging of doors, the hooting of homing cars, the sound of footsteps hurrying up the street towards liberty.

Chapter Two

MR. SMEETH IS REASSURED

I

Mr. Smeeth, still puzzling and pondering over the sullen departure of Goath and the arrival of this mysterious Mr. Golspie, put his books away for the night, and, as his habit was, pulled out his pipe and tobacco pouch. The others had gone, and the office was in darkness except for the solitary light above his desk. His pouch, one of those oilskin affairs, was nearly empty, and he had to take out the last crumbs in order to get a decent pipeful. He had just lit up, blown out the first few delicious clouds, and switched off his light, when the telephone rang sharply, urgently, in the gloom. As he groped back to the receiver, he felt almost frightened. What was coming now? He found himself wishing he had gone earlier, just a little earlier, but nevertheless he had not the strength of mind to ignore the telephone's peremptory challenge.

"Hello?" he began.

A huge voice cut him short, came roaring out of the dark. "Look 'ere, Charlie, what abart makin' it fifty? Carm on, yer gotter do it, ol' son, yer can't get away from it ——"

"Wait a moment," Mr. Smeeth told him. "This is Twigg and Dersingham. Who do you ——"

"I know, *I know*," the voice continued, smashing its way across London and entirely ignoring Mr. Smeeth's protest. "I know wotcher goin' to say, but it'll 'ave to be fifty this time. I been talkin' ter Tommy Rawson s'afternoon, an' 'e says yer'll be lucky if yer get it at that. 'Tell Charlie from me,' 'e says, ' 'e won't touch it under fifty an' 'e'll be lucky if 'e gets it at that.' Tommy's own words them. An' I agree, *I agree.* Nar then, what d'yer say, Charlie?"

"You've got the wrong number," cried Mr. Smeeth.

"What's that? I want Mr. 'Iggins."

"There's no Mr. Higgins here. This is Twigg and Dersingham."

"Wrong number again," said the voice, disgusted. "Ring off—for gord's sake."

Mr. Smeeth, relieved, rang off with pleasure, and departed, chuckling a little. Who was Charlie, and what was it he had to pay fifty for, and why did Tommy Rawson think he'd be lucky if he got it? "Might easily be crooks," he concluded, with a little romantic thrill, worthy of Stanley himself, and then smiled at himself. More likely to be fellows buying second-hand cars, loads of scrap iron, or something like that. At the bottom of the stairs, he ran into the tall fellow with the broad-brimmed hat, who was just coming out of his *Kwik-Work Razor Blade* place.

The tall man nodded. "Turning colder."

"Just a bit," replied Mr. Smeeth heartily. These little encounters and recognitions pleased him, making him feel that he was somebody. "Not so bad, though, for the time of year."

"That's right. Business good?"

"So-so. Not so good as it might be." And then Mr. Smeeth let the tall man stride away down Angel Pavement, for he remembered that he was out of tobacco and so turned into the neighbouring shop, the one occupied by T. Benenden.

Mr. Smeeth was one of T. Benenden's regular customers, a patron (perhaps the only one) of T. Benenden's Own Mixture (*Cool Sweet Smoking*). "No," he liked to tell some fellow pipe-smoker, "I don't fancy your ounce-packet stuff. I like my tobacco freshly mixed, y'know, and so I always get it from a little shop near the office. It's the chap's own mixture and so it's always fresh. Oh, fine stuff!—you try a pipeful—and very reasonable. Been getting it for years now. And the chap I get it from is a bit of a character in his way." Saying this made Mr. Smeeth feel that he was a connoisseur of both tobacco and human nature, and it gave an added flavour to his pipe, which could do with it after being charged with nothing but T. Benenden's own mixture. It was hardly possible that he was right about the tobacco being "freshly mixed," for though mixed—and well mixed—it may have been, it could not come from T. Benenden's little shop, with its hundreds of dusty dummy packets, its row of battered tin canisters, its dilapidated weight scales, its dirty counter, its solitary wheezing gas mantle, its cobwebs and dark corners, and still be fresh. On the other hand, he was certainly right when he described T. Benenden himself as a bit of a character in his way.

T. Benenden's way was that of the philosophical financier turned shopkeeper. He was an oldish man who wore thick glasses (which only magnified eyes that protruded far enough without their help), a straggling pepper-and-salt beard, one of those old-fashioned single high collars and a starched front, and no tie. When Mr. Smeeth first visited the shop, years ago, he was at once startled and amused by this absence of tie, jumping to the conclusion that the man had forgotten his tie. Now, he would have been far more startled to see Benenden *with* a tie. He had often been tempted to ask the chap why he wore these formal collars and fronts and yet no tie, but somehow he had never dared. Benenden himself, though he was ready to talk on many subjects, never mentioned ties. Either he deliberately ignored them or he had never noticed the part these things were now playing in the world, simply did not understand about ties. What he did like to talk about, perhaps because his shop was in the City, was finance, a sort of Arabian Nights finance. He sat there behind his counter, steadily smoking his stock away, and peered at old copies of financial periodicals or the City news of ordinary papers, and out of this reading, and the bits of gossip he heard, and the grandiose muddle of his own mind, he concocted the most astonishing talk. It was difficult to buy an ounce of tobacco from him without his making you feel that the pair of you had just missed a fortune.

As soon as he recognised Mr. Smeeth, T. Benenden very deliberately pulled down his scales and then placed on the counter the particular dirty old canister set apart for his own mixture. "The usual, I suppose, Mr. Smeeth?" he said, picking up the pouch and then smoothing it out on the counter. "I saw your chief this morning, the young fellow—Mr. Dersingham. Came in for some *Sahibs*. Got somebody with him too, new to me, well set up gentleman, with a good cigar in his mouth, a very good cigar. You'll know who I mean?"

"He called this morning at the office," said Mr. Smeeth.

"Well, I didn't say anything," Benenden continued, very seriously as he weighed out the tobacco. "It's not my business to say anything. I *don't* say anything. But I keep my eyes open. And I said to myself, the minute they went out, 'This looks to me as if Twigg and Dersingham's are moving on a bit. This has the look of a merging job, or a syndicate job, or a trust job. And,' I said, 'if Mr. Smeeth does happen to come in for the usual, I'll put it straight to him. It's no concern of mine, but he'll tell *me*. I'll test my judgment,' I said."

"Sorry, Mr. Benenden," said Mr. Smeeth, smiling at him, "but I've nothing to tell you. I don't rightly know what's happening, but you can depend on it, it's nothing in that line."

"Then," cried Benenden, quite passionately, rolling up the pouch and then slapping it down on the counter, "you're wrong. I don't mean you, Mr. Smeeth, I mean the firm. That's the way things are going all the time now, Mr. Smeeth, big combinations—merging away till you don't know where you are—and sweeping the deck, until—dear me—there isn't a picking, not a crumb, left. You see what I mean? Now there's a bit here in one of the papers—I was just reading it when you came in—and I don't suppose you've seen it. Just a minute and I'll find it. Now here it is. Suppose, Mr. Smeeth, just suppose," and here T. Benenden leaned across the counter and his eyes seemed colossal, "I'd come to you a fortnight since, a week since, and said to you, 'What about picking up a bit on South Coast Laundries?'—what would you have said?"

"I'd have said it takes me all my time to pay my own laundry bill," Mr. Smeeth replied, much amused by this retort of his.

T. Benenden made a slight gesture of contempt to show that this was mere trifling. Then he looked very solemn, very impressive. "You'd have said, 'I can't be bothered with South Coast Laundries. I'm not touching 'em—don't want 'em—take your South Coast Laundries away. And you'd have been right—as far as you could see, *then*. But what happens, what happens? Read your paper. It's there, under my very 'and. Along comes a big merger—a bit of syndicate and trust work—and up they go, right up to the top—bang! Now—you see—you can't touch 'em. And there's a feller here—you can see it in the paper—who's been clearing anything out of it—a hundred thousand, two hundred thousand—a clean sweep, made for life. And he's not the only one, not a bit of it! And we sit here, pretending to laugh at South Coast Laundries or whatever it might be, and what are we doing? We're missing it, that's what we're doing, we're missing it." Here, a dramatic pause.

"And if your Mr. Dersingham isn't careful," Benenden concluded, still impressive even if a trifle vague now, "*he's* going to miss it. He wants to keep his eyes open. There's one or two bits in this paper I'd like to show him. Let's see, what was it you gave me? Half a crown, wasn't it? That's right then—one and six change. And good-night to *you*, Mr. Smeeth." And T. Benenden, after stooping down to the tiny gas-jet to relight his pipe, retired to his corner to ruminate.

Mr. Smeeth made his way to Moorgate, where, as usual, he bought an evening paper and then climbed to the upper deck of a tram. There, when he was not being bumped by the conductor, jostled by outgoing and incoming passengers, thrown back or hurled forward by the tram itself, an irritable and only half tamed brute, he stared at the jogging print and tried to acquaint himself with the latest and most important news of the day. An excitable column and a half told him that a young musical comedy actress, whom he had never seen and had no particular desire to see, had got engaged, that it had been quite a romance, that she was very very happy and not sure yet whether she would leave the stage or not. Mr. Smeeth, not caring whether she left the stage or dropped dead on it, turned to another column. This discussed the problem of careers for married women, a problem that had been left absolutely untouched since the morning papers came out, ten hours before. It did not interest Mr. Smeeth, so he tried another column. This reported an action for divorce, in which it appeared that the petitioning wife had only been allowed a hundred and fifty pounds a year on which to dress herself. The judge had said that this seemed to him—a mere bachelor (laughter)—an adequate allowance, but the paper had collected the opinions of well-known society hostesses, who all said it was not adequate. Mr. Smeeth, who found he could not share the editor's passionate interest in this topic, now tried another page, which promptly informed him that evening gowns would certainly be longer this winter, and then went on to tell him, to the tune of three solid columns, that the modern business girl (with her latch-key) had quite a different attitude towards marriage and therefore must not be confused with her grandmother (Victorian, with no latch-key). Mr. Smeeth, feeling sure that he had read all this before, passed on, and arrived at the sports page, where the prospects of certain women golfers were discussed at considerable length. Never having set eyes on any of these Amazons and not being interested in golf, Mr. Smeeth next tried the gossip columns. The tram was swaying now and the print fairly dancing, so that it was at the cost of some eye-strain and a slight headache that he learned from these paragraphs that Lord Winthrop's brother, who was over six feet, intended to spend the winter in the West Indies, that the youngest son of Lady Nether Stowey could not only be seen very frequently at the Blue Pigeon Restaurant but was also renowned for the way in which he painted fans, that the member for the Tewborough Division, who must not be mistaken for Sir Adrian Putter, now in Egypt, had perhaps the best collection of teapots of any man in the House, and that he must not imagine, as so many people did, that Chingley Manor, where the fire had just occurred, was the Chingley Manor mentioned by Disraeli, for it was not, and the paragraphist, who seemed to go about a great deal, knew them both well. Indeed, he and his editor seemed to know all about everybody and everything, except Mr. Smeeth and all the other staring men on the tram, and the people they knew, and all their concerns and all the things in which they were interested. Nevertheless, Mr. Smeeth reflected, as he carefully folded the paper, there were a lot of things in it that his wife would like to read. They seemed to have stopped writing penny papers for men.

Mr. Smeeth occupied a six-roomed house (with bath) in a street full of six-roomed houses (with baths), in that part of Stoke Newington that lies between the High Street and Clissold Park—to be precise, at the postal address: 17, Chaucer Road, N. 16. Why the late Victorian speculative builder had fastened on Chaucer is a mystery, unless he had come to the conclusion that the Canterbury Pilgrims, who have never vanished from this island, might come to rest in the twentieth century behind his brick walls. But there it was, Chaucer Road, and Mr. Smeeth had once tried his hand at Chaucer, but what with one thing and another, the queer spelling and all that, had not made much of him. All that he remembered now was that Chaucer had called birds "Smally foulies," and to this day, when he was in a waggish mood, Mr. Smeeth liked to bring in "smally foulies," only to be countered with "You and your 'smelly foulies!'" from a delighted Mrs. Smeeth. Towards 17, Chaucer Road, Mr. Smeeth now stepped out, swinging his folded newspaper, through the alternating lamplight and gloom, the crisping air, of the autumn evening. Dinner, with a cup of tea to follow, awaited him, for during the week, Mr. Smeeth, like a wise man, preferred to dine when work was done for the day.

II

"Cut some off for George," said Mrs. Smeeth, "and I'll keep it warm for him. He's going to be late again. You're a bit late yourself tonight, Dad."

"I know. We've had a funny day to-day," replied Mr. Smeeth, but for the time being he did not pursue the subject. He was busy carv-

ing, and though it was only cold mutton he was carving, he liked
to give it all of his attention.

"Now then, Edna," cried Mrs. Smeeth to her daughter, "don't sit
there dreaming. Pass the potatoes and the greens—careful, they're
hot. And the mint sauce. Oh, I forgot it. Run and get it, that's a good
girl. All right, don't bother yourself. I can be there and back before
you've got your wits together."

Mr. Smeeth looked up from his carving and eyed Edna severely.
"Why didn't you go and get it when your mother told you. Letting
her do everything."

His daughter pulled down her mouth and wriggled a little. "I'd
have gone," she said, in a whining tone. "Didn't give me time, that's
all."

Mr. Smeeth grunted impatiently. Edna annoyed him these days.
He had been very fond of her when she was a child—and, for that
matter, he was still fond of her—but now she had arrived at what
seemed to him a very silly awkward age. She had a way of acting,
of looking, of talking, all acquired fairly recently, that irritated him.
An outsider might have come to the conclusion that Edna looked
like a slightly soiled and cheapened elf. She was between seventeen
and eighteen, a smallish girl, thin about the neck and shoulders but
with sturdy legs. She had a broad snub nose, a little round mouth that
was nearly always open, and greyish-greenish-blueish eyes set rather
wide apart; and scores of faces exactly like hers, pert, pretty-ish and
under-nourished, may be seen within a stone's-throw of any picture
theatre any evening in any large town. She had left school as soon as
she could, and had wandered in and out of various jobs, the latest
and steadiest of them being one as assistant in a big draper's Finsbury
Park way. At home now, being neither child nor an adult, neither
dependent nor independent, she was at her worst; languid and complaining, shrill and resentful, or sullen and tearful; she would not
eat properly; she did not want to help her mother, to do a bit of
washing-up, to tidy her room; and it was only when one of her silly
little friends called, when she was going out, that she suddenly

sprang into a vivid personal life of her own, became eager and viva-
cious. This contrast, as sharp as a sword, sometimes angered, sometimes saddened her father, who could not imagine how his home,
for which he saw himself for ever planning and working, appeared
in the eyes of fretful, secretive and ambitious adolescence. These
changes in Edna annoyed and worried him far more than they did
Mrs. Smeeth, who only took offence when she had a solid grievance,
and turned a tolerant, sagely feminine eye on what she called Edna's
"airs and graces."

There was a bustle and clatter, and Mrs. Smeeth returned to dump
upon the table a little jug without a handle. "I'm getting properly
mixed up in my old age," she announced, breathlessly. "First I
thought it was there, in front of the bottom shelf. Then when I went,
I thought I couldn't have made any, because it wasn't there. And
then—lo and behold—it was there all the time, right at the back of
the second shelf. Oh, you've given me too much, Dad. Take some
back. I'm not a bit hungry somehow to-night, haven't been all day.
You know how you get sometimes, can't fancy anything. Here, Edna,
you want more than that. Well, I dare say you don't, but you're going
to have it, miss. None of this silly starving yourself, a girl your age!
Because your mother doesn't feel hungry for once in her life, it
doesn't mean you're just going to sit there, pecking worse than a
little sparrow." And here she stopped, to take breath, to snatch Edna's
plate and put some more meat on it, to sit down, to do half a dozen
other things, all in a flash.

According to all the literary formulas, the wife of Mr. Smeeth
should have been a grey and withered suburban drudge, a creature
who had long forgotten to care for anything but a few household
tasks, the welfare of her children, and the opinion of one or two
chapel-going neighbours, a mere husk of womanhood, in whom Mr.
Smeeth could not recognise the girl he had once courted. But Nature,
caring nothing for literary formulas, had gone to work in another
fashion with Mrs. Smeeth. There was nothing grey and withered
about her. She was only in her early forties, and did not look a day

older than her age, by any standards. She was a good deal plumper than the girl Mr. Smeeth had married, twenty-two years before, but she was no worse for that. She still had a great quantity of untidy brown hair, a bright blue eye, rosy cheeks, and a ripe moist lip. She came of robust country stock, and perhaps that is why she had been able to conjure any amount of bad food into healthy and jolly womanhood. By temperament, however, she was a real child of London, a daughter of Cockaigne. She adored oysters, fish and chips, an occasional bottle of stout or glass of port, cheerful gossip, hospitality, noise, jokes, sales, outings, comic songs, entertainments of any kind, in fact, the whole rattling and roaring, laughing and crying world of food and drink and bargaining and adventure and concupiscence. She liked to spend as much money as she could, but apart from that, would have been quite happy if the Smeeths had dropped to a lower social level. She never shared any of her husband's worries, and was indeed rather impatient of them, sometimes openly contemptuous, but she had no contempt, beyond that experienced by all deeply feminine natures for the male, for the man himself. He had been her sweetheart, he was her husband; he had given her innumerable pleasures, had looked after her, had been patient with her, had always been fond of her; and she loved him and was proud of what seemed to her his cleverness. She knew enough about life to realise that Smeeth was a really good husband and that this was something to be thankful for. (North London does not form any part of that small hot-house world in which a good husband or wife is regarded as a bore, perhaps as an obstacle in the path of the partner's self-development.) Chastity for its own sake made no appeal to her, and she recognised with inward pleasure (though not with any outward sign) the glances that flirtatious and challenging males, in buses and shops and tea-rooms, threw in her direction. If Mr. Smeeth had started any little games—as she frankly confessed—she would not have moaned and repined, but would have promptly "shown him" what she could do in that line. As it was, he did not require showing. He grumbled sometimes at her extravagance, her thoughtlessness, her rather slapdash housekeeping, but in spite of all that, in spite too, of the fact that for two-and-twenty years they had been cooped up together in tiny houses, she still seemed to him an adorable person, at once incredible and delightful in the large, wilful, intriguing, mysterious mass of her femininity, the Woman among the almost indistinguishable crowd of mere women.

"And if this pudding tastes like nothing on earth," cried Mrs. Smeeth, rushing it on to the table, "don't blame me, blame Mrs. Newark at number twenty-three. She came charging in, like a fire brigade, just as I was in the middle of mixing it, and shrieked at me —you know what a voice she has?—she said, 'What d'you think, Mrs. Smeeth!' And I said, 'I'm sure I don't know, Mrs. Newark. What is it this time?' I slipped that in just to remind her it wasn't the first time she'd nearly frightened the life out of me, breaking the news about nothing. 'Well,' she said—just a minute, mind your hand, Dad, that's hot. Pass the custard, Edna. Dad wants it. That's right." And Mrs. Smeeth sat down, flushed and panting.

"Bit on the heavy side, p'raps," said Mr. Smeeth, who had now tasted his pudding, "but I've had worse from you, Mother, much worse." Another spoonful. "Not so bad at all."

"No, it isn't, is it?" his wife replied. "But if it isn't, it ought to be. I thought Mrs. Screaming Twenty-three had done it in properly. 'Well,' she said, and nearly bursting she was, 'do you know, Mrs. Smeeth, I've had a letter from Albert, and he's been in hospital in Rangoon, and now he's all right, and the letter came not ten minutes since.' 'You don't say!' I said. 'Where's he been in hospital? And she said, 'Rangoo-oon'—just like that. Reminded me of that Harry Tate sketch, you remember, Dad? Rangoo-oon! I nearly laughed in her face. And talk about sketches! If you want a sketch you couldn't beat this Albert she's making so much fuss about. 'Member him, Edna?—teeth sticking out a yard, and all cross-eyed. They saw something in Rangoo-oon when they saw Albert."

"Oo, he was sorful!" cried Edna, shuddering in a refined way.

"Still, we can't all be oil-paintings," Mrs. Smeeth remarked philosophically. Then she looked mischievous. "And we can't all look like Mr. Ronald Mawlborough either."

"Who's he when he's at home?" Mr. Smeeth inquired.

"There you are, you see, Dad, you're not up in these things. You're behind the times. Matter of fact, you have seen him, 'cos I remember the two of us seeing him together, in that picture at the Empire."

"Oh, one of those movie chaps, is he?" Mr. Smeeth was obviously more interested in pudding than in movie chaps.

"I should think he is. Isn't he, Edna?"

"Oh, do shut up, Mother," cried Edna, crimson now and wriggling.

"What's this about?"

"He's the latest, isn't he, Edna?" said Mrs. Smeeth wickedly. "And I must say he's a good-looking young fellow—curly hair, dark eyes, and all that. Free with his photographs too. Yours sincerely, Ronald Mawlborough, that's him. Nothing stand-offish about him when he addresses his sweet young admirers——"

"Mother!" Edna screamed, nothing now but two imploring eyes in a scarlet face.

"That's what comes of not doing your bedroom out, miss," her mother retorted. "I go up to her bedroom, Dad, and what do I find? Mr. Ronald Mawlborough, hers sincerely, on a big photo. You can nearly count his eyelashes. That's the latest now. Not content with cutting 'em out of these movie papers, they send to Hollywood for them. Darling Mr. Ronald, they write, I shall die if you don't send me your photo, signed in your own sweet handwriting. Yours truly, Edna Smeeth, seventeen Chaucer Road, Stoke Newington, England."

Mr. Smeeth looked severe. "Well, I must say, Edna, I call that a silly game."

"I only did it for fun," she muttered, "just to see what would happen, that's all. Some of our girls have got dozens——"

"Pity they've got nothing better to do," was her father's comment.

"Oh, well, they might be doing worse," said Mrs. Smeeth, rising from the table. "It won't do them any good, but it won't do them any harm either. We've all been a bit silly in our time. I'm sure I was when I was a girl. Girls *are* a bit silly, if you ask me, and it's a good job for the men they are. But that doesn't mean they can't help to clear a table. Come on, Edna, get these things away while I make the tea."

"Oh, all ri-ight," Edna sighed wearily, and rose in slow-motion time. Ten minutes later, after gulping down her tea, she rushed out of the room, leaving her parents sitting at ease, Mrs. Smeeth over her second cup of tea, Mr. Smeeth over his pipe.

The room was small and contained far too much furniture and too many knick-knacks. Nearly everything in it was shoddy and ugly, manufactured hastily, in the mass, to catch a badly-informed eye, to be bought and exhibited for a brief season by the purchaser, and then to be in the way and finally rot out of the way. Nevertheless, the total effect of the room was not displeasing, because it had a cosy, homelike atmosphere, which Mr. Smeeth, whose imagination, heightened by fear, perhaps told him that outside beyond the firelight and the snug walls were stalking poverty, disgrace, shame, disease, and death, enjoyed even more than Mrs. Smeeth. It was probably this feeling, and not so much the strain of the day's work, that made him a man difficult to rouse and get out of the house in the evening, as his wife, who was all for going out somewhere, or, failing that, inviting somebody in, knew to her cost.

"You're an old home-bird, you are," she said, with a sort of affectionate contempt, as she saw him settling deeper now into his chair. "Well, what's been bothering you to-day? You started to tell me and then didn't."

"I got a real fright this morning, I don't mind telling you, Edie," he began. "Not that I hadn't seen it coming the way things were going on," he added, with a gloomy pride.

"Now then, don't start on," she warned him, shaking a teaspoon. "You see too much coming. Always looking into the middle of next week and noticing how black it's getting. Talk about depressions in Iceland! They ought to give you the job, and then there'd be plenty. However, go on, my dear. Mustn't interrupt."

"Well, somebody's got to look, haven't they?" he replied. "And if Mr. Dersingham had looked a bit harder, we'd all be better off."

"Do you mean to say you won't get that rise at Christmas he was talking about?"

"Rise at Christmas! I thought this morning I was in for a rise outside. I tell you, Edie, when he started, my heart went into my boots." And he plunged into an account of the scene in Mr. Dersingham's room that morning and then discussed the mysterious events that followed it, all of which Mrs. Smeeth punctuated with nods and ejaculations, such as "Did he really?" "Well, I never!" and, "Silly old geezer!" She gave him more of her attention than she usually did, because she could see that he was seriously concerned, but at the same time she did not really bother her own head about it, as he knew very well. To her it was all rather unreal, and he was convinced that the idea that he might lose his job, be thrown into the street with only the gloomiest prospect of getting anything half as good, never really entered her head. And this indifference, this childlike confidence in his ability to produce the usual six or seven pounds every week, did nothing to restore his own self-confidence, at least not at such moments as these, but only made him feel that he had to think for two, and in the end left him lonely with his fear.

"All I'm hoping now," he went on, earnestly, "is that this chap who called has got something up his sleeve. It's so funny Goath going like that. Looks to me as if this chap, Golspie, thought Goath wasn't any good—and I've thought so once or twice myself lately—and worked it so that Mr. Dersingham got rid of him. Perhaps he's going to take his place. I must say, it's a funny business. In all my experience——"

"Don't you worry, it'll be all right," cried Mrs. Smeeth. "We're going to be lucky, we are. I don't care if Mr. Dersingham goes mental, we're going to be lucky. Soon too! I don't think I told you, but Mrs. Dalby's sister—the one with the fringe and the jet ear-rings, who reads the cards—told me my fortune the other afternoon, and she said luck was coming, money and good luck, and all through a stranger, a middling-coloured man in a strange bed. Is this man you're talking about middling-coloured?"

"Don't ask me, I never noticed what colour he was. He hadn't any colour. He'd got a big moustache, if that's any use to you. But what puzzles me is this, why did Mr. Dersingham——"

"Don't you worry yourself, Dad, why Mr. Dersingham did anything," his wife interrupted. "Think he's spending his time worrying about you? Not him! And don't you bother your old head about him, either. Let's have a bit o' music. It'll cheer us up." She bounced over to the corner in which George, who had a head for these things, had fixed up that tangle of wires which still passes by the name of "wireless," a loud speaker apparatus. "What starts it? I can never remember," she said, with one hand hovering over the various knobs. "Is it this thing you pull out?"

It must have been, for she pulled it, and immediately a loud, patronising voice filled the room. "Let us turn to anothuh aspect of this problem," it shouted. "As we have already seen—ah—a company cannot barrow unless it is aixpressly authorised—that is, authorised by its memorandum of association—ah—to do so. Let us see what this invalves. Suppose a companay has been formed for the purpose—we will say—ah—of discounting cammercial bills——"

"Oh, help!" cried Mrs. Smeeth, and promptly turned the voice out of the room. "A lot of cheering up you'll do!" she told the loud speaker severely. "Look in the paper and see when the singing and playing comes on."

There was a glimpse of Edna, all dressed up, very white about the nose, very red about the lips.

"Where you're going, Edna?" her mother shrieked.

"Out."

"Who with?"

"Minnie Watson."

"Well, don't be late then, you and your Minnie Watson." A bang of the front door was Edna's only reply. "It's Minnie Watson ev'ry night now," said Mrs. Smeeth. "Next month it'll be all somebody else.

I said to her last night, 'Where's Annie Frost now you used to be so friendly with?'"

"Is that Frost's girl?" inquired Mr. Smeeth. "The chap who keeps the *Hand and Glove?*"

"That's right, Jimmy Frost. So when I said that to her, the little madam turns up her nose at once and says, 'Catch me going with Annie Frost!' Just like that. And it doesn't seem a minute since they were as thick as thieves. I could have died laughing. Just the same, I was, at her age."

"You won't make me believe that," said Mr. Smeeth sturdily. "You'd more sense. Seems to me these young girls now haven't a scrap of sense. The bit they leave school with is knocked out of them by pictures nowadays. They think about pictures—movies and talkies —from morning till night. They're getting jazzed off their little heads."

"That sounds like Georgie," cried Mrs. Smeeth, starting up. "I'll go and get his dinner out of the oven. Come on, boy, hurry up if you want any dinner to-night. It's nearly cinders now."

Left to himself, Mr. Smeeth slowly knocked out his pipe in the coal-scuttle and then stared into the fire, brooding. He was always catching himself grumbling about the children now, and he did not want to be a grumbling father. He had enjoyed them when they were young, but now, although there were times when he felt a touch of pride, he no longer understood them. George especially, the elder of the two, and once a very bright promising boy, was both a disappointment and a mystery. George had had opportunities that he himself had never had. But George had shown an inclination from the first, to go his own way, which seemed to Mr. Smeeth a very poor way. He had no desire to stick to anything, to serve somebody faithfully, to work himself steadily up to a good safe position. He simply tried one thing after another, selling wireless sets, helping some pal in a garage (he was in a garage now, and it was his fourth or fifth), and though he always contrived to earn something and appeared to work hard enough, he was not, in his father's opinion, getting anywhere. He was only twenty, of course, and there was time, but Mr. Smeeth, who knew very well that George would continue to go his own way without any reference to him, did not see any possibility of improvement. The point was, that to George, there was nothing wrong, and his father was well aware of the fact that he could not make him see there was anything wrong. That was the trouble with both his children. There was obviously nothing bad about either of them; they compared very favourably with other people's boys and girls; and he would have been quick to defend them; but nevertheless, they were growing up to be men and women he could not understand, just as if they were foreigners. And it was all very perplexing and vaguely saddening.

The truth was, of course, that Mr. Smeeth's children *were* foreigners, not simply because they belonged to a younger generation but because they belonged to a younger generation that existed in a different world. Mr. Smeeth was perplexed because he applied to them standards they did not recognise. They were the product of a changing civilisation, creatures of the post-war world. They had grown up to the sound of the Ford car rattling down the street, and that Ford car had gone rattling away, to the communal rubbish heap, with a whole load of ideas that seemed still of supreme importance to Mr. Smeeth. They were the children of the Woolworth stores and the moving pictures. Their world was at once larger and shallower than that of their parents. They were less English, more cosmopolitan. Mr. Smeeth could not understand George and Edna, but a host of youths and girls in New York, Paris and Berlin would have understood them at a glance. Edna's appearance, her grimaces and gestures, were temporarily based on those of an Americanised Polish Jewess, who, from her mint in Hollywood, had stamped them on these young girls all over the world. George's knowing eye for a machine, his cigarette and drooping eyelid, his sleek hair, his ties and shoes and suits, the smallest details of his motor-cycling and dancing, his staccato impersonal talk, his huge indifferences, could be matched almost exactly round every corner in any American city or European capital.

Mrs. Smeeth returned with the food, and a minute or two later, George descended from his bedroom, shining, sleek, brushed. He was better looking, better built, tougher in body, than his father had ever been, and he owed far more to his mother, though there was about her a certain generosity of the blood, a suggestion of ruddy mounting sap, that was absent in him: he was drier, more compressed and blanched; and though he was a good-looking youth, who moved easily, quickly, he had hardly any more of the bloom of twenty than had the moving pictures of Mr. Ronald Mawlborough and his kind. In short, he looked too old for an English boy of that age. It was as if the Americanised world he had grown up to discover about him, had contrived to introduce into North London the drying and ageing American climate.

"You're late to-night, George," said his father.

"Been busy," he replied, dispatching his dinner quickly, quietly, efficiently, but with no signs of taking any pleasure in his food. After a few minutes' silence, he continued: "Feller came in with an old *Lumbden*, twelve horse. Could have had it for fifteen quid. Nothing much wrong with it. Wanted new plugs and mag. and brakes re-lining and something doing to the differential, and just cleanin' up a bit. All right then. Take you anywhere. Thought once of sellin' the ol' bike and having a shot at this *Lumbden*."

"I wish you would, Georgie," cried Mrs. Smeeth. "You could take us all out then. See us going out in style, eh, Dad? Besides, I hate that stinking rattling ol' bike of yours. Nasty dangerous things they are too. Get rid of it, Georgie, before it gets rid of you."

"That's all right," said George, "but the ol' bike goes—travels like a bird. This *Lumbden* couldn't look at her. No, me for the little ol' bike, till I can put my hand on something in the super-sports style. And don't worry, I shan't do that in a hurry—costs too much. Doesn't matter, though—Barrett's buying this *Lumbden*. We'll do her up a bit, paint her up, and sell her. There won't be any hurry either, so when we've put a few works in her, if you want a ride, pass the word on, and we'll have a run in her."

"We'll go down to Brighton and see your aunt Flo," cried Mrs. Smeeth, her eyes brightening at the thought of an outing. "Now don't forget, Georgie boy. That's a promise to your old mother. Don't go spending all your time taking the girls out in it. Give your mother a chance. She can enjoy a ride as well as the next."

"Righto," said George briskly. He rose from the table.

"Here, you want some pudding."

"Not to-night. Off pudding to-night. Couldn't look it in the face. 'Sides, I haven't time."

"Time!" cried his mother. "You're never in. Where you going?"

"Out."

"Out where?"

"Just knocking about with some of the fellers."

Mr. Smeeth looked at him, rather gravely. He felt it was his turn to speak now. "Just a minute," he said sharply. "What does 'knocking about' mean exactly, may I ask?"

At this, George looked a shade less confident, a trifle younger, as he stood there tapping his cigarette. "I dunno. Might do one thing, might do another. Might have a game of billiards at the Institute, or look in at the pictures, or go down to the second house at Finsbury Park. Depends what everybody wants to do. No harm in that, Dad." He lit his cigarette.

"Course there isn't," said Mrs. Smeeth. "Your father never said there was."

"No, I didn't," said Mr. Smeeth slowly. "That's all right, George. Only don't take all night about it, that's all. Oh!—there's just another thing." He hesitated a moment. "Somebody told me he'd seen you once or twice with that flash bookie chap—what's his name?—y'know —Shandon. Well, you keep away from that chap, George. I don't interfere—and you know I don't—but that chap's a wrong 'un, and I don't want to see a boy of mine in his company."

"Shandon's no friend of mine," said George, flushing. "I don't knock about with him. He comes into the garage sometimes, that's all. He's a friend of Barrett's."

"Well, if half of what I hear's true," Mr. Smeeth remarked, "he's a friend to nobody, that chap. And you just keep out of his way, George, see?"

"First I've heard of this," said Mrs. Smeeth, looking severely at her son.

"All ri', Dad," George muttered, nodding. "So long, Ma." And he was off.

Mrs. Smeeth promptly rushed the remaining dirty plates into the kitchen, and then returned, five minutes later, to find her husband looking at a battered copy of a detective story that had somehow found its way into the room. You could not say he was reading it. So far, he was merely glancing suspiciously at it. Mrs. Smeeth took up the evening paper, pecked at it here and there, then pottered about a minute or two, then turned on the wireless, which only let loose another patronising gentleman, switched it off, brought two socks and some darning wool from the top of the little bookcase, examined them with distaste, looked across at her husband, then said: "I can't settle down to anything to-night, somehow. How d'you feel about a little walk round? We might look in at Fred's for an hour. What d'you say? Oh no, I thought not—won't stir, the old stick-in-the-mud. One of these days I'll be finding a nice young man to take me to the pictures. Well, if you won't stir, I will. I think I'll just slip round to Mrs. Dalby's for an hour. She asked me if I would."

"You do," said Mr. Smeeth. "I'm all right here."

He lit his pipe again, made up the fire, and tried to settle down with the detective story, which at once hustled him into the library of the old Manor House, where the baronet's body was waiting to be discovered. But he did not make much headway with it. Goath and Mr. Dersingham and this Golspie kept appearing in that library. Angel Pavement was just outside the old Manor House. So he put the book away and tried the wireless. This time the patronising gentlemen had all gone home, and in their place was a rich and adventurous flood of sound. It was not unfamiliar to Mr. Smeeth, and, after a pleasant tussle with his memory, he recognised it as something by Mendelssohn, an overture it was, a sea piece, either Whats-It's Cave or Hebrides or something. Unlike his wife and children and most of his friends, Mr. Smeeth had a genuine, if unambitious, passion for music, and this was the kind of music he knew and liked best. He sank into his chair, and the sharp lines on his face softened as the music came swirling out of the little cone and there arrived with it the old mysterious enchantment of the ear. A phantom sea rolled about his chair: the room was filled with foam and salt air, the green glitter of the waves, the white flash and the crying of great sea birds. And Mr. Smeeth, a magically drowned man, worried no longer, and for a brief space was happy.

III

The next day Mr. Smeeth struggled out of sleep to find himself faced with one of those dark spouting mornings which burst over unhappy London like gigantic bombs filled with dirty water. At the first sign of the approach of one of these outrages, all clocks ought to be put back three hours, so that everybody might stay in bed until their fury is spent. There is no end to their malice. They sweep, lash, and machine-gun the streets with rain; they send up fountains of mud from every passing wheel; they contrive that fires shall not burn and water boil, that tea shall be lukewarm, bacon fat congealed, and warranted fresh eggs change in their very cups to mere eggs and dubious; they make the husband turn on the wife, the father on the child, and thus help to ruin all family life; and they lavishly sow all the ills that townsmen know, colds, indigestion, rheumatism, influenza, bronchitis, pneumonia, and are indeed the industrious hirelings of Death.

"Got your umbrella?" said Mrs. Smeeth. She had been out of bed over an hour, but somehow looked as if her real self was still there, as if this was a mysteriously wrapped wraith of herself she had projected downstairs. "Goo'-bye, then. You'll have to run for it, Dad."

Dad did not run for it, but he managed to trot down Chaucer Road and then along the neighbouring street, but after that he had a pain over his heart and was reduced to a sort of quick shamble. Before he reached the High Street and his tram, the bottom of his trousers were unpleasantly heavy, his boots (one of Mrs. Smeeth's bargains and made of cardboard) gave out a squelching sound, and the newspaper he carried was being rapidly reconverted into its original pulp. The tram, its windows steaming and streaming, was more crowded than usual, of course, and carried its maximum cargo of wet clothes, the wearers of which were simply so many irritable ghosts. After enormous difficulty, Mr. Smeeth succeeded in filling and lighting his morning pipe of T. Benenden's Own, and then—so stubborn is the spirit of man—succeeded in unfolding and examining his pulpy newspaper. Before he had reached the end of City Road, he had learned that the cost of a public school education was too high, that the night clubs on Broadway were not doing the business they had done, that a man in Birmingham had cut his wife's throat, that students in Cairo were again on strike, that an old woman in Hammersmith had died of starvation, that a policeman in Suffolk had found six pound notes in the prisoner's left sock, and that bubonic plague is conveyed to human beings by fleas from infected rats. And Angel Pavement, when he arrived there, looked as if it had been plucked, grey and dripping, from the bottom of an old cistern.

It was an unpleasant morning at the office. To begin with, the situation was more puzzling than ever. Once more, Mr. Dersingham did not appear, but telephoned about half past ten to say that he would not be there until late afternoon and would Mr. Smeeth "just carry on." Goath did not reappear, and Mr. Smeeth felt sure now that he had vanished for ever. Then Miss Matfield was haughtier than usual, and very cross. Young Turgis, who had contrived to get wetter than anybody else on his way up to the office, went slouching about with a long pale face, and every now and then startled and intimidated everybody by sneezing explosively. Stanley, at odds with the weather, the world, and his present destiny, hung about and got in people's way, and when told to get on with his work, pointed out, not very respectfully, that he hadn't any work, and Mr. Smeeth did not find it easy to supply him with any. Several inquiries by telephone could not be properly answered, always an unsatisfactory state of affairs. Mr. Smeeth had sufficient routine work to carry him through the morning, but he felt queerly insecure, not at all happy with his books, his neat little figures, his pencil, rubber, blue ink and red ink, now that he no longer knew what was happening to the firm. It was like trying to post a ledger swinging above a dark gulf.

Lunch time found him at his usual teashop, sitting at a wet marble-topped table and waiting for his poached egg on toast and cup of coffee. The wet morning had perished outside, where there was even a faint gleam of sunshine, but it had found a haven in this teashop, which seemed to be four hours behind the weather in the street, for it was all damp and steaming. Mr. Smeeth was jammed into a corner with another regular patron, a man with a glass eye, bright blue and with such a fixed glare about it that the thing frightened you. Mr. Smeeth was sitting on the same side as the glass eye, and as the owner of it, who was busy eating two portions of baked beans on toast and drinking a glass of cold milk, never turned his head as he talked, the effect was disconcerting and rather horrible.

"Firm we've been doing business with," said the man, disposing of a few beans that had quitted their toast, "has come a nasty cropper —a ve-ery nasty cropper. Claridge and Molton—d'you know 'em? Oh, very nasty."

"Is that so?" said Mr. Smeeth politely, looking from his poached egg at the glaring blue eye and then looking away again. "Don't think I know the firm."

"No, well, you mightn't," the eye continued, as if it had its doubts about that, though. "But they've been a well-known house in the

wholesale umbrella trade for donkeys' years, specially for ribs, han-
dles, and tips. I remember the time when they carried a line of ribs
nobody else could touch—same with the tips. If you'd come to us
ten years ago, or five years ago, or even three years ago, and said,
'We can offer you a line in ribs and tips that'll make Claridge and
Molton look silly,' if you'd said that, we'd have laughed at you."

"No doubt," said Mr. Smeeth, quite seriously.

"And up to eighteen months ago, I'd have told you that Claridge
and Molton was one of the soundest concerns in the business. And
look at 'em now. Properly in Queer Street. Absolutely down the
river."

Mr. Smeeth manfully faced the blue glare. "How d'you account
for it?" he inquired, not out of mere politeness but because he really
wanted to know.

"This milk doesn't taste right this morning," his neighbour remarked mournfully. "They've had it near something. I'm giving it
a miss. What was that?" And here the eye turned balefully. "Oh,
about Claridge and Molton. Well, young Molton's the one that's
upset their little apple-cart. He took charge about a couple of years
ago, then began staying away all day—likes his whisky, y'know—
drew heavily on the firm—sacked their oldest man, old Johnny
Fowler, for something and nothing. Probably tight at the time—
young Molton, I mean, not Johnny Fowler—he never took a drop.
And there you are! You can't do it, y'know, you can't do it. Can
you?"

"No," said Mr. Smeeth sadly, "you can't."

"Course you can't," the eye concluded. "Not nowadays. It's all too
keen, too much competition. You've got to watch yourself all the
time. Isn't that so? Eh, miss, miss! My check, miss. And, I say,
what about this milk?"

Mr. Smeeth finished his coffee, mechanically filled and lit his pipe,
then pushed his way out of the place. He felt miserable. For all he
knew to the contrary, Mr. Dersingham might be following the example of this young Molton. Hadn't Mr. Dersingham just started

staying away from the office all day? Hadn't he just sacked *their* oldest man, Goath? As he moved slowly along, sometimes staring into the windows of shops that meant nothing to him, Mr. Smeeth found himself going over all the possible ways in which a firm might come a nasty cropper, arrive at Queer Street, go down the river, and they seemed so numerous, so inevitable, that he saw himself joining the wretched army of the hangers-on, the dispossessed, at any moment. And, at the corner of Chiswell Street, he gave a man twopence for a box of matches.

When he let himself quietly into the office, he heard loud voices, and thought for a moment that something exciting was happening. But then he caught the words.

"I shaddered him all down Victoria Park Road," Stanley was saying triumphantly, "and he never knew."

"Well, why should he?" Turgis demanded, contemptuously. "He didn't know you were following him, you little chump."

"I know he didn't," cried Stanley. "That's it. That's where shadderin' comes in——"

"Well, shadowing can come out," Mr. Smeeth announced. "And if you don't get on with some work, my boy, you'll be finding yourself shadowing down those steps. Come on, Turgis, you ought to know a bit better. Standing there talking a lot of nonsense!"

"I was telling him it was nonsense," said Turgis, rather sullenly. "He's got this shadowing on the brain. He goes following some chap for miles, and then because this chap doesn't take any notice of him—he doesn't know he's there, of course, and doesn't care, anyhow—he thinks he's a little Sexton Blake."

"No, I don't," said Stanley, wrinkling up his freckled face until it achieved a look of intense disgust.

"The best thing you can do, Stanley," said Mr. Smeeth, sitting down at his desk, "is to drop these silly tricks. They'll get you into trouble one of these days. Why don't you do something sensible in your spare time? Get a hobby. Do a bit of fretwork or collect foreign stamps or butterflies or something like that."

"Huh! Nobody does them things now. Out of date," Stanley muttered.

"Well, work's not out of date, not here, anyhow," Mr. Smeeth retorted, in time-old schoolmaster fashion. "So just get on with a bit."

Miss Matfield arrived, quarter of an hour late, as usual. "Don't talk to me, anybody," she commanded. "I'm furious. Of all the foul lunches I've ever had in this city, to-day's was the foulest. It makes me sick to think about it. Look here, is Mr. Dersingham ever coming here again? It's absurd—I've got umpteen things for him to sign. Can you do anything with them, Mr. Smeeth?"

"I'll have a look at them, Miss Matfield," said Mr. Smeeth wearily. The afternoon dragged on.

IV

At five o'clock, Mr. Dersingham arrived, bursting in like a large pink bomb. He was breathless, perspiring, and all smiles. "Afternoon, ev'rybody," he gasped. "Is there a late spot of tea goin'? Doesn't matter if there isn't. I say, Miss Matfield, just drop ev'rything, will you, and bring your notebook to my room. I want to dictate some letters and a circular. Stanley, you get ready to copy the circular. And, Turgis, you ring up Brown and Gorstein and say I want to speak to Mr. Gorstein. And Smeeth, I shall want you when I'm through with these letters, about a quarter of an hour's time, and will you bring that statement of the outstanding accounts right up to date and let me know all about Gorstein's and Nickman's payments this last year? Good man!"

Mr. Dersingham liked to signalise his arrival in this fashion—it looked as if he was starting the day for everybody, and it still looked like that even if he did it at five o'clock—but now there was a difference. His voice had a triumphant ring, in spite of the fact that he was short of breath. There was about his whole manner a Napoleonic abruptness and self-confidence. He presented the spectacle—rare

enough too—of an Old Worrelian in big business. At one bound the
temperature of the office rose about ten degrees, and Mr. Smeeth,
as he investigated the firm's somewhat melancholy relations with
Brown & Gorstein and Nickman & Sons, was visited once more by
quite wildly optimistic fancies. Undoubtedly, something had
happened.

When at last he was called into Mr. Dersingham's room, he soon
learned what it was that had happened. It was, as he had suspected
more than once, this Mr. Golspie.

"And the position is this, Smeeth," Mr. Dersingham continued.
"He's got the sole agency for all this new Baltic stuff. They won't
sell it to anybody here but Golspie. It's good wood, all of it, quite
up to standard, and he can get it at prices, thirty, forty and fifty
per cent. lower than we've been paying. I don't mind telling you
that when he first explained what he was after, I wasn't keen at all,
not a bit keen. It sounded fishy to me."

"Does seem a bit queer he should come along like that, doesn't
it, sir?"

"It does, Smeeth, and that's what I thought. But we've been going
round with some of his samples at prices we could sell the stuff at
on his figures, and they've been absolutely leaping at them. We can
cut everybody out, absolutely clean cut. We can do more business,
Smeeth, with this new stuff in a fortnight than the firm's ever done,
even in its best days, in a month. And you know what business
we've been doing lately? Awful! A ghastly show! By the way,
Smeeth, Goath was partly to blame for that. Oh yes, he was. Thirty
years in the trade and all that—but the fact is, they were all tired
of seeing his depressing old mug, and he'd given up trying. Golspie
soon showed me that, though I must say I'd had my suspicions for
some time."

"So had I, sir."

"Exactly! Goath had to be booted out, and as it was he booted
himself out. He'll be feeling very sorry for himself soon. Now then,
this is what's happening. Golspie came along here to see me quite

by chance. He'd got this contract, but he wanted some firm already in the trade to join up with. All this is—er—in—y'know—between ourselves, Smeeth."

"I understand, sir," said Mr. Smeeth, flattered and delighted.

"Golspie—Mr. Golspie—doesn't want a partnership, can't be bothered with it. He's coming in here as a sort of general manager, working on a jolly good commission. You'll have to know all about that, of course, because of the books. It's a hefty commission all right, but then he's bringing all the business really, and he'll be responsible for getting the wood over and all that side of it. And the two of us will be working together, running things here. I'll go out a good deal myself for the next few months, and we'll have to get some fellow—somebody young and keen—to take Goath's place."

"You won't be cutting down the office staff then?" said Mr. Smeeth, greatly relieved.

"Cutting it down! We'll have to jolly well increase it, and quickly too. That far sample room will have to be cleared out and tidied up this week, we shall want that. You'd better get another typist to help Miss Matfield—a young girl will do—as soon as possible. This next week or two, Smeeth," and here Mr. Dersingham sprang up and clenched his fists, just as if he had never seen a decent public school, "we've got to drive it hard, go all out, and I'm depending on you for the office side of it. You people have got to stand behind me in this. It's a great chance for all of us, and, of course, a tremendous stroke of luck, Golspie's coming here. He's going all out himself on this—he's that sort of chap, very keen and all that—and we've got to keep pace."

"You can count on me doing my best, Mr. Dersingham," Mr. Smeeth assured him fervently. "There's one or two things I'd like to know about, of course. F'r'instance, what's his arrangement with these foreign people of his about payments?"

"He's going to talk to you about that, Smeeth. We've only just touched on that, so far."

"And another thing, sir," Mr. Smeeth continued, more hesitantly now. "You know how we stand at the bank just now. If we're branching out, we've got to have something behind us there."

"I've been looking into that this afternoon," said Mr. Dersingham. "We can't do anything more with the bank at present, but I think I can borrow a bit to see us through. We've got to have something to jolly well play with, this next month or so, particularly as Mr. Golspie talks about wanting some of his commission in advance, so to speak."

Mr. Smeeth looked grave, then coughed. "Do you think that would be wise, Mr. Dersingham? I mean—er—after all, you've no guarantee——"

"You mean—the whole thing may be just a swindle. Come on, isn't that it?" cried the other, grinning. "Well of course I thought of that. I thought of God knows how many swindles yesterday morning, because, as I said, the whole thing seemed fishy to me, and, between ourselves, I thought Golspie himself a terrible outsider at first. But I've gone into all that. He doesn't draw his commission until the stuff has been delivered to our people, of course, but he wants his money then, without waiting until the account's finally settled. Though, by the way, Smeeth, we're not going to give these fellows so much rope in future. With this new stuff on our hands, we can afford to tighten it up a bit, don't you think?"

"That's so, Mr. Dersingham. I'd like to see one or two of these accounts closed altogether. They're more bother than they're worth." Mr. Smeeth hesitated. "I'm not quite clear yet about this Mr. Golspie, sir. Is he going to be in charge of the office?"

"In a way, yes," the other replied, with the air of a man who had given this question a great deal of thought. "You can take it, he is. Though of course it's still my show——"

"Of course, Mr. Dersingham."

"Suppose, by any chance, you disagree violently with anything he suggests, you'll come to me," said Mr. Dersingham, looking at that moment like a large pink conspirator. "But you needn't tell that to the other people out there."

"I see what you mean, sir," said Mr. Smeeth, who felt that he would see in time.

"Mr. Golspie has a good deal to learn, of course," Mr. Dersingham continued, airily. "He doesn't know the trade, and he doesn't know the City. But—he seems to have knocked up and down all over the place in his time, and he's got ideas, y'know, and colossal push. Rum sort of chap, I must say." Then he became business-like again. "Now look here, Smeeth, I want to push off as soon as I can because I want that money—or some of it—into the bank by to-morrow afternoon. Ask Miss Matfield to hurry up with those letters so that I can sign 'em. And just see those circulars get away to-night, will you?"

"I will, Mr. Dersingham." And Mr. Smeeth turned away, but stopped before he reached the door. "And if you don't mind me saying so, sir, I'm very pleased things are looking up like this. I was beginning to feel worried, very worried, sir."

"Thanks, Smeeth! Good man!" You could not mistake the Old Worrelian now. "Things will be humming here soon, you'll see. Colossal luck, of course, his turning up like this! Oh, by the way, he's probably coming in soon."

Mr. Golspie did come in, but only after Mr. Dersingham had gone and for about half an hour or so, during which he merely asked Mr. Smeeth a few questions. He came again the next morning, and Mr. Smeeth had to join him and Mr. Dersingham in a little conference. Mr. Golspie then returned about half past four, dictated some letters, nosed about the office, examined the far room, and did some telephoning at Mr. Dersingham's table, Mr. Dersingham himself being out visiting Nickman and Sons. The others had gone, and Mr. Smeeth was putting away his books for the night, when Mr. Golspie came out of the private office and began asking more questions, chiefly about accounts. The two of them stayed there another twenty-five minutes, at the end of which Mr. Golspie suggested they should round off the proceedings by having a drink.

When they were at the bottom of the stairs, Mr. Smeeth remembered that he was nearly out of tobacco (he smoked two and a half

ounces of T. Benenden's Own Mixture every week) and said he
would slip in for some. Mr. Golspie followed him in, and T.
Benenden was so surprised to see this massive and large-moustached
stranger again, in company with Mr. Smeeth this time, too, that he
weighed out the tobacco and put it in the pouch without saying
a word.

"You got any good cigars, *good* cigars?" Mr. Golspie demanded in
his resonant bass, at the same time staring hard, even harder than
the tobacconist had stared at him.

"Certainly, I have," replied T. Benenden with dignity. And he.
produced two or three boxes.

Mr. Golspie chose two cigars, cut them, then popped one into his
own mouth, stuck the other into Mr. Smeeth's, and lit the pair of
then, without a word. Then, after blowing a stream of smoke at
Benenden, he said: "How much?"

"Three shillings, for the two."

Mr. Golspie slapped down two half-crowns on the counter. This
was the tobacconist's opportunity.

"What about this big Cement slump, gentlemen?" he began.
"Where's that going to land us——?"

"It's not going to land me anywhere," said Mr. Golspie. "Where's
it going to land you?"

T. Benenden looked rather pained, and still nursed the two shillings change in his hand. "Well, what I mean is this. That's a big
combine, isn't it? A year ago, they were bang at the top, like nearly
all the big combines. All right. But what's happening now? A slump.
And why——?"

"I don't know, and I'll bet you don't know," said Mr. Golspie
heartily. Then he gave a short bellow of a laugh. "Well, I'll be
damned," he roared, "I've been puzzling my head for the last five
minutes wondering what was wrong with you."

"Me?" T. Benenden was startled.

"Yes, you. Didn't you notice I was staring at you?" He turned to
Mr. Smeeth. "Couldn't make it out. I knew there was something

wrong. You see it, don't you?" He now returned to Benenden, at whom he pointed a thick brutal finger. "Why, man, you've forgotten to put your tie on. Have a look at yourself. I *knew* there was something. Is that my change? That's correct—two shillings."

Mr. Smeeth followed him out of the shop, gasping. He had been visiting Benenden's shop two or three times a week, year after year, and never once had he dared mention the word "tie." And now this chap comes along with his "You've forgotten to put your tie on." Mr. Smeeth began to chuckle softly.

Mr. Golspie piloted him across the road and into the private bar of the *White Horse*.

"Give it a name," said Mr. Golspie.

"Thanks, Mr. Golspie. Oh—er—just a glass of bitter," said Mr. Smeeth modestly, from behind his large cigar.

"Don't have a glass of bitter. Too cold a night like this and after a hard day's work, too. Have a whisky. That's right. Two double whiskies and some soda."

It was quiet and cosy in the *White Horse*. Mr. Smeeth had not been in for a long time, and he was enjoying this. The fire winked cheerfully over the grate; the rows of liqueur bottles glimmered and glittered; the glasses shone softly; there was a pleasant hum of talk; the cigars plunged them at once into an atmosphere of rich, fragrant, luxurious conviviality; the whisky tasted good, and washed away that foggy, smoky, railway tunnel flavour of Angel Pavement; and Mr. Golspie, still mysterious and masterful but genial now too, was obviously anxious they should be on friendly terms.

"You've got a fellow working in the Midlands and the North, haven't you?" Mr. Golspie inquired, after they had both taken a pull at their whiskies. "What's he like?"

"Dobson? He's a decent young chap, and he's got a good connection up there. He's not sold much lately, but it's not been for the want of trying."

"We ought to be hearing from him soon, then," said Mr. Golspie. "If he can't sell these new veneers, he'd better be walking. They sell themselves. We've orders pouring in, just pouring. But, mind you, Smeeth, we've got to get a move on. We've got to pile up the orders now—make hay while the sun shines. We want another man for London and district, soon as we can get one. And one that's alive, too, not like that dreary old devil I booted out the first day. You might as well send the dustbin round looking for orders. There ought to be three of us, me, Dersingham, and this other man, who- ever he is, doing London and neighbourhood these next few months. Rush 'em. That's the way, isn't it?"

Mr. Smeeth, taking out his cigar and trying to look keen and aggressive, said it was.

"I'll tell you what I believe in," Mr. Golspie continued, not troubling to lower his voice, or rather to moderate it, for it was low enough. "I believe in working like hell and in playing like hell. If you're going to work, for God's sake—work. And if you're going to enjoy yourself, well, for the love of Mike, enjoy yourself, get on with it."

At this point, Mr. Smeeth started back, for suddenly a head, a large head wearing a very dirty cap, but only about the height of his shoulder, stuck itself between him and Mr. Golspie. "That's all very well, gents," it said, with an impudent whine, "but what if yer can't get work, 'ow yer goin' ter enjoy yerself then, ch? Wotcher goin' ter do then, ch?"

"There's one thing you can do," said Mr. Golspie promptly.

"Wha's that?"

"You can mind your own bloody business," said Mr. Golspie, pushing his face out in a most intimidating and disagreeable fashion. The intruder shrank back at once. "Here y'are," Mr. Golspie said in a milder, contemptuous tone, "here's threepence. Go away and buy yourself something."

"Thank yer, mister." And the head vanished.

"This city's got more and more rats like that in it every time I come back to it."

"There isn't the work, you know," said Mr. Smeeth earnestly. "I don't say they all want it, but there isn't the work. I'll tell you candidly, Mr. Golspie, it frightens me sometimes to see all the chaps looking for work. If we've to take on a few new people, and we advertise for them, you'll see what I mean. Crowds and crowds—ready to work for next to nothing. It's a heart-breaking job interviewing them."

"I dare say," Mr. Golspie replied, in the tone of a man whose heart is not easily broken. "But I know this. A man who's ready to work for next to nothing is no good to me. I wouldn't have him as a gift. And that reminds me, Smeeth. What's this firm paying you?"

Mr. Smeeth hesitated a moment, then told him.

"And do you think that's enough?"

Mr. Smeeth hesitated again. "Well, if business was good, I was going to ask for a rise this Christmas, but as you know, it's not been good."

"No, but it's going to be good, don't make any mistake about that," cried Mr. Golspie. "It's going to be a dam' sight better than Twigg and Dersingham have ever seen it before. Who the devil was Twigg? Never mind about him, though. I'm going to tell you straight out, I don't think you're getting enough. I know a good man when I see one, and when people stand by me—you know what I do?—that's right—I stand by them. And I'm going to stand by you."

"Very good of you, Mr. Golspie," muttered the embarrassed Smeeth.

"The minute these orders that are coming now are turned into solid business—and, mind you, it means more work and responsibility for you all along the line—the minute they do, you're going to get a rise, a good rise a hundred or two a year right off, or I'm not Jimmy Golspie. And we shake hands on that."

Mr. Smeeth, overwhelmed, found himself shaking hands on it.

"And now," Mr. Golspie added masterfully, "we'll just sign and seal that by having a little quick one."

"All right. But—er—it's my turn."

"Not a bit of it. Not to-night. You haven't a turn to-night. Wait till the big rise comes. Two singles, please. Married man, aren't you, Smeeth?"

"I am. Wife and two children, boy just out of his teens and girl nearly eighteen."

"All I've got's a girl. I'm expecting her over soon. Does this girl of yours take much notice of you?"

"Not much. Seems to me they don't, nowadays."

"You're right there. That girl of mine doesn't—the wilful, artful little devil. She's been spoilt all her life, and always will be. Too good-lookin', that's her trouble. Doesn't take after her father, y'know," and here Mr. Golspie disturbed the whole bar with a sudden deep guffaw. "Well, here's the best! This is a dam' rum business, y'know, Smeeth, when you come to think of it. I've had a finger in all sorts of trades, all over the place, and this is a bit more respectable than some of 'em. But when you think of it—it's a dam' rum trade—selling thin bits of wood to glue on to other bits of wood, eh?"

"I've often thought that," said Mr. Smeeth eagerly, the philosopher waking in him too. "I've often thought—well, I dunno—but this trade's like a good deal of the rest of life. Veneers? Well, Mr. Golspie, just think of them. They're only there to make a piece of furniture look as if it was made of better wood than it is made of, a sort of fake. But everybody knows about it. There's no deception. And I've often thought a lot of life's like that, particularly when I've gone into company. You know, everybody setting up to be mahogany and walnut through and through——"

"And the lot of 'em veneered to hell," cried Mr. Golspie jovially. "Never mind, let's see if we can't slap all our stuff on to their rotten chairs and wardrobes and sideboards, and make money and enjoy ourselves. That's the game."

With that, they swung out into the little night of Angel Pavement, where the diapason of Mr. Golspie could be heard thundering out again that it was the game. With rich Havana still in his nostrils, the golden liquor of the glens wandering round his inside like an enchanted Gulf Stream, and Mr. Golspie's promises singing their madrigals in his head, Mr. Smeeth felt for once that it really might be all a game.

Waiting for his tram that night, he bought two evening papers instead of one, and read neither of them.

Chapter Three

THE DERSINGHAMS AT HOME

I

B Y THE middle of the following week, there were several changes at Twigg & Dersingham's. The greatest change was in the atmosphere of the place. Even if you had merely opened the outer door, remaining on that side of the frosted glass partition, you would have felt the difference at once. No doubt the typewriters rattled and *pinged*, the telephone bell rang, voices came through, all in a new and bustling, optimistic fashion. The very chair you were invited to sit on, when you waited behind that partition, had been dusted. Mrs. Cross had not found herself immune from this new influence: she had given the general office a thorough cleaning. There was no question now of anybody not having enough work to do. Stanley still went out, indeed he went out more than ever, but he was compelled to speed up his "shaddering" methods and was only able to follow men who were in a tremendous hurry. Mr. Smeeth among his little figures was as busy and happy as a monk at his manuscript. Turgis, whose duty it was to see that goods were duly forwarded to and from Twigg & Dersingham's, became both hoarse and haughty down the telephone to all manner of forwarding agents, and spoke to railway goods clerks as if they were strange and unwelcome dogs. Miss Matfield rattled off her letters with slightly less contempt and disgust, rather as if they were no longer the effusions of complete lunatics but were now merely the work of village idiots. And she had acquired an assistant. The staff of Twigg & Dersingham had been enlarged at the beginning of this week by the appointment of a second typist. Miss Poppy Sellers had arrived.

The girls who earn their keep by going to offices and working typewriters may be divided into three classes. There are those who, like Miss Matfield, are the daughters of professional gentlemen and so condescend to the office and the typewriter, who work beneath them just as girls once married beneath them. There are those who take it all simply and calmly, because they are in the office tradition, as Mr. Smeeth's daughter would have been. Then there are those who rise to the office and the typewriter, who may not make any more money than their sisters and cousins who work in factories and cheap shops—they may easily make considerably less money—but nevertheless are able to cut superior and ladylike figures in their respective family circles because they have succeeded in becoming typists. Poppy belonged to this third class. Her father worked on the Underground, and he and his family of four occupied half a house not far from Eel Brook Common, Fulham, that south-western wilderness of vanishing mortar and bricks that are coming down in the world. This was not Poppy's first job, for she was twenty and had been steadily improving herself in the commercial world since she was fifteen, but it was easily her most important one. She had been chosen out of a large number of applicants, had been started at two pounds and ten shillings a week, and had been told confidentially by Mr. Smeeth, who seemed to her a terrifying figure, that she had good prospects if she would only learn and work hard. This Poppy fully intended to do, for—as her testimonials were compelled to admit—she was a very industrious and conscientious girl. She was not sufficiently plain to escape entirely the attentions of the youths who hung about the entrance to the Red Hall Cinema in Walham Green (and Poppy frequently visited the Red Hall with her friend, Dora Black, for she liked entertainment), but nobody yet had said that she was pretty. She was small and slight, had dark hair and brown eyes, and she aimed, rather timidly, at a Japanese or Javanese or general Oriental effect, wearing a fringe and all that, but only succeeded in looking vaguely dingy and untidy. Whenever she despairingly made a special effort, plying hard the lipstick, being lavish with the Oriental-effect face-powder, and raising and keeping her eyebrows so high that it hurt, people asked her if she wasn't feeling very well. This failure to achieve the exotic beauty that was— as both she and Dora Black believed—"her type," tended to keep poor Poppy slightly depressed and out of love with herself. During her first few days at Twigg & Dersingham's she was like a mouse. She was overawed by the newness and importance of everything, and she saw that it would be impossible for her to make a friend of the large, superior, infinitely knowledgeable, tremendously conde-scending Miss Matfield. But, like a mouse, she kept her eyes open, missing nothing, with her busy little Cockney mind fastening on every crumb of information and gossip. After three days, Miss Dora Black of Basuto Road, Fulham, knew more, though at second-hand, about the office staff at Twigg & Dersingham than Mr. Dersingham himself had learned in three years.

One of Miss Poppy Sellers' first tasks had been to copy out replies to the letters answering Twigg & Dersingham's advertisement in the *Times* and the *Daily Telegraph*. This was for another man, to take Goath's place, though he would have to spend much of his time further afield. He had to be as unlike Goath as possible in character, but not unlike him in experience. In short, he had to be "young, keen, energetic," and "with some connection in furnishing trade and knowledge of veneers and inlays." And the change brought about by Mr. Golspie was such that Twigg & Dersingham were able to declare that for the right man there was "a good opening."

It has been said that the modern English do not like work. It can-not be said that they do not look for it and ask for it. The day after this advertisement appeared, the postal heavens opened and a hur-ricane of letters fell upon Twigg & Dersingham. Into Angel Pave-ment all that day there poured a bewildering stream of replies. It seemed as if street after street, whole suburbs, had been waiting for this particular opening. There were, it appeared, dozens of men with vast connections in the furnishing trade and the most thorough, the most intimate knowledge of veneers and inlays, and most of these men, though they had apparently refused scores of offers recently, were only too willing to assist Messrs. Twigg & Dersingham. Then there were men who had not perhaps exactly a connection, but had been for years, so to speak, on the fringe of the furnishing trade, men who had sold pianos, who had given removing estimates, who had done a little valuing, who knew something about upholstering. Then there were older men, ex-officers many of them, who knew about all kinds of things and were ready to enclose the most astonishing testimonials, who admitted that the furnishing trade and veneers and inlays were all new to them but who felt that they could soon learn all there was to know, and in the meantime were anxious to show how they could command men and to display their unusual ability to organize. And, last of all, there were the public school men, fellows who knew nothing about veneers and inlays and did not even pretend to care about them, but pointed out that they could drive cars, manage an estate, organise anything or anybody, and were willing to go out East, being evidently under the impression that Twigg & Dersingham had probably a couple of tea plantations as well as a business in veneers and inlays. These correspondents expressed themselves in every imaginable sort of handwriting and on every conceivable kind of notepaper, from superior parchment to dirty little pink bits that had been saved up in a box on the mantelpiece, but in one particular they were all alike: they were all keen, all energetic.

"This tells you something about the old country, doesn't it?" said Mr. Golspie, who always talked as if he came from some newer one. He and Mr. Dersingham and Mr. Smeeth had been going through the pile.

"It's only the slump," said Mr. Dersingham, who was feeling optimistic these days. "It's not so bad as it was, is it, Smeeth?"

"I suppose it isn't, really, Mr. Dersingham." But Mr. Smeeth sounded rather doubtful. These letters had given him another glimpse of the dark gulf. It was a sight that left him feeling shaky.

Mr. Golspie grunted. "Far as I can see from this lot, you can have the pick of England's talent for four or five quid a week. There isn't a dam' thing these fellows can't do—except find work. Well, I've got about four likely ones here. What have you chaps got?"

After a good deal more trouble and talk, they finally narrowed the possible applications down to ten, and these ten were asked to appear at the office in the early afternoon, two days later. They all came at once, and so had to wait their turn on the landing outside, while Stanley, enjoying himself hugely, dashed in and out to summon them. Mr. Smeeth, going round to the bank, had to make his way through this little crowd, and at the first moment, when he stepped outside the office and the two or three of them nearest the door made way for him with almost ostentatious smartness, he felt triumphant, proud, a solid and successful man among a lot of failures. But the very next moment, this feeling disappeared. They were all very well brushed, in their best clothes, and were already looking keen and energetic, especially those nearest the door, who looked the keenest and most energetic, their faces having already taken on the expression most likely to impress the mysterious powers within the office. A few of them were young and had an easy confident look, that of men merely seeking a change of job. Others were older, less confident, tense or wistful. Mr. Smeeth bumped into one, the last in the group, who was standing at the corner near the top of the stairs.

"I beg your pardon," the man cried, eagerly, anxiously. He was indeed an anxious man, about Mr. Smeeth's age and not unlike him, greyish, lined, brittle; a man with a wife and family and vanishing possessions; a man who time after time had found himself the last in the group, waiting at the corner, with the hope inspired by the letter, the letter that came thunderingly, triumphantly, that morning, like an act of deliverance, now dying in him.

"My fault," Mr. Smeeth assured him, stopping, and offering the smile of a polite culprit. But when their eyes met fairly, this smile trembled, then fled, leaving Mr. Smeeth himself grave, anxious. He suddenly felt for this man a swelling sympathy, a deep stir of pity, that he had not known for many a month. They might have been brothers; and, indeed, brothers they were for a second or so, peering at one another in some darkened house of tragedy.

"Good luck!" Mr. Smeeth heard himself saying.

"Thanks," and there came the ghost of a smile.

Mr. Smeeth never saw him again. He had no luck. The successful applicant was very different, much younger, a tall fellow with a remarkably small head, an inquisitive pink nose, and a very wide mouth that opened to show about twice the ordinary number of teeth. His name was Sandycroft, and he knew the trade, for though he had never sold veneers and inlays, he had bought them, having been at one time with Briggs Brothers. This set him apart from all the other applicants. Moreover, he appeared to be all keenness and energy, and threw the most passionate emphasis into the slightest remark he made.

"Mr. Twigg," he cried, addressing Mr. Golspie, "and Mr. Dersingham, you can rely on me. I know the trade. I know the people. I know the ropes, if you don't mind me saying so."

"All right," said Mr. Golspie with his usual genial brutality. "But don't go knowing too many ropes. Eh, Dersingham?"

"Oh, quite!" replied Mr. Dersingham, who did not quite follow this, but looked knowing all the same.

"I understand, sir. I know what you mean. I couldn't do it, sir. It's not in my character. Honesty isn't everything, but I believe it's the first thing. And I'm straight. I believe in being straight, sir."

"Good!" said Mr. Golspie heartily, for he, too, believed in Sandycroft and his like being straight.

"And if it's possible, gentlemen," Sandycroft continued, looking from one to the other of them, "I'd like to stay on now and just pick up the threads, so that I can start right away on the road tomorrow morning. I'm keen to get going, desperately keen. You know what it is, sir. After only a week or two doing nothing much, a man like me feels rusty. I want to get on with it. My wife laughs at me. 'Have a rest,' she says. But no, I'm not like that. I must be getting on with something."

"Good man," said Mr. Dersingham approvingly.

"Well, I think we'll have to be getting on with something, too," said Mr. Golspie. "He'd better come round here in the morning and learn what there is to know about it then, before we send him out."

"I think he had," replied Mr. Dersingham. "Look here, you'd better go home now—break the news to your wife and that sort of thing, eh?—and then be down about nine or so in the morning. If we're not here then, you have a talk to Smeeth—that's the cashier, out there—and he'll be able to tell you something."

"Very good, sir," and you would have thought the speaker was about to salute smartly before retiring. He did not, however, but threw a keen and energetic glance at Mr. Golspie (whom he had recognised at once as the dominant partner), then a keen and ener- getic glance at Mr. Dersingham, picked up his hat (and in such a manner as to suggest that he could do some wonderful things even with that, if he wished to), brought his hat in front of the second button of his overcoat, gave three brisk nods, then wheeled about and made an exit like a torpedo from its tube.

Actually, what Mr. Dersingham and Mr. Golspie did get on with was an invitation to dinner, delivered by Mr. Dersingham and accepted by Mr. Golspie. It had come to that. There were things about Golspie that did not please Mr. Dersingham, for he was dog- matic, rough, domineering, and was apt to jeer and sneer in a way that left Mr. Dersingham's mind bruised and resentful. A few terms at Worrell would obviously have made a great difference to Golspie, who now, in his middle age, showed only too plainly both by word and deed that he was not a gentleman. From that there was no escape: Golspie was not a gentleman. But Dersingham did not think of him as an Englishman who is not a gentleman, a bit of a bounder, an outsider (and there can be no doubt that Golspie at times did talk and act like a bounder, a complete outsider); he contrived to think of him as a kind of foreigner who had acquired an extraordinary command of the English language. This was not difficult, because Golspie did seem to have spent most of his time outside England and to have no roots in this country. And the fact remained that he had presented the firm of Twigg & Dersingham with a new and glorious lease of life, as if he were a god, a commercial god with a baldish head and a large moustache. So the Dersinghams had talked it over and decided that he must be asked to dinner, properly asked to dinner and not merely invited to take pot-luck some Sunday. And this meant something, for though your Old Worrelian who has to hack out his living in the City will smoke a cigar and drink a whisky or share a couple of club chops, if necessary, with any fairly decent sort of fellow he meets in the way of business, he draws the line—his own words—at inviting most of these fellows into his home, to meet his wife and possibly another Old Worrelian or two. Thus it says something for Mr. Golspie's standing that, in spite of certain pronounced defects, he received such an invitation, which, by the way, he accepted calmly enough, with no show of surprise or gratitude.

"There'll be some other people I think you'd like to know," said Mr. Dersingham, "but we won't make it too formal. Just a black tie, y'know, black tie." He said this as people always say it, that is, as if a white tie weighed a ton and they are letting you down lightly.

"What do you mean? Wear a dinner jacket?"

"That's the idea," said Mr. Dersingham, telling himself that really Golspie was extraordinarily out of touch. "And—er—eightish then, next Tuesday, eh?"

"Right you are," replied Mr. Golspie. "Very pleased."

II

The Dersinghams occupied a lower maisonette in that region, eminently respectable but a trifle dreary, between Gloucester Road and Earl's Court Road: 34A, Barkfield Gardens, S.W. 5. Nearly all the people who live in that part of London have the privilege, as the estate agents point out in all their advertisements, of "overlooking gardens," which means that their windows stare down at iron railings, sooty privet and laurel hedges, and lawns and flower-beds that look as if they are only too willing to give up the unequal struggle. Some of these gardens are better than others, but Barkfield Gardens is not one of them. It is one of the smallest and dreariest of the squares, and is rapidly losing caste, its houses slipping through the maisonette and large flat era too quickly and already coming within sight of the small flats, the nursing homes, the boarding houses, the girls' clubs. The Dersinghams did not like Barkfield Gardens. They did not like their maisonette, all the rooms of which seemed higher than they were long or broad and were singularly cheerless. Mr. Dersingham never did anything about it, because he was waiting— as he always said—until he knew where he stood financially. (From which you might gather that he knew where he stood philosophically or socially or politically or artistically.) Now and again, however, Mrs. Dersingham would read all the advertisement columns devoted to desirable residences, rush round to some agents, and even inspect a few houses, but as she had never really decided what it was she wanted, and her husband never succeeded in knowing where he stood financially, they remained at 34A, in the rooms that made them seem like insects at the bottom of a test-tube, grumbling, while a stream of cooks and housemaids, endlessly diverted from four local registries, flowed through the dark basement, leaving as sediment innumerable memories of glum looks, impertinent answers, lying references, missing silk stockings, broken crockery and ruined meals. For some women this state of affairs, making comfort and tranquillity impossible, would have had its compensations, for it would have provided unlimited material for talk, but Mrs. Dersingham prided herself on not being the sort of woman who spends her time discussing the shortcomings of her servants. Most of her friends prided themselves on this fact too, and they told one another what they could

have said had they been that sort of women, and then gave exam-
ples. "I know, but listen to this, my dear," they all cried at once.

At seven-forty-five on the evening of the dinner party to which
Mr. Golspie had been invited, Mr. Dersingham was busy being his
own butler, attending to the wines. He poured some claret into one
decanter, some Sauterne into another, and some port into a third,
then poured a little gin and a great deal of French and Italian ver-
mouth into a cocktail shaker, and carried the shaker and some glasses
into the drawing-room. Having done this, he remembered the cigarettes and filled the silver cigarette box, a wedding present bearing
the Worrell colours in enamel, with *Sahibs* and some Turkish that
his wife always said she preferred to any other, no matter what they
happened to be. Then he presented himself with a cocktail, looked
at the fire, which was blazing cheerfully, looked at the chairs, which
were long, low, fat, and brown, glanced round the room, which
seemed to him a very handsome and friendly place now that the
two shaded lights took away the attention from the great bleak
expanse of wall above, sipped the cocktail, tried to hum a tune, and
began to feel a certain warm glow, a feeling proper to a host.

Mrs. Dersingham, who was in the bedroom, trying to powder the
space between her shoulder blades, was less fortunate. She felt
anxious. Cook had been rather cross all day and might spoil everything, and even when she tried, she was apt to make the soup greasy
and forget the salt in the vegetables. And Agnes, the new maid,
had pretended to understand all about serving, but she was so stupid
that she might easily go sticking vegetable dishes under people's
noses anyhow, and there was bound to be some awful confusion
when it came to clearing the table for dessert. You could laugh it
off, of course, but you got so tired of laughing it off. It was a pity this
sort of thing couldn't be done properly or laughed off altogether.
How terribly tiresome it was! And then, too, all the time you were
so worried and anxious about the food and the serving, you were
expected to be keeping the conversation going, terribly bright and
hostessy.

"I wish," said a silly girl at the back of Mrs. Dersingham's mind, a girl who had always been there but who did not say much except when she was rather tired or cross—"I wish I was a terribly successful actress who lived in a marvellous little flat and had a terribly devoted maid and a dresser and a huge car and nothing much to eat before the performance and then went on and was absolutely marvellous and everybody applauded and then I put on a wonderful Russia sable coat and diamonds and went out to supper and everybody stared. No, I don't. I wish I was a terribly successful woman writer with a villa somewhere on the Riviera with orange trees and mimosa and things and lunch in the sunshine and marvellous distinguished people coming to call. No, I don't. I wish I was terribly rich with a housekeeper and about fifteen servants and a marvellous maid of my own and umpteen Paris model gowns every season and a house in Town and a place in the country and a very attractive dark young man, very aristocratic and a racing motorist or yachtsman or something like that, terribly in love with me but just devoted and respectful all the time and coming and looking so miserable and me saying 'I'm sorry, my dear, but you can see how it is. I can never love anybody but Howard, but we can still be friends, can't we?'"

This silly girl still went rambling idiotically on while there returned into the rest of Mrs. Dersingham's mind various queries and worries about the sauce for the fish and the crême caramel not setting properly and Agnes spilling things. And all the time she was powdering her back or neck, trying on the crystal beads and then the amber, rubbing her cheeks with a tiny reddened pad, and staring at her reflection in the Jacobean mirror that she had bought at Brighton and that turned out to be a poor mirror and not Jacobean at all. The one consolation was that you always knew that you actually looked better than you did in that stupid mirror. Remembering this for the thousandth time, Mrs. Dersingham switched off the light, stood outside the night nursery a moment to discover if the children were quiet, then joined her husband in the drawing-room.

"Oh, thank goodness, nobody's here yet," she said, pulling a cushion or two about, then warming her hands. "It's such a ghastly rush. It's wonderful to have a few minutes' peace and quietness." She was already talking as if company were present.

"Rather," said Mr. Dersingham, loyally.

She stood in front of him now. "I suppose I look a thorough mess," she continued with a relapse into her natural manner.

"Not a bit. Jolly fine," Mr. Dersingham mumbled, feeling awkward as usual. He always had a suspicion that he ought to have said something first: "My word, you're looking jolly fine to-night," something of that sort. But somehow he never did.

"Don't be *too* complimentary, will you, darling? Well, I must say I *feel* a thorough mess tonight. What I'd *really* like is early bed and a book. This rush and seeing people all the time is so terrible." Once more, she was beginning to put on her company manner.

Mrs. Dersingham did not look a thorough mess, but neither did she look as attractive as she hoped she did. She looked like hundreds of other English wives in their earlier thirties, that is, fair, tired, bright, and sagging. She had pleasant blue eyes, a turned-up nose, and a slightly discontented mouth. Her life, apart from the secret saga of the kitchen and nursery, where creatures with the most astoundingly good references were for ever turning out to be lazy, impudent, and thieving, was really rather dull, for she had no strong interests and very few friends in London. But this she would not admit, not even to her husband, except on rare occasions when she lost her temper, broke down, and the truth came blazing through. She pretended that her life was one exciting and multi-coloured whirl of people and social events. She did not actually tell lies, but she created an atmosphere in which every little occurrence was instantly distorted and magnified, like objects dropped into a glass tank full of water. A tea on Monday and a dinner party on Friday were transformed into a week's feasting, a rushing here, there, and everywhere, not enjoyed but endured. If she met a person two or three times, then she had met whole crowds of him or her, day and night. Two matinées (with an old school friend or her mother up from Worcester) coming within one week reduced her to the condition of a dramatic critic at the end of a heavy autumn season. Even when she admitted that she had not attended a certain function, met a person, seen a play, read a book, she contrived to give these confessions a positive instead of a negative flavour, and so strong a positive flavour that somehow she seemed to be in close contact with the function, person, play, or book. She did this partly by throwing the emphasis on the auxiliary verb: "No, I *haven't* seen her," or: "No, I *haven't* seen it," which suggested to the listener that Mrs. Dersingham had attended a series of important committee meetings, had thrashed it out, and had decided with the rest that there should be nothing done about these people, these plays, these books, just yet. Thus, by this and other methods, she created an atmosphere in which a few outings and encounters were transformed into a rich and strenuous social life, which, so strong are our dreams, frequently left her genuinely fatigued. All this puzzled that simple man, her husband, but he never said anything now. The last time he had asked, after the company had gone, why she had complained so much about having to rush about, when he, for his part, could not see she had done much rushing about, she had turned on him quite fiercely and said that if it depended on him she would be sitting moping in the flat, never seeing anybody or anything, from one week's end to another, and that the less he said the better; an answer that left him completely bewildered.

The Dersinghams, standing together now on their bearskin rug, heard the first guest arrive. It must be either Golspie or the Trapes. It could not be the Pearsons, who, living in the maisonette above, always waited until they heard some one else arrive below, before they made their appearance. And Golspie it was, looking strangely unfamiliar to Mr. Dersingham in a rather voluminous dinner jacket and a very narrow black tie. He had hardly been introduced to Mrs. Dersingham before the Pearsons, who were just as anxious not to be late as they were not to be first, came in, breathless and smiling.

"A-ha, good evening!" cried Mr. Pearson, as if he had found them out.

"And how are *you*, my dear?" cried Mrs. Pearson to her hostess, in such a tone of voice that nobody would have imagined that they had met less than four hours ago.

The Pearsons were a middle-aged, childless couple, who had recently retired from Singapore. Mr. Pearson was a tallish man, with a long thin neck on which was perched a pear-shaped head. His cheeks were absurdly plump, a sharp contrast to all the rest of him, so that he always appeared to have just blown them out. He was both nervous and amiable, and consequently he laughed a great deal at nothing in particular, and the sound he made when he laughed can only be set down as *Tee-tee-tee-tee-tee*. Mrs. Pearson, who was altogether plump, had her face framed in a number of mysterious dark curls, and looked vaguely like one of the musical comedy actresses of the picture postcard era, one who had perhaps retired, after queening it in *The Catch of the Season*, to keep a jolly boarding-house. They were a lonely, friendly pair, who obviously did not know what on earth to do to pass the time, so that this was for them an occasion of some importance, to be looked forward to, to be referred to, to be enjoyed to the last syllable of small talk.

They were now all shouting at one another, after the fashion of hosts and guests in Barkfield Gardens and elsewhere.

"Found your way here all right then?" Mr. Dersingham bellowed to Mr. Golspie.

"Came in a taxi," Mr. Golspie boomed over his cocktail.

"That's the best way if you're going to a strange house in London, isn't it?" Mr. Pearson shouted. "We always do it when we can afford it. Tee-tee-tee-tee-tee."

"And how's the little darling to-night?" Mrs. Pearson inquired at the top of her voice, affectionately maternal as usual.

"Oh, we took the infant's temperature, and it was normal. He's all right," Mrs. Dersingham screamed in reply, elaborately unmaternal as usual.

"I'm so glad, *so* glad." And as she said it, Mrs. Pearson looked all beaming and moist. "I was so afraid there might be something really wrong with the dear kiddy. I was telling Walter that you thought it might be a chill. I'm *so* glad it wasn't, my dear. You can't be too careful with them, can you?"

"This Russian business looks pretty queer, doesn't it?" Mr. Dersingham shouted.

"Very queer. What do you make of it?" Mr. Pearson shouted in reply. He made nothing of it himself yet, because the evening paper had not told him what to make of it and he had heard nobody's opinion yet. On any question that had its origin west of Suez, Mr. Pearson liked to agree with his company. When it was east of Suez, he sometimes took a line of his own, and when Singapore itself was actually involved, he had been known to contradict people.

"Well, I'll tell you, Dersingham," said Mr. Golspie who as usual knew his own mind. "It's all a lot of tripe, bosh, bunkum. I know those yarns. Fellows up in Riga trying to earn their money, they send out that stuff."

"That's terribly interesting, Mr. Golspie," Mrs. Dersingham shrieked at him, suddenly looking like a woman of the world who had wanted to get to the bottom of this business for some time. "Of course, you've been up there, haven't you?"

"Round about." And Mr. Golspie gave her a grin, at once sardonic and friendly. It seemed to tell her that she was all right, not a bad-looking girl, but she mustn't try to draw him, for that wasn't her line at all, not at all.

"It makes a difference when you've been there, doesn't it?" cried Mr. Pearson. "You know the facts. Tee-tee-tee-tee-tee."

"And where do you live *now*, Mr. Golspie?" Mrs. Pearson inquired, rather archly and with her head on one side.

"Just got a furnished flat in Maida Vale," replied Mr. Golspie.

"Now I don't think I know that part," Mrs. Pearson said, girlishly reflective.

"There's a lot of London we still don't know. Tee-tee-tee-tee-tee."

"You're not missing much if you don't know Maida Vale, from what I've seen of it," Mr. Golspie boomed away. "Where I live seems to be full of Jews and music-hall turns. Old music-hall turns, not the good-lookin' young uns."

"Tee-tee-tee," Mr. Pearson put it, rather doubtfully.

"Oh, you men!" cried Mrs. Pearson, who had not lived at Singapore for nothing: she knew her cues.

"Tee-tee." Triumphant this time.

Miss Verever was announced, and very resentfully, for already Agnes had had enough of the evening and she had not liked the way this particular guest had walked in and looked at her.

There is something to be said for Agnes. Miss Verever was one of those people who, at a first meeting, demand to be disliked. She was Mrs. Dersingham's mother's cousin, a tall, cadaverous virgin of forty-five or so, who displayed, especially in evening clothes, an uncomfortable amount of sharp gleaming bone, just as if the upper part of her was a relief map done in ivory. In order that she might not be overlooked in company and also to protect herself, she had developed and brought very near to perfection a curiously disturbing manner, which conveyed a boundless suggestion of the malicious, the mocking, the sarcastic, the sardonic, the ironical. What she actually said was harmless enough, but her tone of voice, her expression, her smile, her glance, all these suggested that her words had some devilish inner meaning. In scores of smaller hotels and *pensions* overlooking the Mediterranean, merely by asking what time the post went or inquiring if it had rained during the night, she had made men wonder if they had not shaved properly and women ask themselves if something had gone wrong with their complexions, and compelled members of both sexes to consider if they had just said something very silly. After that, she had only to perform the smallest decent action for people to say that she had a surprisingly kind heart as well as a terrifyingly clever satirical head. This was all very well if people had booked rooms under the same roof for the next three months, but on chance acquaintances, wondering indignantly what on earth she had against *them*, this peculiar manner of hers had an unfortunate effect.

She now advanced, kissed her hostess, shook hands with her host, and then, pursing her lips and screwing up the rest of her features, said: "I hope you've not been waiting for *me*. I'm sure you have, haven't you?" And strange as it may seem, this remark and this simple question immediately made the whole dinner party appear preposterous.

"No, we haven't really," Mr. Dersingham told her, at the same time asking himself why in the name of thunder they had ever thought of inviting her. "Somebody still to come. The Trapes."

"Oh, I'm glad I'm not the last, then," said Miss Verever, with a bitter little smile, which she kept on her face while she was being introduced to the other guests.

A minute later, the Trapes arrived to complete the party. Late guests may be divided into two classes, the repentant, who arrive, perspiring and profusely apologetic, to babble about fogs and ancient taxis and stupid drivers, and the unrepentant, who stalk in haughtily and look somewhat aggrieved when they see all the other guests, their eyebrows registering their disapproval of people who do not know what time their own parties begin. The Trapes were admirable specimens of the unrepentant class. They were both tall, cold, thin, and rather featureless. Trape himself was an Old Worrelian and a contemporary of Dersingham's. He was a partner in a firm of estate agents, but called himself Major Trape because he had held that rank at the end of the war and had become so soldierly training the vast mob of boys who were conscripted then that he could not bring himself to say good-bye to his outworn courtesy title. He was indeed so curt, so military, so imperial, that it was impossible to imagine him letting and selling houses in the ordinary way, and the mind's eye saw him mopping up, with a small raiding party, all flats and bijou residences, and sallying out with an expeditionary force to plant the Union Jack on finely timbered, residential and sporting estates. His wife was a somewhat colourless woman, very English in type, who always looked as if she was always faintly surprised and disgusted by life. Perhaps she was, and perhaps that was why she always talked with a certain ventriloquial effect, producing a voice with hardly any movement of her small iced features.

Leaving them all to shout at one another, Mrs. Dersingham now slipped out of the room, for it was imperative that dinner should be announced as soon as possible. She returned three minutes later, trying not unsuccessfully to look as if she had not a care in the world, a sort of *Arabian Nights* hostess, and then, after the smallest interval, Agnes popped her head into the room, thereby forgetting one of her most urgent instructions, and said, without any enthusiasm at all: "Please, m', dinner's served."

Mrs. Dersingham smiled heroically at her guests, who, with the exception of Mr. Golspie, looked at one another and at the door as if they were hearing about this dinner business for the first time and were mildly interested and amused. Mr. Golspie, for his part, looked like a man who wanted his dinner, and actually took a step or two towards the door. Then began that general stepping forward and stepping backward and smiling and hand-waving which take place at this moment in all those unhappy sections of society that have lost formality and yet have not reached informality. There they were, smiling and dithering round the door.

"Now then, Mrs. Pearson," cried Mr. Golspie in his loudest and most brutal tones. "In you go." And, without more ado, this impatient guest put a hand behind Mrs. Pearson's elbow, and Mrs. Pearson found herself through the door, the leader of the exodus. They crowded into the small dining-room, where the soup was already steaming under the four shaded electric lights.

"Now let me see," Mrs. Dersingham began, as usual, feeling that these guests were not people now but six enormous bodies of which she, the wretched criminal, had to dispose. "Now let me see. Will you sit there, Mrs. Trape. And Mrs. Pearson, there." And then, having disposed of the bodies, she had time to notice that the soup looked horribly greasy.

III

The soup was bad, and Miss Verever left most of hers and contrived to be looking down at it very curiously every time Mrs.
Dersingham glanced across the table at her. As there were eight
of them, Mrs. Dersingham was not sitting at the end of the table,
opposite her husband. Mr. Golspie was there, and very much at
his ease, putting away a very ungentlemanly quantity of bread
under that great moustache of his. On Mr. Golspie's right were Mrs.
Dersingham, Major Trape, and Mrs. Pearson, and on the other side
were Miss Verever, Mr. Pearson, and Mrs. Trape.

"And how," said Miss Verever to Mrs. Dersingham, "did you
enjoy your Norfolk holiday this summer? You never told me that,
and I've been dying to know." The smile that accompanied this
statement announced that Miss Verever could not imagine a more
idiotic or boring topic, that you would be insufferably dull if you
answered her question and terribly rude if you didn't.

"Not bad," Mrs. Dersingham shouted desperately. "In fact, quite
good, on the whole. Rather cold, you know."

"Really, you found it cold?" And you would have sworn that
the speaker meant to suggest that the cold had obviously been
manufactured for you and that it served you right.

At the other end of the table, Major Trape and his host were
talking about football, across Mrs. Pearson, who nodded and smiled
and shook her mysterious curls all the time, to show that she was
not really being left out.

"Do you ever watch rugger, Golspie?" Mr. Dersingham demanded down the table.

"What, Rugby? Haven't seen a match for years," replied Mr.
Golspie. "Prefer the other kind when I do watch one."

Major Trape raised his eyebrows. "What, you a soccah man? Not
this professional stuff? Don't tell me you like that."

"What's the matter with it?"

"Oh, come now! I mean, you can't possibly—I mean, it's a dirty business, selling fellahs for money and so on, very unsporting."

"I must say I agree, Trape," said Mr. Dersingham. "Dashed unsporting business, I call it."

"Oh, certainly," Major Trape continued, "must be amatahs—love of the game. Play the game for its own sake, I say, and not as all these fellahs do—for monay. Can't possibly be a sportsman and play for monay. Oh, dirty business, eh, Dersingham?"

"I'm with you there."

A sound came from Mrs. Trape's face and it seemed to declare that she was with him too.

"Well, I'm not with you," said Mr. Golspie bluntly. He did not care tuppence about it, one way or the other, but there was something in Trape's manner that demanded contradiction, and Mr. Golspie was not the man to ignore such a challenge. "If a poor man can play a game well, why shouldn't he allow that game to keep him? What's the answer to that? A man's as much right to play cricket and football for a living as he has to clean windows or sell tripe ——"

"Tripe indeed! How can you, Mr. Golspie?" cried Mrs. Pearson, girlishly shaking her curls at him.

"My wife hates tripe," said Mr. Pearson. "Tee-tee-tee-tee-tee."

"I disagree," said Major Trape, stiffer than ever now. "Those things are business, quite diff'rent. Games ought to be played for their own sake. That's the proper English way. Love of the game. Clean sport. Don't mind if the other fellahs win. Sport and business, two diff'rent things."

"Not if sport *is* your business," Mr. Golspie returned, looking darkly mischievous. "We can't all be rich amachures. Let the chaps have their six or seven pounds a week. They earn it. If one lot of chaps can earn their living by telling us to be good every Sunday— that is, if you go to listen to 'em: I don't—why shouldn't another lot be paid to knock a ball about every Saturday, without all this talk of dirty business? It beats me. Unless it's snobbery. Lot o' snobbery still about in this country. It pops up all the time."

"What *is* this argument all about?" Miss Verever inquired. And, perhaps feeling that Mr. Golspie needed a rebuke, she put on her most peculiar look and brought out her most disturbing tone of voice, finally throwing in a smile that was a tried veteran, an Old Guard.

But Mr. Golspie returned her gaze quite calmly, and even conveyed a piece of fish, and far too large a piece, to his mouth before replying. "We're arguing about football and cricket. I don't suppose you're interested. I'm not much, myself. I like billiards. That's one thing about coming back to this country, you can always get a good game of billiards. Proper tables, y'know."

"I used to be very fond of a game of billiards, snooker too," said Mr. Pearson, nodding his head so that his fat cheeks shook like beef jellies, "when I was out in Singapore. There were some splendid players at the club there, splendid players, make breaks of forty and fifty. But I wasn't one of them. Tee-tee-tee——"

"We went to see Susie Dean and Jerry Jerningham the other night," said Major Trape, turning to Mrs. Dersingham. "Good show. Very clevah, very clevah. You been to any shows lately, Mrs. Dersingham?"

"That's true," Mrs. Pearson informed her host and anybody else who cared to listen. "When we were out in Singapore, my husband was always going over to the club for billiards. And now he hardly ever plays. I don't think he's had a game this year. Have you, Walter? I'm just saying I don't think you've had a game this year."

"And so what with one thing and another," Mrs. Dersingham told Major Trape, "I've simply not been able to see half the plays I've wanted to see. Something has to go, hasn't it? We were out at the Trevors'—I think you know them, don't you?—the shipbuilding people, you know, only of course these Trevors are out of that—they're terribly in with all that young smart set, Mrs. Dellingham, young Mostyn-Price, Lady Muriel Pagworth, and the famous Ditchways. Well, what with that, and then going to Mrs. Westbury's musical tea-fight—Dossevitch and Rougeot *ought* to have been there and were only prevented from coming at the last minute, but Imogen Farley was there and played divinely. Oh, and then on top of all that, I went to see that new thing at His Majesty's—what's it called? —oh, yes—*The Other Man*. And so I haven't had a single moment for any other show."

"No, by Jove, you haven't, have you?" said Major Trape, with whom this miracle of the social loaves and fishes worked every time. "You're worse than Dorothy, and I tell her she overdoes it. Mustn't overdo it, you know."

Mrs. Dersingham, wondering how long Agnes was going to be bringing up the cutlets, shrugged her shoulders, and did it exactly as she had seen Irene Prince do it in *Smart Women* at the Ambassadors. "It *is* stupid, I know," she confessed charmingly, "and I'm always saying I'll cut most of it out—but—well, you know what happens."

Miss Verever, wearing her most peculiar smile, leaned forward, caught the eye of her hostess, and said, "But what *does* happen, my dear?"

Mrs. Dersingham was able to escape, however, by plunging at once into the talk at the other end of the table, as if she had not heard Miss Verever's inquiry. "Oh, have you been reading that?" she cried across the table to Mrs. Trape, who did not look as if she had spoken for weeks, but nevertheless had actually just conjured out several remarks. "No, I *haven't* read it, and I don't mean to." But did Agnes mean to bring the cutlets?

The talk at Mr. Dersingham's end, as we have guessed, had suddenly turned literary. Mrs. Trape had just read a certain book. It was, she added, apparently throwing her voice into the claret decanter, a very clever book. Mr. Dersingham had not read this book, and did not hesitate to say that it did not sound his kind of book, for after a jolly good hard day in the office he found such books too heavy going and preferred a detective story. Mrs. Pearson was actually reading a book, had been reading it that very afternoon, had nearly finished it and was enjoying it immensely.

"And I'm sure it's a story *you'd* like, Mr. Dersingham," she cried, "even though there aren't any detectives in it. I could hardly put it down. It's all about a girl going to one of those Pacific Islands, one of those lovely coral and lagoon places, you know, and she goes there to stay with an uncle because she's lost all her money and when she gets there she finds that he's drinking terribly, and so she goes to another man—but I mustn't spoil it for you. Do read it, Mrs. Trape."

The claret decanter murmured that it would love to read it, and asked what the name of the book was, so that it might put it down on its library list.

"I'll tell you the title in a moment," and Mrs. Pearson, bringing her curls to rest, bit her lip reflectively. "Now how stupid of me! Do you know, I can't remember. It's a very striking title, too, and that's what made me take it when the girl at the library showed it to me. Now isn't that silly of me?"

"I can never remember the titles either," Mr. Dersingham assured her heartily. "What was the name of the chap who wrote it? Was it a man or a woman?"

"I *think* it was a man's name, in fact I'm nearly sure it was. It was quite a common name, too. Something like Wilson. No, it wasn't, it was Wilkinson. Walter, do you remember the name of the author of that book I'm reading? Wasn't it Wilkinson?"

"You're thinking of the man that came to mend the wireless set," Mr. Pearson replied, shooting his long neck at her. "That was Wilkinson. You know the people, Dersingham—the electricians in Earl's Court Road?"

"Oh, so it was. How silly of me!"

"Tee-tee-tee-tee-tee."

Mrs. Pearson smiled vaguely but amiably, then said: "So you see I can't tell you *now*, but I'll tell Mrs. Dersingham in the morning and then she can tell you."

A sudden silence fell on the table at that moment, perhaps because there was a sort of scratching sound at the door, which opened, but only about an inch or two. That silence was shattered by the most appalling crash of breaking crockery, followed by a short sharp wail. Then silence again for one sinking moment. The cutlets and the vegetables had arrived at last, and a brown stain, creeping beneath the door, told where they were.

"My God!" cried Mr. Golspie to Miss Verever, as Mrs. Dersingham dashed to the door, "there goes our dinner."

"Indeed!"

"You bet your life!" Mr. Golspie, earnest and unabashed, assured her.

Miss Verever and Major Trape exchanged glances, which removed Mr. Golspie once and for all from decent society and handed him over to the social worker and the anthropologist.

Meanwhile, Mrs. Dersingham had disappeared through the doorway, and Mr. Dersingham was trying to follow her example but could not do so because, what with cutlets, vegetables, gravy, broken dishes and plates, a weeping Agnes, and a panic-stricken Mrs. Dersingham, there was no space for him. So he stood there, holding the door open, with his body inside the dining-room and his head outside.

"Oh, do shut the door, Howard," the guests heard Mrs. Dersingham cry.

"All right," the invisible head replied hesitatingly. "But I say—can't I—er—do anything? I mean, do you want me to come out or —er—well, what do you want me to do?"

"Oh, go-in-and-shut-the-door." And there was no doubt that in another moment Mrs. Dersingham would have screamed, for this was the voice of a woman in an extremity.

Mr. Dersingham closed the door and returned to his chair. He looked at Major Trape, and Major Trape looked at him, and no doubt they were both remembering the good old school, Worrelians together.

"Sorry, but—er—" and here Mr. Dersingham looked round apologetically at his guests—"I'm afraid there's been some sort of accident outside."

Immediately, Mrs. Trape, Mrs. Pearson, Major Trape, and Mr. Pearson began talking all at once, not talking about this accident but about accidents in general, with special reference to very queer accidents that had happened to them. Miss Verever merely looked peculiarly at everybody, while Mr. Golspie finished his claret with a certain remote gloom, as if he were a man taking quinine on the summit of a mountain.

Then the door, which had not been properly fastened, swung open again, to admit a mixed knocking and gobbling and guggling noise that suggested that Agnes was now lying on the floor, in hysterics, and drumming her feet. Then came a new voice, very hoarse and resentful, and this voice declared that it was all a crying shame, even if the girl was clumsy with her hands, and that one pair of hands was one pair of hands and could not be expected to be any more, and that while notices were being given right and left, *her* notice could be taken, there and then. In short, the cook had arrived on the scene.

Mr. Dersingham arose miserably, but whether to shut the door again or to make an entrance into the drama outside we shall never know, for Mrs. Pearson, fired with neighbourly solicitude, sprang up, crying, "Poor Mrs. Dersingham! I'm sure I ought to do something," and was outside, with the door closed behind her, before Mr. Dersingham knew what was happening.

And Mrs. Pearson, once outside, did not simply intrude, did not gape and hang about and get in the way, but took charge of the situation, for though Mrs. Pearson may have been a foolish table-talker, may have worn mysterious curls and been old-fashioned and monstrously girlish and affectionate, she was a housewife of experience, who had weathered the most fantastic tropical domestic storms in Singapore.

"I *knew* you wouldn't mind my coming out," she cried, "and I felt I must help, because after all we are neighbours, aren't we? and that makes a difference."

"It's too absurd," Mrs. Dersingham wailed. "This wretched girl's smashed everything and ruined the dinner, and now she's going off into a fit or something out of sheer temper. And it's all her own fault. I engaged her sister to come and help her to-night, and then when her sister couldn't come, at the last minute of course, she wouldn't let me get anybody else, she said she could do it herself."

Mrs. Pearson was looking at Agnes, who was still guggling and drumming on the floor. "Only stupid hysterics. Get up at once, you silly, silly girl. Do you hear? You're in the way. We'll pour cold water over her. That will soon bring her round, you'll see."

The cook, who was standing in the hall, a few yards away, and had been looking on with the air of a complacent prophetess, now began to lose some of her rigidity. The mournful triumph died out of her face. She had no respect for Mrs. Dersingham, but for some strange reason she had almost a veneration for Mrs. Pearson, who was possibly a far more ladylike and commanding figure in her eyes.

"That's so," the cook hoarsely declared now. "A jug of water's what she wants. Accidents will happen and one pair of hands can't be two or three pairs of hands, eight for dinner being out of all reason with them steps and no service lift, but there's no call to be lying there all night, Agnes, having your hysterics and carrying on silly when there's all this mess to be cleared, let alone anything else."

This treacherous withdrawal of a stout ally, combined with the talk of cold water, soon brought the hysterics to mere choking and sniffing, and in a minute or two Agnes was bending over the ruins. "I'll clear these away," she announced between sniffs and chokes, "but I won't bring anything else and serve it, I won't. I couldn't if I tried, I couldn't. I haven't a nerve in me body, not after what's happened, I haven't."

"But I shall have to give them *something*," Mrs. Dersingham was saying. Clearly she no longer included Mrs. Pearson among the guests. Mrs. Pearson had ceased to be one of "them."

"Of course you will, my dear," cried Mrs. Pearson, her eyes gleaming with a happy excitement. "Not that *we'd* mind, of course. It's the men, isn't it? You know what the men are? Now then, what about eggs?"

"Eggs," the cook repeated hoarsely and gloomily. "There's two eggs, an' two eggs only, in that kitchen. Just the two eggs, and them's for the morning."

"Listen, my dear." And Mrs. Pearson clutched at her neighbour affectionately and imploringly. "*Do* leave it to me and I promise you I won't be ten minutes. I won't, really. Now not a word! Don't bother about *anything*. Just you leave it to me." She hurried towards the outer door, pulled herself up before she reached it, and cried over her shoulder, "But warm some plates, that's all."

During the subsequent interval, Mrs. Dersingham had not the heart to return to the dining-room, though she did just look in, put her face round the door and smile apologetically at everybody and say that it was *too* absurd and annoying and that the two of them, she and Mrs. Pearson, would be back in a few minutes. She spent the rest of the time superintending the salvage work outside the dining-room door and helping cook to find enough fresh plates to warm. She felt hot, dishevelled and miserable. She could have cried. Indeed, that was why she did not slip upstairs to her bedroom to look at herself and powder her nose, for once there, really alone with herself, she was sure she would have cried. Oh, it was all too hateful for words!

"There!" And Mrs. Pearson stood before her, breathless, flushed, and happy, and whipped off the lid of a silver dish.

"Oh!" cried Mrs. Dersingham in the very reek of the omelette, a fine large specimen. "You angel! It's absolutely perfect."

"I remembered we had some eggs, and then I remembered we

had a bottle of mushrooms tucked away somewhere, and so I rushed upstairs and made this mushroom omelette. It ought to be nice. I used to be good with omelettes."

"It's marvellous. And I don't know how to begin to thank you, my dear." And Mrs. Dersingham meant it. From that moment, Mrs. Pearson ceased to be a merely foolish if kindly neighbour and became a friend, worthy of the most secret confidences. In the steam of the omelette, rich as the smoke of burnt offerings, this friendship began, and Mrs. Dersingham never tasted a mushroom afterwards without being reminded of it.

"Don't think of it, my dear," said Mrs. Pearson happily, for her own life, after months of the dull routine of time-killing, had suddenly become crimson, rich and glorious. "Now have you got the plates ready? You must have this served at once, mustn't you? Where's that silly girl? Gone to bed? All right, then, make the cook serve the rest of the dinner. She must have everything ready by this time. Call her, my dear. Tell her to bring up the plates." And they returned at last to the dining-room, two sisters out of burning Troy.

Alas, all was not well in there. Something had happened during the interval of waiting. It was not the women, who were all sympathetic smiles and solicitude: Mrs. Trape even dropped the ventriloquial effect, actually disturbed the lower part of her face, in order to explain that she knew, no one better, what it was these days, when anything might be expected of that class; and Miss Verever, though retaining automatically some peculiarities of tone and grimace, contrived to say something reassuring. No, it was not the women; it was the men. Mr. Golspie looked like a man who had already said some brutal things and was fully prepared to say some more; Major Trape looked very stiff and uncompromising, as if he had just sentenced a couple of surveyors to be shot; Mr. Pearson gave the impression that he had been faintly tee-teeing on both sides of a quarrel and was rather tired of it; and Mr. Dersingham looked uneasy, anxious, exasperated. There was no mistaking the atmosphere, in which distant thunder still rolled. The stupid men had had to wait for the more substantial part of dinner; they had felt empty, then they had felt cross; and so they had argued, shouted, quarrelled, not all of them perhaps, but certainly Mr. Golspie and Major Trape. Probably at any moment, they would begin arguing, shouting, quarrelling again. Mrs. Dersingham, very tired now and with a hundred little nerves screaming to be taken out of all this and put to bed, would have liked to bang their silly heads together.

Cook came in, breathing heavily and disapprovingly, and gave them their omelette. There was not a single movement she made during the whole time she was in the room that did not announce, quite plainly, that she was the cook, that the kitchen was her place, that she did not pretend to be able to wait at table and that if they did not like it they could lump it. Her heavy breathing went further, pointing out that when she did condescend to wait at table, she expected to find a better company than this seated round it. Even Mrs. Pearson had apparently lost favour, for she had her plate shoved contemptuously in front of her, like the rest. Real ladies, that plate said, don't rush away and cook omelettes for other people's dinner tables. "P'raps you'll ring when you want the next," the cook wheezed, and then slowly, scornfully, took her departure.

"If you don't mind my saying so, Mrs. Dersingham," said Major Trape, "this omelette's awf'ly good, awf'ly good. And there's nothing I like better than a jolly good omelette."

A voice from Mrs. Trape's direction said that it agreed with him.

"They're right there," said Mr. Golspie to Mrs. Dersingham, as if the Trapes were not often right. "It's as good an omelette as I've had for months and months, and that's saying something, because I've been in places where they can make omelettes. They can't make 'em here in England." And he said this in such a way as to suggest that it was really a challenge to Trape, who was nothing if not patriotic. Obviously, he and Trape had been quarrelling.

Major Trape stiffened, then smiled laboriously at his hostess. "Mr. Golspie seems to think we can't make anything in England. That's where he and I diffah. Isn't it, Dersingham?"

"Well, yes, in a way, I suppose," Mr. Dersingham mumbled unhappily. He felt divided between Worrell and Angel Pavement, between his old and respected school friend, Trape, with whom he instinctively agreed, and the forceful man who was now saving Twigg & Dersingham and making it prosperous, his guest for the first time, too; and it was a wretched situation. He muttered now that there was a lot to be said on both sides.

"There may be," said Major Trape. "But I don't like to hear a man continually runnin' down his own country. Tastes diffah, I suppose. But I feel—well, it isn't done, that's all."

"Time it was done then," said Mr. Golspie aggressively. "Most of the people I meet here these days seem to be living in a fool's paradise ——"

"Now, Mr. Golspie," cried his hostess with desperate vivacity, "you're not to call us all fools. Is he, Mrs. Trape? We won't have it." Then, saving the situation at all cost, she turned to Miss Verever. "My dear, I forgot to tell you, I've had the absurdest letter from Alice. When I read it, I simply howled."

"No, did you?" said Miss Verever.

"A-ha!" cried Mr. Dersingham, doing his best. "What's the latest from Alice? We must all hear about this."

They were all listening now, all at peace for the moment.

"Oh, it was too ridiculous," cried Mrs. Dersingham, despairingly racking her brains to remember something amusing in that letter, or, failing that, something amusing in any letter she had ever had from anybody. "You know what Alice is—at least, you do, my dear, and so do you. I suppose it isn't really funny unless you know her. You see, the minute I read a letter of hers, of course I can see her in my mind and hear her voice and all that sort of thing, and unless you can do that, well I dare say it isn't so funny, after all. But, you see, Alice—she's my youngest sister, I must explain, and they live down in Devon—oh, miles from anywhere. Will you ring, please, darling? Well, Alice has a dog, the absu-u-urdest creature——"

She struggled through with it somehow, and fortunately cook made such a noise clearing and then serving the sweet that most of the anecdote, presumably the funniest part, was lost in the clatter. The cook had been so noisy, so incredibly heavy in her breathing, and so obviously disapproving, when she was serving the sweet, that Mrs. Dersingham dare not have her up again to clear the table for dessert, so as the fruit-plates and the finger-bowls, the port decanter and glasses, were all on the sideboard, she made a joke of it—showing the last gleam of vivacity she felt she would be able to show for months—and she and Dersingham, assisted by Mr. Pearson, who said—tee-tee-tee-tee-tee—that he was used to clearing a table, having been well brought up, did what they could to make the dinner look as if it were coming to a civilised end. Mrs. Dersingham felt that Mr. Golspie, plainly a porty sort of man, and Major Trape might not want to argue so unpleasantly once they had some port inside them. This was the longest and most ghastly dinner she ever remembered. It was not really very late, but it seemed like two in the morning. As she tried to peel a very soft pear, she felt she wanted to throw it at the opposite wall and then scream at the top of her voice.

It was then they heard a ring at the outer door. Perhaps the postman, rather late and with something special to deliver. A minute or so later, there came another and longer ring.

"The only time we were there it rained for a whole week," said Major Trape, concluding his account of the watering places, "and so I said, 'Nevah again.' Can't imagine how these towns get their reputation. These weathah reports they give out——"

Another ring, very determined this time.

"I'm sorry, but do go and see who that is at the door, my dear," Mrs. Dersingham cried, apologetically. "I've just remembered. Agnes has gone to bed, and cook probably can't hear or won't hear. I don't suppose it's anybody but the late post."

Mr. Dersingham was absent several minutes, and somehow during that time nobody appeared to want to talk. Mrs. Dersingham did not press the fruit upon her guests. The moment the last piece was eaten, she intended to rise from the table, and then—oh, thank Heaven!—the worst was over. The men could stay on drinking port and quarrel like cats and dogs if they liked. She would be out of it, among nice, silly, comfortable women in the drawing-room, and so it would all be over. And then, just as she was nearly succeeding in consoling herself, her husband reappeared, and he was not alone. The idiot had brought a complete stranger into the dining-room with him, a girl.

She was a very pretty girl, quite young, and on his face was that fatuous smile which husbands always seem to wear in the company of young and very pretty girls. All wives recognize and detest that fatuous smile. It is bad at any time, but when it accompanies a girl who is a complete stranger into the dining-room at the conclusion of a disastrous dinner, and brings her into the presence of a wife who has not felt even decently presentable for hours and hours and who has been ready to scream for the last forty-five minutes, then it is a catastrophe and a mortal injury. And so Mrs. Dersingham gave Mr. Dersingham one look that sent that fatuous smile trembling into oblivion. And then, half rising from her chair, Mrs. Dersingham looked at the stranger, and decided at once that she had never before seen a girl she disliked' so much at sight as this one.

"I'm afraid—er—I don't——" she began.

But the girl was not even looking at her. She was busy having her left cheek brushed by the large moustache of Mr. Golspie, who had flung an arm round her shoulders.

"Well, hang me, Lena girl," Mr. Golspie was roaring, "if I hadn't forgotten all about you."

"You would," said the girl coolly. "You're a rotten father. I've told you that before. Now introduce me."

IV

"Now this is my fault," Mr. Golspie boomed at the Dersinghams, turning from one to the other, "my fault entirely. I ought to have told you. I meant to, but I forgot. This girl of mine wrote to say she was coming from Paris to-day, but of course she didn't say how and when and what and where, just left it all vague, y'know, as usual, all up in the air. When it got to be half past seven and she hadn't turned up, I began to wonder. What was I to do?" And as he asked this he stared fiercely at Mr. Pearson, who happened to catch his eye.

"Quite so, Mr. Golspie," Mr. Pearson, startled, jerked out.

"Well, I'll tell you what I did do. I left a message with the caretaker of the flats, so that if she did come she'd know where I was ——"

"All right, my dear," his daughter interrupted, "you needn't go on and on. Nobody wants to hear all about it. I got the message. I wasn't going to spend hours all alone in that poisonous flat. So I took a taxi and came here. And that's that." And having thus dismissed the subject, Miss Golspie, who seemed an astonishingly cool and composed young lady, smiled at Mrs. Dersingham, who did not return the smile. Miss Golspie then produced a small mirror from her handbag and carefully examined her features in it.

And even Mrs. Dersingham would have been compelled to admit that they were very charming features. Lena Golspie still remained, after closer inspection, a very pretty girl. She had reddish-gold hair, large brown eyes, an impudent little nose, and a luscious mouth. She looked rather smaller than she actually was. Her neck, shoulders, and arms were slenderly, even too delicately, fashioned, but she had strong, well-shaped legs; and was indeed the complete attractive young female animal. Only in a certain slant of the eye and some movements of the mouth did she resemble her father, though a very acute listener might have found some likeness in their

voices. Their accent, however, was quite different, for Mr. Golspie
spoke with a breadth of vowel sound and roughness of consonants
that suggested the toned-down Lowlander or North-country Englishman, whereas his daughter's English did not properly belong to any
part of England but seemed to be that international English, of a
kind that a clever foreigner might pick up in the Anglo-Saxon col-
ony in Paris and that is sometimes spoken by both English and
Americans on the stage, a language without roots and background,
a language for "the talkies." Indeed, in Lena's company you might
have felt you were taking part in a "talkie."

"And I intended to tell you when I first came in," Mr. Golspie
continued, determined to have his say. "Just to warn you that this
daughter o' mine—who doesn't behave herself as nicely as she looks,
I can tell you—might be landing herself on you."

"Quite all right, of course," said Mr. Dersingham. "I mean—
delighted!"

"Good! No harm done, then." And Mr. Golspie sat down, grinned
at his daughter, noticed the decanter in front of him, and promptly
helped himself to another glass of port.

"But I must say," cried Lena, who had now concluded the exami-
nation of her own features and was busy examining everybody
else's, "I thought you'd have finished dinner hours ago. Did you
begin late or have you been wolfing an awful lot?"

"I think we'd better all go straight into the drawing-room," said
Mrs. Dersingham hurriedly, "unless you men feel you *must* stay and
drink some more port."

"Not a bit," said Mr. Golspie heartily. "Ĭ m ready, for one." And
to show that he was, he drained his glass in one sharp gulp.

"Only too delighted, Mrs. Dersingham," said Major Trape, bowing
and looking very severe, as if indirectly to rebuke the uncouth
Golspie.

"Good work!" said Mr. Dersingham, who obviously felt that
something was still wrong somewhere and was trying in vain to

appear hearty and enthusiastic. He opened the door. "Much better if we all barge in together now."

"Come along, Miss Golspie," and the patient little smile that Mrs. Dersingham contrived to produce was itself a studied insult. "We don't mind a *bit* your not being dressed. It doesn't matter at all, I assure you."

Miss Golspie turned wondering large brown eyes upon her. "Oh, did you want me to change? I would have done if I'd known—specially as I've brought over one or two marvellous new dresses —but it didn't seem worth it. Sorry and all that!"

"Not in the least," replied Mrs. Dersingham, pale with weariness and vexation. Cheerfully—oh, so cheerfully!—she could have murdered this girl.

They trooped rather silently into the drawing-room, which did not seem particularly pleased to see them. It had been neglected itself for some time—so that the fire was low and ashy—and now it did not seem to welcome visitors. Cook arrived with coffee, and put down the tray with the air of a camel exhibiting the last straw. She did not attempt to serve it. She put it down on the rickety little table and immediately made that table seem ten times more rickety. There was no cup for Miss Golspie, who of course said at once that she would have some coffee, and so Mr. Dersingham, with what seemed to his wife a great deal of unnecessary fuss and silliness, insisted that he should go without. And then, having taken the tiniest sip of coffee, this Golspie girl ostentatiously put the cup on one side, and, on being asked by Mr. Pearson, who had also turned silly and officious, if she would have some more, replied that she did not really want any coffee.

"I'll tell you what, though," she declared, in a loud clear voice, "I'd adore a cocktail, if there are any going."

"Oh, would you, Miss Golspie?" Mr. Dersingham began. "Well, I dare say I could rake up ——" But he was not allowed to continue.

"I'm afraid there aren't any cocktails going," said Mrs. Dersingham, in a voice that was if anything louder and clearer, and as frosted as the best Martini.

And the insensitive Mr. Golspie did not improve the situation by chiming in with "I should think not. Don't you take any notice of her, Mrs. Dersingham. I'll give her cocktails!"

"When you get her home, eh?" Mr. Pearson cried, with rash facetiousness. "Tee-tee-tee-tee-tee."

It was easily his least successful "Tee-tee" of the evening. Mrs. Pearson looked surprised at him. Mr. Golspie gave him a glance that told him quite plainly to mind his own business and not try to be funny. Lena herself shot a furious glance at both her father and Mr. Pearson, but did not cast a single look in Mrs. Dersingham's direction—a very ominous sign. As for Mrs. Dersingham, she could not decide which was the more awful, Mr. Golspie or his terrible daughter. She tried to start a conversation with Mrs. Pearson, who was now all embarrassed smiles, and Mrs. Trape, whose face had been completely frost-bound for the last ten minutes.

Miss Verever, every feature in battle order, now bore down on Lena, opening the engagement with a long-range smile of the most sinister peculiarity. "Do I understand, Miss Golspie," she said, with the most mysterious grimace and the most baffling inflections, "that you've just come from Paris? Have you been living there?"

"Hello, hello!" cried Lena's startled expression. "What have I done to you?" But all she actually said in reply was, "Yes, I've just come from there, and I've been living there."

"Oh, you *have* been living there?"

"Yes, for the last eighteen months. With an uncle. You see, he lives there, and I've been living with him."

"Oh, your *uncle* lives there?"

"Yes, he's lived there nearly all his life. He is half French, anyhow. And my aunt's completely French."

"Then is your father—Mr. Golspie—half French?" asked Miss Verever, in one of her strangest whispers.

"No, not at all," said Lena, with a little impatient shake of her head. "You see, this uncle's my mother's brother, not my father's."

"Oh, your *mother's*." And now Miss Verever produced her most famous glance of inquiry, awfully enigmatical in its final meaning and yet immediately challenging. She followed it up with a new smile, crooked, terrible. "Well, then, of course, your mother must be half French, I suppose, just like your uncle?"

"Yes, she was." And then Lena's little nose wrinkled, partly in bewilderment, partly in distaste. Then she looked straight at Miss Verever, who was bending over her and searching her with an unwinking gaze. "But what about it? I mean, there's nothing particularly funny about that, is there? Lots of people are half French, aren't they?"

"Yes, I suppose so." Miss Verever was taken aback.

"Well, then, what are you looking at me like that for?" cried Lena, at once registering a direct hit. "I mean, you look as if there was something terribly weird about it all. There really isn't, you know. It's all quite simple." The shell crashed through and exploded somewhere near the magazine.

Miss Verever was jerked upright by her surprise. Then she turned glacial. "I beg your pardon."

"Oh, I don't mind, but——"

Miss Verever did not wait to hear, but turned away at once and joined the other three women. Lena, after staring after her for a moment, gave a tiny wriggle and then broke into a duet of Old Worrelian talk between Mr. Dersingham and Major Trape, who were merely chivalrous at first but very soon began to wear that fatuous smile. And towards the three of them an icy current began to flow from the group of women. Too tired, too cross, even to pretend to be a good brisk hostess, Mrs. Dersingham let the whole thing slide, and merely prayed for the end. It was not long in coming.

"Shall I?" Miss Golspie was heard to cry to the two men.

They nodded and smiled, a little doubtfully perhaps, but still they nodded and smiled, men under a spell.

"All right, then, I will. Just to cheer us all up. We're getting terribly dismal." And Miss Golspie, with a final and coquettish nod and smile of her own at the other two nodders and smilers, marched across the room, puffing away at one of her host's *Sahibs*. Then she sat down at the baby grand.

"That's the way, Lena," her father shouted approvingly. He had been talking in a corner to Mr. Pearson. "Let's have a tune. Do us good."

Before anybody else could say a word, Lena had begun playing. She played some dance tunes, very sketchily, but with great speed and noise. The first two or three minutes were bad, but the next two or three minutes were much worse, for then her left hand, guessing wildly, began hitting any note roughly in the neighbourhood of the right one, and the very fire irons joined in the din. After ten minutes, she reached a grand *fortissimo*. Mrs. Dersingham could bear it no longer.

"Oh, do *stop* that noise!" she shrieked, rushing forward, white and trembling with fury.

Lena stopped at once. They were all fixed, rooted, in a vast sudden silence.

Mrs. Dersingham bit her lip, recovered herself. "I'm sorry," she said, coldly and curtly, "but I really must ask you to stop playing. I've—got a bad headache."

"I see," replied Lena, getting up from the piano. "Sorry." She walked forward a step or two, then looked at Mrs. Dersingham. "Have you had it all the evening or has it just come on now?" And this was not a polite inquiry, but a challenge. The tone of voice made that obvious.

"Does that matter?" And Mrs. Dersingham turned away.

Into the silence that fell now there came the voice, quavering a little, of Mrs. Pearson. "Now I really think it's time we were going," it began. But nobody took any notice of it.

For Lena burst into a torrent of speech. "No, it doesn't matter, of course. But I just asked because I thought you might have started that headache since I came, because you've just been as rotten as you could be, and I didn't ask to come—I've been travelling half the day and I'm as tired as you are—and I wouldn't have come at all if my father hadn't told me to, and I thought you were friends of his, but from the minute I came in, you've not said a decent word to me or given me a decent look ——"

"Hoy!" roared her father, seizing her by the arm and shaking her a little. "What the blazes is all this? What's the matter with you, girl? That's not the way to behave ——"

"No, and that's not the way to behave either," cried Lena, shaking herself free. "What have I done? I didn't want to push myself into her beastly house." And then she grabbed her father's arm and burst into tears. "I'm going," she sobbed. "Take me home."

Mr. Golspie put an arm round her and she continued her sobbing on his shoulder. "Sorry about this," he said, over her head. "My fault, I expect. I oughtn't to have told her to come. The kid's a bit nervy—tired, y'know."

"Yes, of course—travelling and all that," said Mr. Dersingham, feeling that some reply was expected.

This was Mrs. Dersingham's chance, but she did not take it. She might have accepted the apology if her husband had not been so ready to accept it and make an excuse for the girl. But now she turned her back on Mr. Golspie and his terrible daughter, and said to Mrs. Pearson: "Must you *really* go? It's quite early, you know. Oh, Mrs. Trape, *you're* not going, are you? Why?" And it was well done, bravely done, but it was a mistake, perhaps the biggest mistake she ever made.

Mr. Golspie's face changed its expression, all the good-humour dying out of it at once. "All right," he said shortly. "Come on, Lena, shake yourself up a bit. We're going now. Good-night, all. See you in the morning, Dersingham. Good-night." And immediately he marched himself and his daughter out of the room, and, a minute later, before Dersingham had followed him up, out of the house.

Half an hour later, the Dersinghams were alone, and Mrs. Dersingham was curled up in the largest chair, crying. "I don't care, I don't care," she sobbed. "They were *awful*, both of them. The man was nearly as bad as his terrible daughter. They were ghastly, and I hope to Heaven I never see either of them again. Or any of those people, except Mrs. Pearson. Oh, what a horrible, ghastly evening!"

"I know, I know, my dear," said her husband, hovering about vaguely and trying to be consoling. "Everything went wrong. I know."

"No, you don't, you can't possibly know how awful it was for me. No, don't touch me, leave me *alone*. I just want to go miles and miles away, and never see anybody for months. Don't ever let me see those vile Golspies again. And I don't care what I said or did. It couldn't be too bad for them. Next time, if you want to invite anybody from Angel Pavement, invite the clerks and the typists, anybody before those awful Golspies."

"There, there," said Mr. Dersingham, "there, there, there." And when dialogue is reduced to this, it is time we quitted the scene.

Lena, in the taxi that carried them away from Barkfield Gardens, had stopped crying and was now fiercely resentful, like the spoilt child she was. "Well, they *were* rotten snobs. And it wasn't *my* fault that half her beastly dinner had been dropped outside the door; I didn't even know until you told me; and it was probably a good job for you, it *was* dropped, for I'll bet it was the most awful muck. But there wasn't one of those old cats who gave me a decent look or spoke a decent word to me. You ought to have seen that long thin bony one when I asked her what she was looking so funny about! And you needn't think it was only *me* they didn't like, either. They didn't like you, I could see that. They weren't real friends, any of them."

"Who said they were, young woman?" her father demanded. "Don't make such a palaver about it. I know all about 'em. The best of the lot was that chap with the long neck and the wobbly cheeks—Pearson, the chap from Singapore—and he was only half-baked. If Dersingham's wife doesn't think we're good enough for them, let her go on thinking so. I'll bet she thinks I'm good enough to keep on putting some ginger in that half dead concern of theirs. After what I've seen of the Dersingham end of Twigg and Dersingham, all I can say is that Twigg, whoever he was, must have been a dam' smart chap to have got the firm going at all."

"You don't mean to say you're making money for those blighters?" cried Lena, winding an arm round his.

"The people I'm going to make money for," replied Mr. Golspie grimly, at the same time squeezing the arm, "are these people, these two here. Just you keep quiet and leave it to me, Miss Golspie."

Chapter Four

TURGIS SEES HER

I

Turgis was not lazy and while he was in the office he preferred doing something to doing nothing, but he did not share Mr. Smeeth's enthusiasm for office work and never regarded himself as one of the firm. It was all very well for Twigg & Dersingham to be suddenly busy again, indeed much busier than they had ever been before, but Turgis did not see the fun of going hard at it all day and every day and frequently having to stay an hour later. No doubt somebody was doing well out of it, but he, Turgis, was getting nothing out of it but a great deal more work. He grumbled about this to Mr. Smeeth. It was Saturday morning; he had just received his fortnight's pay, six pound notes, one ten-shilling note, and two florins; and it was a time for such confidences.

"All right, all right," said Mr. Smeeth, with the manner of a person who knew a great deal. "That's your point of view, isn't it?"

Turgis, a little diffidently now, for he had a considerable respect for Mr. Smeeth if no particular liking for him, replied that it was.

"Now let me tell you something, my boy," Mr. Smeeth continued gravely. "Just a week or two ago—I'll tell you exactly what day it was; it was the day Mr. Golspie first called here—Mr. Dersingham was talking things over with me, in that room there. I'm telling you this in confidence, mind. And Mr. Dersingham said the office expenses were too big and somebody would have to go. And it looked as if that somebody would be you."

"Me!" Turgis's mouth, always open a little, was now wide open, for his jaw suddenly dropped.

"You, Turgis," said Mr. Smeeth, with the satisfied air of a man who has produced the desired effect. "It was touch and go whether I told you that very day. I'm glad I didn't because you might have got a fright for nothing. Now it's all right, of course. We're busy, and we need everybody. But when you want to start grumbling about a bit of extra work, my boy, just you remember that. You might have been looking for work now, and I'll bet you wouldn't have liked that, would you?"

"No, I wouldn't, Mr. Smeeth," replied Turgis, humbly enough.

"And I don't blame you." Feeling fairly confident, for once, about his own job, Mr. Smeeth had a great desire to enlarge upon this topic, which had for him a terrible fascination. "Jobs aren't easy to get, are they?"

"Not if you haven't influence and you're not in the know, Mr. Smeeth," said Turgis, who was a great believer in the mysterious power of influence and being in the know, and realised only too well that there were few people in London who had less influence or were further from the know than himself. "That's the trouble. I seen it myself. You can't get a look in. I'd a packet—my words, I'd a packet—before I got taken on here. Trailin' round, queueing up, round again—oh, dear! You know what it's like."

"No, I don't," Mr. Smeeth returned, sharply.

"Beg your pardon, Mr. Smeeth. Of course, you don't. I do, though. Oo, it's sorful," cried Turgis earnestly. "'S'not getting any better either. Well I'm glad you told me, Mr. Smeeth. I'd better keep my mouth shut a bit, hadn't I? It is all right now, isn't it?"

"Quite all right. You do your best for us," Mr. Smeeth added sententiously, "and we'll do our best for you."

Turgis came nearer, and lowered his voice when he spoke. "D'you think, Mr. Smeeth, there'll be any chance of a rise, now I'm getting all this extra work? Ought to be, oughtn't there? I mean, I'm not getting a lot really, am I?"

"You leave it alone a bit, Turgis, and just do your best, and then I'll see what I can do for you."

"I wish you would, Mr. Smeeth. You see, it's not as if I'd got anybody helping me with my work, 'cos this new typist doesn't really help me out much, does she? And if you could—just—you know—say something to Mr. Golspie or Mr. Dersingham, because, you know, Mr. Smeeth, I am doing my best, and you mustn't think I want to grumble, 'cos I don't."

The new typist had been a great disappointment to Turgis, not because she was of no assistance to him in his work but because she was not the attractive young creature his heated fancy had conjured up to fill the post. Miss Poppy Sellers, with her unfortunate Oriental effect which merely resulted in dinginess and untidiness, did not seem to him at all pretty. At the end of the first morning, though he was flattered by her awe of him, he had dismissed her as a very poor bit of girl stuff. When he had heard that the firm was advertising for another typist, a younger girl to help Miss Matfield, he had had instant visions of working side by side with one of those really pretty ones he often noticed making their way about the City. There were one or two good ones in Angel Pavement itself: quite a pretty piece downstairs with the *Kwik-Work Razor Blade Co.*; another not so dusty who went up the stairs next door to *C. Warstein: Tailors' Trimmings*; and a real beauty—one to make your mouth water, a peach—at *Dunbury & Co.: Incandescent Gas Fittings*, at the end of the street. And there were two or three worth looking at, the flashy young Jewessy type, at *Chase & Cohen's Carnival Novelties* place at the end. Any one of these girls, walking into Twigg & Dersingham's, would have lit up the place for him, and the day's routine would have become an adventure. But they must go and choose this dreary-looking kid with the fringe. It was just his luck. Two girls working in the same office, and neither of them any good. Miss Matfield was all right in her way, of course, but then she was too big, too old, and far too "posh" and bossy for him, even if she had ever showed any sign—and, so far,

she hadn't—of being really interested in his existence. This other
one, Polly Sellers, was interested enough, quite ready to be friends,
but then, well—look at her.

The maddening thing about it—and it really was maddening to
Turgis—was that all these other ripe and adorable girls (he thought
of them as "fine bits") were all over the place, walking in and out
of offices, sitting in corners of teashops, elbowing him sometimes
(and he was always there to be elbowed) in buses and tube trains,
so that you might have thought they worked for everybody in the
City but Twigg & Dersingham. And it was no better, perhaps it
was worse, when he was roaming about for pleasure and not simply
going to and from the office. Everywhere he saw them, never missed
seeing them. His mind was for ever busy with their images, for ever
troubled by them. No matter where he went, he was tantalised, the
path underneath his feet a narrow dusty track of wilderness but all
hung about with rich forbidden clusters of feminine fruit, shrinking,
withering, vanishing, at a touch.

Turgis was by temperament a lover. His thoughts never left the
other sex long; happiness had for him a feminine shape; the real
world was illuminated by the bright glances of girls; and at any
moment, one of them might reveal to him an enchanted life they
could share together. It would be easy to see him as a lonely lad
seeking sympathy in that crowd in which he was lost. It would be
just as easy to see him as a figure of furtive lusts, whose mind descended and there lived eagerly in an underworld of tiny mean
contacts, seemingly accidental pressures of the arm and the foot. Yet
behind both these figures was the lover. And this, in spite of his
shabbiness and unprepossessing looks, the shiny baggy suit, and the
frayed tie, the open mouth, that slight pastiness and spottiness, that
faint grey film which seemed to cover and subdue his physical self.
He was no dapper lady-killer. But then if Turgis, even with his
scanty means, did not try very hard to make himself superficially
attractive to the sex that despises crumpled clothes, matted hair,
pasty cheeks, youth that has lost all vividness and glow, it was be-

cause he believed that the cry from within, urgent, never ceasing, must receive an answer. He knew that he had little to offer on the surface, was nothing to look at, nobody in particular, but he felt that inside he was different, he was wonderful, and that sooner or later a girl, a beautiful and passionate girl, caring nothing for the outside show, would recognise this difference, this wonder, within, would cry, "Oh, it's you," and love would immediately follow. Then life would really begin. So far it had not begun; in the tangle, blather, jumble of mere existence, of eating, sleeping, working, journeying and staring, it had only made a number of false starts. In other words, Turgis had had his little adventures but was not yet in love, or rather—for he was perpetually in love—had not yet found the single outlet for all this flood, the one girl.

After returning to his own desk, Turgis thought about these other girls who might so easily have come to work by his side instead of continuing with the *Kwik-Work Razor Blade* or *Dunbury & Co.*, and then, dismissing them reluctantly, he began to tidy up his desk and finish off the week's work. It was after twelve and the week-end was in sight. He leaned forward on his high stool, and breathed hard over communications from the London and North Eastern Railway and the City Transport Company. There was a girl at the City Transport—he had never seen her but she often answered the telephone—who sounded nice, lovely voice she had, and once or twice he had made her laugh. If he had been in the office by himself, he would have talked to her properly, perhaps suggested an appointment—on the pictures they called it a "date" but Turgis thought of it as a "point"—but he was never alone, and even if there was only that silly kid, Stanley, there, it would spoil it. But it was fine to hear her laugh down the telephone. Silvery, that was it—silvery laughter—her silvery laugher—just like in a book.

He was interrupted by a touch on his arm, and he looked round to find the new typist at his elbow, looking up at him with her biggish brown eyes. She had a lot of powder on one side of her nose, and none at all, just shiny skin, on the other side. No good.

"Please," said Miss Sellers in her chirpy little Cockney voice, "please, have you written to the Anglo-What's-It Shipping?"

"No, I haven't," he replied.

She merely stared.

"I haven't written to the Anglo-What's-It Shipping," he continued severely, "because I've never heard of the Anglo-What's-It Shipping. Don't know them—see?"

"Oo, I'm sorry," though she did not sound very sorry. "Have I said something wrong? I can't remember all these names yet. Give me a chance. You know who I mean, don't you? It is Anglo-something, isn't it?"

"If it's the Anglo-Baltic Shipping Co. you're talking about," said Turgis with dignity, "then I have written to them. Wrote yesterday, 's'matter of fact. But to the Anglo-Baltic, mind you. There's no what's-it about it."

The girl looked at him for a moment. "Oo!" she cried softly, "squashed!" And then she promptly walked away.

Turgis glanced after her with distaste. "Getting cheeky now," he told himself. "That's the latest—getting cheeky. And just because she can't make up to me. All right, Miss Dirty Fringe, you'll have to be told off soon, you will. Try it again, that's all, just try it again." And he was filled with a righteous indignation, pointing out to himself that these girls didn't know their place in an office, wouldn't get on with their work properly, and were always trying their little tricks on men who wanted to do their job with no nonsense about it.

There was a familiar scurrying, as of some small animal of the undergrowth that had got itself shod with leather and iron tips; the door burst open; Stanley had returned.

"Come on, boy, come on," said Mr. Smeeth, looking over his eyeglasses. "Get those letters copied, sharp as you can. Don't want us to be here all day, waiting for you, do you?"

"I want to get the one-five from London Bridge, if I can, Mr.

Smeeth," said Miss Matfield. "I'm spending the week-end in the country, thank God."

"You'll get it all right, Miss Matfield," Mr. Smeeth told her. "Plenty of time. Now then, Stanley—bustle about. Sharp's the world, my boy."

"Oo, Miss Matfield," Miss Sellers began, staring at her, "d'you reely like the country this weather? I don't know how you can bear it. I couldn't, not now, when it's winter. It's not as if it was summer, is it?"

"Like it best in winter, if it's not raining too hard. Jolly good! Nothing like so filthy as London is in winter."

"Well, I'm sure it would give me the 'ump," Miss Sellers declared. "But I do like it in summer. It's lovely in summer, I think." You could almost see her looking at the buttercups and daisies. "I like the seaside best, though. Don't you, Miss Matfield? It's lovely at the seaside in summer, I think. I've never been in winter. It's nice in summer even when it rains at the seaside, isn't it?"

Miss Matfield replied, shortly but amiably, that it was, and then began clearing up her papers.

"Here," cried Stanley, in the middle of his copying, "I seen a smash right in Moorgate." He looked round triumphantly.

"I'll bet you didn't," said Turgis.

"I did, and I bet you I did. Anyhow, if I didn't see it, I was there just after, when the bobby was taking names. Oh, what a crowd! I got right to the front. Car and a lorry it was. The lorry was all right, but you oughter seen the car. Oh, no, it wasn't a mess— oh, no!"

"And how many hours did you stand there, eh?" Mr. Smeeth inquired. "That's what takes your time, my boy—doing your bit of nosy-parkering."

"I had to go that way and I couldn't get past, Mr. Smeeth," Stanley cried indignantly. "So I had to see what was up, couldn't help it. I thought the bobby might take my name as a witness, but he didn't. I wish he had done," he added wistfully. "I'd like to be a witness."

"If you don't finish those letters in ten minutes," said Mr. Smeeth, wagging a finger at him, "you'll be in the dock, and never mind being a witness. How are you getting on, Turgis?"

"Nearly finished, Mr. Smeeth," Turgis replied. "I'll just give the City Transport a ring to see if they've heard anything about that lot we sent to Norwich." And he promptly went to the telephone.

There was no silvery laughter this time from the City Transport Company. The voice that answered him was not only a masculine voice but also an irritated, badgered, weary, despairing voice, that of a man who was rapidly coming to the conclusion that he would be spending all Saturday afternoon answering idiotic inquiries. "Yes, I know, I know," it barked. "You rang me up before about it. Well, we're doing our best. We've got the matter in hand. Yes, yes, yes, I've told our Norwich people. I'll let you know on Monday. The first thing, the very first thing, on Monday, I'll let you know." It was pleading now. "Can't do more than that, can I?" And now it was tired of pleading. "All right, all ri-ight, we're doing what we ca-a-an. Ring you on Mo-o-onday."

"They've got through to Norwich about it, Mr. Smeeth," said Turgis, "but they say it'll have to stand over till Monday."

"That's all right then, Turgis. Give them a ring on Monday."

There was now a feeling throughout the office that all manner of things would have to stand over until Monday. This feeling was not confined to Twigg & Dersingham, but could have been discovered operating upstairs at the *Universal Hosiery Co.* and the *London and Counties Supply Stores,* and downstairs at the *Kwik-Work Razor Blade Co.,* and at *Chase & Cohen: Carnival Novelties* on the one side and at *Dunbury & Co.: Incandescent Gas Fittings* on the other side, in fact, all up and down Angel Pavement, and far beyond Angel Pavement, in all the banks and offices and showrooms and warehouses of the City. Very soon the City itself would be standing over until Monday: the crowds of brokers and cashiers and clerks and typists and hawkers would have vanished from its pavements, the bars would be forlorn, the teashops nearly empty or closed; its trams.

and buses, no longer clamouring for a few more yards of space, would come gliding easily through misty blue vacancies like ships going down London River; and the whole place, populated only by caretakers and policemen among the living, would sink slowly into quietness; the very bank-rate would be forgotten; and it would be left to drown itself in reverie, with a drift of smoke and light fog across its old stones like the return of an army of ghosts. Until— with a clatter, a clang, a sudden raw awakening—Monday.

Papers were swept into drawers, letters were stamped in rows, blotters were shut, turned over, put away, ledgers and petty cash boxes were locked up, typewriters were covered, noses were powdered, cigarettes and pipes were lit, doors were banged, and stairs were noisy with hasty feet. The week was done. Out they came in their thousands into Angel Pavement, London Wall, Moorgate Street, Cornhill and Cheapside. They were so thick along Finsbury Pavement that the Moorgate Tube Station seemed like a monster sucking them down into its hot rank inside. Among these vanishing mites was one with a large but not masterful nose, full brown eyes, a slightly open mouth, and a drooping chin. This was Turgis going home.

He had to stand all the way, and though there were at least five nice-looking girls in the same compartment—and one was very close to him, and two of the others he had noticed several times before— not one of them showed the slightest interest in him.

II

When Turgis returned again to the earth's surface, he plunged at once into the noise and litter of High Street, Camden Town, and then turned up the Kentish Town Road, for he lodged in Nathaniel Street, which lies in that conglomeration of short streets between the Kentish Town Road and York Road. He was rather later than usual, for this new Golspie business was having its effect even on Saturday morning, and so he walked quickly for once. He was ready for dinner and he knew that dinner would be ready for him. On Saturdays and Sundays, his landlady provided dinner as well as breakfast, and, indeed, was not averse to laying out a bit of tea, too, if that should be called for, Turgis having been with her now for eighteen months and having proved himself to be—by Nathaniel Street standards, which are based on a bitter knowledge of this world—a good quiet lodger, sober, and punctual in his payments. During the week, he had, officially, nothing but breakfast in the house, and had to shift for himself for his other meals, which followed a descending scale of luxury every fortnight, beginning with the alternate week-ends when he was paid. Thus, every other Monday, Tuesday, Wednesday, Turgis was well fed, and every other Wednesday, Thursday, Friday, he was comparatively half starved. At a pinch, however, his landlady would always give him a little supper. They were all friendly together. They had to be, for they all used the same back room for meals. The bed-sitting-room that Turgis had at the top of the house, so small that the iron bedstead, the yellow washstand, the three deal drawers, the lopsided and groaning basket chair, and the little old gas-fire, a genuine antique among gas-fires, made it seem uncomfortably crowded with furniture and fittings, was no place in which to feed. It did not like being sat in, resented the sight of a cup of tea and a biscuit, and the presence of one good plateful of roast beef, potatoes, Brussels sprouts, and gravy, would have completely finished it.

Number 9, like all the other houses in Nathaniel Street, was small and dark, and its gloomy little hall was haunted by a mixed smell of cabbage, camphor, and old newspapers. Turgis never noticed this smell, but on the very rare occasions when he visited some other and less odorous house, then he noticed the absence of it, his nose declaring at once that it had found itself in an unfamiliar atmosphere. Now he hung up his hat and coat and marched straight into the back room. There he discovered his landlady, who, having finished dinner, was enjoying a cup of tea by the fire. She was not enjoying this cup of tea, however, in an easy leisurely fashion; she

was sitting, almost tense, on the very edge of the chair; and she had
something of the air of a cavalry general between two phases of a
battle.

Mrs. Pelumpton had every right to such an air. She was a short
and very broad woman, with a mop of untidy grey hair and a
withered apple face, and it was easy to see that all her adult life
had been one long struggle, and that unless she suffered a paralytic
stroke or was driven out of her wits, she would die fighting. In her
presence, progress seemed the most absurd myth. If Mrs. Pelumpton
could have been turned into the wife of a marauding viking or one
of the women following Attila's horde, she would have felt she
had been given a well-earned rest and would have been astonished
at, perhaps horrified by, the sudden colour and gaiety of life.

As soon as she saw Turgis she put down her cup and, as it were,
jumped into the saddle again. She placed on the table two covered
plates, her lodger's dinner, meat and vegetables under one cover,
pudding under the other.

"I'm a bit late to-day, Mrs. Pelumpton," said Turgis, settling down.

"Well, I said to myself you might have been or you might not,
according to whether that clock's gone and got fast again, and it
might well have done that, the way he's been playing about with it."

"About quarter of an hour fast, I make it—might be twenty
minutes."

"And that," said Mrs. Pelumpton very decisively, "is what comes
of messing about with it. 'Leave it alone,' I told him. 'Clocks isn't
in your line.' Not that quarter of an hour's going to hurt anybody
in this house—except Edgar, and he's got his own watch with proper
railway time on it." Edgar, her son, who also lived in the house,
worked on the railway down at King's Cross. Turgis rarely saw
him.

"That's a nice bit o' meat you're having there, Mr. Turgis, isn't
it?" Mrs. Pelumpton continued, after taking a noisy sip of tea and
then staring over the cup at him. "Chilled, that is. You'd have
thought that was English if I hadn't told you, wouldn't you?"

"Yes, I would, Mrs. Pelumpton."

"Well, I won't deceive you. It isn't. It's chilled. And it all depends on the picking. Take what they offer, and you don't know where you are. You've got to look about a bit and pick it yourself. They know me now." And here Mrs. Pelumpton produced a short triumphant laugh. "They know me all right. 'Pick where you like, Ma,' he always says to me. 'Oh, I'll watch it,' I tells him. 'I'll watch it.' And I do."

"That's the style. It's a very nice dinner, Mrs. Pelumpton."

A certain shuffling noise indicated that the master of the house, the messer-about with clocks, Mr. Pelumpton, was now approaching. Mr. Pelumpton moved very slowly, partly because he suffered from rheumatism, and partly because he was a man of great dignity. To look at him, at his slack and dingy figure, at his watery eyes, bottle nose, ragged and drooping grey moustache, to mark his leisurely air, was to imagine at once that Mr. Pelumpton was one of those men who do not work themselves but merely see that their wives and children work for them. But this was not the truth. Mr. Pelumpton did work, as his talk would quickly inform you. He was a dealer. He had no shop of his own, but he had some vague connection with a shop, where an astonishing variety of second, third, or fourth hand goods were sold, owned by a friend of his. He passed his time in a dusty underworld in which battered chests of drawers and broken gramophones changed hands and the deals were in shillings and the commission in pence. He interviewed parties who had for sale a cracked toilet set or an old bicycle or five mildewed volumes of *The Stately Homes of England*. He could sometimes be found in the humblest auction rooms, ready to bid up to half a crown for the odds and ends. Every Friday he became a *bona-fide* merchant by making an appearance in Caledonian Market, where, on that grey and windy height, he stood beside a small but very varied stock, consisting perhaps of a Banjo Tutor, two chipped pink vases, a silk underskirt, a large photograph of General Buller, five dirty tennis balls, a zither with most of the strings missing, and the *Letters of Charles Kingsley*. Dealing thus in things that were only one remove from the dustbin, Mr. Pelumpton did not contrive to make much money, and indeed he had been dependent for some time on Mrs. Pelumpton and Edgar; but, on the other hand, you could not say he did not work. He was in the second-hand trade, in the buying and selling line, a legitimate dealer, and took himself and his mysterious business with enormous seriousness. If he was not doing very well, that was because trade was so bad. Mr. Pelumpton had all the deliberation and dignity of an antique merchant prince. He smoked a foul little pipe, liked a glass of beer, was a great reader of newspapers, and always talked in a very solemn and confidential manner. Like many dealers and Caledonian Market men, who have drooping moustaches, very few teeth, and a confidential manner, he softened all the sibilants, putting an "h" behind every "s." There is no doubt that a dealer who can only say "Yes" is not in such a strong position as the dealer who can draw it out into a mysterious "Yersh." Mr. Pelumpton was essentially a "Yersh" man.

He now advanced very slowly into the room, carefully seated himself by the fire, took out his evil little pipe, looked at Turgis in a watery fashion, nodded solemnly, put back his pipe, and waited for somebody to ask him something.

"Well, did you catch him in?" his wife inquired. Mr. Pelumpton was always having to slip round the corner to catch somebody in, even if he had only just finished his own dinner.

"Out till five," replied Mr. Pelumpton. "And a shaúshy ansher for me trouble."

"Who's bin giving you a saucy answer?"

"Hish mishish," said Mr. Pelumpton, "if it ish hish mishish. 'Can't expect to find 'im in on Shaturday arfternoon,' she shaysh to me. 'You'll excuse me, mishish,' I told her, 'but in my bishnish, you've got to work Shaturday arfternoon shame ash any other arfternoon. Yersh,' I told her, 'an' Shunday arfternoon too, if you're not careful.' Jusht telling her politely, shee? All right, what doesh she shay to that? She shaysh, 'Well, we're diff'rent 'ere, shee?' and then shlamsh the door in me faysh."

"The cheeky monkey!" cried Mrs. Pelumpton indignantly. "I'd slam it in *her* face if I'd anything to do with her. It's downright ignorance, that's what it is. There's people round here has no more idea 'ow to behave than a—a—a parrot."

"Ar, well," Mr. Pelumpton continued, philosophically, "we've got a lot to put with in our bishnish. And you can take that from me, Mishter Turgish. But if the shtuff'sh there, we don't mind. All in the day'sh work, shee?"

"After something good, Mr. Pelumpton?" Turgis inquired.

"That'sh right. A lovely piesh he'sh got to shell—a shideboard—oh, a lovely piesh, it ish—only wantsh a bit of polishing and it'sh good enough for anybody, that piesh ish, fit for a palash. I can't 'andle it myshelf, not ash trade ish now, but I know who can. It'sh a commission job."

"That's the idea," said Turgis, with vague approval. He was a youth who liked to agree with his company, not because he felt kindly disposed towards other people, but simply because it was less trouble to agree and applaud. He really thought Mr. Pelumpton a ridiculous old bore.

"Now that's one thing I've always wanted," cried Mrs. Pelumpton. "A sideboard, a proper nice sideboard, cupboards and all, and room for everything. Mahogany, I'd like."

"Ah, that'sh what a lot o' people would like. They're fetching good money them thingsh are. Show me a good shideboard, a sholid piesh—not sho much of your shtuff about it, Mishter Turgish——"

"What's his stuff, for Heaven's sake?" Mrs. Pelumpton demanded. "He hasn't got any stuff, have you, Mr. Turgis? What you talking about, Dad?"

Mr. Pelumpton took out his pipe for this, and looked very reproachfully at his wife. "What am I talking about? I'm talking about what I know, that'sh what I'm talking about. 'Ow many pieshesh of furnisher have been through my handsh? Thoushandsh.

All right then. Don't I know the trade? Ho, no! Ho, no! I don't know the trade." Then he pointed his pipe at Turgis, who was very busy with his treacle pudding, and then said very slowly, very solemnly: "Veneersh. You know what them are. Well, that'sh hish shtuff. Am I right, Mishter Turgish?"

"That's right," said Turgis. "That's what we sell at our place, Mrs. Pelumpton. Veneers for furniture, and inlays, and all that. 'S'matter of fact, I don't have anything to do with 'em personally, 'cos it isn't my particular job, but that's what we sell all right."

"Well, I never did!" Mrs. Pelumpton was filled with honest wonder at a world in which so many different things were bought and sold. "And I never knew that. Thought you was in an office, down in the City, y'know—a clurk."

"Sho he ish," her husband assured her, "but that'sh what hish firm shellsh. He told me long shinsh, didn't you, Mishter Turgish. Well, ash I wash shaying, show me a good shideboard, a sholid piesh, and I'll get you what you like for it—in reashon, in reashon, y'know. Trade may be bad. Trade *ish* bad. But for shome thingsh you 'ave a shteady demand, that'sh what you 'ave—a shteady demand. Where we're feeling it in our bishnish ish in the shmall thingsh——" Mr. Pelumpton was now settling down to a good long monologue, but he reckoned without his audience, both of whom knew these monologues too well. His wife, seeing that Turgis had finished, pounced upon his used plates and bore them off, with a bustle and clatter that brought a frown to her husband's face. He now tried to buttonhole Turgis, who was lighting a cigarette. "Now you take me, Mishter Turgish," he began.

But Turgis refused to take him; he had taken him too often before; and now he promptly escaped upstairs, to his own room. It is difficult for a room to be both stuffy and cold, but this room contrived it somehow, and offered you the choice, if you chose to interfere with it, of being still stuffier or still colder. Turgis, who preferred stuffiness to cold, lit the gas-fire, that tiny antique, which so deeply resented being called into service again that it exploded with an indignant bang and then wheezily complained every other second. After the last breath of raw November had been driven out of the room, Turgis took off his collar and his shoes and stretched himself out on the bed. First, he read all the advertisements in his newspaper, which specialised on Saturdays in the mail-order business. There was a whole page of these advertisements, offering everything from Orientally perfumed cigarettes to electric belts for rheumatism, and Turgis carefully read them all. In public he pretended to be very knowing and cynical about advertisements, but in private he was still their willing victim, and nearly every shilling he spent, whether on clothes, drink, tobacco, or amusement, was conjured out of his pocket by the richest and most artful advertising managers. Perhaps that is why his suits bagged so soon, his shoes soaked up the rain, his cigarettes shredded and split, and his amusements failed to amuse.

When he had done with the newspaper, he took from the mantelpiece (and he could do this without getting up from the bed) the latest issue of a twopenny periodical that was devoted to the films, though more especially to the film actors with the longest eyelashes and the actresses with the largest eyes. He spent the next half-hour staring at the photographs in this paper and reading its scrappy paragraphs, not with any particular enthusiasm. Turgis was not really a film enthusiast. He knew nothing about camera angles and "cutting" and all the intricacies of crowd work, and never in his life had he seriously compared one film with another. He could laugh at the comic men with the rest, but he did not fully appreciate the clowning on the screen, simply because he had not a very strong sense of humour. No, what drew him to the films was the fact that he and they had a common enthusiasm, they had both a passionate interest in sex. In those dim sensuous palaces, filled with throbbing music and shifting coloured lights, Turgis the lover entered his dream kingdom. You could say that the money he paid at their doors was silver tribute to Aphrodite, to whose worship the Phœnicians of the Californian coast have built more temples than ever the old Phœnicians of Cyprus did; and for a few moments, as he sat in the steep darkened galleries, Turgis would be shaken and then intoxicated by the golden presence of the goddess as she flashed through with her train, Eros and the Hours and the Graces, though of all that retinue only two remained with him, to see him home, Pothos and Himeros, shapes of longing and yearning.

The paper slipped from his fingers. His eyes closed; his jaw dropped a little; and his head turned on the pillow, so that the light of the gas-fire, now coming to life in the dwindling daylight, for the window was no brighter than a slate, played faintly but rosily on his features, the pleasant width of the brow, the nose that had missed masterfulness, the round chin that fell away, and as his breathing grew more regular and he slipped into unconsciousness, that light brought something at once grotesque and sad, the red gleam and deep shadow of some Gothic tragedy, into the little room. And for an hour or so Turgis slept, while Saturday went rattling and roaring on, gathering momentum, through the dark little abysses of brick and smoke outside, the streets of London.

III

The Turgis who came out of 9, Nathaniel Street, later that Saturday afternoon, was quite different from the youth we have already met. He was washed, brushed, conscientiously shaved, and he moved briskly. This was for him the best time of all the week. Saturday sang in his heart. If the Great Something ever happened, it would happen on Saturday. The trams, buses, shops, bars, theatres, and picture palaces, they all gleamed and glittered through the rich murk to-day for him. Even now, Adventure—in high heels and silk stockings—might be moving his way. He was making for the West End, for on Saturdays, especially the alternate Saturdays when he received his pay, he despised Camden Town and Islington and Finsbury Park, those little centres that broke the desert of North London with oases of flashing lights and places of entertainment. These were good enough in their way, but if you had a few shillings to spend, the West was a great deal better, offering you the real thing in giant teashops and picture theatres. For this was his usual Saturday night programme, if he had the money: first, tea at one of the big teashops, which were always crowded with girls and always offered a chance of a pick-up; then a visit to one of the great West End cinemas, in which, once inside, he could spin out the whole evening, perhaps on the edge of adventure all the time. And this was his programme for this night, too, though, of course, he was always ready to modify it if anything happened in the teashop, if he found the right sort of girl there and she wanted to do something else.

At the very time he was setting out, hundreds and hundreds of girls, girls with little powdered snub noses, wet crimson mouths, shrill voices, and gleaming calves, were also setting out—nearly all of them, unfortunately, in pairs—to carry out the very same programme. Turgis knew this, or perhaps only a hunter's instinct led him to where the game were thickest; but he did not visualise them, luckily for him, for the tantalising image would have driven him nearly to madness. But there they were, tripping down innumerable dark steps, chirping and laughing together in buses and trams without end, and making for the same small area, the very same buildings, perhaps to jostle him as they passed. It would have been easier for Turgis, as he knew only too well, if he too had had a companion, to match all these pairs of girls, but he had only a few acquaintances, no friends, and, in any event, he preferred to hunt in solitude, to thread his way through the brilliant jungle alone with his hunger and his dream.

A bus took him to the West End, where, among the crazy coloured fountains of illumination, shattering the blue dusk with green and crimson fire, he found the café of his choice, a teashop that had gone mad and turned Babylonian, a white palace with ten thousand lights. It towered above the older buildings like a citadel, which indeed it was, the outpost of a new age, perhaps a new civilisation, perhaps a new barbarism; and behind the thin marble front were concrete and steel, just as behind the careless profusion of luxury were millions of pence, balanced to the last halfpenny. Somewhere in the background, hidden away, behind the ten thousand lights and acres of white napery and bewildering glittering rows of teapots, behind the thousand waitresses and cash-box girls and black-coated floor managers and temperamental long-haired violinists, behind the mounds of shimmering bonbons and multi-coloured Viennese pastries, the cauldrons of stewed steak, the vanloads of harlequin ices, were a few men who went to work juggling with fractions of a farthing, who knew how many units of electricity it took to finish a steak-and-kidney pudding and how many minutes and seconds a waitress (five feet four in height and in average health) would need to carry a tray of given weight from the kitchen lift to the table in the far corner. In short, there was a warm, sensuous, vulgar life flowering in the upper stories, and cold science working in the basement. Such was the gigantic teashop into which Turgis marched, in search not of mere refreshment but of all the enchantment of unfamiliar luxury. Perhaps he knew in his heart that men have conquered half the known world, looted whole kingdoms, and never arrived at such luxury. The place was built for him.

It was built for a great many other people too, and, as usual, they were all there. It steamed with humanity. The marble entrance hall, piled dizzily with bonbons and cakes, was as crowded and bustling as a railway station. The gloom and grime of the streets, the raw air, all November, were at once left behind, forgotten: the atmosphere inside was golden, tropical, belonging to some high mid-summer of confectionery. Disdaining the lifts, Turgis, once more excited by the sight, sound, and smell of it all, climbed the wide staircase until he reached his favourite floor, where an orchestra, led by a young Jewish violinist with wandering lustrous eyes and a passion for tremolo effects, acted as a magnet to a thousand girls. The door was swung open for him by a page; there burst, like a sugary bomb, the clatter of cups, the shrill chatter of white-and-vermilion girls, and, cleaving the golden, scented air, the sensuous clamour of the strings; and, as he stood hesitating a moment, half dazed, there came, bowing, a sleek grave man, older than he was and far more distinguished than he could ever hope to be, who murmured deferentially: "For one, sir? This way, please." Shyly, yet proudly, Turgis followed him.

That was the snag really, though. This place was so crowded that you had to take the seat they offered you; there was no picking and choosing your company at the table. And, as usual, Turgis was not lucky. The vacant seat he was shown, and which he dare not refuse, was at a table already occupied by three people, and not one of them remotely resembled a nice-looking girl. There were two stout middle-aged women, voluble, perspiring, and happy over cream buns, and a middle-aged man, who no doubt had been of no great size even before this expedition started, but was now very small and huddled, and gave the impression that if the party stayed there much longer, he would shrink to nothing but spectacles, a nose, a collar, and a pair of boots. For the first few minutes, Turgis was so disappointed that he was quite angry with these people, hated them. And of course it was impossible to get hold of a waitress. After five minutes or so of glaring and waiting, he began to wish he had gone somewhere else. There was a pretty girl at the next table, but she was obviously with her young man, and so fond of him that every now and then she clutched his arm and held it tight, just as if the young man might be thinking of running away. At another table, not far away, were three girls together, two of whom looked very interesting, with saucy eyes and wide smiling mouths, but they were too busy whispering and giggling to take any notice of him. So Turgis suddenly stopped being a bright youth, shooting amorous glances, and became a stern youth who wanted some tea, who had gone there for no other purpose than to obtain some tea, who was surprised and indignant because no tea was forthcoming.

"And mindjew," cried one of the middle-aged women to the other, "I don't bear malice 'cos it isn't in my nature, as you'll be the first to agree, my dear. But when she let fly with that, I thought to meself, 'All right, my lady, now this time you've gone a bit *too* far. It's my turn.' But mindjew, even then I didn't say what I *could* have said. Not one word about Gravesend crossed my lips to her, though it was there on the tip of my tongue."

Turgis looked at her with disgust. Silly old geezer!

At last the waitress came. She was a girl with a nose so long and so thickly powdered that a great deal of it looked as if it did not belong to her, and she was tired, exasperated, and ready at any moment to be snappy. She took the order—and it was for plaice and chips, tea, bread and butter, and cakes: the great tea of the whole fortnight—without any enthusiasm, but she returned in time to prevent Turgis from losing any more temper. For the next twenty minutes, happily engaged in grappling with this feast, he forgot all about girls, and when the food was done and he was lingering over his third cup of tea and a cigarette, though no possible girls came within sight, he felt dreamily content. His mind swayed vaguely to the tune the orchestra was playing. Adventure would come; and for the moment he was at ease, lingering on its threshold.

From this tropical plateau of tea and cakes, he descended into the street, where the harsh night air suddenly smote him. The pavements were all eyes and thick jostling bodies; at every corner, the newspaper sellers cried out their football editions in wailing voices of the doomed; cars went grinding and snarling and roaring past; and the illuminated signs glittered and rocketed beneath the forgotten faded stars. He arrived at his second destination, the Sovereign Picture Theatre, which towered at the corner like a vast spangled wedding-cake in stone. It might have been a twin of that great teashop he had just left; and indeed it was; another frontier outpost of the new age. Two Jews, born in Poland but now American citizens, had talked over cigars and coffee on the loggia of a crazy Spanish-Italian-American villa, within sight of the Pacific, and out of that talk (a very quiet talk, for one of the two men was in considerable pain and knew that he was dying inch by inch) there had sprouted this monster, together with other monsters that had suddenly appeared in New York, Paris, and Berlin. Across ten thousand miles, those two men had seen the one-and-sixpence in Turgis's pocket, and, with a swift gesture, resolving itself magically into steel and concrete and carpets and velvet-covered seats and pay-boxes, had set it in motion and diverted it to themselves.

He waited now to pay his one-and-sixpence, standing in the queue at the balcony entrance. It was only a little after six and the Saturday night rush had hardly begun, but soon there were at least a hundred of them standing there. Near Turgis, on either side, the sexes were neatly paired off. There were one or two middle-aged women but no unaccompanied girl in sight in the whole queue. The evening was not beginning too well.

When at last they were admitted, they first walked through an enormous entrance hall, richly tricked out in chocolate and gold, illuminated by a huge central candelabra, a vast bunch of russet gold globes. Footmen in chocolate and gold waved them towards the two great marble balustrades, the wide staircases lit with more russet gold globes, the prodigiously thick and opulent chocolate carpets, into which their feet sank as if they were the feet of arch-dukes and duchesses. Up they went, passing a chocolate and gold platoon or two and a portrait gallery of film stars, whose eyelashes seemed to stand out from the walls like stout black wires, until they reached a door that led them to the dim summit of the balcony, which fell dizzily away in a scree of little heads. It was an interval between pictures. Several searchlights were focussed on an organ keyboard that looked like a tiny gilded box, far below, and the organ itself was shaking out cascades of treacly sound, so that the whole place trembled with sugary ecstasies. But while they waited in the gangway, the lights faded out, the gilded box dimmed and sank, the curtains parted to reveal the screen again, and an enormous voice, as inhuman as that of a genie, announced that it would bring the world's news not only to their eyes but to their ears.

"One? This way, sir," and the attendant went down, flashing

his light. This was always an exciting moment for Turgis. He might find himself next to some wonderful girl, as lonely as he was, who would talk to him, squeeze his hand, let him take her home, and kiss him in the darkness of some mysterious suburb. The great adventure might begin at the end of that pointing pencil of light. On the other hand, he might find himself miserably wedged in between two fat middle-aged people. It was all a gamble, with the odds heavily against the wonderful girl, as he knew too well. But still, there was always a chance, and he never walked down these dark steps behind the electric torch without feeling a mounting excitement.

The light pointed along a row, and he followed it, pushing past a dozen indignant knees. The last pair was very stubborn, and he negotiated them without enthusiasm. He had no luck. Here, on one side of him was the owner of the knees, an enormous woman, bulging over her seat, and on the other was a man with a beard and a noisy pipe. And it was too late to change his place now. Once again the miracle had not happened. Gloomily he turned his attention to the news film, and not one single inch or roar of it entertained him. It was followed by a comedy, all about a lot of silly kids, and he sat there, steadily hating it. He also hated the enormous woman, who laughed so much that great lumps of her hit him on the shoulder. He decided, miserably, that he ought not to have come to the Sovereign. Next time he would give the Sovereign a miss. Stiff with fat women and men with stinking pipes, that's what it was—oh, cripes!—awful hole! And another Saturday night going, gone!

Then came the film of the evening, the star feature, and Turgis soon began to take an interest in it and found himself lifted out of his gloom. It was a talkie called "The Glad-Rag Way," and it was all about a beautiful girl (and she was beautiful, for she was Lulu Castellar, one of his favourites) who went to New York to dance in cabarets and for a time forgot all about her sweetheart, a poor young inventor who lived in the most dismal lodgings, like Turgis, but, unlike Turgis, also contrived to have his hair exquisitely waved at regular intervals. This beautiful girl behaved in the most foolish way. She accepted presents from rich men with ugly leering mouths; she went out to supper with them and got tipsy, as well she might, for the whole atmosphere consisted sometimes of champagne bubbles; she attended parties, very late at night, in their flats, and though the rooms in these flats were three hundred feet long and two hundred feet broad, the parties themselves were undoubtedly intimate affairs, at which a girl was able to express herself by dancing on the table and throwing off some of her clothes. Everything this girl wore, every movement she made, only called the attention of these leering fellows to some part of her ravishing figure; and even when she herself had stopped making eyes and smiling at them and undulating round them, with a champagne glass in her hand, her charming legs still insisted on claiming their notice. It was obvious that at any moment these rich cads would make their old mistake, they would assume that she was not a virtuous girl and would act accordingly, to her astonishment and indignation and shame at being so misunderstood, so treated. Meanwhile, the young inventor had received a letter (and you heard him tear it open) asking him to come to New York to meet three heavy men who had just been barking at one another about him in the previous scene. It was, as he himself admitted, his "beeg chaince."

His train was still roaring across the screen when Turgis, whose interest had been thoroughly roused, heard a voice say "'Scuse me" and saw a dim feminine shape that was obviously trying to get past.

"'S'quite all right," he said affably, withdrawing his knees to let her pass.

She dropped into the seat on his left, taking the place of the man with the foul pipe, who must have crept out, towards the other gangway, without Turgis noticing him. This girl who had just arrived was still only a dim shape, but he felt sure she was young and pretty.

" 'Scuse me," she whispered again,. "but is this the big picture?"

"Yes, it is," he replied eagerly.

"Has it been on long?"

"No, not so long. It isn't half through yet, I'm sure," he told her, trying to talk as if he were a confidential old friend. "I'll bet the best's coming on."

"Well, I hope you're right," she said, settling herself in the rather narrow seat and then giving her attention to the screen.

A faint sweet whiff of scent had come his way. His senses did not wait for any more evidence; they reported at once to his imagination, which immediately dowered the vague dark figure beside him with all sweetness and prettiness, not unlike that of Lulu Castellar, who was at the moment absent from the screen, the young inventor, having arrived in New York, being barked at by the three heavy men. Turgis took in all that the film had to offer him, but now he was no longer lost in it; he was living intensely in the tiny darkened space between him and the girl. Instinctively, he edged a little her way. Their elbows touched on the arm of the seat, and even that trifling contact sent a thrill through him. A little later, his left leg encountered something at once firm and soft, another leg, a beautifully rounded feminine leg, and the two remained in contact. This, like the other, may have been casual, but to Turgis the effect was electric. And then it chanced that his hand, hanging loose by his side, touched another hand, which was not withdrawn when it was touched again, this time deliberately. The two hands now met fairly; they grasped one another, squeezed; their fingers were intertwined; they sent and received messages in the dark. Turgis could now regard the graceful antics of Lulu Castellar with a benevolent detachment. The dream life of the screen was nothing compared with the pulsating real life of those contacts in the warm gloom, those little pressures and squeezes that were signals from that other enchanted world. He did not try to talk to her again. That would come later. He said nothing, hardly looked her way, afraid lest he should break the spell.

When the film ended and a kind of soft russet dawn broke as the screen disappeared behind the curtains, they moved away from one another, and he did not even catch a glimpse of her face. A great many people went out, and a great many others came in, but they were not disturbed. Then the curtains moved again; a soft russet twilight came, only to fade into darkness; and the programme artfully continued. But would this other and far more exciting programme continue? His heart bounded in the new darkness. He leaned towards her again; she did not evade him; and hand clasped hand again, stickily perhaps now but still exquisitely, thrillingly. Turgis had not been so happy for months.

It was not until the young inventor's train to New York was again roaring across the screen, after the programme had gone round its full circle, that the girl loosened her hand and began to put on her gloves. Turgis had been waiting for this moment for some time. When she rose, he rose too; and she followed him past the indignant knees and up the stairs. It was when they reached the exit steps, descending into the real world, that he turned and spoke to her. And he knew instinctively that they were not now the two people who had been holding hands for so long in the darkness inside; those two intimates were ghosts now; these two on the steps, in the light, were strangers and would have to begin over again. When he spoke he acted upon this instinctive or intuitive knowledge.

"How did you like the picture then?" he asked, casually.

"I didn't think it was so very good," she replied, just as casually. "I don't like that Lulu Castellar. Pulls herself about a bit too much, she does, if you ask me. Might as well have Saint Vitus' dance and have done with it. Do you like her?"

"Oh—I dunno—she's all right," he muttered. He was recovering from a horrible shock. This girl was not pretty at all, not even reasonably good-looking. She was years older than he was, and she was hideous. He had just caught sight of her face properly for the first time. Her nose was all twisted and she had a bit of a squint. She was thirty if she was a day. Oh, hell—what a wash-out! She was still talking, but he could not bother listening to what she was saying. Sheer vexation made his eyes smart. He kept pace with her down the steps, mumbling an occasional "Yes" and "No," but somewhere inside him was a hot little angry man who screamed and cursed at everything.

"Well," she said, when they reached the bottom door, "I've got my sister to meet, so I'll say good-night to you."

"Good-night," said Turgis miserably.

Saturday night was roaring away outside, but for him the heart had gone out of it. He walked on mechanically, so sorry for himself, so angry with everything, that he could have cried. His head ached from being in that rotten balcony so long. There were queer aches in his body too. Where could he go now? Nowhere worth going to. If you had plenty of money, evening dress and all that, you could go to restaurants and night clubs and dance with beautiful girls with fine bare arms. But he wasn't in that seam. He'd no evening dress; no money; and anyhow he couldn't dance. He couldn't do anything. No, perhaps he couldn't, but he was as good as most of those fat rotten blighters who had the money, who just went chucking it away while he had to count every penny. Look at that lot in the big car, with their fur coats and diamonds and white shirt fronts, probably going somewhere to dance and get boozed up and God knows what before they'd finished! Swine! He was as good as them any day. And better—he did do some work. What did they do? It was enough to make any chap turn Bolshie. He didn't like the other chap who lodged at Mrs. Pelumpton's very much; Park was a dreary, unfriendly sort of devil, and a Sheeny at that; but he didn't blame Park for turning Bolshie. For two pins, he'd turn Bolshie, too. Yes, but what was the good of that?

All this time he had been walking on and on, through a Saturday night with the bottom dropped out of it, and now had left the spangled West End behind him. He stopped at a coffee stall, where several fools were arguing about nothing as usual, and had two buns and a cup of coffee—poor stuff it was too, too sweet and nearly cold. As he turned his back to the counter, he saw a girl, a really nice kid with a red hat and big dark eyes, smiling in his direction, and he smiled back at her hopefully, but then he saw her eyes move slightly and the smile instantly vanish. She had not been looking at him before, when she smiled; she had been looking at the chap standing next to him, who was ordering two coffees. And what a chap to be out with, to be smiling at! If that's what she wanted, she could have him. One vast sneer, Turgis moved away, and boarded the first bus he found that would take him to Camden Town, back to Nathaniel Street with the ruins of his evening.

" 'Ad a good time, boy?" said Mr. Pelumpton, now mellow with beer, as Turgis looked into the back room. "That'sh the way. Yersh. Enjoy yershelf while you're young, I shay, and while you *can* enjoy yershelf. I did when I wash your age an' don't ferget it, boy." Here Mr. Pelumpton chuckled and then coughed. "I 'ad a good time and nobody could shtop me 'aving one."

"What's this about you and your good times?" said his wife, popping out from nowhere.

"I'm jusht telling our friend 'ere that I don't blame him for enjoy-ing himshelf while he'sh young, 'cosh I did the shame thing when I wash young."

"Ar, you was a wicked devil you was," said Mrs. Pelumpton, with reluctant admiration.

"Oh dear, oh dear!" Mr. Pelumpton chuckled. "Lishen to that. Ar well, boy, I don't blame yer. Good old Shaturday night. I've 'ad 'em. I know."

"I'll bet you never had, you silly old fathead," Turgis muttered under his breath.

"Only jusht remember thish, boy. Don'd overdo it, that'sh all. Don'd overdo it. You're only young wunsh. Enjoy yershelf, if yer like, but don'd overdo it."

Turgis looked at him in disgust. "Good-night all," he said, mournfully, and climbed the chilling stairs to his room. So much for Saturday.

IV

Sunday was fine, that is, there was no rain, sleet, or snow falling. There was also very little sunlight falling, and the streets of Camden Town and Kentish Town were like echoing slatey tunnels. Turgis saw them when he went out to buy a paper and a packet of cigarettes, and as usual he disliked the look of them. They were not very cheerful on a weekday, but they were a pantomime and a bean feast then compared with what they were on Sunday. It was on Sunday that Turgis felt his loneliness most keenly.

It must be admitted, though, that on this particular Sunday morning he had received and refused two invitations. The first was from Mr. Pelumpton, who had decided that he must pay a visit to Petticoat Lane—"jusht to shee 'ow the shtuff's goin'," he said, with an impressive professional air. He had suggested, with some condescension, that Turgis might like to go with him. Turgis had promptly declined. He had been to Petticoat Lane before, and he saw quite enough of old Pelumpton in Nathaniel Street and had no desire to go to Whitechapel with him, merely to provide him with a listener and some free beer.

The other invitation came from his fellow lodger, Park, the Bolshie. Park, a neat dark Jewy sort of chap, quiet and civil enough but with something machine-like and vaguely menacing about him, just as if he was not quite human, worked in the printing trade and apparently had to go at all hours, so that Turgis hardly ever saw him. Moreover, he was a tremendous communist worker, for ever attending meetings and conferences and addressing envelopes to distant comrades and circulating what seemed to Turgis, who had inspected it, some terribly dreary literature. The two young men did not like each other very much, but Park always saw in Turgis, who had the depressed look of a faintly class-conscious proletarian, a possible convert. Hence the invitation, which this time was for some communist affair, a meeting or two and coffee and cake for the comrades, somewhere out at Stratford or West Ham. Turgis turned it down, though not ungraciously, for though he did not care much for Park, he had a vague kind of respect for him. But he did not see himself with the comrades. Perhaps the real reason was that he could not imagine any girls, real nice girls, not glaring female comrades, in the picture. He did not tell Park so, did not even admit it to himself; and when Park, with the drab innocence of his kind, accused him of being a timid slave of the bourgeois classes, a would-be bourgeois himself, he had no defence but a grin and a jeering noise.

The paper kept him amused until dinner time. After dinner he went for a walk, which chiefly consisted of penny bus rides. They finally landed him, as they had landed a few thousand other people, at the Marble Arch corner of Hyde Park, where the Sunday orators congregate. Turgis often visited this forum and listened to the orators. He had no intellectual curiosity and never really attended to the arguments, such as they were, but he had a sort of genial contempt for the speakers that was a warming, comforting feeling. He felt that they were a great deal sillier than he was, and that was pleasant. Moreover, any leisurely crowd always had an attraction for him, because there was always a chance that there might be, somewhere in the middle of it, bored and lonely, a wonderful girl who would suddenly smile back at him.

He drifted from speaker to speaker with the crowd, which was largely composed of youths like himself, all feeling pleasantly superior, with a sprinkling of aggressive dialecticians and religious and political fanatics. There was a fantastic old man in a greenish frock coat who banged a large chart and talked in a high sing-song that left five words out of six quite unintelligible. His subject—of all things—was shorthand. Turgis stared at him for a minute or two, concluded that he was mad, and moved on. The next meeting, a large one, was political, and the only words Turgis caught—"What about Russia, where your socialism, my friends, has been put into practice?"—drove him away at once. Then there was a tiny group of people round a harmonium, played by a young man with bulging eyes and a straggling beard. They were drearily singing a hymn, and nobody was taking any notice of them. Next to them, one of those involved discussions, typical of the place, was in heated progress, and the audience, in its own ironical fashion, was enjoying it. All that Turgis, at the back, could hear was the speaker himself, a young man with spectacles and long yellow hair who had something to do with the Catholic Church, who kept crying: "One mewment, my friend, just one mewment! Kindly allow me to speak. Yes, yes, but one mewment! You have asked me if I would considah such a person insane. Now, one mewment!" Turgis lingered for some time at this meeting. There were one or two nice girls in the crowd, but not one of them was by herself. It was no good. He would have to find a pal.

The speaker on the right was being heckled by a woman who looked rather like Mrs. Pelumpton. He was an elderly man, dressed in an old-fashioned black suit, and he was shaking a Bible almost in her face. "Well, what do Ah do?" he cried, his eyes gleaming. "Ah turn once mo-ore to the graa-aate Boo-ook. Yes, Ah've a Bahble text for tha-at." Turgis did not learn what the text was, for there came a tremendous bellow from this man's neighbour, a dirty little fellow with a broad flat nose and an india rubber mouth, who looked like a nasty compromise between Hoxton and Manchuria. "What is thee yighest idee-al of thee yole universe, my friends?" he was screaming, in a lather of oratory. "I'll tell you. Thee yighest idee-al of thee yole universe is Man—Man." And he thumped himself on the chest. Turgis did not like the look of him at all. He also did not like the look of the Salvation Army lasses who were conducting the service on the other side. They were all so pimply. They looked as if they were always eating things that disagreed with them.

Next to the Army was a bony, shabby chap, a Bolshie, possibly

one of Park's pals. Turgis had heard him before, and only stayed
long enough to make sure that he was on the same tack. He was.
"Noo where did communism firrst appearr, ma frien's?" he was
asking. "Noat in Russia—oh no! Noat in England—oh no! Noat in
Frrance—oh no! Bu' in Grreece, ma frien's, in ancient Grreece,
where a mon called Playto wrote a buik called *The Repuiblic*.
Yes, Ah know that this mon should rightly be called Plarto, but if
Ah said Plarto, Ah know everybody would be staring at it an'
wondering who this Plarto was, so Ah call him Playto. An' he was
the firrst communist." It was like listening to a Scots comedian who
had gone sour. Turgis moved on, passing with the merest glance a
very tiny group that everybody had ignored. There were three of
them, two bearded and bare-headed men and a faded woman, and
they were standing close together, apparently praying. Nobody was
taking any notice of them, except a battered and boosy old actor
(he recited a sort of story that introduced the names of all the
successful plays running at the time, and Turgis knew him of old)
who was waiting to claim the pitch. Why did these people come
here? Who were they? What did they do at home? Once more,
Turgis concluded they were all mad, but this time the thought did
not give him any pleasant feeling of superiority. It depressed him.
Suppose he was suddenly taken that way!

But there were roars of laughter coming from the crowd on the
right, and above it Turgis recognised another familiar figure, an
atheist chap, and quite a turn too. He was a fat young man, with
a glittering squint and a nose so resolutely turned up that it could
be described as a snout; and he had a very self-confident perky
manner and a shrill voice. Turgis edged himself into the audience.
"Now, where was Oi? Losing me plice, wasn't Oi?" he cried humorously. "Ow, Oi know. Fish on Froiday, thet was it. Whoi dew the
Catholics eat fish on Froiday? They down't know. They down't—
strite! Yew arsk 'em an' see. They down't know. But Oi know."
Here the crowd roared its approval. "It's in nonner of the old
goddess, Froiyer, goddess of plenty. Froiyer—Froiday—see? Thet's

whoi they eat fish on Froiday. It is—strite." The crowd roared again. "Then there's the Trinity. What's thet? Yew arsk 'em. They down't know. They're not allowed to talk about it. Whoi? Tew sycred. Thet's what they'll tell you—tew sycred. Secret and sycred— come from the sime root—mean the sime thing. They do—strite!" His audience did not care very much if secret and sacred did come from the same root, but it thoroughly approved of the piggy young man. And Turgis shared the general delight.

By the time he had returned down the line of speakers to the place where the old shorthand enthusiast had been (his pitch had been taken by a Christadelphian evangelist, a burly red-faced fellow who looked like a bookie), it was nearly dark and he found himself thinking about tea. He left the park, and walked along Oxford Street. Every teashop he came to was crammed. People were eating and drinking almost in one another's laps. And already there were queues for the pictures. "If they've got homes to go to," Turgis told himself, "why don't they go to 'em." He was sick of them. They were no good to him, these jumbles of faces. Finally, in somewhat low spirits, he found a place just off Oxford Street, one of those humble teashops with tall urns or geysers on the counter, a slatternly girl in attendance, a taxi-driver or two sitting at the first table and three Italians sitting at the back. He had a poor tea and it cost him fourpence-halfpenny more than he thought it would. When he went out again, it was drizzling, and miserably cold and damp. The queues for the pictures were enormous. All the cheaper seats were probably filled for the night.

He crossed Oxford Street and, without thinking where he was going, cut into the streets to the north of it. In one of these, a number of people, mostly women, were hurrying up some lighted steps. A notice informed him that the Higher Thought Alliance, London Circle, was meeting in that hall, to hear a lecture by Mr. Frank Dadds of Los Angeles, and that admission was free and that all would be heartily welcome. He lingered on the steps, where he was sheltered from the thickening drizzle, and wondered whether to go in or not. Now and again, on Sundays, he looked in at various services and meetings (though he had never tried the Higher Thought Alliance before, and had never heard of it), partly for want of something better to do, and partly because he always hoped he might strike up an acquaintance with a girl there, perhaps share the same hymn-book or programme. As he was hesitating, a large middle-aged woman in a fur coat, who had been fussing about in the entrance, noticed him and said: "Do come inside. Everybody is welcome." So he shook the raindrops from his overcoat, clutched at his hat, and, shyly, awkwardly, with his mouth wide open, he entered the hall. There, of course, before he had time to look round and see if there were any vacant seats near any nice-looking girls, an officious little man insisted on showing him to a seat. There were only about four men in the hall, but about two or three hundred women, mostly middle-aged and very dull. His own uncomfortable cane chair was between two of the dullest. On the platform, two women with short grey hair and a strained, gulping sort of expression, played the violin and the piano, and went on playing for the next ten minutes. Turgis began to feel sorry he had come, even though the place was warm and dry and the affair would not cost him anything.

Then the middle-aged woman in the fur coat, who had spoken to him outside, mounted the platform, and announced that they would begin with a hymn. It was not an ordinary sort of hymn—even Turgis could see that—and unfortunately nobody seemed to know the tune. Even the violinist had some difficulty in arriving at it. When the hymn finally trailed away into silence, they all remained standing, and then the woman in the fur coat said: "We affirm health, which is man's divine inheritance. Man's body is his holy temple," and everybody else, except Turgis, looked down at slips of paper and repeated it after her: "We affirm health, which is man's divine inheritance. Man's body is his holy temple." Several of the people near Turgis had some trouble in affirming this, because they were interrupted by fits of coughing, but they did their best. After that, they affirmed all sorts of things, divine love and power and truth and a general sort of oneness in the universe. Then they sat down, and nothing happened for a minute or two, during which time the universe had an opportunity of taking stock of their attitude towards it. Turgis was bewildered and not too happy, for the chair was very uncomfortable and his feet were cold.

He did not listen to what the woman in the fur coat said when she began talking again. She seemed to be reading a poem by a friend of hers, and then leaving a thought with them all. Turgis heard this remark because she repeated it several times and looked straight at him, the last time she said it. "And I'll just leave that great thought with you," she cried, and stared hard at Turgis, who felt embarrassed. The next moment, the two women with short grey hair were playing the violin and piano like mad, and the fussy little man and two others were rushing round with collection boxes. Two hundred and fifty women dived into handbags and then sat bolt upright, trying to look as if they did not know that their right hands were all clutching sixpences. Turgis left his pocket alone, and when the collection box came his way, he gave it a mysterious shake and then passed it on very quickly.

"A few minutes' silent meditation," the woman in the fur coat announced, composing her face meditatively. All the other women composed their faces meditatively too, and then looked down at their shoes. Turgis looked down at his, and noticed that one of them was splitting at the side. He wanted to waggle his toes to warm his feet, but if he began waggling, the shoe might split still more. They were rotten shoes. Everything he ever bought always turned out to be rotten. He was always being taken in. What he ought to buy was a pair of good thick Army boots; there were still some about in those ex-government stores shops; and they were cheap and they would last. But there again, what was a girl going to think of him if she found him clumping about in boots like a navvy's? What girl, though? "Where d'you get your girls from?"

he asked himself, with a sneer. There was a rustle and a shuffle: the silent meditation was over.

"And I'm sure Mr. Frank Dadds needs no introduction from me," the woman in the fur coat was saying. "We are delighted to have him here with us again. We remember the inspiring talks he gave us last time, and we realise that we have a treat in store." And there was an appreciative murmur.

Mr. Frank Dadds of Los Angeles suddenly shot up as the woman in the fur coat sat down. He was a tallish, fattish, fairish American in a light brown suit and a pink tie. He clasped his hands, then rubbed them together. He smiled at them all. He was obviously at home in the universe, and filled with divine love and power and truth and a general sort of oneness. Even Turgis was impressed by him, and all the women sat up and gazed at him with adoration. Then Mr. Frank Dadds burst into speech.

"My friends," he began, without any hesitation, "the title of my lecture this evening is Understanding and Yew. Let me commence by talking about Yew, jast Yew. Perhaps yew don't think much of yourselves. Life doesn't seem to yew to offer very much. There are people—and there may be some of them here with us to-night—who jast haven't got livingness. They think that life is always jast the same old thing. They can even talk of killing time. Killing time!—when every noo moment of time is diamonded with the greatest possibilities of lahv and trewth and bewdy. Once we have got livingness—once we have got understainding—once we are in toon with the in-fy-nyte—then there is a power within us, yes, within every one of us, that can cree-ate the world anoo. Our external selves can easily be fladdered. It is easy to make too much of what we've done. But it is com-pletely im-passible for any words—no matter if the greatest poets utter those words—to fladder what we have within us, our po-tentialities in baddy, mind, and spirrut. We've got to get rid of what some people like to call our in-feriority camplexes. We've got to realise that power within us. That doesn't mean—as some people seem to think—that we should develap sooperiority camplexes. And why? Bee-cause, as Noo Thought shows us, there is a Oneness in the Universe and we are all united in that Oneness. It isn't jast the potes who sing lahv songs. The whole Universe sings a lahv song. The whole Universe *is* a lahv song. If it isn't, the very atoms of which we are composed would disintegrate. I tell you, my friends, there is radiant health, there is power, there is wanderful bewdy, there is lahv, all without stint, without measure, eternal, awaiting all of us, and if we only open our eyes, find the way, develap understainding, get in toon, get livingness, there is not only a heaven above but a heaven here upon earth . . ."

For some twenty-five minutes more, the voice went sounding on, offering them radiant health, power, truth, beauty, and love, without ever once faltering. Turgis could not understand it all, but he listened in a happy dream, forgetting that his chair was uncomfortable and his feet were cold. He realised that he had only to do something or other, get this livingness and oneness and understanding, just turn a corner, and everything would be different, everything would be marvellous. Vaguely he saw himself trim and sleek, with evening clothes, a huge overcoat, white trousers for summer, money in his pocket, money in the bank, an office of his own perhaps, a flat with shaded lights and big chairs and a gramophone and a wireless set, even a car, and by his side, worshipping him, the loveliest and kindest of girls. It was wonderful.

"Come again, young man," said the fussy little man, at the door. "Always glad to see you here."

"Thank you very much," said Turgis earnestly, still glowing.

And then, somehow, outside in the wet streets, among the black figures hurrying home, it all went. Angrily he tried to recapture the glow and the dream, but they would not return. Inside the steaming bus, swaying with the strap he held, he found there was nothing left. He did not know how to get understanding or livingness or oneness or any of those things, could not even imagine what they were. Neither radiant health nor power, truth nor beauty, was coming his way. As for love, well, he had better chuck thinking about it. There was a girl standing next to him, not a bad sort of girl, but every time the bus went swaying round a corner, he bumped into her, not hurting her but just gently bumping into her. He wasn't doing it on purpose, but the third time it happened, she drew back and looked daggers at him—silly little idiot! Oh, yes, the universe was a love song all right!

Park was having a cup of tea and a bite of bread-and-butter with Mrs. Pelumpton in the back room when he got back, and he joined them, telling them where he had been and what he had heard.

"Dope, my friend, that's all you've had," said Park contemptuously, "nothing but dope! Comes from America, doesn't it? Yes, and why? Because the masses there have got to be doped, that's why. You come with me next time and you'll hear something that'll open your eyes a bit; no dope, but the real thing. What's the matter with you, Turgis, is that you don't see how your leg's being pulled, you're not properly class-conscious yet."

Turgis disliked this contemptuous tone. "Are you what-is-it—class-conscious, Park?" he asked.

"Yes, I am."

"Well, you can have it," Turgis retorted, in a voice that told Park pretty plainly that he was a dreary devil.

"All right then, my friend, all right. I will have it. And you keep on with the dope."

"I don't want any dope. Don't believe in it."

"Well, what do you want, then?" demanded Park, who thought he saw in this a chance of a fine long argument.

"I dunno," said Turgis, finishing his tea. "Yes, I do, though. I want to go to bed."

"That's right," said Mrs. Pelumpton approvingly. "Bed. You couldn't go to a better place. I'm sure I'm ready for mine. We're all in now, except Edgar, and I'm not waiting for him."

And then all that was left of Sunday was a walk upstairs.

v

Then, the very next day, on Monday of all days, it happened. It happened in the afternoon. Somebody came in, and, as Stanley was out, Turgis dashed to the other side of the frosted glass partition to see who it was. There, like a being from another world, stood a girl all in bright green, a girl with large brown eyes, the most impudent little nose, and a smiling scarlet mouth, the prettiest girl he had ever seen.

"Good afternoon. Is my father here, please?" She had a queer, fascinating voice.

"Your father?"

"Yes. Mr. Golspie. This is the place, isn't it? He told me to call for him here."

"Oh, yes, he is, Miss—Miss Golspie," cried Turgis eagerly, his eyes devouring her all the time. "He's in that room there. But I think there's somebody with him. Shall I tell him you're here?"

"You needn't yet if he's busy with somebody," said the glorious creature, smiling at him. "I can wait."

"I can tell him now, if you like." He was trembling with eagerness to help, to serve.

"No, it doesn't matter. I know he hates being interrupted. I'll wait for him. I don't suppose he'll be long, will he?"

"I'm sure he won't," he told her fervently. "Will you wait here or in the office? It's warmer in the office."

"This will do," and she made a movement towards the chair.

"Excuse me, Miss Golspie." He brought it stumbling out somehow, and at the same time he dusted the seat of the chair with his handkerchief. "It—it—might be dirty, y'know."

She looked him full in the eyes, deliciously, drowning him in sweetness, and then smiled. "Thank you. I'd hate to spoil my new coat. Everything looks a bit grimy here, doesn't it? It's such a frightfully dark place, too, isn't it?"

He supposed it was, and tried to imagine her walking up Angel Pavement outside. He still lingered. "Is there anything else," he began vaguely, hovering, adoring her.

"Quite happy, thanks."

There was no excuse possible to stay a moment longer. Reluctantly he returned to his desk, with his heart swelling with excitement. The others looked at him inquiringly, but he pretended to be busy with something. He did not even want to explain about a girl like that. He wanted to keep the very thought of her being there to himself. Meanwhile, he was determined to listen hard. The moment that he heard Mr. Golspie's visitor going, he would rush out, tell Mr. Golspie she was there, and thus see her again.

But he was not able to manage it. Mr. Golspie must have shown his visitor out, for immediately after the door was opened, Turgis heard Mr. Golspie's voice booming behind the partition. "Hello, Lena girl!" he heard him say. "Forgotten about you coming. Won't keep you a minute."

Mr. Golspie then came into the office. "I've got to go out," he told Mr. Smeeth, "and I shan't be coming back to-day. Be in about eleven in the morning though, if anybody wants me. Mr. Dersingham'll be back to-morrow afternoon, if anybody wants him. And I say, what's your name—Turgis——"

"Yes, sir," replied Turgis smartly.

"Get hold of the Anglo-Baltic—Mr. Borstein, nobody else, mind, Mr. Borstein—and tell him from me that if we've any more delays like that with the stuff, there's going to be heap big trouble. They said they wouldn't let us down, and they're letting us down like hell. And you can tell him that from me."

"Yes, sir, I will. Did you say Mr. Borstein?" And Turgis stared at Miss Lena Golspie's father, at his massive bald front, at his great moustache, at his big square shoulders. Mr. Golspie had never seemed an ordinary man, but now he had for Turgis the power and fascination of a demi-god. Already his very name spelt sweetness and wonder.

"That's the chap," Mr. Golspie grunted. "Afternoon, everybody." And he departed.

"That was Mr. Golspie's daughter then who came to the door, was it?" said Mr. Smeeth.

"His daughter, eh?" Miss Matfield raised her eyebrows, then looked at Turgis, and said casually: "What was she like? Pretty?"

"Yes," Turgis mumbled, "she was." And he would say no more. He was not going to talk about her. He preferred to think about her. Lena Golspie.

Then, with something like amorous urgency, he went to the telephone, rang up the Anglo-Baltic, and sternly demanded Mr. Borstein. He would tell Mr. Borstein something! He would show him whether he could let them down like hell! Lena Golspie. Lena Golspie. Lena, Lena, Lena. "Hello, is that Mr. Borstein? This is Twigg and Dersingham. Yes, Twigg and Dersingham. Mr. Golspie asked me to ring you up—Mr. Gols-pie, Mr. Gol-spie . . ." Lena's father. Lena, Lena, Lena.

Chapter Five

MISS MATFIELD WONDERS

I

M<small>R</small>. G<small>OLSPIE</small> took the typewritten sheets from Miss Matfield and then spread them out on her table. "All six letters alike, eh? That's the style, Miss Matfield. Hello, is this exactly what I said?"

"As a matter of fact, it isn't." And Miss Matfield raised her eyes and gave him a steady level glance.

"As a matter of fact, it isn't, eh? Then what is it, as a matter of fact? Just a little improvement, eh?"

Miss Matfield coloured slightly. "Well, if you want to know, Mr. Golspie, all I've done is to change *was* into *were* twice, simply for the sake of making it more grammatical. That's all."

"Half a minute, half a minute," Mr. Golspie boomed at her. "Not more grammatical. Just grammatical. You made it grammatical when before it wasn't grammatical. Either it's grammatical or it isn't, d'you see? And now I'm being more grammatical, eh?" He guffawed, suddenly, dreadfully.

"I don't pretend to be particularly marvellous about grammar," she replied, trying to be severe, "but I do happen to know when to use *was* and when to use *were*. It's one of the few things they taught me. And so I thought you wouldn't object if I changed them."

"Much obliged." He regarded her amiably. "By the way, what is it you do pretend to be particularly marvellous at?"

"Does that matter?" This in her best haughty manner. Everybody in the office knew it and respected it.

But Mr. Golspie only gave her a friendly leer. "Of course it mat-

ters," he declared heartily. "Now I like to know these things. Take
me. I used to play a good game at billiards, and I can still play
poker with the best, bridge, too. Oh, and I can crack walnuts between my finger and thumb—fact!" He held up a very large thick
hairy finger and thumb that matched it. "And that's not all either.
Still—we are a bit busy, aren't we?"

"I am." Miss Matfield looked at her typewriter.

"And so," he continued cheerfully, "for the time being, we'll say
it doesn't matter. I'll take these nice grammatical letters away with
me. You've addressed the envelopes, have you? Right." He turned
his broad back on her, gave Mr. Smeeth a wink, whistled softly, and
departed for the private office.

Miss Matfield drew her full lower lip between her teeth and
frowned at her typewriter. As usual, she was left with a vague sense
of defeat. It was, of course, the man's insensitiveness—and she saw
again that large thick hairy finger—that made him so difficult to
snub. Nobody else in the office had dared to talk to her as he did,
not after she had spent her first hour in the building. It was a
nuisance, not being able to put him in his place, as Mr. Dersingham,
Mr. Smeeth, and the others had been put in *their* places. It was
annoying to think that the very next time he spoke to her he would
probably talk in the same strain, not altogether an unfriendly strain,
but disrespectful, jeering, humiliating in a fashion. She could not
really stand up to it, but found herself wanting to lower her eyes,
turn her head away, and almost retreat in maidenly blushes—oh,
gosh! Lilian Matfield feeling like that! How her friends would howl
if they knew! Yet she didn't really dislike him, not now.

A little later, when they were clearing up for the night, she was
presented with this problem of Mr. Golspie again by some artless
questions from the little Sellers girl, who still treated Miss Matfield
with great deference and thus was still in favour.

"He's funny, isn't he?" said Miss Sellers, referring to Mr. Golspie.
"A bit weird."

"I wish you'd tell me, Miss Matfield," Miss Sellers continued, earnestly and deferentially, "d'you reelly *like* him?"

Miss Matfield raised her thick black brows and produced a long *mmm* sound that went up and then down again. Having gone through this little performance, she said, "Do you?"

"Well," said Miss Sellers, wrinkling her little nose in an agony of mental effort, "I do an' I don't—if you see what I mean."

Miss Matfield knew exactly what she meant, but did not say so. She merely gave the other girl an encouraging glance.

"Sometimes I think he's nice," Miss Sellers went on, staring at nothing, "an' sometimes I don't like him a bit. Not that he ever says anything or does anything, y'know—course I don't see as much of him as you do, Miss Matfield—but sometimes I catch a crool look ——"

"A what?"

Miss Sellers' voice had dropped to a whisper. "A crool look," she repeated, her eyes enormous. "An' a reel nasty tone of voice he's got too, sometimes. And then I think 'Well, I don't like you, and I wouldn't like to cross your path, that I wouldn't.' And then the next time, he's as nice as anything. But I don't like him as much as I like Mr. Dersingham. Do you, Miss Matfield? Mr. Dersingham's a reel gentleman, isn't he? I like him best."

"I don't." This came in a hoarse whisper. It was from Stanley, who, free from his letter-copying for a minute, had quietly joined them.

"Now who asked you your opinion?" Miss Sellers demanded. "You go away."

"I like Mr. Golspie best," said Stanley, contriving to introduce an enthusiastic note into his hoarse whisper. "An' I'll tell you why. He's what they call a man's man. I'll bet he's had advenshers."

"You an' your advenshers!" Miss Sellers was very contemptuous. "What d'you know about it?"

"I've heard things, I have," said Stanley, very slowly and impressively.

"What have you heard?"

"Shan't tell you."

"No, because you've got nothing to tell. You run away and get your work done, little boy."

"I'm as big as you are."

"Cheeky! Here, you want to go an' shadder a few manners the next time you go shaddering," Miss Sellers jeered, singling out, with feminine swiftness and accuracy, the weak joint in the other's armour.

"Huh! Shan't learn 'em from you."

"Oh, be quiet, the pair of you," cried Miss Matfield, and began tidying her table. Nothing more was said about Mr. Golspie, but on her way home Miss Matfield could not help thinking about him. She always had a book with her for the journey on the 13 bus to and from the office, but the jogging and the crowding and the changing lights did not make reading easy, especially on the return journey to West Hampstead, and frequently she spent more time with her own thoughts than she did with those of her author. On this particular evening Mr. Golspie claimed her attention, almost to the exclusion of anybody or anything else. She could not make up her mind about him, had no label or pigeonhole ready for him, and this annoyed her, for she liked to know exactly what she felt and thought about people; to be able to dismiss them in a phrase. The fact that Mr. Golspie spoke to her every day, if only for a few minutes, gave her work to do, was sufficient to make her anxious to determine her attitude towards him. Men, with their thick skins and yawning indifference, might be able to work with people for years and not know or care anything about them as persons, but this drab stuff about "governors" and "colleagues" could find no place to stay in Miss Matfield's mind. In the talk among the girls at the Club, all the men who dictated letters to them became immense characters, comic, grotesquely villainous, or heroic and adorable. Their femininity, frozen for a few hours every day at the keyboard of their machines, thawed and gushed out in these perfervid personalities. Behind their lowered eyes, their demure expressions, as they sat with their notebooks on hard little office chairs, these comic and romantic legends buzzed and sang, to be released later in the dining-room, the lounge, the tiny bedrooms, of the Club. Thus, something had to be done about Mr. Golspie, who would have appeared to most of the girls, as Miss Matfield knew only too well, a gigantic find, a mine of glittering material. So far he had merely passed as "weird," but that would not do. It had not sufficed in Miss Matfield's private thoughts since the first two days.

She knew exactly what she thought about the others at the office. Mr. Dersingham she neither liked nor disliked; she merely tolerated him, with a sort of easy contempt; he was "sloppy and a bit feeble," and a familiar type, with nothing at all weird about *him*. Smeeth seemed to her a vaguely pathetic creature who lived a grey life in some grey suburb; the pleasure he got from what seemed to her his drudgery sometimes irritated her, but at other times it roused something like pity; and when she was not despising him, she liked him. Turgis she despised and occasionally resented. She resented his shabbiness and dinginess, his unhealthy skin and open mouth, his whole forlorn air, simply because these things, which were always there in the office, beside her, hurt her own pride by indicating the indignity of her situation. Occasionally, perhaps after a week-end in the country, when the thought of going back to Angel Pavement almost—as she said—made her feel sick, there flashed through her mind an image of Turgis. There had been moments when she had felt sorry for him, but they were very rare. Stanley and the funny little Cockney girl she tolerated and even liked, so long as they behaved themselves, and they might have been a couple of amusing little animals, a pair of spaniels perhaps, inferior and somewhat neglected. All these people were securely in their places. But not Mr. Golspie, the mysterious, large, jocular, brutal man, who always contrived—and for the life of her she could not discover how he did it—to get the best of her in any talk between them, who irritated one half of her, the sensible half, by making the other half feel fluttered and foolish, all girlish—ugh! How she had loathed him at first! Well, she still loathed him, or at least she disliked him, despised him, because he was nothing but a middle-aged bullying lout. He had a ridiculous moustache. He reeked of cigars and whisky, bar parlours. He was at once comic and awful.

As the bus rattled and roared up the long straight slope of Finchley Road on its way to Swiss Cottage, she told herself several times that Golspie was comic and awful and found something comforting in this conclusion. It was not, however, much of a conclusion; it only remained one for a few minutes, for Mr. Golspie, even in memory, even as an image, a faintly illuminated leer in the dark of her mind (like the Cheshire Cat in *Alice*), refused to stay in his place and wear his label. He escaped, and mocked her. It was all too stupid, and when she got up to leave the bus she determined to leave Mr. Golspie behind her, too. She found another girl from the Club waiting for the bus to stop, and when it did stop, they smiled at one another and walked up from the Finchley Road together. Mr. Golspie faded away.

"Do you come all the way from the City in that bus, Matfield?" the other girl inquired languidly. She was a very languid girl, rather affected, and her name was Morrison.

"The whole way."

"How revolting!"

"It is. Absolutely foul! Where do you get it, Morrison? You don't work in the City, do you?"

"No, Bayswater," Miss Morrison sighed. "I get it just in Orchard Street. I have to take another bus first along Bayswater Road. Unless I walk, and I loathe walking, specially on these beastly dark nights. Even then, it seems an awfully long way."

"Nothing to the way I have to come," said Miss Matfield, sternly. When there was any grumbling about, and there usually was some about, she liked to have her share. "Sometimes it takes hours and hours."

"I know. I took a job in the City once and I only stuck it a week." Miss Morrison groaned in the darkness at the thought of it. "I nearly died. Honestly, Matfield, if I'd to go to the City every day and come back here, I'd die, I'd absolutely pass out, I would really. I don't know how you stick it. But then you're so energetic, aren't you?"

Miss Matfield at once denied this terrible charge, and told herself that the Morrison girl was pretty awful. "I'm worn out now," she continued. "Only I'd rather have the City because I can't bear those private secretary jobs. Yours is one of them, isn't it?"

"Yes," with another sigh. "And pretty ghastly. The woman I'm working for now means well, but she's an idiot, she really is, Matfield, a full-sized idiot. No man in any office could ever be such an idiot. She's just dotty."

"Well, here we are at our beautiful home," said Miss Matfield, looking up at the Club entrance.

"I know. Isn't it revolting?"

"Absolutely vile," she replied mechanically, as they walked in. "I don't suppose there are any letters for me. No, of course not. There wouldn't be."

"Mine's a bill," Miss Morrison groaned. "Are you always getting bills? I never seem to get anything else. Just millions of foul bills."

"Foul! Cheerio."

"Oh—er—cheerio."

II

The Burpenfield Club, called after Lady Burpenfield, who had given five thousand pounds to the original fund, was one of the residential clubs or hostels provided for girls who came from good middle-class homes in the country but were compelled, by economic conditions still artfully adjusted to suit the male, to live in London as cheaply as possible. Two fairly large houses had been thrown together and their upper floors converted into a host of tiny bedrooms, and there was accommodation for about sixty girls. For twenty-five to thirty shillings a week the Club gave them a bedroom, breakfast and dinner throughout the week, and all meals on Saturday and Sunday. It was light and well ventilated and very clean, offered an astonishing amount of really hot water, and had a large lounge, a drawing-room (No Smoking), a small reading-room and library (Quiet Please), and a garden stocked with the hardiest annuals. The food was not brilliant—and no doubt it returned to the table too often in the shape of fish-cakes, rissoles, and shepherd's pie— but it was reasonably wholesome and could be eaten with safety if not with positive pleasure. The staff was very efficient and was controlled, as everybody and everything else in the Club was controlled, by the secretary, Miss Tattersby, daughter of the late Dean of Welborough, and perhaps the most respectable woman in all Europe. The rules were not too strict. There were no compulsory religious services. Male visitors could not be entertained in bedrooms, but could be brought to dinner and were allowed in the lounge, where they occasionally might be seen, sitting in abject misery. Intoxicants were not supplied by the Club but could be introduced, in reasonable quantities, into the dining-room when guests were present. Smoking was permitted, except in the dining and drawing-rooms. There were a good many regulations about beds and baths and washing and so forth, but they were not oppressive. In the evenings, throughout the winter months, fires, quite large cheerful fires, brightened all the public rooms. The lighting was good. The beds and chairs were fairly comfortable. Dramatic entertainments and dances were given two or three times a year. All this for less than it would cost to live in some dingy and dismal boarding-house or the pokiest of poky flats.

What more could a girl want? Parents and friends of the family who visited the Burpenfield found themselves compelled to ask this question. The answer was that there was only one thing that most girls at the Burpenfield did want, and that was to get away. It was very odd. You were congratulated on getting into the Burpenfield when you first went there, and you were congratulated even more heartily when you finally left it. During the time you were there, you grumbled, having completely lost sight of the solid advantages of the place. The girls who stayed there year after year until at last they were girls no longer but women growing grey, did stop grumbling and even pointed out to another these solid advantages, but their faces always wore a resigned look.

There was, to begin with, that institution atmosphere, which was rather depressing. The sight of those long tiled corridors did not cheer you when you returned, tired, rather cross, head-achy, from work in the evening. The food was monotonous and the dining-room too noisy. Then, if you were not going out, you had to choose between your little box of a bedroom, the lounge (usually dominated by a clique of young insufferable rowdies), or the silent and inhuman drawing-room. Moreover, Miss Tattersby, known as "Tatters," was terrifying. Very early, Miss Tattersby had arrived at the sound conclusion that a brisk rough sarcasm was her best weapon, and she made full use of it. You felt the weight and force of it even in the notices she was so fond of pinning up: "Need residents who have First Dinner take up *so* much time . . ."; "Some residents seem to have forgotten that the Staff has other duties besides . . ."; "Is it necessary *again* to remind residents that washing stockings in the bathrooms . . ."; that is how they went. But this, after all, was only a pale reflection of her method in direct talk, and some girls, finding themselves involved in an intricate affair concerning a pair of stockings or something of that kind, preferred to conduct their side of the case by correspondence, in the shape of little notes to Miss Tattersby hastily left in her office when she was known to be out. Many a girl, after a little brush with "Tatters," who was immensely tall and bony and staring, and looked like a soured Victorian celebrity, had faced the most infuriated director at her office with a mere shrug. The confident Burpenfield manner in commercial life, of which we have seen something in Miss Matfield in Angel Pavement, was probably the result of various encounters with Miss Tattersby.

But what Miss Matfield, who was cursing the place all over again as she left Miss Morrison and went upstairs to her room, disliked most about the Burpenfield was the presence of all the other members, whose life she had to share. There were too many of them, and their mode of life was like an awful parody of her own. The thought that her own existence would seem to an outsider just like theirs infuriated or saddened her, for she felt that really she was quite different from these others, much superior, a more vital, splendid being. Those whose situation was not at all like her own only annoyed her still more. There were the young girls, all rosy and confident, many of whom were either engaged (to the most hopelessly idiotic young man) or merely filling in a few months of larking about, trying one absurd thing after another, while their doting fathers forwarded generous monthly cheques. Then there were the women older than herself, downright spinsters in their thirties and early forties, who had grown grey and withered at the typewriter and the telephone, who knitted, droned on interminably about dull holidays they had had, took to fancy religions, quietly went mad, whose lives narrowed down to a point at which washing stockings became the supreme interest. Some of them were frankly depressing. You met them drooping about the corridors, kettle in hand, and they seemed to think about nothing but hot water. Others were mechanically and terribly brisk and bright, all nervy jauntiness, laborious slang, and secret orgies of aspirin, and these creatures— poor old things—were if anything more depressing, the very limit. Sometimes, when she was tired and nothing much was happening, Miss Matfield saw in one of these women an awful glimpse of her own future, and then she rushed into her bedroom and made the most fantastic and desperate plans, not one of which she ever attempted to carry out. Meanwhile, time was slipping away and nothing was happening. Soon she would be thirty. Thirty! People could say what they liked—but life was foul.

There was still half an hour before dinner, and, after tidying herself, she sat on her bed trying to repair a ladder in a second-best pair of stockings. She was interrupted by a knock at the door and the entrance of an extraordinary figure. It had a greeny-brown face and was dressed in what appeared to be Oriental costume, and the general effect was that of a seasick Arab chieftain.

"Help!" cried Miss Matfield, but only to her visitor. "What is it? Who are you? It can't be you, Caddie."

The green face never moved a muscle, but a careful voice came from it, and the voice, though muffled and lacking its usual variety of tones, was undoubtedly that of her neighbour, Miss Isabel Cadnam, otherwise "Caddie." She had put a mud pack on her face and had wrapped her head in a towel.

"And you haven't to smile or anything," she announced cautiously, "or it'll crack. But I've come to ask you a favour. Are you in to-night? I mean you're not dressing or anything grand? Well, can I borrow your shawl, the reddy-black one? You promised to lend it to me, if I wanted it terribly some night."

Miss Matfield nodded.

"Well, this is the night. A great do. My dear, Ivor's got tickets for a new cabaret, dance and supper place, opening night to-night, and we're going. Marvellous!" The face did not move, but the eyes rolled and flashed their appreciation.

"All right, you can have the shawl, Caddie," said Miss Matfield, lazily rising to stretch out a hand for it. That is all you have to do to find anything in a Burpenfield bedroom. "It sounds marvellous. But I thought you'd had a row with Ivor, parted for ever for the umpteenth time and all that. Why, it's only last Friday you spent hours and hours telling me about it."

"We made it up this morning," the green mask replied, rolling its eyes. "Started over the telephone, too, my dear. Ivor tried to explain and then I tried to explain and then about forty people in the office went off the deep end, so I said I'd meet him for lunch. We met. And there you are. And now we're going on the razzle."

"Lucky you!"

"I will say that for Ivor. He can be terribly, terribly stupid, almost stupider than anybody I know, except those foul brutes at the office

—honestly, my dear, they *are* the limit—but the minute we've made it up, he always has tickets for something amusing. Free list, you know."

"I believe he waits until he has the tickets, then rings you up that morning and makes it up," said Miss Matfield. "I wouldn't put it past him."

"What a perfectly loathsome idea, Mattie! What a foul mind you have! Still, he might do that. Rather sweet of him, really, when you think about it. Well, I shall have to fly. I've got to get this stuff off. I've been wearing it for hours and I feel I shall never be able to smile again. Thanks for the shawl, and, my dear, I'll take the greatest, the very greatest care of it, and you shall have it back in the morning."

"Have a good time," said Miss Matfield, with no particular enthusiasm. "Give my love to Ivor."

When her visitor had gone, she gave a little impatient shake, sat down again, but threw the stocking on one side. Caddie was really rather a silly creature, but nevertheless she contrived to have quite an amusing, even exciting time. Ivor, a goggly-eyed young man who was with a firm of publicity people, was even sillier than she was, and Miss Matfield admitted to herself at once that she could not possibly endure a single hour of his company, but he pleased Caddie, took her out, quarrelled with her, made it up, took her out more luxuriously, created a continual excitement. It was possible to envy Caddie's state of mind while despising her taste. Miss Matfield's ripe mouth, which hardly needed lipstick, took on a discontented curve. It was a pity that silly young men did not amuse her, for there were plenty of Ivors about, whereas there were very few real grown-up men about, men who could make her feel she was still a mere girl. She was beginning to like, definitely to prefer, middle-aged men—and admitted as much to her intimates—but the trouble was that the really nice attractive ones were nearly always terribly domesticated, up to the neck in wives and families, and had hardly more than an occasional faint gleam of interest to spare for a Miss

Matfield. The middle-aged men who were interested were always the awful ones, with swollen faces and little boiled eyes, dreary rotters. Mr. Golspie? No, he wasn't as bad as that, wasn't quite that type. But quite impossible, of course. Quite absurd.

The gong went clanging below, and as it sounded, a head popped into the room. "You're in, aren't you, Mattie?" it said. "Come on, then. I've got some *News*. Very exciting."

This head, which was decorated with a thick shock of fair hair, horn spectacles, a freckled and turned-up nose, and a wide and amusing mouth, belonged to Evelyn Ansdell, who had had a room close to Miss Matfield's for the last two years, and who was one of the very few friends she had made at the Burpenfield. She was a slap-dash, untidy, scatter-brained sort of girl, younger than Miss Matfield, and though she had all manner of minor faults, she had the two outstanding virtues of being good-hearted and extremely entertaining.

The two girls went down to the dining-room together and were fortunate enough to get a little table to themselves. There, amid the chatter and clatter that went with the mutton stew and the prunes and custard, Miss Ansdell broke the news, in a series of shrieks and gasps.

"I'm nearly dead," she began, impressively. "No, really nearly dead. I've been ringing up parents like mad for the last hour and a half. Don't I sound hoarse? Honestly, I've been screaming and screaming down the telephone."

There was nothing novel about this. Miss Matfield knew all about Evelyn's parents. They were a queer pair, and had been separated for the last four or five years. Mrs. Ansdell roamed about the country, sometimes trying her hand at odd things, while Major Ansdell, no longer in the army but now the representative of some mysterious imperial organisation, roamed about the whole world, completely disappearing for months on end. Now and then, each of them descended upon London and the Burpenfield, and by some odd chance it frequently happened that their London visits coincided, and then Evelyn had to work desperately hard to make sure that they did not arrive at the Club together. Evelyn herself, who had once been sent flying between them like an amused shuttlecock, did not take sides, except perhaps in certain minor differences, but preserved an amiable detachment, not unlike that of a good old referee. Everything was complicated by the fact that all three of them were rather eccentric. All this was strange to Miss Matfield, whose parents adored one another in their dull elderly fashion and were, anyhow, far too sensible and too busy for such alarms and excursions; but the actual novelty of it had passed. So she merely prepared herself to listen to yet another instalment of the Ansdell family row saga.

"It all began with a letter from mother," Miss Ansdell continued, excitedly. "It came this afternoon. My dear, the maddest letter. But the point is, mother's going to run a shop, selling antiques. I forget the name of the place, but anyhow she's actually got the shop and it's a marvellous place, all oak beams and bow windows and all that, and rich motorists stopping every minute. That's not so crazy as it sounds, because mother does really know about antiques and old embroideries and things like that, and could make anybody buy anything if she wanted to. And she wants me to go and live with her, and help her in the shop."

"Oh, Lord!" Miss Matfield groaned. "But you're not going, are you? She's wanted you to go before, hasn't she?"

"Yes, but this is rather different. Quite different, in fact. It really would be rather fun helping her in a shop. I'd much rather do that, swindling the rich motorists, than go on with this secretary rot. You know how I loathe typing and shorthand. And this time she wants me very badly—her own little darling girl by her side sort of thing—you should have seen her letter. So I rang her up—trunk call, my dear, and I'm absolutely broke—to know all about it, and honestly it does sound rather marvellous. Lovely shop, nice old town, lots of nice people, and a car—you have to have a car in this antique business. I must say—even though I know what mother is—I must say it sounds rather marvellous."

"It does," Miss Matfield admitted, grudgingly.

"But wait a minute, wait a minute, Mattie, my dear. That isn't all the excitement. Oh, no! Before I rang off, mother gave me a message to father about some money. He's in town, you know. So I rang him up and then, after I'd given him the message, I told him what mother had suggested. Well, you should have heard him. I thought every minute I should hear him going up in sheets of flame. Then he was very quiet, and I knew he was going to be pathetic. He can do it even better than mother. If he really gets going, I'd agree to anything—while he's there. And he said he had a plan he'd had in his mind for months, been thinking about nothing else, and that he'd have mentioned it before only he thought I was so happy here at the Burpenfield. He's going away again very soon on this Empire rot, and he wants me to go with him as his secretary. He's going to America—Montreal and Toronto and those places—and then on to Australia, and I'd go everywhere with him. What do you think about that? He said he'd been thinking about it for ages, but I believe he'd invented the job five minutes before, just to do mother in the eye. And now they both want an answer at once. Isn't it crazy?"

"Completely mad." But why did nothing like that ever happen to her? "What are you going to do?"

"My dear, I'm going to take *one* of them. Wouldn't you? But which, I don't know. What do you think?"

"Let's get our coffee," said Miss Matfield. "Then we can talk about it afterwards."

This was a blow. Whether Ansdell went off to Canada and Australia or joined her mother at the antique shop, she was lost to the Burpenfield. Another decent and amusing one gone! Something exciting happening to somebody else, as usual! And Miss Matfield was so busy feeling sorry for herself that if her advice had really been demanded over the coffee, she would not have found it easy to give it. Miss Ansdell, however, like many people who ask to be advised, apparently only wanted a listener, for she never stopped talking herself and when she put a question, promptly answered it without giving her friend time to frame a reply.

When they came up from the dining-room, they saw a tall figure standing just inside the entrance hall. "I believe it is," Miss Ansdell gasped. "Yes, it is. It's father. Oh, help!"

And Major Ansdell it was. Miss Matfield had met him, just for a few minutes, two or three times before. He was still a handsome, soldierly looking man, though quite elderly, and was immensely courteous in the Roger de Coverley style to all Evelyn's friends. But there was in him an extraordinary theatrical strain. Quite frequently he behaved as if he were the hero of some old-fashioned melodrama; and was very emotional, very rhetorical, and absurd. He was quite capable of talking just as men talk in bad stories in popular magazines, and Miss Matfield had sometimes wondered whether it was because he had read a great many bad stories or because the stories were nearer the truth than one thought and were worked up, on the fringes of Empire, out of men like Major Ansdell.

Miss Matfield hung back and saw the Ansdells greet one another and then go upstairs, obviously to Evelyn's room. There was no talking to Major Ansdell in a public room; he was far too fond of a scene and was not at all shy. Miss Matfield went into the lounge, to smoke a cigarette, and spent an envious ten minutes glancing through one of those illustrated weeklies that seem to be produced simply to glorify that small section of society which works only to keep itself amused. It showed her photographs of these demigods and goddesses racing and hunting in the cold places, bathing and lounging in the warm places, and eating and drinking and swaggering in places of every temperature. By the time she had finished her cigarette, Miss Matfield quite understood the temptation to start a revolution, and told herself that these papers simply asked for one. Then she too went upstairs to her room.

She had not been there more than a few minutes when Evelyn Ansdell burst in, crying: "My dear, mother's on the phone. Do go in and talk to father until I come back. If you don't, he'll come down and do something absurd. I'll be as quick as I can." And off she went.

Evelyn's bedroom seemed almost entirely filled by her father, who welcomed his daughter's friend—and Miss Matfield felt herself thrust into the part of daughter's friend at once—with his usual grave and elaborate courtesy. He was, she felt, enjoying himself, and was probably the only man who ever had enjoyed himself visiting the Burpenfield. He addressed her as "Miss Mattie," having heard Evelyn refer to her as "Mattie," and Miss Matfield did not feel like correcting him. This only made everything more absurd. It was like taking part in a charade.

"I think you know why I'm here, Miss Mattie," he began, in deep vibrating tones. "I want to persuade this little girl of mine to go overseas with me, to help me with the great work I am doing and to be by my side."

She nodded and made a vague affirmatory noise. It was all she could do, but then he did not want anything more.

"A father has his feelings, Miss Mattie. We don't hear much about them. He keeps them to himself. He hides them, buries them," he continued, with fine emotional effect, clearly enjoying himself. "An Englishman doesn't like to make a display of these things. It's part of the tradition—the great tradition—of our race. If we suffer, Miss Mattie, we like to suffer in silence. Isn't that so? The Britisher— now, just a moment. I know what you're going to say."

"Do you?"

"I do. You're going to say that you don't like that word 'Britisher.'"

"I don't like it much, I must say," Miss Matfield confessed.

"I knew you didn't. I didn't at one time. I detested the term. I wouldn't have it at all. But my work, my travels up and down the Empire have taught me better. We must have something that describes not an Englishman, not a Scotsman, or a Canadian or an Australian, but simply a subject of the great Empire itself, and the only word for that is 'Britisher.' Don't resent it, Miss Mattie. It stands for a great ideal. And I say that the Britisher doesn't wear his heart on his sleeve. But he feels deeply. He may have his work to do, taking him away from his home into the loneliest places, and be glad and proud to do it." Here the Major made a fine gesture and came within an ace of wrecking his daughter's toilet stand. So he sat down on the edge of the bed, where he looked enormous and rather like the White Knight in *Through the Looking Glass*.

"You're my little girl's friend, aren't you, Miss Mattie?" he asked.

Miss Matfield said she was, and added that she would be very sorry to lose her.

"I understand that, I understand that," and he reached over and patted her lightly on the shoulder. "She's a very lovable child, isn't she? And you can understand a father's feelings. I have my work to do, Miss Mattie, and I have many acquaintances, friends if you like, in all parts of the world, but fundamentally, at heart, I'm a lonely man—yes, a lonely man. Evelyn's my only child, and I want her companionship, I want her by my side, unless of course I should be called upon to visit places where one's womenfolk couldn't be taken. If it were a question of our tropical possessions, that would be different, quite different. I don't like to see a white woman, especially a young girl, in such places. They're for men, for us rough fellows who like to clean up some backward part of the globe. If you've any influence with her—and I'm sure you have, and a very good influence too, a steadying influence naturally, being older ——"

"Thank you, Major Ansdell," said Miss Matfield drily. "You make me sound about fifty. It's not very complimentary of you."

"A thousand apologies, my dear Miss Mattie," cried the Major gallantly. "I know very well you're under thirty, a mere girl, and a very charming one, I assure you. But Evelyn's a mere *child*, you see, isn't she?"

Miss Matfield said nothing, but thought that some of the child's antics and talk might possibly astonish him.

"But what I was about to say is this. I want you to use your influence with my little girl to persuade her to come with her old father and join her life with mine. There's some ridiculous talk," he continued hurriedly and more naturally, "of her joining her mother in some wild-cat scheme for selling old furniture and broken crockery and silly knick-knacks down in the country somewhere. You know the sort of place. Ye oldy antique shoppy! Faked warming pans! Rubbish! Even if she won't come with me, I'd fifty times rather see the child staying here and doing her typewriting than embarking on such a gim-crack, nonsensical scheme. Trying to sell faked warming pans to a lot of cads and old women!"

At this moment the door flew open and Evelyn joined them, breathless. The little room was completely full now, and Miss Matfield wanted to escape, to let them talk it out together, but she could not manage it unless she pushed Evelyn out of the way.

"I've been talking to mother," Evelyn began.

The Major jumped up. "Don't tell me she's still trying to persuade you to bury yourself among her fenders and warming pans and go smirking behind a counter. It's the most preposterous idea I ever heard of. It won't even pay. All good money thrown away."

"Oh, I don't know about that, father," Evelyn protested. "Mother really does know a lot about antiques. I know that. I wouldn't be surprised if she didn't make quite a lot out of it."

Neither of them took any notice of Miss Matfield, but nevertheless she could not very well leave the room until she had a good opportunity to push past Evelyn.

"Your mother may or may not know a good deal about antiques," said the Major very impressively, "though I seem to remember her being taken in every day or so by some piece of faked-up rubbish. But she knows nothing whatever about human nature and has no head for business. And if you're going to keep a shop, my child, you have to know something about human nature and business. Now I could keep a shop and make a success out of it, if I wanted to, because I understand people and know how to organise. Your mother knows no more about organisation than a—a prize rabbit."

"Well, listen to me, father, and never mir' about that. I've been talking it over with mother, and I'll tell you what I've decided to do. I'm coming with you on this trip—and, by the way, you'll have to give me some money for clothes, I haven't a thing—and then afterwards, if I don't like it, I shall try mother's scheme, if the shop's still in existence."

"It won't be. But that doesn't matter. This is good news, Evelyn. Just the two of us, side by side——"

It looked as if a magnificent parental embrace were arriving. Miss Matfield, murmuring something about letters, slipped out. The Ansdells were absurd, all three of them, but she could not help envying Evelyn. Major Ansdell might be ridiculous, but if he had asked *her* to go roaming round the Empire with him, she would have accepted like a shot. As it was, she stayed on in Angel Pavement and at the Burpenfield, and would soon have lost an amusing Club neighbour too, almost the only one left with whom she could be friendly and confidential. Foul.

The late post had arrived and there were two letters for her. One was from her mother and was merely the regular hasty bulletin. Dad was working too hard as usual, looking after everybody for miles around except himself, and not looking at all well. The Wesleys' little girl was down with pneumonia. Those new people, the Milfords, the elderly people who had taken Rogerson's old house, had a son and his wife home from India, quite nice. There was no chance of her getting up to town this next month but Dad said he might have to come up and would let her know in good time. And when did Lilian think she could manage another week-end at home? Oh—and Mary Fernhill, the quite plain one who went out to South Africa last year and came back so suddenly, well, she was engaged. There was nothing very exciting in all that. Just the usual stuff. Poor mother, poor dad! He did work too hard, and he was beginning to have a terribly pinched look. That was the trouble about being a doctor, you never bothered, went on until you dropped. That was pretty foul too. There didn't seem to be much good luck going in life, and what there was completely escaped the Matfield family.

The other letter was more interesting, and she kept it until she reached her own room again. It was dated from the Chestervern Agricultural College:

> Dear Lilian,
>
> I have to be in London to-morrow (the 16th) and am wondering if you would care to spend the evening with me, have dinner and then go somewhere. It would be a great treat for me. I'm sorry the notice is so short, but couldn't help that. Will you let me know at once—c/o Holborn Palace Hotel—and tell me what time to call for you if you are free.
>
> Yours sincerely,
>
> Norman Birtley.

So Norman Birtley hadn't forgotten her existence. She sent a dashing note to him at his rather ghastly Holborn Palace Hotel, telling him she was free and could be called for at the Burpenfield at seven o'clock. And after slipping out to post it, she felt slightly better.

Ansdell looked in, having disposed of her father, not without first making him promise her a new outfit. "And we sail in a fortnight, my dear," she crowed. "And to-morrow I give those beastly people the sack, after which I hand out the same to Tatters *in person too*. Yes, I am. That will probably close the dear old Burp to me for ever, and not a bad thing too. Except I shall be very sorry to leave you, Mattie. I will really. After all, we've had some great conferences in these queer little dens, haven't we? I'll have to tell father he must have two secretaries, and then we'll both go out, slip away and marry big brown men from the West and the great open spaces. What do you say?"

"I'd love it," said Miss Matfield, forcing a smile. "I'm terribly sorry you're going. They'll put some awful creature into your room, either one of the old hot water brigade or some devastatingly bright young person from the lounge set. I suppose it's nearly time I joined the hot water school, the kettle fillers ——"

"Don't be absurd. You're one of the very few people here who are really alive—and look it. Let's change the subject. I believe it's depressing you. Had any letters?"

"One from mother, very dull, and one from a man I've known off and on for years. He's coming up to town to-morrow and wants me to spend the evening with him, seeing the sights."

"A-ha! Is he a big brown man? Do you like him?"

"He's not bad," Miss Matfield replied, indifferently. "A bit feeble. He's from my part of the world and used to hang about a lot at one time, but we haven't seen much of one another for ages."

"I scent a roam-a-ance," cried Miss Ansdell. "His sweetheart when a boy. And you have cared all these yee-ars and I never knew ——"

"Don't be an ape. You're making me feel sick."

"But seriously, Mattie. Is he going to ask you to marry him, after the coffee has been served in a shaded corner?"

Miss Matfield smiled, but thought this over. "He might, you know," she admitted, staring into nothing, her eyes growing sombre. "And if I thought I was doomed to stay in this place much longer, spending my evenings washing stockings and pattering round with kettles, I'd marry him next week. But I haven't the least desire to marry him. He's quite decent, but—oh—he's just rather feeble. Most young men seem rather feeble, these days. I suppose most of the other sort were killed in the war. I hate feeble men, don't you? I mean, I like a man to have plenty of character, a solid lump of it, and I don't even care if it isn't a terribly good character so long as there's plenty of it. There's a man in my office ——"

"You don't mean Mr. Dirty—Dersy—what's it?" Miss Ansdell asked.

"No. He's rather sloppy too. Not a bit amusing. But there's a man who's just come lately, Golspie ——"

"I know. But you said he was awful."

"So he is," Miss Matfield admitted hastily. "I told you about him, didn't I? I don't say I like him. He's rather a brute, and looks it, or at any rate looks weird. But he has got some character, and could do something without asking everybody's permission. That's all I meant. Of course, from every other point of view, even poor Norman Birtley, who really isn't so bad, is worth fifty of him. Imagine going out to dinner with Golspie!" And she laughed aloud at the thought.

They talked of other things, yawned, stared, talked again, more idly, yawned again, and then went to bed.

III

Miss Matfield awoke next morning with a vague feeling that something pleasant and rather exciting was about to happen. Norman Birtley. So that was it. She could think of nothing else, and was rather disappointed, slightly cross with herself, when it all dwindled to Norman. That showed the sort of existence she led, these days. There had been a time when Norman Birtley was only a joke. When he became serious she had brushed him aside. After that, when he turned into the attentive admirer, popping up at odd intervals and popping down again wistfully, it is true she had liked him better. But now, the very thought of an evening with him could bring her out of sleep in a vague sense of excitement. It was absurd. It was pathetic. No, it was simply revolting.

Before she reached the office, she had completely reversed this judgment. There was nothing revolting about it. Perfectly right and natural. Norman Birtley was quite decent; he liked her, admired her, perhaps was in love with her; and she had every right to look forward to an evening with him, to an evening out with anybody (except girls from the Club, sharing Pit seats and sandwiches), for that matter. The 13 bus, grinding away through the slight fog, agreed with this conclusion, hinted that she was too proud, and seemed to say that for its part it took all it could get, like the stout-hearted Cockney it was. There was some fog too in the City, and it was a raw yellow morning for Angel Pavement. Everybody in the office yawned a good deal and was rather irritable for the first two hours. It was that sort of morning. The rest of the day was more comfortable, but dull and slow, lumbering towards five-thirty like a stupefied elephant. Miss Matfield had not much to do. Mr. Golspie was out all day, and it was he who usually kept her busy. Mr. Dersingham, who found himself getting pink and flustered when Miss Matfield coolly stared at him and waited, with a kind of ironic resignation, for his next halting sentence, preferred to dictate his letters, whenever possible, to little Poppy Sellers, in whose eyes, as he rightly suspected, he was a large fine gentleman. The only amusing thing that happened in the afternoon was that poor Mr. Smeeth, returning importantly and fussily from the bank, tried to tell them a funny story he had heard there and completely failed to bring out the point. He was rather pathetic, Mr. Smeeth. After that there were huge blank spaces, during which yellow wisps of fog seemed to creep into one's mind. But she was able to get away early and have a really good Burpenfield bath, tons of hot water, before changing.

She was quite ready when the message came that Mr. Birtley was waiting below. In the corridor she ran into Kersey, one of the depressing old inhabitants who, as usual, was trailing along with a kettle. She meant well—poor old thing—but she had a horrid trick of saying things that depressed you at once.

"Hello, Matfield," she droned damply. "Going out, are you? That's the way. You have to enjoy yourself sometimes, haven't you? That's right, dee-ar."

This was Kersey's usual speech if she saw that you were dressed to go out. She had another speech ready for you if she saw you were not dressed. "Not going out to-night, eh, Matfield? No, I thought not. Well, you can't expect to go out every night, can you, dee-ar?" And you left her drooping there, with her kettle, but not before she had set your spirits drooping too, whether you were staying in or going out. It was as if the horrible future addressed a few remarks to you.

Norman Birtley was waiting in the lounge, looking very tall, very awkward, very uncomfortable. Round the fire was the usual set, two or three of the bright young ones with Ingleton-Dodd lounging in the middle of them. Ingleton-Dodd was a large woman, about forty, with a curious white face, her hair plastered back, severe mannish clothes, and a bass voice. She seemed to have more money than anybody else in the Club, and owned quite a good little car, about which she talked a great deal. She was talking about it, or about some car, when Miss Matfield walked in.

"Oh, the man was a complete fool," she was saying, in that deep bass voice of hers. "I told him to have a look at the mag. 'Put the mag right,' I told him, 'and the whole thing will be right. Clean those points a bit, to start with.' By this time, he'd taken the mag out and was staring at it like a stuck pig."

"Marvellous!" cried one of the bright children. They all thought Ingleton-Dodd "the very last word."

" 'Oh, give it to me,' I said, and snatched it out of his hand. Then I sent for the manager. 'Look here,' I said to him, 'does anybody in this place know how to time a mag?' You should have seen his face."

Awful creature! *She* ought to have seen Norman Birtley's face. He was looking at Ingleton-Dodd with fascinated repulsion written clearly on his simple and expressive features. He greeted Miss Matfield confusedly, dropping his hat when he shook hands. His hands were hot and damp, and there was a glint of perspiration on his pink forehead. He had not changed at all, except that he now wore rimless eyeglasses and his sandy moustache was a trifle more in evidence. He was only a year or so older than Miss Matfield and, as he was far less sophisticated than she was, not at all at home in London, which he only visited at long intervals, she felt the older of the two.

"How are you, Lilian?" he inquired, smiling nervously. "You're looking very well."

"Am I? I don't feel it. I'm feeling pretty foul."

"You're not, are you?" He looked at her anxiously. "What's

wrong? You haven't got anything the matter with you, have you? Are you seeing a doctor?"

This obvious concern ought to have pleased her, for it was very flattering. But these questions, demanding as they did a definite answer, a disease or two, only irritated her. It was understood at the Burpenfield that you were nearly always pretty foul, with nothing exactly wrong with you perhaps, but nevertheless in a fairly permanent state of being worn out, nerve-racked, tottering on the brink of something ghastly. Miss Matfield had forgotten that this simple visitor from the country knew nothing of this convention.

"Oh, I'm all right really, I suppose," she replied, dismissing the subject. "Shall we go now? Where do you propose to take me, Norman? Have you any plans?" She moved to the door.

"Well, I didn't know exactly what to do. I suppose I ought to have asked you first, but there wasn't time. There seems to be a rather good show on at the Co'ladium this week, so I got two seats for that, second house. Do you like music halls?"

"Not bad. It all depends."

"A fellow I was talking to at the hotel said it was a very good show, so I thought that would be all right. But if you don't want to go, I suppose I can get rid of the tickets, can't I?"

"No, that will be all right. I'd like to go," she told him. They were walking down the hill now, towards Finchley Road.

"Good. And about dinner," he continued, struggling laboriously with his duties as host. "I thought we might go to a place in Soho. Old Warwick—he's our principal at the Chestervern Agricultural, and he's been here a good deal—told me there was a good little place, one of those French or Italian places, you know, a bit bohemian but very good cooking—I've got the name and address in my book and I'll find it in a minute. Anyhow, I thought, if you didn't mind, we might go there."

"All right," she replied, not very enthusiastically. Some of those little Soho places were rather foul, and old Warwick of the Chestervern Agricultural might not be a very good judge. "Let's go there, and you can dig out the name and address on the way. We'll hurry and catch a bus."

"Oh, will a bus be all right?" he cried, obviously relieved. "I thought perhaps we might have to take a taxi."

"No, a bus will do," she told him. A taxi, though, would have done a great deal better. She loved riding in taxis. Perhaps—who knows? —if Mr. Birtley had insisted upon their having a taxi, the whole evening might have been different.

Once again she went jogging down the long hill, past the sudden sparkle of Swiss Cottage, the genteel gloom of St. John's Wood, and a Baker Street that was now like a series of captivating peepshows. They did not talk much inside the bus, which was full and uncommonly noisy, but he shouted a few questions about the Club and Ingleton-Dodd (whom he regarded with horror) and the office and her father and mother, and she screamed fairly adequate if brief replies. Her spirits rose when they actually arrived in Soho, for though she had some mournful memories of its *table d'hôte* and had been in London long enough to be sceptical about its romantic bohemianism, she could not resist the place itself, the glimpses of foreign interiors, the windows filled with outlandish foodstuffs, chianti flasks, and bundles of long cheroots, the happy foolish little decorations, the strange speech, the dark faces, the girls leaning out of the first-floor windows. It was quite a long time since she had last walked along Old Compton Street. It made her sigh for an adventure. Meanwhile, that very evening took on a faint colouring of adventure while they were still searching for old Warwick's restaurant, though, with all the good will in the world, she could not transform Norman Birtley, fresh from the Chestervern Agricultural College, into a romantic and adventurous companion.

At last, they found old Warwick's restaurant. It might have been French or Italian or even Spanish or Hungarian; there was no telling; but it was determinedly foreign in a de-nationalised fashion, rather as if the League of Nations had invented it. No sooner was Norman's hand on the door than a very fierce-looking, moustachioed, square-jawed Latin flung it open very quickly and with a great flourish, so that they were almost sucked in. The place was very small, rather warm, and smelt of oil. The lights were shaded with coloured crinkly paper. There were only four other people there, two oldish tired girls masticating rather hopelessly in the far corner, and a queer middle-aged couple sitting almost in the window. The fierce Latin swept them across to a tiny table, thrust menus into their hands, rubbed his hands, changed all the cutlery round and then put it all back again, rubbed his hands once more and then suddenly lost all interest in them, as if his business was simply to drag people in and then, having got them seated, to create a momentary illusion of brisk service before they had time to change their minds.

"You can have the whole dinner for three and sixpence," said Norman, looking up from his menu. "Wonderful how they do it in these places, isn't it? I mean to say, what would you get in an English restaurant for that? Nothing worth eating, I'll bet. But these foreigners can do it. Of course, it's their job. They know how to cook. Shall we have the dinner?"

Miss Matfield thought that they might, and looked about her, not very hopefully, while Norman gave the order to a waitress, a very tall fat girl with a chalky face and no features, who had just appeared. The queer middle-aged couple looked queerer still now, for the man appeared to be dyed and the woman enamelled and it was incredible that they should ever eat food at all. You felt they ought to feed on wood and paint.

Having given the order, Mr. Birtley was now looking about him too, and when he had finished doing this and had obviously noted the more picturesque details for the benefit of the other members of the staff of the Chestervern Agricultural College, he beamed at her through his rimless eyeglasses. "Nothing I enjoy better than studying these queer types," he whispered. "A place like this is a treat to me, if only for that reason. Old Warwick told me I'd enjoy that part of it. He's had some very funny experiences in his time. I must try to remember some of the yarns he's told me, once or twice when I've been sitting up with him over a pipe at the Chestervern."

While Miss Matfield was asking idly what sort of man Mr. Warwick was and Norman was telling her, the waitress had brought them the two halves of a grapefruit, the juice of which had apparently been used some time before. They had not finished with old Warwick, who seemed to Miss Matfield a silly old man, when the waitress returned to give them some mysterious thick soup, which looked like gum but had a rather less pronounced flavour.

Miss Matfield tried three spoonfuls and then looked with horror at her plate. Something was there, something small, dark, squashed. There were legs. She pushed the plate away.

"What's the matter, Lilian? Don't you like the soup?"

She pointed with her spoon at the alien body.

Mr. Birtley leaned across and peered at it through his glasses. "No, by George, it isn't, is it? Is it really? Oh, I say, that's not good enough, is it? That's the worst of these foreigners. Do you think I ought to tell them about it?"

"If you don't, I will," said Miss Matfield indignantly. "Absolutely revolting!"

But there was nobody to tell. Even the fierce Latin had disappeared. It seemed as if when soup was served, the whole staff hid in the kitchen. Miss Matfield was sure now that her first instinctive disapproval had been right, as usual. This was a foul little place. Unfortunately, she was really hungry, having had a very small lunch.

The next member of the staff they did see obviously could not be blamed for the soup, for he was the wine waiter, an ancient gloomy foreigner. He padded across to Mr. Birtley, who was trying not very successfully to explain a very funny thing that had happened last term at the College, held out a wine list decorated with dirty thumb marks, and waited apathetically.

"A-ha!" cried Mr. Birtley jovially. "Let's have something to drink, shall we? Do you think we could manage a whole bottle? I think we could. Yes, let's have a whole bottle. Now then, what is there? Will you have red or white wine, Lilian? It's all the same to me."

"I'd like red, I think," she replied. "Burgundy perhaps." It was more sustaining. After all, with bread and butter and some burgundy, it might be possible to stun one's appetite. She had no hopes of the dinner.

"Burgundy it is," cried Mr. Birtley, with the air of a reckless musketeer. "All right, then. A bottle of Number Eleven. Beaune."

"You geef me moanay," murmured the ancient foreigner.

"Righto. Money. There you are." And then he gave Miss Matfield a wink and smiled at her. She smiled back, softening towards him a little, for he was so obviously enjoying himself and thinking it all so wonderful. Poor Norman!

"You ought to come and see us at the College next time you're home, Lilian," he said. "You'd like it. We've got one or two amusing fellows on the staff, and the students aren't a bad crowd. We have little dances sometimes, and tennis in the summer. It's growing too. In a year or two, if I can scrape up some money, I may get a partnership. Not bad, eh? The fact is," and he lowered his voice, as if to keep these confidences away from the waitress, who had just deposited some microscopic pieces of fish in front of them and was still standing near, as if to see if they would have the audacity to eat them, "the fact is, I can get on better with old Warwick than any of the other fellows. He's taken rather a fancy to me, thinks I've got more drive than the others. And as a matter of fact," he added, looking earnestly at her, "I have. And I wish you'd come and look me up down there."

She said she would, if she could manage it, and then explained, while the ancient foreigner poured out the wine, how difficult it was to do all one wanted to do, what with one thing and another, and then, fortified by the burgundy and determined to drive old Warwick out of the conversation for a time, she went on to tell him more about the office and the Club. He listened attentively, though with just the faintest suggestion of patronage. Obviously he thought a good deal more of himself these days, now that he had made such a hit with his old Warwick of the Chestervern Agricultural. But then all men were alike in that: they all thought they were marvellous. However, she could tell from the way he looked at her that he still thought she was marvellous too, which was very pleasant. She could feel herself getting steadily better looking and more attractive.

This could not be said about the dinner. The chicken was not marvellous, was not even pleasant. Like many other places in Soho, this restaurant evidently had a contract that compelled it to accept only those parts of a chicken that could not be called breast, wing, or leg. It specialised in chicken skin. The salad could be eaten, but its green stuff seemed to have been grown in some London back garden behind a sooty privet hedge. The sweet was composed of a very small ice, the paper in which it had been delivered from the van at the back door, and some coloured water that might have been part of the ice two hours before. That was the dinner, a miserable affair. Even Norman seemed to have a suspicion that it had not been very good, but he did not apologise for it, perhaps out of loyalty to old Warwick. Miss Matfield, in despair, had had two full glasses of the burgundy, a raw and potent concoction, which had produced at once a rather muzzy effect in her mind so that everything seemed a little larger and noisier than usual. Once, just before the coffee, she had found herself wanting to giggle at the thought of Norman taking his sandy moustache back to Chestervern and old Warwick. The coffee, black and bitter, stopped all that nonsense. They smoked a cigarette together over it, and Norman, with tiny beads of perspiration on his ruddy forehead and his glasses slightly misty, talked about old times and smiled sentimentally across the cruet at her.

It was time to be gone. The Latin suddenly decided to notice their existence again, brought the bill, accepted money, proffered change, swept away the tip, and then apparently threw them both into the street, where the air seemed at once remarkably pure and unusually cold. They arrived at the Colladium just at the right moment, a few minutes after the doors had been opened for the second house. The place was, as usual, besieged by a mob of pleasure seekers who all looked like demons in the red glare of the lights at the entrance. Norman led the way, a little uncertainly, and they went swarming down thick-carpeted corridors.

"Didn't that man say 'Round to the left and up the stairs'?" Miss Matfield asked. She had a slight headache now. Those peculiar red lights outside the Colladium look exactly like a headache, and perhaps they had inspired the burgundy. "I'm sure he did, you know."

"I didn't hear him," replied Norman, not too amiably. He was somewhat fussed. "Talking to somebody else, p'raps."

Feeling a little dubious, she followed him down the gangway on the ground floor of the auditorium, which looked as if it were recovering from a fire, there was so much smoke about. There were programme girls showing people to their seats, but you had to wait your turn and Norman, anxious to secure his two beautiful seats, would not wait his turn. He marched on, glancing at his tickets and the lettered rows of stalls, then finally found the row he wanted, and they pushed past a few people, sought and found the right numbers, and sank into their seats.

"This is all right, isn't it?" said Norman, after breathing a sigh of relief. "Jolly good seats, eh?" He looked round triumphantly. More lights were being turned on; the orchestra was beginning to tune up again; and the place was filling rapidly. Miss Matfield's headache retreated, dwindled to an occasional twinge.

"What about a programme?" said Norman, and began to make vague, fussy, ineffectual signs.

Then two large determined men, coarse-looking fellows with heavy jowls and cigars stuck in the corners of their insensitive mouths, came pushing down the row. They stopped when they came to Mr. Birtley and Miss Matfield. "Here, I say," the first one called back to the programme girl, after looking at his ticket, "is this the right row?" Apparently it was, for now he turned his attention to Norman.

"I think you're sitting in the wrong seats, my friend," he said, not unpleasantly.

"I don't think so," replied Norman, rather sharply. He brought out his own tickets and gave them a reassuring glance.

"Well, I do," said the other. He had a loud voice, the kind of voice that attracts attention. "Row F, fourteen and fifteen. Isn't that right? Well, those are my seats, bought and paid for. Ask the girl. She sent us here."

"I don't see that," said Norman stiffly. "Mine are Row F, fourteen and fifteen. And we were here first. They must have made a mistake at the box office."

Miss Matfield had risen from her seat. People were looking round at them. If there was anything she hated, it was this stupid sort of scene.

The second large determined man, who had nothing like the amount of room to stand in his bulk demanded and deserved, now made a number of impatient noises. These noises goaded his friend into more direct action.

"Here, come on," he said roughly, "let's have a look at your tickets. Here are mine. Now let's have a look at yours." He almost snatched them out of Norman's hand. The instant he saw them, he cried triumphantly: "There y'are. Balcony Stalls, *Bal-cony* Stalls. These aren't Balcony Stalls. Cor!—you're in the wrong part of the theatre, boy, in the wrong part of the theatre."

"Wouldjer believe it!" cried the second man contemptuously.

"Cor! Up there you want to be, right up there, boy."

"Sorry. I didn't know." Poor Norman was very flustered now. Miss Matfield might have been sorry for him, but she wasn't. She was furious. Even after they had left the seats and were pushing their way back to the gangway, the two brutes were still talking about it and laughing and making contemptuous noises. Then as she arrived, scarlet, in the gangway, she ran into a little party of three that was waiting to be shown to its place. The first was a tall man with a bristling moustache, obviously a foreigner; the second was a youngish girl, very smart and pretty; and the third, who was still interviewing the girl with the chocolates was—yes, no other—Mr. Golspie, rather flushed, very jovial. There was some congestion in this part of the gangway; they had to stop; and he looked up and saw her.

"Evening, Miss Matfield," he said, grinning at her in his usual fashion. "So this is where we come, is it?"

She stammered something.

"Had a good day at the office? You'll see me there to-morrow. Half a minute, Lena. Well, Miss Matfield, see you enjoy yourself. Here, take one of these."

She found one of the boxes of chocolates in her hand. Before she could do anything or even say anything, he had given her another of his vast grins and had turned away. As she followed Norman up the gangway, most of the lights were lowered and the overture blared out. Their seats were in the first tier and by the time they found them, the curtain had risen and the stage was occupied by three very grave young men who were busy throwing one another about.

"That was a bit of a mix-up, wasn't it?" said Norman, when they had settled themselves. "But it wasn't really my fault. They should give their seats proper names. I've never heard of stalls being up here."

"Well, you might have asked. I told you what that man said."

"By George, so you did. Sorry! But, I say, who was that rum looking chap you were talking to down there?"

"He's a man who's just joined the firm I'm working with. I do his letters."

"Didn't he give you that box of chocolates?"

"Yes, he did. As a matter of fact, he just shoved it into my hand."

"Funny thing to do," Norman continued, half resentfully. "What did he want to do that for?"

"I don't know. You'd better ask him." She stared at the three young men, who were now climbing on to piles of chairs and tables in order to throw one another a greater distance.

"I must say I didn't like the look of him very much."

"That's sad, isn't it, Norman?" replied Miss Matfield. "Hadn't you better call at the office to-morrow morning and tell him so? What had I better do? Get another job?"

"You don't mean to tell me you like that chap?"

"I don't know whether I do or not," she told him, with perfect truth. But her voice betrayed irritation. "It doesn't matter, anyhow. I'll admit, though," she added, more amiably, "that he does look a bit weird. But he's rather amusing. Have one of his chocolates, seeing that they're here, and don't talk so much."

The subject was dropped and when they talked again, as they did at odd moments throughout the performance, Mr. Golspie was not mentioned. The show itself was neither better nor worse than the others she had seen there. She liked the white-faced clown with the squeaky voice who nearly fell into the orchestra pit, and the two men who got involved in the most passionate argument all about nothing, and the Spanish dancers, and the wildly ridiculous school-master. On the other hand, she did not like the American cross-talking and dancing pair, or the two girls who sang at the piano or the various acrobats and trick cyclists. Norman, who soon recovered from the ticket scene and settled down to enjoy himself, to like as much as he could of the show and to patronise the rest, was rather more human than he had been during the misery of dinner. Old Warwick was banished at last, and the dull shade of Chestervern never fell on the talk.

When they came out of the Colladium into the astonishing sanity of the night, and Norman not only suggested a taxi but actually found one, she felt she was beginning to feel friendly towards him again. And if he had said, "You know, Lilian, I *am* rather feeble and a bit of an ass, and I know you're marvellous and far above my style, but I've been in love with you a jolly long time and still am, honestly I am, worse than ever in fact, so will you marry me? I'm not doing anything very wonderful, I know, and you might easily find it dull at first down at Chestervern, but we'd have some fun and things would get better all the time"; if he had said something like that, in the proper tone of voice—rather wistful—and with a dumbly devoted look in his eyes, she felt there was no telling what she might reply. She could just see herself marrying him.

But he made no such speech, and was clearly not in that dumbly devoted mood at all. All the way home, he was vaguely sentimental —what fun they'd had in the old tennis club days and what good pals they'd been!—and was timidly amorous, like some faint-hearted Don Juan taking one home after a dance. Unluckily, Miss Matfield was not sentimental, at least not on conventional or Christmas card lines, and she heartily despised and disliked the timidly amorous male, who could not let one alone but had not passion enough, or courage, to make him risk a sound snubbing. He would slip an arm round her waist and she would tell him to take it away because it was uncomfortable, as indeed it was. And then he would say, "Ah, Lilian, you're not very kind to me," in a ridiculous mooing voice, like a farm hand trying to ape the artful philanderer. It was all terribly irritating. When at last, as the taxi began grinding up the last hilly half mile, she was so tired of this that she actually asked him questions about his prospects at Chestervern, dropping into the part of the cool interested woman friend with a sound business head, he turned rather sulky and answered her in a poor half-hearted fashion.

"I suppose I can get a bus back?" he said as they stood at the entrance to the Burpenfield and the taxi departed.

"Oh, yes, of course. Just at the bottom there, on the Finchley Road. They run until after twelve, and they're much quicker at this time of night, too. You're going back to-morrow, aren't you?"

"Yes, on the 10.20. I suppose I'd better be getting along now. Rather cold standing here, isn't it?"

"Well, Norman," she said, trying to look bright and friendly and not ungrateful, "it's been nice seeing you again. And thanks awfully for the dinner and everything. I adored that clown with the chairs, didn't you? Good-bye."

He shook hands. "Good-bye. I'm glad you liked it," he muttered. "Good-bye."

She stood in the entrance a minute or two after he had gone, fumbling for her key, and suddenly from that great ocean of deep depression which she always felt was not far away, rose in the dark a great breaker and swept her away. She could have cried. It was not Norman Birtley—he was a feeble fool who was rapidly getting worse —but the endless cheating of life itself that frightened her and stifled her. She was Lilian Matfield, Lilian Matfield, the same that had gone playing and laughing and singing and looking forward to everything only a few years ago, no different now except a little older and more sensible, and yet she felt, obscurely, darkly, that somehow she was being conjured into somebody miserably different, somebody stiff and faded and dull.

Another girl came up. Miss Matfield steadied herself, found her key, and walked in. Isabel Cadnam was just coming out of the lounge, and they met.

"Hello, Matfield. Been on the razzle? Look here, I hope you didn't want that shawl I borrowed. I didn't get in last night until the crack of dawn, and then I was in such a hurry this morning, I forgot about it."

"No, it didn't matter, thanks, Caddie. I'm going up. I'm tired."

"So am I. Had a good night. That show that Ivor took me to last night was rather a wash-out, I must say. The most ghastly people, and millions of them. And Ivor wanted to join in with some of the ghastliest, and I didn't, of course, and that started it all over again. Another row, my dear. Isn't it foul?"

Miss Matfield said dispiritedly that it was.

"What did you do to-night, Matfield? Anything thrilling?"

"Not very. Rather dull, in fact. I've got a headache. I think I've eaten too many chocolates. I'll try some aspirin."

"Nothing like it," said Miss Cadnam. "Look here, I'll fetch your shawl and bring it round, and then, if you have any to spare, I'll borrow a couple of aspirins. If I don't take *something*, I'll never get a wink of sleep all night. It's always the same after I've had a row with Ivor. I begin *arguing* with him the minute I get to bed, and then I go on and on all night until I think my head's going to burst. Isn't it foul?"

"Completely," said Miss Matfield, opening her door. "All right, then. Hurry up with the shawl and I'll get you the aspirin." She closed the door behind her.

IV

It was rather queer seeing Mr. Golspie again, in the grey light of Angel Pavement, after that strange meeting at the Colladium. It was rather like seeing someone you had just met in a vivid dream. She did some letters for him the next morning, and when he had finished them, he dropped his impersonal stare and tone of voice, grinned at her, and said: "Enjoy the show last night?"

"Not very much," she told him. "Did you?"

"No, I didn't," he boomed. "Dead as mutton. Not a patch on the old halls. They call it Variety now, but that's about all the variety you get. All the same, isn't it? I keep trying it, but it's poor stuff. That girl of mine likes to go. She enjoys it all right. Did you see her last night? She was there with me."

"I wondered if it was your daughter. She's awfully pretty, isn't she?"

"Think so?" He was pleased at this. "Well, she's pretty enough, and knows it, the little monkey. Was that the young man, the one I saw you with?"

He really had some ghastly expressions. The young man! "Good Lord, no!" she cried. "He was just an old friend who comes from my part of the world. Shall I bring these letters in to sign as soon as I've done them?"

"I'd like them as soon as possible, Miss Matfield. I want to be off before lunch. I've got several members of the Chosen Race to see this afternoon."

That was all. The awful "young man" question was, of course, in his favourite vein, but apart from that, he was much quieter and pleasanter than usual in this little talk. For once he had dropped the jeering and leering style that made her feel so uncomfortable. He was friendlier. And she had never thanked him for the chocolates. She would have to do that when she went back with the letters.

"Oh, Mr. Golspie," she cried, when he had finished signing the letters, "I forgot to thank you for the lovely box of chocolates. I don't know why you gave them to me—so suddenly, like that ——"

"Just to celebrate the little meeting, that's all," he replied, waving a hand. " 'Here's our Miss Matfield,' I thought, 'looking a bit uncomfortable because her young man's landed in the wrong seats.' "

"Oh, did you notice that? It was a stupid business."

"Bit of a box-up, certainly," he said, grinning at her. "Yes, I saw you all right. You looked very annoyed, too. Anyhow, I thought something ought to be done about it."

"Well, it was very nice of you," she said, though she was not altogether pleased at the turn the conversation had taken.

"Ah, but I'm a very nice man," he assured her, looking very solemn for a moment. Then he produced a short disconcerting guffaw, and waved his hand again. She turned away. "And another thing," he called out. She stopped. "You never catch me getting into the wrong seats, you try me sometime, Miss Matfield, you just try me. You'd be surprised." He chuckled a little as she went out. This time she felt hot and uncomfortable again, and felt ready to dislike him just as much as she had done when he first came. It was odd how uncomfortable he could make her feel. After all, she had worked for unpleasant men before to-day. But this was rather different.

Messrs. Twigg & Dersingham were now busy making what Mr. Dersingham, who was beginning to wear a look of great self-importance, called a "big drive." He and Mr. Golspie and the two travellers were visiting as many firms as they could, showing the new stuff that Mr. Golspie had introduced and piling up the orders. Apparently, it was important that as many orders as possible should be obtained during this little period, for some reason that was not made plain to the office staff, and perhaps was not plain to anybody but Mr. Golspie. It meant a great deal of work for everybody. Miss Matfield was kept at her machine nearly all day making out lists, invoices, and advices. It was not difficult work but it was rather close work and very dreary, and it left her fagged and feeling quite unfit to plan some amusement for herself. There were plenty of mildly amusing things that could be done with a little planning, but she was too tired to bother, like so many of the girls at the Club. Going anywhere, even if it was only attending a concert or doing a theatre, always meant so much fuss and arranging that she let it all slide, not excepting the week-end. If somebody had come along with a cut and dried plan for doing something entertaining, that would have been quite different, indeed heavenly; but nobody did. She spent a good deal of her time at the Club listening to Evelyn Ansdell, who was in the thick of her preparations for the Empire tour with the Major and talked at great length about every single thing she had to buy. Evelyn was quite amusing about it, of course, but it was distinctly depressing to think that very soon she would be gone, probably for ever. On the Sunday they both went round to have tea with Major Ansdell who was quite absurd and provided them with an enormous sticky tea—bless him!—but it was really all rather sad. And on Monday and Tuesday there was quite a frantic bustle at the office. Mr. Smeeth turned himself into a faintly apologetic slave-driver, and Mr. Dersingham ran in and out like a large pink fox terrier.

The next morning they learned the reason for all this fuss. Mr. Smeeth, after visiting the private office, came back looking rather important, and said, "Mr. Golspie's leaving us to-day."

Every one of them looked surprised, and three of them, Miss Matfield, Turgis, and Stanley, looked either startled or disappointed.

"He's not going for good, is he, Mr. Smeeth?" asked Turgis, before anyone else could speak.

He had spoken for Miss Matfield, who felt, she did not know why, the most acute anxiety. For some strange reason, which had certainly nothing to do with business, for at heart she did not care a rap whether Twigg & Dersingham sold all the veneers and inlays in England or drifted into bankruptcy, she hated the thought of Mr. Golspie leaving them. At one stroke it flattened the whole life of Angel Pavement.

"He's not going for good, I'm glad to say," Mr. Smeeth replied, enjoying their suspense. "He's only going back for a short visit, on our business, to the place he came from, up there in the Baltic. I don't know how long he'll be away. He doesn't know exactly himself yet. But he's sailing this afternoon, going the whole way by boat on the Anglo-Baltic. And," here Mr. Smeeth glanced out of the window at the raw damp morning, "I don't envy him. It'll be a cold job crossing the North Sea, this weather. I remember I once had a sail on a boat at Yarmouth one Easter, not very far out, y'know, but—my word!—it was perishing. I was glad to get back. Well, what's it going to be like right in the middle, this time of year. I wouldn't be paid, wouldn't be paid, to do it."

"I'll bet he doesn't care," said Stanley boastfully. Mr. Golspie was still one of Stanley's heroes—though nobody could discover why, except that he looked rather like a detective—and Stanley had no half measures in the heroic. "I'll bet he likes it. I would. I wish he'd take me with him. I wouldn't go. Oh no, oh no! Wouldn't I just!"

"You get on with your work, Stanley," said Mr. Smeeth mechanically. "We all know what you'd do and what you wouldn't do. Well, he's sailing this afternoon, all the way to the Baltic Sea, and, as I say, I don't envy him." And Mr. Smeeth returned, well content, to his cosy desk and his neat little rows of figures.

Half an hour afterwards, Mr. Golspie, wearing an enormous ulster, looked in on them. "You won't see me for a week or two," he announced cheerfully. "Keep it going. Shoulders to the wheel! Full steam ahead, as people say—though why they say it, God only knows, because nobody in a ship ever said it—doesn't mean anything. Make 'em all pay up, Smeeth. Keep your eye on that cut rate with the Anglo-Baltic, Turgis. Just remember me in your prayers, you girls, if you do pray. Do you pray, Miss Matfield? Never mind, tell me another time. And, Stanley——"

"Yes, sir," said Stanley, springing to attention.

"Run down and get me a taxi, sharp as you can. Good-bye, everybody."

When they had all said good-bye, too, and he had gone and they had heard the outer door slam behind him, in the sudden quiet that followed, the whole office had appeared to shrink and darken a little. Miss Matfield, aware of this, resented it, and, compressing her lips, threw herself into what work she had on hand with a sort of grey determination, never looking up and only speaking when compelled to answer a question. By lunch time she felt so discontented that, instead of spending the usual ninepence or so at the little teashop not far away, she went further afield, to a superior place just off Cannon Street, and had cutlet and peas, apple tart and cream, and a cup of coffee, paying her half-crown manfully. After that she was more cheerful and more honest. She had been depressed because though all kinds of things seemed to be happening to other people, nothing was happening to her. It was hard luck losing Evelyn Ansdell. It was hard luck losing Mr. Golspie, if only for a week or two. She could not say yet whether she really liked the man, but at least he made Angel Pavement more amusing. It would be terriby flat now without him. Everything, it seemed, was sinking into dullness. Well, she must make an effort and think of something amusing to do. When she returned to the office, quarter of an hour late, as usual, she was cheerful and comparatively friendly with everybody.

Perhaps the little gods who look after these minor affairs decided that she must be encouraged, for at once they found something amusing for her to do. Shortly after three, Mr. Smeeth took a telephone message and then called Miss Matfield to him.

"That was Mr. Golspie, Miss Matfield," he began, in his pleasantly fussy and important way. "He says they're sailing later than he thought, about five or so, and he wants you to go down to the ship and take down a few important letters he's just remembered about. And you've also got to take that sample book—it's in the private office—he forgot it. I haven't got Mr. Dersingham's permission for you to go, and I can't get it, because he's out, but of course it's all right. I accept all responsibility. You don't mind going, do you?"

"I'd love it," cried Miss Matfield. "But where exactly do I go?"

Mr. Smeeth adjusted his eyeglasses and then examined the slip of paper he had been carrying. "You go to Hay's Wharf, that's on the south side of the river between London Bridge and the Tower Bridge, you go over London Bridge and turn straight to the left to get there. And the ship's the *L-e-m-m-a-l-a, Lemmala.* Can you remember that, Miss Matfield? And he says, 'Take a taxi,' so I'd better give you half a crown out of the petty cash for that—I'll have to put it down as travelling expenses. Now you get your notebook and pencil and your things on, and I'll get that sample book out of the private office for you. It'll be a little jaunt for you, something out of the common, won't it? Stanley'd give his ears to go, wouldn't you, Stanley? Oh, he's not there. Where is that lad?"

Yes, it was a little jaunt for her. It was great fun. First, Moorgate Street, the Bank, then King William Street, went rattling past the taxi window; then came London Bridge, with leaden gleams of the river far below on either side; then a slow progress along a narrow street on the other side, a turn to the left up a street still narrower, a mere passage, at the end of which the taxi had to stop altogether. She dodged up another dark lane, asked a pleasant large policeman if she was going the right way, and finally found herself at the water's edge, where men were busy loading and running about with papers and shouting to one another. There, about fifty yards further down, was the *Lemmala,* a steamship with one tall thin funnel, not very large and rather dingy but nevertheless a fine romantic sight. A flag she had never seen before drooped from its little mast. As she drew nearer, she heard some of the men shouting down from the deck, and they were speaking in a language she had never heard before, a tremendously foreign language. Up to that moment, business had been for her an affair of clerks and desks and telephones and stupid letters that always began and ended in the same dull way, but now, in a flash, she suddenly realised that it was all very romantic. It was as if Mr. Dersingham had stalked into the office in Elizabethan costume. The wood they sold in Angel Pavement came in boats like this, indeed in this very ship, and at the other end, where the veneers began, there was quite a different sort of life going on, huge forests, thick snow and frosts all winter, wolves on the prowl, bearded men wearing high boots, women in strange bright shawls, scenes out of the Russian Ballet. Miss Matfield, like most members of the English middle classes, was incurably romantic at heart, and now she was genuinely thrilled, and could hardly have been more astonished and delighted if a few nightingales had suddenly burst into song in one of the dark archways. London was really marvellous, and the wonder of it rushed up in her mind and burst there like a rocket, scattering a multi-coloured host of vague but rich associations, a glittering jumble of history and nonsense and poetry, Dick Whittington and galleons, Muscovy and Cathay, East Indiamen, the doldrums far away, and the Pool of London, lapping here only a stone's throw from the shops and offices and buses.

She had arrived now at the foot of a gangway that came down steeply from the rusty side of the *Lemmala*. She looked up, hesitating. Somebody was calling. It was Mr. Golspie above, and he was waving her up. When she reached the head of the gangway he was there, waiting for her.

"We've a couple of hours at least before she moves," he explained, piloting her along the deck, then up a short flight of stairs to the deck above, "but I shan't keep you so long, y'know. Awkward if she moved off and you were still aboard, eh? Have to take a trip then, eh?"

"I don't know that I'd mind very much," she told him, looking about her on the upper deck. "It would be rather amusing."

"Oh, you wouldn't have a bad time at all, so long as you weren't seasick. These fellows here would make a great fuss of you, I can tell you."

"Well, that would be rather a nice change."

"Would it now?" He grinned. "Well, we won't kidnap you this time. We'll go in here." And he led the way into a little saloon, quite neat and cheerful. On the table, which was covered with a hideously bright cloth, were some cigars, a mysterious tall bottle of a shape she had never seen before, and several small glasses. Some newspapers and illustrated papers, printed in fantastic characters, were scattered about, and these helped more than anything else, unless it was the tall bottle, to make it all seem very foreign. Yet through the windows at each side she could see the roofs and spires, the familiar smoky mass, of London.

"Ah, I'd better look after that sample book," said Mr. Golspie. "Now then, you sit down there, Miss Matfield, with your notebook."

She sat down and tried to pull the chair nearer to the table, but of course it would not move, or at least would only swing round. She was forgetting that she was on board a ship. It was all very odd and delightful.

The letters were not difficult and were all more or less alike, and in half an hour they had done. Once or twice, while they were at work, various faces, foreign faces, had peeped in at them, had nodded, smiled, and then disappeared. The only other interruptions were occasional shouts and hootings outside.

"I think that's all," said Mr. Golspie, lighting a cigar and pouring himself out a drink from the tall bottle. "But just you read through what you've done while I try to think if there's anything else. There's plenty of time. D'you smoke? That's right. Well, have a cigarette. Here, have one of these." And he threw over a very fancy cardboard box, from which she took a long cigarette that was half stiff paper, like a Russian. It was a fine romantic cigarette and she enjoyed it.

"Can't think of anything else," said Mr. Golspie, puffing out a cloud of smoke. "Just run through that lot quickly, will you?" She did, and there was only one change to be made. "I'll sign some sheets now for you," he continued, "and then you can take 'em back with you to the office. I brought plenty of the firm's stationery with me. Always do, wherever I am. That's the worst of being on your own. Have to buy your own stationery. It's a thing I hate doing. Funny, isn't it? I'd spend money like water on all sorts of silly rubbish and never turn a hair, but I hate spending money on paper. Expect you're the same, aren't you, about something?"

"Pencils," replied Miss Matfield promptly. "I loathe and detest having to buy pencils. If I can't borrow or steal one, and actually have to go to a shop and pay money for one of the wretched things, I simply hate it."

"Ah, we're all a queer lot, even the best-looking of us," Mr. Golspie ruminated while he signed the blank sheets. "We're all both crooks and old washerwomen rolled into one, though I expect you'll tell me that *you* aren't, eh?"

"No, I shan't. I know exactly what you mean."

If they were on the very edge of a pleasant sympathetic talk, as it appeared at that moment, then Mr. Golspie only yanked them miles away at one swoop with his next remark. "Well, if you do," he said, "you know more than I do. And that's a nuisance." He looked up, having finished with the sheets. "Here, you're shivering."

"Am I? I didn't know I was. But I am rather cold now," she admitted. She was still wearing her thick coat, but the little saloon was not warmed and there was a nipping air along the river.

"You've finished here now," said Mr. Golspie, looking at her, "but if you'll take my tip you won't go like that, you'll have a drink of something to warm you up first. Might get a cold before you could say 'knife.' "

This was Mr. Golspie in a new and unsuspected vein. She could have laughed in his face.

"If the steward's about," he continued, "I could get some tea for you. These people aren't great on tea but they can make it all right.

Or coffee, if you'd rather have that. It just depends if he's handy."
He got up, passing the signed sheets to her.

"Oh, don't bother, Mr. Golspie. They're probably all frightfully
busy now, and I'd rather not, thanks. I can get some tea on my way
back to the office."

"Well, you must have something. You can't leave the ship shivering like that. Have some of this stuff," and he pointed to the tall
bottle. "It'll warm you up. I'm going to have some. You join me."
He poured out two small glasses of the colourless liquor.

"Shall I? What is it?"

"Vodka. It's the favourite tipple in these ships."

Vodka! She picked up the glass and put her nose to it. She had
never tasted vodka before, never remembered ever having seen it
before, but of course it was richly associated with her memories of
romantic fiction of various kinds, and was tremendously thrilling,
the final completing thrill of the afternoon's adventure. At once she
could hear herself bringing the vodka into her account of the adventure at the Club. "And then, my dear," it would run, "I was
given some vodka. There I was, in the cabin, swilling vodka like
mad. Marvellous!"

"Come along, Miss Matfield," said Mr. Golspie, looking at her over
his raised glass. "Down it goes. Happy days!" And he emptied his
glass with one turn of the wrist.

"All right," she cried, raising hers. "What do I say? Cheerio?"
Boldly she drained her glass, too, in one gulp. For a second or so
nothing happened but a curious aniseedy taste as the liquor slipped
over her palate, but then, suddenly, it was as if an incendiary bomb
had burst in her throat and sent white fire racing down every channel of her body. She gasped, laughed, coughed, all at once.

"That's the way, Miss Matfield. You put it down in great style.
Try another. I'm going to have one. Just another for good luck."
He filled the glasses again.

She floated easily now on a warm tide. It was very pleasant. She
took the glass, hesitated, then looked up at him. "I'm not going to be

tight, am I? If you make me drunk I shan't be able to type your letters, you know."

"Don't you worry about that," he told her, grinning amiably and then patting her shoulder. "You couldn't be soused on two glasses of this stuff, and you'll be as sober as a judge by the time you get back to Angel Pavement. It'll just make you feel warm and comfortable, and keep the cold out. Now then. Here she goes."

"Happy days!" cried Miss Matfield, smiling at him, and once more there came the aniseedy taste, the incendiary bomb, the racing white fire, and the final warm tide.

"Now I like you, Miss Matfield," he told her, with a full stare of approval. "That was done in real style, like a good sport. You've got some character, not like most of these pink little ninnies of girls you see here. I noticed that right at the start. I said to myself, 'That girl's not only got looks, but she's got character, too.' I wish you were coming with us."

"Thank you."

"Well, it's a real compliment. Though I don't know that you'd like it. It'll be perishingly cold, and by tomorrow she'll be rolling like the devil all the way across the North Sea, and she'll start rolling again when we get into the Baltic. I know her of old. How d'you feel now?"

"Marvellous!" And she did. She rose and gathered her things together. "Not too sober, though."

When they went out on to the upper deck, she stopped and looked down the river. Daylight had dwindled to a faint silver above and an occasional cold gleam on the water, and at any other time she would probably have been depressed or half frightened by the leaden swell of the river itself, the uncertain lights beyond, and the melancholy hooting, but now it all seemed wonderfully mysterious and romantic. For a minute or so, she lost herself in it. She was quite happy and yet she felt close to tears. It was probably the vodka.

"Sort of hypnotises you, doesn't it?" said Mr. Golspie gruffly, at her elbow.

"It does, doesn't it?" she said softly. At that moment, she decided that she liked Mr. Golspie and that he was an unusual and fascinating man. She also felt that she herself was fascinating, really rather wonderful. Then she gave a quick shiver.

"Hello, you're not starting again?" he said, humorous but concerned too, and he took hold of her arm and drew her closer to his side. They stayed like that for a few moments. She did not mind being there. All that she felt was a sudden sense of warmth and safety.

She stepped aside, and announced that she must go. He made no effort to detain her, said nothing, but simply led the way back to the lower deck and the gangway. There he stopped and held out his hand.

"Very pleased to have met you, Miss Matfield," he said, taking her hand and, for once, smiling rather than grinning.

"I hope you have a good trip, Mr. Golspie," she told him hurriedly, "and it isn't too cold and the crossing isn't too bad." Then, without knowing why, she added: "And don't forget to come back."

He gave a sudden deep laugh. "Not I. You'll be seeing me again soon. I'll be back in Angel Pavement before you can turn round." And he gave her hand a huge squeeze, then released it.

She turned round once and waved, though it was almost impossible to see if he was still there, then hurried down the narrow lane, which brought her gradually back into the ordinary world. By the time she crossed London Bridge again and looked through the bus window, there was hardly anything to be seen of that other world, only a glimmer of lights. By the time she was back at her table, holding her notebook up to the nearest shaded electric light, that other world was infinitely remote and might never have existed outside a daydream in the November dusk. Yet there, on the very paper she slipped behind the typewriter roller, was the sign that it was there, the sprawling *J. Golspie* of the signature. And it was queer now to think that he would be coming back, returning from his tall bottle and rolling ship and the snow and forests of the Baltic place, to walk through that swing door there, not a yard from Smeeth's elbow. It was queer and it was also rather exciting, which was more than could be said of the 13 bus and the lounge at the Burpenfield and her room there and the aspirin and the hot water. She sent the typewriter carriage flying along. It gave a sharp *ping*.

Chapter Six

MR. SMEETH GETS HIS RISE

I

M R. SMEETH was happier than he had been for some time. The shadow of dismissal, unemployment, degradation, ruin, had gone, except in occasional dreams, when, after a bit of fried liver or toasted cheese had refused to be digested, he had found himself out of a job for ever and walking down vague dark streets with nothing on but his vest and pants. It had vanished from his waking hours. The firm had not only staved off bankruptcy, but it was doing a brisk trade—you might almost call it a roaring trade—in these new Baltic veneers and inlays. This meant that Mr. Smeeth had more and more columns of neat little figures to enter and then add up, and that no matter how hard he worked during the day he had to put in an extra half hour or so with the ledger and day books in the evening. He did not mind that, though sometimes when it was nearer seven than six and the electric light above his desk had been burning half the day and any real air there might have been in Angel Pavement during the morning had been used over and over again, well, he did find himself with a bit of a headache. Once or twice too he had that nasty little ticking sensation somewhere in his inside, but it never went on long, so he never said anything about it to anybody. If he had mentioned it to his wife, she would have dosed him with half a dozen different patent medicines and would have rushed out for half a dozen more. She did not care for doctors, but she loved patent medicines and would try one after another, not as an attempt to cure some definite ailment, for she could not claim to have one, but simply in the hope that there would be some mysterious magic in the bottle. Mrs. Smeeth called at the chemist's in the same spirit in which she called on her fortune-telling friends. Mr. Smeeth was sceptical about both, though not so sceptical as he imagined himself to be.

Occasional little pains, however, were nothing compared with the relief of seeing the firm busy again. There had been times when he had almost hated going to the bank, for he felt that even the cashiers were telling one another that Twigg & Dersingham were looking pretty rocky, but now it was a pleasure again. "Just going round to the bank, Turgis," he would say, trying not to sound too important. (Not that it mattered with Turgis, who really thought Mr. Smeeth *was* important. But once or twice, when he had said something like this, he had caught a certain look, a kind of gleam, in Miss Matfield's eye. With that young madam you never knew.) Then he would button up his old brown overcoat, which had lasted very well but would have to be replaced as soon as he got a rise, put on his hat, fill his pipe as he went down the steps, stop and light it outside the *Kwik-Work Razor Blade* place, and then march cosily with it down the chilled and smoky length of Angel Pavement. Everywhere there would be a bustle and a jostling, with the roadway a bedlam of hooting and clanging and grinding gears, but he had his place in it all, his work to do, his position to occupy, and so he did not mind but turned on it a friendly eye and indulgent ear. The bank, secure in its marble and mahogany, would shut out the raw day and the raw sounds, and he would quietly, comfortably wait his turn, sending an occasional jet of fragrant *T. Benenden* towards the ornamental grill. "Morning, Mr. Smeeth," they would say. "A bit nippy, this morning. How are things with you?" And then, if there was time for it, one of them might have a little story to tell, about one of those queer things that happen in the City. Then back again in the office, at his desk, and very cosy it was after the streets. The very sight of the blue ink, the red ink, the pencils and pens, the rubber, the paper fasteners, the pad and rubber stamps, all the paraphernalia of his desk, all there in their places, at his service, gave him a feeling of deep satisfaction. He felt dimly too that this was a satisfaction that none of the others there, Turgis, the girls, young Stanley, would ever know, simply because they never came to work in the right spirit. His own two children were just the same. They were all alike now. Earn a bit, grab it, rush out and spend it, that was their lives.

"And it beats me, Mr. Dersingham," he said to that gentleman, one morning, "who is going to be responsible in this lot, when the time comes. And the time must come, mustn't it? I mean, they can't be young and careless all their lives."

"Don't you worry, Smeeth. They'll all settle down," replied Mr. Dersingham, who felt that he stood between these two different generations, and also felt that anyhow he knew a lot more about everything than Smeeth. "I can remember the time, and not so long ago, when I felt just the same," he continued, evidently under the impression that he was now a tremendously responsible person. "When the time comes, we take the responsibility all right. That's the English way, you know, Smeeth."

"I hope that is so, Mr. Dersingham," said Mr. Smeeth doubtfully, "but this new lot does seem different, I must say. I know from my own two. Anything for tuppence, that's their style, and let next week look after itself. It frightens me to hear them talk, though I say their mother's always been a bit like that and they may have got it from her."

Both George and Edna, however, unsatisfactory as their general outlook might be, seemed to be going on all right just then, and this too was a great source of pleasure to Mr. Smeeth, who saw them—and had seen them ever since they were babies—surrounded by snares and pitfalls without number. He had to worry for two, for their mother never seemed to worry about them or anything else, for all her fortune tellings and bottles from the chemist's, and to listen to her, you might think life was a fairy tale. To Mr. Smeeth— though he did not say so—life was a journey, unarmed and without guide or compass, through a jungle where poisonous snakes were lurking and man-eating tigers might spring out of every thicket. Only when he saw a little clear space in front of him could he be easy in mind. His was a naturally apprehensive nature, and in a religious age he would never have overlooked the least comforting observance. But he did not live in a religious age, and he had no faith of his own. In his universe, the gods had been banished but not the devils. He saw clearly enough all the signs and marks of evil in the world, having a mind that could foreshadow every stroke of malice out of the dark, and so was surrounded by demons that he was powerless either to placate or to vanquish. If, desiring as he did to be honest, decent, kind, good and happy, his courage failed, he could call upon nobody, nothing—but the police. Thus he lived, this man who went so cosily from his little house to his little office, more apprehensively, more dangerously, than one of Edward the Third's bowmen. He touched wood, and desperately hoped for the best. Just now, it seemed to be arriving. He was happier than he had been for some time.

II

The morning after Mr. Golspie's departure, two things happened to Mr. Smeeth. The first seemed of little importance at the time, though afterwards he remembered it only too well. George rang up from his garage, with a message from his mother. "She's here now, only she doesn't fancy herself at the phone," said George. "So I've got to give you the message. This is it. Do you remember hearing her talk about her cousin, Fred Mitty? Well, he's here in London with his wife. She's just had a letter from them, and they want her to go round and see them to-night, somewhere Islington way. She didn't think you'd want to go."

"No, I don't want to go," Mr. Smeeth told him. "But that's all right."

"Yes, I know it is," said George, "but the point is this. She's going there to tea, and she'll be gone some time before you get home.

What she wants to know is this, has she to leave something for you, she says, or will you have your tea out somewhere and amuse yourself for once ——"

"Now then, George," his father cried down the telephone sharply, "that's enough of that."

"I'm only telling you what she says," George's voice explained. "Keep cool, Dad. Nothing to do with me. You can either have your tea out and amuse yourself ——"

"I don't want to amuse myself. As I've told some of you before," he added rather grimly, "I like a quiet life."

"All right then, she can leave something for you. You'll only have to warm it up yourself. I shan't be in and Edna won't be either."

"Here, all right," said Mr. Smeeth, who was not fond of warming things up for himself. "I'll stop out for once. Tell your mother that's all right. And tell her I hope she enjoys herself with Mr. Mitty."

He had heard his wife talk about her cousin, Fred Mitty—she was rather given to talking about her relations—but he had never met him. Mitty had been living in one of the big provincial towns, Birmingham or Manchester, for the last few years. He could have stopped there, for all Mr. Smeeth cared. However, his wife would enjoy herself. She liked nothing better than going out for the evening and having a good old gas with somebody fairly lively, and Mr. Smeeth remembered now that Fred Mitty—what a name!—was supposed to be very lively, one of the dashing members of his wife's family, the chief comedian at all the weddings, and all the funerals, too, for that matter. So long as Mrs. Smeeth's lot could all get together and eat and drink and gas and kiss one another, they didn't much care whether they were marrying them or burying them. The Smeeths, what was left of them, were different. When they met, it meant business. Four of them had not spoken to one another for ten years, all because of two cottage houses in Highbury. His wife's lot would have sold the pair and eaten and drunk away the proceeds in less than a week.

"But it wouldn't do for us all to be alike, would it, young lady?"

he cried, almost gaily, to Miss Poppy Sellers, who came up to him at that moment with some invoices she had just typed.

"That's what my dad's always saying, Mr. Smeeth," she replied in her own queer fashion, half perky half shy. "And my mother always says, 'Well, you might try a bit anyway.'"

"And what does she mean by that?" asked Mr. Smeeth, amused.

Miss Sellers shook her dark little head. "I might be able to give a guess, and then again I mightn't. I've done all these, Mr. Smeeth. Are they all right?"

"Well, now, let's have a look," he said, adjusting his eyeglasses. "I might be able to tell you—and then again I mightn't."

She laughed. She was a nice little thing, even though Turgis had kept on grumbling about her. But he had not grumbled so much lately. He had not done anything much lately, except get on with his work—he had done that all right—and then sit mooning. The only time he looked lively and brisk and up-to-the-minute was when Mr. Golspie came in and asked him to do something. A queer lad, Turgis. But he was beginning to smarten himself up a bit, that was something; he had taken to brushing his hair and his clothes and changing his collars a little more often; and about time too. Mr. Smeeth shot a glance at him over his glasses, then read through the invoices.

"Please, Mr. Smeeth," said Stanley, returning from the private office, "Mr. Dersingham wants to see you."

And this was the second thing that happened that morning, this little interview with Mr. Dersingham.

"What I feel, Smeeth," said Mr. Dersingham, after a few preliminaries, "is that you've been doing your bit for the firm, and the firm now ought to do its bit for you. You've had a good deal of extra work lately, haven't you, just as we all have?"

"I have, Mr. Dersingham. It's been a very busy time for me—and I'm glad to say so, sir."

"For me too, I can tell you. I've been putting my back into it these last few weeks. Jolly heavy going, if you ask me. Particularly this last week, with the big drive—and it's not over yet, not by a long chalk it isn't. However, what I wanted to say is this, you've stood by the firm, done your best and all that, and now I propose to give you a rise." He paused, and looked at his employee.

"Thank you very much, sir," cried Mr. Smeeth, flushing. "I didn't want to say anything just yet, knowing how things have been, but Mr. Golspie did say something, just after he came——"

"Well, of course, this isn't Golspie's show at all. I mean to say, he has his work here and, to a certain extent, he's in charge, but whether you get a rise or not or anybody else gets a rise or not has nothing to do with him. It's my affair entirely."

"Quite so, Mr. Dersingham. I quite understand that," said Mr. Smeeth apologetically, though he was already silently thanking Mr. Golspie for this.

"Though it's—er—only fair to tell you that Mr. Golspie did mention it to me. But, as a matter of fact, I'd practically made up my mind then. He mentioned you, and he also mentioned Miss Matfield. He seemed to think she had been doing some very good work."

"Miss Matfield's been working very well, sir. And she certainly isn't getting as much as she might. We promised her a rise, if possible, after the first six months, when she was taken on."

"Well, I thought from now on we'd give her three ten instead of three pounds. Perhaps you'll tell her, Smeeth. Do it quietly. I don't think I can give Turgis any more yet."

"He's improving, Mr. Dersingham."

"He'll have to wait, though. As for you, Smeeth, I thought we'd make it three seventy-five for you."

This was a fine rise, well over a pound a week. "Thank you very much, Mr. Dersingham. I'm sure I'll do my best——"

But Mr. Dersingham, large, pink, benevolent, cut him short with a friendly wave of the hand. "That's all right, Smeeth. I hope it won't be the last, either. You'll rise with the firm, and at the present rate there's no telling where we shall land. Mr. Golspie has suggested several side-lines, quite profitable, handled properly, and I propose to look into our end of it while he's away. Oh—by the way—I think those increases, both yours and Miss Matfield's, had better begin this fortnight, eh?"

At odd intervals throughout the day, Mr. Smeeth thought about this extra money and delightedly considered what might be done with it. He was, of course, all in favour of saving it. They lived comfortably as they were but they saved little or nothing, and now at last they had a chance of really putting something away. Insurance? That ought to be looked into, for they had all kinds of schemes. National Savings? A good safe investment. They might buy a house through one of the Building Societies. He saw himself looking into all these things, smoking his pipe over them and then making notes and putting down a few rows of neat little figures. It almost made his mouth water.

It was not until late afternoon, when they were finishing off, that he began to tackle the major problem, for, like most people, he preferred to examine the little problems, the pleasant, cheerful little fellows, first. Plump in the middle of this major problem was Mrs. Smeeth. If she was told about this extra money, she would want to spend it. That was her nature; she was a born spender. She was not a grabber and she was not a grumbler; if the money was not there, she made no complaint, and could make a little go a long way with the best of them, if there was no help for it. Tell her there was more money coming into the house, and she would never rest until it had been all frittered away, on clothes and orna-ments and meals in cafés and visits to the theatre and the pictures and trips to the seaside and chocolate and bottles of port wine. Insurance and National Savings and Building Societies!—he could hear her telling him what she thought about *them*, and what she thought about him too for suggesting such a miserable way of spending their money. (She never understood the idea of saving, except when it merely meant putting a few shillings in a vase until Saturday. Giving money to an insurance company or a bank seemed to her simply spending it and getting nothing in return.) She would make him appear a mean ageing sort of chap, almost an old miser, cutting a contemptible figure in her eyes, and would refer to other men of her acquaintance, big, open-handed, dashing fellows. That would be so hateful that, finally, he would give in, and then what would they have for the future, for the rainy day? Empty bottles and chocolate boxes and old programmes and souvenirs of Clacton. It wasn't good enough. He saw one way out, of course, and that was not to tell her at all, to say nothing about his rise until he had made a good start with his savings; but he hated the thought of doing that. It meant lying to her, not once but perhaps scores of times. It would be all for the best, but he had an idea that he would feel mean all the time. Some chaps seemed to think of their wives as people you always felt mean with, and to hear them talk you would think they had married their worst enemies, but though he and Edie were often pulling different ways, that wasn't their style at all. So what was he to do?

His mind was still busy with this problem when he left the office for the night and called in T. Benenden's, round the corner. As he watched Benenden take down the familiar canister, he wondered if Benenden was married. He had exchanged remarks with him all these years and never found that out. Surely Benenden couldn't be married. A man who never wore a tie couldn't possibly have a wife, unless of course he left home with a tie and then took it off in the shop.

"You a married man, Mr. Benenden?" he inquired casually.

T. Benenden stopped his weighing at once. "Now that's a queer question," he said, staring.

"I beg your pardon, I'm sure," said Mr. Smeeth, rather embarrassed. "No business of mine at all."

"Not at all, not at all," said T. Benenden, still staring. "No offence taken, I assure you. What I really meant was it's a queer question for me to answer. You say to me 'Are you a married man, Mr. Benenden?' Well, the only answer I can give to that is, I *am*— and then again I'm *not*. What do you make of that?"

Before Mr. Smeeth had time to make anything of it, a youth rushed in, flung some coppers on the counter, and cried "Packet o' gaspers. Ten."

Mr. Benenden contemptuously threw down a packet of cigarettes, contemptuously swept the coppers away, and watched the youth rush out again with even greater contempt.

"You saw that, you 'eard it?" he said scornfully. "'Packet o' gaspers. *Packet o' gaspers.*' Rushes in, rushes out, never stops to say *please* or *thank you*, never stops to think. Just—packet o' gaspers. Can't even say *of*. A packet *of* gaspers. Now that," he continued gravely, his eyes fixed on Mr. Smeeth's apparently without once winking, "is the ruin of the tobacco trade to-day. I don't mean there's no money in it. There *is* money in it. That's where the big for-chewns 'ave been made—packets o' gaspers. If you and me had had the sense to realise, when the War started, that this packet-o'-gasper business was bound to come, *bound* to come—men smoking 'em, women smoking 'em, boys and girls smoking 'em—we could have made out forchewns, as easy as that. You watch for the big dividends in our trade—where are they? It isn't tobacco that's behind 'em—it's packets o' gaspers. Same with the shops. Quick turnover, in and out, throw 'em down, pick 'em up, outchew go. Easy money. All right. But I say it's the ruin of the tobacconist to-day. And why? It takes the 'eart out of the business. Some of 'em have started putting rows of automatic machines outside at closing time. You've seen 'em. Well, I say they might as well keep 'em all day and have done with it. Packet o' gaspers. Ten. There's your sixpence. Twenty. There's your shilling. Am I a man or am I an automatic machine?"

"Quite so," said Mr. Smeeth, nodding his head.

"I'm a man, and what's more, I'm a man with expert knowledge, I am. You come to me, and you say, 'I want such and such a smoke, a bit of Virginia, a bit of Lati-kee-ya'—or you mightn't say that because you mightn't know so much about it—but anyhow you've got your idea of what you want and you come to me and I fix you up, just as I've fixed *you* up with this mixture of mine.

There's some pleasure in that. But this packet o' gasper business. I might as well stand in the door there, and every time you put sixpence in my mouth, a packet of ten drops out of my waistcoat."

"You'd look well, wouldn't you?" Mr. Smeeth watched him filling the pouch, and could not help thinking that T. Benenden's Own looked dustier than usual.

"Getting a bit down with that," T. Benenden admitted, rolling up the pouch, "though if you ask me, I'd tell you to give me the bottom of the tin every time. That's not ordinary dust, y'know. That's good short stuff, best Oriental. It's rich, that, and the Prince of Wales wouldn't want anything better than that in his pipe—and I believe he smokes one."

"I believe he does," said Mr. Smeeth, handing over his money. "But what was that you were saying about being married?"

"Ar, yes," said T. Benenden, preparing to consume some of his own stock. "Well, my answer to that question of yours was, 'I *am* and I'm *not.*' And how do you puzzle that out?" he asked with the air of a man who had produced a rare riddle. "Bit of a facer that, eh?"

"Oh, I don't know. I'd say—offhand—that you say you *are* married because you're still legally married and have a wife living, but at the same time you say you're not married because you're not living the life of a married man. In fact, you're separated from your wife. How's that Mr. Benenden?"

The other's face fell at being robbed so quickly of the chance of explaining himself. "That was a bit of smart thinking on your part, Mr. Smeeth," he said, brightening up. "There aren't many men about here who could have got on to it like that. And you're right. I've been separated for nearly ten years. She goes her way, and I go mine. We were only married three years, and that was quite enough for me, a regular cat-and-dog life that was. If she wanted to go out, I wanted to stay in, and if she wanted to stay in, I wanted to go out. Well, that's all right, isn't it? If she wants to go out, let her go out. If she wants to stay in, let her stay in. What's the matter with that? Ar, but that's a man's point of view. This is where the unfairness of the sex comes in. I was ready to let her go out or stay in, just as she pleased. But what about her? Had she the same fair-minded attitude, the same broad principles?" Mr. Benenden here removed his pipe to make room for a short bitter laugh. "When she wanted to go out, I'd to go out too, and when she wanted to stay in, I'd to stay in as well. That was her idear. Dog in the manger, she was, all the time, and specially on Saturdays and Sundays, just when you wanted a bit of give and take. We didn't get on. Why some men like to tell you they get on well with women's a mystery to me. I never did get on with 'em, and I don't care who knows it."

"That's the spirit," said Mr. Smeeth, for no particular reason except that he felt Benenden ought to be encouraged.

"Yes, well, as I say, we'd three years of it, and she left me three times and I left her twice during them three years. Interfering relations always 'brought us together'—as they called it—but it was a miserable business. One of us was always packing up. I never knew whether I was going home to find a bit of supper or a note to say she'd gone to her sister's at Saffron Walden. So the last time, I left a note saying she'd better stay for good at Saffron Walden and I went into lodgings down Camberwell way for a week and didn't go back for over a week. When I did go back, she'd just gone again to Saffron Walden—she'd been back, you see, and waited a few days—and she stayed there."

"And don't you ever see her now?"

"Let me see," said T. Benenden, tickling his beard with the stem of his pipe. "Last time I ran across her by accident, a year or two ago, or it might be three years ago. I was walking round the Confectionery and Grocery Exhibition at the Agricultural Hall, and I suddenly saw her and her sister—they're in that line—and another woman all eating free samples of custard or jelly or potted meat or something, which is what I might have known they *would* be doing. I gave them one look and then went the other way."

"Didn't you stop at all?" said Mr. Smeeth.

"If I'd gone up to them there," said Mr. Benenden earnestly, "what would have happened? A lot of argument. 'You did this—Oh, did I?—Well, you did that.' What she wouldn't have said, her sister'ud said for her. Her sister had a tongue a yard long, noted for it up in Saffron Walden. I know that because a man from there came into this very shop one morning. Well, you can't have that sort of argument at a free custard and jelly stall, can you? I had a picture postcard from her last year, from Cromer—all show-off, y'know. No, I'm better without them. Let's see, Mr. Smeeth, I think you're married, aren't you? I seem to recollect you're a family man."

"That's right," said Mr. Smeeth, feeling very much at that moment the affectionate father and husband. "And I like it."

"Oh, it suits some people," said Mr. Benenden judicially. "They have the knack or an inclination that way. I'm not laying down any rules about it. But it never suited *me*. I like a quiet life of my own, to do *what* I like *when* I like, and have time to think things over. Good-night."

As Mr. Smeeth walked away, he came to the conclusion that he had solved the mystery of the absent tie. Benenden did not wear a tie just to show his independence. Mr. Smeeth, however, did not envy him, although the question of Mrs. Smeeth and the extra money had yet to be settled. He was glad that he was not going home for once and would not have to meet his wife until late that night. He dismissed the problem and asked himself instead how he should spend the evening. The first thing to do was to have a meal and as he had once or twice had a respectable sort of high tea in a place in Holborn, he decided to go there again, so turned down Aldermanbury and Milk Street, caught a bus in Cheapside and, ten minutes later, was seated snugly at a little table in the teashop.

He could not help feeling richer than he had done that morning. Now he was practically a four-hundred-a-year man instead of a three-hundred-a-year man. He felt that he was entitled to celebrate this promotion in his own quiet way. So he began by ordering a good solid high tea, and then searched his paper to discover what was happening that night in the world of entertainment. There was a symphony concert at the Queen's Hall. He would go there. He had never been to the Queen's Hall, had always thought of the concerts there as being a bit above his head. Symphony concerts at the Queen's Hall—it did sound rather heavy, rather alarming too, but he would try it. After all, though he didn't pretend to know much about it, he did like music, indeed liked nothing better than music, and there would sure to be something he could enjoy, and the Queen's Hall, expensive and highbrow as it sounded, couldn't kill him. So far, he had got his music from gramophone records and the wireless, bands in the park or at the seaside, popular concerts in North London or occasionally at the Kingsway Hall and the Central Hall, and nights in the gallery in the old days to hear the Carl Rosa Company do *Carmen* and *Rigoletto* and that one about the pierrots, *Pag-lee-atchy* he supposed they called it. Well, this would be a new move, this symphony concert in the Queen's Hall, a bit of an adventure. He ate his tea deliberately, as usual, but with a little inner glow of excitement.

He arrived at the Queen's Hall in what he imagined to be very good time, but was surprised to find, after paying what seemed to him a stiffish price, that there was only just room for him in the gallery. Another ten minutes and he would have been too late, a thought that gave him a good deal of pleasure as he climbed the steps, among all the eager, chattering symphony concert-goers.

III

His seat was not very comfortable, high up too, but he liked the look of the place, with its bluey-green walls and gilded organ-pipes and lights shining through holes in the roof like fierce sunlight, its rows of little chairs and music stands, all ready for business. It was fine. He did not buy a programme—they were asking a shilling each for them, and a man must draw a line somewhere—but spent his time looking at the other people and listening to snatches of their talk. They were a queer mixture, quite different from anybody you were likely to see either in Stoke Newington or Angel Pavement; a good many foreigners (the kind with brown baggy stains under their eyes), Jewy people, a few wild-looking young fellows with dark khaki shirts and longish hair, a sprinkling of quiet middle-aged men like himself, and any number of pleasant young girls and refined ladies; and he studied them all with interest. On one side of him were several dark foreigners in a little party, a brown wrinkled oldish woman who never stopped talking Spanish or Italian or Greek or some such language, a thin young man who was carefully reading the programme, which seemed to be full of music itself, and, on the far side, two yellow girls. On the other side, his neighbour was a large man whose wiry grey hair stood straight up above a broad red face, obviously an Englishman but a chap rather out of the common, a bit cranky perhaps and fierce in his opinions.

This man, moving restlessly in the cramped space, bumped against Mr. Smeeth and muttered an apology.

"Not much room, is there?" said Mr. Smeeth amiably.

"Never is here, sir," the man replied fiercely.

"Is that so," said Mr. Smeeth. "I don't often come here." He felt it would not do to admit that this was the very first time.

"Always crowded at these concerts, full up, packed out, not an inch of spare room anywhere. And always the same. What the devil do they mean when they say they can't make these concerts pay? Whose fault is it?" he demanded fiercely, just as if Mr. Smeeth were partly responsible. "We pay what they ask us to pay. We fill the place, don't we? What do they want? Do they want people to hang down from the roof or sit on the organ pipes? They should build a bigger hall or stop talking nonsense."

Mr. Smeeth agreed, feeling glad there was no necessity for him to do anything else.

"Say that to some people," continued the fierce man, who needed no encouragement, "and they say, 'Well, what about the Albert Hall?

That's big enough, isn't it?' The Albert Hall! The place is ridiculous. I was silly enough to go and hear Kreisler there, a few weeks ago. Monstrous! They might as well have used a race course and sent him up to play in a captive balloon. If it had been a gramophone in the next house but one, it couldn't have been worse. Here you do get the music, I will say that. But it's damnably cramped up here."

The orchestral players were now swarming in like black beetles, and Mr. Smeeth amused himself trying to decide what all the various instruments were. Violins, 'cellos, double-basses, flutes, clarinets, bassoons, trumpets or cornets, trombones, he knew them, but he was not sure about some of the others—were those curly brass things the horns?—and it was hard to see them at all from where he was. When they had all settled down, he solemnly counted them, and there were nearly a hundred. Something like a band, that! This was going to be good, he told himself. At that moment, everybody began clapping. The conductor, a tall foreign-looking chap with a shock of grey hair that stood out all round his head, had arrived at his little railed-in platform, and was giving the audience a series of short jerky bows. He gave two little taps. All the players brought their instruments up and looked at him. He slowly raised his arms, then brought them down sharply and the concert began.

First, all the violins made a shivery sort of noise that you could feel travelling up and down your spine. Some of the clarinets and bassoons squeaked and gibbered a little, and the brass instruments made a few unpleasant remarks. Then all the violins went rushing up and up, and when they got to the top, the stout man at the back hit a gong, the two men near him attacked their drums, and the next moment every man jack of them, all the hundred, went at it for all they were worth, and the conductor was so energetic that it looked as if his cuffs were about to fly up to the organ. The noise was terrible, shattering: hundreds of tin buckets were being kicked down flights of stone steps; walls of houses were falling in; ships were going down; ten thousand people were screaming with toothache; steam hammers were breaking loose; whole warehouses of oilcloth were being stormed and the oilcloth all torn into shreds; and there were railway accidents innumerable. Then suddenly the noise stopped; one of the clarinets, all by itself, went slithering and gurgling; the violins began their shivery sound again and at last shivered away into silence. The conductor dropped his arms to his side. Nearly everybody clapped.

Neither Mr. Smeeth nor his neighbour joined in the applause. Indeed, the fierce man snorted a good deal, obviously to show his disapproval.

"I didn't care for that much, did you?" said Mr. Smeeth, who felt he could risk it after those snorts.

"That? Muck. Absolute muck," the fierce man bellowed into Mr. Smeeth's left ear. "If they'll swallow that they'll swallow anything, any mortal thing. Downright sheer muck. Listen to 'em." And as the applause continued, the fierce man, in despair, buried his huge head in his hands and groaned.

The next item seemed to Mr. Smeeth to be a member of the same unpleasant family as the first, only instead of being the rowdy one, it was the thin sneering one. He had never heard a piece of music before that gave such an impression of thinness, boniness, scragginess, and scratchiness. It was like having thin wires pushed into your ears. You felt as if you were trying to chew ice-cream. The violins hated the sight of you and of one another; the reedy instruments were reedier than they had ever been before but expressed nothing but a general loathing; the brass only came in to blow strange hollow sounds; and the stout man and his friends at the top hit things that had all gone flat, dead, as if their drums were burst. Very tall thin people sat about drinking quinine and sneering at one another, and in the middle of them, on the cold floor, was an idiot child than ran its finger-nail up and down a slate. One last scratch from the slate, and the horror was over. Once more, the conductor, after wiping his brow, was acknowledging the applause.

This time, Mr. Smeeth did not hesitate. "And I don't like that either," he said to his neighbour.

"You don't?" The fierce man was almost staggered. "You don't like it? You surprise me, sir, you do indeed. If you don't like that, what in the name of thunder *are* you going to like—in modern music. Come, come, you've got to give the moderns a chance. You can't refuse them a hearing altogether, can you?"

Mr. Smeeth admitted that you couldn't, but said it in such a way as to suggest that he was doing his best to keep them quiet.

"Very well, then," the fierce man continued, "you've got to confess that you've just listened to one of the two or three things written during these last ten years or so that is going to *live*. Come now, you must admit that."

"Well, I dare say," said Mr. Smeeth, knitting his brows.

Here the fierce man began tapping him on the arm. "Form? Well, of course, the thing hasn't got it, and it's no good pretending it has, and that's where you and I"—Mr. Smeeth was given a heavier tap, almost a bang, to emphasise this—"find ourselves being cheated. But we're asking for something that isn't there. But the tone values, the pure orchestral colouring—superb! Damn it, it's got poetry in it. Romantic, of course. Romantic as you like—ultra-romantic. All these fellows now are beginning to tell us they're classical, but they're all romantic really, the whole boiling of 'em, and Berlioz is their man only they don't know it, or won't admit it. What do *you* say?"

Mr. Smeeth observed very cautiously that he had no doubt there was a lot to be said for that point of view. When the interval came and he went out to smoke a pipe, he took care to keep moving so that the fierce man, who appeared to be on the prowl, did not find him.

The concert was much better after the interval. It began with a longish thing in which a piano played about one half, and most of the orchestra, for some of them never touched their instruments, played the other half. A little dark chap played the piano and there could be no doubt about it, he *could* play the piano. Terrum, ter-*rum*, terrum, terrum, trum, trum, trrrrr, the orchestra would go, and the little chap would lean back, looking idly at the conductor. But the second the orchestra stopped he would hurl himself at the piano and crash out his own Terrum, ter-*rum*, terrum, terrum, trum trum trrr. Sometimes the violins would play very softly and sadly, and the piano would join in, scattering silver showers of notes or perhaps wandering up and down a ladder of quiet chords, and then Mr. Smeeth would feel himself very quiet and happy and sad all at the same time. In the end, they had a pell-mell race, and the piano shouted to the orchestra and then went scampering away, and the orchestra thundered at the piano and went charging after it, and they went up hill and down dale, shouting and thundering, scampering and charging, until one big bang, during which the little chap seemed to be almost sitting on the piano and the conductor appeared to be holding the whole orchestra up in his two arms, brought it to an end. This time Mr. Smeeth clapped furiously, and so did the fierce man, and so did everybody else, even the violin players in the orchestra; and the little chap, now purple in the face, ran in and out a dozen times, bowing all the way. But he would not play again, no matter how long and loud they clapped, and Mr. Smeeth, for his part, could not blame him. The little chap had done his share. My word, there was talent for you!

"Our old friend now," said the fierce man, turning abruptly.

"Where?" cried Mr. Smeeth, startled.

"On the programme," the other replied. "It's the Brahms Number One next."

"Is it really," said Mr. Smith. "That ought to be good." He had heard of Brahms, knew him as the chap who had written some Hungarian dances. But, unless he was mistaken, these dances were only a bit of fun for Brahms, who was one of your very heavy classical men. The Number One part of it he did not understand, and did not like to ask about it, but as the elderly foreign woman on his right happened to be examining the programme, he had a peep

at it and had just time to discover that it was a symphony, Brahms'
First Symphony in fact, they were about to hear. It would probably be clean above his head, but it could not possibly be so horrible
to listen to as that modern stuff in the first half of the programme.

It was some time before he made much out of it. The Brahms
of this symphony seemed a very gloomy, ponderous, rumbling sort
of chap, who might now and then show a flash of temper or go
in a corner and feel sorry for himself, but for the most part simply
went on gloomily rumbling and grumbling. There were moments,
however, when there came a sudden gush of melody, something
infinitely tender swelling out of the strings or a ripple of laughter
from the flutes and clarinets or a fine flare up by the whole orchestra, and for these moments Mr. Smeeth waited, puzzled but excited,
like a man catching glimpses of some delectable strange valley
through the swirling mists of a mountain side. As the symphony
went on, he began to get the hang of it more and more, and these
moments returned more frequently, until at last, in the final section,
the great moment arrived and justified everything, the whole symphony concert.

It began, this last part, with some muffled and doleful sounds
from the brass instruments. He had heard some of those grim
snatches of tune earlier on in the symphony, and now when they
were repeated in this fashion they had a very queer effect on him,
almost frightened him. It was as if all the workhouses and hospitals
and cemeteries of North London had been flashed past his eyes.
Those brass instruments didn't think Smeeth had much of a chance.
All the violins were sorry about it; they protested, they shook, they
wept; but the horns and trumpets and trombones came back and
blew them away. Then the whole orchestra became tumultuous,
and one voice after another raised itself above the menacing din,
cried in anger, cried in sorrow, and was lost again. There were queer
little intervals, during one of which only the strings played, and
they twanged and plucked instead of using their bows, and the
twanging and plucking, quite soft and slow at first, got louder and

faster until it seemed as if there was danger everywhere. Then, just when it seemed as if something was going to burst, the twanging and plucking was over, and great mournful sounds came reeling out again, like doomed giants. After that the whole thing seemed to be slithering into hopelessness, as if Brahms had got stuck in a bog and the light was going. But then the great moment arrived. Brahms jumped clean out of his bog, set his foot on the hard road, and swept the orchestra and the fierce man and the three foreigners and Mr. Smeeth and the whole Queen's Hall along with him, in a noble stride. This was a great tune. Ta *tum* ta ta *tum* tum, ta *tum* ta-ta *tum* ta *tum*. He could have shouted at the splendour of it. The strings in a rich deep unison sweeping on, and you were ten feet high and had a thousand glorious years to live. But in a minute or two it had gone, this glory of sound, and there was muddle and gloom, a sudden sweetness of violins, then harsh voices from the brass. Mr. Smeeth had given it up, when back it came again, swelling his heart until it nearly choked him, and then it was lost once more and everything began to be put in its place and settled, abruptly, fiercely, as if old Brahms had made up his mind to stand no nonsense from anybody or anything under the sun. There, there, there there, *There*. It was done. They were all clapping and clapping and the conductor was mopping his forehead and bowing and then' signalling to the band to stand up, and old Brahms had slipped away, into the blue.

There was a cold drizzle of rain outside in Langham Place, where the big cars of the rich were nosing one another like shiny monsters, and it was a long and dreary way to Chaucer Road, Stoke Newington, but odd bits of the magic kept floating back into his mind, and he felt more excited and happy than he had done when he had heard about the rise that morning. Undoubtedly a lot of this symphony concert stuff was either right above his head or just simply didn't mean anything to anybody. But what was good *was* good. Ta *tum* ta ta—now how did that go? All the way from the High Street to Chaucer Road, as he hurried down the darkening streets and tried to make his overcoat collar reach the back of his hat, he was also trying to capture that tune. He could feel it still beating and glowing somewhere inside him.

His wife and Edna were in. He heard their voices as he shut the front door. George was probably still out. "Hello, there. Only me," he shouted. "George in yet?" They told him that George was in bed (George was always out very late or in bed quite early. A puzzling lad), so he carefully locked and bolted the front door.

"Well, here's the wanderer," cried Mrs. Smeeth gaily. She had still got her hat and coat on, and was refreshing herself with a piece of cake and half a tumbler of stout. "And where did you get to, Dad?"

"Went to a concert," he replied, a trifle self-consciously. He drew nearer the fire and began taking off his boots.

"Get your dad his slippers, Edna, that's a good girl," said her mother. "And where was this concert then?"

"Queen's Hall."

"Oo! classy, aren't we?" cried Mrs. Smeeth. "Did you like it?"

"I'll bet he didn't," said Edna, an aggressive low-brow.

"How do you know he didn't, miss. Some people like a bit of good music, even if you don't. We're not all jazz-mad. There's nobody round here who enjoys good music, classical pieces, better than your father. Isn't that so, Dad? Nobody knows that better than I do, the times I've had to listen to it as well, and a little bit goes a long way with me. Now you get off to bed, Edna, now, else you won't be getting up in the morning and then you'll be in a bit more trouble at the shop."

"What's this?" asked Mr. Smeeth, looking at his wife and then at his daughter. "Has she been getting into any trouble?"

"It wasn't my fault at all, and you needn't have mentioned it, Mother," Edna began, but she was cut short by her mother.

"I didn't say it was, but it will be if you don't pop off upstairs." She waited then until Edna had disappeared. "Tells me she's had some bother with the buyer or floor manager, all something and nothing, but she thinks one or two of them there are getting their knife into her, and I've just been telling her to keep quiet a bit and not give any back answers until it's blown over. Well," she continued, settling back in her chair, after disposing of the stout, "I think George told you I was going to see Fred Mitty and his wife."

"He did," said Mr. Smeeth. "And how's Cousin Fred? What's brought him here?"

"I can't quite make out what it is. Something to do with advertising and something to do with picture theatres and all that. He didn't explain it properly. But he's looking well, and so is his wife, and the daughter. Quite grown up, she is, about Edna's age but bigger than Edna. But laugh!" Her face lit up. "Laugh! I thought I'd have died. I wish you'd been there, Dad. Oh, dear, dear, dear! Fred was always a lively card, never knew him when he wasn't, but he gets funnier as he gets older, and he set us off to-night and I thought we'd never have stopped. He started taking off a man he knew in Birmingham—I believe he worked for him—and it seems this man talks on one side of his mouth, can't help it, you see, and Fred started——"

"I think, if you don't mind, we'll have all this to-morrow, Edie," said Mr. Smeeth, standing up. "I feel like going to bed. I'm tired."

"Oh, all right, Mister Methodical," cried Mrs. Smeeth good-humouredly. "Fat lot of good it is saving a joke for you, isn't it? Never mind, you'll see for yourself on Saturday. I'll ask Fred to do it again. They're all coming up on Saturday night."

"Oh, they are, are they," said Mr. Smeeth with an entire lack of enthusiasm.

"Oh, I know what you'd like to say," she told him, as they moved to the door. "But I had to ask them back, hadn't I? Besides, we've got to have a bit of life sometime."

That was true enough. He didn't want to spoil her fun. He hadn't told her about the rise yet, and he wasn't sure if he was going to tell her. Somebody had to do the worrying and saving at 17, Chaucer

Road. Tum *tum* tum tum—no, he couldn't get it. He turned out
the light and followed his wife upstairs.

IV

All the following day, he told himself that he would not say a
word to Mrs. Smeeth about the extra money until he had made
arrangements to save most of it. Once he had committed himself,
it would be safe—though not pleasant—to tell her. In the meantime,
if she asked him why he wasn't getting the rise he had been promised, he would have to put her off with some tale or other. That
wouldn't be very pleasant either and not at all simple. To look at
Mrs. Smeeth, with her free and easy style, you would think she
was easy to lie to, but she wasn't—or so it seemed to Mr. Smeeth.
Whenever he tried he found himself, at his age too, still blushing
and stammering. But there it was; that was the plan. And he spent
some of his lunch time, all that could be spared from the usual
poached egg and cup of coffee, "looking into" one or two things,
insurance and National Savings chiefly, and when he returned to
the office and made a few notes and calculations in his neat little
script, he felt vaguely rich and rather important for once in his life.

The only person in the office who noticed any change in him was
Stanley. Stanley's interest in the affairs of Twigg and Dersingham,
never strong at any time, had almost entirely lapsed now that Mr.
Golspie was away, and that afternoon he found Mr. Smeeth un-
bearably tyrannical. He had to comfort himself by imagining a
certain dramatic scene in the future, in which Mr. Smeeth, now the
victim of a desperate gang, called in despair on the great detective,
S. Poole, only to discover, after bowing humbly, that he was face
to face with Stanley, the boy he had once bullied and despised.
"Yes, Smeeth," said S. Poole, lighting another cigar, you little
imagined then who it was copying your letters and filling your inkwells. But we will let bygones be bygones. Come, I will rid you of
these pests." And the great S. Poole, after slipping a revolver into

the pocket of his fur coat, strode out, followed by an amazed and trembling Smeeth. "Courage, man, courage," said S. Poole, as he climbed into the driving seat of his powerful roadster. "I can never thank you enough, Mr. Poole ——"

"And just get on with your work, Stanley," said the same voice. But oh!—the difference in intonation. "I told you those letters have to catch the country post. Be ready to slip out with them. Got the envelopes there?"

On his tram, going home, Mr. Smeeth turned the pages of his evening paper, looking for those appeals to "The Saving Man" and "The Small Investor." One of the advertisements asked him, not for the first time, what he was going to do in the Evening of Life, and though he still had no answer ready, for once he could look at it without feeling himself shrinking somewhere. Already he carried a good insurance for a man in his position; he had a bit, for emergencies, in the Post Office Savings Bank; and now he would have over a pound a week to put away. Now if he did that for ten years, fifteen years, perhaps increased it if the firm went on doing so well and gave him another rise, why, then, surely—and he lost himself in pleasant speculations.

He arrived home to find Edna sitting over the fire, hugging herself in misery, and red and swollen about the eyes.

"Hello, hello," he cried. "What's the matter here?"

"Lost my job," Edna mumbled into the fire.

"Yes, she's a fine one, isn't she?" And Mrs. Smeeth bounced into the room with a saucepan in her hand. "I told her to be careful, last night, the way they were getting their knife into her, and in she comes, half an hour ago, and tells me they've had a regular dust-up and the long and short of it all is, my lady's sacked."

"It wasn't my fault," said Edna, who had obviously said this a great many times before.

"Just you go upstairs and tidy yourself up," cried her mother. "Dinner will be ready in a minute and the face you've got now isn't fit to be seen at a table. It would put us off our food. And don't start telling me you don't want any dinner, just because you've got sacked. Get along upstairs and don't keep us waiting all night when you do get up."

"What's all this about?" Mr. Smeeth asked, with the quiet despair of a man who has known something like it happen before, and not a few times before. He put on that look familiar to all wives, who are left wondering why men should imagine that domestic life, unlike any other kind of life, ought really to be entirely lacking in disturbing events.

"Look at me with this saucepan in my hand," cried Mrs. Smeeth, laughing at herself. "Just you sit down and keep calm, and I'll have dinner on the table in a minute, though what it'll be like, Lord only knows, the way I've been badgered and rushed."

Left to himself, Mr. Smeeth came to the conclusion once again that his wife was to be envied. She made a great fuss, far more noise than he ever did, but she didn't really dislike these disturbances and strokes of bad luck. Any sort of happening, even an apparent misfortune, braced her up and left her really enjoying it. What she didn't like was a quiet life, the same thing day after day.

She came in now like a savoury whirlwind. "Draw up, Dad. We won't wait for Edna. She'll be down in a minute. Help yourself to that stew and take plenty of it because the meat's nearly all bone. Dig down and you'll get the barley, and that'll do your old inside good."

"What's this about Edna, then?"

"Far as I can see, you can't really blame her, though she's probably been acting a bit too independent. Edna *is* independent, though better that, in the long run, than too much the other way. But she's only a child, when all's said and done, and I know she liked the work and wanted to stop on there. For two pins, I'd slip down to Finsbury Park to-morrow and give that floor manager or whoever he is a piece of my mind. All favouritism really, that's what it boils down to, and of course Edna hadn't been there long and ought to have kept quiet—though a girl's a right to speak up for herself, and I'd be the last to say she hasn't—but they begin picking on her and she stands up for herself and lets out one or two things she oughtn't to and the next thing is, she's told to go."

This was not a very clear account of how a girl came to be suddenly dismissed from an important firm of retail drapers, but it seemed to satisfy Mr. Smeeth, who did not ask for any details. The truth is, he had gone through this scene before, and he knew now that it was not worth trying to discover exactly what had happened. Edna returned, looking her usual self except that she wore a slightly tragic air.

"When do you finish then, Edna?" her father asked.

"This week. And the sooner the better. I wouldn't go to-morrow if I hadn't to get my week's money. Lot of pigs, they are. I knew one or two girls—Ivy Armitage, for one—who's been there and they told me what it was like, but of course I wouldn't believe 'em but it didn't take me long to see they weren't talking so silly as I thought."

"And what's the next move, then?" demanded Mr. Smeeth rather wearily.

"Don't you worry, Dad. I'm not going to stick about home long. I'll find something."

"What she'd like to do is to go to Madame Rivoli's in the High Street," Mrs. Smeeth explained, "and learn the business properly."

"What business? I'll trouble you for the greens, Edna."

"Millinery. You know Madame Rivoli's in the High Street, the place where I got that very nice purple hat of mine that fell into the water at Hastings that time? Mrs. Talbot keeps it now. You know, her husband died of eating oysters about four years ago, and nobody round here would touch 'em for months—well, that's Mrs. Talbot, a little woman, looks a bit Frenchified—smart, y'know, Dad, but overdoes it a bit. I pointed her out to you one day, and you said if you'd legs as thin as that you'd take the trouble to hide 'em and I thought she heard you."

"And then you talk about *me* talking," cried Edna. "That's a nice way to talk, isn't it? And about Mrs. Talbot, too. You couldn't want anybody nicer than Mrs. Talbot."

"All we want is for you to mind your own business," said Mrs. Smeeth, forgetting that this really was Edna's business. "But if you want something to do, you can be fetching that pudding in and making yourself useful, while I finish this. And be careful getting it out. Use the cloth."

"And where does Madame Rivoli come in?" asked Mr. Smeeth.

"She doesn't come in. It's just a *name*, y'see, Dad. Miss Murgatroyd had it before Mrs. Talbot. It catches people, makes them think all the hats are Paris models. For all that, it's the best little hat shop we've got about here. If you know of a better one in Stoke Newington, I'd like to know where it is, I would really. Only thing that keeps *me* away from that shop is the prices they ask—oh, wicked, they are—you might as well go to the West End and have done with it. But Mrs. Talbot does a fine business—I don't think it's altogether her shop, I think she just manages it, and somebody told me two Jews really owned it. Now then, Edna," and Mrs. Smeeth sprang to her feet and took the pudding from her daughter, "just nip back for the plates and then we're all right. There we are. It'll taste better than it looks. This pudding always does. Plenty for you, Dad?"

"Just middling, Mother," said Mr. Smeeth.

"Well, if that isn't enough, you can always come again, can't you? What about you, Edna? Don't want any, I suppose? Well, you're going to have some. You eat that and see if it doesn't make you feel better."

"I've tasted worse," said Mr. Smeeth judicially. "Bit heavy, though, isn't it?"

"Oo, Mother, you can't have mixed it properly," cried the fastidious Edna. "It's like lead. It is really. I'll have a bit more of the apple, please. I can't eat the crust."

"Now if you'd been me and I'd been *my* mother," said Mrs. Smeeth with an attempt at severity, "you'd have been made to eat what was on your plate and not gone picking and choosing like that. But it's not come out as well as it might, I must say."

"Well, to get back to what we were talking about," said Mr. Smeeth, laying down his spoon and shaking his head at an offer of more pudding. "Where does this Mrs. Talbot or Madame Rivoli or whoever it is come in? What's she got to do with us? I've forgotten how it all started. You go on and on and what with purple hats and oysters and legs and Jews, I don't know where I am. Now then, start again, if we *must* have it."

"Oh, you tell him, Edna, while I go and make the tea. And for goodness' sake be careful you don't mention purple hats and oysters or else your father will be leaving home. Old silly!" And Mrs. Smeeth, as deft as a juggler, swept herself and half a dozen plates and a few dishes out of the room.

"It's like this, Dad," Edna began. "My friend, Minnie Watson, knows this Mrs. Talbot who's managing Madame Rivoli's because her mother has known her a long time and Minnie Watson introduced me to Mrs. Talbot and we got on talking and Minnie Watson told her afterwards I wanted to go in for the millinery if I could ——"

"Ah, we're coming to it at last, are we?"

"Well, the point is, Mrs. Talbot told Minnie Watson that she liked the look of me and that if I wanted to go as an apprentice, I could do, and they'd teach me the business. Only I'd have to go for six months first without getting any money at all, and then they'd pay me something after that—not much at the start, but afterwards I could earn a lot, because you can if you're a proper milliner and know the business."

"That's the idea now, you see, Dad," said Mrs. Smeeth, coming in with the tea. "Learning the millinery. I don't say it's a bad idea, because it's not, and, if you ask me, I should say Edna had as good a chance of making something out of it as any girl I know, because she's good with her fingers—when she cares to use 'em and that's not often in the house—and she likes altering hats, which is more than I ever did."

"Everybody says I'm clever at it," said Edna, looking rather defiant.

"I don't know what you mean by 'everybody,' but if you mean your Minnie Watsons and such like, I don't think whatever they say amounts to much. They'd tell you anything for tuppence. But still, Dad, it's not a bad idea—but, as I told her, this apprenticeship business is coming a bit hard on us because it's working for nothing and now that she's been earning money, she's used to having it to spend, and we've got to keep her looking decent and she'll still want to be spending something and she'll be bringing nothing in for a long time. You say I haven't a head for business, Dad—and I dare say I haven't and I don't know that I want to have—but I saw that as soon as she mentioned it and asked her what she thought we were going to get out of it."

"Dad can't talk," cried Edna, looking across at him triumphantly, " 'cos he wanted me to be a teacher and if I'd started to be a teacher, I'd have been going to college now, and then he'd have had to be paying for me, never mind me not earning anything."

"Yes, but you didn't want to be a teacher, did you?" said Mrs. Smeeth, as if that somehow settled the matter.

"Besides, my girl," Mr. Smeeth began, rather pompously.

"Take your tea, Dad." It was a curious thing, but whenever Mr. Smeeth had some really dignified statement to make, Mrs. Smeeth invariably broke in to hand him a cup or a plate or to ask him to put some coal on the fire or to see if there was somebody at the front door.

"Go on, Dad, what were you saying?" said Mrs. Smeeth, observing that he was frowning a little at his cup.

"I was going to say that teaching's one thing and millinery's another thing. If you'd have decided to be a teacher, Edna, I was ready to make a sacrifice to see that you became one. Teaching's a profession. Safe, too. Once you become a teacher, you're safe for the rest of your life ——"

"Awful old maids they look too, some of the old ones. Lord help us, what a life!" Mrs. Smeeth shuddered, shook her head, then smiled at her husband, encouraging him to continue with his little speech.

"But this millinery business is quite a different thing. There may be money in it and there may not—I don't know. What I do know is, it's in a different class altogether, not the same standing at all. I'd do for one what I wouldn't do for the other. So don't throw that teaching affair in my face because it's outside the argument altogether."

"Oh, all right." Edna wriggled her shoulders. "Don't go on and on about it. If I can't go, I suppose I can't, that's all." She pushed her cup away and rose from the table. Then she stopped and looked at them, and Mr. Smeeth saw, to his dismay, that her eyes were filling with tears. Like that, she looked hardly a day older than she had done when he still played childish games with her. "But I did want to go. It's the only thing I've really wanted to do since I left school. And if I went, I might be earning quite a lot in a year or two and some day I might be able to have a shop of my own. If George had wanted to do something like this, you wouldn't have said no to him—oh ——"

She was making for the door, but her father's shout stopped her.

"Here, wait a minute," he called out. Then, when she halted, he threw a quick glance at her streaming little face, looked across at her mother and then down at the table-cloth, and said: "Well, I suppose you'd better have a try at it then, Edna."

"Oo, can I?" She was all delighted eagerness now, and darted across to him. "I can, can't I?"

Awkward, a trifle shamefaced, Mr. Smeeth made a movement as if to put his arm round her, but apparently thought better of it and merely patted her nearest shoulder-blade. "That's all right," he muttered. "That's all right."

"Can I go round and see her now?" said Edna, her eyes shining and her feet dancing with impatience. Then she flew out of the room.

"Well, Dad," said Mrs. Smeeth. "I won't say I'm sorry you've decided that way, because I'm not. I believe it's what she's wanted some time. She doesn't know whether she's on her head or her heels now. Ah!—" and she gave a tremendous sigh—"I like to see them happy. After all, we've only got to live once——"

"How do you know?" demanded her husband.

"Well, I don't know, if it comes to that, Mister Clever," she retorted good-humouredly. "All the same, I've a very good idea. But what I wanted to say is this, Dad. I wasn't going to give her permission to start this business. And don't say I persuaded you, because I didn't. You did it yourself. You know what it means. She'll be earning next to nothing for a year or two, and though she'll have to pull herself in a bit now she's not earning anything, she can't be kept on nothing. So don't you turn round on me and tell me I don't know that twelve pennies make a shilling or something of that sort. It's your own doing, this time. I made up my mind I wouldn't say a word. And if you think you can do it all right, well and good; I'm glad."

"Of course I can do it," he told her, rather indignantly. Then out it came. "Matter of fact, I've got that rise."

"You've not?"

"Yes, I have."

"How much?"

"I've been put up to three seventy-five, that's more than a pound a week more than I've been getting." And as he said it, Mr. Smeeth asked himself if he wasn't behaving like a complete fool.

Mrs. Smeeth descended on him impetuously and gave him a resounding kiss. "I knew there was something coming," she cried jubilantly. "I told you about Mrs. Dalby's sister, didn't I? She told me again that money and good luck were coming through a stranger, a middling-coloured man in a strange bed. And that was this Mr. Golspie of yours, I'll bet. Nearly four hundred a year, isn't it, now? That's something like. My cousin, Fred Mitty, was boasting the other night about what he could make sometimes, and now this will be something to tell him to-morrow night. And fancy you just sitting there as if nothing had happened and never saying a word! I never knew anybody so close, you old oyster you! But that shows what they think of you, doesn't it? And you always worrying about your job and talking as if you were going to be out in the street next minute!" She ran on and on, happy and excited, while he filled his pipe and tried to appear very cool and collected. Actually he was being pulled two ways. One half of him was gratified, no, more than gratified, delighted by her pleasure and her pride in him, and the other half was dubious and demanded to know if he realised what he had done.

"Now look here, Dad," said Mrs. Smeeth, "we must celebrate the great occasion somehow to-night. It's no good luck coming to the house if we're not going to take any notice of it. Let's go out somewhere. Let's enjoy ourselves."

"I thought we were going to do that to-morrow," he told her drily, "when Fred Mitty and company arrive."

"But that's different. I mean, just ourselves, just you and me. Let's go and see a good picture or down to the second house at Finsbury Park or something like that, and sit in the best seats, and you buy yourself a cigar and buy me some chocolates for once, and let's do it properly. Come on, boy. What do you say?"

The Saving Man and the Small Investor in Mr. Smeeth went down before the affectionate husband and the proud male. When she looked at him like that, it would be a sin and a shame to refuse her. "All right, Edie. You decide where you want to go, and we'll go."

"I'll just put George's dinner out and put the dirty things under the tap," she announced breathlessly, flushed and bright-eyed, a girl again, "and while I'm doing that, you look at the paper and see where you'd like to go. Give me those two cups. No, I can manage. You just sit there and have a quiet smoke."

He could hear her singing, in her own cheerful vague fashion, above the faint clatter of crockery in the kitchen, while he had his quiet smoke. He did not look at the paper to see where he would like to go. She could decide that, and she would soon enough when she had washed up. For a week or two, she would be feeling rich and would be bringing out all sorts of plans. If by the end of this night she had not thought of twenty different ways of getting rid of a good deal more than an extra pound or so a week, he would be surprised. She had a weakness for hire purchase schemes, to begin with, and he detested them, both as a man of business and a careful householder. Well, after the first excitement had gone he would have to put his foot down; no more of these fairy tale views of life; somebody had to do the thinking. Now his thoughts took on a sombre colouring. He had never envied the rich their luxurious pleasures; he was a simple chap, and their way of life seemed to him ridiculous; he did not want a great deal for himself; but what he did want—and for this he was prepared to envy anybody—was security, to know that decency and self-respect were his to the end of his days. To be safe in his job while he was fit for it, and after that to have a little place of his own, with a garden (he had never done any real gardening, but he always found it easy to imagine himself doing it very well and enjoying it) and a bit of music whenever he wanted it—that was not asking much, and yet, for all the firm's increased turnover and its rises, he could not help thinking it was really like asking for the moon.

"'Lo, Dad," cried George, entering briskly. "How's things?"

"Pretty good, boy. How's the car trade?"

"Not so dusty. You don't know anybody who'd like to lend me sixty quid, do you, Dad?"

"I don't," replied Mr. Smeeth very decidedly.

"Pity," said George, who showed no signs of disappointment. "If I could put my hand on sixty quid this minute, I could make money. A cert. Sounds like horse racing, doesn't it, but it isn't——"

"And I should hope not," said his father, looking at him severely.

"Second-hand car deal. Money for nothing. Ah, well—you wait a bit."

"Well, you be careful, with your money for nothing."

"Leave it to me, Dad," said George coolly.

Mr. Smeeth looked wonderingly at him. It seemed only yesterday when he was filling his stocking and putting the Meccano set by the boy's bedside. And now—leave it to him, sixty quid, a cert! Mr. Smeeth took his pipe out, stared at it, and then whistled softly.

v

"Come along, Dad," cried Mrs. Smeeth, pouring out the Rich Ruby Port for the ladies. "Buck up. Join in the fun." She had herself a rich ruby look, for what with eating and drinking and shouting and laughing and singing, her face was crimson and almost steaming.

Unfortunately, Mr. Mitty overheard her. "That's right," he roared, drowning every other voice in the room. "Come on, Pa. Take your turn. No shirking. Take your turn, Pa. Show us a conjuring trick."

"Oh, shut up, Fred," Mrs. Mitty screamed, pretending to chide him, as usual, and really drawing attention to his astonishing drollery. "You've gone far enough."

Mr. Smeeth could not do any conjuring, but if he had been given unlimited powers, he knew one trick he would have liked to perform that instant, a trick that involved the immediate disappearance of Mr. Fred Mitty. It was Saturday night, the little party was in full swing, and they were all in the front room, all, that is except the Mitty girl and Edna, who had gone out together for an hour or so, probably round to the pictures. In addition to the Mitty pair, there were Dalby and Mrs. Dalby (whose sister told fortunes with cards). Mr. Smeeth had seen the room when it had had more people in it, but he had never known it when it had seemed so full. He had always thought of Dalby, who lived at 11, Chaucer Road, was a bandy-legged insurance agent, and fancied himself as a wag and a

great hand at parties, as a noisy chap, but compared with Fred
Mitty he was quiet and decent and merely another Smeeth. It had
not taken Mr. Smeeth ten minutes to discover that he disliked Mitty
intensely, and every thing that Mitty had done and said since (and
for the last hour or so he had insisted on calling Mr. Smeeth "Pa")
had only increased that dislike, which did not stop short at Fred,
but extended to Mrs. Mitty and the girl, Dot. He had never known
three people he had disliked more.

Mrs. Smeeth's cousin was a fellow in his early forties who had
probably not been bad-looking once in a cheap flashy style. He had
curly fair hair, very small, light-coloured greedy eyes, a broken nose,
and a large loose mouth that went all out to one side when he
talked. He reminded Mr. Smeeth at once of those cheap auctioneer
chaps who take an empty shop for a week or two and pretend they
are giving everything away. Mr. Mitty's complexion seemed to be
permanently rich and ruby, and it had evidently cost somebody a
good deal in its time, though—as Mr. Smeeth assured himself,
vindictively—not necessarily Mr. Mitty himself, who clearly brought
out visiting with him a colossal thirst and appetite. He was a funny
man, a determined wag, and the noisiest Mr. Smeeth had ever
known. He shouted all the time, just like one of those cheap auc-
tioneers. His jokes gave you a pain in the stomach and his voice
a headache. Moreover, he seemed to Mr. Smeeth quite obviously a
silly boaster, a liar, and a man not to be trusted a yard. Such men
frequently ally themselves to quiet little women, but Fred Mitty—
fortunately for some quiet little woman—had found a female of his
own kind. Mrs. Mitty, who had a long blue nose and hair that was
bright auburn at the ends and grey-brown near the roots, was as
brassy as her husband. Her scream accompanied his roar. If she
said anything playful to you, she hit your nearest rib with her bony
elbow; and if you said anything playful to her, she slapped you on
the arm. Here she differed from Fred, who banged you on the back
and poked you in the ribs, unless you were a woman and not too
old, and then he hugged you or invited you to sit on his knee. Dot,

the solitary offspring of this brassy pair, was about Edna's age and was all legs and golden curls and a hard blue stare. She talked of becoming a film actress. Mr. Smeeth, who did not know much about Hollywood, but nevertheless had a horror of the place, told her quite sincerely that he hoped she would get there, and added, with perfect truth, that she reminded him of those Broadway girls on the pictures. Edna of course—the silly child—had been fascinated at once by Dot; and as for Mrs. Smeeth, who really had no more sense about people at times than a baby, she seemed to be infatuated with all three of them.

"Will you have a little port wine, Mrs. Dalby?" said Mr. Smeeth, who felt that he must do something.

"Just the tiniest, weeniest sip, Mr. Smeeth," she replied. And when he had brought her the Rich Ruby she continued, "Lively to-night, aren't we?"

"Very," he told her.

She gave him a quick look. "Well, it's nice to see people enjoying themselves. But you look a bit tired to-night, Mr. Smeeth."

"Oh, I don't know. Do I? Feel all right, y'know, Mrs. Dalby." Did he feel all right? What about that little tick-tick of pain somewhere inside him? "I've been working hard just lately. We've been busy, for once."

"You're inside all the time, aren't you?" said Mrs. Dalby seriously and sympathetically. "And that's what tells on you. Tom works very hard—though you wouldn't think so, to hear him talk—but he's out most of the time, on his round, you know, and so it's not so bad for him, unless we get a spell of nasty damp weather and then he begins to feel it in the chest. He's had chest trouble before."

"Has he really?" said Mr. Smeeth. This was not a very cheerful conversation, but nevertheless it pleased him. Mrs. Dalby was a nice, quiet, ladylike sort of woman, and talking to her in this company was like having a few words with a sane person in a madhouse.

"That's right, Fred," Mrs. Smeeth shouted. "Do help yourself."

"Trust me!" roared Fred, who was pouring himself out some whisky. Yes, there was a bottle of whisky, as well as some beer and the Rich Ruby. So far as Mr. Smeeth could see, half the week's housekeeping money must have been spent on this racket.

"Yes, trust '*im*," screamed Mrs. Fred, putting down her empty glass. "If you don't take that bottle away from him, he'll have it all before you know where you are."

"Ah like ma droap o' Scoatch, d'ye ken," Fred bellowed in a very hoarse voice and in what he imagined to be a Scots accent. "Wha' day ye say, Meesees Macphairson? Hoch aye!"

"Oh, stop it, Fred," cried his wife.

"Good as a turn, you are, Fred," said Mrs. Smeeth admiringly.

"Reminds me of the chap from Aberdeen," Dalby began. But it was no use. It was not his evening.

"There was a Scottie I knew in Brum," Fred shouted.

Mrs. Fred let out a piercing shriek. "Oh, yes, tell 'em about him." Fred did, but Mr. Smeeth, by a tremendous effort, contrived not to listen, although Fred's voice more than filled the room. Indeed, there was so much of it that it was possible not to take it in properly. Mr. Smeeth thought about other things, and paid no attention until he suddenly discovered that he was being addressed.

"Yes, do let's have that," cried Mrs. Smeeth, her face very red and her eyes moist with laughter. "Y'know, that one you did the other night for me—that man in Birmingham. Laugh! I thought I'd have died. Dad, you remember me telling you? Do listen to this."

"That's right, Pa," roared Fred, with mock severity. "A little of your attention, please, while I endeavour to give you a slight impersonation of—Mis-ter Snook-um of Brum."

"That wasn't his real name, you know," Mrs. Fred screamed, turning on Mr. Smeeth so that he got the full force of it. "That was the name these chaps gave him. Do it properly, Fred, this time. Dress up for it."

"Shall I? What about it?"

"Yes, go on, do. Like you did that time at Mr. Slingsby's. I'll tell you all about that night in a minute," Mrs. Fred added, with the air of one about to confer a great favour. "That *was* a night. But go on, Fred."

"All right," replied Fred, noisily finishing his whisky. "I will—by special request."

"Looks as though we're going to have a performance," said Dalby, not very pleasantly. There had been rather too much of Fred for his taste.

"That's right," Fred shouted at him, not too pleasantly either. "Any objections?"

"Hurry up, Fred," cried Mrs. Smeeth beaming at him. "We're all waiting."

"Allow me one minute in which to change my costume," Fred replied, "and I will oblige." And out he went, and the others were moved about to allow a clear space near the door, and Mrs. Dalby and Mrs. Mitty were pressed to take a little more of the Rich Ruby or to have a sandwich or a piece of cake, and Mrs. Dalby had a sandwich and Mrs. Mitty, whose long nose was a much deeper shade of blue than it had originally been, accepted another glass of the Rich Ruby.

"I ought to tell you that this chap he's going to take off," Mrs. Fred explained to them, "was a chap Fred had some business dealings with in Birmingham. He owned one of the picture theatres there. He wasn't a bad sort of chap really, but he was an absolute comic— didn't mean to be, y'know, didn't know he was funny—but he *was*, and Fred and the other fellows used to make game of him. To start with, he always talked, you see, with his mouth on one side ——"

"Well, so does Fred," said Mr. Smeeth, bluntly and boldly.

"Now, Dad," cried Mrs. Smeeth, "how can you say that!"

"That's right, Mrs. Smeeth," said Dalby. "He does talk with his mouth on one side. I noticed it myself. Just a habit, you know. Easy to get into. Probably you never notice it now," he remarked considerately to Mrs. Fred. "You've got used to it."

"Oh, that's quite different," she said stiffly. But she did not continue with her explanation. "Wait till he comes in. You'll see what I mean."

What Mr. Smeeth did see when Fred came in was that Fred was wearing his best overcoat and hat. He must have chosen these things because they were obviously too small for him and so added to the comic effect. The coat was strained across his shoulders, and the hat, a good grey soft felt, which Mr. Smeeth only wore at the week-end and for special occasions, had been jammed on his head and punched in at the top in a horrible manner. Mr. Smeeth was so annoyed he could hardly sit still.

"Good evening, you people," said Fred, speaking in a queer voice and throwing his mouth round to the other side. "I'm Mister Snookums of Brum, and I'd loike you to understand that I'm the propreeotor of the Luxydrome Peecture Palaice, situated in one of our main thoroughfares of the city and built ree-gardless of expense. Hem!" Here Fred coughed in a silly way, with a quick movement of one hand to his mouth, a movement that nearly split the seams of the overcoat. His wife and Mrs. Smeeth shrieked with laughter; Dalby and his wife smiled; and Mr. Smeeth merely looked glum. This went on for several minutes, at the end of which, Fred, in a frantic attempt to capture the whole audience, was shouting at the top of his voice, nearly bursting the overcoat, and punching the hat out of any recognisable shape. At last, Mr. Smeeth could stand it no longer.

"Just a minute," he said, advancing upon Fred. "I'm sorry to interrupt, if you've not finished. But, y'know, that's my hat, my *best* hat—when you've done with it." And he held out his hand for it.

"All right, old sport," said Fred, giving it to him and resuming his normal appearance. "No damage done. And ber-lieve me, people," he added, mopping his brow, "that's nearly like work. Yes, I think I will, Cousin Edie." And he made for the whisky.

Edna and Dot returned now from the pictures. It was Dot's turn to entertain the company. "Oo, I say," she cried, like a suddenly galvanised doll, "oo, I say, you oughter see Ducie Dellwood in this picture we've just seen. A college girl, what they call over there a co-ed."

"I thought she was sorful," said Edna. "Didn't you, Dot?"

"I didn't like her much. This was her. Watch me, everybody. Just watch me a minute. This was her." And Dot, after screaming everybody into attention, began jazzing about and rolling her eyes and flinging herself into a chair and then jumping out of it again. "That song's in this picture, mother," she gasped. "You know— what is it?—*It's Necking or Nothing Now*—and Ducie Dellwood sings it—like this." She stood facing them with her legs apart and knees bent, crooked her elbows, spread out her fingers, then swayed as she sang, or tried to sing in a little nasal voice, what she remembered of the song. Mr. Smeeth, after noticing that Edna was regarding this performance with open admiration, told himself that in spite of the fact that he was a quiet and good-tempered man, he would dearly like to get up and give this Dot girl a good box on the ears and then pack her off to bed.

"Well, I really think we'd better be getting along now," said Mrs. Dalby.

"Yes, time to be off," said her husband.

"No, don't go yet, Mrs. Dalby," cried Mrs. Smeeth.

"The night is yet young," roared Fred. "I thought you London people kept it up till all hours. Why, up in Brum, when a few of us got together, some of the bo-hoys and some of the ger-hirls, we used to be settling down to it now, I give you my word."

"And how much longer does he think he's going to stay here?" Mr. Smeeth asked himself bitterly, as the irrepressible Fred went roaring on. Mrs. Dalby was firm about going and edged towards the door, smiling at her hostess; Dalby followed her and when they did finally go, Mr. Smeeth, glad to escape even for a minute or two, saw them to the door. The night was beautifully dark and quiet, delighted in its entire lack of Mitties.

"Lively card, all right," said Dalby, as they halted a moment.

"A bit too lively for me," said Mr. Smeeth in a low, confidential tone. "A little of him goes a long way, it seems to me. Mrs. Smeeth's cousin, y'know," he added, disclaiming all responsibility.

"Well, to be quite truthful, Mr. Smeeth," Mrs. Dalby declared, "I must say I thought the way they allowed that girl to carry on was ridiculous. My words, if she'd been a girl of mine ——!"

"Or mine," said Mr. Smeeth grimly.

"Still, we've had a very enjoyable evening, haven't we, Tom?" said Mrs. Dalby, who had plainly had nothing of the kind but was a polite woman.

After they had said good night, Mr. Smeeth remained at the door for a few minutes, enjoying the quiet and the cool fresh air. When he returned to the others he made straight for the fire and raked it together with the poker, but did not put any more coal on it. Then he yawned once or twice, and did not try very hard to pretend he was not yawning. Ten minutes later, he told Edna to get upstairs to bed, pointing out very firmly that on any other night she would have been there some time. There were signs then, after Edna had reluctantly and with much wriggling of shoulders taken her departure, that the Mitty family was about to go, but unfortunately George made his appearance and that kept them another half-hour, towards the end of which Mr. Smeeth merely stared at them in despair. When they did go Mrs. Smeeth and George saw them to the door, and Mr. Smeeth stayed where he was.

Somehow the room looked as if fifty people had been eating and drinking and smoking in it for days. There were two sandwiches and a flattened cigarette end on the carpet; somebody had spilled some port on the little table; there was the glass that Fred had broken; there were the forlorn bottles, the dirty glasses, the remnants of food, the cigarette ash, the smoke rapidly going stale: the whole room, the pride of the house and as nice a parlour as you would find in the length of Chaucer Road, looked tipsy, bedraggled, and forlorn, and as its disgusted owner wearily moved about, throwing bits of stuff into the fire and straightening things, he felt as if the Mitty crew had left their sign and mark on it for ever. He threw open the windows and was just in time to hear from outside the last good nights.

His wife came in. "George has gone to bed," she announced. "I was telling him he seemed quite struck with young Dot."

Mr. Smeeth grunted.

She followed her usual practice on these occasions, sitting down by the fire with a last sandwich, prepared for a cosy little gossip about the evening. "I'm not going to touch a thing to-night. It'll have to wait until the morning. Well, well, I must say I've enjoyed myself to-night; whether other people have or not." For a moment her face was alight with reminiscent mirth, that pleasant afterglow of jolly evenings, but it died out as she looked at her husband. "But I must say, too, Dad, I never saw you in such a mood. I expect you thought I wasn't noticing you, but I was. Couldn't help it. Quite grumpy you were, half the time, and downright rude, if you ask me, once or twice. Fred's wife noticed it, too."

Mr. Smeeth mumbled something to the effect that he did not much care what Fred's wife noticed.

"Perhaps you're tired. Are you, boy?" she said, her manner changing. "I thought once or twice you looked tired, and Mrs. Dalby told me *she* thought you were looking a bit tired to-night."

"I expect I am," said Mr. Smeeth.

"Ah, well, that's different, isn't it, when you're tired and you don't feel in the humour for it? Never mind, next time I expect you'll be ready to join in the fun. They've asked us all down for one night next week—they'll let us know which night—to meet some people they know who used to be in Birmingham, too."

"Well, I hope you told them I wasn't going."

"Of course I didn't, Dad. The very idea!"

"Well, I'm not going."

"Why, what for?"

"Because I'm *not*. If you want to know," Mr. Smeeth added, his voice trembling, "I've had quite enough of 'em here to-night, without going to look for some more."

His wife looked at him indignantly and sat up straight. "That's a nice way to talk, isn't it? What harm have they done you? It's not Fred's fault—or his wife's fault—if you didn't enjoy yourself to-night."

"It is. If it's not their fault, whose fault is it?" Mr. Smeeth retorted. "I can't stand him—and I can't stand his wife—and I can't stand that jazzing girl of theirs either. And the less Edna, or George, for that matter, sees of that little ——"

"Now just you be careful what you're saying," cried Mrs. Smeeth. "You'll be saying something in a minute you'll be sorry for afterwards. Now, Dad, you're tired to-night, and I expect they were a bit too noisy for you. Fred does get noisy when he gets going, I'll admit. But you'll feel different about it in the morning. Let's go to bed."

"All right. I'm ready. But understand this, Edie. I'm not going down to Fred Mitty's this next week or any other week. If you want to go, I can't stop you, and if you want to ask them here again, I suppose I can't stop you—though if he starts coming here regularly, drinking the amount of whisky he drank to-night, I'm going to have something to say. But he doesn't see *me* again for a long time, I can tell you that."

"The way you talk!" said Mrs. Smeeth on her way to the door. "But I'm not going to argue with you to-night. I'm tired myself and I'm sure you're so tired you don't know what you *are* saying. I'll leave you to lock up, Dad."

No doubt he *was* tired. He was still trembling a little as he went round, turning off the lights and seeing that both outside doors were locked and bolted; but his mind was made up on the Mitty question. There is a certain pleasure in making up your mind, putting your foot down, taking a firm stand, especially if, like

Mr. Smeeth, you do it very rarely, not being a wilful or autocratic man; and as he walked along the dark little hall and climbed the stairs, Mr. Smeeth experienced that pleasure, and the hand that he placed on the banisters was that of a strong determined man, the natural head of a house. Yet even before he had reached the bedroom door there was mixed with that pleasure, absorbing it gradually, an uneasiness, a faint foreboding, a sense of worse things to come.

Chapter Seven

ARABIAN NIGHTS FOR TURGIS

I

"Yersh," said Mr. Pelumpton, staring at Turgis and pulling hard at his little pipe, which replied with a sickening gurgle—"yersh, that'sh what you want, boy, shome short of 'obby, to parsh the time—shee?"

"That's right," cried little Mrs. Pelumpton, sitting down but only on the edge of the chair to show that this was a mere breathing-space in the long battle with beds and stairs and dirty plates and potatoes and legs of mutton. "You oughter get out of yourself more, Mr. Turgis—if you catch my meaning. That's what you're telling him, isn't it?"

"Yersh," said Mr. Pelumpton, who was busy now poking at his pipe with a very large hairpin.

"Oh—I dunno," said Turgis, vaguely and mournfully.

"Look at Edgar," Mrs. Pelumpton continued. "What with 'ar-riering—y'know, a lot of 'em all running together, miles and miles, and not as much on as you might go in the water with if you was at the seaside—though he 'asn't done much of that lately——"

"Don't blame him," Turgis muttered, shuddering. The last thing on earth he wanted was to be a harrier, who not only ran and ran until he nearly dropped but also contrived to look silly. Ugh!

"What with that and now these racing dog dirt tracks——"

"Hear that," Mr. Pelumpton broke in, pointing a derisive pipe-stem, "d'hear that, Mishter Turgish? Dog dirt tracksh! That'sh a good one. You've got it wrong, Mother. Nobody'd pay to shee a dog dirt tracksh; you can shee them any time, outshide in the shtreet. Plenty of 'em round 'er. That makesh me laugh, that doesh." And to show that it did, he cackled a little.

"It wouldn't take much to make you laugh. But you know what I mean?" and she turned to Turgis.

"Greyhound racing."

"That's right," cried Mrs. Pelumpton triumphantly. "He goes to see 'em once or twice a week—never misses—and though it costs money——"

"Yersh," said Mr. Pelumpton. "Think it doesh. It'sh a betting bishnish—shame ash 'orsh racing, a betting bishnish."

"Oh, is it?" Mrs. Pelumpton was thoughtful. "Well, that's not as good as it might be, is it? I don't want Edgar starting with them betting tricks—two to one each way and all that. Never any good came of *that*, in *my* opinion."

"A mug's game," said Turgis, with the air of a rather gloomy man of the world.

"I thought they just went to see the dogs run about, just a bit of fun," Mrs. Pelumpton continued, dubiously. Then she brightened. "But I can trust Edgar to behave and not do anything silly."

"Yersh, yersh. Matter of a bob or two, that'sh all. The boy'sh all right. Mindjew, for *my* part, I never cared for thish betting game, neither 'orshesh or anything elsh. Wouldn't touch it. Fellersh 'ave shaid to me, 'You put all you've got on sho-an'-sho—it'sh a shert,' —but I've told 'em, 'No.' Matter of prinshiple, shee? I don't want the bookiesh' money and they're not going to 'ave my money. What I've made," Mr. Pelumpton added, apparently under the impression that he had made whole fortunes in his time, "I've honeshtly earned. There'sh quite enough gambling in the dealing bishnish for me, quite enough."

"Well, I'd rather see Edgar going up there, even if it means he's putting his shillings on now and then," said Mrs. Pelumpton, getting up, "than see him going round the pubs. That's an expensive 'obby, if you like. And you can't say you've never had a try at that,

Dad. If you ever had any principles against the publicans 'aving your money, all I can say is they never took you very far. What you've honestly earned you've mostly honestly spent, too." And Mrs. Pelumpton waddled into the kitchen.

"Yersh," said Mr. Pelumpton, completely ignoring his wife's speech and now fixing Turgis with his watery stare, "quite enough gambling in the dealing bishnish for me. Now here'sh an inshtansh."

"Oh, blow you and your instances!" Turgis cried to himself.

"Chesht o' drawersh going up in Holloway and I'm requeshted to 'ave a look at it. Very pretty piesh, very pretty piesh. Worth money, that piesh. I'm tellin' you now what I thought, at the time. I went back and shaw Mishter Peek an' tellsh him that piesh'sh worth a ten pound note if it'sh worth a penny. 'Go back,' he shaysh, 'and go right up to sheven if nesheshary.' I go back and thish piesh'sh gone. Old Craggy up the road there had bought it—'ad to pay sheven too—an' I could have kicked myshelf. Well, that'sh what?—oh, eight munsh, ten munsh, a year ago. All right. I'm looking round in old Craggy'sh the other day and what do I shee—the very shame piesh. I shaysh to 'im 'I know that piesh' and I told him 'ow and why I did know it. Then I shaysh to him, 'What you wanting now for that piesh?' An' what do you think he shaid?"

"Fifty pounds," said Turgis promptly. He had heard this type of story many, many times from Mr. Pelumpton.

"Now that'sh jusht where you're wrong, boy," cried Mr. Pelumpton, delighted. "Jusht where you're wrong. Not fifty poundsh but *five* poundsh, two lesh than he'd given for it. Couldn't get rid of it—shee?—and had pulled it down and down—and I give you my word, I believe I could have 'ad that piesh from him for *four*—he was sho shick of sheeing it about the shop. And I'd have bought it for sheven, sho would Mishter Peek, sho would you, sho would anybody. It jusht showsh you. The dealing bishnish ish a gamble."

"If you ask me," said Turgis, all gloomy and profound, "it's all a gamble."

"Well, don't loosh 'eart, boy, don't loosh 'eart. Take a ninterest in thingsh like I do. Shtart a nobby ——"

"What's your hobby?" asked Turgis, not too graciously. And he immediately gave himself the answer silently, "Finding free beer, you old soak, that's your hobby."

"My work ish my 'obby now," replied Mr. Pelumpton very solemnly. "In my time I've 'ad all manner of 'obbiesh, from pigeonsh to joining the volunteersh, but now my work ish my 'obby. It'sh not only my work but my play, ash you might shay. And if you're going to make anything at all out of dealing, if you're going to be a *real* dealer, that'sh the only way to do it—make it a full time job, wherever you are, be on the look-out, keep your eyesh open, your earsh open, turn thingsh over in your mind. If you'd a bit more money, d'you know what I'd shay to you?"

Turgis could think of several things that Mr. Pelumpton would say to him, the very minute he had some more money, but he was certain that not one of them was in Mr. Pelumpton's thoughts at the moment. So he merely shook his head.

"What I'd shay to you ish—shtart collecting. In a shmall way, y'know, to begin with. Doeshn't matter what you collect. And I'd put you on to thingsh. That'sh where you'd be lucky 'cosh you'd 'ave the benefit of my experiensh and knowledge of the trade."

Turgis did not think he would care very much for collecting, and Mrs. Pelumpton, returning at that moment, wiping her hands on an apron, said that she didn't think of collecting either. "Just wasting your money and littering the place up, that would be," she added. "So don't you go and put ideas into his head, Dad. I'd sooner see you taking an interest in these politics, same as Mr. Park."

"You know what he ish, Mishter Park?" said her husband. "He'sh a Bolshie, that'sh what he ish."

"Well, it keeps him quiet enough," Mrs. Pelumpton retorted. "And sober, too. Never makes any noise or trouble. Nobody will make me believe he's a real Bolshie, a nice quiet young chap like that. And he's never been to Russia, never once set eyes on it. He told me so himself."

"That doeshn't matter," said Mr. Pelumpton.

"What does matter then?" asked Mrs. Pelumpton triumphantly.

No doubt her husband could have told her, but he did not choose to; he merely made a contemptuous noise, and then took up the evening paper. Turgis decided to go to bed. It was not late, but there was nothing to do. He was tired of talking to the Pelumptons, though he felt vaguely grateful to them, or at least to Mrs. Pelumpton, for taking an interest in him. What they actually said did not mean much to him—for he did not want any of their silly hobbies and had not the slightest desire to be like either Edgar or Park—but it was pleasant to feel that somebody was interested in him. His father took no interest in him, hadn't done for years, and he had no other near relations. They didn't care much about him at the office. Even Poppy-with-the-fringe had kept away from him lately, and the others simply took him for granted. He had no friends. He was just a chap in the crowd. Nearly all his time away from the office was spent in a crowd somewhere, getting back to his lodgings in the packed Tube, returning to the thronged streets afterwards, perhaps eating in some crowded place, then waiting in a queue to get in a picture theatre, making one of a huge audience, wandering along the lamp-lit pavements, and he was for ever surrounded by strange, indifferent or hostile faces, looking into millions of eyes that never lit up with any gleam of recognition, and spending hour after hour in the very thick of packed humanity without exchanging a single word with anybody. His existence was noticed only when he bought something, when he turned himself into a customer.

And yet, of course, this was not entirely true. There were innumerable people in London who were not only ready to make the acquaintance of Turgis, but were actually longing for him. There were Park's comrades, the communists, who would be only too glad to obtain another recruit; possibly the Socialists; and certainly the Anti-Socialists, who would have been delighted to show him how to mount a soap-box. There were clergymen of all denominations and sects on the prowl for him, willing to lead him in prayer, to instruct him in the Scriptures, to teach him anthems, to show him lantern slides of the Norfolk Broads, to smoke a manly pipe at him, to play a game of chess, draughts, dominoes, bagatelle, or billiards with him, to give him a right hook and then a straight left with the gloves on, according to their varied tastes and dispositions. There were men who were not clergymen, but had the habits and outlook of clergymen, leaders of ethical societies and the like, who would be pleased to talk to him about their own particular universes, lend him a few books, and welcome him twice a week at their philosophical-literary-musical services. No doubt there were criminals who could have made good use of a youth with such a guileless air. There were thousands of other young men in lodgings and offices, young men who were not very clever or strong or handsome or brave or artful, young men who were for ever packing themselves into tubes and buses, eating hastily in corners of crowded teashops, and then using the music-halls, picture theatres, saloon bars, and lighted streets as their drawing-rooms, studies, and clubs, who would soon have been overjoyed, once the mumbling preliminaries were passed, to spend their evenings with Turgis.

But then he did not really want any of these people, did not want company for company's sake. What he really wanted was Love, Romance, a Wonderful Girl of His Own. And these had lately all been assuming the same shape in his mind, that of Miss Lena Golspie. He had never spoken to her, had never seen her except once, at a distance, since that day she appeared at the office, but he had thought a great deal about her. To say that he had fallen in love with her at sight would be to exaggerate. If an attractive girl—and she need not have been anything like so pretty as Miss Golspie—had turned up and had been kind to him, no doubt he would soon have forgotten all about Lena. But no such girl turned up; indeed no girl of any kind appeared. If Lena Golspie was not the prettiest girl he had ever seen (and he could not remember a prettier, not even if he included the beautiful shadow people, Lulu Castellar and the other film stars), she was certainly the prettiest girl he had ever spoken to, and the fact that she had actually made her appearance at the office door in Angel Pavement somehow brought her definitely into his own world. That she was not really a creature of that world only made her more fascinating, mysterious, romantic, like the beautiful heroine of a love story of the films. She was a lovely bird of passage. He imagined her against a background of strange places and fantastic luxuries. It was as if Lulu Castellar had stepped out of the screen, taken on colour and solid shape, and had actually spoken to him, smiled at him. And yet, there it was, her father worked in the very same business, in the very same office, with him. No wonder he could not get the girl out of his head, which for a long time now had been haunted by a vague but infinitely desirable feminine shape. It was vague no longer; it had definite form and features; it had a name.

It had also an address, and Turgis, his wits suddenly sharpened, had contrived to learn it at the office. The Golspies lived 4a, Carrington Villas, Maida Vale, W. 9. He had seen the very house, or rather the upper half of the house, in which they lived. He had, in fact, seen it several times, and had actually been watching when lights were being turned on and off there. Before this, Maida Vale had been for him a mere name, but now he was rapidly becoming familiar with the district, and it had for him a most curious fascination. He had never really decided what he would do if he was lucky enough to run into Miss Golspie. She had been friendly that day she came to the office, though condescending to him, of course, as she had every right to do; but on the strength of that, he did not see how he could very well stop her, perhaps in one of the darkest parts of Carrington Villas, and say: "Do you remember me. I'm Turgis and I'm the clerk at Twigg and Dersingham's. And how are you, Miss Golspie?" And if he wasn't to do that, what was he to do? He did not know, and so left it to the inspiration of the moment. That moment never arrived. He was not very surprised or disappointed. He went across to Maida Vale several nights, not so much because he felt he had a good chance of meeting her there or even of seeing her, but because on these particular evenings every other part of London seemed terribly dreary, and Maida Vale drew him across these desolated spaces like a magnet. He only went when it was fine, and then he took a turn or two up and down Carrington Villas, sometimes stopping near the house to see if anything was happening there (it was a detached house with two pillars before the door and three steps leading up to it, and there was a broken statue in the dingy bit of garden in front), perhaps walked along the street at the top a little way, towards the main road, then did the same at the bottom, had a last saunter along Carrington Villas, perhaps ended up with a glass of bitter at the high-class little pub just round the corner at the top, and went home. The first few evenings he had spent like that he had enjoyed; there was to him something enchantingly mysterious and romantic in the winter-evening gloom of this Maida Vale; as he moved about the quiet streets, a shadow among shadows, he became aware of an intense secret inner life of his own; but the pleasure rapidly decreased. Too often the upper half of the house was all dark, and then of course the whole neighbourhood lost its charm, which was transferred to some other, unknown, part of the city, where she was spending the evening. Probably in the West End, that brilliant jungle, where you might meet anybody, the last person in the world you expected to meet, and where you might miss for ever the one person you wanted to meet. It was in the West End he caught sight of her. He had been to a picture theatre and it was late, and he saw her with her father and another man. Mr. Golspie was shouting for a taxi, and in another moment he had got one and they were gone. But he saw her distinctly, and it was strange seeing her, for though he had thought so much about her, she had almost stopped being real.

He was beginning to mope now, for he was tired of going over to Maida Vale, and yet could not settle down to spend his evenings in the old way, and that was why the Pelumptons, seeing him hanging about and looking vaguely miserable, had begun to give him advice about hobbies. They did not understand, he told himself gloomily, that he wasn't simply another Edgar or Park. But he admitted once again that it was decent of them to take an interest in him, even if they missed the great fact about him—namely, that he was entirely different from Edgar or Park or anybody else they knew. The innermost self of Turgis was always being surprised and hurt by the general ignorance of this simple fact. Having reached his little room, he now did what he had done many hundreds of times before: he examined his face carefully in the tiny cracked mirror to see if there were any signs of this difference written there; and once again he came to the conclusion that there were, only you had to look closely and sympathetically at him, not just give a hard stare and then march off, to notice them.

For once, the little gas-fire did not explode when the match came near and then wheezily complain. It gave only a soft pop and then merely murmured. Its master knew that that meant that the meter demanded another shilling, and as he had not got a shilling and was too lazy to return to the back room for possible change, he let it murmur and sink, until its flames were like tiny blue flowers. Then he did something he had not done hundreds of times before. He began brushing his clothes. Mr. Smeeth had already noticed, as we saw, that Turgis had smartened himself up. We are now behind the scenes of this smartening. It had occurred to Turgis that his next meeting with Lena Golspie, if there ever was one, might easily take place in the office, like the first meeting, and then he realised at once that he would have to take some trouble with his appearance during the day. He went to the length of spending one-and-threepence on a clothes brush of his own. A day or two later, he went to the further length of buying a few collars, very smart soft collars with long points on them, and was quite surprised at the difference they made. Then he had taken to folding his trousers and putting them under the mattress, and had even taken his better pair downstairs once and ironed them. Now, after brushing the coat and waistcoat and doing a little scratching here and there with his penknife, he took these trousers from under the mattress and thoroughly examined them.

He sat down on the edge of his bed, the trousers over his arm, staring at the large hole in the old rug. But he was not looking at the hole, but through it, into Angel Pavement, into the office. Mr. Golspie had just gone away, and now Turgis suddenly realised that that fact was tremendously important. It might mean that there was no chance whatever of Lena coming near the office, now that her father was not there. On the other hand, it might mean just the opposite, that there was a very good chance of her visiting the office, just because her father *was* away. She might want something; she might be in trouble; and Mr. Golspie might easily have told her to come to the office. And now he remembered hearing *something*, something that Mr. Golspie, at the outer door, had shouted to Mr. Dersingham sitting in the private office, a something that had to do with Lena and "you people here," as Mr. Golspie had called them. Turgis knew definitely that Lena was being left behind. Well then, she might call at the office any day. There was quite a chance, anyhow. So there and then, he decided that for the next twelve days or so, while Mr. Golspie was away, he would shave carefully every morning, put on his better suit and wear a clean collar, and have his hair cut at lunch time on the following day. Having thus made up his mind, he felt quite excited, and, as people do, if they have drifted for a long time and then suddenly come to a decision and adopted a programme, he found himself visited obscurely by a conviction that something was bound to happen, just as if by drawing a firm straight line he could compel circumstance to come and toe it.

The gas-fire retired from service with a very sad little pop. He moved and the bed immediately gave a groan. (Everything in the room creaked and groaned and constantly complained. It was tired of people, that little room.) Very carefully he raised the mattress and replaced the trousers underneath. Then, with something like an air of sheer dandyism, he put out an absolutely clean collar for the morning. He went to the little dormer window and stared through the few inches of open space at the dark and the faint glimmer of the town. Here he was, high up above Camden Town, in his own little room. There she was, Lena Golspie, perhaps in *her* little room in Maida Vale, perhaps just above those two pillars he had seen, peering through the open gate, perhaps looking down on that broken statue in the front garden. It made his eyes water, staring there like that, but still he remained. His lips moved. "Listen, Lena," he began; but then stopped. "Listen, Miss Golspie, Miss Lena Golspie. Listen. Do come to the office, do come to the office. And make it something I can do. Turgis, you know, the one you saw that day. Do come to the office."

As soon as he stepped back into the little room, it told him, in its various creaky voices, not to be a damned fool.

"Oh!—you!" he said to it, aloud, and then made haste to undress and get the light out.

II

Turgis kept his word to himself. Every day he appeared at the office all shaved and brushed and as spruce as it was possible for him to be. The others congratulated him and chaffed him and invented the most elaborate reasons for the change. Sandycroft, the tall traveller with the small head, the inquisitive nose, and the extraordinary number of teeth, paid one of his flying visits to headquarters and pretended, possibly at the instigation of Mr. Smeeth, not to know Turgis.

"I say, Smeeth," Sandycroft barked—and he really did bark; it was like having an enormous terrier about the place when Sandycroft arrived—"what's become of that other chap—you know, what's his name—that chap who used to wear the dark brown collars ——?"

"Now who was that, Sandycroft?" said Smeeth, frowning and putting his head on one side. Smeeth was as conscientious and painstaking a wag as he was a cashier. It was not often that he joined in a joke, but when he did he was almost alarmingly thorough.

"You *know* the chap I mean, Smeeth," replied Sandycroft, sniffing with that queer little nose of his. "Never had his hair cut—wore a beard—looked like a Spring Poet in the autumn. Sat at the desk over there," he continued, lowering his voice, "where that smart young feller is. Oh, what *was* his name?"

Here Stanley gurgled and spluttered, not perhaps because he thought this was very brilliant humour, but because he thought comic relief in any form should be encouraged. Miss Poppy Sellers was giggling a little, too, and Miss Matfield smiled at them, not without condescension.

"Oh, don't be so funny," Turgis mumbled, giving Stanley a ferocious scowl.

"That's queer, Smeeth. The same voice—the very same voice."

"I believe you're right, Sandycroft. I believe you're right," said Mr. Smeeth, with the air of a dutiful cross-talk comedian.

"Sure I am," the other barked. Then he stepped forward, with a large polite smile on his face, displaying at least a hundred teeth. "Not Mr. Turgis? Surely it can't be Mr. Turgis?"

"No," said Turgis, who was not very good at this sort of thing, "it's Charlie Chaplin."

"Well, Mr. Charlie Chaplin Turgis," said Sandycroft, "I must congratulate you, I really must. All in favour, show in the usual way. Thank you very much, ladies and gentlemen." And he turned away, grinning.

"Ah, well," said Mr. Smeeth, settling down to his books again, rather as if he had just come to the end of some great gusty epic of humour, "a bit of fun won't do any of us any harm now and again. Here, Stanley, slip round to Nickman and Sons with this and say it's for Mr. Broadhurst—for Mr. Broadhurst, mind. And hurry up, don't take all morning about it. Don't go shadowing somebody all round London."

A week had passed, and though news of Mr. Golspie himself had trickled through into the general office, Turgis had heard nothing about Lena. It seemed as if he was making a fool of himself—and being laughed at by the others for his pains—and he was beginning to feel very disheartened. On two evenings, he had returned to Maida Vale and had hung about the neighbourhood of 4a, Carrington Villas, but had been rewarded by nothing more than a glimpse of a shadow on a curtain. He had been tempted then to walk boldly up to 4a and offer some wild excuse for trying to see Miss Golspie. But he could think of nothing that did not sound insane, and, realising that this crazy step might spoil everything and get him into trouble at the office, he dismissed the notion. The other evenings went very heavily. He had begun to tell himself that he was silly to bother his head about the girl at all, but it was one thing to tell himself that and quite another thing to stop bothering.

Stanley returned, and was sent out again. Mr. Smeeth departed for the bank. Turgis and the two girls worked away quietly; there was not a lot to do that morning. Then Poppy Sellers came over to Turgis with some advice notes she had just typed.

"Are these all right?" she asked.

He looked them over. "Yes, they're all right. You've got into it now, haven't you?" he added, deciding to give her a good word for once. She wasn't a bad kid, really. "Wish I could type as neat as that. I used to have to do it sometimes, before you came, but I used to make a nasty mess of it, I did."

Her sallow little face brightened at once at such praise. But her manner was as perky as ever. "My word! we are coming on, aren't we! What have I done to deserve this? But I say," and here she became more confidential in tone, "you didn't mind what they said —y'know when they were trying to pull your leg. I had to laugh, and I thought you looked a bit mad."

"If it amuses 'em, I don't care," replied Turgis loftily. "Bit silly, I call it, all the same. I don't go round making personal remarks about other people. Matter of fact, I don't mind what old Smeethy says, 'cos he's a decent sort and anyhow it isn't often *he* breaks loose. But I don't like that chap Sandycroft. He's a cocky devil, he is. And, anyhow, he's only just come here—what does he want to be trying to be funny for?"

"That's right," said Poppy, nodding her head. "I don't think much of him, either. Not my style at all, he isn't. Too many teeth, if you ask me. And I don't like them noses that turn up the way his does. If he worked here all the time, he'd have that nose and teeth into everything. I know that sort."

"So do I. We'd a school teacher the very image of him when I was a kid, and he used to try it on with us—oh, what a hope!"

"Mind you," Poppy continued, looking at him a little uncertainly, "you do look diff'rent—smarter, y'know."

"Well, that's nobody else's business but mine," Turgis declared. "What's it got to do with anybody else?"

"Oo, all right, don't jump at me. I only meant—well, you look a lot nicer now. In fact, I think you look very nice."

Turgis did not know what reply to make to this, so he merely grunted.

"You don't mind me saying so, I hope?"

"No, 's all right," he replied awkwardly.

"I say, listen. Are you going anywhere to-night?" She stopped for a moment, but then, before he had time to answer, went on with a rush. "'Cos if you aren't—well, it's like this, my friend—her father's a policeman—and she got two tickets given for the Police Minstrels to-night and now she can't go 'cos she's in bed with the flu and I've got the tickets and I wondered if you'd like to come with me." And she drew a deep breath.

"Well, thanks very much," he stammered, "but—I don't know —you see——"

"Have you fixed up already to go somewhere?"

"Well, I have—*really*——"

"Oh, sorry." Her face fell. She was silent for a moment, then looked up—rather cheekily, he thought—and said, "Going out with your girl, p'raps?"

This annoyed him, just as if she had jabbed at some sore place. "Well, that's my business, isn't it?"

"Oo, sorry, sorry, sorry! Squashed again. I'd better shut up." And she marched away, a compact little figure, and began typing with great vigour and noise. Miss Matfield threw a curious glance at her.

Turgis wondered if he had been foolish to pretend that he wasn't free to go to that entertainment. It would be a lot better than doing nothing. He supposed it was too late to change his mind, particularly now that she had walked off in a huff. He would wish, when the evening did come and he had nothing to do but mope about, that he had accepted her offer. She really hadn't a bad face when you took a good look at it. Yes, perhaps he'd been silly not to accept.

But when the evening did come and he suddenly remembered how he had refused this other engagement, how glad he was! It seemed like fate. And afterwards, when he suddenly remembered yet again how he had refused this other engagement, how sorry he was! And still it seemed like fate.

He and Miss Matfield came back from lunch at the same time that afternoon (Miss Matfield had gone out first, but then she always took quarter of an hour longer than anybody else), running into one another in Angel Pavement, near T. Benenden's. "You know, Turgis," she announced, in that clear hard voice of hers which always rather frightened him, "I do think you're beastly rude to little Miss Sellers."

"Why, what have I done to her?" he demanded.

"I saw this morning you'd hurt her feelings again," Miss Matfield continued. "And why you should, I can't imagine. She's quite a nice child, really, underneath that silly perky manner of hers, and I think she's rather lonely, and you could be quite good friends. You see, she happens to think you're rather marvellous."

"And you don't, Miss Matfield," said Turgis, bold for once with her. "Go on, you might as well put that in properly. I could hear it in your tone of voice."

"I certainly don't think you're at all marvellous," she said coolly. "Why should I? What I do think is that you're being very rude to somebody who is prepared to like you a good deal. And when people really like you," she added severely, "you ought to be specially nice to them and not rude. Now don't say anything to her about what I've just said or I shall be really annoyed."

"All right," said Turgis sulkily, wondering why he couldn't say something sharp to her, for her cool cheek. "But I don't see what I've done to her. She takes offence too quickly, that's it. And whose fault's that? And for that matter, who's ever considered *my* feelings in the office?"

"You're different," she said airily, "or if you're not, you ought to be. You're a man."

Turgis, pleased by this statement that he was a man, but still labouring under a grievance, could do nothing but mumble and mutter, and Miss Matfield, taking no further notice of him, led the way upstairs. The next time he saw Miss Sellers, Turgis looked curiously at her. So she thought he was "rather marvellous," did she? He found himself returning to this, and to her, several times during the afternoon.

But then something happened, something so important that it promptly blew away all thought of Miss Sellers or anybody or anything in that office. Mr. Dersingham, who had only been there long enough in the morning to go through the first post, returned about four to examine the later posts, and he had not been in ten minutes before he sent for Mr. Smeeth. After a short interval, during which one of them telephoned to somebody from the private office, Mr. Smeeth came out, looking fussy, as he always did when he had something special to do.

"Let's see," he said, looking round the office, "does anybody here live Maida Vale way?"

What was this? Turgis's heart jumped and knocked.

"Well, I live in Hampstead and that's roughly the same way," Miss Matfield began, dubiously.

"What is it, Mr. Smeeth?" cried Turgis eagerly. "I know Maida Vale very well."

"Thought you lived Camden Town way?" said Mr. Smeeth.

"Yes, I do, but—er—I know somebody in Maida Vale, often go there. Is it anything I can do, Mr. Smeeth?"

"Yes, I think you'd better have the job, Turgis," said the unconscious Mr. Smeeth, little knowing what effect his words were having. "You see, Mr. Golspie's got a daughter living with him—well, you know that, because she came here one day, didn't she?"

Oh, my gosh!—didn't she!

"She hasn't got a bank account," Mr. Smeeth continued, "and apparently the girl's got through all the money her father left her—these girls, my word, they think we're made of money!—wait till you're a father, Turgis, and then you'll know—and he's arranged with us to let her have some from his account here. She wants it at once, to-day, and we've just telephoned to see if she'll be in, and she will—trust her!—they'll always be in if they get something for it—so somebody had better take it up to her, Mr. Dersingham says. I'd make the young madam wait if I'd anything to do with it," he went on, maddeningly, "because this is only encouraging extravagance, upon my word it is—but Mr. Dersingham says she'd better have it now."

"Well, I'll take it, Mr. Smeeth." Oh, wouldn't he just!

"All right, then. You'd better clear off that work you've got on hand, Turgis, and then when you go, you needn't come back. If you leave here about five, you'll get there about half-past five, and that'll leave her ample time to put in a full evening spending it. I've got the address here all ready."

Got the address! If old Smeethy only knew! Turgis could have banged his desk and sent all his advice notes and bills of lading and railway and shipping accounts flying about the office. He did contrive to clear up a few odd jobs, but he did not do as much work as he pretended to do, for it was impossible to keep his mind crawling there, among the papers, and to prevent it from taking a wild leap now and then. At a few minutes to five, he cleared his desk ruthlessly, so that it looked as if the last crumb of work had been gobbled up. "I'm ready now, Mr. Smeeth," he announced.

"Right you are," said Mr. Smeeth. "I'm putting twelve pounds, twelve pound notes, into this envelope, and it has the name and address on, you see—Miss Golspie, 4a Carrington Villas, Maida Vale. I'll seal that. Now here's a form of receipt I've made out, and you must get her to sign that, so that there's no possible mistake. You understand that?"

Turgis assured him fervently that he did. He was delighted at the receipt idea. Once or twice he had thought what a dismal ending it would be if he merely handed over the money at the door—"Is that the money? Thank you. Good afternoon." But signing a receipt was a different matter; it could not be done properly at the door; you should read a receipt carefully before you sign it; you might want to have it explained; you must ask the messenger in, and then of course he might have a chance to talk. The receipt made it a piece of real business. Good old Smeethy! It was just like him to insist on a proper receipt.

"And you needn't come back, of course," said Mr. Smeeth. "Just pop off home. I'll just tell Mr. Dersingham I've fixed it all up."

"What's all this about?" Miss Matfield asked, as he was taking his overcoat from its peg.

He explained shortly.

"Where do they live?"

"In Maida Vale. 4a, Carrington Villas," he told her.

"I say, listen," cried Miss Sellers, sweeping away her grievance. "If you get a chance of going in, go in, and then tell us what it's like to-morrow. I'd like to know what sort of place Mr. Golspie lives in. Wouldn't you, Miss Matfield?"

Miss Matfield, to Turgis's surprise, for he expected her to be disdainful of such idle curiosity, admitted at once that she would. "I'm rather sorry I didn't ask for the job," she added. "It would be amusing to see what the daughter's like. I have just seen her, but that's all. And I can't imagine what sort of place Mr. Golspie lives in, though it's probably some furnished maisonette they're camping in. Maida Vale's stiff with them."

"Well, I can't fancy that Mr. Golspie having a 'ome at all," Miss Sellers put in. "Seems a 'omeless sort of man to me."

"I'll say 'Good afternoon,'" cried Turgis loudly and cheerfully, and off he went, the money and the receipt form snugly tucked away in the inside pocket of his coat, the best coat he had and all brushed and as natty as you like. Now for Maida Vale, and no hanging about this time, but straight as a shot from a gun through the front gate of 4, Carrington Villas. He hurried out, running down the stairs, in fear of Mr. Dersingham or Mr. Smeeth or Miss Golspie or the gods suffering a change of mind at the last minute and dragging him back to his desk.

III

There was just light enough, and time enough, for him to notice that the broken statue, really a plaster thing, was that of a little boy playing with two large fishes, and that the two pillars were peeling badly. There were two bells, one for 4, the other for 4a. He was careful to press the 4a one. He pressed it several times and altogether waited nearly five minutes, but nobody came. It looked as if she was out, after all. In despair, he tried the bell for 4. Instantly a light was switched on in the hall, and the door—there was only one door for both flats—flung open.

"Is it you here again, young man," cried an enormous woman in an apron, standing there. "Because if it is, I've to give you the mistress's word that she's paying out no more money for the machine because the girl that could work it has left and it's no use to us at all the way we are now, and not another penny will she pay out for it, so take it itself and leave us in peace."

"I don't know anything about your machine," Turgis told her.

"Aren't you the same young man? Well, you're the very image of him."

"I want to see Miss Golspie."

"The young lady above, isn't it? Then ring the other bell, with the *a* on it, and she'll hear it soon enough."

"But I've been ringing it," he explained. "I've rung it about six times."

"For the love of God!" cried the enormous woman, coming out and looking at the bell-push, as if that might explain something. "Haven't they got that bell of theirs ringing yet? Every time it's us, it's really them. Come inside, young man, come inside, or if we stand here talking another minute the mistress'll be raising Cain the way she'll say she's destroyed with the draught. Does she know you're coming at all?"

"Yes, she does," replied Turgis, following her into the hall. "I've been sent to see her on business. It's very important. I hope she's in."

"Ah, she's in, too, because I heard the mistress say she was going to see her. At the top of the stairs you'll see a bit of a door—it may be open and it may be shut—and if you knock on it, you'll make her hear. The servant they have is out to-day because I met her here myself this afternoon, all dressed up and telling me she's to meet her young man, a sailor in the Royal Navy. Up the stairs then, it is, and a hard knock on the door."

Just beyond the head of the stairs, there *was* a door, and it was open a little, so that he could plainly hear the sound of a gramophone playing jazz. He knocked hard. The gramophone stopped abruptly.

It was Miss Lena herself who came to the door. She was dressed in a shimmering greenish-blue, and she was prettier than ever. At the sight of her standing there, solid and real again at last, his heart bumped and his mouth went suddenly dry.

"I've come from Twigg and Dersingham's, Miss Golspie," he announced, stammering a little.

Her face lit up at once. "Oh, have you brought that money?" she cried, in that same queer fascinating voice he remembered so well. "How much is it? Come in, though. This way."

The room was very exciting. It was a big room, but in spite of its size it was full of things. Turgis had never seen, except on the pictures, so many cushions; there seemed to be dozens of them, huge bright cushions, piled up on a big deep sofa sort of thing, stuffed into armchairs, and even scattered about the floor. And then there were gramophone records and books and magazines all over the place, and bottles and tins of biscuits and fancy boxes heaped together on little tables, and then enough glasses and fruit and cigarettes and ash-trays for a whist drive or a social; and all in this one rich bewildering room. It was lit with two big, crimson and yellow, shaded lamps, and it was very cosy and warm; almost too warm, even though it was a cold afternoon, for an excited young man who had hurried there from the bus.

"It's twelve pounds," he explained, "and I have a receipt here that you have to sign."

"Good! I could do with it, I don't mind telling you. I adore having money. Don't you? It's beastly when you suddenly find you haven't got any, and can't go anywhere or buy anything. Oh, I remember you. You're the one I spoke to that day when I called at the office, aren't you? Do you remember me?"

Turgis assured her fervently that he did. He was still standing, awkwardly, with his hat in his hand and his overcoat hanging loose from his shoulders, and he felt rather hot and uncomfortable.

"You seem jolly sure about it," she said lightly. "How did you remember so well?"

"You won't be annoyed with me if I tell you, will you, Miss Golspie?" he said humbly.

She stared at him. "Why, what is it?"

"Well, I remembered you," he replied, gasping a little, "because I thought you were the prettiest girl I'd ever spoken to in all my life."

"You didn't, did you? Are you serious?" She shrieked with laughter. "What a marvellous thing to say! Is that why *you* brought the money?"

"Yes, it is," he said earnestly.

"It isn't. You were just sent here. I believe you're pulling my leg."

"No, I'm not, Miss Golspie. The minute I knew some one had to come here," he continued with sudden recklessness, "I specially asked to be sent—just to see you again." The hand that was still in his overcoat pocket tried to make a sweeping gesture, with the result that his overcoat brushed the top of one of the little tables and emptied a box of cigarettes on to the floor.

"Look what you've done now," cried Miss Golspie, greatly entertained.

"Oh, I'm sorry," muttered Turgis, confused and sweating now with sheer awkwardness and shyness. "I'll pick them up."

"Wait a minute. Take your overcoat off and put your hat down, and then you'll feel much better. That's right. Dump them down there—anywhere. Now you can pick the cigarettes up and you can also give me one of them. Take one yourself." Unsteadily he lit her cigarette, picked up the others, and then lit his own. "Now what about the money?" she continued. "What do I have to do to get it?"

"Only sign this receipt," he explained. "You ought to count it first to see if it's all right."

When they had concluded this little transaction, she said suddenly, "Have you had any tea?"

"No, I haven't," said Turgis promptly.

"Well, I haven't, either. I was too lazy to make it. The maid's out today. Let's have some. Shall we? Most of it's ready on a tray, but I just couldn't bother boiling some water and making the tea. You come and help and then you shall have some. He followed her into the little kitchen, where he filled a kettle and watched it come to the boil while she chattered in a drifting haze of cigarette smoke and languidly produced another cup and saucer and some things to eat. Then, when everything was ready, he carried the tray into the other room and set it down on a low table in front of the fire.

Lena reclined, like a lovely lazy animal, on a pile of cushions, while Turgis, at the other side of the low table, sat in a low, fat arm-chair. It was a wonderful tea. The tea itself was good, for there were little sandwiches and all kinds of rich creamy chocolate cakes and biscuits, all piled up anyhow, like everything in this careless and sumptuous place. And then, far more important than sandwiches and cake, there was Lena herself, so real, so close, so magically illuminated there in the firelight and shaded lamplight. She asked him all manner of questions, beginning with "What's your name?"

"Turgis," he told her shyly.

"What's your first name?"

"Harold," he mumbled. It was years since anybody (anybody, that is, who didn't merely want him to fill up a form) had asked him what his Christian name was. He brought it out with desperate embarrassment, but when it came out, he felt better.

"I don't like Harold much. Do you? Mine's Lena."

"Yes, I know it is."

"It seems to me you know everything about me," she cried, laughing. "You'll be telling me next how old I am and where I was born and all the rest of it. Who do you think you are—a detective?"

This was a good opportunity to be bright and entertaining, so he told her all about Stanley at the office and how Stanley wanted to be a detective and went about "shaddering" people. After which, Lena, who seemed to enjoy Stanley, asked him about the other people at the office.

"You don't like it there, do you?" she said, wrinkling her nose in distaste. "I'd die if I had to work every day in a place like that. So dark and dismal, isn't it? And they call that street Angel Pavement! What a name for it! I nearly passed straight out when my father told me. If ever I have to work for my living, I'd rather work in a shop than in an office like that. I wouldn't mind being a mannequin. Or go on the stage. That would be best of all. I want to go on the stage. I nearly went on when I was in Paris. And a man

wanted me to go in for film work—he said he'd get me a part
right away. Do you think I'd be any good for the films?"

"Yes, I'm sure you would," said Turgis earnestly, all solemn
adoration. "You'd be wonderful on the pictures—like Lulu Castellar
or one of those stars—only better. I'd go anywhere to see you."

If he had thought about it for days, he could not have produced a
speech more calculated to please her than this, because it chimed
with her own innermost aspirations and beliefs. And his solemn
adoration, a change from the usual obvious gallantry, was very pleasant. She smiled at him, slowly, with a kind of sweet deliberation,
and he sat looking at her, silent, intoxicated.

The silence was broken by a sharp *rat-tat-tat*. "Oh, damn!" cried
Lena. "Who's that?" and went out to see. She returned, raising her
eyebrows comically at Turgis, followed by a very strange figure.
It was an old woman who looked like a dressed up and painted
witch. She had an enormous nose, hollow cheeks, deeply sunken
eyes, but, nevertheless, her face had the pink and white colouring
of youth. This was because it was thickly painted, and when it
caught the light, it shone, just as if it was enamelled and varnished.
She was wearing, above a purple dress, a gigantic yellow shawl with
a pattern of scarlet flowers on it, and she glittered with brooches,
necklaces and rings. Never in his life before had Turgis been in
the same room with anybody as fantastic as this old woman, and
suddenly he felt frightened. For a second or so, he even forgot about
Lena, and simply wished he was not there, wished he was somewhere familiar, sensible and safe. It was a queer moment, and he
remembered it long afterwards.

Lena introduced him, in an off-hand, slap-dash fashion, so that he
never caught the name of this extraordinary visitor. All he knew
was that it was something foreign; and he guessed that she was the
woman who lived downstairs, the mistress mentioned by the fat
Irish cook, or whatever she was who had admitted him into the
house.

"No, no, no, my dee-air," cried the old woman in a cracked foreign voice, "I'll not stay at oll, onlee one seengle minute. I haf asked my nephew and hees vife and hees friend from de Legation to com' to me to-night because I am again in vairy great troble. Yes, yes, yes, yes, yes—in vairy, vairy great troble again. Dere ees no end of eet." At this point she sat down, shot out a claw-like hand and took a cake, and promptly gobbled it up. Turgis stared at her, fascinated.

"What's the matter?" asked Lena, trying to sound concerned, but obviously ready to giggle at any moment.

"Aw!" cried the old woman, repeating this "Aw" a great many times and wagging her head as she did so. "My daughtair again, *of course*—need you ask? Always de same—onlee a deef'rent troble." She swooped down upon a cigarette, and popped it in her mouth and lit it with uncommon dexterity. After blowing a cloud of smoke in Lena's direction, she resumed: "I haf com', my dee-air, for two t'ings. First, here are de plomss I said to you I would geef you. No, no, no, no. Dey are noding, noding, noding at oll. Steel, dey are vairy, vairy nice plomss." Apparently these plums were in the little box she now handed to Lena. "Next, I ask your fadair, Meestair Colspie—does he say ven he com' back 'ere?"

"He didn't say exactly," said Lena. "I don't think he quite knows yet. But it ought to be some time next week. Perhaps you know, do you?" And she looked at Turgis.

"That's all I've heard, Miss Golspie," replied Turgis, very conscious of the fact that the old woman was staring at him. "We expect him back some time next week."

"No, no, no, no. I should like to ask your fadair about dees troble for my daughtair—dat ees oll—and eenoff! Aw yes!—eenoff. My nephew's friend from de Legation, he may do somet'ing. Eef not, I ask your fadair next veek." She threw her cigarette into the fireplace, and got up from her chair surprisingly quickly. "Aw, my dee-air, dat ees a nice, a vairy nice dress you 'ave on now. Aw yes, eet ees." She ran a be-ringed claw over some of it. Then she looked at Turgis, who immediately wished she wouldn't. "Eesn't eet a nice dress, eh? You t'eenk so?"

The embarrassed Turgis said it was.

"She ees vairy preety, Mees Colspie? Aw, yes—loffly, you t'eenk, eh?"

"Yes, I think she is," replied Turgis, after clearing his throat.

"You are in loff wit' her, eh?"

These foreigners! What a question to put to a chap? What had it got to do with her, the nosy old hag? He made some sort of noise in his throat, and it was enough to stop her staring at him and to set her moving towards the door, chuckling just as if she was a witch. "The young man ees afraid of me. He ees in loff. Geef 'im a plom, dee-air."

When Lena came back, after closing the outer door behind the old woman, a new feeling, of friendly ease and lightness, immediately descended upon them both. They were young together. They laughed at the old woman, whom Lena imitated with some skill.

"She's our landlady," she explained. "Not a bad old thing, really —she's always giving me things—but quite cracked, of course. And the daughter she talks about, the one who's in 'troble'—she's some sort of a countess—seems to be completely dippy. Everybody who ever comes downstairs is a bit mad, and they're the only people I've spoken to these last few days, so you can tell the sort of time I've had. It's just my damnable luck!—when my father's away and I could do what I liked—three friends, all three, take it into *their* heads to go away, too, this week. I could have screamed, I've been so bored." She lounged over to the window and looked out. "Looks very thick now. Another fog coming, I suppose. That's the worst of London, all these foul fogs. What shall we do now? You haven't to go home or anything, have you?"

Turgis, looking his devotion, said at once that he hadn't to go home or anywhere.

"Let's go to the movies. We can go to the place near here. It's not bad. Just wait; I shan't be long. Or, look here, you could take these tea things back into the kitchen."

He had taken them all in and had seriously begun to think of washing them long before Miss Golspie appeared again. What he did, when she did appear, was to wash himself in a bathroom that had more towels and bottles and jars and tins in it than all the other half-dozen bathrooms he had ever seen put together. And now they were ready for the pictures.

It was not far, but they had to grope their way through a mist that was rapidly turning into a thick fog, and once or twice Lena put her hand on his arm, and they were cosy together in the blank woolly night, and it was all rather wonderful. It was better still when they were sitting, close, cosier than ever, in the scented and deep rose-shaded dimness of the balcony in the picture theatre. (Turgis had paid for these best seats, and was left with exactly three-and-threepence to take him through the rest of the week.) They were both enthusiastic and knowing patrons of the films, so that they had a good deal to talk about, and frequently as they whispered, her head came close to his and her hair even brushed his cheek. It was tremendously exciting. The chief picture, a talkie —it was *Her Dearest Enemy*, with Mary Meriden and Hunter York —was good stuff, but it was nothing compared to merely sitting in that balcony with Lena Golspie, who, incidentally, was much prettier than Mary Meriden. She herself thought she was just as pretty, but Turgis was sure that she was much prettier, and told her so several times. On this occasion he abandoned his usual tactics. He did not even try to hold her hand. He was content to sit there, to whisper, to be so near to this fragrant dim loveliness, with his hunger, which he had taken into so many picture theatres, momentarily appeased. A dream had come true. He reminded himself of this, time after time, if only because the dream, which had been haunting him so long, was still more real than this sudden actuality. He longed to make everything stand still, knowing only too well that it was all flowing away from him. Every photograph that leaped on to the screen and then leaped away again was nibbling at the evening. Very soon the programme would be completing its circle, and she would be wanting to go, and it would be all over. Turgis felt all this, even if he did not find phrases to express it, so that he was not completely and perfectly happy. He was, as we have seen, a born lover, and a romantic, and what he wanted at heart was not ordinary human happiness, but a golden immortality, a balcony seat high above Time and Change.

"You can come back and have some supper, if you like," said Miss Golspie casually, when they descended into the gloom of Maida Vale again. "You can help me to make it. I'm hungry. Aren't you?"

He *was* hungry, and if she didn't mind, he would like to help her with supper. He could have shouted for joy at the thought that he had not to leave her yet, that the evening was being thus magically extended. All the way back, they talked about pictures and film actors and actresses they liked and disliked, and as there was not really much difference in their points of view, for they both went to the films in search of an amorous dream life and the mere difference of sex only added spice to the discussion, they got on very well indeed. After the fog, the room at 4a seemed richer and cosier than ever, and as Turgis helped to put odds and ends of food, mostly out of tins, on the little table in front of the fire, he felt as if he had wandered into a glorious film.

"Can you mix a cocktail?" asked Lena.

"No," he replied. Cocktails were not a part of real life at all to him, and in a sudden burst of candour he added: "Matter of fact, I've never tasted one in my life."

"Don't be silly," she screamed at him. "You're trying to be funny. You *must* have had."

"I haven't really," he assured her. "I've had beer and whisky and port wine and sherry and all that, but I've never had a cocktail."

"All right, my good little boy," said Lena gaily, "you're going to have one now—one of the special Golspie Smashers."

He watched her take bottle after bottle from the sideboard and then shake a tall silver flask, just as he had seen people do on the stage and in films. "Now just you taste that, Mr. Angel Pavement," she commanded, giving him a little glass. It had a queer flavour, rather sweet at first, then slightly bitter, and ending with a sort of golden glow, which seemed to travel all over him.

"Like it?" and she put her own glass down.

"It's fine."

"Have another then. We'll just have one more and then we'll eat."

After the second one, he felt larger and more important and even happier than he had done before. He insisted upon showing her a trick with three pennies. He knew three tricks, one with the pennies and the other two with cards. The other two could wait; it would not do to show her everything at once. She thought the trick with pennies very smart, and they postponed eating until he had shown her how to do it and she had practised it several times. They were better friends than ever when they sat down to eat the sardines and the two salads in the cardboard jars and the sliced veal loaf and the fruit salad and chocolate cake. Lena ate very quickly and left things and started again on them and pushed them aside and altogether dined in a delightfully fussy extravagant fashion that was quite new to Turgis, who was used to seeing people walk through a meal at a good round pace.

When she had finished eating, Lena lit a cigarette and then darted to the large gramophone in the corner. Having wound it up, she could not find the record she wanted (there seemed to be records all up and down the room), and he had to help her, when she had told him half the name and tried to whistle a bit of it at him. At last they found it, and the gramophone came gloriously to life, filling the room with the lilt and throb of this fashionable tune.

"Can you dance?" she asked him, gliding and twirling to the music.

"Not much," he mumbled, ashamed of himself.

"Well, let's see. Shove that rug back, there. That's enough. Now then." And she came up to him. "Not that way. Like this. That's it. Go on, you can hold me tighter than that."

He could, and he did. If they had been standing still, it would have been a rapturous moment, but though he was delightedly conscious of the body against one arm and of the hand that gripped his, he had to try and dance, and he was very awkward.

"You're ghastly," she told him, with lips that were not four inches from his, "but you'll improve. I've known worse. You've got some idea of the rhythm, and some men never even get that. Now—left —right—left—that's better. Only you're so stiff—put some pep into it. Oh, hell!—the gramophone's stopped. Shove another dance record on and we'll try again."

They tried several times, with an interval during which they had another cocktail each, and Turgis improved considerably, and towards the end was holding her as she wanted to be held, close to him, and had time to enjoy the situation. When they stopped, his arm left her waist reluctantly and she did not seem to resent it. She told him all about the dances she had been to in Paris, and then, having come to the end of them, suddenly yawned. He glanced at the clock.

"Well," he said slowly, "I suppose I'd better be going now."

"All right," she replied, yawning again. "I suppose you had. I'm tired all at once—must be this rotten heavy weather."

"What about all this stuff?" He pointed to the little table.

"Oh, they don't matter. The maid will clear them in the morning. She'll be in soon—unless her sailor boy's persuaded her to stay out all night. And that would be nice for *me*, wouldn't it?—here all night by myself. No, she'll be in soon. I thought I heard her then."

Very slowly, reluctantly, Turgis put on his coat, carefully buttoning it and lingering over every button. While he did this, he stared at her, wondering how he could possibly say what was in his mind.

She, too, had been thoughtful. "Look here," she cried at last. "Have you been to the Colladium this week? Well, I haven't either, and I want to go, and I hate going by myself. If I can get two seats for the first house to-morrow night, will you come with me? I might go down and get them to-morrow afternoon if I feel like it. I want to spend some of that twelve pounds, anyhow."

Would he go? Oh, my gosh!

"All right then," she continued, walking towards the door with him. "Listen. I'll telephone to you at the office some time in the afternoon if it's all right. I'll tell you where to meet me and all that then."

They were standing at the door now, and he was still holding her hand, as if he were about to shake it, but was at the moment too busy trying to stammer out a few adequate phrases. Nor was he merely holding the hand, for, involuntarily, he was pulling it too, so that there was less and less space between them as his little speech floundered on. This made Lena impatient.

"I don't know what on earth you're trying to say," she told him, "so don't bother. And you might as well go now before the girl does get back. And I'll telephone to-morrow. Oh, don't dither so much, silly. There!" And with that she leaned against him, putting a hand on each shoulder, kissed him swiftly on the mouth, drew back, laughed, and then shut the door on him.

Turgis stared at the door, drew a long breath, and then wandered down the stairs and through the hall below like a man drifting drunkenly out of some Arabian Night. He walked up to Kilburn, where he caught a 31 bus that took him most of the way home. The fog was not very thick, but it was wretchedly cold damp stuff that made people shiver and cough and wipe their eyes and blow their noses and look miserable. But Turgis did not care. As he sat gazing at nothing in the bus or marched along the blackened pavements, he was warmed by the fire inside him and cheered by a host of coloured fancies that were rocketing in his mind.

IV

When he awoke next morning, he knew at once that he was in possession of an exquisite secret and was quite different from the Turgis who had rubbed his eyes so often in that little room. He was the chap who had been kissed by Miss Lena Golspie the night before. He was also the chap she was going to telephone to this very day and take to the Colladium this very night. He jumped out of bed and then jumped into the part of this new and splendid chap. The fact that he still looked like the old Turgis, to whom nothing wonderful had ever happened, only made it all the more amusing.

"Another raw morning, my word," said Mrs. Pelumpton, as she handed him his breakfast. "Them's best off this morning who has to stay in. Edgar's been gone these two hours, and a nasty cold job it must be in that station this morning."

"Yes, it must, Mrs. Pelumpton," said Turgis heartily. "I'm sorry for Edgar." And so he was. Edgar would never be kissed by a girl like Lena Golspie, not if he lived to be a thousand. Poor dreary devil!

Old Pelumpton shuffled in, unwashed, blue about the nose, and wearing a greasy muffler. Turgis had seen him like that many times before, but this morning he resented the appearance of this dirty apparition. If Lena Golspie knew that he had to eat his breakfast looking at that nasty old mess, who might have just crawled out of the dust-bin, she would probably never speak to him again.

"No letter, I shee," said Mr. Pelumpton, going to the fire and warming his hands. "That meansh he doeshn't want me to go and shee the shtuff thish morning. I'll go round jusht before dinner and catch 'im in then. That'sh the idear."

"Yes, that is the idea," said his wife sharply, as she bustled about. "Wait till the pubs is open and then catch him in. I know that idea. It's a good idea, that is. If it wasn't for that idea, I don't know why the pubs 'ud ever open at dinner time, 'cos they wouldn't have any custom."

"You hear that," Mr. Pelumpton said to Turgis, who was putting away his breakfast as fast as he could. "Deary me, they've got pubsh on the brain, the women 'ave. If a man shtops in a bit, they want to know when he'sh going to do a bit o' work, an' if he goesh out, then it'sh the pubsh."

"And you don't go in the pubs, do you, Mr. Pelumpton?" said Turgis, with a very marked ironical inflection.

"Oh no! He 'ates them, he does," cried Mrs. Pelumpton. "You couldn't get him to go near one."

"What shome o' you people don't realishe," retorted Mr. Pelumpton with dignity, "ish that the pub may be nesheshary in bishnish. And until you've been in bishnish—a bishnish like mine, I mean—it'sh shomething you don't undershtand. The amount of bishnish transhacted in pubsh, my wordsh——"

" 'Morning, Mrs. Pelumpton," cried Turgis, wiping his mouth and dashing out. What a life the Pelumptons had! It seemed incredible that anybody could find so dingy an existence worth living. Hurrying down to the Camden Town Tube Station, cramming himself into the lift, waiting for a City train, swaying near the doors among a mass of elbows, newspapers and parcels all the way to Moorgate, he hugged his grand secret. When he arrived at the office, he swelled exultantly, for this was where Mr. Golspie gave his orders, and they all knew Mr. Golspie and they had heard about his daughter, but they did not know what Turgis knew. It was a delightful feeling. He wanted to laugh out loud every time one of the others spoke to him or even looked at him. Ah, little did they know!

"You got that receipt all right, did you, Turgis?" said Mr. Smeeth.

It was extraordinary. He had forgotten all about the money and the receipt. But he had the receipt in his pocket, nevertheless, and when he handed it over he found himself swelling again inside, nearly bursting with secret knowledge and happiness.

"Did you go inside?" said Mr. Smeeth casually.

"Yes," replied Turgis. Did he go inside!

"Oo, did you?" cried Poppy Sellers, who missed nothing. "Tell us what it was like? What did you say to his daughter? Is she nice? Tell us all about it—go on."

Not a bad kid, really, though that fringe effect was a distinct mess. And she thought him—what was it?—rather marvellous. (And so *she* ought. Why, if Lena Golspie—oh, well, I-mean-to-say!) Poor kid—a bit pathetic, when you came to consider it. And she had wanted him to go with her to the Police Minstrels last night! And he had half thought of going! Dear, dear, dear!

"Well, Miss Sellers, if you really want to know," he said, "I'll tell you."

"My words, aren't we getting grand!" cried Poppy. "Go on. Very good of your lordship, I'm sure."

"They live in the top half of a detached house," said Turgis, "and the room I went into was a large room, bigger than this office here, and it had all sorts of things in it, and shaded lights and a big gramophone and dozens of cushions all over the room——"

"Did it look like a furnished flat?" asked Miss Matfield.

"I suppose so. I don't know. I don't know anything about furnished flats."

"Well, what about his daughter?" Miss Sellers enquired. "What's she like?"

"I've seen her—for a minute," said Miss Matfield. "She's rather pretty, isn't she?"

"Yes, she is," replied Turgis, keeping a hold on himself. He was bubbling inside.

"Yes, but what's she *like*?" Miss Sellers persisted, staring at him. And when he made no reply, but turned away and pretended to be suddenly busy with some work, she gave him a curious look before she herself turned away too. He never saw it, and if he had seen it, he would not have been interested.

Fortunately, both for him and for Twigg & Dersingham, he was not very busy that afternoon. Otherwise, he might have muddled every consignment of veneers and inlays, and so confused the whole trade that it might not have recovered for a fortnight. The disadvantage of pinning your whole afternoon on a possible telephone call in an office is that the telephone is ringing every few minutes and you are for ever on the jump. Up to three-thirty, Turgis was comparatively calm; from three-thirty to four, he was on the tiptoe of expectation; from four to four-fifteen he was desperate; from four-fifteen to four-thirty he was swaying on the brink of a vast abyss of misery, only to be plucked back by every ring of the bell and then hurled forward again by each unwelcome voice ("And if you ask me," said the girl at Brown & Gorstein's, after making one of these calls, "I think it's time Twigg and Dersinghams just veneered a few manners on. The way they snap your head off!"); and, at four-thirty-five he was sitting staring at a desk in hell, all hope gone, and at four-forty-five he was breathing heavily down a telephone receiver in heaven. Yes, she had got the tickets and would he meet her just inside the entrance to the Colladium at twenty-five past six.

Even now, there was no peace for him. The instant he had put down the receiver he had realized that it would not be easy for him to be at the Colladium at twenty-five past six. Sometimes they did not finish until nearly that time, and indeed, on really busy nights, it was often considerably later. He had to get from Angel Pavement to the Colladium, and if possible he had to have some tea.

"What time do you think we'll be finishing to-night, Mr. Smeeth?" he enquired respectfully.

Mr. Smeeth looked up from his neat little wonderland of figures. "Oh, I dunno, Turgis. Just after six, I suppose. Why, have you got something special on?"

"I've got to be up in the West End at twenty-five past six," said Turgis. ("And if you knew who I'm going to meet, Smeethy, old man, you'd have a fit.") Then he thought for a moment. "Would you mind if I sent Stanley out for some tea for me, Mr. Smeeth?"

"Well, as long as you do it now, before he's busy copying the letters, it'll be all right."

So Stanley was dispatched to the Pavement Dining Rooms for one pot of tea, one buttered teacake, and a bun—total eightpence. "And do I keep the change?" asked Stanley, who had been given a shilling.

"I should think you don't, my lad!" cried Turgis, whose finances were now in a desperate state. The pictures last night had left him with three and threepence; the bus going home had cost him twopence; lunch had been ninepence (it cost him nothing travelling to the office because he had a pass on the Underground); and now, after paying out this eightpence, he would be left with one and eight. On that one and eight, he would have to travel to the Colladium and get home afterwards, and then exist all the next day, Friday. And he had only two cigarettes left. If Lena wanted anything in the Colladium—and he could imagine her asking for chocolates and cigarettes and ices—he was in a hole.

He got away at five minutes past six, after having a very thorough wash-and-brush-up in the little office lavatory, hurled himself into the flood of west-bound travellers, and arrived, breathless and triumphant, under the red glare of the Colladium entrance exactly on time. He had ten minutes in which to cool off before Miss Golspie appeared, wearing a handsome coat with a huge fur collar and cuffs and looking so rich and beautiful that he was almost too shy to talk to her. Their seats were down at the front—Turgis had never sat in such seats before—and it would all have been perfect if it had not been for two little incidents. The first occurred when Lena, during the second turn, a silent juggling affair, announced that she would like some chocolates. "Can you get hold of that girl there," she said. "She always has some nice boxes."

Nice boxes! "How much are they?" he asked her, miserably.

"Well, you are a mean pig! How much are they? I like that, and after I've paid for the seats, too!"

"I'm sorry," he stammered, "but—you see—I've only got one and sixpence." He had paid tuppence on the bus, getting there.

"One and six!" Lena laughed. It was not an unfriendly laugh, but it was not a very sympathetic one either. "That's worse than I was, before you brought that money, yesterday. It doesn't matter, though. I don't know that I do want any chocolates. But would you spend your wonderful one and six if I asked you to?"

"Yes, I would. Of course I would. If I'd," he added, as the curtains swept down on the smiling jugglers, "if I'd hundreds and hundreds of pounds, I'd spend them all if you asked me to. I would, honestly."

"Oh, it's easy to say that," said Lena, not displeased, however, at his fervent tone. She gave him a brilliant glance, and no doubt remarked that his face was flushed and his eyes were at once hot and moist, as if he stared through a steam of embarrassed adoration.

Unfortunately, not all her brilliant glances were reserved for him, and that fact formed the basis of the second disturbing incident. There was a young man, a rather tall handsome chap with wavy hair, who was sitting with a girl in the row in front of them and a little to their right. Turgis had noticed that this fellow was turning round a good deal whenever the lights went up and that every time he did so his glance always came to rest finally on Lena. After this had happened several times he noticed that she was returning this glance. At last, during the interval, he caught her smiling, yes, actually smiling, at the chap. Instantly, he felt miserable, then angry, then miserable again.

He could stand it no longer. "Do you know that chap there?" he asked, trying to appear light and easy.

"Which one? What are you talking about?"

"Well, you keep smiling at him—I mean, that one there, the chap who's just had a permanent wave, by the look of him."

"Oh, the one who keeps looking round. He seems to think he knows me, doesn't he? He's rather attractive, as a matter of fact."

"Well, I suppose as long as you think so, it's all right, isn't it?"

said Turgis bitterly. He could feel a pain, a real pain, as bad as toothache, somewhere inside him. "He doesn't attract me," he mumbled. "If you ask me, he looks a rotten twister—bit of a crook or something." But in his heart he knew that the chap was taller and stronger and better-looking and better-dressed and altogether more important than he was, and he could have killed him for it.

"He doesn't at all," said Lena. Then she laughed and made a face at him. "You're jealous, that's all. And you oughtn't to be jealous, it isn't nice. I'll smile at him again now. I think he's lovely."

When she said that and looked so determinedly in that fellow's direction, Turgis was filled with a desire to take hold of her there and then, dig his nails into her soft flesh, and hurt her until she screamed. He was suddenly shaken with the force of this desire, which was like nothing he had known before. But at that moment this little game of glancing and smiling came to an end, and the person who put a stop to it was the girl with the other man. She turned round too—and good luck to her, thought Turgis—then frowned and said something to her companion, and after that there was no more turning round and Lena divided her attention between the stage and Turgis, who was left in a queer state of mind and body.

"You can come and have some supper again, if you like," said Lena, when it was all over. "The maid wanted to go out again, so I said she could, and if you'd like to come and help me again, you can."

"I should think I would like to," he cried enthusiastically. "And I'm sorry if I was silly—y'know, in there."

"Jealous boy," she said, smiling. "That's what you are, aren't you? Oh, it's cold out here, isn't it. Let's get a taxi. Oh, never mind about your precious one and six—I'll pay. I want to get home quick, out of the cold. Come on. Stop that one, there."

Turgis had only been in a taxi once before in all his life. As he sat close to Lena in the dark leathery interior and saw the familiar crowded streets go reeling past the window, this effortless journey-

ing seemed magical. They were in Maida Vale in no time. It made
life seem at once wonderfully rich and simple. When they entered
the house, they heard a tremendous babble of talk coming from
the lower flat. It sounded as if that fantastic old foreign woman
had summoned all her relations and friends and all their friends
and relations to discuss her "troble." In the room above, there
appeared to be even more cushions, gramophone records, boxes
and bottles than there were the day before. Once more, Lena mixed
some cocktails, and Turgis encountered the queer flavour, sweet
at first, then slightly bitter, and ending with a sudden glow. Once
more, he had a second and bigger one, and found everything enlarged, including himself. Once more, they sat down to supper at
the little table in front of the fire, though this time there was more
luxurious food and it all seemed to come out of little cardboard
containers. They were very friendly over the cocktails and the food,
and Lena, dressed in bright green, a colour that seemed to throw
her red-gold hair and light brown eyes, her scarlet mouth and white
neck, into brilliant relief, was lovelier than ever. It was wonderful.

"Do you know Mrs. Dersingham?" she asked him.

He shook his head. "She came to the office once, and I just saw
her, that's all."

"She's not as pretty as I am, is she? Or do you think she is?"

"Pretty as you!" Turgis gave a gasp, and meant it. "Why, there's
no comparison. She's just ordinary—and you're lovely. Yes, you are,
really."

"You don't mean it. You're just teasing me."

"I'm not," he said, solemnly. Teasing her indeed! A fat chance
he would ever have of teasing *her*. "I've never known any girl as
pretty as you—never seen one—in all my life before—and I never
shall, never, never."

She rewarded him with a smile. Then she frowned. "I don't like
Mrs. Dersingham. I met her once. I loathe her. She's a snob and a
rotten cat."

"Is she?" Turgis didn't care what Mrs. Dersingham was.

"Yes, she is. I hate her. My father doesn't like her either. He doesn't like Mr. Dersingham much either. He thinks he's a fool."

"I don't think he's a bad chap though," said Turgis thoughtfully. "I've never really had much to do with him. But I don't believe he's much good at business. I know the business was in a rotten state just before your father came. Good job for us he did come. I don't pretend to know much about it, but I do know that. Mr. Golspie's clever, isn't he?"

She nodded. "He's always making a lot of money, but he usually spends it all or loses it in some mad scheme. He hates staying in one place long, and if it wasn't for that, he could have made a lot more money and been really rich. But he doesn't care about that. When he wrote to tell me he was coming to London, he said I'd have to come, too, because he was going to stay a long time and make a proper home for us, but now he's here, he says he doesn't like London, and he's going away again soon."

"Is he?" Turgis stared at her. "What—how do you mean 'soon'?"

"Oh, quite soon," she replied carelessly. Then she remembered something. "Look here, I may be wrong, though. And you mustn't say anything to anybody, will you? Promise you won't."

"All right, I won't. But if he went," Turgis continued, regarding her earnestly, "would you go too?"

"Oh, that's it, is it?"

"Yes, it is. You wouldn't be going, would you?"

"I might—pass me a cigarette, will you?—and then again, I might not. It all depends. But, look here, if my father knew I'd been saying anything, he'd be furious, and though he usually lets me have my own way, when he's really furious, he's hellish, I can tell you."

"I'll bet he is," said Turgis, who had never had any doubts about that. "I wouldn't like to see him in a temper."

"What a dreary depressing conversation!" she cried, getting up. "Let's have another drink. Have you ever been tight? I expect you have. I got tight once or twice in Paris, with some Americans. We were drinking champagne and liqueurs all night. I fell on the floor once and rolled under a table and went to sleep for hours and hours. Shove the gramophone on, with something decent on. Then come and have this drink and I'll see if you can dance yet."

They did not dance long, however, for Lena announced that she was too tired and that he was too clumsy. She turned off one of the two shaded lights and went and stood by the fire. He joined her there, standing quite close, trembling a little. He put his arm round her tentatively and when she did not move away, he tightened it. She half turned so that she was lightly pressing against him, and then she lifted her glamorous face, looked at him with huge mysterious eyes, raised her lips to within an inch or two of his, and whispered, "Wouldn't you like to kiss me?"

"Yes," and he made a quick movement.

But she was quicker still, and in a second had broken away from him and was laughing. "Well, you can't then—unless you say you adore me and are madly in love with me and that I'm the most wonderful person you've ever met and that you'll do anything in the world I ask. Now then."

"But you are. Oh, you are," he stammered, all his heart trying to break through. "I've thought that ever since I saw you that day in the office. I've never thought about anything else. I used to come and stand outside this house, hoping to see you again, just to look at you."

"You didn't." There was a faint suggestion of giggling in her voice. "You didn't."

"Yes, I did. Lots of nights. I did, really. Oh, Lena ——"

"Oh, funny boy!" she cried, mocking him. "Well, you can kiss me—if you can catch me."

And she dodged behind enormous armchairs and round the various tables and he went almost blindly after her, until at last she darted across to the big deep sofa thing, and there sank down among the cushions. "No, no," she cried, laughing and breathless, as he came up, "you didn't catch me."

But now he bent over her, clasped her fiercely in his arms, and kissed her hard. When he drew back, she began laughing and protesting again, but in another minute her arms were about his neck and her body was crushed against his and they were kissing again. After a few minutes of this, she pushed him away and sat up, but she gave him her hand and he knelt there, holding it, with great roaring tides sounding in his ears.

"And now you've got to behave yourself," she said, strangely calm.

"Yes," he said humbly, looking up at her. If she had spoken kindly to him then he would have cried.

She smiled at him, and then, leaning forward, rubbed his cheek gently with her other hand. She brought her face nearer his, so that her mouth flamed again in his misty sight, but as he raised his head, she retreated, until at last he sprang up and clasped her to him as fiercely as before, and they were kissing again. For an hour she kept him swaying and lunging and beating about in this wild dark tide, and sometimes he was only gripping her hand and pressing it to his cheek and at other times she was completely in his arms for a few moments, answering his drive of passion with sudden bright flares of her own. And then, strangely calm again, she told him he must go.

Dazed and aching, he leaned against the back of a chair and stared at her with hot pricking eyes.

She looked at herself in the mirror above the fireplace, humming a little dance tune. Then she turned round, met his stare with a slight frown, and pointed out again that he really must go.

He wanted to say all manner of wonderful things to her, but could not find words for them. He tried to put them into the look he gave her. "Can I see you to-morrow?" he said at last.

"Mmmm?" She pretended to look very thoughtful. "Well, perhaps. What do you want to do?"

"I don't mind what it is so long as I'm with you," he assured her, trying to smile, but finding his face all stiff, so stiff that a smile would crack it. "What would you like to do? Can't I take you somewhere?"

"Yes. I'll tell you what. I'd like to see that Ronald Mawlborough talkie, that new one, you know—where is it? at the Sovereign. Isn't that it—the Sovereign? I believe it's terribly crowded, so you'd have to book seats."

"I'll do that if you'll only come," said Turgis stoutly.

"All right. We'll go there, then. And you get the seats, don't forget."

"I shan't forget. What time?"

"Let me see. Oh, I'll meet you just outside at quarter to eight. I believe that's just before the Ronald Mawlborough picture starts, because I looked it up in the paper, this morning."

"Quarter to eight. All right then. And—I say—Lena——"

But she pointed to his hat and coat, and when he had got them on she took his arm and led him to the door. "You can tell me all that to-morrow. But just tell me this. Am I nice?"

"Oh, Lena—you're the most marvellous girl—oh, I don't know what to say ——"

"Don't you, dar-ling?" she replied, laughing at him. She came very close, held up her mouth, drew it back suddenly, laughed again, but finally allowed herself to be kissed.

Turgis was still dazed, still aching, still hot and pricking about the eyes, as he went out into the street and turned to have a last look at the enchanted window above; and desire burned and raged in him as it had never done when he had vainly searched the long lighted streets for an answering smile, had stared at red mouths, soft chins, rounded arms and legs in tube trains and buses and teashops, had felt those exciting little pressures in the darkness of the picture thea-tres, had returned to his little room, tired in body but with a heated imagination, as he had done so many times, to see its dim corners conjure themselves tantalisingly into the shapes of lovely beckoning girls. The flame of this desire was fed from the heart. He was now in love, terribly in love. The miracle had happened; the one girl had arrived; and with this single magical stroke, life was completed. He merely existed no longer; but now he lived, and, a lover at last, was at last himself. Love had only to be kind to him, and there was nothing he would not do in return; he was ready to lie, to beg, to steal, to slave day and night, to rise to astounding heights of courage; all these trifles, so long as he could still love and be loved.

The conductor of the 31 bus, noticing the young man with the rather large nose, the open mouth and irregular teeth, the drooping chin, whose full brown eyes shone as they stared into vacancy, whose face had a queer glowing pallor, might easily have concluded that there was a chap who was sickening for something. But Turgis was alight with love. He sat there in a dream ecstasy of devotion, in which remembered kisses glittered like stars.

v

"Please, Mr. Smeeth," he said, next morning, "could you let me have a pound to-day?"

Mr. Smeeth rubbed his chin irritably. "Well, you know, Turgis, I don't like doing this," he said, fussily. "It's not so much the thing itself ——"

"It's only till to-morrow morning," Turgis pointed out, for the next day, Saturday, was the fortnightly pay day.

"Yes, I know that, and it's a small thing in itself, but it's a bad system. Once you start doing that sort of thing, you don't know where you're going to end. When I was with the Imperial Trading Company, before the war, they'd a very easy-going cashier there, an old chap called Hornsea, and we used to be paid every month. The result was, some of the fellows, particularly one or two of the lively sparks, were subbing all the time and old Hornsea would let them have it out of the petty cash. What happened in the long run? He got let down, badly let down. Now I don't mean to say you're going to let me down ——"

"You know I wouldn't do that, Mr. Smeeth."

"Well, you couldn't, not even if you tried," said Mr. Smeeth with great emphasis. "It wouldn't work here at all. I'm not old Hornsea. But, believe me, my boy, it's a bad system. Can't you last out until to-morrow morning? I could lend you a bob or two myself, for that matter."

"No, thank you, Mr. Smeeth. I'd rather have the pound on account, if you don't mind. It's something special I have on to-night." And he added to himself that old Smeethy would be just about dumb with surprise if he knew too.

"Oh, well, in that case, I suppose you'd better have it. But it's a special case, mind. And don't forget you'll have a pound less to-morrow morning." He carefully made out a slip, *Sub. H. Turgis—£1 os. od.*, placed it in the petty cashbox, and then handed over the pound note.

"Thank you very much, Mr. Smeeth," said Turgis, quietly, humbly. That was the first thing done. The next was to book the seats at the Sovereign. He could have telephoned and then paid for them in the evening, but this did not occur to him, for he did not belong to the seat-booking classes, and even if it had occurred to him, he would have rejected it as being too precarious. To make certain of getting good seats, he curtailed his lunch to a mere gobble and gulp, then hurried off to the West End and the Sovereign, which was already open. Indeed, for the last hour or so, the Sovereign had been doing excellent business, chiefly with young wives who had come in from distant suburbs to buy three and a half yards of curtain material and, having saved ninepence, felt they were entitled to a glimpse or two of Ronald Mawlborough. Early as it was, there were several people in front of Turgis at the advance booking office, but he was able to get two fairly good seats at four and sixpence each. Nine bob for the pictures! This was easily his record, and it certainly seemed a lot of money, nearly as much as he earned in a whole day. Nevertheless he paid it gladly. With the tickets in his pocket, to say nothing of eleven shillings to meet emergencies, he had nothing to do now but quietly exist until quarter to eight, and then—Lena.

It was not worth while going back to his lodgings after he had finished at the office, so he went to a teashop not very far from the Sovereign and there spun out his meal as long as he decently could. Even then, however, it was only half-past seven when he arrived at the Sovereign; but he did not mind that, for it would be pleasant just standing there, watching the crowd, and knowing that every minute brought Lena nearer to him. There was a queue waiting for the cheaper seats. Turgis had stood in that queue many a time. Now he looked at it with a mingling of pity and scorn. It seemed to belong to some ancient and desiccated past. In the entrance hall, under the russet globes, the footmen and pageboys in chocolate and gold were handing the people on to one another and sending them, in two jerky dark streams, up the two great marble staircases. For the first ten minutes, Turgis merely lounged about, but after that, when he knew that Lena might arrive any moment, he carefully planted himself in the centre, in sight of all the doors in front, so that there was no chance of missing her. Hundreds of girls passed in with their young men, but not one of them as pretty as Lena. A few days ago he would have envied a good many of those fellows, but now he could afford to pity them. They didn't know what a girl was. "Wait till you see Lena," he told them, under his breath, as they passed, unconscious, smiling.

At five minutes to eight, he pointed out to himself that Lena had been ten minutes late the night before at the Colladium. Girls always kept a chap waiting. They were famous for it. At eight o'clock he began to be anxious. He wondered if he was waiting in the wrong place, and he hastily searched the whole breadth of the entrance. At quarter past eight, his eyes began to smart. Time, which had passed so slowly at first, was now rushing away. The Ronald Mawlborough picture had started long ago. A lump, compact of sheer misery, rose in his throat and then wobbled up and down there, trying to choke him. Half-a-dozen times he stepped forward eagerly, only to retire again, under the stare of strange girls who thought they were about to be accosted, and to pretend to himself that it was still worth while staying there a little longer. The last half-hour was nothing but a dismal farce, for he knew that she could not be coming now, yet somehow his feet refused to move more than a yard or two away. It was nine o'clock when he finally left the place, with two useless tickets in his pocket. One of them he could have used, but he never thought for a moment of doing so. It was Lena he wanted to see. not Ronald Mawlborough.

He thought of a hundred excuses for her. She might have been taken ill quite suddenly, for girls often were, he believed. Something might have happened at the house. Her father might have come back unexpectedly. What he could not believe was that there was any mistake about the meeting itself, for she had suggested both the time and the place. Still struggling with his disappointment, he hurried along, through the stupid idiotic crowds, and caught the first bus that would take him to Maida Vale. More excited every minute, he turned at last into Carrington Villas, and almost ran to get a sight of 4a. There was no light coming from the sitting-room. She was not there. Nevertheless, he came to the conclusion that somebody was in, for after waiting a few minutes, he thought he saw a light go on in one of the other windows. Once he had made up his mind, he did not hesitate at all, but marched straight up to the door and rang the bell. He remembered then that it was probably out of order. Still, he rang again.

"Yes," said a voice, as the door opened a few inches, "what is it?"

"Is Miss Golspie in, please?"

The girl, obviously the maid who had been out the two previous nights, now opened the door properly and came forward to have a look at him. "Oo no, she isn't."

"Do you know where she's gone?"

"Oo no, I don't."

"Oh—I see," said Turgis miserably. "I was hoping to see her to-night."

"Well," said the girl confidentially, "I think she went out with a friend, because she got all dressed up just after seven and she told me she wouldn't be back till very late, and then about half-past seven a young gentleman called for her in a motor-car. And that's all I can tell you. Would you like to leave a message?"

No, no message. He walked slowly down the garden, out of the gate, across the road. He had to stop at the corner, because he was biting his handkerchief, which he had screwed into a ball. Then, when at last he was quiet and had put his handkerchief away, he walked on and on through a blank misery of a night.

Mr. Pelumpton was sitting up alone, just finishing his last pipe and a mouthful of beer, when Turgis burst into the back room.

"Can you lend me some ink, please?" he asked.

"Yersh, I think sho. I got a drop shomewhere. But you're not going to shtart writing lettersh thish time o' night, boy, are yer? If I wash like you, clerking all day in a norfish, writing lettersh about thish, that, an' the other, never shtopping, why, deary me!—you wouldn't catch me wanting to write lettersh thish time o' night, my wordsh you wouldn't——"

"Oh, for God's sake," Turgis screamed at him, "let me have the ink if you've got any and stop yapping."

" 'Ere, 'ere, 'ere, 'ere, 'ere! Thatsh a way to talk now, ishn't it!" Mr. Pelumpton, offended and on his dignity, produced the ink-bottle and put it down on the table and then promptly turned his back on it. "There'sh shuch a thing," he continued, still with his back turned, "ash mannersh an' ashkin' for a thing in a proper way. And you can't 'ave everything you want the minute you want it, not in thish world you can't, and it'sh no good you or any other man——"

But Turgis had banged the door behind him and was on his way upstairs. He sat in his little room, a pen in his hand, a writing pad on his knee, but at the end of half-an-hour there were only a few stiff sentences down on the paper, although a torrent of phrases, angry, reproachful, bitter, appealing, had gone raging through his head. When, in despair, he crumpled the paper and flung down his pen and then wandered wretchedly to the window, the night out there was filled with tall handsome young men with wavy hair and evening clothes, all with Lena in their arms. They were laughing at him. She was laughing at him. He left the window, and told himself that perhaps she wasn't, though, perhaps she was sorry now. He wished he had waited in Carrington Villas until she had returned, no matter how late that might have been. He smoothed out the writing pad and tried to decide whether he should write something short and forceful or long and appealing. Oh, but what was the use of writing! He would see her, speak to her, tell her what he thought while looking her straight in the eyes. He would show her she wasn't dealing with a kid now, but with a Man.

He undressed, and, as usual emptied his pockets. Two tickets, four and six each, for the Sovereign Picture Theatre. And it was she who had suggested it, and she had never even bothered letting him know she wasn't coming, but had just gone out with somebody else, had dressed up, got into a car, and laughed at him or forgotten his existence. He turned out the light, got into bed, and found himself in a hot salty darkness, his eyes filling with tears.

Chapter Eight

MISS MATFIELD'S NEW YEAR

I

A DAY or two before Mr. Golspie returned, Miss Matfield, sitting with cold feet and a novel she disliked in the 13 bus, realised with a shock that it was nearly Christmas. The shops she passed every day in the bus along Regent Street and Oxford Street had been celebrating Christmas for some time; and it was weeks since they had first broken out into their annual crimson rash of holly berries, robins, and Father Christmasses. The shops, followed by the illustrated papers, began it so early, with their full chorus of advertising managers and window dressers, shouting "Christmas Is Here," at a time when it obviously wasn't, that when it did actually come creeping up, you had forgotten about it. Miss Matfield told herself this, and then remembered that every year her mother used to cry, "What, nearly Christmas already! I never thought it was so near. It's taken me completely by surprise, this year." Yes, every year she used to say that, and year after year, Miss Matfield would tease her about it. And now, Miss Matfield told herself, she had begun to say it, just as if she was on the point of becoming forgetful and absurd and middle-aged. Oh—foul! She stared out of the window. Those two miles of *Xmas Gifts* and lavish electric lighting and artificial holly leaves and cotton wool snow were still rolling past. The festive season— help! It was all an elaborate stunt to persuade everybody to spend money buying useless things for everybody else. She tried her novel again: *The months passed, and still Jeffrey made no sign. He had not forgiven her. In despair, Jenifer accepted an invitation to join*

*the Mainwarings in Madeira, returned to a gay but feverish fort-
night in Chelsea (where John Anderson sought her out everywhere
and never left her side), and then appeared, still smiling, still audacious, but with a vaguely haunted look, at Cap d'Antibes. It was
there she heard that Jeffrey had been seen at Miami—"And with
Gloria Judge, my dear."* And that was quite enough of that. Who
cared what happened to Jenifer and Jeffrey, the pair of ninnies? And
why were all these novels always filled with people who spent all
their time travelling about to mere resorts and spas, and deciding
whom to live with next? Nobody ever did any work in them.

She returned to the subject of Christmas. It was, on the whole,
she decided, revolting. You gave people a lot of silly things, diaries
and calendars and rot, or useful things that were not right, gloves
of the wrong size and stockings of the wrong shade (and she
would have to be thinking out her presents now, and she was terribly
hard up); and they in their turn gave you silly things and the useful
things that were not right. You ate masses of food you didn't want
(and even Dr. Matfield, who had ideas about diet, said it didn't
matter at Christmas), and then you sat about, pretending to be jolly,
but really stodged, sleepy, headachy, and in urgent need of bicar-
bonate of soda. If you stayed at home, you yawned, tried to convince
your mother that you hadn't a rich secret life you were hiding from
her, and drearily sampled the family supply of literature. If you went
out, you had to pretend you were having a marvellous time because
you were wearing hats from crackers and playing pencil and paper
games ("Let me see, a river beginning with 'V'?"). And what was
so terribly depressing and revolting about it all was that it was possible to imagine a really good Christmas, the adult equivalent of
the enchanting Christmasses of childhood, the sort of Christmas that
people always thought they were going to have and never did have.
As the bus stopped by the dark desolation of Lord's cricket-ground,
swallowed two women who were all parcels, comic hats, and fuss (a
sure sign this that Christmas was near, for you never saw these
parcels-and-comic-hat women any other time), and then rolled on,

Miss Matfield took out from its secret recess that dream of a Christmas. She was in an old house in the country somewhere, with firelight and candlelight reflected in the polished wood surfaces; by her side, adoring her, was a vague figure, a husband, tall, strong, not handsome perhaps but distinguished; two or three children, vague too, nothing but laughter and a gleam of curls; friends arriving, delightful people—"Hello," they cried, "What a marvellous place you've got here! I *say*, Lilian!"; some smiling servants; logs on the fires, snow falling outside, old silver shining on the mahogany dining table, and "Darling, you look wonderful in that thing," said the masculine shadow in his deep thrilling voice. "Oh, you *fool*, stop it," Miss Matfield cried to herself. She had only brought out that nonsensical stuff to annoy herself. She liked reminding herself how silly she could be. It braced her.

She would go home, as usual, for Christmas, and on the way there she would look forward to it and imagine that *this* time it was going to be rather nice, and once she was there she would wonder how she could have thought it would be anything but depressing. All as usual. Still, it would be a change, a break in what had lately been the very dull round of the office and the Burpenfield. Never had the round been duller. The Burpenfield was getting worse; Evelyn Ansdell—lucky child!—had gone off with her absurd father; and nobody amusing had arrived. She had not met a single interesting new person for ages. Then, life in Angel Pavement had merely been so much typewriter-pounding since the one amusing person there, Mr. Golspie, had been away. Mr. Golspie, she admitted to herself, with unusual candour, *was* amusing, easily the most amusing person on the horizon—bless him!—and she would be glad when he came back. It would be fun, if only one had the cheek and courage to do it, to bring Mr. Golspie into the Club, to introduce him to Tatters, to say "Miss Tattersby, this is the *only* amusing man I know just now." But—O Lord!—she must keep off Tatters. In the Club, they talked about Tatters day and night.

She had further proof of this, if she had wanted it, when she reached the Club, for on the landing outside her room she met the depressing Miss Kersey. "Is that you, Matfield?" Kersey wailed, all damp and droopy as usual. "Don't, *don't,* go near Tatters to-night, whatever you do. I went in to ask her about sub-letting my room and she simply snapped my head off, didn't give me an earthly chance to tell her when I wanted to sub-let or anything. She just *flew* at me, Matfield, as if I'd been caught stealing or something. Isn't Tatters really *awful?* And yet the last time I went in, she was as nice as anything and even asked me about my sister, the one who's gone to Burma. I won't go near her now for months," she added, really enjoying the fact that Miss Tattersby could be so ferocious, so unpredictable in manner. "I'll send her notes as some of the others always do. Don't you go near her to-night."

Miss Matfield said she had no intention of doing so, and then hurried into her room, where she came to the conclusion, as she tidied herself for dinner, that it was really Tatters who made the Burpenfield endurable for people like Kersey, for she gave their lives a colouring of danger and drama, poor old things. At dinner, she had to share a table with Isabel Cadnam, the languid Morrison, and a recent arrival who had taken Evelyn Ansdell's old room, and annoyed Miss Matfield just because she was not Evelyn Ansdell. But, apart from that, this new girl was an irritating creature. Her name was Snaresbrook; she had untidy dark hair, huge staring eyes (heavily made up), and white, flabby, sagging cheeks; and she was soulful, gushing and psychic. So far she had been a great success because she went round talking to people about themselves very sympathetically, offering to tell their fortunes, and going in tremendously for this heart-to-heart business. Miss Matfield, a tougher subject than most, refused to be taken in. When she sat down the other three were already there, and were talking about work.

"I'll bet you'll agree, Mattie," said Miss Cadnam.

"What's that?" inquired Miss Matfield.

"I was just saying that it's part of the cussedness of everything that nearly every girl here has the wrong job. I mean, if you like *one* kind of thing, then it's ten to one you have to work in a place where it's all another kind of thing. I've just discovered that Snaresbrook here works for a film renting show, and she loathes it——"

"I wouldn't say that," Miss Snaresbrook put in softly in her soulful contralto, "because I don't loathe anybody. I don't think one ought to——"

"I do," said Miss Morrison. "I loathe nearly everybody. I think the world's full of people who are absolutely foul."

"No, I don't loathe these film people. But I do feel they're not my own kind. I don't feel really sympathetic towards them, and I feel there is work of a better kind waiting for me." And Miss Snaresbrook turned her huge staring eyes, like the headlights of a car, round the table.

"That's just what I'm saying," cried the excitable Caddie. "Now I'd adore to work at a film place; just my style. And here I am, assistant secretary to the League of the Divine Lotus, and I'm sure you'd adore that, wouldn't you, Snaresbrook? Whereas, if you don't mind my saying so, I think these Divine Lotus people are all too sloppy to live, and the minute they begin to talk now, they get on my nerves. If I stay there much longer I'll go potty too and break out into robes and mystic stars and Wisdom from the East. If anybody mentions the East now, I want to scream. A lot of fat film men smoking cigars would be a marvellous change. And to go to trade shows if you want to—marvellous!"

"You two ought to swop jobs," said Miss Matfield. "Then you'd both be satisfied. What about that, Caddie?"

"That's just where the cussedness comes in. They'd never have the right ones. It's the same with nearly everybody here. If you're heavily West End, you're landed with a job at a wholesale cheap milliner's somewhere in the City——"

"Revolting!" murmured Miss Morrison.

"And if you're a wild Socialist or something, like that Colenberg girl, you find yourself secretary to Lady Thomson-Greggs in Berkeley Square and grumble like anything because the place is stiff with footmen. I told Ivor about that, the other night, and he said I ought to write an article about it for the papers."

"Why don't you?" said Miss Snaresbrook. "I'm sure you could write. You have the gift of expression. I don't think I've looked at your hand yet, have I? I'm sure it's written in your hand."

Miss Matfield looked across the table in time to catch a disgusted glance from Morrison, whose grey eyes had also the gift of expression and announced quite clearly that Snaresbrook was revolting. "Well, I don't think much of my job," said Miss Matfield, "but I don't know that I particularly want anybody else's here. The fact is, they're all pretty rotten, and that's the real trouble. We don't any of us get a chance to do anything really important. They're all silly little mechanical jobs. If we were men, we'd be doing something decent now. What chance has a girl? The rot they talk about women working! The men jolly well see where all the decent jobs go to. And you know it."

"True, Miss Matfield," said Miss Snaresbrook, turning on all the sympathetic stops. "I feel it's particularly unjust in your case. A girl with a strong character like you is entitled to an important, responsible post. We have a long way to go yet. Men are still trying to hold women back, to keep them in inferior places. And their attitude! The things some of those film men have said to me!" She sighed, then switched on the headlights.

"Yes, I'll bet they're a tough crowd," said Caddie cheerfully, "but that ought to make it amusing. Men are easy enough to handle. It's women who are so awful. There are some frightful old cats among those Lotus creatures. They come swarming and drooping all over you, and all the time they're poking their long noses into your affairs and making up the most fiendish lies. Give me men. I wish there were some in this club."

"Miss Cadnam, you don't really," said Miss Snaresbrook reproachfully.

"Yes, she does, and so do I," said Miss Morrison, roused for once from her languid disgust, "and so will you when you've been here as long as we have. I'm not so terribly keen on men—most of them are pretty foul, so far as I can see—but a few here would be a pleasant change. The ones we do get as visitors are usually fairly hopeless, but even then I like to see them down here, trying to pretend they don't mind the foul food. There are too many girls here. Ugh! Too much feminine slush and slop. Too much powder and lipstick and cold cream. Too many stockings and silk jumpers. Too many hot-water bottles and bedroom slippers. Too much messiness and brightness and depressingness and sympathy. Every time I hear some man clumping about here, and see him sit down, all solid and thick, I'm delighted—I don't care how terrible he is. Too many women about. Revolting!"

"Whoops!" cried Caddie. "Go on, my dear. Don't stop now."

"Talk about girls living their own independent lives!" Miss Morrison continued, pink and defiant. "It's a marvel to me that after living here a year or two and being faced with the prospect of living here for donkey's years like some of the poor old things ——"

"Oh, don't!" Miss Matfield groaned.

"I say that it's a marvel to me we don't just marry anybody, anybody at all, or, failing that, run away with somebody. A place like this simply encourages wild matrimony and risky adventures. And if there isn't more of it, I'll tell you why. It's not just because we're all such ni-ice, ni-ice girls, so ni-icely brought up, but because there aren't many chances going about."

"Oh, aren't there, Morrison?" said Caddie. "Speak for yourself."

"I'm not speaking for myself or for anybody in particular ——"

"You're certainly not speaking for *me*, Miss Morrison," said Miss Snaresbrook, with large, sweet, forgiving smile. "I like the society of men, but I like the society of other girls too. Whoever they are, I find they interest me, and we have something to say to one another, very often some little secret to share, some confession to make. Of course, I admit those little clairvoyant gifts of mine have helped me a great deal, and have brought me friends, dear friends, among girls who probably imagined at first that they and I hadn't much in com-

mon. And I'm sure I intend to enjoy *my-self* at the Burpenfield."
And, smiling sympathetically at them all, she rose and left the table.

"And I hope it keeps fine for you," muttered Miss Morrison to her
retreating back. "You know, of the many ghastly specimens who
have turned up here this year, I think that one the worst."

"Oh, I don't know," said Miss Cadnam. "She's not so bad,
really ——"

"That's because she's going to read Caddie's palm to find her gift
of expression," Miss Matfield explained.

"Of course it is," said Miss Morrison. "You're feeble, Caddie. I
saw you swallowing the bait, as if you'd just been born. Vile!"

"Have you people realised that it's nearly Christmas?" said Miss
Matfield as they moved upstairs, where they could smoke.

"My dear Mattie," cried Miss Cadnam, "you don't mean to say
you've only just found that out! I've bought all my presents and
sent half of them off. If I don't send some of my people very early
presents, they never remember to send me anything."

"Christmas, yes," said Miss Morrison, with lanquid distaste. "Isn't
it foul? I haven't bought a thing yet, haven't even made out a list.
Anyhow, I haven't any money. I loathe Christmas, even though one
does have a holiday. What good is it? Are you going home,
Matfield?"

"Yes. I always do."

"So am I. It's pretty ghastly. It wasn't so bad before my brother
went out to the Sudan. We used to have rather an amusing time."

"But you've another brother, haven't you, Morrison? I thought I
saw him here once."

"Yes, Anthony. He's at Cambridge, researching. By the way,"
Miss Morrison continued, "he wants to come along early next week
and bring his researching friend Jiggs or Hoggs or something and
take me and any lady friend o' mine out for what passes for a gay
evening up in the Cambridge research labs. If either of you is dying
to come, you can, but I don't advise it. I'm trying to get out of it."

"I thought you were bursting to go round with a few men, Morrison."

"No, it's not as bad as all that. I've tried this before. Anthony, my brother, is pretty glum and dumb—quite different from Tom, the Sudan one—and his researching friend, Higgs or Joggs, is the limit. He's frightfully tall and awkward, with very short hair, a very long nose, and spectacles, and when you try to make conversation with him, he thinks you're asking scientific questions. If he doesn't know exactly, he just says 'I don't know'; but if he does know, he explains all about it, gives you a short lecture, and then completely shuts up. It's like being back at school, only worse. He's a horror. Anthony, of course, adores him, and thinks he's conferring an immense favour on you by bringing this monster. He said to me, 'One day you'll be proud to think you've talked to Jiggs'—or Hoggs. And so I told him I wasn't ambitious and I'd risk having missed the great Higgs. No, on second thoughts, you can't come. I'm definitely going to put him off. Talking about Joggs has brought it all back too clearly."

"Hello!" cried Miss Cadnam, looking at her watch. "I must fly."

"Ivor?"

"Ivor—thank God! We're supposed to be in the middle of another row, but I know he'll be there."

"What a ridiculous pair!" said Miss Matfield, smiling, as she watched Caddie leave the lounge.

"Who? Caddie and her Ivor? Oh, quite mad, of course, from what I've heard about them. Still," said Miss Morrison carefully, "it does pass the time for her, doesn't it?"

"Oh, it does a lot more than that. Caddie lives a wonderfully dramatic life. She probably would, anyhow, if there wasn't Ivor to quarrel with and then make it up with. She and Evelyn Ansdell were the only two people here I've ever envied, because they both contrived to have an exciting life all the time, even if they *were* absurd. I think I shall have to find a nice little Ivor." And Miss Matfield gave a short laugh.

"You don't lead a double life or anything of that kind, do you, Matfield?" Miss Morrison inquired, almost wistfully.

"Heavens, no! What do you mean?"

"Let's have another cigarette, shall we? Make a night of it. I only meant—well, it's a compliment, really ——"

"It doesn't sound like one."

"Well, I meant that you looked as if you had a more interesting sort of life going on *somewhere*. You go down to your office in the City—it is in the City, isn't it?—yes, I remember your telling me it was—and you come back here and don't seem to do anything much, but at the same time you look quite alive, as if something's happening somewhere."

"It isn't." Miss Matfield laughed, then lit her cigarette. "I wish it was. All perfectly dull, respectable, ordinary. A typical Burpenfield existence."

"Oh, foul! Well, I'm disappointed in you, I really am, Matfield. I've been suspecting some time that you were a dark horse. Tell me, what sort of men are there in that office of yours. Did I ever tell you I was in the City once? I nearly died. I don't believe it was a typical City place at all, though I was only there a week. There were four men there, two young ones with adenoids and whiny voices, who always called me 'Miss,' and two older ones with red faces and waxed moustaches who either shouted at me at the top of their voices or came over slimy and breathed down my neck and put their hot hands on my shoulder. Revolting! Don't tell me they're all like that. What are your lot like?"

They were in a quiet corner of the lounge, which was not so full as usual, indeed almost empty, and Miss Matfield found herself drifting into a fairly detailed description of the people in Angel Pavement, concluding at some length with the newest arrival there, Mr. Golspie. She ended with an account of her visit to the *Lemmala*, the foreign sailors, the cabin, the vodka, all the strange romantic accessories. She described it well, and Miss Morrison, who appeared to have dropped her usual attitude of languid disdain towards this life, listened eagerly.

"But, my dear Matfield," she cried when it was done, "I think that was a most amusing adventure. I like the sound of that man, even if he is middle-aged and what not. Now, if I met people like that when I went to work, I wouldn't grumble. No such luck, not in Anglo-Catholic and ladies' bridge circles in Bayswater—nothing but old tabbies. I think I shall have to try the City again, after all. I didn't know there were such entertaining, mysterious, brigandish sort of men down there."

"That's exactly what Mr. Golspie is—brigandish."

"Quite right, too. I'm all for it. You ought to lure him in here, so that I can meet him. But tell him to shave off that large moustache first."

"Why should I? It doesn't matter to me. I'm not going to kiss him," Miss Matfield added quickly, without thinking what she was saying.

"No, I suppose you're not," said Miss Morrison meditatively. "By the way, has he suggested you should?"

"No, of course not. Don't be ridiculous. I believe you're suffering from a complex, Morrison. Why should he?"

"Oh, I don't know. He sounds vaguely like it to me. I don't mean he sounded like those awful creatures with waxed moustaches that I worked for—not a bit. Quite a different type. But still —— How ever, I'll say no more. Did you say he was away, this mystery man? When is he coming back? Quite soon? All right, Matfield, you must tell me more about this, you really must. I'm interested for once in my young but embittered life. You must tell me more."

"There won't be anything to tell," said Miss Matfield casually. "I think I'll write home, think about Christmas presents, have a bath, and go to bed early. Good-night, Morrison." No, of course, there wouldn't be anything to tell. And if there was, it was no business of Morrison's. (But Morrison was not a bad sort, much better than she used to appear to be.) But then, there wouldn't be. Absurd

II

"Just read that over, please, Miss Matfield," said Mr. Dersingham, and then listened self-consciously. "Does that sound all right to you?" he inquired, when she had done. "I want to send them—y'know—a jolly stiff letter. They've asked for it, by George!"

"I think it sounds rather feeble," replied Miss Matfield. She had no respect for Mr. Dersingham; he was too vague, pink, and flabby; he was like too many men she had met at home, the sort who cry "Shooting!" when somebody makes a good stroke at tennis; he did not really exist, in her eyes, as an individual at all; there were hundreds, thousands of him. She knew that though he might be her employer he was really frightened of her. Impossible for her to have any respect for him. Quite a decent fellow, of course, but then the place is stiff with dull, decent fellows; a few fascinating crooks would be a change.

"Oh, I don't know about that, Miss Matfield," he said. "Seems to me to touch 'em up a bit. What's wrong with it exactly?"

"I should change it—there"—she pointed—"and there, don't you think so?" What was it like being Mrs. Dersingham, she wondered, and came to the conclusion that it must be rather fussing half the day, boring the other half, but on the whole pleasanter than being Lilian Matfield at the Burpenfield. But that was leaving out Dersingham himself. She couldn't marry him. Help! She stared at his nose, which was quite a healthy, sound nose, slightly bulbous, a shiny pink deepening to a fishy red at the blunted tip; there was really nothing wrong with it; nevertheless, it annoyed her; it was a silly nose. What was Mrs. Dersingham's real opinion now, of that nose? Did she think it was marvellous? Was she indifferent to it? Had she been irritated by it so long that she was ready to scream at the very thought of that nose?

Happily unconscious of what was buzzing about in the dark head so close to his, Mr. Dersingham frowned down upon the letter he was answering, an evasive, slinking, slimy letter from the mysterious fellow who ran the Alexander Imperial Furnishing Company. "He's a dirty dog, y'know, Miss Matfield," he mused. "This is the fourth letter he's sent explaining why he can't pay, and every time it's a different excuse. By the way, remind me to send Sandycroft a note, telling him not to call there any more. All right, I'll write something shorter and stronger. 'Unless our account is settled within the next fourteen days, we shall be obliged to take—what is it?—proceedings.' Something like that, eh? Right you are, then. Cancel that one. We'll start again."

That did not take long. The note to Sandycroft could be left to Miss Matfield. She was given several letters that Mr. Smeeth could attend to, and then there was nothing left. "I'm expecting Mr. Golspie back this morning," said Mr. Dersingham. "He'll probably have some letters for you. He rang me up last night, at home, to say he'd just arrived and would be down this morning. Just take this lot, will you? Half a minute, though, I must have another look at that North-Western and Trades Furnishing letter. Hang on a minute."

Miss Matfield, hanging on, found she was quite excited by the prospect of seeing Mr. Golspie again so soon, though they had been expecting him to return any time these last few days. It was not quite three weeks since she had stood by his side on the deck of that steamer in the Thames, but, nevertheless, Mr. Golspie, strictly as a person, a face, a body, a voice, had become curiously dim and unreal, though as a figure in outline and as a mass of character he had been constantly in her thoughts, where he had appeared, especially during the last few days, hardly as a real person she knew, but rather as a particularly vivid and memorable character in a play she had seen or a novel she had recently read. It was queer and exciting to think that he would actually walk into the office at any moment.

"I think I'd better have a talk to Mr. Smeeth about that letter," said Mr. Dersingham, putting it on one side. "You might tell him,

Miss Matfield ——" But now two doors were flung open and banged to in rapid succession. Mr. Golspie had arrived.

"Hello, Dersingham," he boomed, clapping and rubbing his hands. "Hello, Miss Matfield. Brrrrr—but it's devilish cold here. I can feel it creeping up and down my bones. Funny thing, but it's colder here than it ever is in places that pretend to be really cold, twenty below and all the rest of it. Damp, I suppose. Ten years of this would do me in. Well, how's everything? Making money?"

"All right, Miss Matfield," said Mr. Dersingham.

Miss Matfield could not decide whether she had exaggerated the size of Mr. Golspie's moustache or whether he had had it trimmed. The fact remained that it seemed considerably smaller. Another fact remained, and that was that she felt disappointed. She walked out of the room feeling absurdly disappointed. It was quite unreasonable, but there it was.

This feeling persisted throughout the day. Mr. Golspie came into the general office and shouted genial greetings at everybody. Afterwards, when Mr. Dersingham had gone, he dictated a few letters to her, but he said little or nothing, and neither that day nor any of the days before Christmas did he once refer to her visit to the *Lemmala*. There was no particular reason why he should, but still it was disappointing, and he was disappointing, and everything was disappointing.

Those last few days before Christmas were so awful that she found herself looking forward more and more eagerly to the holiday at home, to that train which would take her away, on Christmas Eve, from the vast glittering muddle of London. Mr. Golspie, who was apparently going to spend Christmas in Paris with his daughter, and Mr. Dersingham, whose spirits rose at the approach of all holidays, were in a good temper, but everybody else in the office seemed unusually gloomy. Mr. Smeeth was not exactly gloomy, but he was worried and fussy, as if something was troubling his grey and shrinking little mind. Turgis, who was not very cheerful at any time, was simply terrible; he went slouching about the place, sat at his desk staring out of the window at the black roofs, made a mess of his work, and almost snarled his replies to any civil question. Several times she had to speak to him quite sharply, the lout. The little Sellers girl, perhaps because Turgis was either so aloof or so rude, was not her usual perky self, and even Stanley, though ready to give Christmas or any other holiday the warmest welcome, had suffered so much lately from the moods of Mr. Smeeth and Turgis, who accused him unjustly of dawdling over every errand, that he was now turning into quite a sulky boy. And although Miss Matfield, who considered herself merely a visitor to Angel Pavement, *in* it but not *of* it, had always preserved her independence, she had to sit in the same room all day with these others, to work with them, and could not help being influenced by the prevailing outlook and their various attitudes. It was depressing.

Outside the office it was as bad, if not worse. She had her presents to buy, which meant frantic rushes to the shops during lunchtime or the short space left to her in the evening before they closed. They were packed out with people, and, of course, you could never find the things you wanted, and if you went late, the assistants, who had not drawn a proper breath for several hours, hated the sight of you and would not help. At last the army of advertising managers, copy writers, commercial artists, colour printers, window dressers, bill posters, which had been screaming "Buy, buy. Christmas is coming. Buy, buy, buy" for weeks and weeks, was charging to victory. London was looting itself. Those damp dark afternoons seemed to rain people down into the shopping streets; whole suburbs burst upon Oxford Street, Holborn, Regent Street; the shops themselves were full, the pavements were jammed, and the vehicles on the crowded road could hold no more. Never before had Miss Matfield seen so many boxes of figs and dates, obscenely naked fowls, cheeses, puddings in basins, beribboned cakes, and crackers, so much morocco and limp leather and suede and pig-skin, so many calendars, diaries, engagement books, bridge-scorers, fountain-pens, pencils, patent lighters, cigarette-holders, dressing-cases, slippers,

handbags, manicure sets, powder-bowls, and "latest novelties." There
were several brigades of Santa Clauses, tons and tons of imitation
holly, and enough cotton-wool piled in the windows and dabbed on
the glass to keep the hospitals supplied for the next ten years. Between those festive windows and a line of hawkers, street musicians,
beggars, there passed a million women dragging after them a million children, who, after a brief space in some enchanted wonderland
were dazed, tired, peevish, wanting nothing but a rest and another
bun. From a million bags, bags of every conceivable shape and colour, money, wads of clean pound notes straight from the bank, dirty
notes from the vase on the mantelpiece, half-crowns and florins from
the tin box in the bedroom, money that had come showering down
out of the blue, money that had been stolen, money that had been
earned, begged, hoarded up, was being pushed over counters and
under little glass windows and then conjured into parcels, parcels,
parcels, with whole acres of brown paper and miles of string called
into service every few minutes. Hundreds of these parcels, especially
the huge three-cornered ones, seemed to find their way into every
bus that Miss Matfield, after waiting and running forward and returning and waiting again, contrived to board. She felt like a shivering and bruised ant. Never had she hated London so much. She
wanted to scream at it. When she got back to the Club, the only
thing she wished to do was to have a long hot soak in the bath, and
of course it was precisely the thing that everybody else wanted to
do too, so she would find herself hanging about, still waiting, after
waiting to leave the office, waiting to get a bus, waiting to be served
in the shop, waiting at the cash desk, waiting for her parcel, waiting
for another bus; and then Kersey would come up and say: "Going
out to-night, Matfield? No? Well, you can't expect to go out every
night, can you, dee-ar?" Hell!

Mr. Golspie left for Paris—lucky man—on the morning of Christmas Eve; Mr. Dersingham wished them all a merry Christmas and
departed early; Mr. Smeeth gave them all an extra week's money,
brightened up a little, and hoped they would have a very good time.

Miss Matfield, after working miracles, arrived at Paddington, a Paddington that suggested that some invading army had already reached the Bank and that shells were falling into Hyde Park and that the seat of government had already been transferred to Bristol, and she was just in time to get three-quarters of a seat and no leg space in the 5.46. The lights of Westbourne Park and Kensal Green, such as they were, blinked at her and then were gone. Thank God she was done with this nightmare of a London for a few days! Perhaps Christmas at home this time would be amusing. At any rate, it would be reasonable and quiet, and her father and mother would be glad to see her, and she would be glad to see them. As the train gathered speed, shrugging off the outer western suburbs, she thought of her parents with affection, and for a little time felt nearer the child she had once been, the child who had thought her father and mother so wonderful and had found Christmas the most radiant and magical season than she had done for many a month. She closed her eyes; her mouth gradually lost its discontented curve; her whole face softened. Angel Pavement would hardly have recognized her.

III

"Hello, Matfield! What sort of a Christmas did *you* have?"

"Oh, the usual thing, you know—rather feeble."

"Do anything special?"

"No, just stodged and sat about and yawned. Stayed in bed every morning for breakfast and never got up till nearly lunch time. That was about the best thing that happened. What about you?"

"Oh, awful!" replied the other girl, Miss Preston, who worked at the Levantine Bank, but based her claim to attention at the Club on the fact that her brother, under another name, was a well-known actor. He had visited the Club twice, and each time Preston's reputation had soared. "The minute I got home I started the vilest cold, and then Archie—my brother, you know, the actor—had promised to come for Christmas, but wired at the last second that he couldn't."

"Hard luck!" cried Miss Matfield, but not with much conviction. You had to give out so much sympathy at the Burpenfield that you were apt to become very mechanical, and if something really terrible and tragic had happened there, if, for example, half a dozen girls had gone down with ptomaine poisoning, the other girls would probably have been struck dumb, having over-worked so long all the possible expressions of pity and horror.

Now they were all discussing their holidays. The youngish ones, who had probably enjoyed themselves thoroughly, were mostly going about crying "Vile! Absolutely ghastly, my dear!" The oldish ones, the lonely hot water bottle enthusiasts, who had probably had nothing but a mocking shadow of a Christmas, were busy pretending, with a strained creaking brightness, that they had had a wonderful time. The members in between these two groups, such as Miss Matfield, gave fairly truthful accounts. The entrance hall, the lounge, the stairs and the corridors above, all buzzed with these descriptions. The Burpenfield Club was returning to its normal life. With admirable forethought, Miss Tattersby had pinned up half a dozen new notices all written in her most exclamatory and sardonic style, and already these notices, especially a very bitter and tyrannical one about washing stockings and handkerchiefs, were feeding the mounting flames of talk. "My dear, but *have* you seen Tatters' latest?" they cried, along the landings and in and out of their little bedrooms.

Miss Matfield went up to her little room, found a space on the wall for two framed Medici prints she had brought back from home, cleared out of her tiny bookshelf several books she had borrowed and forgotten to return, and put in their place some books she had contrived to borrow during the holidays. There were two travel books and three novels or romances, and all three stories had for their settings such places as Borneo and the South Seas. This was not a mere coincidence. Miss Matfield liked her fiction to be full of jungles, coral reefs, plantations, lagoons, hibiscus flowers, the scent of vanilla, schooners on the wide Pacific, tropical nights. So long as the young man was first shown to her dressed in white and lounging on a verandah, while a noiseless brown figure brought him something long and cool to drink, she was ready to follow his love story to the end. If the story had no love in it but had the right exotic setting, she would read it, but she preferred a fairly strong love interest. She had not bad taste, and if the story was written for her by Joseph Conrad, so much the better; but she was ready to endure if not to delight in authors of a very different cut from Conrad if they would only give her the jungles and lagoons and coral reefs and mysterious brown faces. The worst story about Malaysia was preferable to the best story about Marylebone. She did all her reading on the bus to and from the office, in some teashop at lunch time, and in bed, and as her one desire was to escape from any further consideration of buses, teashops, and girls' club bedrooms, these stories of the other end of the world, strange, savage, beautiful, might have been specially created for her; indeed, many of them were. She never admitted that she had a passion for these exotic and adventurous tales. She did homage to them negatively by looking through other and very different novels, novels about London and Worcestershire, and then sneering heavily at them. A long acquaintance with these heroes in bungalows and schooners and bars run by Chinese had gradually shaped and coloured her attitude towards men, though here again she admitted nothing and only paid these distant creatures a negative tribute, by criticizing adversely the fellows who were quite different and much nearer home. The idea of a man that warmed her secret heart was that of the strong, adventurous, roving male with a background of alien scenes, of little ships and fantastic drinking haunts. If she married him, she might want to domesticate him in that beautiful old country house in which she had spent so many imaginary Christmasses, but he would have to be that kind of man first, and not born in captivity.

It was not possible to change her room very much—though she

always tried after being away—because it was far too small; it was like trying to re-arrange three or four toys in a boot-box; but now, as before, she did what she could. She had come back determined, as she told herself, to fight against the Burpenfield atmosphere. No more drooping and whining, no more waiting for something to turn up while you knew all the time it wouldn't, no more wistful hanging about on the roadside of life! She would lead a real life of her own, full, adventurous, gay. This was not the first time—alas!—she had come back to the Club with such a resolution and had promptly tried to change her room about as an early outward sign of it; but now it was different; she was older, more experienced, and this time she meant it. Moreover, she had now a total of five pounds a week instead of four pounds ten, for they had given her a ten-shilling rise at the office, and though she had told her father, he had only congratulated her (with that tired smile and that faint irony which frequently accompany long experience of a general medical practice, that constant round of births and deaths), and had not proposed cutting down his allowance of six pounds a month. Any girl at the Burpenfield would have instantly appreciated the profound distinction between five pounds a week and four pounds ten shillings, for whereas on four pounds ten you have still to be careful, on five pounds you can really begin to splash about a bit.

"Well, if you ask me, Mattie," said Miss Cadnam, who had looked in and had been promptly told about this new mood, "you're absolutely *rolling*. I only get four, you know, including what I get from home, when they don't forget, and I know if I suddenly got an extra pound, I'd simply break out in all directions. Do you know, Ivor only gets six pounds a week, that's all. Don't say anything, of course. He'd be furious if he knew I'd told anybody—men are awfully silly about things like that, aren't they?—terribly secretive—but honestly that's all he gets, and he seems to have an awful lot to spend."

Miss Matfield shut a drawer with a bang, turned to face her

visitor, and looked very determined. "I always think this time that's coming now—the next two months or so—the foulest part of the whole year. Awful weather, cold and slush and everything, and Easter and spring a long time away, and nothing happening very much, and it's just the time when, if you let yourself go, you get depressed beyond words."

"I absolutely agree," said Miss Cadnam earnestly.

"Well, I've made up my mind this time I'm not going to have it. If things don't happen, I'll *make* them happen. If anybody asks me to go anywhere or do anything that's at all decent, I shall accept. I shall go to theatres and concerts more, and if there's any dancing about, I'm having it. By the way, mother's given me what seems to me *rather* a nice dress. I'll show it to you. The only thing I'm not certain about is the length at the front. What do you think?"

There was a short interlude, during which the dress was held up, pulled down, examined, and finally approved.

"Anyhow, that's *my* programme, Caddie," said Miss Matfield, after the dress had been put away again. "I've come to the conclusion that one gives in too much—I don't mean that you do, my dear, because you're one of the very few people here who definitely don't—it's something in the Burpenfield atmosphere that does it, sort of saps your initiative and makes you frightened—and if you let yourself drift here, it's fatal. I'm not going to have it. And that's to-day's great thought and resolution, Caddie."

"Good! I always come back feeling like that. You know, feeling I must start all over again *somehow*, whether it's leading a gay life or leading a quiet life or what it is."

There was a tap on the door, which opened to admit the head of Miss Morrison. "Hello, Matfield. Hello, Cadnam. Is this terribly private? Sure?" She came in. "This is to announce that I've changed my room and am now your neighbour, four doors down on the other side."

"That's Spilsby's room," said Miss Matfield.

"It was, but is Spilsby's no longer. Spilsby is not coming back.

She's going to New Zealand or Australia, I forget which, and it's just the place for her, whichever it is. I've discovered Spilsby's secret vice—reading those American magazines that you can buy cheap at Woolworth's and other places, you know the kind—Western Yarns with a Punch."

"I know," cried Miss Cadnam. "But not Spilsby?"

"Spilsby. She'd bought hundreds of them. I've just had them turfed out. You couldn't move for them. All Westerns or the big wild North-West or the red-blooded Yukon, all bunches of gripping yarns with a punch. Spilsby was a red-blooded Western addict— Revolting! Are you sure you wouldn't like some, Matfield, before they're all gone? You look a bit fierce to-night."

"She is," said Miss Cadnam. "Aren't you, Mattie? She's just been telling me that she's come back full of grand resolutions."

"Ugh!" Miss Morrison looked disgusted. "Don't tell me you've made up your mind to spend all your evenings learning Italian and German or something like that."

"You're quite wrong."

"Quite."

"Thank the Lord for that," said Miss Morrison. "It would have been completely foul. Besides, you're not young enough and not old enough, if you see what I mean, for that sort of thing. When I was a few years younger, I used to come back full of good intentions and ambition and tell myself I was going to learn commercial Spanish or qualify as an accountant or something equally crazy. You feel like that after the holidays. But what's this new attitude?"

It was explained to her, and she listened with a dubious smile on her smooth pale face. "Ah, my children," she said, "I like to hear you talk. I, too, have felt like that in my time. It won't work."

"In your time! Why, Morrison, I'm two years older than you at least," cried Miss Matfield.

"And I'm nearly as old as you, Morrison," said Miss Cadnam. "I'm getting terribly old."

"It isn't just the years, little ones. It's the experience. You make me feel old with your charming youthful illusions. However, I'm all for you leading a dashing worldly life, Matfield. I'm all in favour of you going to the devil, for that matter. How do you do it, by the way? I used to hear an awful lot of vague talk about the temptations of a poor girl's life in London. Where do they come in? Nobody ever tempts me. The only temptations I have are to steal some of my worthy employeress's terribly expensive bath salts when I'm allowed to enter her bathroom to wash my hands, and—there must be something else—yes, not to give the bus conductor my penny when he doesn't ask for it. What chance have I then to be really virtuous or to be wicked either? I admit, Matfield, that you're different. You go down to the great City, to begin with, and meet mysterious men on romantic ships——"

"When was this?" cried Miss Cadnam. "Did you, Mattie, or is she making it up?"

"Quiet, child! You will understand in time. And then again, my dear Matfield, you have a *look*. I don't say you look terribly marvellous, my dear——"

"I don't pretend to," Miss Matfield told her.

"But there's a *something*—a hint, you might say, of dark, wild forces. I don't suppose you have any, really, but there's a *look*. That's where you completely beat me. I haven't that look at all, whereas if people only knew what I was *really* like—— Well, never mind. But you have it, though if I were you—particularly now, when you've made up your mind to be a One—I should do my hair rather differently. You ought to have it out at the side more. I'll show you what I mean. You watch, Cadnam, and see if you don't agree."

"Ye-es, I think you're probably right," said Miss Matfield finally.

"By the way," said Miss Morrison, "there's a dance here on New Year's Eve. And as nobody has asked me anywhere else, I think I'll go, and I might be able to persuade a couple of men I know vaguely to look in. They're not very bright lads, but they're energetic and harmless and better than nothing. What about you, Matfield? A dance at the Burpenfield is perhaps hardly a proper start on the downward path—but still, you never know."

"Oh yes, I'll be there," said Miss Matfield. But she wasn't.

IV

Many a time afterwards Miss Matfield wondered if Mr. Golspie deliberately engineered that staying late on New Year's Eve. She never asked him and never made up her own mind about it. At the time, it seemed accidental enough. He had looked in at the office during the morning, had gone out quite soon and had not returned until six o'clock, when they were all busy clearing off the last odds and ends of work. Mr. Dersingham had already gone. Mr. Golspie arrived, shouted for her, and went into the private office.

"Sorry, Miss Matfield," he began, "but I'll have to ask you to do a bit of work for me at once."

"What, now?"

"Yes, now. Don't look at me like that, Miss Matfield—spoiling your handsome features. It can't be helped, and an extra hour for once isn't going to hurt you, is it?"

"I suppose not, Mr. Golspie. It's only—well, it's New Year's Eve, isn't it?"

"So it is. I'd clean forgotten. Old Year's Night, we always used to call it. Still, there'll be plenty of it left when we've finished."

"Yes, that's all right—only, I'd arranged to go to a dance to-night."

"O-ho, the gay life, eh?" he boomed, grinning at her. "Now I remember, my daughter's going to one to-night. One of these balloon, confetti, and false noses affairs, eh? Champagne at midnight, eh?"

"No such luck. It's only a dance at the girls' club where I live, a very modest affair."

"Oh, a dance at a girls' club, eh? That's nothing. You're as well off here with me as at a dance at a girls' club. What time does it start?"

"About nine, I suppose."

"I shan't keep you here until nine, unless you want me to. Now you go back and finish what you were doing, and you can tell the rest of 'em they can go when they like, as far as I'm concerned. Then come back here, bring your notebook, and we'll get down to it. I've some letters I must get off to-night. Somebody's got to earn some money for this firm, y'know."

When she returned to the private office, Mr. Golspie, meditating over a cigar and occasionally jotting down some figures, motioned her towards a chair and did not speak for several minutes. She heard the outer door bang behind the other people, going home, heard other doors banging and noisy footsteps on the stairs, and then everything suddenly sank into silence.

"Now then," said Mr. Golspie, "let's make a start. You can take the whole lot down at once, if you like, or you can take two or three, go and type 'em, then come back for more, just as you please. All I care about is that they go to-night."

She took down several letters, then went to type them out while he looked at his figures and thought about the rest of them. It was very strange to be at work in the deserted general office, to go back to the private office and find Mr. Golspie there, almost lost in his cigar smoke, to return again to her machine under the solitary light. As the quarters of an hour slipped by, so many little noises from outside disappeared into the silence that at last she did not seem to be working in a place she knew at all. The instant the familiar and now cheerful clatter and *ping* of her typewriter stopped, everything turned ghostly, until she found herself again in the private office, which was not at all ghostly. There was nothing spectral about Mr. Golspie.

"But what about copying them?" she cried, when they were all done, all signed, and ready for their envelopes.

"They can stay uncopied," replied Mr. Golspie.

"But, you know, we always copy all letters."

"Well, this time we don't. It isn't worth the bother. I know what

I've said to these people, and they're my letters, not Dersingham's. Help me to put them into their envelopes and bring some stamps, then we've done. That's the way. A good job of work, that, Miss Matfield. I'm much obliged. Most girls would have kicked up a fuss and then done the work dam' badly just to show their independence. What time is it? Would you believe it?—nearly eight! I thought I was hungry."

Miss Matfield had given a little cry of dismay.

"Hello, what's the matter with you?"

"I'd no idea it was so late, though I feel terribly hungry, too. Dinner will be over at the Club when I get back there now, though I suppose I shall be in time to get something."

"You're hungry, too, are you? What did you have for lunch?"

"I never had much lunch, you see," said Miss Matfield. "I had an egg and a roll and butter and a cup of coffee."

"And then you had a cup of tea and a biscuit, and now it's nearly eight and you feel hungry and you think if you run all the way back to your Club they'll give you a bite of something there—that's it, isn't it? Well, that's no good at all. That's the way you girls do yourselves in. You don't feed. It's all wrong. If you don't have at least one thumping big meal a day in this town at this time o' the year, you might as well send for the doctor at once and have done with it. Now, Miss Matfield," and he rose and put a hand on her shoulder, "you're not one of those half-starved wizened little monkeys of creatures that pass for girls nowadays; you're a fine upstanding girl, a real woman; and you can't play those tricks with yourself. Now listen—you're coming to feed with me. We've both been working; we're both hungry; and we're going to feed together."

"Oh, are we?" It was all she could find to reply at the moment.

"If you want me to make a favour of it, I'll do it," he continued. "Here I am—on the last night of the year, too—going to have dinner all by myself, and here are you, as hungry as I am, and we've been working together, and you won't join me to cheer me up a bit. How's that?"

She laughed. "All right, I will. Thank you. Only I can't go anywhere very marvellous, looking like this, you know."

"You could go anywhere looking like that, believe me," he
assured her. "But I suppose you mean you're not all dressed up.
That doesn't matter. We're not going where they're slinging the
confetti at one another, we're going where the food is. You go and
get ready while I stamp these letters."

It was a clear cold night. Angel Pavement looked strangely dark
and deserted, a little black gulf with a faint spangle of stars above it.

"Do you know why I came to your place?" said Mr. Golspie, as
they walked along. "I looked up the names of the firms in this
line of business, and Twigg and Dersingham took my fancy not because of *their* name, but because of the address. Angel Pavement did
it. I was so tickled by that name, I said to myself, 'I must have a
look at that lot, first of all.' And if I hadn't said that, I shouldn't
have been here, and you wouldn't have been trotting along here
with me, would you?"

"Didn't you know anything about this business before?" she
asked.

"Not a thing. But I've picked up a good many different sorts
of business in my time, and I haven't finished yet, not by a long
chalk. But I don't call this veneer trade a proper business. It's a
side-line. There's no size to it. You might as well be selling sets o'
chessmen or rocking-horses. No size to it, no chance of real
growth, you see? It's all right for Dersingham—it's about his mark
—but then he's not really in business. He's only got one leg in it
instead of being up to the neck in it. He thinks he's a gentleman
amusing himself. Too many of his sort in the City here. That's how
the Jews get on, and the Americans. None of that nonsense about
them."

The main road, into which they had turned now, still showed
a few lighted windows, behind which the last orders of the year
were being booked and the last entries made in the ledgers, and
there were still a few belated clerks and typists hurrying away on

each side; but compared with its usual appearance, the hooting muddle of the day and early evening, its appearance now was that of a
lighted stone wilderness. A tram came grinding down, looking as if
it expected nothing. A bus slipped through, curiously swift and
noiseless. They walked down to the end of the road, past the
narrow openings of little streets and alleys already sunk into midnight and the mouths of wider streets that were illuminated emptiness. At the bottom they turned to the right. A taxi came jogging
along at that moment, and Mr. Golspie at once claimed it, shouted
"Bundle's" to the driver, and then sat very close to Miss Matfield.

"Thought we'd go to Bundle's," he said, "if it's all the same to
you. D'you know it?"

"I've heard of it, of course," she told him, "but I've never been
there. It's more a restaurant for men, isn't it?"

"More men than women there certainly, but women do go. And
if they'd more sense, they'd go oftener. Bundle's is the place if
you're really hungry and you want a good solid feed. It's English,
too, and I like it for that—good old-fashioned tack. I don't suppose
there'll be a lot of people there now—lunch is the crowded time at
Bundle's—and there's no need to dress up to go there."

"Thank Heaven for that!" cried Miss Matfield.

"Mind you, Bundle's isn't a cheap place, by any means," Mr.
Golspie continued, apparently anxious to suggest that he was not
skimping his hospitality. "Don't get that idea into your head. It's
plain, but it works out as expensive as most places, even though the
other places are giving you ten courses and a band and rattles and
confetti and God knows what else. There's nothing like that at
Bundle's, but there's real food and some good drink."

"Well, Mr. Golspie, I'll be quite candid, and confess that I could
do with both at this very moment. Even," she added mischievously,
"if they will cost you a lot of money."

"I didn't say that, Miss Matfield," he said, pinching her arm. "All
I said was that Bundle's isn't cheap. As for costing me a lot of
money, I don't honestly think you could do if you tried, not at

Bundle's. You'd be sick before you could eat that amount, and drunk long before you could drink it. I took a feller there, just before Christmas, and he *did* cost me money. He found they had some Waterloo brandy there, and fancied a few goes of that after lunch."

"Well, suppose I do, too," said Miss Matfield, as St. Paul's went jogging past the window on her side of the cab. "What about that?"

"I'll promise you one, though, if you ask me, it's a waste of beautiful stuff, because I'm sure you can't appreciate it. But you won't get any more out of me. If you did, you'd turn round afterwards and tell me I made you drunk. No, no."

"Don't be absurd. I was only joking. I don't like brandy, as a matter of fact; the taste of it always reminds me of being ill. I loathe whisky, too. I like wine, though, you'll perhaps be glad to know. You will also be glad to know that I can drink quite a lot of it—if it's good—without feeling tight."

"All right. Now I know. The sooner he gets there now, the better it will be. I'm getting hungrier and hungrier."

"So am I. If I'd gone back to the Club, I'd never have been able to find enough to satisfy my appetite to-night. The food's not really too bad there, but it isn't quite real—if you know what I mean. It's like the food you get in cheap hotels."

"I know," said Mr. Golspie grimly. "You can't tell me anything about cheap hotels and bad grub. And when you say it's not real, you mean it all tastes alike and never quite leaves you satisfied. Nothing like that about Mr. Bundle. And here he is."

Mr. Bundle, whoever he was, had remembered one simple fact when he first established his tradition of catering, and that was that Man is one of the larger *carnivora*. You went to Bundle's to eat meat. The kitchen turned out acceptable soups, vegetables, puddings, tarts, savouries, and the like, but all these were as nothing compared with the meat. The place was a vegetarian's nightmare. It seemed to be perpetually celebrating the victory of some medieval baron. Whole beeves and droves must have been slaughtered daily in its name. If you asked for roast beef at Bundle's, they took you at your word, and promptly wheeled up to you the red dripping half of a roasted ox, and after the waiter had implored you to examine it and had asked you a few solemn questions about fat and lean, under-done and over-done, he cut you off a pound or two here, a pound or two there. A request for mutton was not treated perhaps with the same high seriousness, but even that meant that legs and shoulders came trundling up from all directions, and you found yourself facing a few assorted pounds of it on your plate. The waiters them-selves had a roasted jointy look, though most of them were lean and under-done, whereas most of the guests were obviously fat and over-done and suffering from gigantic blood pressures that took an-other leap upward every time they went out of these doors. It was the meatiest place Miss Matfield had ever seen, and she had a sus-picion that if she had not been feeling really hungry, it might have made her feel rather sick. As it was, she welcomed the look of it and smell of it, and enjoyed, too, its very definite masculine atmosphere.

Mutton was wheeled at Miss Matfield and beef was wheeled at Mr. Golspie, and, while acolytes brought vegetables, the high priests gravely pointed to fat and lean and under-done and over-done, and then sliced away with their exquisite long narrow knives. Mr. Gol-spie, after consulting briefly with her, ordered a good rich burgundy. Then, after Mr. Golspie, a true Bundle's man, had polished off his gigantic helping of beef, and Miss Matfield had eaten about a third of her mutton, he had a savoury and she had some apple tart and cream.

"We'll finish the wine before we have coffee," said Mr. Golspie, pointing the bottle at her glass, which she had emptied. "It's a good burgundy this."

"Only about half a glass, please. It's lovely rich sunshiny stuff, but I daren't drink much more. I feel as if I'd had about fifteen of my Club dinners rolled into one. I don't believe I shall ever be hungry again."

"You look well on it," said Mr. Golspie, who perhaps looked a shade too well on it himself. "You've a fine colour, Miss Matfield, and your eyes are sparkling, and altogether you look full of fight and fun, too good for Angel Pavement, I can tell you."

"Oh, but I am," she cried humorously. She suddenly felt that life was rich and gay.

"Of course you are. I said that to myself the first time I set eyes on you. There's a girl with some spirit and sense, I thought—she's alive, not like these other poor devils. 'She don't belong,' I said to myself. That's why I kept my eye on you. Did you notice me keeping my eye on you?"

"Mmmm, ye-es," looking at him and hoping that her eyes were still sparkling. "Sometimes I thought you seemed quite human."

"Human!" he roared, so that a waiter jumped forward. "I'm human enough, I can tell you. I'm a dam' sight too human."

"If you're in the City, you can't be *too* human, Mr. Golspie. Not for me. I've spent months there sometimes and never spoken to anyone who seemed to me really human. Awful creatures. Then people like Mr. Smeeth, all grey and withered and not bad really, but just—pathetic."

"No, Smeeth's not a bad feller. But he's not pathetic. He doesn't make me weep, anyhow. All he wants is to be safe, that's what's the matter with him. Anything to be safe—that's his line. Pay him a pound or two a week, give him some little cash-books to play with, tell him he's safe, and he's as happy as a king. But he's better than that dreary youngster you have in there—what's his name?— Turgis."

"Oh, he's hopeless, I agree."

"Not your style, eh?"

"What, Turgis! Help!"

"He's a typical specimen of what they're breeding here now—no sense, no guts, no anything. I can't even remember the look of the lad, although I see him nearly every day. That shows you what impression *he* makes. He might be a shadow flickering about the place."

"I know. And yet that funny little Cockney girl, Poppy Sellers, thinks he's marvellous. I've watched her worshipping him at a distance. Isn't it strange—I mean, the way everybody amounts to something different to everybody else?"

"Well, a lad like that'ull never mean anything to me, never amount to anything to anybody, I should think, no more than a bit of straw or paper blowing about the streets," said Mr. Golspie.

The waiter who had jumped forward was still waiting expectantly a few yards away. Mr. Golspie called him. "You'll have some coffee, won't you? And I'm going to have some brandy, not the Waterloo, though. Will you have a liqueur? Have one of the sweet ones. What about a Benedictine or a Kümmel? What do you say? Here, look at the list."

She examined it. What fascinating names they had, these liqueurs! "I don't know. Shall I? All right then, I'll have a Green Chartreuse."

Mr. Golspie lit a cigar and then, over the coffee and liqueurs, answered some questions she asked about his recent trip abroad, and went rambling on about his experiences in those Baltic countries and in other places still more mysterious and romantic to her. As she listened, feeling very gay and confident inside, his blunt staccato talk seemed to open a series of little windows upon a magical world she had always known to be somewhere about, although she had never walked in it herself, and his own figure took colour from the blue and golden lights flashing through these little windows. He talked in the way she had always felt a man should talk. He was so tremendously and refreshingly un-Burpenfieldish. And he was interested in her; he was not merely filling in an idle hour; she attracted him, had attracted him, she felt now, for some time; and—oh!—it was all amusing and exciting.

"It's quarter to ten," Mr. Golspie suddenly announced. "What about that dance of yours?"

"O Lord!—I don't know. It's hardly worth it now. What a nuisance!"

"Like dancing, eh?"

"Adore it."

"All right. You listen to me. I remember now I had an invitation from one or two of those Anglo-Baltic chaps; they weren't giving the show, but a friend of theirs was, and a lot of people I know were going to be there. Dancing, too. We'll go there, and then you won't be able to say I've done you out of your Old Year's Night celebration. What d'you say? Good! I've got the telephone number down in my notebook, and now I'll just ring up to make sure. Shan't be a minute."

He returned, smiling, with the news that the party had just begun. "Yes, I know what you're trying to say now," he continued. "What about clothes, eh? Well, any clothes are right for this affair. They're not a dressy lot. If you went without clothes, they wouldn't care. We'll have to stop on the way to buy something—a bottle or two and something to eat—to take with us. It's not necessary, but it'll be appreciated. These people will be a change for you—not the sort you meet in a girls' club at all—and it'll amuse you, if you're the girl I take you to be."

There wasn't even time to ask him then what exactly was the girl he took her to be.

v

They went in a taxi and the place was somewhere Notting Hill way, but that was as near as she ever came to knowing where it was. She could have asked, of course, but she preferred to be without exact information; it was more amusing. The road in which they finally stopped looked one of those dingy, shabby-genteel streets, but she could not be sure even about that. They walked up a garden path, but instead of going up the steps to the house itself, they turned to the right, by the side of the house, until they came to a lighted door and a great deal of noise. Apparently the party was being held in one of those large detached studios.

She found herself shaking hands with a very small woman with frizzy black hair, tiny black eyes that seemed to jump and snap, a long humorous nose, and an outrageous purple dress. After that she shook hands with a very tall fair man who looked like a retired Siegfried. These were obviously the host and hostess, and they were both foreigners, but she never caught their names. Clearly it was the sort of party at which names were of little importance. The studio was filled with people; most of whom had a foreign look. None of the men wore evening dress, and among the women, she was glad to see, there was an astonishing variety of clothes, so that she was not at all conspicuous. Mr. Golspie recognised a good many acquaintances, and she was introduced to some of them, mostly youngish men of a nondescript foreign appearance who drew themselves up sharply, looked grave for a moment, then suddenly smiled and widened their eyes, as if to say: "I am being introduced to a lady, by my friend Mr. Golspie. This is serious, important. Ah, but how charming, how beautiful a lady!" It was a pleasure being introduced to men with such a manner. One of them, the youngest, a nice, smiling boy with bright hazel eyes, called Something-insky, insisted upon her smoking a long cigarette, and brought her a mysterious, greeny-yellow drink. Mr. Golspie, who had found a whisky and soda, grinned at her, and exchanged knowing remarks in a mixed language with various men, who patted him on the shoulder and slapped him on the back and were patted and slapped in return.

The little hostess, her eyes snapping furiously, came rushing through and screamed in an unknown tongue at two young men in a corner, a small crooked Jew, almost a hunchback, and a thin red-haired young man, very serious behind enormous spectacles. When she finished screaming at them and had held out both her arms in an imploring gesture, these two bowed gravely, and then the Jew sat down at the grand piano and the red-haired spectacled

one seated himself behind some drums. They began playing—and
very well they played, too—and in a moment the centre of the room
was cleared for dancing.

"You veel danz, eh? Pleass?" said Something-insky.

He was a good dancer, and though he was not quite tall enough
for her, they got on very well together. As he piloted her in and
out, for nearly everybody was dancing and the floor was crowded,
he talked the whole time. "I study here ee-conom-eegs," he told her,
"at Lon-don School of Ee-conom-eegs," and he was very serious
about his economics, but it was difficult to understand much of what
he said about them. Very soon he passed to more intimate matters.
"Yes, I like Eng-lish girls vairy moch. Oh, but I am vairy saad,
vairy, vairy saad now," he told her, his hazel eyes dancing with
pleasure. "I leef in High-gate and in High-gate I have a girl, an
Eng-lish girl, vairy beautiful—Flora. She leefs, too, in High-gate,
Flora, and she has blue eyess and golden hair. For two veeks, you
see, we have a quarrel. Oh yes, it is vairy seely, but it is vairy saad,
too. One night I go to movees. I ask Flora to go too, but no—she
cannot go. So I go-by-myself. I am standing outside and I see a girl
I know, a girl from High-gate. Vairy nice girl—but—aw, she is
noding to me. But I am pol-ite, I say to her, 'Good-evening, mees.
You go to movees too?' I am by-myself. I take her weet me into
movees. Noding, noding at all. But after, she tell Flora—at High-
gate—'Oh, I go weet your foreign friend to movees.' Flora comes
to me and we have a beeg quarrel." He squeezed Miss Matfield's
hand as if he felt that at this point he must have sympathy or die.
"Yes, a beeg quarrel. For two veeks, I do not see Flora at all. I am
vairy saad now."

Miss Matfield said it was rather sad, but told herself that in its
mixture of Highgate and foreign-ness it was really quite absurd and
wonderlandish, and somehow it gave the key to the whole evening.
Nobody in this studio, except herself and Mr. Golspie (and she was
not sure about him), was quite real. Something-insky and his friends
were very charming, but it was rather a relief when Mr. Golspie

marched up, very solid and dominating, and said, "Well, what about a dance with me?"

"Of course," she told him. "I thought perhaps you didn't dance. You've not been dancing, have you?"

"No. I thought I'd wait for you, Miss Matfield. You're the partner I want. I can dance all right, but, mind you, I don't pretend to be good at it, not like some of these lads. Have another drink before we start, eh?"

"If I have another drink to-night, I shall probably be quite drunk. I feel hazy now."

"No harm in feeling hazier. I'll look after you, don't you worry."

But she shook her head. The music started again, the little Jew wagging his black locks over the piano and his companion solemnly nodding above his drums, and Mr. Golspie grasped her masterfully. He was obviously not a very good dancer, but even if he had been, there would not have been much chance for him to show what he could do in that crowded space, for now there seemed to be twice as many people on the floor.

"How d'you like this show?" he asked, grinning at her.

"I do like it. It's amusing."

"I'm glad you think so."

"You sound as if you don't care for it very much."

"It's not bad," he told her. "But too much of a crowd for my liking. Just the pair of us somewhere would please me better."

Afterwards there was an interval, during which everybody ate and drank and smoked and talked all at once, and a girl who appeared to be a secretary at some legation came up with Something-insky and another, older man, and the girl who was a secretary was very giddy and gay and apparently rather tight, though not unpleasantly so, and then a little foreign girl with a hideous fur-trimmed jacket joined them, and the six of them made a little group in one corner, where they ate and drank and smoked and talked as hard as anybody. Then the little hostess screamed again, and this time the tall host produced a number of astonishing syllables in a rasping tenor and then put on a colossal smile, and at once everybody sat down somewhere and most of the lights were turned out. Only the corner where the Jew still sat at the piano was fully illuminated. Then there appeared in front of the piano a smallish plump man with an enormous bald head and a yellow fat face, who stood there, smiling vaguely at them while they applauded, like another but alien Humpty-Dumpty. The Jew played a few sonorous and melancholy chords. Humpty-Dumpty put his hand to his mouth, as if to press a button, for when he lowered his hand, his face was quite different; the smile had been wiped off; his eyebrows had descended at least an inch and a half; and his eyes stared tragically out of deep hollows. Miss Matfield noticed all these details. It was queer, but though things in general were curiously hazy, she had only to concentrate her attention upon anything and every detail of it, like Humpty-Dumpty's lips and eyebrows, stood out in clear relief. This made everything seem tremendously amusing, and she was very happy. Humpty-Dumpty began singing now in a great rich bass voice, which immediately plunged Miss Matfield, who delighted in rich bass voices, into a dreamy ecstasy. He sang one song after another, sometimes sinking into the profoundest melancholy and the bitterness of death, and at other times breaking into high spirits that were as strange and wild as a revolution. With her eyes fixed on that great yellow moon of a face from which these entrancing sounds came, Miss Matfield allowed her mind to be carried floating away on these changing currents of music, and her body to rest against the stalwart arm and shoulder of Mr. Golspie. She was sorry when it came to an end, and Humpty-Dumpty, after bowing, smiling, frowning, shaking his head in an amazingly rapid succession, walked away to eat a whole plateful of sandwiches, wash them down with lager beer, and talk to five people at once with his mouth full.

There was just time for another dance and then it was twelve o'clock. Everybody was silent for a moment. At the end of that moment, they all behaved like men and women who had been reprieved in the very shadow of the gallows, which is perhaps how they saw themselves. Never before had Miss Matfield seen such a raising and clinking of glasses, so much back-slapping, hand-shaking, embracing, and kissing. Something-insky kissed the little girl in the fur-trimmed jacket and the secretary girl from the legation, and then kissed Miss Matfield's hand fifteen times while the girl in the fur-trimmed coat, who had suddenly burst into tears, kissed her on the cheek. Mr. Golspie shook her by the hand, then gave her a big hug. It was at this moment that the only unpleasant event of the evening occurred. Once or twice before, Miss Matfield had had to escape from a tall bleary-eyed man, one of the very few Englishmen there, who was rather drunk and had been bent on dancing with her. Now he suddenly lurched into the middle of their little group, murmuring something about a happy New Year, and tried to embrace her. Mr. Golspie, however, stepped forward smartly and with one shove of his heavy shoulder sent the man reeling back.

"I think I'd better go now," she said to Mr. Golspie. "I'm terribly late as it is."

"All right. I'll come with you." Taking no notice of the unpleasant fellow, who was mumbling threats just behind them, he took her by the arm, marched her through the crowd to shake hands with the host and hostess, and then led her towards the door. There they separated to look for their things. When Miss Matfield returned to the little entrance hall of the studio, the unpleasant man was there. Fortunately, Mr. Golspie appeared, too.

"Now wha's the idea, eh?" said the unpleasant one, thickly and truculently to Mr. Golspie, trying to put a hand on his shoulder.

"The idea is—you go home to bed," replied Mr. Golspie, giving him one contemptuous glance.

"Home to bed!" the other sneered. "T-t-t-t-t-talk like a dam' fool. Bed!" Then he recollected himself. "All I wanner do is to wish thish young lady a Hap-py New Year." And he made a clutch at her.

This time Mr. Golspie instantly pinned both the man's arms to his side with so powerful a grasp that the man cried out. "Talk like a dam' fool, do I?" said Mr. Golspie, pushing his face forward. "If you don't make yourself scarce, you'll start the worst new year you ever remembered. See?" And he shook the man. "See?" And with that, he sent the man flying back, took three or four steps forward to see if any more persuasion was needed, and when he saw it was not—for the man had obviously had quite enough of Mr. Golspie—he returned to Miss Matfield's side. "I've rung up for a taxi," he said calmly. "There's a telephone in there where I had my hat and coat. It'll be here in a minute. We'll wait just outside and get a breath of fresh air."

Miss Matfield, who had been half frightened, half elated by the little scene, and now, what with the wine and the dancing and the music and the embracing and the general excitement of the long evening, was in a fantastic condition, tired and excited and timid and audacious and thrilled all at once, followed her brutal or heroic friend out of the studio and into the shadow of the neighbouring house. Just before the shadow ended, he stopped. "We can wait here as well as anywhere," he said.

She did not tell him that it would be still more sensible to wait at the front gate. She stopped, and said nothing.

"Well, that wasn't bad," he said, "though I'd had enough of it when you said you had to go. They'll keep it up till the milk comes. I shouldn't have gone, though, if you hadn't said you'd come with me. If you want to know my opinion, we've had a good Old Year's Night. We've got to see more of each other."

"Oh, have we?" She was in no condition to be femininely cool and mocking, but she did her best.

"Yes, of course we have," he replied coolly. "You're the sort of girl I like, and I don't often find one."

"Thank you for the compliment," she said, and was instantly annoyed with herself for sounding so feeble.

"Well, Miss Matfield—oh, damn it, I can't keep calling you Miss Matfield, not out of the office, anyhow. What's your other name?"

"Lilian," she replied, in a tiny voice.

"That's good—Lilian. Well, Lilian, now that we're out of that monkey house in there, with everybody snatching and pecking at each other, I can wish you a proper Happy New Year." And, saying no more, he swept her to him, kissed her several times, and held her close, so close that she could hardly breathe.

She could not have described it as being either pleasant or unpleasant. It was not an experience that could fall into such easy categories. It could not be tasted, examined, reported on, like most of Miss Matfield's experiences. If it belonged anywhere, it belonged to the fire, flood and earthquake department. Her quickening blood faced and replied to this huge masculine onslaught, but the rest of her was simply dazed and shaken.

"There's our taxi," he said, breathing hard, but otherwise cool enough. "What's the address?"

Inside the taxi, she suddenly felt very tired and quite disinclined to talk. She drooped, leaned against him, and could only repeat to herself that it was all quite absurd, though all the time she knew very well that whatever else it might be, it was not absurd. Mr. Golspie was quiet too, though in that little enclosed space he seemed now a gigantically vital creature, a being essentially different from herself, a huge throbbing engine of a man.

"Getting near your place?" he inquired, as the taxi began to mount the hill.

"Yes, it's only about half-way up this hill."

"We'll have some more nights out together, shall we? Not all like this, y'know. Just the two of us, roaming round a bit, going to a show or two, and so on. What d'you say?"

"Yes, I'd like to. In fact—I'd love it." She glanced out of the window, then rapped on it. "We're just outside now. Please, don't come out. No, no more. All right then—there! Good-bye—and—and thank you for my nice big dinner."

The dance was over at the Club and most of the lights were out, but a few girls were still drifting about the hall and chattering softly on their way upstairs.

"Hello, Matfield!" somebody cried. "Happy New Year!"

Would it be? It had begun strangely enough. Now that she was back in the familiar and despised Burpenfield atmosphere, the night's antics ought to have appeared in retrospect gayer and more delightfully adventurous than ever, with Mr. Golspie directing them like a droll and massive fairy prince; but oddly enough, they cut no such figure and she found herself wanting to avoid the thought of them. As she slowly climbed the darkening stairs she shivered a little. She was tired, rather cold, and her head ached. There floated into her mind, as if borne there by white virginal sails, the comforting thought of aspirin and her hot water bottle.

VI

When he asked her, two days later, to spend another evening with him, she gladly accepted, although she had told herself several times before that she would refuse; and after that they spent a good deal of time together. They would have dinner somewhere, and then amuse themselves by visiting some show of his choice. They saw the new Jerry Jerningham musical comedy and a crook play; they went twice to the Colladium; they tried a Talkie or two; and one exciting night he took her to a big boxing match. She never really learned a great deal about him; he would talk about odd experiences he had had by the hour, but he remained mysterious; she never discovered what his plans were, and at times she suspected that he did not intend to stay in England much longer, but this suspicion was only based on casual vague remarks; she never went near his flat, never met his daughter, and never heard a single word from him about his dead wife, if indeed she was dead; and yet she felt she knew him as she had never known a man before. Sometimes he was simply friendly or uncle-ish, dismissing her with a pat on the shoulder or a squeeze of the arm; sometimes he turned cynically and grossly amorous, and when he tried to paw her and she repulsed him, he jeered at her and said things that were all the more brutal because there was in them a hard core of truth, and then she saw him as a gross middle-aged toper, loathed him, and despised herself for having anything to do with him; but then, at other times, after a happy exciting evening, he would reach out to her in sudden passion and her own mood would flare up to match with his, and in some little patch of darkness or in the taxi going home, they would kiss and clutch and strain to one another, without a single word of love passing between them, and she would be left shaken and gasping, unable to decide whether she was a woman who was falling in love with this strange unlikely man or a crazy little fool who had just had too much excitement and wine, who ought to go and have a good hot bath and learn sense and decency. And that was all, so far, though even she guessed it could not go on like that. Meanwhile, between these curious expeditions, she chatted and grumbled as usual at the Club, wrote home in the old strain once a week, and quietly worked away at the office, where nobody knew what was happening to her.

Then, one night, as he took her back to the Club, he said, quite casually: "I see they're having a nice fine spell on the South Coast. What about a trip down there next week-end, Lilian? Might get hold of a car."

"Oh yes," she cried at once, without thinking, for week-ends out of London were her dream, even in January. "Let's do that."

"Is it a bargain?" he said quickly, triumphantly.

And then she realised what it meant. "No, no. I'm sorry. I spoke without thinking."

"Ah, she spoke without thinking, did she? You do far too much thinking. Girls shouldn't think too much, not good-looking ones, anyhow. When I first met you, you'd done nothing but think for a long time, and you weren't looking too cheerful on it."

She made no reply. She was annoyed, partly because she was compelled to recognise the truth behind this little jeer. When he talked about her in his casual, rather brutal fashion, he had a strange knack of fastening upon some unpleasant truth. He seemed to take aim quite wildly, but somewhere in her mind, a bell rang nearly every time.

He changed his tone now. "Oh, come on. Nobody's going to hurt you. Let's enjoy ourselves while we're here."

"No, thank you," she said quietly, though she found it far more difficult to resist this kind of appeal.

He pressed her.

"No, I won't. Sometime, perhaps. But not now. No, I mean it."

"Well, I'm disappointed in you. Still, I'll try again. Otherwise, y'know, you might regret saying that, some day. Oh, you can laugh——"

"I might well laugh. I think men are the limit. You just want your own way, no matter what it costs—to me, and you're quite hurt and disappointed because you can't have it, and anybody would think to hear you that you'd been spending weeks thinking it all out purely for my benefit."

"That's right," said Mr. Golspie cheerfully, and she knew, though she could not see him properly, that he was grinning. "Just what I have been doing. That's why I'm disappointed."

"And that's why I'm laughing," she retorted, though she did not feel like laughing now. "At your impudent selfishness. Marvellous!"

"And I tell you, young woman, you might regret it one day. I'm going to ask you again. You think it over."

"I won't."

But she did think it over, and unfortunately she began that very night, so that it was hours and hours before she got to sleep. Her angry taut body refused to relax; her head was a huge hot ring round which her thoughts went galloping dustily; and as she turned in the uneasy darkness she heard the late taxis and cars go hooting far away, melancholy hateful sounds in the deep night, like flying rumours of disaster.

Chapter Nine

MR. SMEETH IS WORRIED

I

WHERE you going to?" asked Mr. Smeeth, turning round in his chair to look at his wife, who had suddenly made her appearance in the doorway, wearing her hat and coat. She was still flushed with temper. It was surprising how young and smart she looked. Still, she could not go on like that, no matter how young and smart she looked.

"Out," she replied, with that special look and special voice she had for him when they had quarrelled. Oh dear!

"Yes, I know that," he pointed out, "but where you going to?"

Up she blazed then, with her colour flaming and her fine blue eyes flashing at him: "Just *out*, and that's enough for you. Begrudge every penny you give me, keep me as short as you possibly can, tell me I mustn't buy this and mustn't buy that, go peeping and spying about and then lose your silly temper because you've seen something you don't like to see—though—goodness me!—there can't be a woman in this street who hasn't a few bills like that in the house, and most of them a lot more and instalments, too, to pay and their husbands not bringing in anything like what you are——" Here Mrs. Smeeth stopped, not because this fine rhetorical sentence had got out of control (it had, but she was capable of finishing it somehow), but simply because she wanted to draw a deep breath. "And then you want to know where I'm going! I suppose you'd like me to give an account of that as well, wouldn't you? Yes, of course. Oh, of course!" Her head wagged as she brought out these vast

356

sneers. "That would be very nice for you, wouldn't it? I'll come and ask if I can spend a penny or tuppence. Then I'll ask if I can walk down the road——"

"Oh, don't be so silly, Edie," cried Mr. Smeeth, who hated this sort of wild ridiculous talk and could not see what good it did. Even after all these years, he was still innocent enough to imagine that his wife was trying to argue and failing absurdly, and he did not realise that she was merely exploding into speech.

"Don't be so silly!" she repeated indignantly, at the same time coming forward into the room. "I'd like to ask anybody who's the silly one here. They'd soon tell you. And I'd rather be silly than mean. Yes—*mean*. If you're not careful, Herbert Smeeth, you'll soon be too mean to live. Pinching and scraping as if you didn't know where the next penny was coming from! And the more money you're getting, the worse you are. It's growing on you, this mean-ness. My words, I'd like you to be married to some women, that's all. They'd teach you something about spending."

"No, they wouldn't," he said crossly, "'cos I wouldn't have it, wouldn't have it for a single minute. I'd soon put a stop to *their* little games. As for being mean, you know as well as I do, Edie, I'm not mean, and never have been. There's nothing you've ever really wanted, or the children either, you haven't had. But somebody's got to be careful, that's all. We're not made of money. When I got this rise, I hoped we'd begin to save properly. Anybody'd think to hear you talk they'd given me the Bank of England instead of another pound a week. Have a bit of sense, Edie. If we're going to spend every penny we have now and get into debt, where are we going to be if anything happens to us? Just tell me that."

"And what is going to happen to us? Bless me, the way you talk! A proper old Jonah you're turning into! You give me the pip, Dad, honestly you do. Anybody'd think to hear *you* talk that we'll have to sell up any day. You can't enjoy yourself a minute for thinking about what might happen to you the year after next or sometime.

We've only got to live once and we've only got to die once, and for heaven's sake let's enjoy ourselves while we can, I say."

"Yes, and when we can't—what then? I've heard this kind of talk before, and I know where it lands people. And anyhow, I can enjoy myself as well as the next, only I can do it sensibly and I don't need to spend every penny we get and go and ask any Fred Mittys to help me to do it."

"That's right. Bring him in. I've been waiting for that, I've just been waiting for that. I wondered how long you'd be able to keep Fred Mitty out of this. That's you all over. You got your knife into him the first time he came here, and after that of course he had to be blamed for everything. Go on. Don't mind me. Why don't you say I give him all my housekeeping money, and have done with it. Go on."

"Well, I'll say this," said Mr. Smeeth, his temper rising. "That bill from Sorley's there's been all this bother about wouldn't have been that size and would have been paid before now, if you hadn't taken it into your head to ask Mitty and his wife and their guzzling pals up here those two nights round Christmas. It's bad enough them coming here at all—most men wouldn't have it for a minute, not if they couldn't stand the sight of 'em and never stayed in the house when they were there, like me—but it's fifty times worse when you go and run yourself into debt to do it, just so they can all swill it down at my expense. It's not good enough, and you know it isn't."

"Oh, isn't it? Well, next time Christmas comes round, I'll tell Fred and everybody else to keep away, and we'll all go into the workhouse, and then you'll be satisfied. If you wasn't getting too mean to live, you'd have thought nothing about it. You talk as if I owed Sorley's about fifty pounds. Three pounds fifteen, that's all it is, and you make all this bother."

"Well, it's three pound fifteen more than you can pay, it seems," he retorted.

"Who says it is? I haven't even asked you to pay it yet. Keep your money. I can pay it all right in time. Sorley's can wait, for all I care."

"Well, they can't for all I care. I believe in paying cash down and no debts running on, always have done, and you know it. And I'll have that to pay, just because you've decided to open a free pub for Mitty and his fine little lot. That's what it amounts to."

"That's right, start again now. You can argue with yourself for an hour or two, and see how you like it. I'm going out. And if you want to know, I'll tell you where I'm going. I'm going," she added deliberately, "down to Fred Mitty's."

He was furious, but he knew that he could not prevent her from going. He looked at her, and he had to twist round in his chair, for she had retreated towards the door: "Well, see you come back sober," he said.

"What's that?"

But he did not repeat it. He wished it unsaid. The instant after it had slipped out, he wanted to call it back. And, for all her "What's that?" she had heard him all right; she was staring at him now, with some of her high colour gone and her mouth curiously drawn down; her whole attitude was different from what it had been during their noisy argument; she was really hurt, this time; he had gone too far, miles and miles too far.

"Yes, I heard you, though," she said quietly, "and it's the nastiest thing, by a long, long way, that you've said to me in twenty years. Did you ever know me come back in any other way but sober?"

"No, no," he muttered. "I'm sorry . . . bit of a joke." He couldn't look her in the face.

"Bit of a joke! I wish it was. But it wasn't. You meant it, Herbert Smeeth. You meant to be as nasty as you could be. There's only another thing worse you could say to your wife, and you'd better hurry up and get that said."

"I tell you, I'm sorry." He got up from his chair now, and looked at her, mumbling something about "going too far."

"Yes, and I'm sorry too," she said bitterly. "I didn't think you'd

got a nasty thing like that in your head to say. Oh, I know it slipped
out, and now you wish it hadn't. But it oughtn't to have been there
to slip out. That's what hurts me."

"Well, after all, you've as good as called me a miser—or at any
rate, a mean devil—half a dozen times to-night," he told her, but
not with much confidence.

"Oh!—that's different—and you know it is."

"I don't see that. Still, if you think so, all I can say, Edie, is—
I'm sorry."

But before he had finished, she had gone, slamming the door contemptuously behind her. A few seconds later, she was outside the
house. Mr. Smeeth returned wretchedly to his chair by the fire. There
was nothing he disliked more than a quarrel with his wife, and this
looked like being a particularly bad one. That remark of his would,
he knew, take some living down. If she had been a woman who
never took a drink at all, there would have been nothing in that
remark; but she liked a drink or two, especially in company, and
was liable at times to get flushed and excited, as she well knew
herself; and if he had thought for months, he could not have said
a thing that would have hurt her more. He was still sorry that he
had said it, though there was one part of him that could not help
enjoying the fact that the shot had told so well. "That got home on
her all right, didn't it?" it chuckled, even while the rest of him, the
part that loved Mrs. Smeeth and was her willing slave, grieved and
repented. Mr. Smeeth did not often swear, but now he called Fred
Mitty, under his breath, every foul name at his command. That
earlier argument would not have taken such a bad turn if it had not
been for Mitty. They had had these little squabbles about money
before, like most couples, he imagined, one of whom is nearly
always a spender and the other a saver. This had been a bit more
serious than most of their squabbles, if only because the extra money
had made her all the more eager to spend and had made him all
the more anxious to begin saving. But Mitty and his wife even came
into this part of the quarrel, for the whole thing began when he

came across that bill from Sorley's for three pounds fifteen, which she had not paid and couldn't pay, and Sorley's off licence and Mr. and Mrs. Swilling Mitty and their bright pals had been responsible for that bill. He had not seen what they had had because on both occasions, being duly warned, he had taken himself off, once to hear "The Messiah," and the other time to play whist with Saunders, and had taken care each time, being a peaceable man, to arrive back home as late as possible, when Mitty and Co. were no longer there. He didn't believe for a moment that his wife was so tremendously fond of the Mitty lot as all that, but just because he had grumbled at first and been a bit heavy-handed about them, she had kept it up, out of devilment and to show her independence. She was like that, if you took the wrong line with her, and he had admitted to himself for a week or two now that, if it was peace and quietness he wanted and not a tussle to decide who was master, he had certainly taken the wrong line.

After brooding over it all for about quarter of an hour, he felt so uncomfortable that if his wife had gone anywhere else but the Mitty's, he would have gone after her, to call for her and then to try and make it up on the way home. But he had his pride, and it refused to allow him to call for her at the Mitty's. He tried to dismiss the whole wretched business. He lit his pipe and picked up the evening paper. There was nothing in it he wanted to read and had not read before. He tried the wireless, and the first station plunged him into the middle of a talk on modern sculpture by a young gentleman who was apparently very tired. Finding no satisfaction in him, Mr. Smeeth went over to the other station, which was running a sort of pierrot show. The pierrots themselves seemed to be enjoying themselves immensely and so did their audience, who laughed and clapped unceasingly, but Mr. Smeeth merely felt rather out of it and thought the jokes not good enough, for all that laughing, and the songs not worth all that applause. "Overdoing it," he muttered darkly at the loud speaker, which replied by bombarding him with more tinny laughter and applause. But he was the master;

he had only to make a little movement and the pierrots and their cackling friends were banished at once, simply hurled into silence; and now he made this little movement, and the loud speaker was at once emptied of sound, nothing more than a bit of a horn. He had a book from the Public Library somewhere about, and now, in despair, he found it and began reading. It was *My Singing Years* by the great soprano, Madame Regina Sarisbury, whom he had once heard in an oratorio years ago, and the young woman at the Library had told him it was a most interesting book, on the word of her sister, who was taking singing lessons and had two or three professional engagements. But so far it had not appealed to him very much. As a matter of fact, he was a reluctant and unenterprising reader, one of those people who hold their books almost at arm's-length and examine them in a very guarded manner, as if at any moment a sentence might explode with a loud report; and he had probably returned more books half-read than any other member of the local Public Library. Nevertheless, he liked to have a Library book about, and to be discovered reading it.

He was discovered now. Edna came in, pulling off her close-fitting little hat, and fussy and breathless, as usual. In a few minutes, she would swing completely round, becoming slack, indifferent, languid, as if the house bored her. Mr. Smeeth knew this, and it irritated him, though he was very fond of the girl.

"Where's mother?"

"Your mother's out."

"Where's she gone to? She said she wasn't going out to-night!"

"The question is, not where she's gone to, but where you've been too," he said, rather severely, looking at her over the top of his eyeglasses.

Edna did not stop to examine the logic of this, or if she did, she did not comment upon it, being still young enough to recognize the right of parents to talk in this fashion. "Been to the pictures—first house," she replied.

"What again! I'm surprised you don't go and live there. You've been once this week, haven't you? Yes, I thought so. And I suppose you'll be wanting to go on Saturday. That'll be three times in one week—three times. Paid ninepence too, I suppose. And who gave you the money to go to-night?"

"Mother did." And Edna looked slightly confused. Her father, noticing this, jumped at once to the wrong conclusion, namely, that Edna had been told to say nothing about this extra visit to the pictures to him and had suddenly realized what she had done. The truth was, however, that Edna was confused, not because she had spent another ninepence, but because the money was still in her possession, for she had gone to the pictures as the guest of one Harry Gibson, Minnie Watson's friend's friend, who, in his turn, was supposed, by his parents in their turn, to have been attending an evening class in accountancy on this particular night.

Mr. Smeeth nodded grimly and tightened his lips. "There'll have to be something said about this, Edna. When I agreed to let you go and learn this millinery business, I didn't agree to let you go to the pictures every night in the week, too."

"I don't go every night, and you know very well I don't, Dad. Some weeks I only go once."

"It's a funny thing I never seem to notice those weeks," said Mr. Smeeth with fine irony. It would have been still finer irony if he had stopped to consider that it really was not funny at all but quite natural. "But apart from the waste of money, I don't like all this picture-going. Doing you no good at all. Doing you harm. I don't object to a girl having her amusement," he continued, dropping into that noble, broad-minded tone of voice that all parents, schoolmasters, clergymen, and other public moralists have at their command. "I go to the pictures now and again myself. But going to the pictures now and again's one thing, and *living* for pictures is another thing altogether. Teaches you nothing but silliness. Get false ideas into your head. Why don't you settle down with a book?" He held out his own book. "Do a bit of quiet reading. Amuse yourself and learn something about the world at the same time. Take this book I'm reading, f'r'instance—*My Singing Years* by Madame Regina Sarisbury—this is a book that tells you something worth knowing, all about the—er—musical career."

"I read a book last week," Edna announced.

"Yes, and been to the pictures three times since then," said her father, who was determined to have his grievance. "Too much going out and amusing yourself altogether, my girl. Why, you're worse than George was at your age. It's my belief you girls are worse than the boys nowadays, more set on having amusement, pictures and dances and what not. I walked from the tram to-night with Mr. Gibson, who lives in the corner house at the bottom of the next street, and he was telling me that his son—I forget his name, but he's about your age, perhaps a year or so older——"

"Do you mean Harry Gibson?" asked Edna.

"Is it Harry? Yes, I think it is. Well, Mr. Gibson was telling me that this boy of his is attending three evening classes a week —accountancy, book-keeping, and something else—three evening classes. That boy means to get on and be somebody in the world. He's not wasting all his time, he's using it to some purpose. I'm not saying that you ought to go to evening classes——"

Here he broke off because he noticed that a mysterious smile that had been hovering for the last minute now seemed to have definitely settled on Edna's face. This smile made him angry, or rather gave him an excuse for exploding the anger that had been waiting inside him. "And for goodness' sake, Edna, take that silly grin off your face when I'm trying to talk sense to you," he shouted, making her jump. "You're not at the pictures now. You're nothing but a great silly baby."

"What have I done now?" she began indignantly.

"Any more of that impudence from you," Mr. Smeeth shouted at her, glaring. But there was no more of that impudence, which suddenly melted to tears. Edna, not a strong character at any time and now completely taken aback by her father's sudden rage, hastily left the room, whimpering.

Mr. Smeeth spent the next few minutes telling himself all the things that were wrong with his daughter and that justified any man getting angry with her now and then. He worked hard, but he did not succeed in convincing himself. He put away *My Singing Years* and turned the wireless on again. At half-past ten, George came in, got a grunt or two from his father (who was, in truth, afraid of talking), retired to the kitchen in search of food and then went to bed. At eleven Mrs. Smeeth returned.

"Have you had anything to eat?" she asked. Sometimes he had a little snack just before going to bed.

He shook his head.

"Can I get you something?" she enquired politely.

He knew now that he was in for a serious quarrel. Mrs. Smeeth easily lost her temper and squabbled, but she recovered it with equal swiftness and ease. If she had marched in and called him a few names and looked as if she was about to throw something at him, he would have known that the whole thing could have been settled before they went to sleep. But when Mrs. Smeeth was quietly polite to him, it meant that for once she had really hardened her heart. She would now turn herself into a very efficient housewife. Nothing would be allowed to go wrong; every meal would be on the table at the proper time and every dish done to a turn; he would not be given the slightest chance to grumble. But as a wife, a real wife, she would cease to exist. Not a smile, not a friendly glance, would come his way; and they would be estranged for days, perhaps weeks.

"No, thanks. I don't want anything. Don't feel like it." Which was true enough, but he hoped it would suggest that he was not very well. She remained quite stony, however.

"Both the children in?" she asked.

"Look here, Edie," he began desperately, "don't be silly."

"I'm not silly. I'm going to bed now." And off she went.

He was in for it now, days of it, perhaps weeks of it; and in order to get out of it, not only would he have to apologize at great length, but he would probably have to buy something as well, in short to spend more money. Yet the root of the whole trouble was that too much money was being spent already. He wished he had never set eyes on Sorley's miserable bill. He wished he had gone out and paid it without a word. He wished—"Oh, damn and blast!" he cried, and in his sudden spasm of fury he screwed up his face so hard and shook his head so violently that his eyeglasses fell off and he spent several minutes groping about the black wool rug before he could find them. Oh—a miserable evening!

II

Between Thursday evening, when hostilities began, and Saturday morning, Mr. Smeeth had tried unsuccessfully once or twice to make his peace and to replace this strange polite woman by his real wife. On Saturday morning he determined to do no more; she could have her sulk, if she wanted it; he would simply make the best of his position as a sort of super-lodger. He trotted down Chaucer Road, on his way to the tram, hardening his heart. The morning, which already had a companionable Saturday look about it, smiled upon him, if only faintly. For a day in late January, it was beginning well; no fog, snow or rain; but a slight sparkle and nip of frost and the early ghost of a sun somewhere above. Mr. Smeeth was very fond of Saturday; he liked the morning in the office (he always had a pipe at about half-past eleven, unless he was very busy), and he liked the afternoon out of the office. It was difficult for him to forget that his wife had quarrelled with him, but he hardened his heart and did his best to forget. Unfortunately—as he knew only too well, for he had said it often enough—it never rains but it pours. This treacherous Saturday was destined to give him a series of shocks, of varying degrees of severity.

The first, and slightest, of these shocks arrived when he walked over to his desk, rubbing his hands as usual and exchanging a remark or two with everybody. His inkwells had not been filled up, and no fresh blotting-paper had been put on his desk.

"Hello!" he cried, looking round. "Where's Stanley?"

"Hasn't turned up," replied Turgis.

"Well, well, well, well," said Mr. Smeeth fussily. "Does anybody know what's happened to him? Is he ill or something?"

Nobody knew. Miss Sellers thought he had probably caught a cold, because she was sure she had heard him sneeze several times while he was copying the letters the night before. Turgis said with gloomy satisfaction that he had probably been knocked down and run over while trying to shadow somebody on his way to the office.

"I don't suppose for a minute he has," said Mr. Smeeth sharply. "But you needn't seem so pleased about it, Turgis. Not a nice way of saying a thing like that at all. I don't like to hear anybody talking like that in this office. Don't know what has come over you lately, Turgis." And it was true. He hadn't liked the way Turgis had looked and talked for some time now.

The mystery of Stanley was cleared up when Mr. Dersingham, very much the Saturday man in plus fours, arrived to go through the letters, for among these was one from Stanley's father, apparently a man of few words, who announced that Stanley was needed badly by his uncle, just returned to the ironmongering in Homerton, where the boy would be nearer home and have a better chance of getting on than in Angel Pavement—and sorry no better notice given but half fortnight's wages due could be kept but please send Insurance Card all filled in—*Yrs truly, Thos. Poole.*

"That means getting another boy," said Mr. Dersingham. "I'm sorry about that one, too. He was a lazy little devil like all of 'em, but he looked rather bright, didn't he?"

"Wasn't a bad boy at all, Mr. Dersingham," said Mr. Smeeth, meditatively. "I'm sorry he's left us, too. We might get a lot worse. He fancied himself as a budding detective, Stanley did—we used to pull his leg about shadowing people and all that."

"Did he? A detective, eh? And I never knew that. He'd got that from reading about 'em, you know. I'm fond of a good detective yarn myself. But I never wanted to be one when I was a boy. They weren't quite so much the thing then, were they? I remember I wanted to be an explorer—you know, expeditions across the desert and all that sort of thing. All the exploring I've done lately, Smeeth, has been looking for some of those mouldy Jew cabinet-making places in back streets in North London. Ah—well!" And for a moment the large pink face of Mr. Dersingham looked clouded, as if he had suddenly discovered that life was quite different from what he imagined it would be when he was in the Fourth at Worrell.

"We live and learn, sir, don't we?" said Mr. Smeeth vaguely.

"Do we? I dunno. People always say we do, don't they? But I dunno. I doubt it sometimes, I do, Smeeth, honestly," the other replied, first glancing at Mr. Smeeth and then looking out of the window, through which nothing could be seen but a ramshackle roof and a few chimney pots beyond. A queer melancholy, quite unlike the proper spirit of any office on Saturday morning, invaded the room, and for a minute the pair of them were lost in it.

"Well, well," cried Mr. Dersingham with a sudden briskness, "you'll have to see about getting another boy. I'm sorry about that, though. That boy might have been a useful chap later on. He's missed a good opening. If that other fellow, Turgis, had gone, I don't think I'd have minded very much. How's he getting on, that fellow? I don't see much of him, but I must say I don't like the look of him these days. He slouches about, looking like nothing on earth. What's the matter with him?"

"I don't know, Mr. Dersingham. I've noticed it, too. There's been something wrong with him lately. He does his work, but only after a fashion, and it's not a fashion I like, I must say. Something on his mind, I should say."

"And a thoroughly nasty mind too, by the look of him! Well, look here, Smeeth, you'd better take him on one side and have a good talk to him. Tell him I'm not satisfied with him and you're not satisfied with him, and that if he doesn't buck up pretty soon, he'll have to clear out. Tell him he's a fool to himself, too, with the business growing as it is and all sorts of chances coming along for smart fellows. You know the kind of thing to say. Threaten him with the sack, if you like; I don't mind. I shouldn't care if I saw the last of the fellow this morning. I never did think much of him. Got a Bolshie look about him. All right, then, Smeeth—see about that, and about getting another boy. And I shall be off in about half an hour or so, and Mr. Golspie won't be in, this morning. So just—er—carry on, will you."

Mr. Smeeth was really sorry that Stanley had gone, and not merely because it meant getting another boy and showing him what to do. He realized now that he had liked Stanley and would miss that freckled snub nose of his, that sandy bullet head, and all the ridiculous detective talk. But that was not all. Nobody knew better than Mr. Smeeth that office boys come and go, are here to-day and gone to-morrow, but nevertheless this sudden departure of Stanley troubled him, if only because he disliked change of any kind and found himself visited by a vague mistrust, a flicker or two of apprehension, whenever it occurred. Stanley had become part of the office for him, and now Stanley had gone. It was not important, but still, he did not like it.

"If we finish in good time this morning," he said to Turgis, after he had told them all about Stanley and had handed over the copying and posting of the letters to little Poppy Sellers, "I want to have a little talk with you, Turgis. You're not in a great hurry to get away, are you?"

Turgis wasn't. Indeed, the outside world appeared to have lost as much favour with him as the office had.

It was an easy morning. At twelve, Miss Matfield had nothing more to do, and was allowed to go, looking rather more pleased with herself and the world than she usually did. Turgis lounged up and gave Miss Sellers a hand with the copying, for which he received several grateful glances from the brown eyes beneath the fringe. Mr. Smeeth, sending out a fragrant drift of Benenden's Own

Mixture, fussed about and locked up, then gave the letters to Poppy and packed her off.

"Now then," he said to Turgis, as soon as they were alone.

"Yes, Mr. Smeeth?" replied Turgis mournfully.

Mr. Smeeth looked at him, and perhaps saw him clearly for the first time for weeks. There were dark rings under his eyes, and the eyes themselves had a queer reddish look, as if their owner was not getting enough sleep. He never had much colour, but now he was very pale, and the bony ridge of his rather large nose shone as it caught the light, as if the skin had been drawn back from it at each side. The lad didn't look at all well. Mr. Smeeth, who knew that Turgis lived in lodgings and was a lonely sort of chap, felt sorry for him.

"Here, Turgis," he said, "there's plenty of time. We'll go out and talk there. Can you drink a glass of beer?"

Turgis, pleased and flattered by this invitation, said that he could.

"Well, we'll go across the road and have a glass of beer there. Do us no harm. Everything's locked up, I think, isn't it? All right, then. We'll go." And so they went down the stairs, Mr. Smeeth kept up a cheerful clatter of talk: "I'll just pop round the corner to Benenden's to get some tobacco first. Always get my tobacco there, have done for years. His own mixture, y'know—mixes it himself. Better than this ounce packet stuff. You get it fresh. You don't smoke a pipe, do you? Cigarettes, eh? You ought to try a pipe. Cheaper and a better smoke and better for your health, too. I've tried to get my boy George to start a pipe, but he won't drop his cigarettes. Gaspers all the time. Too much trouble just to fill and light a pipe, that's it. I wonder how these *Kwik-Work* people are going on? Always seem to be busy enough, but I never knew anybody that used their blades. I stick to the old-fashioned razor. I've used the same two for twenty years. I call it a silly waste of money buying these safety razor blades. No wonder they give the razors away nowadays. They know once you've got the razor you'll have to keep on buying their blades. That's the catch, you see. Well, just wait a minute. I'll call on my old friend, Mr. Benenden."

But he didn't, because his old friend Mr. Benenden was not there. Behind the counter was a plump young woman with bright ginger hair, and if Cleopatra herself in full regalia had been standing there, Mr. Smeeth could not have stared at her in greater astonishment.

"Yes?" said the plump young woman.

To explain what he wanted in T. Benenden's, when year after year he had merely had to put his pouch on the counter, was in itself so novel an action that Mr. Smeeth found himself at a loss to perform it. "But—where's Mr. Benenden?"

The young woman smiled. "You a regular customer here?" she asked.

"I should think I am," said Mr. Smeeth. "I've been coming in here, week in and week out, for Mr. Benenden's Own Mixture for years. It made me jump to see anybody else here. What's happened? He's not given it up, has he?"

"No, he's not given it up," she explained. "He's in hospital. He got knocked down by a car last night in Cheapside, and they took him to St. Bartholomew's."

"Well, you surprise me! I'm sorry to hear that. Is he bad?"

"We don't know yet. He didn't seem so bad last night, because he got a message through to my mother and she went to see him and he gave her the key here and asked if I'd look after the shop for him, because he knew I wasn't doing anything and I'd worked once in a tobacconist's before—well, tobacconist's and sweets', it was, not like this, y'know—so it didn't sound as if it was bad, with him being able to talk and arrange things like that, but the doctor told my mother it was worse than it looked, for all that, and it might be a nasty long job, and she's going again to-day. I'm his niece, you see."

"Poor old chap! I *am* sorry about this," said Mr. Smeeth, who was indeed genuinely distressed. "You must let me know how he goes on." He had to point out to her the tin canister that held T. Benen-

den's Own Mixture and had even to tell her the price of it. When
he rejoined Turgis outside, he could talk of nothing else for the next
five minutes. This one morning, not content with removing Stanley
from Angel Pavement for ever, had gone and swept Benenden out
of sight, put a plump young woman with ginger hair behind that
counter, and turned Benenden into a mysterious suffering figure
in a hospital. Benenden and Angel Pavement had been inseparable
in his mind for years, and now the thought of Benenden not being
there, no longer waiting, tie-less, behind his dusty counter, gave
the whole place a queer look. Turgis had been in the shop many
a time for cigarettes, but, being one of the "packet o' gaspers"
customers, he could not really claim to be acquainted with Benenden.
By the time Mr. Smeeth had finished talking to him about the
tobacconist, the pair of them were in the private bar of the *White
Horse* across the road and had two glasses of bitter placed in front
of them.

Mr. Smeeth had not been in this bar since that night, two or
three months before, when Mr. Golspie took him in, gave him a
double whisky and a cigar, and talked about the business. It was
still as cosy as ever, but this time it was not so quiet. It was entirely
dominated by a large man with an enormous red face, who roared
and spluttered and coughed and wheezed very loudly at his two
companions, men of ordinary size, who could only make ordinary
noises back at him. All conversation in the bar was provided with
a thundering accompaniment by this large man. There was no
escaping him.

"You see, Turgis," said Mr. Smeeth, "I thought I'd better have
a little talk to you, because, for one thing, I've been noticing a few
little things myself, and for another thing, Mr. Dersingham's been
saying something to me about you. If you remember, I said something when we had a little talk a month or two ago."

"I remember that, Mr. Smeeth. When you said they'd been thinking of giving me the push."

"That's right. Well, Mr. Dersingham talked to me about you this morning—rather in the same strain, Turgis, and I said I'd have a talk to you."

"But what have I done wrong?" cried Turgis bitterly. "Why's he always picking on me? I do my work all right, don't I? You've never said anything about it to me, Mr. Smeeth. Seems to me they want to get rid of me whether I've done anything wrong or not——"

"Outch-ch-ch-ch," went the large man. "Wait a minute, Charlie, wait a minute, let me tell it. Oh dear, oh dear, oh dear, oh dear. 'Ere, this is it. Simmy come up to me, that morning, and I'm standing as I might be 'ere, see—and old Simmy—— Just a minute, Charlie, let me tell it——"

"This is the point, Turgis," said Mr. Smeeth earnestly. "And, mind you, I'm talking in a friendly way. Nobody's got anything against you at all. Put that out of your head. But as Mr. Dersingham says—you've got to buck up. Just lately, you've not been taking your work in the right spirit at all. I know you're not a lazy chap and I know you can do your work all right, but if I hadn't known it, I don't mind telling you, I might have come to a wrong conclusion just lately. Now, we all have our troubles. I've plenty of my own, I can tell you," he continued, with the air of a modest hero, "though you mightn't think it. That's because I've learned not to bring 'em to the office with me. I'm old enough and experienced enough not to let my troubles interfere with my work. You're not, and it's nothing to be ashamed of. My opinion is, Turgis— you've not been feeling up to the mark lately."

"That is so, Mr. Smeeth," said Turgis. "You're right there. I haven't."

"Didn't he, Charlie?" roared the large man, drowning everybody. "He did. It's as true as I'm standing 'ere. Next time you see Simmy, you say to 'im 'What price Lady Flatiron at Newbury?'—that's all. Just say that. Laugh! O Gord! Outch-ch-ch-ch-ch." The enormous face was purple now.

"It's no business of mine, Turgis," said Mr. Smeeth in his ear, "and I'm only asking in a friendly spirit. But it's my opinion you've got yourself into trouble somehow. If it isn't that, you'd better go round and see a doctor. Perhaps you're just not feeling well."

"I'm not feeling so well, Mr. Smeeth, but it isn't that, really. It's just—oh, I dunno—well, you see, Mr. Smeeth, it's a girl. That's what's been bothering me just lately."

"Oh, that's it, is it? Ought you to be marrying her or something of that sort? No? Nothing like that, eh? Oh, well, had a bit of a quarrel, eh?"

"Yes, in a way," replied Turgis, guardedly, looking very uncomfortable.

"Oh, well, don't you let that bother you," cried Mr. Smeeth, astonished to discover that this was nothing but a lovers' tiff. "I know what it is, of course. You're talking to an old married man now, my boy. I've got a son nearly as old as you. It doesn't matter how you've quarrelled, you don't want to take it as hard as that. Bless me!—you'll be making yourself ill over it."

"That's what I think sometimes," said Turgis bitterly.

"Ridiculous! It'll soon blow over. And if it doesn't, why, go and find another girl who isn't so quarrelsome. I can tell you this, if she's quarrelsome now, she'll be past living with, if you're not careful, later on. You're too sensitive about it, Turgis—that's your trouble."

Turgis produced a smile that was abject misery itself, the tortured ghost of a grin.

"No, no, not at all," the large man shouted. "We've ten minutes yet. Plenty of time for another. What is it? Same again? Three double Scotches, miss. I 'aven't told you yet what 'appened the other night, 'ave I? I mean, with Jack Pearce and old Joe, down at Staines —oh dear!—splooch-ooch-ooch-ooch-ooch!"

"He seems to be enjoying himself all right," said Turgis. "I don't know how some of these chaps do it—spending money all day, no work, knocking about all the time, and not giving a damn for anybody. How do they do it, Mr. Smeeth?"

"Don't ask me," replied Mr. Smeeth, a trifle irritably, as if he too had felt a sudden spasm of envy at the thought of this rich careless life, but would not admit it to himself. "Racing chaps, I suppose. Easy come and easy go—that's their motto. All right while it lasts—but how long does it last?"

"How long does anything last?" Turgis muttered.

"Now that's silly talk from a young fellow like you," said Mr. Smeeth. "It's that sort of talk that lets you down with everybody. Now listen to me. I believe if you'll only smarten yourself up a bit, don't be so gloomy, look as if you didn't hate the sight of every-body ——"

"I don't, Mr. Smeeth, honestly I don't."

"—and settle down to your work properly, there's a good steady job waiting for you with Twigg and Dersingham. As Mr. Dersingham said, only this morning, what with all this new business, the firm'll be growing and expanding, and that'll be just the opportunity for a young fellow like yourself."

Turgis swallowed desperately. "I'm not so sure about that," he declared.

"What d'you mean?" cried Mr. Smeeth, staring at him.

"I don't think it's all so rosy as all that. I've been thinking it over. All this new business—and as far as I can see, it's about all the business we're doing—came with Mr. Golspie." He brought out this name with a sudden jerk.

"Well, what if it did? You're not telling me anything now, Turgis. I know that as well as you do—and better."

"If he goes, what happens then, Mr. Smeeth?"

"If he goes? That would depend. A lot might happen, or nothing might happen. But, anyhow, Mr. Golspie's not going."

"I think he is—soon, too."

Mr. Smeeth stared at him. Turgis was obviously quite serious. "Where did you get that idea from?"

"I think he is."

"What's the good of talking like that! You think he is! Why should he now? What's the object? He's making plenty of money out of the business, as I know better than you do. He's making a surprising amount, for a trade like this—I don't mind telling you. He'd been a fool if he did go, unless, of course—well——" And Mr. Smeeth thought of several possibilities, but kept them to himself. "No, that's silly talk, Turgis. What put that into your head?"

"It isn't silly, Mr. Smeeth," cried Turgis, goaded into saying more than he had ever intended to say. "I *know* he's going. At least, I know he's not staying with the firm long. I know he doesn't think much of Mr. Dersingham either. I know that, too."

"But where have you got all this from?" Mr. Smeeth was more angry than alarmed. "This is the first I've heard of it. How did you learn it? You're not trying to be funny, are you?"

"Well," roared the large man. "Get a move on, eh? You coming to eat with me, Charlie? That's right. See you Monday, Tom, eh? Course I'll be there. You betcher life, boy! Wouldn't miss it. Am I what? Oh—you wicked feller, Tom, you wicked feller! So long, boy. Morning, miss. Morning, Sam." And the silence he left behind him was almost startling.

In this silence, Mr. Smeeth and Turgis looked at one another. Then Turgis turned his eyes elsewhere, but Mr. Smeeth continued looking at him.

"I don't make head or tail of this, Turgis."

Turgis frowned, shut his mouth tight for once, and moved uneasily. Finally, he said: "I—heard something, Mr. Smeeth, that's all. I can't tell where I heard it or anything. I'm sorry I spoke now."

Mr. Smeeth saw that Turgis was terribly in earnest. There could be no doubt about that. "Do you mean to say you won't tell me where you heard it, how you heard it, or anything?"

"I'm sorry, Mr. Smeeth. I oughtn't to have said anything. I can't tell you any more, honestly I can't. Don't mention it to anybody, please, Mr. Smeeth. If you do, you might get me into trouble, though I haven't done anything really wrong, I haven't, honestly. Only I did hear that about Mr. Golspie."

"When was that? You can tell me so much, anyhow."

"Not long before Christmas, a week or two."

"Mr. Golspie was away then, was he?"

"Yes," Turgis admitted sullenly. "It was while he was away."

"Then somebody told you while Mr. Golspie was away," said Mr. Smeeth sharply, not taking his eyes off the unhappy Turgis for a second. He thought quickly. "It must have been his daughter, that time when you took the money to her. You got talking and then she told you. Is that it?"

Turgis said nothing, but he had no need to, for his face replied for him. "Well, what did she say exactly?" Mr. Smeeth continued, far more concerned now that he knew Mr. Golspie's daughter was the informant. "Come on, Turgis, you might as well tell me now. What did she say?"

"I don't remember any more," Turgis mumbled miserably. "That was all. It was nothing. I oughtn't to have said anything. Mr. Smeeth, please don't you say anything, please don't, will you? Promise."

"All right. I don't suppose there's anything in it. I know what these girls are. They'll say anything. Well ——"

"Yes, I must be getting on now," said Turgis. "And thank you for telling me—you know about what Mr. Dersingham said. I'll do my best, Mr. Smeeth. I'm a bit worried just now, that's all."

As his tram climbed the swarming City Road, Mr. Smeeth considered this Golspie gossip. It made him feel uneasy, although he was still ready to dismiss it as girls' nonsense. It seemed unlikely that Mr. Golspie would leave them, but then it seemed unlikely that Stanley would be spirited away by an uncle in Homerton and that Benenden would be lying in Bart's Hospital. There was no connection between these events, as Mr. Smeeth knew very well, but the sudden disappearance of Stanley and Benenden had left him with a feeling of insecurity. They made him realise the fact that things simply happened and that he had no control over them, no more than he would have if the tram suddenly left the lines and charged the nearest shop. In the dark hollows of his mind, apprehension stirred again. He decided to talk all this over with his wife, who, perhaps because she was so unreasonable, had got something that he had never had, a large confidence in life. With all her faults, there was nobody like Edie for him at these times, when he felt a bit down in the mouth. Then he remembered that they were still not on proper speaking terms, and that, in her present state of mind, he could no more talk to her about what he felt than he could talk to the strange woman sitting in front of him in the tram. "We just would be quarrelling now, wouldn't we!" he cried to himself, with that gloomy satisfaction, that faint sweetness which comes with the last bitter drop, known only to the pessimist. Life could do many dreadful things to Herbert Norman Smeeth, but it couldn't take him in. He was one of those people who are always there first, who are standing at the grave before the doctor has even begun shaking his head.

III

This treacherous Saturday, however, was still capable of giving him another shock, from an unexpected quarter. Mrs. Smeeth was out when he arrived home, and he had a solitary dinner, with Edna flitting about and trying to keep out of his way. After dinner, he smoked his pipe and pottered about for half an hour or so, and then, as the afternoon sent some gleams of pale sunlight creeping, like a returned convalescent, into Chaucer Road, he went out for a walk. Fate, which had for once an easy task, directed him to Clissold Park, where his shock was awaiting him.

The fifty green acres of Clissold Park are surrounded by miles and miles of slates and bricks, chimney-pots and paving stones, and so, in the middle of it, placed there perhaps as a sign that the round green world of mountains, forests and oceans still exists somewhere, or at least once had an existence, there are a number of animals and bright birds. If you are a Stoke Newington ratepayer, you have only to turn a corner or two to catch the soft shining glances of deer, to meditate upon the spectacle of birds so fantastically fashioned and coloured that it is impossible to believe that both they and North London are equally real, that one or the other is not a crazy dream. You stand there, a litter of peanut shells and paper bags all round you, with a Stoke Newington dinner inside you struggling with your digestive juices, and you suddenly hear a scream from the jungle and a green and scarlet wing from the Orinoco is flashed at you.

There are links, however, between these two worlds. One of them was standing beside Mr. Smeeth, and wore a short grey beard and a dusty bowler. "Yus," he remarked, looking at the gorgeous birds, then at Mr. Smeeth, then at the birds again, and doing it masterfully, as if to keep both the birds and Mr. Smeeth there, "yus, I been where them things comes from. Common as sparrers there, yer might say. Bigger than these, too—yus, and brighter colours on 'em. Yus, I been where them birds comes from."

"Is that so?" said Mr. Smeeth. "And when was this? Not lately, I'll bet."

"And you'd win, mister. Forty years ago, that was, in good old Queen Victoria's time. Ah, yer little devils!" he cried, addressing the birds now. "What d'yer think o' that, eh? Forty years ago. I left the sea thirty-five years ago, mister, but I'd stopped going to them places five years before I left the sea for good an' all. Yus, the last five years I was on the North Atlantic run, and you don't see any o' them little dazzlers up there—fog and icebergs is what you see up there, mister. But I've seen the time when I've brought them things 'ome, proper old sailor style. Yus, I have. If yer don't believe me, ask the pleece; they know everything there is to know, isn't that so, Sergeant?"

Mr. Smeeth discovered that an acquaintance of his, a Stoke Newington man and a very good hand at a whist drive, Sergeant Gailey of the local division, had strolled up. "Now then, Mr. Lee, telling lies again! Dear, dear, dear! Oh, it's you, Mr. Smeeth, is it? You're the victim, this time."

"That'll do, Sergeant," retorted Mr. Lee amiably, "yer only giving away your ignorance. Yer've seen nothing yet, and I don't think yer ever will now. Good afternoon." And off he toddled.

"You know him, don't you, Mr. Smeeth?" said Sergeant Gailey. "Oh, he's a rum old devil. Keeps a second-hand shop—furniture and curios and all that stuff—down by the Green. His daughter runs it now, but it's his shop, and he's better off than you'd think, that old devil is. Won't part with nothing, you know, but his reminiscences and good advice. He's a character."

"When he started, I thought he was going to try and cadge a bob," said Mr. Smeeth, moving away slowly with the sergeant.

"He'd have it all right if you offered it him, though he could buy you and me up, Mr. Smeeth, a good many times. But how are you getting on, these days? Here, what's the name of that boy of yours?"

"You mean George?"

"That's right. George Smeeth, Chaucer Road—eh? I saw the name a day or two ago, and thought it must be that boy of yours. We're having him up at the North London next week, Tuesday, I think."

"At the North London!" Mr. Smeeth stopped, and gaped at him. "Do you mean the police court?"

"That's right. Case comes on on Tuesday, I think. What, didn't you know?"

"No, of course, I didn't know," cried Mr. Smeeth in horrified amazement. "Do you mean—my boy George?"

"Here, steady, steady, Mr. Smeeth! We're not charging him. He's only up as a witness."

Mr. Smeeth breathed again, but he was still puzzled and worried, and the sergeant, noticing this, began to explain.

"I don't know why he's not told you. It's one of these car stealing jobs. We're always getting 'em now. What with cars running over people and then skipping off, and cars in these smash-and-grab outfits, and cars being lost and pinched—coo!—we get a proper packet of cars! I don't know what the Force did in the old horse traffic days. 'Owever, this is one of the car stealing jobs and by a bit o' luck *and* judgment, we traced this particular car to that garage where your lad's been working lately. Chap o' the name of Barrett runs it, and between you and me, we've had an eye on him for some time. Well, he bought this car—a good car, nearly new; I don't remember the make, but it was a *good* car, worth money—for fifteen quid. He doesn't deny it. Now we're taking the line that he bought that car knowing it to be stolen, not the property o' the chap that offered it to him. It's our belief he's done this before, and a good many times, too. As I say, we've had an eye on him. If he's not a wrong 'un, I give it up. Whether we'll get him this time or not, I don't know. I wasn't on the case myself. But that fifteen quid'll take a bit of explaining. They'll be saying they get cars given 'em soon."

"But where does George come in?" said Mr. Smeeth, who did not care what happened in the car-stealing world, but cared a great deal about his son.

"Oh, that's nothing. He worked there, see, and was there when the car went into the garage, and so on. We've nothing against him, of course. He'll only be asked to say what he saw."

"Thank goodness for that! You gave me a fright, I can tell you, Sergeant. I don't mean by that, mind you, that I thought for a minute my boy'd be mixed up in anything dishonest. I don't see as much of him as I ought these days, and he just goes his own way, but I know the boy's as straight as you like."

"I'll bet he is," said Sergeant Gailey with a certain forced heartiness, which he immediately dropped for a more serious, cautionary tone. "But, all the same, Mr. Smeeth, he ought to have told you, you know. And another thing. You get him away from that garage and that chap Barrett. He's in bad company there. Doesn't matter if Barrett walks out of that court next Tuesday with the case against him in bits; never mind about that; you get your boy out of it and away from that chap. If we can't prove it this time, we'll prove it next time, and there always is a next time with those cocky birds. I wouldn't let a boy of mine put his nose in a dump like that."

"Don't you worry about that, Sergeant," cried Mr. Smeeth, his voice trembling with excitement. "George doesn't stay there another day. I should think not! And I'm very much obliged to you for telling me, Sergeant, very much obliged."

"That's all right, Mr. Smeeth. Thought you ought to know. Which way you going now?"

"Straight home. That's my way now," replied Mr. Smeeth, and he went as fast as he could go to Chaucer Road. He was still rather alarmed and astonished, for police court affairs were remote from his experience and he had a horror of them, but he was chiefly indignant, indignant at the thought that this business, which took George to court and might take his employer to gaol, should have been kept from him. Did his wife know all about it, and had she deliberately hidden it out of his sight? He could hear her saying to George, "Now don't you say a word to your father about this. You know what he is." Yes, something like that. If she really had done that, then they *would* have a quarrel. This was serious. My word, what a life! You never knew what was happening.

He arrived home to find his wife still absent and Edna and her friend, Minnie Watson, screaming with laughter in the dining-room. "Just a minute, Edna, I want you," he said sternly. She followed him into the other room.

"Where's George?"

"I don't know, Dad. Working, I suppose, down at the garage. What's the matter?"

"Did you know anything about this police court business?"

Edna stared at him, her chocolate-stained mouth open. "What police court business? What are you talking about, Dad? Has it something to do with George?"

"Never mind about that. You don't know anything about it, eh?" It certainly didn't look as if she did, but Mr. Smeeth told himself wearily that you could never tell, not with children like these, such a strange secretive lot. "All right, it doesn't matter. Where is this garage? You can tell me that, I suppose?"

She gave him precise directions, and ten minutes later he was there, confronting a queer George in greasy overalls, who was doing something incomprehensible to the inside of a car. He was probably astonished to see his father, but he only raised his eyebrows and grinned. George had ceased for some time to show any signs of surprise.

Telling himself that this was his son, who had been a child only yesterday, Mr. Smeeth looked sternly at him, and summoning all the forces of parental authority, he said curtly: "Just clean yourself up and get your hat and coat on, George."

"What d'you mean, Dad? What's up? Anything wrong at home?"

"No, there isn't, but just do what I tell you."

"Well, I don't understand."

"Oh, come outside if you're going to argue about it," said Mr. Smeeth impatiently, and led the way out into the street. "It's the police court business. I've just heard all about it."

"Oh—I see," said George slowly.

"I'm glad you do see. I'd like to have seen a bit earlier," said his father bitterly. "Why didn't you tell me? Have to have a police sergeant telling me what's happening to my own son!"

"Well, you needn't go at me, Dad. I've done nothing, and they'll tell you I haven't."

"I know all about that. And you're not going to do anything either. That's why I came round. You're finishing here now, George. I was warned not to let you stop on—though I didn't need any warning. I'm not going to have you mixed up with this sort of business. So you can just tell them you're finishing now, this minute."

"Oh, I can't do that, Dad. We're busy."

"I don't care how busy you are, George. You've got to stop."

"Oh, all right—if you feel like that about it. But look here, Dad, I must finish that job I'm doing now."

"How long will that take you?"

"Ten minutes. Quarter of an hour. Shouldn't be longer."

"All right," said Mr. Smeeth grimly, "I'll wait." And he waited twenty minutes; but at the end of that time George came out, washed and brushed and without his overalls.

"I might have lost the week's money, walking out like that," he told his father, "but they paid up—like good sports."

"Who are 'they'?"

"There's another chap running this besides Barrett, a chap called McGrath—proper motor mechanic, he is."

"And is he a wrong 'un, too?"

"Not more than most. McGrath's all right."

"Tell me this, George," said Mr. Smeeth, halting and looking very earnestly at his son, "did your mother know anything about this police court business?"

"Course she didn't, Dad. I wasn't going to tell *her*."

"I see," said Mr. Smeeth, relieved to find there had been no general conspiracy. "But why didn't you tell *me*, boy? I can't understand you keeping a thing like this to yourself."

They were walking on again now. "Oh, I didn't want to bother you about it," replied George coolly. "I knew there'd be a lot of gassing and fussing if I did. And there was nothing to get excited about. I hadn't done anything. They weren't running *me* in, were they?"

It was incredible. Mr. Smeeth gave it up. Here was this boy of his, who had been playing with clockwork trains on the floor only the day before yesterday, so to speak, and now he could talk in this strain, as cool as you please, as if he were Sergeant Gailey or somebody! Mr. Smeeth waited a minute or two, then said very quietly: "About that car, George—did you know it was stolen?"

George grinned; no wincing, shrinking, anything of that kind;

just a plain grin. "I didn't *know*, but I had a few ideas of my own about it. And about one or two others, too."

"Do you mean to tell me that you'd a good idea of what was going on there and you didn't do anything about it?" Mr. Smeeth was shocked and astounded.

"What could I do about it, Dad? If I'd been dragged into it, that would have been different. But they didn't try. And you needn't worry—I wouldn't have had it. Buying cars that have been pinched like that is a mug's game, if you ask me. Barrett's a fool, though he's not a bad sort, really, and he's treated me all right. Doesn't know anything about cars though, not like McGrath does. I believe he *had* to take over some of those cars. I saw one or two fellows who called to see him, and I didn't like the look of them at all—real toughs, they were. But mind you, Dad, I don't *know* anything about those cars, don't forget that."

The boy talked about buying stolen cars as if it was simply a little weakness on Barrett's part, a silly hobby. He didn't seem to be in the least shocked or frightened. Mr. Smeeth could not make it out at all. It was just as if he had brought up a boy who had suddenly turned into an Indian. The boy was all right, really; he had left the garage without making a fuss; but, nevertheless, his point of view appeared to be whole worlds away from anything his father could understand. "I must say I don't like to hear you talking like that, George," he said. "Seems to me you don't understand the seriousness of this business. It's criminal, this is, work for the police, and you talk about it as if it was a tea-party or something. Talk like that, and you don't know where you'll land yourself."

"That's all right, Dad," said George tolerantly. "Don't you worry. I can look after myself."

"Well, you're going to do it outside that place now," Mr. Smeeth told him.

"Oh, I meant to leave there soon, anyhow," George remarked airily.

"I should think so! And the next job you find for yourself, I hope, will be in a concern that the police aren't interested in. You'd better tell me something about it, first. Easy to get yourself a bad name, y'know, boy, even if you don't do anything wrong yourself."

George, who seemed to live in a world in which bad names didn't count, a world his father didn't know, made no reply, but merely whistled softly as he walked along. When they arrived home, tea was waiting for them, with Mrs. Smeeth sitting behind the teapot. She was surprised to see George walk in with his father. Mr. Smeeth gave her a look that said "Quarrel or no quarrel, you've got to recognize that this is serious," and cut short her inquiries by remarking, "We'll have a talk about this afterwards, Mother."

As soon as the two children were out of the room, he told her what had happened, and she gave him all her attention, realizing at once that this affair transcended any quarrel.

"You did right, Dad," she told him, when he had finished.

"I hope you realize," he added, not without bitterness, "that this means the boy may be out of a job for some time, and that means both of them earning nothing. It's all right, of course, but still— we'll have to be careful."

"George'll soon get something. He always does," she said confidently. "I shouldn't wonder if he hasn't got a better job in his eye now. You were right to do what you did, but you leave him alone now and don't worry. He'll find something."

This seemed a good opportunity to tell what had happened during the earlier part of this eventful day, with special reference to the disturbing rumour about Mr. Golspie. But she wouldn't listen. She turned herself again into a woman who had quarrelled with him, merely listened to a few words with a distant politeness, excused herself and then gathered up the tea things in a very grand, dignified manner, rather like a duchess visiting a poor cottager. Mr. Smeeth was left to smoke his pipe, alone, a solitary little figure in a huge, dark, mysterious world of cracking walls and slithering foundations, with echoes and rumours of catastrophe in every wind.

IV

On Tuesday morning, Mr. Golspie and Mr. Dersingham spent more than an hour talking together in the private office, and Mr. Smeeth, whose chief duty during that time was to examine a number of replies to Twigg & Dersingham's advertisement for an office boy, found it difficult to concentrate his attention upon these rather monotonous letters, all in round handwriting that began well, but always wobbled towards the end. He was curious to know what was happening in the private office. Now and again he had heard voices raised, and once the door had opened, so that Mr. Golspie's booming tones had come flying out into the general office, but the next minute the door had been closed again. Just after half-past eleven, the bell in the private office rang dramatically. Miss Sellers, now the junior, answered it, and came back to say: "Mr. Smeeth, Mr. Dersingham wants to see you."

The private office was filled with cigar and cigarette smoke, and Mr. Golspie, who stood in front of the fire, his legs wide apart, clearly dominating the scene. Mr. Dersingham, sitting at his table, was rather rumpled and flushed and obviously not at ease.

"A-ha!" Mr. Golspie cried, "here's Smeeth. He's the man. He'll tidy us up a bit. You know, Smeeth, if I'd been as tidy as you, as good at putting down little figures every day, never forgetting 'em, adding 'em up, I'd have been a rich man now."

"Well, I'm not a rich man, Mr. Golspie," said Mr. Smeeth, smiling nervously.

"No, but I didn't say—if I could do that and nothing else, d'you follow me? What I meant was, if I could do what you do, *plus* what I can already do. I'd be a very rich man now, and you wouldn't find me in a dust-bin, eh? Now if you want to make money, Dersingham, *really* make money, pile up a big fortune, you've only to be like me and like Smeeth here both together, two in one. Quite simple."

Mr. Dersingham nodded vaguely. He was not interested in this talk and did not like the sound of it, for Mr. Golspie's voice had dropped into a jeering tone. He caught Mr. Smeeth's eye, and then began: "Look here, Smeeth, Mr. Golspie and I have come to a new arrangement. I'll just explain it——"

"Oh, I'll explain it," Mr. Golspie broke in roughly. "It's simple enough. Up to now, I've been drawing commission on all this Baltic stuff as soon as it's delivered to your customers, haven't I? That's right. Well, that's too slow for me. I don't want to have to wait for my money like that. Some of these new orders are spread over months."

"Yes, and don't forget how long we'll have to wait for our money, Golspie," said Mr. Dersingham, "or rather, I'll have to wait for mine."

"Quite so, sir," said Mr. Smeeth, who knew how long it took to get accounts settled better than they did.

"That's up to you," Mr. Golspie replied, in his hearty brutal way. "I don't want to point out again that if it hadn't been for me there'd have been no orders and no money to come in, whether it comes in this year or next."

"Yes, yes, that's all right, Golspie. I agree. You needn't harp on it, needn't rub it in."

"Rub it in!" Golspie laughed. "You're talking now as if you were sore somewhere. There's nothing to rub in but a lot of good new business. Anyhow, Smeeth, this is the point. I can't wait now for all this big lot of orders to be delivered. I want my commission on the orders as they stand. They've gone through; the stuff's on the other side all right, as you know; and your people are here all right; so I want my cut now. I'm not as good as you at figures, but that's what I make it, right up to date." He handed over a slip of paper. "That's a rough total, of course."

It may have been a rough total, but what leaped to Mr. Smeeth's eye was the fact that it was a surprisingly large total.

"Pretty big, eh? Bigger than you thought, eh? That shows you the business that's come into this office just lately."

"It does, Mr. Golspie," said Smeeth, glancing down at the figure again.

"Yes, that's true." Mr. Dersingham's face cleared at the thought. "Jolly good. Of course, it's—what-is-it?—phenomenal—a sudden rush, y'know, because they've been booking this stuff of yours ahead as fast as they can."

"Don't blame 'em," said Mr. Golspie, looking at his cigar.

"You want me to check this, I suppose?" said Mr. Smeeth, glancing from one to the other.

Mr. Golspie yawned. "That's it. When can you have it done, with the figures right bang up to date, Smeeth? By to-morrow morning, eh? All right. And you'll see how you can arrange the payment, Dersingham, eh? Yes, yes, I know how it is—you told me—but if you can split it into three, say, and let me have the first cheque this week and the other two as soon as you can, that'll do me. I'll leave you to work it out. I'll be looking in this afternoon."

They said nothing until they heard the outer door close behind him and his footsteps die away on the landing. They seemed to be in a much larger room now. Mr. Dersingham himself was much larger. "Get a chair, Smeeth," he said, and lit another cigarette. They looked at one another through the sudden spurt of smoke from it.

Mr. Dersingham gave a short laugh. "Friend Golspie's putting the screw on this morning. My God! Smeeth—I'll tell you candidly— and this is very much between ourselves, you understand—that chap's getting on my nerves. He's such a damned outsider, he really is. He's brought all this business here, it's true, but—my God!—he doesn't let you forget it either. If we hadn't been in such a rotten bad way before he came, well—I don't know—I think I'd have told him to take his stuff somewhere else. Don't repeat a word of this, Smeeth, for the love of Mike! But that's just how I feel, and I must let steam off for a minute. He gets worse. Talk about rough riding or whatever they call it! He's the complete bouncing bounder.

Business may be business, but give me a gentleman to deal with in it, every time. Friend of mine, Major Trape—we were at Worrell together—met the chap at my house, just after he came and I asked him to dinner, the first *and* the last time, and Trape summed him up after half an hour, and several times since he's said to me that he wouldn't have a chap like that working with him, sharing the same office, not if he brought a quarter of a million pounds' worth of business in his pocket. He's getting worse, too. Ouf!"

"Well, Mr. Dersingham, you've got to meet all kinds in business, haven't you?" said Mr. Smeeth, astonished at this outburst.

"Looks like it," replied Mr. Dersingham bitterly. He remained silent for a minute, and his face gradually cleared. "Still, there's no doubt we're doing the business. Golspie's total—and I don't suppose it's far out, even though it is rough—surprised me, and of course he's drawn a fair amount of commission, on the actual deliveries here, already, hasn't he?"

"I suppose this new arrangement's all right," said Mr. Smeeth dubiously.

"If you mean it's a damned nuisance, I agree with you, Smeeth. It's that all right. Look what we've got to pay him, and he wants it all these next two or three weeks—says he's a lot of old debts to meet, though God knows where they are. That's what I want to talk to you about. We'll have to go into this pretty carefully. I don't know how much you expect to get in these next two weeks, but I imagine we'll have to ask the bank to help us out. That'll be all right, of course, because I can explain to Townley there how we stand."

Mr. Smeeth nodded. "Well, I suppose it's all right, sir," he said once more, still dubiously.

"What do you mean, Smeeth?" Mr. Dersingham was impatient.

"Well," he hesitated, "I don't quite know. I'm just wondering if it's all right."

"Oh, don't keep saying that," cried Dersingham angrily. "Of course it's all right. I'm not a fool. It's a nuisance, and I wouldn't do it if I could help it, but it's all right. Plenty of fellows who work on commission have this arrangement and get their money as soon as the order goes through."

"I suppose they do, Mr. Dersingham. But you're thinking of ordinary travellers, aren't you, sir, chaps who just get a very small commission, not like this?"

"No, I'm not. I'm thinking of other fellows who—er—work in a big way," said Mr. Dersingham rather vaguely.

"Suppose Mr. Golspie leaves us? I can't help thinking about that, you know, sir."

"Why should he? My hat!—he's doing well, isn't he? He's making more out of this firm than I am, just now. No, I know what you're thinking, Smeeth, and I know what you're going to say. You mean, there's nothing to prevent him walking over to some other firm in our business, if they made it worth his while. Or another thing. He might sell out the whole agency—he's got a tight grip on that, y'know, Smeeth; I know that for a fact—for this Baltic stuff to somebody else, and then clear out."

"That's right, sir. I thought of both those things."

"And so did I, Smeeth. Don't you worry about that. I don't blame you for being cautious—does you credit, and I know you're a good safe chap—but you mustn't think I was born yesterday, you know. I don't pretend to be one of these born City men, the real old cunning sharks—that's not my style at all, Smeeth, and if I could afford it, I'd be out of business to-morrow and be in some snug little country place—but I've had some experience and I'm no fool, y'know. Oh no!" he cried confidently to Mr. Smeeth and perhaps to the listening gods. "I've thought about that for some time, and this morning, when he brought up this commission idea and wanted to clear our account at one swoop, for that's what it amounts to—though he's earned it fairly, y'know, we must admit that—I tackled him on those points."

"Oh, I'm glad about that, Mr. Dersingham," said Mr. Smeeth, greatly relieved.

"Yes, and he agreed to meet me half-way. I agree to pay this commission over to him as soon as possible, and he'll sign an agreement, promising not to take the agency elsewhere and to see that we keep the agency on here if he decides to clear out. That's fair enough, isn't it? You can't get away from that. In fact, we stand to gain by this new arrangement, don't we? We're only paying out, a little in advance, what's due to him, and on the other hand, we make the business safe for ourselves. If Golspie goes after he's signed this agreement—and I'm going over to my solicitors this afternoon to have it drafted out; we'll do it properly—then he leaves us with the new business in our hands, and all I can say is, the sooner he goes the better. And I'll tell you another thing, Smeeth. When he's signed this agreement, he's going to drop some of his little blighter-ish tricks, that nasty jeering tone of his, because I'm not going to put up with it any longer. I shan't need to, after this. By George!" and Mr. Dersingham's voice had a triumphant ring now and he tried to look like a very crafty man of affairs. "I'd never thought of that, not properly. It didn't occur to me that, after this, if he doesn't like it, he can lump it, if you see what I mean. He'll have to change his tune, thank God!"

"Yes, I see, Mr. Dersingham," said Mr. Smeeth slowly. "It's funny he didn't think of that, too, isn't it?"

"Oh, he wants his money in his pocket. That's what he's thinking about. And then he probably imagines I like that nice cheerful manner of his, and like to be told every day or so that if it hadn't been for him the firm wouldn't be paying its way. I tell you, these loud bounders never think what's going on in other people's minds."

"I shouldn't think Mr. Golspie cared very much, certainly," said Mr. Smeeth thoughtfully. "But I don't know that I quite see him in that light, though you know him better than I do, I'll admit that, Mr. Dersingham. But—I don't know——"

"If you don't mind my saying so, Smeeth," said Mr. Dersingham, grinning at him, "there are times when you're just a bit of an old washerwoman, and I'm not sure this isn't one of them. No, no, don't mind that—I know you're a good chap, and I can honestly say I wouldn't like to run this show without you. Now, look here, will you work out that total properly, as soon as you can, and let me know what we're likely to get in these next two weeks, what we've got in hand, and so on, and then we'll settle the whole thing. Right you are."

The latter part of this speech was all so friendly that Mr. Smeeth could not take offence at the "bit of an old washerwoman." He left the room feeling that he ought to be convinced, and almost ashamed of himself because he could not share Mr. Dersingham's sudden burst of confidence. The fact remained, though, that he still felt dubious. There was something in Mr. Dersingham's tone of voice that made him wince. He did not like this easy dismissal of Mr. Golspie; there was a catch in it somewhere; and he felt that Mr. Dersingham was taking the wrong line with Mr. Golspie. What was it that Turgis had said, reporting the daughter? He wondered if he ought to have mentioned that, but then quickly dismissed the possibility. Mr. Dersingham knew what he was doing. He talked as if he did. Indeed, he talked too much as if he did. Mr. Smeeth, with his apprehensive mind, always felt a slight alarm when anybody was triumphantly confident. You had to be careful.

He settled down at his desk, with the various books in front of him, to work out the exact figures. For the next hour he was lost in them, quite happy, at home in this familiar little world of unchanging numerals and balancing columns, this world in which you had only to have patience enough and everything worked out beautifully, perfectly.

v

"And how's Mr. Benenden?" Mr. Smeeth asked. He had called in the shop as he returned from lunch on Wednesday, and had found the plump niece still behind the counter there.

She remembered him, and at once smiled at the prospect of a

little chat and then looked sad because the subject would be her
stricken uncle. After that, she compromised neatly between the two.
"He's not as well as he might be, thank you," she replied. "Now
they've got him in there and had a good look at him, they've found
a lot of things wrong with him. He never would go to a doctor
himself, didn't believe in them, he said—you know—silly. No, it
isn't just with him being knocked down like that, though that was
bad enough, but they examined him, you see, and now they say
he's not in a good way at all. They may have to operate."

"That's bad, isn't it? What's wrong exactly?"

"Now I couldn't tell you. You know what they are in these
hospitals. If they know themselves, they don't let on. I went to see
him on Sunday, and I told him about the shop and who'd been in
and all that. You're not Mr. Bromfield, are you?"

"No. My name's Smeeth."

"Mr. Smeeth. Yes, that's right. He mentioned you as well."

"Did he now?" Mr. Smeeth felt all the gratification of a person
who has been singled out, no matter by whom. "Asked if I'd been
in, I suppose, eh? Well, I wish you'd tell him how sorry I am to
hear he's laid up. Tell him I say that Angel Pavement doesn't seem
the same place without him. And I hope he's stirring again soon."

"Yes, I will." The plump young woman hesitated a moment.
"I'll tell you what, Mr. Smeeth, if you just happened to have a
spare half-hour this afternoon, perhaps you might like to go and see
him. It's visiting day up there to-day, you know. Three to four. My
mother's going about half-past three, but if you could have a look
at him, just to give him a word or two and pass the time of day,
sometime before then, just after three, he'd be ever so pleased. But
perhaps you're busy."

"I don't know." Mr. Smeeth thought it over, then looked at
his watch. "I think I will, you know. It wouldn't take me long to
slip round to Bart's. Where shall I find him?"

She gave him elaborate directions. He remembered then that he
had wanted to have a word with Brown & Gorstein, whose place

was just off Old Street. He could go round to Bart's first, and then up to Brown & Gorstein's. It did not look like being a very busy afternoon, and he had still three-quarters of an hour in which to clear up a few odds and ends of jobs in the office before he went.

At three o'clock he came out into Little Britain, beneath the innumerable blue-curtained windows of Bart's new building. As he crossed the road, something huge in the sky, to the left, caught his eye and made him stop and look that way when he reached the other pavement. It was the dome of St. Paul's, and never before had he seen it look so massive and majestic; it was almost frightening. He had never seen the dome from that distance and that particular angle before, and it was as if he was seeing it for the first time. He might have been in a strange city. For once his sense of wonder was quickened, and after that, throughout the afternoon, until he returned to the office, it never slept. The wide space between the main entrance to the hospital and Smithfield Market was filled with carts coming from the market, a very decided smell of meat, and a narrowing stream of people, mostly women carrying paper bags and little bunches of flowers, who were pouring into the hospital entrance. It was all very strange to him, for he had not been near a hospital for years and had never visited one of this size before. It was like walking into a fantastic little town, a strange city within the city. He went through an archway and found himself in a great courtyard or quadrangle with a fountain in it. Here there was all the bustle of a market-place, but not of any marketplace he had ever seen before. Doctors in white coats and bare-headed students ran in and out of the many doorways; nurses fluttered snowily across the quadrangle; and now and then he caught a glimpse of a patient, strapped and rigid on a stretcher, being wheeled away to God knows where. One passed him close, and he saw a face cut out of yellow bone and staring unfathomable eyes. It was terrifying. The whole place, this little town of white uniforms and mysterious silent traffic within the roaring city, terrified him. He could have sworn that the little pain somewhere inside began tick-

ticking again; and for a moment or two it seemed to him astonishing that he should still be one of the uneasy invaders swarming in here, one of the workers, eaters, drinkers, smokers, pleasure lovers, movers about, from outside. Any day now, he felt, he would be on one of those stretchers.

Somehow it had never occurred to him that he would see Benenden actually in bed. He had vaguely imagined a hospital and had imagined Benenden in it, but he had really thought of him as being still behind a counter, the familiar half-length figure, beginning about the second button of the waistcoat and then going on to the old-fashioned high collar and stiff front (with no tie), the straggling sandy-grey beard and the thick glasses. In all the time he had known him, Mr. Smeeth had never once seen Benenden away from his counter; and for all he knew to the contrary, Benenden might have had no legs at all. Now, as he approached the white-enamelled iron bed, he saw less of Benenden than ever, but what he did see gave him a shock. It was not that Benenden looked very ill (for that matter, he had never looked very well), but simply that he looked quite different. Mr. Smeeth wanted to laugh. That head of Benenden's above the sheet looked idiotic. It was as if Benenden had taken to wild joking.

"Hello, Mr. Benenden. Your niece in the shop suggested I might call and see you. How are you feeling now?"

The enormous eyes behind the glasses had slowly swivelled round, and now there was a slow faint creasing of the face that did duty for a smile. "Very pleased to see you, Mr. Smeeth. Very good of you to call." This came in tiny high explosions of sound, as if Benenden's ordinary tones had been raised an octave or two and only allowed to emerge in separate little puffs.

Mr. Smeeth could see that he really was ill. Every movement of the face and his speech were so slow, as if they had to be thought out first. And though he had been away from his shop such a little time, he gave the impression that he had been away for years and years, had gone round and round the world, had even changed his nationality. He did not belong any more to the workers and bustlers and movers about. He was now a citizen of this inner city.

"Not a bit," said Mr. Smeeth, wanting to be cheerful and hearty, but not outrageously so, "not a bit. I'm only too glad. I've missed you at the shop. Quite a shock to hear what had happened to you. How are you feeling then?"

"Not good, Mr. Smeeth. No, not good. Baddish."

"I'm sorry to hear that, Mr. Benenden. I suppose that accident of yours was a shock to the system, eh?"

"That was nothing, that wasn't," replied Benenden, speaking in a slow, oracular fashion. "They say there's all sorts o' things wrong with me. Heart bad. Kidneys bad. Inside all wrong. They don't tell me much. When they do, they think they're teaching me something." The eyes behind the thick glasses seemed to gleam with pride. "They're not teaching me anything. I could have told 'em that, Mr. Smeeth. I could have told 'em that—yes, and a bit more—a long time since. I've known all about it for years, years and years."

"You don't say so!" Mr. Smeeth looked concerned.

"Yes, I've known it for years. They can't tell me anything about that heart of mine. It's rotten. There's many and many a man—and I've known some of 'em—who's dropped in the street with a heart not so bad as mine. Been missing the beat for years, missing it all over the place. Same with the kidneys. They're rotten, too. But, mind you, Mr. Smeeth, it's not all the kidneys. There's the liver to be taken into consideration. They're overlooking that, so far they are, but I'm just waiting for 'em to come round to my opinion. I'm not saying anything. I'm just letting 'em find out a few things for themselves. One of these days, that young doctor's going to notice my liver and then he's going to have another surprise. And that isn't all, either." Here the astonishing image, after a little effort, produced something like a chuckle. T. Benenden was exiled from his shop and his financial columns and his chats with customers, but now he had discovered in his ailments and dubious organs a new and absorbing interest, and, stretched out there, he saw himself as a romantic and exciting figure. Within sight of death, he was beginning life all over again.

Mr. Smeeth caught a fleeting glimpse of this fact, but he was in no mood to appreciate it. The spectacle of Benenden, suddenly transformed from a familiar Angel Pavement character, and comic at that, to this infirm shadow of himself, filled him with dismay and foreboding. Try as he might, he could not help believing that he would never see T. Benenden behind that counter again. As he listened—for Benenden did most of the talking, slowly boasting of the severity and complication of his ailments—Mr. Smeeth told himself that never again would the tobacconist bring out the canister of Benenden's Own Mixture for him.

Yet there was no real evidence for this. "How is he?" he asked the nurse who had first shown him the bed.

"Who? Seventy-five? Oh, getting along all right," she replied briskly. "We're operating at the end of this week or early next week. He'll be all right."

She sounded confident enough, but Mr. Smeeth did not know whether to believe her or not. As he left the hospital, a clammy air of dissolution and mortality clung to him. Barbican and Golden Lane, through which he passed on his way to Old Street and Brown & Gorstein's, spoke to him only of decay. It was a curious afternoon, belonging to one of those days that are in the very dead heart of winter. The air was chilled and leaden. The sky above the City was a low ceiling of tarnished brass. All the usual noises were there, and the trams and carts that went along Old Street made as much din as ever, yet it seemed as if every sound was besieged by a tremendous thick silence. Cold as it was, it was not an afternoon that made a man want to move sharply, to hurry about his business; there was something about it, something slowed down and muffled in the heavy air, the brooding yellowish sky, the stone buildings that seemed to be retreating into their native rock again, that impelled a man to linger and stare and lose himself in shadowy thought.

Mr. Smeeth found himself doing this, after he had left Brown &

Gorstein's, and had turned down Bunhill Row on his way back to the office. He halted opposite that large building boldly labelled *The Star Works*, and wondered what was made there and whether it had anything starry about it. Then he turned round, idly, and stared through the iron railings at the old graves there. He had been this way before, many a time, in fact, but he never remembered noticing before that the earth of the burying-ground was high above the street. The railings were fastened into a wall between two or three feet high, and the ground of the cemetery was as high as the top of this little wall. There was something very mournful about the sooty soil, through which only a few miserable blades of grass found their way. It was very untidy. There were bits of paper there, broken twigs, rope ends, squashed cigarettes, dried orange peel, and a battered tin that apparently had once contained Palm Chocolate Nougat. This dingy litter at the foot of the grave-stones made him feel sad. It was as if the paper and cigarette ends and the empty tin, there in the old cemetery, only marked in their shabby fashion the passing of a later life, as if the twentieth century was burying itself in there too, and not even doing it decently. He moved a step or two, then stopped near the open space, where there is a public path across the burying-ground. He stared at the mouldering headstones. Many of them were curiously bright, as if their stone were faintly luminous in the gathering darkness, but it was hard to decipher their lettering. One of them, which attracted his attention because it was not upright in the ground but leaned over at a very decided angle, he found he could read: *In Memory of Mr. John Willm. Hill, who died May 26th, 1790, in the eighteenth year of his age.* That had been a poor look-out for somebody.

" 'Aving a look at the good old graves, mister?" said a voice. It belonged to an elderly and shabby idler, one of those dreamy and dilapidated men who seem to haunt all such places in London, and who will offer to guide you, if you are obviously a stranger and well-to-do, but are quite prepared to pour out information for nothing to a fellow-citizen.

"Yes, just having a look," said Mr. Smeeth.

"Ar, there's some pretty work 'ere, if yer know where to look for it, mister. I know the Fields well, I do. Some big men's buried 'ere. An' I'll tell yer one of 'em. Daniel Defow's buried in 'ere, boy, and I could take yer straight to the plice. Yers, the grite Daniel Defow."

"Is that so? Now, let me see, who was he exactly?"

"Oo was 'e? Daniel Defow! Yer know Rawbinson Crusoe, doncher? Rawbinson Crusoe on the island and Man Friday an' all that? Thet's 'im. Defow—'e wrote that. Cor!—think 'e did! Known all over the world, that piece, all over the wide world. Well, 'e's in 'ere, Daniel Defow, and I could take yer straight to the plice. Yers, that's right. Monument, too—ee-rected by the boys and girls of England to Daniel Defow 'cos 'e wrote Rawbinson Crusoe—in 'ere. I tell yer, boy, there's some big men in there—what's left of 'em."

Mr. Smeeth nodded and continued to stare idly through the railings of Bunhill Fields, where the old Nonconformists are buried in mouldering eighteenth century elegance, to which they had at least conformed in death if not in life; and where, among the divines and elders, not only Defoe, but also Bunyan and Blake, the two God-haunted men, lie in the sooty earth, while their dreams and ecstasies still light the world. As Mr. Smeeth stared, something floated down, touched the crumbled corner of the nearest headstone, and perished there. A moment later, on the curved top of the little wall beside him was a fading white crystal. He looked up and saw against the brassy sky a number of moving dark spots. He looked down and saw the white flakes floating towards the black pavement. In all his life, he had never been so surprised by the appearance of snow, and for one absurd moment he found himself wondering who had made it and who was responsible for tumbling it into the City. He hurried away now, and as he went the snow came faster and shook down larger and larger flakes upon the town. Before he had reached Angel Pavement, not only had it whitened every cranny, but it had stolen away, behind its soft curtains, half the noises of the City, which only roared and hooted now through the white magic as if in an uneasy dream.

It was so thick that Mr. Smeeth was no longer one of ten thousand hurrying little figures, but a man alone with the whirling flakes. The snow was storming the City and all London. In Twigg & Dersingham's, they had turned on the lights, but they could still see a queer dim scurrying through the windows. Mrs. Smeeth, in her little dining-room up at Stoke Newlington, watched it with delight and remembered her childhood, when they had cried, "Snow, snow faster, White alabaster." Mrs. Dersingham, who had been shopping in Kensington High Street, had to shelter from it in a doorway, and was wondering if it had caught the children. The Pearsons, secure in their warm maisonette in Barkfield Gardens, stood at the window for quarter of an hour, calling one another's attention to the size of the flakes, for there had never been anything like this in Singapore. Miss Verever, who had missed her usual visit to the Italian Riviera, wrote another angry little note to her solicitor, because it was he who had insisted upon her staying in London. Lena Golspie, in Maida Vale, watched it for a minute or two, then switched on one of the big shaded lights and curled among the cushions, with a magazine, voluptuously, like a sleek blonde cat. Mr. Pelumpton was just prevented in time from making a bid of twelve and six for a marble clock (out of order), and stayed at home, in Mrs. Pelumpton's way. Benenden, having dozed off, never knew it was there. For an hour it was unceasing, and all the open spaces on the hills, from Hampstead Heath on one side to Wimbledon Common on the other, were thickly carpeted, and everything in the city, except the busier roadways and the gutters, was magically muffled and whitened and plumed with winter, just as if it had been some old town in a fairy-tale.

Chapter Ten

THE LAST ARABIAN NIGHT

I

THE outward changes in Turgis, already noticed by Miss Matfield and Mr. Smeeth, were only tiny scattered hints and clues, and by no means in proportion to the changes within, for during these last seven weeks, ever since that night when Lena Golspie had failed to keep her appointment with him, his life had been like a bad dream. There are some dreams, trembling on the edge of nightmare, in which the dreamer goes rushing frantically through dismal reeling phantasmagoria of familiar scenes and places trying to find a lost somebody or something. This had been Turgis's real life. He had got up as usual, bolted his breakfast and exchanged a word or two with the Pelumptons, hurried down to the Tube, climbed into the City, sent and received advice notes, telephoned to this firm and that, fed variously in teashops and dining-rooms, looked at newspapers, even gone to the pictures, all as usual; but these customary activities had merely been a dream within a dream, a shadowy routine of existence. His real life had been this pursuit of Lena, and so far it had had all the urgency and dark bewilderment of a bad dream.

He had been able to call again at the flat before her father had returned, but she had only spent half an hour with him and had been vague and shifty in her excuses. He had flung away his resentment, had made the most abject apologies, and at last had made her promise to meet him again. She had kept him waiting twenty minutes on this occasion, and when she did come, she only turned the evening into a misery. She had been cold, had criticized his appearance, his manners, and had made him jealous. When he had tried to kiss her, she had laughed at him and evaded him. Then her father had returned, Christmas came, and the two of them had gone to Paris, leaving Turgis to imagine, with a vividness and force that brought a curious mingling of pain and pleasure, a host of scenes in which Lena went smiling in the arms of rich and handsome Frenchmen and Americans. But at least he could not see her, and so he was free for a few days to make what he could of life by himself. He made nothing of it. He could not forget her for a single minute. London was a jumble of silly meaningless faces. Before he had met her he had spent most of his leisure looking for adventures with girls and hardly ever finding them, but now, of course, they were offered at every turn, thrust on him, and they had no interest at all. He tried once—a girl outside one of the smaller picture houses had smiled at him and he had taken her in—but it was merely dull and savourless, like trying to eat sawdust. After that, he never bothered, living entirely in his thought of Lena and in the memory of those two first rapturous nights. He could not believe—how should he? —that those two nights did not mean as much, or nearly as much, to her as they meant to him, and so he was ready, was eager, to see in everything she had done since merely so many mysterious feminine moods, a queenly wilfulness and waywardness that would gradually be consumed in the mounting fires of passion. He knew that this was what happened with these wonderful creatures: he had seen it happen many a time on the pictures.

At first, he had realized, with wonder and humility, that it was all miraculous, that he was nobody in particular, with nothing very much to offer. But she herself had changed that. She had kissed him into being somebody, and now he had a great deal to offer—his love, his life. Very soon, being a born lover and romantic, it seemed to him that no girl could want more than that. Living over and over again as he did that hour or so of passionate embraces and kisses, he could look back on what appeared to him a long intimacy with her, far removed from any casual encounter (for he knew all about them, and this was quite different), so that he felt he had a claim, a right, and that when she avoided him or in any way challenged that claim, she was trying to escape from the very condition of life itself. Thus, if it was not wilfulness and waywardness, then it was something abominably wicked stirring in her to be regarded as a bigoted and militant priest would regard a heresy. None of this, of course, moved on the surface of his mind, but it coiled and uncoiled below that surface and obscurely determined what did eventually move there or what at last came bursting through, exploding beyond thought, into action.

When the Golspies came back, after Christmas, it took two imploring letters and a final telephone call (he rang up from the nearest call box to the office during a time when Mr. Golspie was safely away from the flat) to induce her to agree to another meeting, and even then, after all the crescendo of excitement, she never turned up. He was left in a hot and salted misery of shame and resentment, but he could no more turn his mind away from her than he could walk about with his eyes closed. And now all London and every familiar way of life were like the flickering background of a film, a film in which he pursued and she evaded him. He could think of nothing, nobody, but Lena.

The sleep that would not come to him at night hovered perilously near him during the morning at the office, when, heavy, drowsy, brooding, he would lean forward, chin in hand, one elbow on the desk, and leave his work untouched until his attention was called to it. He spoke little, and hardly let his dull gaze rest for a moment on one of the others there. They told one another that he seemed stupid, and stupid he was too, in everything that did not concern Lena. In what did concern her, he developed a wonderful acuteness and foresight. Thus, for example, any telephone call from the private office could be overheard at the receiver in the general office, if the little switchboard was rightly manipulated; and it often happened that the Golspies talked over the telephone to one another, usually with reference to what one or other of them proposed doing during the evening; and Turgis became expert at catching these talks while pretending to be at the receiver waiting for some number to be given him. He was able, too, to work on the least hint that might be dropped in Mr. Golspie's casual talk. Then he would wait hours, even on cold, sleety nights, in the neighbourhood of 4a, Carrington Villas; sometimes in time to see her come out, perhaps with a young man, perhaps with her father and one of his friends, and then to stalk her down the road to the bus or the taxi rank; sometimes late enough to see her returning home, to hear her laughter suddenly break the silence. Twice, he had watched her, with an escort, go into a large expensive restaurant, where he could not possibly follow her. Once he had been able to get to the same theatre, and had sat in the corner of the gallery, looking down at her in the stalls. He had often jeered at young Stanley and his "shaddering," but now, inspired by his jealous misery, he suddenly turned himself into a master shadower. Icy winds pierced and smote him; his feet ached in the slush; his hands grew numb and his eyes watered; he caught colds that ought to have sent him to bed, but he never heeded them and somehow they disappeared; and all this discomfort hardly troubled him at the time, for he carried a fire inside him, a burning excitement. It was only afterwards, when he trailed back to Nathaniel Street, sat in his little room pulling off his wet boots, turned and tossed and coughed in his bed hour after hour, dragged himself out in the leaden mornings, that he suffered in the body.

His mind, however, lived as it had never lived before, knowing exquisite agonies, finding pleasure and pain inextricably confused in these hours of waiting and shadowing. Sometimes when he was returning to his lodgings, cold, tired out, hopeless, or rose to meet another heavy blank morning, he would tell himself that he had done with it all, and then he might creep through a day or two trying to live a life of his own, but everything would seem then so dull, so savourless, that he hurried back to Carrington Villas, to the waiting and dodging and hurrying round corners. He discovered, too, that when he knew where Lena was, what she was actually doing, his jealous feelings were less strong and sharply barbed than when he did not know where she was and whom she was with: it was bad to realise that for the next two or three hours she would be dancing with that tall fellow who sometimes brought a car, but it was much worse to be miles away from her and to know nothing. When he was pursuing her, though only in this strange, shadowy fashion, Lena and he alone were real, the only real human beings in a city that had been turned, with all its winter magnificence of lighted lamps and shop windows, golden buses, glittering night signs, and shining wet pavements, into an illuminated jungle. When he tried to put her out of his mind, however, there was nothing in the whole city that would let him forget. It had been tantalising, maddening enough before he had met Lena, when he had gone wandering about the streets in an amorous hunger, but now it was a hundred times worse. Everything he saw spoke to him of women and love. The shops he passed were brilliant with hats and clothes that Lena might wear; they showed him her stockings and underclothes; they were piled high with her entrancing little shoes; they invited him to look at her powder-bowls, her lipstick, her scent bottles; there was nothing she wore, nothing she touched, they did not thrust under their blazing electric lights. The theatres and picture houses shouted to him their knowledge of girls and love. The hoardings were covered with illustrations, nine feet high, of happy romances. The very newspapers, under cover of a pretended interest in Palm Beach or feminine athletics, gave him day by day photographs of nearly naked girls with figures like Lena's. And in and out of the buses, tube trains, theatres, dance-halls, restaurants, teashops, public-houses, taxis, villas, flats, went boys and their sweethearts, girls and their lovers, men and their wives, smiling at one another, laughing together, holding arms, clasping hands, kissing. Slinking through this Venusberg, like a shabby young wolf, he could not forget. It never gave him a chance. He had never given himself a chance. He had nothing to put in the way, no ambition, no interests, no friends; so far he had asked for little, merely food, shelter, and trifling amusement, except love. In his heart of hearts, he did not want to forget.

That first phase of unusual smartness, brushed hair, clean collars, creased trousers, had passed; he could not bother with that any more; if Lena wanted him to be smart again, well and good, she could tell him so, but meanwhile, he was his old shabby self, indeed shabbier than ever. Mr. Dersingham, Mr. Smeeth, Miss Matfield were beginning to give him some queer glances at the office. Well, they could look; so long as he kept the job at all (and that was certainly important), it did not matter to him; he was careless of all that. He was careless of most things these days. His finances, always difficult, had now drifted into a very bad state, and he owed Mrs. Pelumpton a pound or two, and even then he had to cut his ordinary expenses down to the lowest level, which meant that he had to feed cheaply and scantily. That did not matter either, for only now and then did he feel really hungry. Mr. Pelumpton, the old fool, had told him several times he ought to see a doctor, and even Mrs. Pelumpton was beginning to ask him if he hadn't a pain anywhere, he looked "that bad," she said. He told her that he hadn't a pain, though this was not true, for very often now he had a sort of pain, not easy to describe, but roughly amounting to a tender hollowness, in his head. He tried one or two things at the chemist's, just to make him sleep, for the nights following these vigils were the worst, when he turned and tossed and his eyes burned and the hollow place in his head enlarged itself; but these things did not do him much good, and what sleep he got, he paid for in the morning, when he felt heavy and shivery, so that the scantiest wash and shave was a hard drudgery. His work in the office was that too, though after Mr. Smeeth had taken him into the "White Horse," he tried to appear a bit more energetic, for he knew very well that if he lost his job, he was in a hopeless situation. All these things, however, were only on the dream-like fringe of life. What was there in the centre, though this was like a dream too, a very different dream, dark, urgent, and with a terrible beauty, was his pursuit of Lena, the outward Lena who was behaving so strangely to him, whom she had welcomed and kissed and held so close. Even yet he believed that she was merely teasing him, holding him off for a little space, and that soon all would be well.

At last, after seeing her several times in one week, at a distance and never once alone, he made a desperate throw and spoke to her. It was a queer night, unlike any other he had seen during the time he had haunted Maida Vale, for during the afternoon, a Wednesday, there had been a sudden heavy fall of snow, so sudden, so heavy, that for once it had remained as snow and had not changed immediately into a black slush. The roofs and gardens and privet hedges in Carrington Villas were still white with it; even the gates and railings here and there were snow lined; and the night was at once curiously light and muffled. He did not pay any close attention to these details, did not consciously observe the brilliance of the stars, the unusually solid velvety black of the houses, the white-blanketed spaces, the sudden crystal glitter now and again, the crunch of the trodden snow as the night crispened; but nevertheless they stole into his consciousness and worked obscurely there. He thought of his boyhood, which he had not left behind him long, though usually it seemed a hundred years away, a faded muddle. Now it returned to him vividly, evoked by the unfamiliar sight of the snow. He had not had a very happy boyhood, but in this hour, when it came back purged of its shame and distresses, it seemed magical and the thought of it warmed and melted him, so that something suspicious, something grudging, something in his mind that matched a certain furtive look he had, shook itself free and then vanished. It left him feeling confident, eager, a young man in a world full of friends.

Then he saw her coming up the street, the tall fellow by her side. He was not sure at first, but then he heard her voice. He hurried forward to meet them before they could turn in the entrance to 4a, and he contrived it so easily that he was able to slow up and then come face to face with them before they had reached the gate. He stopped, raised his hat, and cried: "Good evening." He did not know whether to add "Miss Golspie" or "Lena," had no time to decide, but felt that something must be added, so ended with a mumble that might have been anything. His heart knocked painfully. She looked lovelier than ever in the mysterious snowy half-light.

The tall young man stopped at once, raising his hat, too, and smiling.

"Oh!" Lena's soft little cry was charged with meaning; there was dismay, irritation, disgust in it. She hesitated a moment, threw him a quick frowning glance, then said, coldly: "Oh—good evening," and at once moved away, leaving the tall young man staring after her for a second or two. Then he gave Turgis a nod and hurried away.

Turgis saw them turn in at the gate. He heard the young man's short gruff laugh and then an exclamation of some sort followed by a little trill from Lena. The door closed behind them, and it might have been banged to in his face. For several minutes he never moved. Then he slowly walked past the house, and, looking up, saw the light in the window above, in that room where she had given him supper and danced with him and kissed him. For a moment he thought wildly of marching up there, striding in and demanding to know this and that; but he knew there was no sense in that, for not only was the tall young man there, but also Mr. Golspie himself might be there. He crossed the road, turned to look at the lighted window again, stared at it until at last it was nothing but a vague crimson blur, then walked away, his shoulders humped in misery.

"Yersh," said Mr. Pelumpton, as he shuffled into the conjugal bed-room, three-quarters of an hour later, "e'sh jusht come in, proper blue look on 'im, too. No, I didn't arshk 'im where 'e'd been. I like ter get a shivil arnsher when I arshksh a man a shivil queshen, I do. 'Leave you alone, boy,' I shaysh to myshelf. 'You go your way an' I go mine. Yersh.' What you shay, Mother?"

"I say it's a pity, too," replied Mrs. Pelumpton, above the bed-clothes. "Worries me, it does, to see a quiet young feller goin' the wrong way like that. 'E's got a nasty broodin' look. And if you want *my* opinion, 'e's got 'imself into trouble with some girl—one of these flappers, as they call 'em. My words, I'd give 'em flapper if I'd anything to do with 'em!"

"Oh, I dare shay, I dare shay," said Mr. Pelumpton, with philosophic melancholy. "If it'sh bother yer want, that'sh where to find it, that'sh my ecshperiensh. Oo, I got a narshty pain in my back tonight. It'sh the cold, yer know."

II

"Is that Mr. Levy?" Turgis cried down the telephone. "Yes, this is Twigg and Dersingham's. It's about the next delivery—you know, you were asking. Well, I'm sorry, but we can't manage it for Tuesday. No, they say they can't do it. I've been on to them. But they'll manage it for Thursday—yes, the whole lot. Yes, Thursday certain, Mr. Levy—you can depend on that. Yes, I'll advise you. All right."

He put down the receiver and returned to his desk. He was shaking a little. There had been something queer about his voice when he had been speaking to Levy. As he left the telephone, he had noticed both Miss Matfield and little Poppy Sellers glancing curiously at him. Let them look, silly fools, and then mind their own business! He had come to a sudden decision, and the very thought of it made him shake with excitement, though that was not very difficult, because he was not feeling at all well. That great hollow inside his head was filled now with jagging hot wires; his bones ached vaguely; his hands shook a little as he wrote; and his face kept twitching, as if it disliked the feel of his heavy burning eyes. Yet he had not the least desire to go to bed or to see a doctor; he did not feel ill in the ordinary way at all; it was only nerves, he concluded, just imagination. He had only to sleep better and eat more and all would be well.

His decision was to see Lena and have it out with her that very night, if by chance he could find her in the flat. He knew that her father would not be there, because when he had gone to the telephone to ring up Levy, Mr. Golspie had put a call through from the private office, and it had been to book a table for two at a restaurant. On this the cunning shadower in Turgis pounced at once. Mr. Golspie sometimes took his daughter out for the evening, but Turgis was certain that he would not trouble to book a table for her. He had not sounded like a man who was spending the evening with his daughter. If Lena was out, then she was out, and Turgis would have to wait, but he knew she did not go out every night and this was a chance not to be missed. At eight o'clock or just after, when Mr. Golspie was well out of the way, sitting down in his West End restaurant, he would go to the flat and, if Lena was there, he would see her and talk to her in that room of theirs again. He would see her, whatever happened. *Whatever happens, whatever happens*—a voice inside him said it over and over again as the Friday afternoon, fussy and irritable because of its week-end rush of things-that-must-be-settled-at-once, dragged on, with the last dripping traces of snow fading outside the window.

"Finished that copying, Miss Sellers?" said Mr. Smeeth, as he began to put away his books. "That's the way. We'll have that new boy here on Monday, and then you'll have it easier, eh? You cleared up, Turgis? Did you have a word with Ockley and Sons—y'know, I mentioned it to you this morning?"

"Yes, I did, Mr. Smeeth. It's all right."

"You're through, then, eh?"

"All I can do to-night, Mr. Smeeth. One or two things I've had to leave till to-morrow morning—couldn't help it."

"Quite so," said Mr. Smeeth, taking out his pipe and pouch. "Well, I don't think there'll be much fear of you not turning up here to-morrow morning. What do you say? Pay day, eh, Turgis? That's one of the days we *don't* like to miss."

Turgis smiled faintly. "No, I'll be sure not to miss that, Mr. Smeeth. You can count on me for that."

"It's as well we can count on somebody for something these days," Mr. Smeeth remarked jocularly, "Well, you can get away now, Turgis—you, too, Miss Matfield, of course—and I'll see you in the morning."

"That's right," said Turgis. But as he was taking down his hat and coat, he said to himself, for no particular reason: "How does he know he'll see me in the morning? He doesn't want to be so jolly sure about it." Then as he was putting his overcoat on, he looked across at Smeeth, who was now lighting his pipe, and said to himself: "Old Smeethy there, with his eyeglasses and his pipe and his nice clean collar every day and his nice home with his wife and kids and his walk round to the bank and his seven or eight quid a week, he's all right and he deserves it, for all his fussing about, 'cos he's not a bad old stick. But he's a bit of a dreary devil for all that, and he thinks everything's settled the way it is with him, and he knows no more really about what's going on than an old charwoman. Still, if I got on a bit and Lena married me and we'd a nice little home the same as his, I'd like to ask him in sometimes with his wife and we'd have a smoke and a drink."

And Mr. Smeeth, looking up from his pipe and catching Turgis's eye, said to himself: "That lad's looking bad, my words he is, worse than ever to-day. He ought to knock off for a day or two, even if we are short-handed. Doesn't look after himself, that's the trouble. And nobody to look after him—in lodgings. Bit miserable that. But then he's no responsibilities, no worries, only himself to provide for, and he could have a good life—go to concerts and all that—if he only set about it properly. Probably doesn't know how to look after himself. I ought to ask him up to tea or supper one of these week-ends—be a nice change for him—bit of home life. Yes, I'll do that when we're a bit more settled and Edie's in a good temper."

Thus, with these thoughts buzzing in their heads, they looked at one another, almost staring as people stare at a familiar word that has suddenly grown strange. Then, with a sober nod across the office, they turned away, Turgis to the door and Smeeth to his desk.

III

It was fine that night, and in the slight stir of wind there was a faint warmth that hurried the black slush into the gutters. Once out of the main road, where the bright lamps and the passing cars and buses were crazily mirrored in the wet stone, Turgis turned into a Maida Vale that was quite unlike the one he had seen two nights before, when the snow lay thick on the ground. Now it was close, dark, and dripping. Carrington Villas was one great gloomy *drip-drip* and it smelt slightly of wet grass. Turgis, shivering a little, not with cold, but from excitement, never gave these things a thought, but nevertheless he noticed them. He noticed everything that night. The least thing, a shadow moving on a curtain, a boy's whistle far down the road, stood out clearly, rammed itself home. At No. 2 somebody was playing the piano, and he recognised the very piece; he had heard it many a time at the pictures.

He stood outside the gate. There was a light up there. She was in, that was certain. Some one might be with her, but he would have to risk that. He did not care very much now if there was somebody there, for he could go up and say something. He waited a moment. Then, as he waited, he was suddenly visited by an impulse to go away, to drop it all then and there and never to think about the girl again. He felt for a second as if he had only to turn on his heel and walk straight forwards until he reached the top of the street, just the top of the street, that was all, and he was free and a different kind of fellow, stronger and happier. It was almost as if a voice whispered sharply in his ear: "Come on. Have done with it. Come away, *now*." There was a cold emptiness somewhere in his stomach. He wasn't well. He could easily have cried. If that light up there had suddenly vanished from the window, he could have turned away without regret. The faint crimson glow remained, however, and he could not leave it now for a safe but empty world.

Once again, he passed the broken statue of the little boy playing with two large fishes, climbed the steps between the two peeling pillars, and carefully rang the bell marked *4a*. When nobody seemed to hear it, he remembered what had happened before, and tried the other bell. The door was opened by the enormous woman in the apron.

"Do you know if Miss Golspie's in, please?"

"Oh, I'm wearing me feet out for them people!" cried the woman. "Up and down, and every time our own bell rings, it's for them. Miss Golspie, is it? I believe she's in too, though it's no business of mine whether she's in or out or gone to the devil, young man. Would she be expecting you coming at all?"

"No, she isn't. Do you know if she's by herself—I mean, is there anybody else there?"

"I'll see, I'll see. I'll give her a shout. Just come inside and close the door gently behind you, so there's no draught in the place, and then I'll give her a shout." And the woman went down the hall, climbed a few stairs, and gave a shout that soon opened the door above. "Miss Golspie, there's a young man here, known to you—I've seen him before meself—he wants to know if you're alone up there and can he come up to see you."

"Yes, I'm all on my lonesome tonight," Turgis heard Lena cry. "Tell him to come up, please, and I won't be a minute." She sounded as if she was pleased. It was wonderful to hear her like that.

"You've to go up and then when you get there, she says she won't keep you a minute, meaning you'll wait while she tidies herself and makes herself pretty."

"Thanks very much," said Turgis fervently, and up he went. The door was open and he walked forward, straight into the big sitting-room, which he had revisited so many times in his imagination these last few weeks that it was quite strange to see waiting quietly there for him, the very same room, with the very same piles of bright cushions, the same deep sofa thing, the same gramophone records, books, magazines, bottles, fancy boxes, fruit, and glasses all over the place, the same two big shaded lamps. He shook to see it there, solid, real. He did not sit down, but stood in the middle of the room, holding his hat, glancing quickly, nervously, at this thing and that.

"Hel-*lo!*" cried Lena gaily in the doorway. Then the sound was cut short. He turned to face her.

"Oh!" she cried, staring at him. "It's you." And her face fell, her voice dropped.

He tried to say something.

"Do you want to see my father about something?" she demanded.

"No, I don't. I want to see you—Lena."

"What do you want to see me about?"

"Oh!—you know, Lena. Everything."

She came forward a little now. "I don't know. My father will be coming back soon—any minute."

"He won't," he told her sullenly.

"How do you know he won't? You don't know anything about it!"

"I do. I know where he is, and I know he won't be back for some time."

"Yes, you *would!* That's why you're here. You've been spying and following me about, haven't you? Making me look a fool! *You* look a fool too, let me tell you that, a nasty fool."

"Well, what if I have? I wanted to see you."

"Well, I didn't want to see you," she cried, furious now. "And you ought to have known I didn't. You can't take a hint. I told you as plainly as I could I didn't want to see you any more."

"Lena, why don't you?"

"Because I *don't*, and that's why. If I don't want to see you, why don't you go away and stop away? I don't want you hanging about me and coming slinking in here, looking like nothing on earth. Just because I felt sorry for you once and hadn't anything much to do and was nice to you, do you think I've got to spend all my time trailing round to the pictures with you?"

"But, Lena, listen——"

"I tell you I won't listen. I don't want to hear. If you only *saw* yourself! Go away. I won't listen. I didn't want to be rude to you, but you're so *stupid* and you just make me look silly too."

"Lena, please, please, just listen a minute——"

"Oh, go away, can't you! Fool!"

"You'll have to listen," he screamed. He sprang forward, dropping his hat, and seized both her wrists and held them tight. As she struggled to break loose, he poured it all out in a wild unbroken rush of short phrases, the whole story of his first distant adoration, his desire and his passion, all the ecstasies and miseries of his love. As he came to the end, his grasp suddenly slackened and she was able to free her wrists. She had not listened to him. She was in a fury.

"You damned rotten rotten——" she gasped, fighting for breath. Then she flared up into a shriek: "Keep your filthy hands off me," and she flung her own hands into his face, pushing him away.

Things were snapping inside him now like taut fiddle-strings. "All right, I'll kiss you for that," he cried, and caught hold of her before she could get away. He was not a muscular youth, but he was strong enough now. He pressed her body to his and forced a few brief kisses upon her before she had a chance to do anything but push and wriggle. The feel of her body, the soft cheek burning beneath his lips, the scent of her hair, touched a spring inside him; all tenderness for her vanished; his blood leaped and sent a murderous cataract roaring in his ears. He still held her, but hardly noticed her hands on his face.

She gave a violent twist, partly freeing herself. "You dirty, filthy pig!" she cried. "Let me go. I hate you. If you touch me again, I'll scream and scream until somebody comes."

He looked at her and there came, like a flash of lightning, the conviction that she was hateful, and something broke, and a great blinding tide of anger swept over him. Her scream was cut short, for his hands were round her soft white throat, pressing and pressing it as he shook her savagely. Her head wobbled like a silly mechanical doll's. Her mouth was open and her eyes were bulging, and so she wasn't even nice to look at any more, but just silly and ugly, so silly and ugly that his hands, which had an independent life of their own now and were strong and masterful, pressed harder than ever.

A horrible rusty noise came from that open mouth. She suddenly went limp, and, as his hands released their grip, her eyes closed and she slipped backwards, striking her head against the corner of the divan as she fell and then rolling over on to the floor, a huddle of clothes and white flesh. She made no movement at all, not a twitch, not a tremor. He crept forward, his eyes fixed on what could be seen of her face, purply-white and still. The whole figure was completely motionless. He waited a minute, raising his eyes in a slow strained fashion until they took in nothing but the shape and colour of a fancy box of cigarettes on the little table by the divan. There was a gay picture of a Turkish woman on the box. He had had some cigarettes from that box; they were very good; they were foreign cigarettes; Turkish, of course, but not sold in England; foreign words just above the picture of the Turkish woman, foreign words. Very slowly his eyes left the box and returned to the figure on the floor. Lena. Not a movement. No, that wasn't Lena any more; that was a body. You couldn't lie there like that unless you were dead. Lena was dead.

He stopped thinking then; no more thoughts came, not one. He picked up his hat and shambled quickly out of the room, out of the flat, leaving the door wide open behind him. When he reached the hall below, somebody came out from somewhere, perhaps spoke to him, but he took no notice. He left the house. It was better outside, in the dark.

IV

Down the straight length of Maida Vale, past the detached villas, past the great blocks of flats that were like illuminated fortresses, he moved at a steady pace, never lingering, just as if he were a young man who knew exactly where he was going and knew exactly how long it would take him to get there. But he wasn't going anywhere;

he was only moving on, simply leaving that room with the bright
cushions and the fancy boxes and the quiet huddle of clothes and
limbs by the end of the deep sofa. He wasn't quite real. He was
a young man walking in a film. Somebody spoke to him once. It
was a big man in a cap and mackintosh, and he planted himself
squarely in front of the dazed Turgis and said, almost angrily:
"Here, I say, how do I find Nugent Terrace?" And when Turgis
muttered that he didn't know, that he was a stranger in that district,
the big man said that he was a stranger too and that everybody he
asked was a stranger, that they were all bloody strangers. When
Turgis was walking on again, he kept repeating that—"all bloody
strangers." He noticed things as he went along, though they weren't
very real, only like the things you see in the background of a film.
Maida Vale turned itself into Edgware Road, and immediately became bright and crowded, a gleaming medley of shop windows,
pubs, picture theatre entrances, hawkers' barrows, and pale faces.
There was a shop where you could get sixpenny packets of gaspers
for fivepence. A woman was shouting at a pub door; she was drunk.
A lot of people were waiting to see the pictures, and a fellow with
a banjo was singing to them. Two Chinamen came out of a sweet
shop: *All These Chocolates Our Own Make*. That fried fish smelt
bad. Two men starting a row, and a woman trying to pull one of
them away. A good raincoat for 25/6. Funny what a lot of these
imitation bunches of bananas there were, and didn't look a bit like
the real ones either. That chap standing in the shop doorway was
just like Smeeth, might be his double. It streamed on and on, like
a coloured film, a film with heavy bumping bodies and real eyes in
it. Marble Arch, and some people waiting for buses.

Now, quite suddenly, he felt sick and terribly tired. There was
nothing left of his body but some tiny aching old bones, but his
head was enormous and there was more screeching and grinding
and dull roaring in the great hollow inside it than there was among
the cars in the road. He tried to think. Had he really gone there
and done that? He had gone to that room so many times in his

imagination, had so many scenes there, so many vivid encounters with Lena, that perhaps this last visit wasn't real either. Had he done that? His fingers, closing round ghostly flesh, sent a sharp message to say he had done it. Yes, he had. Then there was no changing it at all. It was there. As if curtains had suddenly parted and been drawn up, he saw the room again; he was back in it; a Turkish woman on a box of cigarettes, and then—on the floor, not a movement. Something inside him, a little wild thing, trapped, mad, sent up a scream. Something else muttered over and over again that it was an accident, only an accident, a pure accident, just an accident, all accidental, simply an accident; and then it said that he wasn't well, not at all well, ill in fact, nerves and all that, yes nerves, quite ill, not healthy, not well. The tears came into his eyes as he thought how true this was, for lots of people had said that he wasn't well and he knew he wasn't well. Then a bus came up and everybody got on it, so he got on it too, and sat inside. The man next to him had a big swelling at the back of his neck, and for a moment Turgis was sorry for him, but after that he forgot all about him, forgot about all the other people in the bus, forgot all about Oxford Street and Regent Street that rolled past like a gleaming and glittering frieze. He did not notice where the bus was going; he did not care; he sank into a sick stupor.

" 'Ere, come along," said the conductor. "Fares, please."

Mechanically, vacantly, Turgis handed him twopence and received his ticket.

Nobody else bothered about him at all. They glanced in his direction and then looked indifferently away. Yet in a week or two perhaps they might all of them be talking about him. But then he would not be Turgis any more, Mrs. Pelumpton's lodger and the railway and shipping clerk at Twigg & Dersingham's; he would be the Maida Vale Flat Murderer; and as that he could set huge machines in motion, send men running here and there, men with notebooks, men with cameras; news editors would mention him at conferences; sub-editors would rack their brains for good headlines for him; reporters would describe his little room in Nathaniel Street and interview Mrs. Pelumpton; columns on his "ill-fated romance" would be commissioned for the Sunday papers; good money would be paid for the smallest snapshot of him; every detail of his past would be sent roaring through the printing machines; men who had known him would boast of it; special contributors would comment on his story and his fate for twenty guineas a thousand words; scholarly criminologists would make a note of his case for future reference; novelists and dramatists would see if he could be worked up into anything good; millions would talk about him, would denounce him, would cry for his execution, would sign petitions, or perhaps pray for his soul; if he were set free, ten thousand women would be ready to marry him, and any halting sentences he could produce about himself would be handsomely paid for and conjured into The Story of My Life, announced on innumerable placards and hoardings: he would be somebody at last—the Maida Vale Flat Murderer. As yet, however, he was only a shabby, hollow-eyed youth with a vacant look, huddled in a seat that slowly moved round Piccadilly Circus, where, against the night sky, commerce was clowning it royally in a multi-coloured fantasy of lights. Nobody bothered about him yet; they were, as the big man had said, all strangers.

At the corner of the Strand and Wellington Street the bus turned and then stopped, and there he left it and began walking eastward. He had no destination, no plan; his mind issued no commands to his body to move, this way or that; his legs simply went on; while his mind was half in a dream and, for the rest, a vague jangle of conflicting voices. It was quieter now, less crowded, for he was going along Fleet Street, where later, perhaps, the machines would pound him into brisk news just as the other machines had pulped the tall trees into paper for such news. They were waiting, just round the corner, down the dark alleys, these machines, ready to pounce on some unhappy morsel of humanity. But as yet he was still only Turgis, Mrs. Pelumpton's, Twigg & Dersingham's, and now he drifted on, up Ludgate Hill, turning his face towards the old grey ghost of St. Paul's, then curving in its shadow round Church Yard, up Old Change, down Cheapside, along Milk Street and Aldermanbury. It was better here in the City; not so much glare and noise, not so many people; it was huge, dark, and wettish, like a big cellar, a cave. It made his head feel better; and at last he could think a bit, though it was like trying to think in a nightmare. His legs were taking him somewhere now. There was no sense in it, but then there was no sense in anything. Oh, what had he done, what had he done? A street lamp, set queerly at the side of a great blank wall, threw its uncertain light on to a short curving flight of stone steps. While he questioned himself, his feet sought these steps and trod them with an ease that suggested familiarity. His hand touched the stout little iron post at the top, as it had done many and many a time before, for the blank wall belonged to *Chase & Cohen: Carnival Novelties,* and these were the steps that prevented Angel Pavement from being a *cul de sac.*

Two little yellow lights flickered at him, like a dubious pair of eyes, from somewhere down the little street. He walked towards them, quite slowly now, as if at last his mind was attempting to control his legs. The lights were those of a car. They were the feeble headlights of a taxi. And above this taxi, there was one lighted window, on the first floor, and on the first floor of No. 8. Somebody was in the office, Twigg & Dersingham's, at this time, ten o'clock. He had to tell himself so very slowly and clearly, and he did it while he was standing in front of the waiting taxi.

He put his head round the corner, to look in the driver's seat. "I say," he began, with difficulty as if his voice was rusty, "I say——"

"Hel-lo, hel-lo!" the driver suddenly shouted, so that Turgis jumped back. "What the hel-lo! You give me a start, mate. I must ha' dropped off."

"I say," said Turgis, returning to look at him earnestly, "did you bring somebody here? In there, I mean."

"I did," replied the driver. "And I'm waiting for the party to come out."

"Who was it? I mean, what was he like?"

The driver pushed forward a wrinkled red face. "Now I should say—that's my business. Who d'you think you are, young feller? Scotland Yard or what?"

"No, but you see, I happened to be passing, you see," he hesitated a moment, "and, well, I work up there—where the light is—in that office, and I wondered who it was."

"Your place—like?"

"Yes." Turgis gulped. He felt sick; he was trembling; he couldn't talk like this long. "My place, where I work."

"I see. Well, matter of fact, there's two of 'em in there, and I brought 'em here from a restaurant in Greek Street. There's a young lady and a stiffish gent—big moustache. That's who's in there, mate. Now are you satisfied?"

"Yes—thanks."

" 'Ere," said the driver, after a pause, pushing his face over the edge of his door and staring at Turgis, " 'ere, half a minute, boy, what's the matter? You're not crying, are you? Got the jim-jams, boy, or what?"

But Turgis had disappeared into the dark doorway.

v

The office door was slightly open, so that a thin pencil of light pointed across the landing. Turgis waited a minute, staring at it from the shadow. He passed a hand roughly over his wet face. Then, summoning all the courage left him in the world, he blundered in, almost flinging himself into the private office beyond.

"Now who the hell are you?" roared Mr. Golspie, jumping up from his chair at the table. Somebody gave a scream. It was Miss Matfield, in the corner.

"Lena," said Turgis, choking over the name.

"Well, I'll be damned! If it isn't What's-his-name—Turgis." Mr. Golspie glared at him, and advanced ferociously. "And what the devil do you want charging in here like this, eh? What's the game, eh?"

"Lena. Lena."

"Do you mean my daughter, Lena? What are you talking about? What about her? What the blazes has she got to do with you?"

"I think—I've killed her."

"*Killed* her?"

"Yes." And Turgis stumbled to a chair and began sobbing.

"My God! he's mad, he's clean mad," cried Mr. Golspie to Miss Matfield, who had risen from her chair and was looking from Turgis to Mr. Golspie in startled bewilderment. "Here, you, stop that blubbering, and try to talk sense. What do you know about my daughter, Lena? You've never even set eyes on her."

"I have," cried Turgis, almost indignantly. "I was with her tonight, in your flat. I've been there before. I took some money there first——" He hesitated.

"That's right, he did take some money there," said Miss Matfield quickly. "Oh!—I believe it's true."

Mr. Golspie pounced on him at once, clapping a heavy hand on his shoulder. "Come on, then. What happened? Get it out, quick."

Turgis blurted out a few sentences, broken and confused, but they were quite enough.

"My God, if she is, I'll kill *you*. Come on, get up, you—you bloody little rat, you—we're going straight into that taxi and we're going to see, and you're coming with us."

"But can't you telephone?" cried Miss Matfield, wildly.

"Yes, of course—no, I can't. I knew I'd have thought of it. The rotten telephone's out of order—been out of order for two days. Come on, let's get away. You turn the lights out, Lilian; I'm going to look after this fellow. Hurry up, for God's sake."

It was a long long journey. For the first five minutes or so, nothing was said, but after that Mr. Golspie, out of sheer impatience, began to ask questions, and piece by wretched piece, he dragged the whole miserable story out of Turgis, who sat facing him, on one of the little seats, trembling, afraid every minute that Mr. Golspie was going to hurl himself across the tiny space at him. His misery was so great, now that his brain was clearer, that he felt that he would not mind being killed, but nevertheless Mr. Golspie's huge violence, repressed but apparently ready to burst out any moment, terrified him. Miss Matfield hardly spoke a word the whole time, and when she did it was in a very soft shaky voice. But she stared at Turgis, and when the lights flashed in he saw that her face was pale. It never occurred to him to wonder what she was doing there so late with Mr. Golspie.

"It just shows you, doesn't it?" said Mr. Golspie to Miss Matfield. "If I hadn't suddenly thought during dinner I ought to slip back there for quarter of an hour, to tot those figures up to show that chap in the morning, we'd never have seen this fellow. What were you doing there anyhow? I don't know if it's much good asking you, because you seem to me wrong in your damned head—but what were you doing there?"

"I don't know," Turgis muttered. "I just went there. I didn't know where I was going. I suppose when I got to the City, well, I just went to Angel Pavement—sort of force of habit."

"Another ten minutes and we shouldn't have been there, and then I shouldn't have got back home till twelve. What time is it now? Quarter past ten, eh? What time did you leave my place?"

"I don't know really. I'm all mixed up ——"

"My God!—you are," said Mr. Golspie bitterly. "And you're going to be a worse mix up soon, let me tell you."

"I think—it couldn't have been much after eight—I don't know, though—might have been half-past eight."

"Nearly two hours—och!" Mr. Golspie groaned. "Here, this fellow's got to drive faster than this, or we'll be all the damned night getting there."

It was horrible stumbling back up that garden path again, going through the hall and climbing the stairs once more. It was worse inside the flat. "You go in there and wait, you," said Mr. Golspie, and gave him a mighty shove that landed him in the middle of the sitting-room, which seemed to him now, of all the places he had ever known, the most horrible, the most closely packed with misery, and the very sight of its cushions and fancy boxes made him feel sick. Nevertheless, he had not been there more than a minute before he knew somehow that Lena was not dead. Then, after a few more minutes, voices came through the open door behind him, and he turned and crept nearer to it.

"No, no, no!" cried a voice, and he recognised it at once as that of the foreign, witch-like old woman who lived downstairs, "she would not 'ave a doctair. I loosen her dress and geef her cognac and do dees teeng and odair teengs, and ven I say, 'You 'ave a vairy great shock, my dee-air, ve call a doctair,' she say: 'No, no, no. No doctair.' Vell den, eet does not mattair. But I say, 'You go to bed. Aw, yes, you go to bed, at vonce, my dee-air.' And she deed not vant to go to bed, but I make her go."

"Little monkey!" Mr. Golspie rumbled. "Good job you thought something was up, though, and came in. I'm much obliged. Very grateful. Just take Miss Matfield here in to her, will you, and I'll be back in a minute or two."

"Is she all right?" cried Turgis, as Mr. Golspie came into the room.

"I don't know about that," he replied grimly, "but she's a damned sight better than she was when you left her lying here, you crazy little skunk. Come here."

"Oh!—thank God!"

"Come here. You can do your thanking afterwards." And he grabbed Turgis by the lapel of his coat and yanked him nearer. "Just listen to me. There are one or two things I could do to you. To start with, I could give you such a damned good hiding you'd never want to look at a girl, never mind put your hands on her, for the next six months. See?" And he shook Turgis with a sort of menacing playfulness, like a terrier with a rat. "And while I'm about it, here's a bit of good advice for you. Keep away from 'em. You're not a lady-killer, y'know—though, by God, you nearly were to-night—and if you take a good look at yourself, you'll see why. Drop it. You're no good at it. And another thing I could do to you, mister half-starved caveman, is to hand you over to the police. I could do that all right, couldn't I?" he demanded, looking sternly at his wretched prisoner, who, hearing that tone and meeting that look, had every excuse for not realising that this was the last thing Mr. Golspie had any idea of doing.

"Yes, you could, Mr. Golspie," he replied miserably. He saw himself marched off, locked in a cell.

"Well, I'm not going to, not yet, anyhow. But, listen—if I ever set eyes on you again, I will. If you come within a mile of this place——"

"Oh, I won't, I won't." And Turgis certainly meant it.

"And you don't go back to that office, understand? You don't go near it again. Keep right away from it. Keep away from me altogether, see?"

"Yes, yes, yes," Turgis gasped, for now Mr. Golspie had stopped shaking him, but was pulling him backwards through the sitting-room doorway, almost lifting him bodily with that huge powerful grasp on his coat shoulder.

"I don't ever want to see you again, unless it's in the dock or the madhouse," said Mr. Golspie, throwing open the door of the flat with one hand while with the other he gave a violent twist and brought Turgis round in front of him. "The very sight of you turns my stomach, see? You understand? You're not going back to that office, and you're not coming within a mile of this flat, and you're going to keep out of my sight and you're going to keep your nasty mouth shut, too. You've been lucky to-night, my God you have! But if ever I see you again, you won't be lucky. So get out and bloody well stay out. There!" And Mr. Golspie, spinning him round, released his coat collar, put a hand in the small of his back, and with a short run and a tremendous heave sent him sprawling down the stairs. He pitched forward badly, banged his nose so hard that it bled, and was bruised, but managed to pick himself up at the bottom and go blindly along the hall to the front door.

He waited a minute outside, leaning dizzily against one of the pillars. The cool darkness rocked round him. In the garden, just by the broken statue of the boy and the two fishes, he was violently sick.

VI

Nearly all Nathaniel Street was in darkness when he returned there that night. At No. 5 they were still up, and he could hear them singing; a rum lot at No. 5. Across the street there was a light or two and a gramophone going somewhere. But that was all. No. 9 was in complete darkness; obviously they had all gone to bed, Edgar too, for when Edgar was out, Mrs. Pelumpton always left a light in the hall for him, a courtesy she did not extend to her two lodgers, Park and Turgis. If they were so late, they had to grope. Very quietly, slowly and painfully, for he had walked all the way from Maida Vale, partly because he wanted to arrive late and so avoid any questions, and was tired out, aching all over, Turgis crawled upstairs to his room at the top. There he lit the tiny gas mantle, and then sat down on his bed, resting his head in his hands.

All his face felt stiff. Laboriously, he removed his soaking shoes, and was not surprised to find that his socks were wet. He put a match to the little gas-fire, which exploded with a startling bang in that stillness. He did not take his socks off, but held out in turn the sole of each foot towards the gas-fire and watched it steam. He had no slippers; he was always meaning to buy some, but never did. He stared at his reflection, holding the cracked little mirror in the wooden frame near the gaslight. There was a bruise on the ridge of his rather prominent nose; dried blood caked about the nostrils; a long smear down one cheek and just above one eyebrow. The eyes, red-rimmed, stared back at him in despair. In all his life he had never hated himself as much as he did then. The cracked face in the black wooden frame began to twitch a little, and he banished it. The water he had used before going out was still in the basin, and now he soaped his hands in it and rubbed them over his face, until his eyes smarted. When he had finished wiping his face, he looked at it again in the mirror, and found that the smears and dried blood had gone, but that the bruise was more marked than before. He did not look long. His face, pale and silly, disgusted him. Going through his pockets, he discovered a crumpled cigarette and had the first smoke for several hours. He remembered the last one, when he was on his way to Maida Vale, not five hours ago. Not five hours ago! A hundred years ago.

The haze had completely vanished from his mind, leaving a dreadful clarity. He saw himself quite clearly, and loathed what he saw. He knew now that Lena was simply a little flirt, who had happened to be bored, her friends being away, when he first called at the flat with the money, and had amused herself with him for a few hours because she had nothing better to do and, for the time being, his obvious worship entertained her. Then the minute somebody better came along, she had dropped him at once, and had afterwards been so annoyed that she had disliked the very sight of him. Now it seemed all quite clear, and it was unbelievable that he could not see it like that before, that he could have gone on dreaming away and hanging about to see her and deluding himself. He did not even hate her now. She simply did not interest him.

What did interest him, however, was the figure he cut himself, and that was what he saw with such terrible clearness. As he sat drooping on the bed, pulling away mechanically at the last inch of the cigarette, he put himself through a pitiless cross-examination. How could he ever have thought that he could make a girl like Lena fall in love with him, a girl who was pretty, who could meet all kinds of fellows, who had lived in places like Paris, who had a father with money? The very thought of Mr. Golspie crushed the last grains of self-respect in him. What had he, Harold Turgis, been fancying himself for? What was he? What could he do? What had he got? Nothing, nothing, nothing. Only a silly face, with a big useless nose and a trembling mouth and eyes that began to water almost if anybody looked hard at them. He threw the stump of his cigarette at the dirty saucer in front of the gas-fire, missed it, and had to go down painfully on his knees and retrieve the glowing end.

He returned to the bed and curled up on it, his eyes fixed on some photographs, cut out of a film weekly, pinned up on the opposite wall; but he did not see the photographs, for he was staring through them, through the wall, into the future, a vague darkness, in which he, a small lonely figure, moved obscurely. His job was gone. He had finished with Twigg & Dersingham and Angel Pavement. Perhaps they might have given him a rise soon; he might have had Smeeth's job and seven or eight pounds a week before long, a proper home and carpets and armchairs and a big wireless set of his own; and now it might be a long time before he got a job as good as the one he had just lost. What could he do? A bit of typing and clerking, that was all, and anybody could do that; even girls could do it; some of them, really educated ones like Miss Matfield (yes, and what had she been doing with Mr. Golspie?), just as well as he could. And when he had queued up and looked at advertisements and written letters and trailed round and waited and got a job at last, what then? What would he get out of it? Nothing. He saw the world before him with no happiness in it, only foolish work and weariness, and unnamed fears, a place of jagged stones, shadows, dim menacing giants.

Having got so far, he could go no further. A little voice, like that of some tiny erect indignant figure in a great gloomy assembly, spoke up now, protesting. It was not right. It was not fair. There had been a time when it had looked as if everything was going to be quite different. Something had gone wrong. Where, how had it gone wrong? He could be happy; he could be as happy as anybody, if only he had a chance to be; and why hadn't he a chance to be? Here!—if he'd a chance, he could be a lot happier than Park or Smeeth or even Mr. Dersingham—yes, he could! Then why shouldn't he be? What was wrong? What *was* it, what *was* it? The little voice asked these questions, but no answer came. No answer. It was as if the erect figure suddenly collapsed and the gloomy assembly remained untroubled, unstirring.

It was no good. Every bit of him, from the damp soles of his feet to his tangled hair (which seemed to have a separate and equally miserable existence of its own, this night), agreed that it was no good. He stood up. He looked about him, as if searching the little room in despair for something to touch, to hold, to cling to, now that the night was pouring in, through the decayed woodwork of the window frame, through the cracked mortar and the foul old stone, its malevolent influences, its beckoning and gibbering ghosts. The calm, the clarity, were gone; the dream fumes rose and drifted again; but when he moved, he still moved slowly, as if led here and there by uncertain spectral hands. He fastened the window tight, and stuffed paper in its various crevices. The door fitted badly, and he had to stuff more paper, indeed all the paper he had, between the door and the frame, and then in the keyhole. He turned off the gas from the tiny mantle, leaving the room uncertainly illuminated by the gas-fire. For a moment he considered the dying glow of the mantle. Could he use that gas? If he had a tube he could, but he hadn't a tube; and if he turned it on full, it gave out so little gas that it would be painfully, horribly slow doing anything to him. No, the gas-fire was the thing. He had only to turn it out now, wait a minute or two until the burners had cooled, then put a hand to that tap again, lie on his bed and hear the gas hissing out for a minute or two, fall asleep and all would be over.

He sat on the floor, in front of the fire, leaning his elbow against the side of his bed. Staring at the three twisted glowing pillars of the fire, he contemplated with sombre satisfaction his approaching end. It would be painless, that he knew, for he had once talked to a man in the Pavement Dining Rooms, and this man had a brother who was a policeman, and this policeman had had a lot of experience with people who had done it with gas and he gave it as his opinion that they all passed quietly away in their sleep without a bit of pain and fuss and worry: it was far easier getting out of the world altogether than taking a train to the City at Camden Town Tube Station. They would find him in the morning, peacefully asleep. There would be an inquest and it would get into the papers. Some of them, Mr. Golspie and Lena, perhaps, would have to give evidence. Mrs. Pelumpton, too. Had the deceased been strange in his actions lately, had he something on his mind? A promising young fellow—would anybody say that? Tragic End, Young Clerk's Fatal Romance. Who would be really sorry? Nobody. No, no, one or two, perhaps a lot of people; you never knew. Poppy Sellers, for instance; Miss Matfield had said that little Poppy, poor kid, was keen on him; so that she ought to be sorry, very sorry; perhaps it would be the great sorrow of her life—"He meant everything to me, that boy. I worshipped him"—he could hear these, and other heart-broken phrases from the pictures, coming from a rather vague Poppy Sellers, very pale and dressed in black. It made him feel sorry himself, and it was the pleasantest feeling he had had for hours, quite warm and luxuriant.

"A very sad case, gentlemen," said the coroner, mournfully. "Here you have a young man full of promise ——" Turgis interrupted him, for somehow Turgis was there too: "It's all right saying that *now*," he cried to them all, triumphant in his bitterness, "but why didn't you do something about it before? It's too late now, and you know it is. Too late, too late! Let this," he continued sternly, "be a warning to you." But that was silly. He would be dead and gone. Perhaps he ought to leave a letter; they usually left letters; but he hated writing letters, and he knew there was no ink in the room. No, of course, he hadn't any ink! He'd nothing! He might as well finish it off now, and show them all, the rotten swine!

As he arrived at this savage conclusion, he noticed for the first time that the three little glowing pillars of the gas-fire were dwindling. They shrank rapidly until they were nothing but quivering blue blobs that shot up once and popped, shot up again and popped, then popped out altogether. No more gas. He hadn't a shilling, he had only eightpence. He couldn't even commit suicide, couldn't afford it.

After a short silence, an unusual sound, a most strange sound, a fantastic and incredible sound, came from the side of the bed and travelled round the dark little room. It came from Turgis, and he may have been crying, he may have been laughing, or doing both at once. He was certainly not committing suicide.

He made a great deal of noise now. Putting out a hand, quite instinctively, to the tap of the gas-fire, he touched something hot in the darkness there, gave a sharp cry, and banged his hand on the floor. Then he stumbled to the window to pull out the paper, and somehow the window stuck and he pushed so hard that when it did open, the rotten old woodwork of the frame partly gave way, and as it suddenly flew open and the night air rushed in, there was a loud crack. The door was noisier still. He was determined to get all the paper away, but it was not easy and he was impatient, and he began pulling away at the knob of the door until at last the door suddenly swung in and he sat down with a bump, the knob still in his hand. It was then that he heard sounds from below, and saw through the open door a light travelling jerkily upwards. The next minute he was looking at the extraordinary figure of Mr. Pelumpton, who was standing outside in his nightshirt, holding a candle.

"Now let'sh 'ave reashon, let'sh 'ave reashon," said Mr. Pelumpton reproachfully. "Bangin' and knocking the housh about like that! The mishish thought shomebody was breakin' in. 'Ave a bit o' shensh, boy, jusht 'ave a bit o' shensh! Can't go on like that, thish time o' night. It'sh all very well going out an' 'aving a pint or two an' coming in late—done it myshelf in me time—but that'sh no reashon for carrying on like that, ish it? Blesh me shoul!—like a nearthquake, jusht like a nearthquake. Now jusht get yourshelf to bed quietly, boy, and let other people shleep even if you can't."

"I'm sorry," Turgis told him. "It was an accident. I'm all right. I'm not drunk or anything."

"Well, you might be in the ratsh, properly in the ratsh, green sherpentsh all round you, the way yer going on," said Mr. Pelumpton severely, as he withdrew.

In ten minutes, Turgis was fast asleep.

VII

"Well, we'll have to see," said Mrs. Pelumpton dubiously. "That's what we'll have to do, we'll have to see."

Turgis had been trying to explain, without any reference to the real facts, why he hadn't gone to the office that Saturday morning, why he wasn't going there again, and why he couldn't immediately pay Mrs. Pelumpton what he owed her. He had not come down to breakfast until late, and both Pelumptons were convinced that he had been uproariously drunk on the previous night, when he had made all that noise.

"I'm sure they'll let me have this fortnight's money all right, Mrs. Pelumpton," he told her. "And then I'll settle up at once, before I do anything else."

Mrs. Pelumpton stopped bustling about for a minute, stood and looked at him, making herself as compact as possible, so that she seemed exactly square from the front; and suddenly said in a startlingly deep voice: "Will you promise me one thing?"

Turgis said he would. He was ready to promise anything to her.

"Well, it's this. Promise me to keep right off the drink this next week or two."

"I promise," he replied promptly. Two glasses of bitter a week were usually enough for him at any time. The Pelumptons were positive, however, that he had been drinking heavily for weeks. Mr. Pelumpton, a beer man himself, said that whisky made you look and behave like that, if you could only get enough of it.

"In or out of work, that 'abit's bad," Mrs. Pelumpton continued. "But far, far worse it is, out of work. Keep off it for a bit. Don't touch a drop. I'm not one of these prohibiters and temperancers—though I did sign the pledge when I was a girl, but then I wouldn't

'ave touched a drop then anyhow, didn't like the taste of it—but
I do say that a young feller like yourself who's going to 'ave to
look for a job is better without a single drop, if only for the sake of
not being smelt."

"I'm sure you're right, Mrs. Pelumpton," said Turgis, who was
hoping that this good advice meant that she was willing to let him
stay on while he was looking for another job.

"I know I am. And what's just 'appened—'cos you can talk about
business until you're blue in the face, but you won't make me
believe you haven't got into trouble with your little goings-on lately
and that's why they've given you the sack—but I say, what's just
'appened ought to be a lesson. You can't afford it and you 'aven't
got the 'ead for it, so you've just got to let the booze alone. Pa
can't afford it, but I will say 'e's got the 'ead for it. You 'aven't.
That's why it's a lesson. Promise me that, and I'll let you run on a
bit, paying me what you can, while you're out of a job. We've got
to live and let live in these times, and I will say that up to lately
you've been as quiet and reg'lar paying a young chap as I've ever
let to. And just you keep on Pa's right side too, for 'e won't like it,
being in business himself you might say and a bit of a stickler, but
I've got a softer nature and I'm not for turning a young chap out
just 'cos he's got his bit of trouble and can't pay all he's agreed
to pay——"

"Thanks very much, Mrs. Pelumpton," said Turgis warmly.

"—For a few weeks anyhow," she added cautiously.

Turgis thanked her again, but with considerable less warmth this
time. It might be more than any few weeks before he saw another
three pounds a week or anything like it, and the way Mrs. Pelumpton talked before she said that, he had imagined she was ready to
let him stay on for months. Still, a few weeks were something. He
had dreaded telling her that he had lost his job, had not even got
this fortnight's money, and would have to keep her waiting. He
felt a bit better now that he had told her, but nevertheless he was
still feeling pretty miserable. He wondered what was happening

in the office, whether Mr. Golspie had explained to Mr. Dersingham what had occurred last night, whether they would send his money on to him, whether they would give him a reference. He had exactly eightpence now and he wanted a cigarette badly this morning. It was no use, he would have to have a smoke. So he went down the road for a packet of ten gaspers, and then decided to go and look at some advertisements of jobs and perhaps have a peep at the Labour Exchange. It was one of those uncomfortable streaky days, a minute or two of sunshine, then clouds and a bitter east wind. It was miserable walking about in it with just twopence in your pocket, no job, a terrifying Mr. Golspie (with possible police) somewhere about, and no hope in any direction. When he saw the Labour Exchange, he was sorry he had gone that way, for the very look of it made him feel still more wretched. He hated Labour Exchanges.

It was late when he had dinner, and when it was over and Mrs. Pelumpton was washing and tidying up in that despairing fury at which she always arrived on Saturday, Mr. Pelumpton returned from the pub down the road, immensely oracular, and insisted on talking to Turgis for the next hour. This time Turgis was compelled to stay there and listen, for already he was beginning to feel that he was there on sufferance. Moreover, with only twopence in his pocket, and an east wind blowing outside, he was better off there than he would be anywhere else. Something must have told Mr. Pelumpton this, for he never took his dim boiled eyes off Turgis, and droned on and on, sometimes touching on the dusty mysteries of "dealing," sometimes offering ridiculous good advice. It was awful. Turgis sat there, steadily hating the old bore. "That's right, Mr. Pelumpton," he would say, with dreary politeness, adding to himself: "You silly old devil, you ought to give those whiskers of yours a good wash and brush up." But there was not much satisfaction in that.

At about half-past three, Mr. Pelumpton's steady flow was suddenly checked. Somebody was at the front door. Mrs. Pelumpton immediately made a dramatic appearance from nowhere, crying, "You go and see, Pa. It might be Maggie," and then waited, tense, with lifted brows and open mouth, while Pa shuffled out of the room and along the hall.

"Yersh, that'sh right," they heard him say. "Come inshide. Jusht a minute." And then he came shuffling back, so maddeningly deliberate that his wife's eyes began rolling round with sheer impatience. "Is it Mrs. Foster?" she cried.

"No, it ishn't Mishish Foshter," he replied, with dignity. He looked at Turgis. "It'sh a young lady from your offish who'sh been shent to shee you."

"Take her in the front," said Mrs. Pelumpton, before Turgis could get out of the room.

It was little Poppy Sellers, and Turgis took her into the front; which only made it all the more queer, for he hardly ever went into that room. It was used only on the most special occasions, and for about three hundred and sixty days of the year it remained a shrouded and mysterious chamber. It housed, behind faded lace curtains, some of Mr. Pelumpton's best bargains in "pieshesh," a piano with a pleated silk front, two armchairs that were very shiny and plushy, half a bearskin rug, several books in one glass case, dozens of butterflies in another case, two real oil paintings of waterfalls, and a fine collection of shells, glass paper-weights, wool mats, marble ash-trays, and souvenirs of all the South-Eastern seaside resorts. Above the mantelpiece, and flanked by two tall mirrors that had storks painted on them, Mrs. Pelumpton's father, so immensely enlarged in sepia that at a first glance he seemed to be a generous view of the Alps, stared down in mild astonishment. The air inside this room was quite different from that of the rest of the house; it did not smell of food at all; it was unlived-in, chilly, with hints of wool and varnish in it. There was a large paper fan in the fireplace, and immediately the two human beings entered the room, a host of indignant specks ran down the folds of this fan, making a queer little flicker of movement and sound in that dim quiet place.

"I've brought your money," said Poppy, bringing an envelope out of her scarlet handbag. She was very smart, this afternoon, in a black and white check coat, a hat nearly the same colour as her handbag, a yellow scarf with red dots in it, and dark silky stockings and shiny black shoes. Not the Japanese style this time—more French. She looked well in that front parlour, sitting in one of the plushy armchairs. "Yes, this is it," she continued, handing it over. "I think you'll find that all right. Mr. Smeeth said somebody had better take it, and I said I would, 'cos I have a cousin that lives up here, in Bartholomew Road, and I sometimes come up here, so I said I didn't mind bringing it, 'cos I know the district, even if I do live a long way off, and I hadn't anything special to do to-day." She rattled this off very quickly, as if it were a set piece she had rehearsed a good many times on the way.

"Thanks very much," said Turgis. Recent events had left him with an imagination that was capable of leaping into life very suddenly. It leaped now. Here was Poppy Sellers bringing his money to him just as he had taken the money to Lena Golspie. She had been ready with a good excuse just as he had. This thought did not immediately pluck him out of his despondency, but it certainly made him feel several inches taller at once. Besides, the kid had made herself look so neat and smart, quite pretty in fact.

"Aren't you well?" she asked him, looking at him very earnestly.

"I'm not too bright," he admitted. "Matter of fact, I've been a bit off colour for some time. Nothing much, y'know. Nerves, really, that's what it is. I'm one of those highly strung people I am."

"You look pale, and you've got a mark on your nose, haven't you?" She examined his face in that special detached way that all women seem to have at times, looking at your face as if it was not part of you, but something you were showing them, like a picture or a piece of china. Then she nodded wisely at it. "I believe something's been up. Here, listen," she continued eagerly, "something's happened, hasn't it? I mean, you're not coming back, are you?"

Turgis admitted sadly that he was not.

"I've been puzzling and puzzling my head about it," she told him, a mounting excitement in her face and voice. "When you didn't come this morning, Mr. Smeeth said you must be ill, and he wasn't surprised. And I thought so, too. And Miss Matfield didn't say anything, and I thought she looked a bit queer, as if she knew something. She does, too, I'm sure, though I don't know what. She doesn't tell me much—bit stand-offish, you know, though she's nice, she really is—but she knows a lot, and something's been going on with her some time, if you ask me. But, anyhow, Mr. Golspie came in, later on, and he was talking to Mr. Dersingham, and then they sent for Mr. Smeeth, and after a bit, Mr. Smeeth came back and said later on, y'know, just trying to be ordinary like, as if nothing special had happened, that you weren't coming back. I knew all the time there was something funny about it. And I didn't see how they'd told you, 'cos you didn't know last night, did you? Course it's not my business, I know," she added, with a wistful note, "but I couldn't help wondering. And I'm sorry, too."

"You're sorry I'm not coming back?"

"Yes, I am," she declared, tightening her lips, nodding, then looking him full in the face. "I don't care what anybody says—I am."

"I'm sorry, too. Can't be helped, I suppose. I've been in trouble." His voice trembled slightly as a wave of self-pity swept over him.

She kept her eyes fixed on his, and they were dark and round. "Did you—do something?"

He nodded. Already, even in this nod, there was a certain gloomy romantic suggestion.

"Course you needn't tell me if you don't want," she said hastily, "but p'r'aps you'd like to, 'cos I'm not trying to poke my nose in— it's not that—but I'd reelly, reelly, like to know—'cos—well, it doesn't seem a bit fair, turning you off like that, and I said so this morning. You've always done your work all right, and you knew a lot about it, didn't you? I'm sure you've helped me a lot, and I don't care who knows it. And I said so straight out. I spoke up for you. They can say what they like about me, but I do stick up for my friends and anybody I like." Then she lowered her voice. "You didn't take something, did you?"

"D'you mean—pinch some money?"

"Yes," she replied, looking down at her brilliant handbag.

"I should think I didn't. Nothing like that. It wasn't anything to do with Twigg and Dersingham's at all. It was something—quite different."

"I see." She ran a finger up and down the bag. Nothing was said for a minute. As the room, chill and shuttered, waited for somebody to speak, there stole into it all the Saturday afternoon noises of Nathaniel Street, but all faint, muffled. Mrs. Pelumpton's father stared down at them with mild astonishment. Turgis, sitting up in the other armchair, tapped a foot, and a few more specks stirred in the paper fan. This front room made him feel miserable, hopeless. He looked at the girl, and though she was so quiet now, she seemed delightfully vivid, warm, alive, human. He did not tell himself that, but he felt it.

"Well, I suppose," she began, grasping her bag properly and making a movement of her body.

"Listen, I'll tell you what happened," he said quickly.

"You needn't if you don't want, y'know."

He did want. He told her almost the whole story, as he saw it then, and he did not see it then quite as he had seen it when he had returned in abject misery to his room the previous night. It took on a certain romantic colouring, and, as the history of a poor, virtuous, infatuated young man and a rich, wicked syren, it was not unlike a good many films that both the narrator and his hearer had seen and admired. She listened enthralled, exclaiming now and then, her eyes round with wonder.

Her first question, when he had done, was about Lena. What was she like, and did he still think she was as pretty as all that? This was not an easy question to answer, for he had to convey the impression that Lena was immensely seductive and at the same time to suggest that she had no further attraction for him. But he contrived to answer it, a trifle awkwardly, perhaps, but he satisfied Poppy.

"Course you never ought to have done that," she cried, thinking of his terrible assault upon the jeering "vamp." The glance she gave him, however, had more wonder and awe in it than disgust. It made him feel that he was not a man to be trifled with. "That was awful, that was. You didn't reelly know what you were doing at the time, did you?"

"That's it. I didn't. Nerves, y'know. Highly strung. A sort of madness, it was. Can't imagine now how I did it, 'cos I've never been that sort of chap, though, mind you, I've always had a temper if I got properly roused. Still, I don't know how I came to do it, I don't, really I don't. Must have been properly mad at the time. Seems strange now, I can tell you, 'cos I don't feel anything about it now, nothing at all."

"Well, I don't say you ought to have done it, 'cos you oughtn't, and it's turned out lucky the way it has." She had a moment of real distress, imagining how it might have turned out. Then she went on to consider other aspects of the matter. "But I must say she very near deserved it, whatever happened, going on the way she did." She had throughout shown the greatest indignation with Lena. "Horrible, I call it. Some girls haven't any real feelings at all. Girl I know—she lives near us, and she's one of these manicurists—she's just the same. Treats boys and talks about them, too, in the most awful way. If they only heard what she said about them, they'd never look at her again. She's asking for trouble too, and she'll get it before long, and it'll serve her right—I haven't a bit of sympathy for her. I wouldn't behave to a boy like that, I don't care who he was, not if I'd never liked him at all and he was always follering me round and all that. And look at the way she went and encouraged you at first, making herself as cheap as anything— that ought to have told you, but of course boys can never see that."

"I can see it now," said Turgis, with the air of a man purged and purified by great suffering, a pale romantic figure.

"Boys haven't a bit of sense like that," she cried indignantly. "And you were just as silly as the rest, in that business. Mind you, I can see there's a good excuse for you, 'cos a girl like that, with her father so well off and able to have all the clothes she wants and make herself look nice all the time—course you think it's all natural, her looking like that, but it's having the money and nothing else to do that does it—well, there is some excuse, and I admit it. Fancy you going on with Mr. Golspie's daughter like that! And I never knew! Doesn't it just show you?"

Undoubtedly it did. They continued a little longer, dramatically and not unpleasantly, in this strain, and then Miss Sellers asked what time it was, and Turgis, instead of telling her the time, said: "Just a minute. Don't go. I want to give my landlady some of this money, and I'd rather not keep her waiting for it. I'll be back in half a minute."

Mrs. Pelumpton, who was making tea, was very pleased to see the money.

"This young lady works in the same office, you see," Turgis explained, "and they sent her up with it. We've been having a good talk about all the business and all that."

"Quite so," said Mrs. Pelumpton, affably but with dignity, as if the very presence of a strange member of her own sex in the house, even though not in the same room, made her put on a special manner, affable, dignified, lady-like. "Perhaps the young lady would like a cup of tea, with yourself—that is, if she cares to take us as she finds us?"

"Thanks very much, Mrs. Pelumpton," cried Turgis. "I'll go and ask her."

Miss Sellers was easily persuaded to abandon a projected visit to her cousin in Bartholomew Road, and stayed to tea, during which she and Mrs. Pelumpton discovered, after a great deal of elaborate cross-questioning, that Miss Sellers and her sister had actually stayed for a week in a boarding-house at Clacton that had been kept, three years before they went there, by Mrs. Pelumpton's sister, whom therefore, they had only missed meeting by two years and ten months. Delighted to discover once more they were living in a world so small, so cosy, Miss Sellers and Mrs. Pelumpton were very pleased with one another. After tea, when the Pelumptons were out of the way, Turgis, though still the same young man, without prospects, without hope, actually went to the length of indulging in that mysterious badinage which is the signal of sexual attraction and interest among the young inarticulate creatures of this country. "What d'you mean?" they cried to one another. "Oh, I don't mean what *you* mean!"

Then, at the end of half an hour or so of this, "Well, I *half* promised to see a girl friend to-night."

"Oh, well, don't bother," he told her. "She can do without you, can't she, just for to-night?"

"Just for to-night, eh? Well, can't you do without me too, Mister Cheeky?"

"No, I can't. I want somebody to cheer me up."

"Oh, that's it, is it? Thanks for the compliment. Anybody will do, eh?"

"No, I didn't say that. You know I didn't."

"Well, you meant it."

"No, I didn't. Reelly, I didn't. Come on. What d'you say?"

"All right then," she said, turning her perky little head on one side and smiling. Then she looked serious. "Listen, though. If we do go, I must pay for myself. Yes, I must. I believe in that," she added earnestly, as if she had thought about it for years and had not just invented this rule for herself, knowing only too well that he would be hard up in the near future and that every extra shilling would make a great difference. "I'll come if you'll let me pay for myself. There now!"

As they walked down Nathaniel Street, they decided that it must be one of the big West End picture theatres, but could not settle which it should be, and argued pleasantly about it, and she pretended to care more about it than she actually did and he pretended to care less; she was the eager, excited, imploring female, and he was the large, knowing, tolerant, protective male. Out in the smoky blue and gold of the lighted streets, they were more at ease than they had been in the house. Already they may have felt that they were going further together now than the way to the remotest picture theatre could take them. Perhaps this was the best day's work in one or other of their lives; perhaps the worst. Saturday night: the children of the pavements and chimney-pots came pouring out, seeking adventure, entertainment, profit or forgetfulness in the vast impersonal thunder and glare of the city; and soon these two were lost in the crowd.

Chapter Eleven

THEY GO HOME

I

IT WAS coming to a close like any other Friday afternoon. They were short-handed, for though the new boy, Gregory Thorpe from Hatcham, S.E., a lad with a singularly long face and spectacles, far more conscientious than Stanley but not so engaging, had been with them since Monday, Turgis had been absent since Monday too, and his place had not yet been filled. Fortunately, they had not been very busy this last day or two; the rush of a few weeks before appeared to be over now; Mr. Golspie had not been near the office since Tuesday, and had not sent in any new orders; and the next Anglo-Baltic boat was not due in until the following Monday; so that things were easier. Even without Turgis, they were getting through the work at the usual pace. Mr. Smeeth, glancing round over the top of his desk, thought they ought to have finished in another half-hour or three-quarters. He would get away about six, have his tea in comfort, with plenty of time to spare before the concert began. He was going to hear that symphony by Brahms, the same symphony he had heard before, the one that suddenly and gloriously broke into Ta *tum* ta ta *tum* tum. Another orchestra was playing it this time. It was lucky that the advertisement of the concert had caught his eye: Brahms' Symphony No. 1. He had been looking forward all the week to hearing that symphony again, especially to that moment when the great melody would come sweeping out of the strings again. He had tried to remember it for weeks and weeks, and then suddenly it had returned to him—Ta *tum* ta ta *tum* tum. Brahms might be as classical and highbrow as they said he was (and Mr. Smeeth had been making a few inquiries), but the fact remained that the thought of his first symphony, that dark but splendid adventure, now warmed the heart of Herbert Norman Smeeth. Ta *tum* ta ta *tum* tum—but no, he must get on with his work, finish off and see that the others were finishing off too.

"Miss Matfield, have you anything for Mr. Dersingham to sign? Have you, Miss Sellers? Take them in now if you have."

Mr. Dersingham was in the private office. He had been there most of the day. This was unusual, and rather queer because Mr. Dersingham did not appear to be very busy. He seemed to be waiting for something or somebody. Several times during the afternoon, when the outer door had opened, Mr. Smeeth had heard Mr. Dersingham come out of the private office, as if he could not bear to wait an extra half minute or so. He seemed to be jumpy, too, about telephone calls. Very unusual, rather queer, not like Mr. Dersingham. Mr. Smeeth came to the conclusion that it must be some private business, and therefore no affair of his.

"Now where's that letter from Poppett and Sons?" he demanded. "It was on this desk an hour ago, I'll swear. It's a letter about their account, and I told one of you this morning we'd have to answer it to-day. It was you, wasn't it, Miss Sellers? Well, have you taken their letter away, then? Just see if you have. Yes, there you are— that's it. Bring it here and I'll answer it now. Poppett and Sons, Poppett and Sons," Mr. Smeeth repeated idly as he re-read their letter. "Ye-es. Are you ready? No, half a minute, though—my mistake. I'll have to check that figure. Fi-ifty-fo-our pounds, thi-irte-een shillings—yes, yes, that's all right. Now then——" and here Mr. Smeeth adjusted his eyeglasses and cleared his throat, giving a faintly pompous little cough. Even now, the thought that he, Herbert Norman Smeeth, was sitting there, a cashier, dictating letters to this firm and that, gave him a thrill. "—er—We are in receipt of your— er—communication—put the date in there, Miss Sellers—respecting our statement of account dated so-and-so—and beg to point out that this account was quite in order. You asked us to send down the goods by special road delivery and agreed that the extra carriage, paid by us, should be added to our account—no, just a minute—extra carriage, which had to be paid by us in the first place, should be charged to you, and this we accordingly did. We refer you to your letter—I have a note of that letter—ah! here it is—to your letter of the 4th of December last ——"

Mr. Smeeth rounded off his letter and Miss Sellers hurried it away to her machine. Miss Matfield, who appeared to be in a great hurry, pulled a sheet of paper out of her typewriter with one fine sweep of the hand, and then furiously tidied a little pile of typewritten sheets. The new boy, Gregory, laboriously worked away at his letter copying, with the air of a man engaged in not very hopeful bacterial research. It was wearing away like any other Friday afternoon. There was nothing to suggest that it might blow up any minute, unless the unusual activities of Mr. Dersingham, who appeared to be moving uneasily now in the private office, were considered to be fantastically significant.

"Who was that?" Mr. Smeeth asked, after several doors had banged and Gregory had returned from behind the frosted glass partition.

"I think it was a telegraph boy, sir," replied Gregory sadly.

"How d'you mean—you *think* it was?"

"Mr. Dersingham was there, sir. He got there first, and he was holding the door open and taking something, so I couldn't see who it was properly. I only saw an arm, and it looked like a telegraph boy. You see what I mean about the door, sir? It comes back, inside, when it opens, and Mr. Dersingham was holding it with one hand, and so the door was in the way, you see——"

"Yes, yes, yes, I see. No need to make such a song about it, boy." There was a sad earnestness about this new boy that had been rather impressive at first, but now it only irritated Mr. Smeeth. He liked a boy to be conscientious with his work, but this one was too dolefully dutiful. You could not even relieve your feelings by telling him sharply to get on with his work, because he never stopped doing something, toiling away like a spectacled young sheep. Mr. Smeeth wished now he had chosen a brighter boy, even if the lad would have larked about a bit.

"Smeeth. Smeeth."

"Yes, Mr. Dersingham," Mr. Smeeth called back, frowning a little. He did not like to be summoned in this fashion, by a shout from the door of the private office; it was not dignified. He hurried in, however, for Mr. Dersingham sounded as if he had something important he wanted to say.

"Shut the door, Smeeth," said Mr. Dersingham, who did not look so pink and cheerful as usual. "Oh, look here—have they nearly finished out there?"

"Just clearing up, sir."

"All right, then," said Mr. Dersingham wearily. "Have I signed everything? Tell 'em to let me have everything that must go off to-night, will you? I want 'em to clear out, and leave us alone. Do that now. Just get them to finish up as quick as possible."

Wondering, rather apprehensive now, Mr. Smeeth bustled to and fro with letters to be signed, hurried on Miss Sellers and the boy, and in ten minutes had everything signed, copied, sealed up, and stamped. "Yes, yes," he told them, "that'll be all. You can go now. That's right. Good-night, Miss Matfield. What's that? Yes, I remember. Mr. Dersingham said you could have to-morrow morning off, didn't he? Off for the week-end, eh? Lucky to be some people, Miss Matfield. Yes, yes, quite all right. Good-night. Good-night, Miss Sellers. And—what's your name—Gregory, don't forget you've got three registereds there; bring me the receipts in the morning. No, that'll do. Good-night, good-night." He returned to the private office. "All finished now, Mr. Dersingham. Yes, all gone."

"All right, Smeeth. Bring the order book in, then the other books. Bring the order book in first."

It looked as if he was going to have a little stock-taking and general survey of the business, a very wise thing to do too, now and again. Mr. Smeeth hoped that he would not be kept long, but otherwise he was quite pleased and proud, for there was nothing he liked better than these confidential talks about the business, and he was glad to see that Mr. Dersingham was taking himself seriously now as the head of a very flourishing little concern.

"Nothing wrong, I hope, Mr. Dersingham?" he said, when he had brought in all the books.

Mr. Dersingham gave a short laugh, and it was a very unpleasant sound. It startled Mr. Smeeth.

"Everything's wrong, Smeeth, every damned thing, unless you can see a way out. Sit down, man, sit down. We're going to be hours and hours on this job."

Mr. Smeeth sat down, staring at him.

"Golspie's cleared out," Mr. Dersingham continued, "and he's done us in, absolutely done us in. Oh, the rotten swine! God, I was a fool to trust that chap a yard! I ought to have known, I ought to have known. And now he's gone. I rushed up to that flat of his in Maida Vale at lunch time, hoping to catch him in and have it out with him, but he'd gone—at least, the maid said he had, and it was only a furnished place he'd taken, and she'd been taken over with it, so I suppose she wasn't lying about it. He's going abroad, if he isn't already gone. Clearing out properly, the rotten crook! This isn't the only dirty game he's been playing here, if you ask me. I always thought he had a few more irons in the fire besides his work here. He never spent more than half his time with our business. But he's had plenty of time to do us down." He was out of his chair now, kicking a ball of crumpled paper about the room.

"But what's happened, Mr. Dersingham? I thought you knew he might leave us. You told me so a week or two ago, and you said you were getting him to sign an agreement, when he drew all that forward commission, so that you would have the agency."

"Oh, we've got the agency all right," cried Mr. Dersingham, with great bitterness. "No mistake about that. Only it's not worth having now, that's all. Mikorsky's have raised all their prices. They say it's owing to the increased cost of their new process and to some labour troubles and to some new government tax—oh, they've got all kinds of reasons, and they may be true and they may not, but the fact remains they've raised all their prices. They're all up fifty and sixty and even seventy per cent."

"As much as that? Good Lord, Mr. Dersingham, that's a ridiculous advance. It makes them as dear as the most expensive of the old firms we were dealing with before, doesn't it? I see, now."

"No, you don't see, you don't see at all yet," Mr. Dersingham yelled at him. "It's a lot worse than that. Look at that telegram. Just look at it."

"I don't understand this, sir," said Mr. Smeeth, after carefully reading the telegram. "Why did they send it?"

"They sent it because I'd wired to them asking if what Golspie had written to me was true. I thought he might have been bluffing, just out of devilish spite. But he wasn't. They're all in league together, of course, if you want my opinion, just a lot of rotten foreign swindlers with this chap Golspie the worst of the lot."

"I'm sorry, Mr. Dersingham. I can see it's a bad business. But I don't quite get the hang of it yet. They can't have raised their prices already."

"My God!—that's just what they have done, and that filthy telegram confirms it." Mr. Dersingham banged it so hard with his fist that he hurt his hand. Then he became quieter and sat down again. "I'm getting too excited. Sorry I yelled like that, Smeeth, though it's enough to make any man shout his head off. I'll explain. I got a letter from Golspie this morning, saying that he was clearing out. Here, you can read it for yourself."

Mr. Smeeth read it through twice. It pretended to be an ordinary business letter, but there was a good deal of unpleasant irony in it. One phrase, which practically said that Mr. Dersingham had tried to sneak the agency for himself and had not succeeded, made Mr.

Smeeth look up and ask a question. "Did you really write to those people and try to get the agency yourself, sir?" he asked.

Mr. Dersingham nodded.

Mr. Smeeth hesitated a moment. "I don't think you ought to have done that, sir," he said finally, respectful but reproachful.

"That's my business, Smeeth."

Mr. Smeeth looked down and remained silent. Neither of them spoke for a minute or two, and the room was strangely quiet.

"Oh well," cried Mr. Dersingham, struggling with his embarrassment, "perhaps I oughtn't to. As it's turned out, it was a bad move. But I wasn't really trying anything underhand, y'know, Smeeth. It wasn't as if I was trying to take a fellow's living away from him, working behind his back. I know it might look a bit like that, to anybody who didn't know the circumstances, but it wasn't. This chap Golspie was obviously one of these here-to-day-and-gone-to-morrow fellows—didn't make any secret of it, boasted of it—and I never liked the look of him and I didn't know what tricks he might be up to. He came here, made use of our connection with the trade and our organisation and everything and drew a heavy commission, as you know, and all the time he walked about the place as if he owned it. As I told you before, I couldn't stand the chap—a terrible bounder. I tried to be as friendly as possible at first, but it wouldn't work. And my wife took a strong dislike to him—she only met him once, but you know what women are, and she saw what he was in five minutes—and she was always telling me to have nothing more to do with him, to get rid of him. So I just wrote a confidential letter to Mikorsky's, saying it would pay them to have the agency properly in the hands of a wholesale firm here like ours, and that the—er—present arrangement wasn't really satisfactory to them or to us either, and that they ought to consider it. All in confidence, mind. That was just before he went over there, and of course they told him all about it. I didn't know they were friends of his. I thought they had an ordinary business agreement, and I considered I was entitled to suggest another business agreement, leaving Golspie out."

"Yes, I see that," said Mr. Smeeth, still a little doubtful. "And I suppose they told him then, and that's what put his back up?"

"Oh, they did that, but I think he'd been ready to play any dirty little trick right from the first. He isn't a gentleman—never looked like one—and he isn't even an ordinary decent business man. He's just an adventurer, trying his hand at anything for tuppence. No wonder he never stopped anywhere long—too crooked! But you see what he says there, that he encloses a little document that had—what is it?—escaped his memory. Well, there's the little document, there—that statement of Mikorsky's, dated when he was there, raising all the prices. There's the full list of 'em—up fifty to seventy per cent."

"But—but," Mr. Smeeth stammered, as he looked at this list, "we can't be expected to pay these prices. We've already bought heavily on the old prices."

"Have we? Golspie did the buying, and I can't find any acknowledgment from them."

"Well, can't we cancel the last orders then, Mr. Dersingham? I never heard of such a thing. It's not reasonable. Here their prices have been up for weeks and weeks, and we've been thinking we were buying at the old rates. They can't force us to take the stuff at these prices, surely."

"I don't know. That side of it doesn't matter, anyhow. The point is, Smeeth—don't you see?—whether we've bought the stuff or not, we've *sold it.*"

Mr. Smeeth did see: he saw with fatal clearness; and his dismay must have been written on his face.

"Yes," Mr. Dersingham continued, "we've sold it, stacks and stacks of it, thousands of square feet, big orders, Smeeth, big orders, all those orders we paid Golspie that commission on. You might well look like that. I've been feeling like that all day, even though I still hoped there might be a mistake—before that telegram came."

"But, Mr. Dersingham—it's—it's ruination, sheer ruination."

"And it's damnably, damnably unfair, Smeeth. We've simply been swindled. Listen, d'you think there's any chance of us getting all those orders cancelled here?"

Mr. Smeeth thought for a minute, then slowly shook his head. "We've undertaken to deliver the stuff, Mr. Dersingham, and there's no getting out of that. I mean to say, if our customers say 'We want it,' then they'll have to have it and they can compel us to let them have it at the price we sold it, or compel us to go out of business. No argument about that at all, sir."

"What I'm wondering is this, Smeeth. It's not our fault this has happened. I mean to say, it's not the ordinary case of selling the stuff before you've bought it, hoping for a fall in prices, and then getting nipped because the price goes up when you have to deliver the stuff. It's nothing like that, you see. We've been let down by sheer rotten trickery. Not our fault at all. Now I'm wondering if our customers would agree to cancel the orders if I explained the situation to them, told them straight out that Golspie was a wrong 'un and we've been let down. It's worth trying, isn't it? Where's that order book? I want to see who are about the biggest buyers of these last lots that I can get hold of at once. What about Brown and Gorstein? They're not far away."

"And they've bought as much as anybody," said Mr. Smeeth. "We've a lot to deliver to them. You might get hold of Mr. Gorstein."

"I'll ring up and see if he's there." And while he waited, receiver in hand, he added: "Jot down what Brown and Gorstein have bought, will you, Smeeth?" By the time Mr. Smeeth had done this, Mr. Dersingham had learned that Gorstein was still there and was willing to see him at once. "I'll go over at once," said Mr. Dersingham. "I'll just tell my wife first not to expect me back in a hurry. I believe we were going out to play bridge with somebody. My hat! —I feel as much like playing bridge to-night as I do like—like— spinning tops."

When the other had finished his telephoning, Mr. Smeeth had the order book and some paper in front of him. "While you're there,

Mr. Dersingham, I'll try and work out the whole thing on the new prices."

"I was going to tell you to do that," said Mr. Dersingham, as he took down his hat and coat. "Get it all worked out while I'm up at Brown and Gorstein's. God!—we're in a mess. I'll be back as soon as I can."

Left to himself, Mr. Smeeth did not think. He refused to think. He applied himself sternly to the task before him, and for the next quarter of an hour never looked up from his books and his calculations. He was not Herbert Norman Smeeth, but simply the master of the neat little figures, and he added and subtracted and multiplied them without letting his mind wander away from their austere but calculable world, in which he had spent so many pleasant hours. He had plenty to do. All the orders of the last few weeks, back to the early part of December, in fact, had to be estimated on the basis of these new prices, and he had to add the usual costs and then the commission already paid to Golspie. He did it with his usual neatness, accuracy, thoroughness, producing a statement that could be understood at a glance. At the end of quarter of an hour, the telephone rang and disturbed him, but it was not a call for them. Mechanically, then, he filled his pipe, and spent a minute or two listening idly to the various sounds that came from the steps outside, from Angel Pavement, from the City beyond, a sort of vague symphony, and the only one, it seemed, that he would hear that night. He put his pipe in his mouth unlit, and bent over his figures again. Time slipped away as the totals mounted up on the statement, and soon half an hour had gone. He turned now to other books, to the general financial side of the matter, estimating what they had in hand and what was due to them.

Mr. Dersingham came bursting in, large and active, but a figure of misery. "It's no use, Smeeth. We're absolutely done."

"What did Mr. Gorstein say?"

"I told them as much as I could, and they laughed at me, they did, honestly they did, they just laughed at me. Pretended not to, pretended to be very sympathetic and all that, but I knew. That fellow Gorstein's another rotter, if you ask me. Very sorry and all that, hard luck on us, but of course they'd bought what we'd offered them, and they'd undertaken to supply *their* customers and made contracts on what they'd bought from us, and we'd have to deliver, and no nonsense about it. And they practically told me that every-body else in the trade would say the same thing, but only be a bit more damned insolent about it. No, I see that now, plainly enough. There's no getting out of it."

"But, Mr. Dersingham, it's a terrible position we're in, it really is."

"Good God! man, you've no need to tell me that. It's the foulest mess I ever dreamed of, and all because of that dirty crook. Honestly, Smeeth, I don't pretend to be a bruiser or anything of that sort, but if I saw that chap now, I'd go for him. I'd either knock him down or he'd have to knock me down. Have you been working it all out? What does it look like?"

Mr. Smeeth now considered his totals and the full implication of them for the first time. He handed the papers across the table.

Mr. Dersingham, running a finger across his teeth and allowing his jaw to drop, stared at them for several minutes without saying a word. Then he queried one or two figures, and Mr. Smeeth worked them out again, for his benefit. The order book was referred to several times. But there was no escaping from those totals.

"I've just been working out how we stand, too, Mr. Dersingham. I thought you'd want to know now. This is the position, counting everything in."

They went over that now, spending about half an hour in what was mostly futile discussion, as Mr. Smeeth, sick at heart, knew only too well.

"It's no good, Smeeth," the other said finally, "there's no getting away from it. It was a tight squeeze paying that swine all that com-mission in advance, and now we've got to sell every square foot of stuff at a loss, on all those orders."

"It's a terrible loss. The business as it is will never stand it, Mr. Dersingham."

"I know that. And what's left of the business, even supposing I could borrow enough to see me through this mess? Where should we be? Only back where we were before we began handling this stuff, before Golspie came, doing just about enough trade to pay expenses, and on top of that I'd be up to the neck in debt. I couldn't carry on a month. I've borrowed as much as I can, and even if I could borrow any more, I wouldn't—it's only throwing money away. Honestly, Smeeth, how can I go on?"

Mr. Smeeth looked through the papers again, though there was no real meaning in the glances he gave them. He was trying to think of a way out, but it was impossible to find one.

"What are you going to do, then, Mr. Dersingham?" he asked, miserably.

"Nothing. Finish. What else can I do? I'll buy what I can of this lot, deliver it, and then finish. And if they bankrupt the firm, they bankrupt it, and there's the end of it. If they don't, I close down and clear out, anyhow, and that's the end of it, too. I don't suppose it's the first time a dam' fool's been robbed clean out of a business, is it?"

"I don't know what to say, Mr. Dersingham." And Mr. Smeeth didn't. He was staring at the opposite wall in utter dejection.

"What's the good of saying anything? But what makes me sick is the way that rotter Golspie has cleared out——"

"I thought at the time it was a bit fishy, sir, when he wanted all that commission in advance."

"Well, if you thought so, why the devil didn't you say so at the time. No good saying so now."

"I did say something at the time, Mr. Dersingham, I did really."

"Well, I must say I don't remember you saying anything. Anyhow, it's too late now. You know, Smeeth, that fellow's robbed me just as much as if he'd broken into my flat—it's worse, when you think of it. And there isn't even a charge against him. All he's done is to collect some commission and keep a letter back. You can't go to the police about that. The swine! That's what maddens me. What's the time? Quarter past eight? Come on, let's get out of this."

They walked down the stairs and out of the building together. Across the way, the only sign of life came from the bar of the "White Horse." "I don't know about you, Smeeth," said Mr. Dersingham, stopping, "but I want a drink. It's a long time since I wanted one so badly. You could do with a spot, couldn't you? Of course you could. Let's have one, while we can still pay for it."

The private bar was completely deserted, except for a long, grey cat that stretched itself arrogantly in front of the little fire. The barmaid came round the corner, swept away several glasses, polished a foot or two of counter, said, "Tom, Tom, Tom, Tom, Tom," to the cat, then smiled at the gentlemen in the way a lady ought to smile, and, "Good evening. Nicer now, iserntit?"

"Two double whiskies, please, and two small sodas," said Mr. Dersingham.

"Two doubles," murmured the barmaid.

Mr. Smeeth could not help being reminded of the time when Mr. Golspie had brought him in here and had insisted on his having a double whisky. That was the night when Mr. Golspie had told him that he ought to have a rise. Everything was going too wonderful that night.

"Here's luck, Smeeth," said Mr. Dersingham, raising his glass, "and I'm sorry for your sake it's turned out like this, though you're not losing what I'm losing, not by a long chalk. But here's luck— here's to your next job, and I hope it's a better one than Twigg and Dersingham ever gave you."

"Thank you, Mr. Dersingham," said Mr. Smeeth shyly. "And here's luck to you too, sir ——"

"You'd think that cat, to look at it," said the barmaid, "was a good mouser if ever a cat was. Wouldn't you now? Well, it isn't. No good at all. Won't touch a mouse. Will you, Tom? No, you won't, you lazy old rascal. Don't earn your keep at all, you don't. Come here, Tom. Tom, Tom, Tom."

"I'm going to try for a job out East as soon as I've straightened things up," said Mr. Dersingham confidentially. "No more City for me. I never did care for it. Not really my style at all, y'know, Smeeth. I always wanted to go out East. You get a gentleman's life out there. A man I know—he's just retired and he's a neighbour of mine—told me some time ago he could get me a good job out there any time. I shall have a shot at it."

Mr. Smeeth nodded and looked gloomy. There was no job out East for him, and these remarks of Mr. Dersingham's suddenly opened out a vast, dreary prospect. At the moment, he preferred not to think about the future.

"Look at him, the silly old thing," said the barmaid, who had the long cat in her arms now. "Aren't you a silly old thing, Tom? He's got nice markings though, hasn't he? Reg'lar, aren't they? Go on then, go down then, if you want to, Tom. There! Boo! Boo! Just watch him. He can open the door by himself. Artful as anything, I can tell you."

Mr. Dersingham gulped down the rest of his whisky and soda. "Rotten luck. The worst possible. Where I made the mistake though, Smeeth, was not trusting to what's-it—instinct, intuition, you know. About Golspie, I mean. I was trying to be the smart City bounder, with an eye for a tricky bit of business and nothing else—y'know, like that awful fellow, Gorstein, and all the rest of 'em. Not my style at all, really. I didn't like the chap and I ought to have known he'd do me down. Never mind, he'll come to a sticky finish before he's done. And so will that daughter of his. You never met her, did you, Smeeth? Very good looking, in the film and chorus girl style, but a terrible little minx. You ought to hear my wife on Miss Golspie! She came to my place once—but never again, never again. That was a queer business, y'know, Smeeth, about Turgis and that girl, when Golspie came and said Turgis would have to be sacked because he'd been up to some mysterious games with the daughter.

I never really understood what it was all about—though I'd like to bet that Golspie's daughter was up to her tricks there—she looked ̣hat sort."

"I never understood that business," said Mr. Smeeth mournfully. "I wasn't properly told about it."

"Neither was I, for that matter. But I didn't bother much, because I never thought that chap Turgis was much good, anyhow, and was rather glad to get rid of him. Thinking it over now, though, I feel a bit sorry for the poor devil. Have you heard anything about him, Smeeth?"

"Miss Sellers has seen him once or twice, I believe. I fancy she's a bit sweet on him. He's not got another job yet, of course, and it's not likely he will for some time." He breathed hard, like a man who wants to sigh but has forgotten how to do it, looked down at the remainder of his drink, and slowly finished it.

"Well, I'd better be getting along," said Mr. Dersingham. "That drink's made me feel hungry. I'll stop at the club and see if I can get a bite. I might see a fellow there who could give me one or two tips about this miserable business. Then I'll go home, and that's the part I'm not looking forward to, I can tell you. Are you going home now?"

"Yes," said Mr. Smeeth slowly, buttoning his overcoat. "I'm going home."

II

As her bus turned into that hive of buses in front of Victoria station, Miss Matfield shivered a little. She was nervous; she was excited; and her mind was facing two different ways. She spent the next few minutes getting from the bus to the station, which was very crowded and week-endy, and then to the place where she had arranged to meet Mr. Golspie, which was on the departure side, between the bookstall and that large clock with four faces. Mr. Golspie was not to be seen. This did not surprise her, for she was rather

early. She was somewhat relieved to find that he was not there. It
left her with a welcome breathing space. She was by no means single-
minded about this adventure.

It had been planned, if a few hasty and last-minute questions and
answers can be called planning, three days before, on Tuesday night,
which was the last time she had seen him. He had not been to the
office since and she had had no message from him, but that did not
worry her. She had a strong suspicion that he was going away very
soon, but she did not know when he would be going and she did
not believe that he knew. Last Tuesday, just before they parted, he
had asked her once again to go away for the week-end with him,
anywhere she pleased, and this time, moved obscurely by many
different feelings and forces, something genuinely eager and passionate in the man's voice, a sudden desire to clutch at experience, to
throw herself upon life, a contempt for her qualms and misgivings
and timidities, she had agreed to go. An hotel on the Sussex coast
she had once seen was to be their destination, and the time and
meeting place were hastily settled. Several times since, she had been
tempted to write to him or ring him up, to say that she had changed
her mind. Her pride, however, would not let her do this. She had
said she would go, and now she would carry it through. She had
wanted adventure, and though she would not have admitted it,
there was always a man in this adventure, and now that it offered
itself and she had accepted it, she could not run away. Yet there was
a creature in her, and not merely a brain phantom, but a creature
that had some of her rich blood flowing through it, that very blood
which this coarse, middle-aged man could so inspire that it dazzled
and inflamed her, a shrinking and fastidious creature that cried to
run away, to run away and hide. It protested against the shabbiness
and furtiveness of this adventure, and pounced upon the sinister lack
of fairness in it. It loathed the cheap imitation wedding ring that
was now tucked away in her bag, a ring that was part of the adventure, and that had seemed rather a joke when it first had been
mentioned last Tuesday. She had heard about those rings before,

and they had always seemed rather a joke, perky, glittering little stage properties in amusing escapades, and it was not difficult for her to force herself to see that ring in her bag in the same theatrical light; but, nevertheless, the protest was not silenced and the loathing remained. If Golspie had asked her to marry him, no matter if he had told her that they would have to settle in the most outlandish place, she would have agreed; but he had not asked her to marry him. Yet he wanted her, not idly either, and, when all was said and done, that was a heartening and exciting fact; and after this, he might want her still more, the last traces of self-sufficiency in him (and he had appeared unusually self-sufficient at first, and that had made him all the more attractive) might vanish, and then—well, everything might be different.

If you delight in movement and change, the appeal of a large railway station is irresistible; you are still in the dark cocoon of the city, but one end is splintering already and you can see the blue beyond; the rumbles and shrieks and snortings are only part of the tuning up; and even the smoky smell has the savour of adventure. There had been moments during the last two days when this week-end, this arrival at Victoria, had loomed in Miss Matfield's mind like some unusually desperate appointment at the dentist's, and at the thought of it something coldly writhed inside her. Now that she was here, however, she was less introspective and her spirits gradually rose. It was almost better that something extremely unpleasant should happen than that nothing at all should happen; and it was very unlikely that anything extremely unpleasant *would* happen. She responded to the lively and adventurous bustle of the station. As she strolled over to the bookstall, carrying her small suitcase, she felt tall, healthy, strong, a fine woman of the world. One or two middle-aged men had smiled in her direction and several young men had looked earnestly at her, all of which meant that she was looking her best. The bookstall offered her an almost unlimited choice of reading matter, light periodicals, heavy periodicals, books that were "amazing successes," books that were "very outspoken," books that were simply "great bargains." She did not accept any of them, but the knowledge that they were there somehow gave her pleasure. It was impossible to resist a holiday feeling. The sight of all the fussy and bewildered people, of whom there were an unusually large number, the people who went rushing up to any man in a railway uniform, who looked in despair at the notice-boards, who mopped their brows and snapped at one another, who blankly surveyed great mounds of luggage, who flitted like uneasy ghosts from one platform entrance to another, only brought her a pleasing sense of her own superiority. They were nothing to do with her; she was not behaving like that; and so she looked on, amused, contemptuous, failing to see in this spectacle of the harassed and inexperienced travellers any symbol of this life of ours.

There were two trains, and they had hoped to catch the earlier one. It was now only a few minutes from the time of starting. She returned to her former place, nearer the clock, and looked about her anxiously. He would get the tickets, of course, before he came on to the main platform, so that there was still plenty of time for them to catch the train if he appeared at all. There seemed to be more and more people about, though round her there was a small clear space. It was just possible that he might have missed her. Only two minutes now. She hurried over to the entrance to No. 17 platform and looked over the barrier down the waiting train. Then she returned, even more hastily, to her place near the clock. From there she heard the train go out.

It was annoying. They would have more than three-quarters of an hour to wait now. It was her turn to keep him waiting. Very deliberately, she made her way to the tearoom, which was not very full though it looked vaguely as if it had just been wrecked by a revolutionary mob, and she spent ten minutes over a cup of tea and a cigarette. She would have liked to have stayed longer, but it is almost impossible to linger successfully with only a sheet of glass between you and a host of trains and passengers. She tried to loiter on her way back to the four-faced clock and the bookstall, but an inner restlessness prevented her, and she arrived there as if her train might start any moment. He was not there. Now she began making little circular tours with the clock as their centre. After quarter of an hour of these, she returned to the meeting place and remained there, her suitcase at her feet, erect, motionless, sullen. She was there, and he must find her. People came and went, bought papers and books, looked at the clock, looked at the departure board, glanced at her; porters wheeled their loaded barrows and trucks at this side of her and that; the trains snorted and puffed and sent red gleams to the glass roof; but now she paid no attention at all. She was tired of Victoria, tired of waiting. This time, when the later train was nearly due to start, she stayed where she was and made no attempt to discover if he was already on the platform. When the train had gone, she stood quite still for a minute or two longer, then walked away.

She had to wait again before she could get a telephone call put through to his flat. The telephone boxes were in brisk demand. She knew his telephone number and knew, too, that the instrument at his flat, which had been out of order the week before, was all right now. But she would not have been surprised to find that there was no reply to her call, for she was sure at least that he would not be there. Something had gone wrong; and even now he was probably trying to get to Victoria. There was a reply, however, and it obviously came from a maid.

"Is Mr. Golspie there, please?"

"No, he's not. He's gone. So has Miss Golspie. They've both gone," said the voice.

"Gone? Do you mean—he's out?"

"No, gone. Gone for good."

"But—I don't understand. Are you sure? I had an appointment with him to-night."

"All I know is—he's gone, Miss Golspie too. They've gone to South Africa or South America or one of them places. In a boat, I *do* know. I helped 'em to pack, and a job it was too, and a nice mess they've left this place in, I can tell you. I'm cleaning it up now, after 'em, 'cos they only took it furnished and I stayed on with the place. There was a gentleman came when I was having my dinner," the voice continued, as if it was rather pleased to have a little chat with somebody, "and he wanted Mr. Golspie badly, but I couldn't tell him anything except they'd gone, went this morning, luggage and everything, and you never saw such a pile."

"Did Mr. Golspie leave any message—for anybody?"

"No, he just went ——"

"All right, thank you," said Miss Matfield, interrupting and then ringing off.

He had gone, left the country, without even telling her he was going, without even telling her he could not keep this appointment at the station. He had simply tossed the week-end away, and her with it, as if it had been a crumpled bit of paper. If he had not forgotten all about it, then he had not cared enough to see her for the last time or even to send a message. And this was the man—oh, the humiliation of it all! She left the station, burning with shame and resentment. An hour earlier she might have felt relieved if Mr. Golspie had come and told her that it would be impossible for them to go away this week-end. But she had waited there, suitcase in hand, that filthy little ring in her bag, had waited there, and all the time he was miles away, not caring if she spent the rest of her life standing in Victoria station. Never before had she felt such bitter contempt for herself. She could have cried and cried, not because he had gone and she would probably never set eyes on him again, but because his sudden indifference, at this time of all times, left her feeling pitiably small and silly. The misery of it was like the onslaught of some unexpected, terrible disease. Her mangled pride bled and ached inside her, so that she felt faint.

That was why she did not return, as a sudden impulse commanded her to do, to the station and take the first train anywhere, to get away for the week-end at any cost from London and the Club. She could not do it; all energy and initiative were drained away; she was too tired. She found a No. 2 bus, climbed on top, and then watched, with smarting eyes that refused to see anything properly, the glitter and blue murk of half London go lumbering past, Hyde Park Corner, Park Lane, Oxford Street, Baker Street, Finchley Road, all a meaningless jumble of light and dark, offering nothing to Lilian Matfield, no more than if it had been some Chinese river flickering past on a cinema screen.

Once in the Club, she hurried upstairs, as if she had stolen the suitcase she carried. Hastily, mechanically, she washed, tidied her hair, changed her dress, powdered her face, and then went down to the dining-room. She did not really want food, but something impelled her to throw herself back into the routine of the Club. But she was careful to find one of those nondescript tables for late-comers, at which there was little talk, and what talk there was merely the occasional impersonal remarks of acquaintances. She ate little, and the sight and smell of the food, the look of everybody there, the high chatter and clatter of the room, made her feel sick. Nevertheless, she stayed on, and had her coffee with the rest. When she got back to her room, she began examining all her clothes and grimly set aside some stockings to be mended. Then she remembered something.

"*Can* I come in?" said Miss Morrison. "Hello, Matfield, what on earth are you doing? Something desperate, by the look of you."

"Hello, Morrison. I was only throwing something away," she replied, closing the window. Somewhere out there was a cheap imitation of a wedding ring.

Miss Morrison, who was wearing bedroom slippers, contrived to shuffle elegantly—for she never quite lost her slim elegance—into the room, and hoisted herself on to the bottom of the bed, resting her back against the wall. "Oh, by the way," she cried, "you oughtn't to be here. Weren't you going away for the week-end?"

"I was," said Miss Matfield shortly, hanging a dress up, "but I changed my mind."

"Good!" And that was all Miss Morrison had to say about that. It was one of her virtues, as Miss Matfield had begun to notice, that she did not ask questions when they were obviously unwelcome, made no attempt, except in fun, to nose things out of you. Most girls at the Burpenfield, if you were on room-visiting terms with them, did not allow you to have any private life of your own. "I ought to have gone out to-night," Miss Morrison continued, in her usual languid manner, "but I can't bother to. I feel foul. I never remember feeling more completely foul, except when I've had 'flu or something like that. I'd go and see a doctor only I can't afford to, and then again I disapprove of the way we females run after doctors and worship them. Cadnam's just been raving to me about some doctor she's just been to. 'He's fifty, of course, and heavily married,' she said, 'but the most marvellously attractive man, my dear.' She went raving on and on. I think it's revolting the way these young females adore their doctors and dentists. I refuse to join in, don't you? After that it'll be vicars and curates and dear, dear doggies—vile! But, as I said before, I feel thoroughly ill. It's partly the idiocy of my respected employer, who really is the silliest woman there ever was—she gets sillier—and then again it's partly the time of year. Don't you honestly think this is the very, very foulest time of all the year? It's such a long way from anything or anywhere interesting, isn't it? Just fiendishly dull. I don't blame all those illustrated paper people—Lady Chagworth, Colonel Mush, and Friend—for going away and slacking about on the Riviera or in Madeira, or wherever it is they do go. I say 'good luck to them!'—don't you? Though I must say it oughtn't to be the same people who go every year and the same people who stay at home, like us, and push into buses on wet nights. They ought to change round a bit. Your turn this year. Our turn next year. That sort of thing."

"I should think so," said Miss Matfield, somewhat indifferently. She was still busy putting clothes away. "I call it beastly unfair. I think I'll turn Bolshie."

"I've often thought of turning *something*," said Miss Morrison meditatively. "Have you got a cigarette, by the way?"

"Some over there somewhere. Can you reach over and get them? I'll have one, too."

Having found the cigarettes, Miss Morrison handed one over, accompanying it with a curious glance. "I went to that Chehov play, last night. I didn't tell you, did I? My dear, don't go. I wept and wept—yes, honestly I did. It was just like the Burpenfield with the lid off, really it was—awful! When I got back last night, I said to myself, 'I can't bear it. I can't bear it.'"

"I think that's stupid, Morrison," said Miss Matfield, sitting in the only chair.

"What's stupid?"

"All that—about not bearing it and about the Club being the Chehov play. It's not a bit like it."

"How do you know, my dear? You haven't seen the play."

"I've read it."

"I don't suppose it's the same, just reading it. I admit it's not like this at all on the surface, but honestly it's got the same what-is-it—atmosphere."

"It hasn't a bit, I tell you," said Miss Matfield earnestly. "And I really think it's stupid talking like that about this place. It's ridiculous—all silly exaggeration. When you talk like that, Morrison, you annoy me——"

"Since when, my dear?"

"Well, I've made up my mind that it's simply absurd, besides being terribly depressing, going about talking like that about the life we lead here. It makes it seem fifty times worse than it is. And, anyhow, it's not bad really. It's our own fault if it is. Yes it is."

"My dear, you can't mean it."

"Yes, I do mean it."

Having said this, Miss Matfield put down her cigarette, looked at the floor for a minute, then quite suddenly and unaccountably burst into tears.

"Sorry!" she cried, five minutes later, when it was all over. "I'm not going mad, though I dare say it seemed like it. I think—I've been feeling rotten too, all strung up, you know."

"My dear," said Miss Morrison, who had been very tactful, "if I hadn't wept buckets last night at that play, I don't know what I'd be doing to-night."

"Listen," cried Miss Matfield, jumping to her feet and smiling damply. "I've made up my mind now. Yes, I have. It's serious. Listen. I'm going to work properly, and I'm going to get a better job and make more money."

"You're not going to leave your present job, are you?"

"The Lord forbid! If I did, the scheme wouldn't work at all. No, but I'm going to tell them there isn't anything in the office, or connected with it, I won't and can't do, if they'll only give me a chance. I'm going to be *really* in business, not just sort of hanging on there. I've got a jolly good chance because my firm's very busy now and we're short-handed, and the man who really sold all the veneers and inlays has just left us——"

"Not the man you told me about, the fascinating one?"

"Yes," Miss Matfield continued hurriedly. "He's gone, and that means there'll be an awful lot to do and they'll have to get new people. Well, I'm going down to Angel Pavement in the morning—and I needn't go if I don't want, because I got the morning off when I thought I was going away for the week-end——"

"Wait a minute. Do you mean to say that you've actually got the morning off and yet you're going all the same? You do? My dear, it sounds desperate."

"Yes, I am. And I'm going to Mr. Dersingham, and I shall tell him that I believe I could do anything that any man could do—and I don't care if it's going round to the weirdest Jewy East End furniture places selling veneers—and that he ought to give me a chance. I believe he will too, particularly now, when business is so good and he's so short of people. He could easily get another girl to do my typing, and that sort of thing, and I'd go and do some real work and then ask for more money. Very soon, I might have a real job, with a decent salary and proper responsibility and everything."

"Quite crazy! Though I believe you could do it, if they'd give you a chance."

"They'll have to give me a chance, and I'm sure I could do it."

She kept returning to the subject for the next hour, and then, when Miss Morrison had gone, she made up her mind all over again, and saw Messrs. Twigg & Dersingham growing more and more prosperous and herself, a real member of the firm, growing more and more prosperous with it. She arrived at Angel Pavement in a neat little car, and stepped out of it a cool, capable business woman, dressed with a certain austerity, but still attractive. Before she finally got to sleep, she had furnished not only her tiny flat in town, but also her little week-end cottage, which was the delighted admiration of her mother and other occasional guests. "Lilian, you *are* lucky," they cried; but she told them it was all the result of sheer hard work. This was the last dream of the day, and it was very pleasant. The dreams that followed in the night, the dreams that came without being asked, were curiously different, all dark and troubled, like the dreams of a child who has been hurried away to a strange place.

III

Mrs. Dersingham, Miss Verever and Mr. and Mrs. Pearson were playing bridge upstairs at 34, Barkfield Gardens, in the Pearsons' drawing-room. Mr. Dersingham should have been there, but he had telephoned to say that urgent business kept him at the office, so Miss Verever, who was usually abroad at this time of the year but had stayed in London because she was quarrelling with her solicitors, had taken his place. She was always ready to take anybody's place at any dining or bridge tables, though she never gave the least sign that she was enjoying herself. The card table was in the middle of the room, and there was only just space enough for it and its four players, in spite of the fact that this was a large room, larger than any of the Dersinghams' downstairs. The trouble was that the Pearsons had so many things. They had furnished the room first with good solid late Victorian furniture, and then they had poured into it the glittering East, all the loot of Singapore. If the Federated Malay

States had been destroyed by an earthquake and a great tidal wave, their life could have been re-constructed out of that room, which put any missionary exhibition to shame. Everybody looked out of place in it, and nobody more out of place than the Pearsons themselves.

They were now playing their third rubber of auction. Mrs. Dersingham had Mr. Pearson for her partner, and they were not badly paired, for she was rather a bold, slap-dash player, while he was very dull, cautious, obvious, though he always tried to give the impression of immense cunning. Nobody believed in this cunning of his except his wife, who would shake her mysterious dark curls at him and girlishly protest against his sinister subtlety. "Isn't he dreadful?" she would cry, after Mr. Pearson, with much stroking of his chin and narrowing of his eyes, had succeeded in some commonplace *finesse*. Mrs. Pearson, though she had been sitting at bridge tables for years, was one of those cheerfully bad players who continually ask for and receive advice, but have not the slightest intention of improving their play. Probably she only saw the cards as so many vague pieces of pasteboard, and what was real to her was simply the social scene, the faces round the green cloth and the pleasant chatter between games. If somebody had suggested playing *Snap* with the cards or telling fortunes with them, she would have been delighted, but as people seemed to prefer bridge, whether in Singapore or in London, she gladly made one at the table. And if all Barkfield Gardens had been combed, it would have been impossible to find a worse partner for Miss Verever, who played a good, keen, close, give-no-quarter game, and loathed all idle chatterers at the table, all idiots who would *not* get trumps out, all the fools who clung to their wretched aces, all the witless monsters who said, "Have you seen her lately? I haven't seen her for weeks and weeks. Let me see, *what* are trumps?" Mrs. Pearson combined smilingly every fault in bridge-playing known to Miss Verever, and Miss Verever's glances and tone of voice, queer and disturbing at any time, were now more queer and disturbing than ever, so that Mrs. Dersingham felt quite frightened and wished she had never asked her to take Howard's place. On Mrs. Pearson herself, however, these very peculiar glances, these biting accents seemed to have no effect.

"Well," said Mr. Pearson, picking up his pencil, "that's three down, doubled—three hundred to us. Simple honours to you, eighteen. Didn't do badly that time, eh partner? Must make something while we can. Tee-tee-tee-tee-tee."

"Isn't he dreadful?" cried Mrs. Pearson. "And you're nearly as bad, my dear, you're encouraging him. You see what it is, playing against my husband, Miss Verever. He's a dreadful man. Never mind, we'll do better next time, won't we?"

"But was it necessary to go Three Spades?" Miss Verever enquired bitterly.

"Well, wasn't it? Oh, do tell me if it wasn't. When you'd gone One, you see, and I had some spades, I thought we might win the rubber if we played the spades. If you think I did anything wrong, Miss Verever, don't be afraid of telling me, because I know you're ever so much better than I am. Should I have played that king first?"

Miss Verever drew a deep breath, but Mrs. Dersingham was too quick for her. "Oh, don't let's have post-mortems," she cried. "Whose deal is it? Mine, isn't it?"

"I suppose Mr. Dersingham will come up when he gets back, won't he?" said Mrs. Pearson, who never failed to snatch at any little opportunity for a chat. "He's late, isn't he? It must be so tiring for him, poor man. We know what it is, don't we?"

"We do," replied her husband. "At least I do, my dear. Tee-tee-tee-tee-tee."

"He used to work terribly late sometimes out in Singapore," Mrs. Pearson explained. "Night after night, sometimes in the hot season, too."

"Couldn't grumble though," said Mr. Pearson. "It meant that business was good."

"Yes, of course, that's what I feel," said Mrs. Dersingham, pausing in her dealing. "I suppose they've had a sudden rush or something."

"That's splendid, isn't it?" cried Mrs. Pearson. "I do like to hear of anybody I know doing so well. So many people don't now, do they?"

"It's made a great difference to Howard, being so busy," said Mrs. Dersingham, still with the cards motionless in her hand. "He really likes being in the City now. He was getting very depressed about it some time ago. Now let me see——"

"The next card should be mine," said Miss Verever coldly.

"Oh, should it? That's all right, then." And she continued dealing.

"Well, I didn't want to say anything at the time, my dear," Mrs. Pearson began, but she was cut short. Mrs. Dersingham looked up to see Miss Verever, on her right, giving her a terrible glance, and so she hastily declared "Pass."

"But I thought he seemed rather depressed about it, too," Mrs. Pearson continued. "About six months ago, wasn't it?"

"*One Heart,*" said Miss Verever, quietly, but with a fearful intonation. "*One Heart.*"

"Oh dear, have you started bidding already? How quick you are with your cards!" Mrs. Pearson began sorting hers in a frantic fashion. "Did you say One Heart? You did, didn't you? Well, after last time, I shall say—nothing."

"But it's not your turn to say anything," Mr. Pearson pointed out. "In this game, your husband for once gets a chance to speak. And I say—One No Trumps. Yes, this is where your husband's allowed to speak, my dear. Tee-tee-tee-tee-tee."

They were a game all in this rubber, so Miss Verever struggled up to Three Hearts, but her opponents went Three No Trumps, got them, won the rubber, and put her down eight hundred points.

"Is there time for another rubber?" said Mrs. Pearson, who was always quite willing to go on playing, perhaps because she never really started.

"I hardly think there is," said Miss Verever, with one of her peculiar smiles.

"No, let's stop now," cried Mrs. Dersingham.

"Somebody owes me four and ninepence," Mr. Pearson pointed out.

"Listen to him! Isn't he really a dreadful man when he plays this game? I believe I've lost four and nine—or is it five and nine?" Mrs. Pearson shook her curls at the score. "But I refuse to pay *you* anything, so there!"

"Tee-tee-tee-tee-tee."

"Well, I suppose I must pay *my* debts," said Miss Verever, looking at her score as if it was composed of something filthy, then glancing round without removing all the last expression from her face. "I pay you, I think, my dear. I'm afraid—yes, I'm afraid—I shall have to ask you for change."

"It doesn't matter," said Mrs. Dersingham hastily. "I haven't got any change."

"Please remind me then, the next time." Miss Verever said this as if they would soon be meeting in some torture chamber.

Somebody had arrived. It must be—it was—Mr. Dersingham. He came forward, blinking a little. His wife did not like the look of him. He was flushed and rather untidy.

Mrs. Pearson rushed at him. "Come along, you poor, poor man! Sit down here. Make yourself comfortable. You've been working all this time while we've been enjoying ourselves. Walter, give poor Mr. Dersingham a drink this minute. I'm sure you'd like one, wouldn't you?"

Mr. Dersingham said that he would, and the next minute he was taking a good swig of a large whisky and soda. When he put the glass down, he caught his wife's eye, and for a moment he just stared at her. She liked the look of him now less than ever. To begin with, this was by no means the first large whisky he had had that night. She saw that at once. But that was not all. There was something wrong. She glanced round and saw Miss Verever staring at him, and decided immediately that the sooner Miss Verever left them the better. She did not mind much about the Pearsons, who were kind and homely people, but she did not want Maud Verever to see or hear anything. She was about to suggest that they must go, when Mr. Pearson spoke.

"Had a long day, Dersingham, eh?" said Mr. Pearson, his cheeks wobbling sympathetically. "We were just talking about it. I know what it is. I've had these rushes, you know, working half the night—in the hot season too, not a breath of air. Takes it out of you, I'll tell you. Still, it's good for business, isn't it? Better than the other way round, eh? Tee-tee-tee-tee-tee."

"I think I really ought to be going now," said Miss Verever, with one of her dreadful smiles.

"Enjoyed yourself?" said Mr. Dersingham.

She started back. "Oh—of course," she replied, keeping her eyes fixed on him.

"Good. I'm glad to hear it. I like to hear of anybody enjoying themselves, and specially you, Miss Verever."

There was something very extraordinary about this, but Miss Verever did not care to stop and investigate it. She began saying Good-night. Mrs. Dersingham said that they must go too, but Mr. Dersingham refused to stir, so Miss Verever left by herself, though Mrs. Dersingham accompanied her down the stairs.

"Howard doesn't seem to be very well to-night, does he?" said Miss Verever, when they reached the hall below, in the Dersingham half of the building.

"He's tired, that's all. I don't think he's very well. He's been working tremendously hard. It's terribly tiring working late like this down in the City."

"I suppose it is." And it would be impossible to cram a larger amount of dubiety into four words than Miss Verever did into those four.

"Of course it is," cried Mrs. Dersingham, a trifle impatiently. "You just try it and see."

"Why, have you tried it, my dear? If you have, it's news to me. However, I hope Howard's better soon. He shouldn't tire himself out like that. It must be very bad for him. Don't you think so? Well, it was very nice of you to ask me to make the four up and play with Mrs. Pearson. Good-bye, my dear."

Mrs. Dersingham hurried back to the Pearsons, slightly alarmed and considerably annoyed. It looked as if Howard had not been kept late at the office at all, but had sneaked off to his club, where he had had more drinks than were good for him. There was always just a little, a little, danger of that with Howard. She found him sitting with his legs stretched out straight in front of him, listening to the Pearsons, who were still talking about Singapore.

"Taking it all round, y'know, the good with the bad," Mr. Pearson concluded, "it's not such a bad life out there, though it's not so good as it was. It isn't anywhere in the East. Still, even so, I believe if I'd my time over again, I'd go out there again, I really believe I would."

"Good!" said Mr. Dersingham, with a kind of dreary solemnity. "All right then, Pearson, what about that job out there you promised to get me?"

"Any time, any time! Tee-tee-tee-tee-tee. When would you like it? Tee-tee-tee." Mr. Pearson evidently regarded this as a great joke.

"You can start getting it for me now, old man."

Mrs. Pearson joined in the joke. "You'd better be getting your clothes ready, my dear," she told Mrs. Dersingham, who smiled, though not very brightly. She did not see anything very funny in all this, and her husband was behaving very stupidly. It was time she got him away.

"I'm serious, y'know," he declared now, with the same dreary solemnity. "I'm not joking. You get me that job out there as soon as you can. I'm serious."

"That's right. So are we. When would you like it then? Tee-tee-tee-tee-tee."

Mr. Dersingham drained his glass, then examined what was left in it, the last golden drops, with a thoroughness that suggested he was conducting a chemical experiment.

"We *really* must go, yes, really we must," cried Mrs. Dersingham, with a forced brightness; and in less than two minutes she had said all there was to say and had hustled her husband and herself out of the room. There was no fire in the drawing-room below, but there was the whitening ruin of one in the dining-room, and immediately he stumped in there in a heavy sort of way and sat down. She walked in after him, but did not sit down.

"I'm going to bed," she announced coldly.

"Just a minute," he said in a muffled voice.

"I prefer to go to bed. I'm tired, even if you're not." And she turned away.

"No, don't go," he cried, quite sharply now, with hardly anything of that thickness in his voice that had been there before. "You mustn't, Pongo. I've got something to tell you."

She closed the door and came back. "Pongo" was his old specially silly delightful name for her, and even now, when she was annoyed with him, when he was a large, pink, sagging creature, whose every stupidity she knew by heart, when he was sitting there, flushed and thick with whisky, not at all the sort of man she ever imagined she was marrying, a hundred times less attentive and considerate and clever and courageous, even now, the sound of that "Pongo" gave her a little thrill. She was annoyed with herself for feeling it. If he imagined he was going to be forgiven at once, simply because he had called her by that name, he was sadly mistaken.

She took up a position on the other side of the hearth, and stood looking down on him. "I should think you have something to say! Have you been to the club?"

He nodded and waved an impatient hand. "That was nothing," he muttered.

"No, but if you *must* pretend you have to work late and then you go on to the club and fuddle yourself with drinks, you might at least have the sense to keep out of the way, instead of barging in like that and behaving so stupidly. No, Howard, I'm really disgusted. You know I'm not silly about drinking, as some women are. But there's a limit. I believe you're drinking a jolly sight too much these days, a lot more than is good for you. Yes, I mean it. Anybody could see what was the matter with you to-night, up there."

"Oh, could they?" He gave a little laugh.

"Yes, of course they could."

"Well, believe me, my dear, they *couldn't*. Not one of 'em. Not you, even. No, not you."

"Oh, don't be silly, Howard."

"I'm not being silly. I wish to God I was. You know when I asked Pearson about that job? I suppose you thought I was being funny then, didn't you?"

"I didn't think you were being particularly funny," she told him, "though you obviously thought you were. If you want to know what I thought, it was that you were just being rather stupid."

"Well, I wasn't, Pongo," he said quietly. "I was quite serious. No, listen. We're absolutely done—I mean the firm, Twigg and Dersingham—completely finished."

"Howard, you don't mean it?"

"Yes, I do. That's what kept me to-night. I had a drink or two just because I felt played out, and I suppose I did show it—sorry about that—but I've had a hell of a day. Golspie's cleared out and left us ——"

"But you told me the other day that even if Golspie did go, it wouldn't matter and you'd arranged everything so that you could do without him."

"I know, but the rotten swine did me down ——"

"But how? I don't understand. Howard, you don't really mean it's as serious as all that? The firm can go on, can't it?"

He shook his head, and kept his face turned away. He looked like a great foolish baby. She swept down on him. "Tell me what's happened. Why didn't you tell me at once? I'm sorry I was cross with you. I didn't know it was anything serious—naturally. Now tell me."

He told her the whole wretched story.

"But do you mean to say that brute has gone and you can't do anything, anything at all? But it's ridiculous. Can't you tell the police? Why, it's just as bad as burglary or swindling. It *is* swindling. But I knew, I *knew* all the time that something would happen because of that man. He hated us after that night he came here and I lost my temper with that vile little minx of a daughter. I felt all the time he did. I told you to get rid of him, didn't I? Oh, Howard, you have been stupid. Yes, you have. I'll never believe in you again as a business man. You used to tell me I didn't understand about these things, but I'm sure I understand about people—and that's the main thing—better than you. But what's going to happen now?"

"I don't know," he mumbled miserably, and he explained as best he could the position they were in. As she listened, she suddenly saw the four walls enclosing them, the table and chairs and sideboard, everything in sight, no longer as solid objects, fixed, rooted in a secure existence, but as things brittle as glass, unstable and wavering as water. Nor did her imagination stop there. It explored the whole maisonette, the drawing-room, the kitchen below, the nursery and bedrooms, and discovered nothing substantial there, except the two children asleep upstairs and a few personal possessions that had long ceased to be mere things. She realised now, with a shock of dismay, that something absurd and fantastic could happen in Angel Pavement, far away, that could change all this. Their life here in Barkfield Gardens, not their personal life, but everything else, all the cleaning and cooking and shopping and visiting, was a mere candle-flame—one puff of wind, a wind that came from nowhere, and it was gone. She understood how millions of people live. It was a moment of revelation.

"What are we going to do?" she asked.

"I don't know yet," he replied wearily. "Give me time. I haven't had a chance to think yet. Hang it all, this has all been dropped on me like a ton of bricks. God!—I'm tired."

He sounded helpless, looked helpless. Her mind began working furiously now, and the effect, after months and months of stagnation, of pretending and dreaming and vague discontent, was curiously exhilarating. "Do you think Mr. Pearson could get you a job out East?"

"No, I don't."

"But why? You haven't asked him properly. He doesn't know you want one—if you really do want one, and I'm not sure about that."

"I know he doesn't, my dear. But I'm sure when he does he'll change his tune. I felt that when he was talking to-night. It's all right," he added bitterly, as if he had suddenly discovered what the world was like and what men were made of, "while it's still a joke. The minute he finds I'm serious, he'll pull a long face. I don't mean he's not a decent chap and all that. But he thinks he's talking to a prosperous business man who doesn't really want a job. That's the difference."

"I must have some tea," she announced. "It's no good; we must talk it over; if I went to bed I shouldn't sleep a wink—and if we're going to stay up, I must have some tea. I'll go down and make some. No, I can do it by myself. You stay here, and, Howard, do, do try and think of something. Try and find out how much money we'll have left—and everything."

When she returned with the tea, he was still sitting in the same huddled fashion. "Listen, I've been thinking," she began, almost gaily. But seeing him there, a large melancholy heap of man, she put down the tray, came across, pushed him back in his chair, and stood looking down at him, her hands still on his shoulders.

"Do you love me?" she asked.

He found this question as difficult as ever, but this time there was none of that masculine impatience or grinning intolerance. "As a matter of fact, I do," he told her in a shamefaced mumble, "but I don't feel this is the time to say so."

"Of course it is. Why not?"

"Well, I've let you down. I've let you down badly. I've been a fool. I'll admit I have. But I never liked the business, you know that, don't you? If it hadn't been for the cursed War, I'd never have gone into it. Not my style at all. I always hated it really—Angel Pavement and all those damned furniture places and sniffling East End Jews, and the whole thing. I've tried my best, but it's always gone against the grain. I'm not excusing myself, mind, though honestly I think anybody might have been let down the same way by that artful devil. Smeeth—and he's been in business all his life—never had a suspicion. He was more surprised than I was. And a fellow I talked to at the Club said he'd never heard of such a thing, said I couldn't be blamed at all. But there it is. What bothers me is that there's some of your money gone, too. I'm sorry, Pongo. I seem to have made a mess of it."

"I have some money left, though."

"Not much," he told her gloomily. "About twelve hundred, perhaps. No, not quite that."

"Well, that's something, isn't it? It's quite a lot, really. And after all you've had very good business experience now. Then—you remember what Uncle Phil said? Just a minute; I'll pour out the tea. Yes, you must have some." She did not sound at all depressed.

She was not depressed. In a few weeks, she might be miserable—she knew that too; she seemed to know everything to-night—but now, at this moment, she might have just had good news instead of very bad. Unlike her husband, who appeared to be only half the man he usually was, a listless lump, she felt twice her customary self. The footlights had blazed out, the curtain had shot up, and she had responded at once to the call of the drama. But there was more in it than that. She was no longer playing and pretending in the background. The situation, leaving him crushed, challenged her, and there was something exhilarating in accepting the challenge. Everything was suddenly real and exciting. Plans by the score, some of them born of old idle day-dreams, were stirring in her mind, and now while he listened, sometimes shaking his head, sometimes looking at her hopefully, they came tumbling out. "Of course, we'll give this place up as soon as we can—we ought to get a decent premium too—look what we've spent on the decoration—and then I'm sure mother would take the children for a few months. . . ."

IV

Yes, Mr. Smeeth was going home. It never occurred to him to go and hear what was left of the concert. He had done with Brahms & Co. for a long time, perhaps for ever. As he waited for his tram, he remembered that tune again—Ta *tum* ta ta *tum* tum—and now it seemed like something that was going on a long, long way off, like a birthday party in Australia. He said good-bye to that tune. As the tram went lumbering and groaning up the City Road, he said good-bye to many things.

He was feeling rather queer. He had missed his usual evening meal and was empty; that double whisky had had its effect; there was undoubtedly a pain somewhere in his side; and then of course there was the shock of the bad news. He had for years moved gingerly, apprehensively, through a world in which the worst might happen at any moment. The worst had happened. He could have said to himself, with satisfaction, "What did I tell you?" Perhaps there ought not to have been any shock. But it was not so simple as that. He had never expected to be hurled out of his job in this fashion. He had always seen danger coming from many quarters, but nevertheless this blow had arrived from quite an unexpected quarter. The more he thought about it, the angrier he grew. His anger was not directed against Mr. Dersingham, not even against Golspie, but against the whole world, the very nature of things.

You go on for years and years building up a position for yourself until at last you have a place of your own, a little world of your own, in which the figures do what you tell them to do, the books reveal their secrets, the fellows at the bank say "Good morning, Mr. Smeeth," and everything is snug and sensible. Then a chap turns up from nowhere, looks at a trade directory and happens to choose your firm, wanders in to Angel Pavement, and then, in less than six months' time, without your having any hand or say in it, he blows you clean out of it all, without even knowing or caring a thing about

it. You are quietly finishing off for the day, and then suddenly—
bang! What was the good of trams going up and down the City
Road and conductors taking fares and nobody smoking inside or
spitting on top under penalty of a fine? What was the good of having
a City Road at all and lighting it with street lamps and opening shops
and sending policemen to walk up and down it; what was the good
of paying rates and taxes and shaving yourself and seeing that you
had a clean collar and going round to doctors and dentists and reading the newspapers and voting, if this is what could happen any
minute? My God!—what was the good of it all?

This blanched middle-aged man, sitting in a corner of the moving
tram, an unlighted pipe trembling beneath his grey moustache, the
wrinkles on his face deeper than ever, peered through his glasses
now at the familiar panorama of the North London roads and saw
not a glimmer of it. His gaze was really fixed on the crazy structure
of things, and of that he could make neither head nor tail. He was
shaking a little, not with fear, but with indignation. For years
there had been a great shadow haunting and terrifying him, for he
had seen all the little lighted things of his life menaced by it. Now
the lights had gone, blown out; he sat in the shadow itself; the tram
was crawling through it; the Stoke Newington Road was in it; and
all his fear had been used up before by that shadow, when he had
been a man who had something precious to lose. Now he had lost
it. In a week or two, he would have to start again, and at a time
when even the boys were lining up in their hundreds for a chance of
a mere beginning at ten shillings a week. It wasn't good enough.
That was the phrase he used, the first that sprang into his mind, and
he repeated it over and over again with tremendous emphasis. "Not
good enough," he said as he left the tram. "Not good enough," as he
made his way to Chaucer Road, "not good enough."

It was only too evident, he told himself grimly, that they were not
expecting him back so soon at 17, Chaucer Road. Everything seemed
to be in full swing there. You might have thought somebody had
just been left a fortune. He heard a great noise coming from the

front room, and he saw a light in the dining-room. He chose the dining-room, and found George there, tinkering about with the wireless set.

"Who's in there?" asked Mr. Smeeth.

"The Mitty crowd," said George, with a tiny grin. "I came in here out of the way. I've had enough of that lot. Mitty owes me a quid, too. He's no good." He looked curiously at his father. "Anything up, Dad?"

"You got anything to do yet, George?"

"Not yet. I thought I was on to something to-day, but it was no go. I'm going round to see a chap to-morrow morning, big garage up at Stamford Hill. Why? Anything wrong?"

"Yes. I look like being out of a job within the next fortnight, and you know what that means."

It was not the tragedy to George that it was to his father, not merely because George was much younger, but also because his whole outlook was different, for he lived in a newer world in which jobs came and went and nobody troubled to spend years consolidating a position. Nevertheless, the youth had sufficient imagination to realise what this meant to his father. "I'm sorry about that, Dad— by gosh, I am! Rotten luck, isn't it? How'd it happen? They'd never sack you, would they? Has the firm gone broke?"

"That's it. Try and get something as soon as you can, George. You know how we'll be fixed."

"Don't worry, Dad, I'll get something soon, something good, too. Edna's not earning anything now, either, is she? She'd better make another start, too, hadn't she?"

"I'll attend to that. We'll all have to make another start now, if you ask me," said Mr. Smeeth grimly. They looked at one another, with approval on both sides, in silence for a moment. They could hear sounds of merriment from the other room. "Seem to be enjoying themselves in there," said Mr. Smeeth, his temper rising.

George came nearer. "Dad, boot 'em out. I would if it was my house. I told mother so, too ——"

"Taking something on yourself, boy, aren't you, these days?"

"Well, I did. I can't stand that lot. That's why I came in here."

Mr. Smeeth nodded. "That's just what I'm going to do, George. I want some peace and quietness to-night, and I'm going to have it." He walked out, and his son followed him.

The front room was just as it had been the first time the Mitty family visited them. There were only five people in it, Mitty and his wife and daughter, Mrs. Smeeth and Edna, but it seemed quite crowded and as thick, hot, and smelly, as if people had been eating, drinking and smoking in it for weeks. It made Mr. Smeeth feel very angry and disgusted.

Mrs. Smeeth stared at him, and looked uneasy. "Hello, Dad," she cried. "I didn't expect you back so soon."

"So it seems."

"Didn't you go to the concert?"

Fred Mitty, very flushed, was about to help himself from a bottle that stood, with other bottles, glasses, and some cake and biscuits, on a little table in the centre of the room. He was leaning forward, but straightened himself when he saw Mr. Smeeth standing there. "Thought you was having some classical music to-night, Pa," he roared. "Gave it a miss, eh?"

Mr. Smeeth advanced into the room, breathing hard. He looked at Mitty. "I've been working hard," he said pointedly, "and I want some peace and quietness now. So I'll say Good-night."

"What d'you mean, Dad?" cried Mrs. Smeeth.

But the irrepressible Fred could not resist this. "Well, night-night, Pa," he yelled, "if you're going to bed. Don't let me keep you." He looked round with a grin, asking for applause, and got it from the two girls, who giggled. Then he made a move towards the bottle again.

"I'm not going to bed, just yet," said Mr. Smeeth, his voice trembling. "But you're going home. That's what I meant."

"Here, half a minute, Dad." Mrs. Smeeth's voice rose in indignation. "What a way to talk!"

"I should think so indeed," cried Mrs. Mitty, sitting up sharply.

"For the more we are too-gether," Fred sang, as his hand closed round the whisky bottle, "the merrier we will bee-yer."

The fuse had been burning briskly for some time, and now its travelling spark reached the explosive. Mr. Smeeth blew up. "Get out!" he screamed at Mitty. "Get out of here! Go on! Get out!"

"That's the stuff," shouted George from the doorway.

But that scream was not enough for such an explosion of wrath. Two seconds later, Mr. Smeeth had flung down the little table and sent whisky and port and dirty glasses and cake and biscuits and oranges flying about the room. All was roaring chaos, with Fred Mitty shouting, the two wives screaming, Dot Mitty shrieking with laughter, Edna bursting into tears, George charging forward, and Mr. Smeeth standing in the middle, bellowing and stamping among the ruins. All the others jumped up and there was a pushing and jostling and Mr. Smeeth lost his eyeglasses and had no hope of finding them in the scrimmage. Nothing could be plainly heard in the din, and now, for Mr. Smeeth, robbed of his glasses, nothing could be plainly seen. His wife seemed to be shaking his arm and shrieking at him; Mrs. Mitty seemed to have hurled herself at Fred, to prevent further violence; and George appeared to be taking a hand in all the proceedings. But in another minute, he was alone in the room, and all the others seemed to be talking at the top of their voices outside. Feeling shaky, he made a step or two towards a chair, and trod on some glass. His own eyeglasses were still on the floor somewhere, and no doubt somebody had trodden on them. He collapsed into the chair, and in a dazed fashion removed a strange soggy substance from his left bootsole. It was what had once been a very generous slice of sandwich cake. Then a piece of broken glass, a jagged fragment of tumbler, cut his hand. He felt ill. It would not have been very difficult for him to have been sick on the spot. The sound of the voices outside did not abate for several minutes, but he stayed where he was. They could argue it out between them, could say and do what they liked; he didn't care.

The door had been left open, and he heard the Mitty family go, and then he heard George say something to Mrs. Smeeth and Edna. The three of them went into the dining-room and closed the door behind them, but the sound of their voices, raised in heated discussion, came to him in his armchair. He had groped about a little with the hand that was not cut, but all he had found were two biscuits and these he had eaten in that mechanical fashion in which biscuits are nearly always eaten. The voices were lower now and suggested that their owners were no longer merely shouting at one another, but were really talking. More minutes passed, and then he heard Edna go upstairs to bed. Then, after a short interval, during which he listened intently, shakily, to every sound, his wife came into the room. She did not burst in, as he had expected her to do; she came in quietly and shut the door after her. But this did not necessarily mean that there would not be a storm, and he braced himself to meet it.

There was no storm, however. Mrs. Smeeth's first fury had passed, though she was still very agitated. "If it hadn't been for George, I was going to say something to you, Herbert, you wouldn't forget for a long, long time. But he says you're very upset about your work."

"I am," said Mr. Smeeth in a very low voice.

"He says you're going to lose your job. Is that right?"

"That's right, Edie. It's all up with Twigg and Dersingham. In a week or two I'll be finding myself without a job."

"You're sure this time, Dad? I mean—it's not one of your false alarms, is it?"

"I wish it was. No, there's no false alarm about it this time."

"Mind you," cried Mrs. Smeeth hastily, shakily, "that's no reason why you should have gone and behaved like this. My word, if anybody'd told me you'd have gone and done a thing like that—you of all men—my word, I'd have told *them* something! Smashing the place up, too! Look at this room! Look at yourself! But I suppose if you were upset, you weren't responsible. Here, Dad, are you sure, really sure, about your job? You're not—you're not trying to frighten me again, are you?"

"No, of course I'm not."

"I can't believe it. Here, what happened?"

He tried to tell her what had happened, and at least succeeded in convincing her that he was entirely serious. "And if you think I'm going to get another job as good as that, or a job worth having at all, in a hurry, you're mistaken, Edie. I know what it is, with office jobs; and it'll have to be an office job because that's what I've always done. I'm nearly fifty, and I look it. I dare say I look older——"

"That you don't, Dad."

"Well, that's your opinion, but you won't be employing me. I know what it is." And there came back to him suddenly, poignantly, the memory of that tiny scene outside the office door, several months ago, when he had said to that anxious man, the last in the line of applicants, "Good luck!" and had received the ghost of a smile. "There are four of us here. George is out of work, though he might get something soon. He's a good lad, really. There's Edna. She's earning nothing now."

"She will be before this time next week," said Mrs. Smeeth quickly. "I'll see to that."

"She might be, and then again, she might not. And in a week or two I'll be among the unemployed. And we've got about forty odd pounds saved up, that's what we've got, all told, unless you count this furniture."

"I can work," cried Mrs. Smeeth fiercely. "You needn't think there'll be me to keep in idleness. I'll get something. I'll go out charring first."

"But I don't want you to go out charring," Mr. Smeeth told her, almost shouting. "I didn't marry you and I haven't worked all this time, never missing a minute if I could help it, and we didn't save and plan to get this home together, so you could go out charring. My God, it's not good enough. When I think of the way I've worked and planned and gone without things to get us a decent position ——!" His voice dropped.

"We'll manage somehow." And having said this, Mrs. Smeeth, the gay and confident partner, suddenly and astonishingly burst into tears.

"Manage? We'll have to manage," Mr. Smeeth had begun, grimly. Then he changed his tone. "Here, Edie. That's all right, that's all right. Now then, now then. I'm sorry I lost my temper too ——"

"It was my fault," she sobbed. "Yes, it is. I deserved it. I know I've spent too much money. Yes, I have."

"Oh, never mind. You weren't to know the firm was going broke like that. I didn't know myself. Never more surprised in my life. Here, Edie. Now then, now then." He was standing beside her now.

"Oh dear," she gasped, a few minutes later, trying to wipe her eyes. She was both laughing and crying now. "Oh, dear, dear, dear, dear!"

He looked at her solemnly.

"Oh dear, dear, you do look a sight, Dad. I don't know who looks the worst, you or this room. I never saw such a sketch, though I expect I'm bad enough, goodness knows!"

"I've dropped my eyeglasses, that's all that's wrong with me," Mr. Smeeth announced, not without dignity.

"I can see that, Dad, I can see that," she told him, dabbing at her face. "Here, I'll look for them. You sit down. But, mind you, if they're broken, don't blame me. It wasn't me that started throwing things about to-night, was it? Here they are."

"Broken?"

"Yes, somebody made no mistake when they trod on them. You'll have to wear your old ones for a day or two, that's all. I'll go and get them for you, and then you can help me to clear this mess up."

"All right, Edie." Mr. Smeeth hesitated. "Is there anything to eat in the house? I'm getting hungry now."

"Didn't you have anything? Haven't you had anything at all to-night? You silly man, why didn't you say so? I'll go and get you something now. You go and get your glasses, you know where they are—in the drawer upstairs. If you can't see them, you can feel for them. Yes, in the top drawer. And I'll get you something to eat while you're finding them. Oh dear, what a life! Still, it's the only one we've got, I suppose, so we'd better make what we can out of it.'

She bustled out and Mr. Smeeth followed her. He was very short-sighted, almost helpless without his glasses, and after he had stumbled upstairs to their bedroom he spent some time groping about for the old pair. Annoyed by the dim shapelessness of everything, he told himself that he ought to have been wearing his glasses before he started on such a search. Then he saw the irony of it and was quite entertained for a few moments, during which he felt for the first time for a long while a curiously reassuring detachment from things, and when he found the old glasses and put them on, he seemed, for one brief interval, to be staring at another and smaller world, and it was a world that could play all manner of tricks with Herbert Norman Smeeth but could never capture, swallow, and digest the whole of him. The newly-born ironist then returned down-stairs, to eat his supper.

Epilogue

M R. GOLSPIE, pottering about in his cabin, would not have known she was moving off if he had not suddenly seen a blue funnel go wandering across the open porthole. He could feel no motion, but then she was not moving under her own steam, but was being taken out of the docks by tugs. Mr. Golspie put his head into the next cabin, where his daughter was still fussing about with her things. "We're off," he said, grinning at her. Lena showed no sign of excitement. You might have thought she had been travelling to the River Plate all her life.

"Coming out?" said her father.

"Not yet. Are we really going? There doesn't seem to be any excitement."

"There isn't. If that's what you want, we ought to have gone on a liner, and then you'd have had palaver enough—kissing and crying and cheering and God knows what. These boats do it quietly."

"Well, I'm disappointed. But I'll come out when there's something to see and I've put these things away. I'm rather tired of staring at these silly docks, though. Tell me when anything happens."

He nodded, grinned again at her, then withdrew, and went out on to the main deck, where several of the other passengers were standing. There were only a dozen passengers all told, for this was primarily a cargo boat. One of these fellow travellers caught Mr. Golspie's eye, nodded, and then came nearer. They had exchanged a few remarks already, each having recognised in the other an old hand and a kindred spirit. They knew even now that the moment the steward was at liberty to dispense his liquors, they would be having a drink together, the first of many, many drinks. This other man, Sugden, was a tallish fellow with a long bony face and a vast shaven upper lip, a Lancashire man who travelled for some chemical firm. He had one of those hard, flat, Lancashire voices that give every statement they make a lugubrious and disillusioned air.

"Moving," that voice announced now, to Mr. Golspie.

"Moving," said Mr. Golspie.

They stood together, two solid middle-aged men, and together they watched the long line of masts and funnels in the Royal Albert Dock go sliding away. They were still in London, and no great distance from the buses and trams, the teashops and the pubs, yet all that London seemed to have disappeared long ago. Here was another city with streets and squares of dark water, a city of wharves and sheds, masts and funnels and cranes, barges, tugs, and lighters. Wherever you looked there appeared to be nothing but these things, though in the far distance a haze of smoke, hanging above the multitudinous chimney-pots of Poplar and Bow, suggested that the other London, the brick and paving-stone London, was still there. It was not a bad morning for the time of year. Now and then the sunlight struggled through and set the water glittering or brought out ghostly rainbow hues on the darker oilier patches.

"This is where they bring all the meat," said Sugden. "This, and Liverpool. If you blocked this place up for a week or two, a lot o' people would find themselves without their Sunday dinners. Not me, though. Give me English meat, when I can get it. And when I'm at home, I insist on having it. Get enough o' the other sort when I'm away."

"You've been on these boats before, haven't you?"

"I have. I've been on this very ship twice before. They know me here. You ask 'em."

"Food all right?"

"Suits me," replied Sugden. "Should suit you, too. Good quality and plenty of it. Nothing fancy, y'know—not like these liners, with their chefs and what not—but plenty o' good solid stuff. That's what I like."

Apparently it was what Mr. Golspie liked too. He produced a

cigar case, and the two men lit up and through a fragrant dribble of smoke regarded the moving docks with half-closed eyes and a vague air of patronage.

"This port of London's a bit of an eye-opener to me," Mr. Golspie remarked.

"Ever been all round it? Tremendous—oh tremendous! There's the West India Docks further up here, and then the Surrey Commercial on the other side. You never saw such a place. It's a hard day's work looking round the Surrey Commercial. Chap tried to show me once, but I gave it up. And then you've got the London Docks further up still. And Tilbury, of course. If you go out on one of the regular liners and mail boats, you get on down at Tilbury. I've done that once or twice, but this suits me better. When I'm aboard a ship, I like to travel quietly. I don't like all this floating hotel, song-and-dance, fancy-dress ball business. What d'you say?"

"Haven't been on one of those big ships for donkeys' years," Mr. Golspie confessed. "I've never been out to South America before, as a matter of fact. I've been to the States, in my time, and I've been to Central America, but not to south. But an old pal of mine's out there—Montevideo's his headquarters—and he's put up a good proposition, so I'm going to see what it looks like."

"Plenty o' money there, plenty. Only place where there is now, there and the States. I shouldn't like to live there though. Wouldn't suit me."

"And where do you live when you're at home?"

"St. Helens. That's where my firm is, and that's where I live. Been there all my life. D'you know it?"

"Saw it once from the train," Mr. Golspie replied. "Bit ugly, isn't it?"

Mr. Sugden was not surprised. Obviously he had heard this before. "Yes, it's a bit ugly, if you're not used to it. But I'm a bit ugly myself. And if it comes to that, you're no beauty." And he roared with laughter.

Mr. Golspie laughed too, companionably. They strolled round the deck, on which Miss Lena Golspie, in a fur coat and with a scarlet scarf about her neck, soon made an appearance, to the delight of several of the younger male passengers and ship's officers, who had been waiting for this moment, after hoping, with the despair born of many previous disappointments, that she was not merely a fleeting vision, one of those lovely creatures who come aboard for an hour or two and then depart, leaving the whole ship under a shadow. She joined her father and was introduced to Mr. Sugden (not an impressionable man), and then wandered away, to stare with disdainful interest at the other ships and to gather out of the corners of her brilliant eyes a good deal of exciting preliminary information about her fellow passengers. The scene before her—the ship had stopped now in that unaccountable fashion that ships have—seemed to her very ugly and dull, and it was incredible that this dirty water and drab messiness should be the beginning of a voyage to South America, of which her fancy entertained the liveliest and most exciting pictures, chiefly derived from the films. After that awful night with the boy from the office, she had been only too glad to leave London, which seemed to her, on the whole, a stupid place, but she could hardly believe now that in a fortnight or so she would be staring at South American young men with black side-whiskers and absurd hats. She was annoyed with the ship for stopping like this, as if it had nothing better to do than loiter about these dingy sheds and flat boats full of barrels, and when one of the officers hung about, looking as if he wanted to pour out information, she gave him a haughty glance and walked away.

Her father and his new acquaintance, having finished their cigars, leaned over the rail, and decided that they were ready for lunch. Meanwhile, they talked idly.

"I don't blame you," said Mr. Sugden. "I don't like London myself—never did. I had a year there once. Didn't like it at all. I couldn't get on with the Londoners—too much of this haw-haw-haw stuff and the striped trousers and black coat and white spat business. Didn't suit me, I can tell you. They thought they were smart, too."

"They're not—most of 'em," said Mr. Golspie. "I soon found that out."

"So did I," the other continued in his curiously flat mournful voice, "and when I did find it out and told 'em as much, they didn't like it. No, they didn't like it." Mr. Sugden did not go on to explain why they should have liked it. He merely repeated several times more that they didn't like it. But he was yawning rather than talking.

"Well, I've just had about four or five months of it," said Mr. Golspie, indifferently, "and that was quite enough for me. They're half dead, most of 'em—half dead. No dash. No guts. I want a place where everybody's alive, where there's something doing."

"Where were you in London?"

"What—working? Well, my headquarters were in a funny little street—I don't suppose you've heard of it—down in the City it is."

"I know the City fairly well."

"I wonder if you know this place. I'd never heard of it before. Angel Pavement."

"Angel Pavement? No, I never heard of that. You win. Well, I must say I'm ready for my lunch. I think I'll slip down and wash my hands. Well, *well*, well, we-ell." He sang these, at the same time stifling a yawn. "Meet any angels there?"

"What, in Angel Pavement? I can't say I did."

"Not on view, eh?"

"Not while I was there. I met somebody who nearly turned into one, but not quite. No, they were all just human, and they hadn't got too dam' much of that. I was sorry for the poor devils—some of 'em."

"All I'm sorry for just now is my inside," said Mr. Sugden, with great deliberation. "It's crying out for a piece of steak nicely done and a few chips. Hello, there go the Customs chaps. We ought to be moving again soon. And—my word!—it's time they thought about a bit o' lunch. Look at the time. Let's go down."

"Listen. That's it," said Mr. Golspie. "Come on. Oh, I'll get hold of that daughter of mine."

When they returned after lunch, they found that they had left the docks behind and were now in the river. There was a new chill freshness in the air and a vague hint of the sea. On one side, the last of Woolwich was straggling past, with a misty Shooters Hill behind; and on the other side there were some old piers and a gas works.

"Better take a last look at London," said Mr. Golspie to his daughter, as they walked round the deck. "There it is, see?"

"There's nothing to see," said Lena, looking back at the glistening streaky water and the haze and shadows beyond. "Not worth looking at."

"All gone in smoke, eh? I mean the proper London. As a matter of fact, we're not out of London yet. That's right, isn't it?"

"Not quite out of it yet," replied Mr. Sugden, "but you've seen all there is to see. I think I'll go down and have my little afternoon snooze."

A string of barges passed them, moving slowly on to the very heart of the city. A gull dropped, wheeled, flashed, was gone, and with it went what little sun there was. The gleam faded from the face of the river; a chill wind stirred; the distant banks, a higgledy-piggledy of little buildings and green patches, retreated; and even the smoky haze of London city slipped away from them, thinning out into grey sky. "Well, the sun's gone in," said Mr. Golspie, "so I'll go in, too." Somewhere a steamer hooted twice out of the ghostliness. He gave a last look, then turned away. "And that's that."

THE END